'THE THIRD

STALEMATE

COLIN GEE

1

'Stalemate'

The third book in the 'Red Gambit Series'.

WRITTEN BY COLIN GEE

Dedication for the Red Gambit Series.

This series of books is dedicated to my grandfather, the boss-fellah, Jack 'Chalky' White, Chief Petty Officer [Engine Room] RN, my de facto father until his untimely death from cancer in 1983 and who, along with many millions of others, participated in the epic of history that we know as World War Two, and by their efforts and sacrifices made it possible for us to read of it, in freedom, today.

Thank you, for everything.

Foreword by Author Colin Gee

There has been some suggestion that the action sequences contain descriptions that are too graphic, and in some quarters, I have heard the key word 'gratuitous' whispered.

It is my habit to think about what my readers have to say on the content; to do otherwise would be foolhardy in my view.

Therefore, in reply to those who find the sequences too powerful, I make the following observations.

I have never been in combat, but have spoken with those who endured a great deal of it, in all its horrible forms. Listening to descriptions of hand-to-hand combat, I very quickly formed the opinion that it was wholly bestial, and without qualms or rules of any kind.

My time in the Fire Service exposed me to some of the worst traumas imaginable, and some that went beyond that threshold.

Together, I believe that the two experiences permit me to give some air of reality to my action sequences, and not portray the standard format that carries other authors successfully through their own literary confrontations.

Some of what I present is my interpretation of historical fact, as recanted to me by men who were there. Some of what I present comes from my own knowledge of the events of World War Two. Yet more is a product of my own dealings with the horrible ways that our fellow man can find to leave this planet.

In some ways, I would apologise to any reader who is unsettled by reading such sections, and in some ways, I find that I cannot.

I would not wish to disturb anyone, but similarly, why should readers be hidden away from the awfulness of combat?

Such avoidance could leave the reader with all the tastes of glory, and none of the true cost of battle.

After all, we still send our young men and women into foreign fields, and they all return in one way or another; alive and well, alive but scarred forever, both mentally and/or physically or, as in the case of far too many, dead, returned home for their loved ones to intern.

4

In my view, to wrap up combat in the traditional glorifying and sanitised way would do them, and all those who went before, an injustice.

I do not believe that what I write is gratuitous violence, and it is not my plan to shock. I firmly believe that what I present to the reader is my best effort at telling combat how it was, and, to focus on one of the main points of my books, how it was for the soldiers on either side of the divide.

There has been some criticism of spelling, so I would ask the reader to remember that I am an Englishman, and therefore, honour is just that, as is valour. I have been extremely surprised to find just how many words have been varied between the USA and the UK. However, I have tried to use Americanism's where dealing with American figures and scenarios, and the reader will find some, such as 'armored', 'honor' and 'valor', where appropriate.

Again, I have deliberately written nothing that can be attributed to that greatest of Englishmen, Sir Winston Churchill. I considered myself neither capable nor worthy to attempt to convey what he might have thought or said in my own words.

My grateful thanks to all those who have contributed to this project in whatever way, as every little piece of help brought me closer to my goal.

My profound thanks to all those who have contributed in whatever way to this project, as every little piece of help brought me closer to my goal.

In no particular order, I would like to record my thanks to all of the following for their contributions. Gary Wild, Jan Wild, Mario Wildenauer, Loren Weaver, Pat Walsh, Elena Schuster, Stilla Fendt, Luitpold Krieger, Paul Dryden, Mark Lambert, Greg Winton, Greg Percival, Robert Prideaux, Tyler Weaver, Giselle Janiszewski, Brian Proctor, Steve Bailey, Bruce Towers, Victoria Coling, Alexandra Coling, Heather Coling, Isabel Pierce Ward, Ahmed Al-Obeidi, Hany Hamouda, and finally, the members of the 'Red Gambit' facebook group.

Again, one name is missing on the request of the party involved, whose desire to remain in the background on all things means I have to observe his wish not to name him.

Once more, to you, my oldest friend, thank you.

The cover image work has been done by my brother, Jason Litchfield, and his efforts have given the finished article a professional polish beyond my dreams. Thanks bro.

Quotes have been obtained from a number of sources, which have included brainyquote.com and quotegarden.com. I encourage the reader to visit and explore both sites.

Wikipedia is a wonderful thing and I have used it as my first port of call for much of the research for the series. Use it and support it.

My thanks to the US Army Center of Military History website for providing some of the out of copyright images. Many of the images are my own handiwork.

All map work is original, save for the Château outline, which derives from a public domain handout.

Particular thanks go to Steen Ammentorp, who is responsible for the wonderful www.generals.dk site, which is a superb place to visit in search of details on generals of all nations. The site had proven invaluable in compiling many of the biographies dealing with the senior officers found in these books.

If I have missed anyone, or any agency, I apologise and promise to rectify the omission at the earliest opportunity.

This then is the third offering to satisfy the 'what if's' of those times.

Book #1 - Opening Moves [Chapters 1-54]
Book#2 – Domination [Chapters 55-77]
Book#3 - Stalemate [Chapters 78-102]

Author's note.

The correlation between the Allied and Soviet forces is difficult to assess for a number of reasons.

Neither side could claim that their units were all at full strength, and information on the relevant strengths over the period this book is set in is limited as far as the Allies are concerned, and relatively non-existent for the Soviet forces.

I have had to use some licence regarding force strengths and I hope that the critics will not be too harsh with me if I get things wrong in that regard. A Soviet Rifle Division could vary in strength from the size of two thousand men to be as high as nine thousand men, and in some special cases could be even more.

Indeed, the very names used do not help the reader to understand unless they are already knowledgeable.

A prime example is the Corps. For the British and US forces, a Corps was a collection of Divisions and Brigades directly subservient to an Army. A Soviet Corps, such as the 2nd Guards Tank Corps, bore no relation to a unit such as British XXX Corps. The 2nd G.T.C. was a Tank Division by another name and this difference in 'naming' continues to the Soviet Army, which was more akin to the Allied Corps.

The Army Group was mirrored by the Soviet Front.

Going down from the Corps, the differences continue, where a Russian rifle division should probably be more looked at as the equivalent of a US Infantry regiment or British Infantry Brigade, although this was not always the case. The decision to leave the correct nomenclature in place was made early on. In that, I felt that those who already possess knowledge would not become disillusioned, and that those who were new to the concept could acquire knowledge that would stand them in good stead when reading factual accounts of WW2.

There are also some difficulties encountered with ranks. Some readers may feel that a certain battle would have been left in the command of a more senior rank, and the reverse case where seniors seem to have few forces under their authority. Casualties will have played their part but, particularly in the Soviet Army, seniority and rank was a complicated affair, sometimes with Colonels in charge of Divisions larger than those commanded by a General.

SOVIET UNION	WAFFEN-SS	WEHRMACHT	UNITED STATES	UK/COMMONWEALTH	FRANCE
KA - SOLDIER	SCHÜTZE	SCHÜTZE	PRIVATE	PRIVATE	SOLDAT DEUXIEME CLASSE
YEFREYTOR	STURMANN	GEFREITER	PRIVATE 1ST CLASS	LANCE-CORPORAL	CAPORAL
MLADSHIY SERZHANT	ROTTENFUHRER	OBERGEFREITER	CORPORAL	CORPORAL	CAPORAL-CHEF
SERZHANT	UNTERSCHARFUHRER	UNTEROFFIZIER	SERGEANT	SERGEANT	SERGENT-CHEF
STARSHIY SERZHANT	OBERSCHARFUHRER	FELDWEBEL	SERGEANT 1ST CLASS	C.S.M.	ADJUDANT-CHEF
STARSHINA	STURMSCHARFUHRER	STABSFELDWEBEL	SERGEANT-MAJOR [WO/CWO]	R.S.M.	MAJOR
MLADSHIY LEYTENANT	UNTERSTURMFUHRER	LEUTNANT	2ND LIEUTENANT	2ND LIEUTENANT	SOUS-LIEUTENANT
LEYTENANT	OBERSTURMFUHRER	OBERLEUTNANT	1ST LIEUTENANT	LIEUTENANT	LIEUTENANT
STARSHIY LEYTENANT					
KAPITAN	HAUPTSTURMFUHRER	HAUPTMANN	CAPTAIN	CAPTAIN	CAPITAINE
MAYOR	STURMBANNFUHRER	MAJOR	MAJOR	MAJOR	COMMANDANT 1
PODPOLKOVNIK	OBERSTURMBANNFUHRER	OBERSTLEUTNANT	LIEUTENANT-COLONEL	LIEUTENANT-COLONEL	LIEUTENANT-COLONEL 2
POLKOVNIK	STANDARTENFUHRER	OBERST	COLONEL	COLONEL	COLONEL 3
GENERAL-MAYOR	BRIGADEFUHRER	GENERALMAJOR	BRIGADIER GENERAL	BRIGADIER	GENERAL DE BRIGADE
GENERAL-LEYTENANT	GRUPPENFUHRER	GENERALLEUTNANT	MAJOR GENERAL	MAJOR GENERAL	GENERAL DE DIVISION
GENERAL-POLKOVNIK	OBERGRUPPENFUHRER	GENERAL DER INFANTERIE¹	LIEUTENANT GENERAL	LIEUTENANT GENERAL	GENERAL DE CORPS D'ARMEE
GENERAL-ARMII	OBERSTGRUPPENFUHRER	GENERALOBERST	GENERAL	GENERAL	GENERAL DE ARMEE
MARSHALL		GENERALFELDMARSCHALL	GENERAL OF THE ARMY	FIELD-MARSHALL	MARECHAL DE FRANCE
		* OR ARTILLERY, PANZERTRUPPEN ETC			

1 CAPITAINE de CORVETTE   2 CAPITAINE de FREGATE   3 CAPITAINE de VAISSEAU

ROUGH GUIDE TO THE RANKS OF COMBATANT NATIONS.

8

Stalemate

The third book in the 'Red Gambit' series.

7TH SEPTEMBER TO 27TH OCTOBER
1945

Book Dedication

This book is not dedicated to a specific person by name, but to a national icon, a figure that represents something different, and very personal, to each of us.

He or she is an institution, and an object of great affection for the British nation.

He stood behind the wooden stakes at Agincourt, and knelt in an infantry square at Waterloo. He rode a charger into the Valley of Death at Balaclava, and suffered in the heat at Spion Kop.

A whole generation went to war and walked into a hail of bullets on the Somme, manned a battlecruiser at Jutland, or drove a tank at Cambrai.

The next generation took their own mounts into the skies over Britain in 1940, or stood on the Imjin River in Korea.

Their issue went forth into the South Atlantic, and found immortality on, and around, a barren windswept island.

Their sons and daughters now give their all in the combat zones of the world; in Afghanistan, Iraq, and everywhere that the flag is raised, and people need protecting.

* * * * *

This book is humbly dedicated to the ordinary British soldier.

God bless 'em.

Although I never served in the Armed forces, I wore a uniform with pride, and carry my own long-term injuries from my service. My admiration for our young servicemen and women serving in all our names in dangerous areas throughout the world is limitless. As a result, **'Blesma'** is a charity that is extremely close to my heart. My fictitious characters carry no real-life heartache with them, whereas every news bulletin from the military stations abroad brings a terrible reality with its own impact, angst, and personal challenges for those who wear our country's uniform. Therefore, I make regular donations to **'Blesma'** and would encourage you to do so too.

Index

Contents

13

21

23

My thanks to...

The events that brought me to write the 'Red Gambit' series have been outlined previously, as have the major contributions of some of the more important characters.

I have already offered up my thanks to a large number of helpers, but I must now include the following.

The personal diaries and papers of Brigadier John Bracewell were invaluable, and helped me better understand the events at Barnstorf, as well as providing valuable insight into many of the subsequent Northern German operations. My thanks to his son, Major General Lawrence Bracewell MC OBE, and his granddaughter, Lieutenant Colonel Victoria Childs MBE, both for the access, and the additional knowledge they provided.

Major Andrew Charles, Grenadier Guards, provided me with huge amounts of personal testimony and physical information, and I thank him and his wife Christine for their enthusiastic support.

The memoirs of RSM Neville Griffiths CGM, MM and bar proved a mine of information. Alas Neville passed away the day before we were due to meet.

Pieter de Villiers provided me with an array of details, by way of recollection or the written word, and I am indebted to him for providing me with insight into the Soviet POW camps, and some specific events at Sarov during September 1947.

I am indebted to the guardians of the affairs of General Benoit Hugues Kelly Plummer, former French Defence Minister, who provided me with full access to the incredible private collection he established, the contents of which deal with so much more than just French affairs, and which provided me with a great deal of information not previously in the public domain.

The granddaughter of Gisela Jourdan provided me with her personal diaries, and they have been of great assistance. At her own request, she wishes to remain anonymous.

Generalleutnant Willibald Trannel provided me with insight into the operations of the Special Air Group that assisted with the Allies' covert operations in Europe, and was particularly helpful in piecing together the details of the SAG during the last months of the war.

I was privileged to meet with Marquis Ito Hirohata and receive, at first hand, the full story of the Rainbow Brigade. I am indebted to his son, Isoroku, for help with translations, on the occasions that my Japanese, or his father's English, failed to measure up.

Finally for this volume, I met with Egon Nakhimov, who was able to provide so many details on the Chateau assault, and the subsequent activities of Makarenko's unit of survivors, one of the greatest untold stories of WW3.

With the help of all these documents, the personal memories of the above, and others, I have been able to put together a story of the last two years of World War Two, or as they became known, World War Three, years which cost many lives, and which left such an indelible mark on those who fought on both sides.

I have tried to combine the human stories with the historical facts, and to do so in an even and unbiased manner. In my humble opinion, the heroes wear different uniforms and only in one specific area are they on common ground.

They are all ordinary human beings.

The story so far.....

As this book forms part of a series, I would recommend that you read all books in sequence.

'Opening Moves' deals with the political decision making behind the Soviet attack, and the first assaults into Allied occupied Europe.

'Breakthrough' deals with the development of the second phase of the Soviet plan.

This is the story so far.

The Soviets have been presented with reasons, seemingly substantial, to suspect treachery from the Allies.

Stalin and his cronies harness the indignation of the Soviet Officer Corps for their own Imperial intentions, and plan a lightning attack on the Western Allies in Germany.

Elsewhere, the US Atomic Bomb test was a failure, and Soviet intelligence secures American information that permits their own Atomic project to advance.

Rumours of a Soviet attack do not arrive in time, despite the best efforts of some German POW's, who work out what is happening, and make a daring bid to get to the Allied forces in Austria.

The war starts, commando attacks and assassination squads preceding the ground forces, Soviet air force missions reaping huge benefits and reducing the Allied air superiority to parity at best. Initial Soviet advances are made, but the resilience of the Allies is unexpected, and the Soviet leadership develops a sudden respect for the 'soft' capitalist troops. The war descends into a gutter fight, not the free flowing fight that the Soviet High Command had envisaged would take place, once they broke through the front lines.

The USSR's new ally, Imperial Japan, rearmed with captured German weapons, starts making inroads in China, as well as taking advantage of subterfuge to deal heavy blows to the US Pacific Fleet and Pacific ground forces.

The casualties are horrendous on both sides, and Allied commanders find themselves unable to regain the initiative, constantly responding to the Soviet assaults.

The German Army, displaying incredible resilience, commences reforming, promising to commit substantial numbers to the Allied forces.

The Soviet Navy plays its part, its submarines, many of which are former U-Boats, wreaking havoc on the Atlantic reinforcement programme.

However, the American war machine begins to whirr again, once more underestimated by an enemy.

Men and weapons, slowly at first, begin to flow from the camps and factories.

Also, the Allied Air forces recover, showing great resilience and taking the Air War back to the Soviets.

In particular, the Soviets have failed to appreciate the heavy bomber force, a mistake of immense proportions, but perhaps understandable, given their own bomber force's capabilities and the rushed nature of their strategic planning.

None the less, the Red Army continues to make inroads into the Allied defences, and the rate of attrition is awful.

Whole divisions can be swallowed up in the smallest of battles for the most insignificant of locations.

The Soviet plan has allowed for a number of phases of attack, with substantial reinforcements under central command, ready to be fed in when needed.

Despite some serious setbacks, the Red Army launches its second phase on 13th August 1945.

The assaults reap good rewards, and Allied divisions are ravaged from the Danish Border to the Alps.

The Allies plan to withdraw, fighting all the way, intent on standing in defensive positions established on the Rhine.

Amid rumours of Soviet supply issues, the Allied units bleed the assault formations at every opportunity, but constantly lose ground.

The Allies fight a number of encirclement battles, breaking out valuable troops, but at a cost in men and equipment.

An unwise decision by the British Prime Minister Attlee brings a crisis to the Allied cause, and encourages the Red Army to concentrate its efforts against the British and Dominion forces in Northern Germany.

Attlee is ousted and replaced by Churchill.

The Red Army renews its efforts.

Fig #51 - European locations of 'Stalemate'.

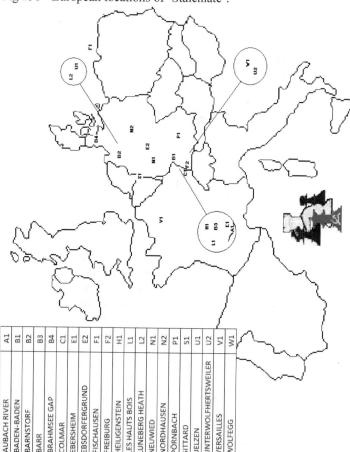

A1	AUBACH RIVER
B1	BADEN-BADEN
B2	BARNSTORF
B3	BARR
B4	BRAHMSEE GAP
C1	COLMAR
E1	EBERSHEIM
E2	EBSDORFERGRUND
F1	FISCHAUSEN
F2	FREIBURG
H1	HEILIGENSTEIN
L1	LES HAUTS BOIS
L2	LUNEBERG HEATH
N1	NEUWIED
N2	NORDHAUSEN
P1	PORNBACH
S1	SITTARD
U1	UELZEN
U2	UNTERWOLFHERTSWEILER
V1	VERSAILLES
W1	WOLFEGG

I appreciate that Kindle readers have had difficulty with the maps. I trust that the technology will one day catch up, as existing users have complained that they are difficult to display.

I can only apologise for that, but they do work within the paper version, so they must remain.

None the less, all maps, charts and graphics are available to the reader as a free download from www.redgambitseries.com, www.redgambitseries.co.uk, and www.redgambitseries.eu .

Use them how you will.

For all those that take up the sword shall perish by the sword.

Matthew 26:52

Chapter 78 - THE TERROR

<u>1017hrs, Friday 7th September 1945, Headquarters, Red Banner Forces of Europe, Kohnstein, Nordhausen, Germany.</u>

Colonel-General Mikhail Malinin consumed the GRU report dealing with the dishonoured British peace negotiations.

Zhukov sat peeling an apple, having already read the document.

He spoke, rushing the words, anticipating the taste of the first slice.

"Your thoughts, Comrade?"

"I see no reason to doubt her report, Comrade Marshal. Even though it is hard to imagine such an act without a mandate, Comrade Nazarbayeva sets out the reasons quite clearly, and the reinstatement of Churchill seems to bear out all she states."

"So we lost many men for no good reason, Mikhail. Bagramyan is hopping mad and threatens our lives, so I'm told."

Whilst Zhukov delivered that with humour, both men understood that the old Armenian Marshal was extremely upset at having lost so many good men for something that, in the end, produced no advantage.

In fact, it had produced some advantages, in that the British and Dominion formations had been given a very hard time and, by all accounts, were exhausted beyond measure.

That at least three times as many casualties had been suffered by the attacking forces was of no comfort to the British, but they had not folded under the pressure and now, with the return of Churchill, they seemed almost inspired to higher things.

"We must send the Armenian Fox some more troops. Draw up a list of units we can release for his use."

Malinin raised an eyebrow at his superior, knowing he was husbanding his reserve forces for the right moment.

By way of reply, Zhukov adopted a conspiratorial voice to try to suit the moment, but he did not carry it off.

"Just enough to shut him up, Comrade. Just enough to shut him up, and not a soldier more."

Malinin looked at his commander, realising for the first time that the strain of command was laying heavier than normal on his shoulders.

1957hrs, Friday 7th September 1945, Allied defensive line, east of Unterankenreute, Germany.

The 4th Indian Division had given up Bergatreute and Wolfegg under pressure, dropping back into the woods to the west, protecting the major highways that led to the remaining parts of Germany still under Allied control.

They had yet to take serious casualties, their retreat caused by logistical problems that saw some frontline units without more than a few minutes worth of ammunition.

Food was also just beginning to be a problem, the restrictions of their various faiths meaning that it was less easy to scavenge, or accept gifts from the friendly population.

A serious enemy thrust on Vogt had been bloodied and repulsed, the combination of British tanks, Indian artillery and USAAF ground attack proving too much for a large mechanized force that withdrew in disarray.

Nonetheless, the position was still precarious and the withdrawal continued.

Those units melting into the cool shadows of the trees found ample munitions and hard supplies waiting, the result of a magnificent effort by the Division's logistical chain, meaning that this was a line that they could hold. Bullets and explosive had taken priority over bread and meat, so only modest amounts of food reached some units, whilst others waited in vain

Many men went hungry that evening.

Partially because of the absence of food.

Partially because of the presence of the enemy.

They were known as the 'Red Eagles', a homage to their divisional badge.

Their service during the Second World War was exemplary, from the 1940 campaigns in the Western Desert, through East Africa and the rout of the larger Italian Forces, Syria, and finally Italy.

Italy, where the division earned undying glory in and around the bloodbath that was Monte Cassino.

The 4th was considered an elite formation, but it had taken heavy casualties in the process of acquiring its illustrious reputation.

Returned from a stint of armed policing in Greece, the Indian Division had slotted back into the Allied order of battle alongside sister units with whom they had shared the excesses of combat, only to be swiftly transferred north, and into the cauldron of the new German war.

It performed well against the new enemy and swiftly relieved the exhausted 101st Airborne.

The new positions assigned to the 7th Indian infantry Brigade covered the routes out of Wolfegg and the approaches to Vogt.

The 4th/16th Punjab Regiment, ably supported by two platoons of the 6th Rajputana MG Battalion, had stood firm in and around Vogt, British tanks from the 26th Armoured Brigade causing heavy casualties amongst the attacking T34's.

As the Soviet probes continued, the 2nd/11th Sikhs were pushed hard along their defensive line, set in parallel with Route 324 to the north of Vogt.

On Route 314 to the north, British soldiers of the 1st Royal Sussex Regiment folded back but did not give, forcing the attacking Soviet infantry and cavalry to retreat leaving scores of dead on the field.

An unusual error in Soviet attack scheduling had delayed the central assault, enabling the defending artillery to concentrate on assisting the Sussex Regiment before switching to the aid of the forces defending Routes 317 and 323.

Fig #52 - Junction of Routes 317 & 323, near Wolfegg, Germany.

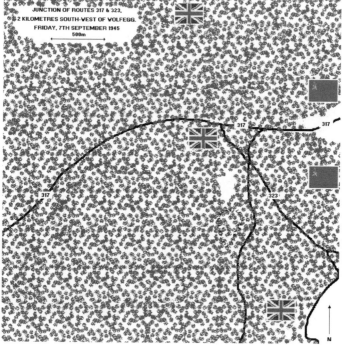

<u>2007hrs, Friday 7th September 1945, Junction of Routes 317 & 323, two kilometres south-west of Wolfegg, Germany.</u>

Company Havildar Major Dhankumar Gurung looked around him, able to make out the shape of one of his men here, a weapon manned and ready there.

8th Platoon was quiet, safely hidden behind their tree trunks, protected by the hastily scraped foxholes, or comfortable in the old German trench.

Not one man had suffered any injury as the Soviet artillery, weak by comparison to normal, had probed the defensive positions of the Sirmoor Rifles.

Part of their line was a trench that was eight foot deep, wood reinforced, and with firing steps along its length. Some fading graffiti marked it as German, and a relic of the previous conflict.

32

Gurung's soldiers had extended the trench, and taken advantage of natural depressions in the ground, as well as fallen tree trunks, creating a strong position from which to resist.

Thus far, the battalion had not seen an enemy, apart from the occasional flash of an aircraft overhead.

According to the legends of the British Army, no enemy relished fighting these wiry hill men from Nepal, and, to a man, they were keen to get to close quarters with the new foe to put their martial skills to the test against a strong and cunning enemy.

The Sirmoor Rifles, also known as the 1st/2nd [King Edward VII's Own] Gurkha Rifles, waited in anticipation of the battle to come.

Allied forces – 1st/2nd [King Edward VII's Own] Gurkha Rifles, and 2nd Platoon of 'A' Company of 6th Rajputana MG Battalion, both of 7th Indian Infantry Brigade, 3rd Royal Horse Artillery, and 11th Field Regiment, Royal Artillery, all of 4th Indian Division, directly attached to US 12th Army Group.

Soviet Forces – 3rd Battalion of 22nd Guards Cavalry Regiment of 5th Guards Cavalry Division, and 2nd Company, 1814th Self-Propelled Gun Regiment, and Special Group Orlov, 7th Guards Horse Artillery Regiment, all of 3rd Guards Cavalry Corps, 5th Guards Tank Army, 3rd Red Banner Central European Front.

"Are you fucking kidding, Comrade Kapitan?"

"No, I am not, Comrade Serzhant, and what's more, we go in fifteen minutes because staff already fucked it up once."

The old Cossack shook his head.

"They are fucking it up again then, Comrade Kapitan."

He pointed in the direction of advance, emphasising his words.

"Those boys down there are proper infantry, with machine guns. They want us to charge them? Mudaks!"

"Calm yourself, Kazakov. Apparently this is not your first action."

"That is why I question this order, Comrade Kapitan. It's total fucking lunacy!"

Captain Babaev moved like a striking snake, the flat of his hand wiping itself loudly across the older man's face.

"You shut your mouth, Serzhant, or I will shoot you myself!"

All around, the younger Cossacks froze at the sound of flesh striking flesh, their eyes drawn to the growing red weal on Kazakov's cheek, the ferocity of the blow becoming more apparent with the darkening of the skin.

Kazakov froze, controlling his breathing, his mind racing.

Babaev looked at him with unconcealed contempt.

"You boast constantly of the action you have seen and the men you have killed, and yet all I hear from you is whining about being sent to fight."

The officer cleared his throat, intent on completing the NCO's humiliation.

"I say enough of it, Kazakov! I demote you to Private immediately, and you will lead the attack!"

To the watchers, it seemed that a strange peace settled on Kazakov. The few that really knew the man understood that a white fury was consuming the 'former' sergeant.

Finishing the job, Babaev summoned one of the observers to him.

"Comrade Levadniy, you are now Serzhant. Don't let us down."

"Thank you, Comrade Kapitan."

The new sergeant saluted respectfully, avoiding the burning eyes of the previous incumbent, slipping quickly away to find some rank markings.

Kapitan Babaev poked his finger into Kazakov's right breast, hard enough to cause the man to sway under the blow. His finger flicked up at the medal that was the pride and joy of the man he had come to despise.

"The Order of the Red Star, for which I have been unable to find any proof of entitlement I might add!"

Kazakov's eyes moved upwards, making the eye contact that he had been trying hard to avoid.

"The divisional records are meticulous, except when it comes to you it seems."

Kazakov exhaled slowly in an effort to control himself.

"I wanted to strip you of it, but the Colonel prevented it."

The former Sergeant's eyes blazed openly, his fury feeding on the officer's words.

"So we have agreed to give you the chance to earn it. That is why you are leading the attack."

Stepping half a pace closer, Babaev leaned his head forward so that the distance between their faces was the length of a cigarette.

"And you fuck up in any way, any way at all Kazakov, and I will shoot you down like the cowardly dog you are. Clear, Comrade?"

Babaev misunderstood the delay for compliance, whereas it was a moment of debate for the ex-sergeant. He decided against his preferred course of action and replied, coolly and softly.

"Understood completely, Comrade Kapitan."

"Excellent. Now fuck off and get yourself ready, Comrade Private Kazakov."

Babaev smiled openly as the defeated man strode off, removing his epaulettes as he went.

The officer checked his watch, noting that he still had twelve minutes before the attack commenced.

He lit a cigarette and consumed the rich smoke avidly, happily unaware that it was the last he would ever smoke, and that his life had seventeen minutes to run.

22nd Regiment had not conducted a horsed charge for over two years, the fighting mainly being done on foot with a few disappointed Cossacks left behind to restrain their mounts.

The general plan was to deliver a horsed cavalry charge into the positions of the Indian troopers, using the woods as a cover, accepting that the upright trunks would both conceal and break up the advance, slowing it to a modest running pace at times.

A small probe had already established that both roads were mined and to be avoided.

The woods were heavy, but gaps between trees were wide, and there was little thick undergrowth to halt the surge. The Pine trees had no low-lying branches to foul the riders, and so the normally unthinkable seemed feasible, at least to those who ordered the attack.

It would require excellent horsemanship, something that actually stimulated many of the men who would make the charge, as the challenge appealed to their sense of showmanship, creating a stage for them to demonstrate their riding skills to each other.

Some wiser heads agreed with Kazakov, as horsed cavalry and machine-guns made for a bad mix, but a message from the new Major assured them that the enemy troops were ready to fold, and that a full-blooded Cossack charge would break them in an instant.

At 2025hrs, Soviet artillery commenced a brief but violent barrage on the enemy positions, partially to cause damage but also to mask the sound of harnesses and sabres rattling as the assault company got ready.

At 2030hrs, the 3rd Cossack Battalion commenced its advance.

[Author's note. Indian Army ranks. Lance-Naik = Lance-Corporal, Naik = Corporal, Havildar = Sergeant, CSM = Company Havildar Major, Jemadar = Lieutenant]

Sudden cries from the section on his right drew the attention of Company Havildar Major Dhankumar Gurung.

Some piece of artillery shell had found soft flesh, and one of his men was screaming loudly.

A reliable Naik, Gajhang Rai, was already scrambling across the defensive position, and the medical orderlies were ready to move, once the bombardment stopped.

To the right, another shell found its mark, but this time there were no sounds from pained throats, the three men blotted out in an instant, and their Bren gun silenced forever.

Making a note to adjust his reserve Bren gun team, Gurung found himself showered with earth as a round landed nearby.

Fortunately, for the Gurkhas, the Soviet artillery was only of modest calibre, otherwise the accurate fire would have reaped more bloody rewards.

As it was, a small number of them had been killed and a handful more wounded.

So far.

36

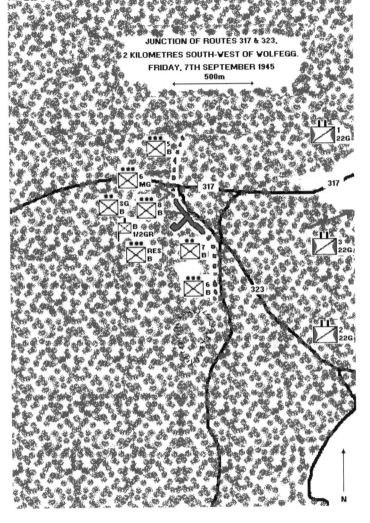

One of the last shells tossed over by the 76.2mm guns hit on thick branch directly central to the company's position, exploding thirty feet above the ground, transforming the shell into deadly shrapnel and the tree into wooden splinters, equally capable of taking a man's life.

37

Directly below a Vickers machine-gun team from the 6th Rajputs died, fast moving metal and wood taking the lives of every man in the position, metal alone responsible for perforating the water-cooler jacket on the big machine-gun.

Captain Graham, the Gurkha company commander, recognized the problem immediately and gestured at his senior non-com.

Grabbing three of 8th Platoon's men, Gurung sprang from cover to cover, making it to the silent Vickers position as the Soviet guns fell silent.

Graham immediately shouted at his men to make ready.

The Company Havildar Major quickly organized the recovery of the Vickers, aware that an unusual sound was steadily growing from the direction of the enemy.

The signaller with Captain Graham cursed, his radio another victim of the shrapnel. A small piece had somehow missed the man, who had protected it with his body, creating an insignificant hole in the top casing, but causing significant damage within.

The Indian artillery could not be called in until it was fixed, the spare radios already consumed in the earlier fighting.

The summer light was fading, but what there was illuminated the battlefield from behind the Gurkha positions, drawing the Cossacks forward.

The Gurkhas were straining to identify the sounds, allocating many identities to the enemy, until one horse planted its leg in a small hole, snapping the bone in an instant.

The cry of distress was easily identifiable.

"Jesus Christ! It's cavalry! Pass the word, Jemadar!"

Captain Graham looked upon cavalry as a ceremonial necessity with no place on the modern battlefield.

But now that he was faced by the reality of approaching horse, he found himself unexpectedly challenged.

The Gurkha Jemadar saluted formally, reporting that the company was aware of the enemy to their front.

"Fix bayonets if you please."

The Jemadar passed the order on once more, despite the fact that he and his men preferred to do their close work with the kukri.

The noise of approaching cavalry was increasing and Graham's bayonet order undoubtedly eased some of the tensions growing amongst the Nepalese hill men.

Amongst the trees to their front, the shadows flitted as the day drew to a close, and the Cossacks pushed their horses hard.

In front of Graham's eyes, the shadows became real, and dangerous.

"Fire!"

All along B Company's positions weapons fired, filling the air with .303" bullets. Vickers heavy machine guns and Bren guns, held in competent hands, punched out their own version of death in deadly streams of bullets.

Lee-Enfields, bolts being worked furiously, added their own .303" rounds to the wall of metal into which the Cossacks of the 3rd Battalion charged.

A bugle sounded, bringing to the battlefield a feeling of days long gone by, of times when Napoleon and his peers had held sway in matters of war.

Many bullets found trees or occasionally nothing, hurtling on into the approaching night beyond.

Those that were left found flesh, horse and man, in equal measure.

Two hundred and ninety-one riders and mounts had started the attack, the remaining strength of the experienced cavalry unit.

Now, dead men and horses filled the woods in front of the Gurkha positions, the attack losing momentum as the trees restricted alternative manoeuvre and obstructed the second wave.

A Soviet officer rode forward, picking his way through a number of wounded beasts, commanding his men to dismount and fight on foot until a rifle round plucked him from the saddle.

Angered more by the loss of their mounts than the deaths of their comrades, small groups of Cossacks started to organize and push forward, their superiority in numbers finally coming into play.

Soviet mortars were quickly brought into firing position, and accurate shells dropped on the defensive lines once more, buying time for the attack to be restarted.

Some cavalrymen deployed their own machine-guns, and a deadly exchange commenced, lives being claimed on both sides.

Kazakov opened his eyes, the effects of his collision with the ground heavy on him still.

His horse had been chopped from underneath him and collapsed immediately, throwing the old Cossack into the forest floor face first, temporarily stunning him.

Spitting out a combination of blood, earth, and teeth, Kazakov tried to orient himself, whilst the self-preservation part of his brain checked that he was in some sort of reasonable cover.

Babaev watched him, desperate to attract his attention but unable to move, unable to shout, unable to cry out for release.

His mount had also been shot down in the charge and the Captain had been thrown off as the dying animal fell forward, hurling him against a tree.

That would have been painful enough, but Babaev was still on that tree, transfixed by a stubby branch root that stood proudly out of his back.

Hanging two feet off the ground, the Cossack officer was dying in excruciating pain, but his damaged lungs and windpipe did not permit him the release of screaming.

He tried to speak, and managed a tortured sound, enough to attract the attention of the man he had recently humiliated.

Kazakov examined the apparition, noting the large amount of blood and protruding wood with a detached professional interest.

Shaking his head to rid himself of the final effects of his fall, he rolled over to the base of Babaev's tree.

The officer's eyes were streaming with tears, blood trickling from his nose and mouth, occasionally surging, fresh and crimson, occasionally absent.

"Shoot me, you bastard. For fuck's sake, shoot me."

The act of speaking almost achieved the same result, as the effort induced coughing that brought on more bleeding.

The former Sergeant opened his holster, extracting a Tokarev pistol.

"That's right, you fucking bastard, shoot me!"

Checking that he was unobserved, Kazakov spoke quietly to the Captain.

"The pleasure is all mine, Kapitan, all mine."

He pulled the trigger, sending a single bullet into his nemesis.

Not quite as Babaev intended, for the muzzle of the pistol was against the officer's genitalia, which was destroyed by the passage of the heavy bullet.

Leaving the horribly wounded man to die, Kazakov looked around for a place to hide until the attack was over.

One rush of Cossacks had made it across the road to the 7th Platoon position, withering and dying in the direct fire from Brens and Stens, the brave Russians hacked down to a man.

The position around the damaged Vickers seemed vulnerable, so Captain Graham, the company second in command, moved his handpicked reserve group there to bolster it before another thrust was made.

That attack came two minutes later, and what resulted was a fight more reminiscent of an older age, of bloody Cannae, or of Alexander at Gaugamela.

The cavalrymen had gathered and launched a disciplined and focussed attack, centering on the position adjacent to Gurung's Vickers.

A flurry of grenades had caused heavy casualties in the centre and Soviet left side, and DP light machine guns lashed into the machine-gun position just as Graham arrived. Smoke from the Soviet mortars completed the hasty preparation for a rush.

The experienced Nepalese prepared themselves, the remaining Brens parting the smoke with small bursts of fire, the gunners unable to see if their efforts were bearing fruit.

As more grenades emerged from the smoke, others, hurled by the Gurkhas, flew in the reverse direction.

Shrapnel flayed the wearers of both uniforms, flesh and bone giving way to hot metal, the defenders ravaged by heavy casualties, the offensive force decimated in turn.

The combination of the failing light, the woods, and the flash of weapons, made for a surreal atmosphere.

A riderless horse, wounded and panicked, ran through the no man's land, its body struck by the bullets from both sides before it dropped in front of the old German trench and coughed out its final seconds.

Suddenly, Allied control was lost, as Graham was felled by a stone thrown up by a grenade, and the Jemadar shot down and killed by a speculative burst from the other side of the smoky divide.

CHM Gurung was already down, a bullet in his left shoulder as he had directed the Vickers' fire against a large group of cavalrymen.

The Cossacks charged forward on foot, firing as they ran.

Again, the Gurkhas claimed lives with their accurate fire, but lost men in return.

The Vickers, swiftly relocated to a secondary position, stuttered back into life, and stopped the assault in its tracks, carving the leaders into pieces and driving the survivors into cover.

Soviet cavalrymen fired back, but the Vickers pinned them in place.

One Cossack officer attempted to relocate one of his own machine-gun teams, but he and they were betrayed by their muzzle flash, and they permanently lost interest in the battle.

The Vickers kept firing, swivelling from left to right, its damaged cooling jacket losing hot water and steam as the constant firing increased the temperature.

A DP burst struck home and the gunner rolled away, clutching his stomach.

One of the loaders kept the weapon going, preventing the Cossacks from rising up and continuing the assault.

Gurung moved gingerly, his wounded shoulder reminding him of its wretched state. He took over firing the gun whilst the loader went back to his task of joining the ammo belts together, so the gun could keep firing.

An enterprising Cossack had crawled forward to attempt a grenade at the new Vickers position. As he pulled back his arm, a rifleman shot him in the face, the primed grenade dropping back to earth, and putting the brave man out of his misery.

The Soviet battalion commander ordered his mortars into one last effort, the last of their rounds to be fired off on to the 7th and 8th Platoon positions. He organised as much of his available manpower as time permitted, and focussed them on the intended breakthrough point.

A salvo of 82mm shells fell amongst Gurkha positions, one spectacularly striking an ammunition stash, sending a shower of .303, and unarmed grenades, in all directions.

A few fires started, illuminating the defenders from behind.

The third salvo saw a high-explosive round drop close to the Vickers, knocking the weapon over, killing one of the loaders, and throwing both Gurung and the other man off their feet.

The Cossacks rose up again and this time they were not going to be stopped.

Submachine guns spewed out streams of bullets one way, Bren and Sten guns replying, each second the volume of fire dropping as another man was silenced by a bullet strike.

B Company's commander, an experienced Major, had realised the difficulty and committed his final reserve to 8th Platoon's aid. Screaming like a mad man, he led forward a special forty-man group, consisting of men from the Battalion carrier platoon and B Company headquarters, and completed by the some members of the battalion pipe band.

They arrived at the same moment as the Cossacks penetrated the front line positions and a gutter fight commenced, the Major knocked down immediately by SVT rounds, dying silently as his men swept forward and into the Cossacks.

A sudden surge in one of the fires illuminated part of the battlefield.

CHM Gurung saw the danger and reached for a nearby Enfield. Picking up the weapon, he fought the pain in his shoulder and fired into a group of Soviet cavalrymen sneaking around the left side of the main position.

The survivors withdrew, dragging two of their number with them, leaving a third motionless behind them.

Successfully seeking out his own Thompson, Gurung discarded the rifle and checked that the men around him were ready to go.

The melee to his front was growing in intensity, and on the left side, hand-to-hand combat had developed.

The Cossacks were lovers of their long Shashkas, and remembering how the deadly blades had given them the edge in many such encounters with the Germanski, a number of men bared their weapons and rushed in close, whirling the sabres in time-honoured fashion.

Starting on the Gurkha right, the front positions started to descend into chaos. Men, too close for modern weapons of war to do their jobs, fell back on more ancient tools for the close-in killing.

At first, rifle butts and bayonets responded to Shashkas, but it was not long before the Gurkhas discarded their guns for their weapon of choice, and the Kukris flashed in the last light of the dying sun.

The Shashka was a superb weapon, slightly curved and very strong, as well as legendary for its sharpness. It was also designed to be nothing but a killing machine, a job it performed extremely efficiently in the hands of an experienced swordsman.

The Kukri was beaten on length at seventeen and a half inches, being just about half the length of the Soviet blade. Its origins were as a work knife but, historically, the tool had converted easily into a wholly efficient weapon of war, and the strangely shaped blade meant that it delivered optimum cutting power when in the hand of a proficient soldier.

Both the Cossacks and the Gurkhas knew their craft and whilst bullets and butts still claimed lives, it was the sharp blades of the Shashka and Kukri that did most of the killing in the awful close-quarter fighting.

Graham, recovering, but still groggy, assessed the situation and summoned men to him. He rushed them forward to the position that was under most pressure. Halting behind it, he ordered rapid fire and bullets smashed into the cavalrymen who were gaining the upper hand there, reducing the numerical superiority of the enemy to his front.

The English Captain had mastered all facets of his command, from the language and culture through to being able to hold his own in the Gurkha skills, and to that end, he carried his own Kukri.

With his Webley revolver in his left hand, he raised his right hand high. Brandishing his blade, he shouted the battle cry loud enough to hearten the men fighting to his front.

"Ayo Gurkhali! Jai Mahakali! Ayo Gurkhali!"

His small group plunged forward into the fighting, immediately driving back the nearest cavalry troopers.

The sides fell briefly apart, and firing grew as blades were substituted for guns, both sides shocked by the nature of the fighting.

A burst from a PPSh knocked over a number of Gurkhas to the left of Gurung's position.

In the centre, it seemed that Graham's counter-attack had succeeded in restoring stability.

On the right, part of the mixed force had rushed to bolster the sagging 6th Platoon, but the fighting was hard and bloody.

The CSM made a quick assessment of where the next attack would focus.

It seemed obvious to the experienced NCO.

It would be on the left, where he was positioned, so Gurung readied his men for the charge.

The PPSh's did more work, and another two riflemen fell, encouraging the Cossacks to push in once more.

Gurung gave the order and charged forward, the pain in his wounded shoulder now forgotten. Despite the hammering of the Thompson in his left hand, his mind was focussed on his right hand, now occupied by the weapon of his youth.

Blinking rapidly to clear the tears brought on by the smoke, the CHM sought another target. The Thompson yielded its last bullets, smashing down a panicky cavalryman as he reloaded his PPSh.

Tossing the empty weapon to one side, Dhankumar Gurung threw himself forward, rolling under the thrust of a Soviet bayonet, coming up into the crouch and ramming his kukri home, point first, the tip exiting the back of his screaming opponent.

Releasing the blade, he rolled again, avoiding a massive swipe from a bearded Cossack, the tip of the shashka kissing the rim of his helmet and creating a ringing metallic sound.

Slipping as he tried to rise, Gurung's wounded shoulder impacted with a discarded ammo box, and he cried out in pain.

Seeing weakness in his opponent, the bearded Russian attacked once more, intent on using his strength and reach to batter the Gurkha down.

Blade met blade as Gurung fended off the blows, but the Gurkha was being penned back, acting solely defensively, as the big Cossack pressed harder still.

Suddenly, the man halted in mid swipe, his face demonstrating a lack of understanding, whilst his body knew very well that it was dying.

A second shot from Graham's Webley dropped him lifeless to the earth.

The captain bore all the hallmarks of a man drunk on blood, his wild eyes and grinning face betraying his combat madness.

In his right hand, he now carried a bloodied shashka, the former owner having no further use for it. Graham's kukri remained deeply embedded in his skull.

"Up and at 'em, Havildar-Major, up and at 'em I say."

In an instant, he was gone, gobbled up by the steadily increasing fight.

Securing the position, Gurung installed a Bren gun team with back up to prop up the left flank, and pushed back into the throng to help secure the centre.

More Cossacks entered the fight, the organised remnants of the 3rd Battalion focussing on the perceived weak point, desperate to break through.

Some Cossacks were learning the hard way that a trench was not the best place to be when the enemy has a kukri, its lack of length suddenly becoming a strength, as the longer shashkas fouled the wooden boarded sides of the old German earthwork.

The sun disappeared, leaving the illumination to the flames and flashes from explosives and weapons.

A group of cavalrymen became isolated and pressed on both flanks, the heavy bladed kukris carving men into pieces, until the Gurkhas met in the middle over the dead bodies of their enemy.

A Soviet grenade exacted a price from the victors of that small battle, levelling the score in an instant.

Parts of the wooden trench began to burn, slowly at first, but then gathering in ferocity.

One group of Gurkhas, under the command of Naik Rai, stepped back from the close fight and started to pour fire into the approaching Cossack reinforcements, forcing them into cover and delaying the support they tried to bring to their fellows.

5th Platoon's commander attempted to turn the right flank of the Cossack attack, advancing two sections to the southeast.

As they rushed the road, the Gurkhas fell foul of Soviet machine-gunners, positioned to cover just such an effort.

5th Platoon lost a dozen men and failed to affect the fighting on the other side of Route 317.

The Captain commanding the Soviet machine-gunners sent up a magnesium flare to help see. It deflected off an overhanging branch, slamming back into the ground and illuminated his own positions long enough for a Bren gunner to extract some revenge.

The remaining men of 6th, 7th and 8th Platoons fought harder in an attempt to throw the enemy out of their positions, but they were fighting high calibre troops who had no intention of giving ground.

It made for a bloodbath.

The final portion of Major Graham's reserve launched itself forward and fell in behind the close combat zone, firing at targets of opportunity, careful to avoid their own side.

Rai, the Naik, was down, legs smashed by a burst from a DP, but he still encouraged his men, directing their fire, and keeping them focussed with his shouted encouragement.

Graham appeared on the edge of the position, his loud voice immediately getting the attention of the carrier platoon's Havildar commanding the adjacent reserve. He followed the officer's gesture, spotting a group of enemy pressing hard to the left of centre.

The Havildar's group switched their fire, dropping a few Cossacks, but the cavalrymen refused to halt, speeding up to get to the doubtful safety of close quarters.

Ordering his men forward, the Havildar fell in mid-shout, a single rifle bullet instantly taking his life.

None the less, his men plunged into the fray, driving hard into the flank of the new Soviet arrivals and, once again, balancing the numbers in the frontline position.

Gurung, his wounded shoulder aching badly, watched as the battle temporarily moved away from him. He permitted himself to take a few deep breaths before seeking further involvement elsewhere.

He spotted Graham fighting like a man possessed, lashing out with the Cossack blade and his empty Webley.

Horror overtook him, for his leader had not seen the approaching danger.

Gurung screamed a warning at his officer.

"Sahib! Behind you!"

Throwing a kukri was an acquired and delicate skill, and CHM Gurung was renowned as an able practitioner and excellent shot.

The bloodied kukri flew through the air.

It missed.

On hearing the warning, Captain Graham had turned, just in time for a bayonet to slam into his solar plexus, punching through gristle and bone, folding him in two with the weight of the thrust.

The dying officer tried to swing the sabre, but he was robbed of his strength, rolling away to the left as the Cossack twisted his rifle, causing unspeakable agony.

The rifle spoke once, blasting a larger hole in Graham's chest, stopping his heart in the briefest of moments.

Beside himself with rage, partially at the death of the popular British officer, and partially because of his own failure, the maddened Gurung threw himself forward, crashing into the Cossack, and sending both men flying.

His shoulder wound forgotten, the wiry Gurkha dodged the knife aimed at his body and slipped inside the thrust, knocking the man down again and breaking the Cossack's wrist when he fell on top of his arm.

The knife fell away from his useless fingers, and was instantly retrieved by Gurung.

He stabbed quickly into the man's side and stomach and was about to finish him off when a sixth sense warned him and he rolled away.

A sabre cut the air where his head had been the briefest moment before.

Another blow made contact, slamming into his midriff, but failing to cause him damage, the blade eating into his webbing and pouches and halting at the buckle.

One of his younger platoon members saw his senior NCO in difficulty and sprang forward, only to receive a deadly blow as his kukri was brushed aside, and the sabre left free to kill.

The dead man's kukri dropped invitingly to the ground, but the Cossack understood the situation, and made sure he stayed between it and Gurung.

Swinging the shashka, he advanced again, his wounded adversary having no choice but to retreat, the knife useless against such a heavy attack.

A burst of firing, close at hand, marked a momentary separation between some of the combatants, a space that some of the Cossacks exploited, using PPSh's to slay a number of Gurkhas.

The firing distracted the cavalryman, only for a split-second, but enough for Gurung to spring.

Attention back on the fight, the Cossack slashed at the moving shape, nicking an arm as the Gurkha rolled low and right, slipping under the attack, and jamming the knife in the meat of the cavalryman's thigh.

It jarred into the bone, causing a horrendous pain that momentarily paralysed the Cossack, until it passed just as quickly and he turned to deal the Gurkha a deadly blow.

"Ayo Gurkhali!"

Gurung led with a powerful thrusting straight arm, moving inside the latest sabre cut, the retrieved kukri smashing, point first, straight through the man's upper teeth, before penetrating the roof of his mouth and into the brain beyond.

Regardless of the absence of verification in the Divisional records, Kazakov actually had been awarded the Red Star for valour, back in the days when he was a patriot, prepared to risk his life for the Rodina.

That had long since passed, and the butchery to which his unit had been subjected, often by orders of doubtful military worth, had left him with only self-preservation of immediate concern.

Or so he thought.

Watching from his position, he observed men he had lived with these past four years, comrades and friends, dying and bleeding for the same cause he had forsaken.

Something clicked inside.

"Blyad!"

Substituting his weapon for a discarded SVT rifle with spare magazines, he slipped forward in the half-crouching run that marked out the veterans from the cannon fodder.

Arriving at the old German trench section, he calmly picked off Gurkhas, saving more than one of comrade's life in the process.

Tossing an empty magazine away, he saw the movement and turned, dropping the new mag as he raised the rifle to stop the blow.

A bloodied Gurkha brought down his kukri and found only the rifle. The blade bit into the wood and metal and lodged there, the weakened man tugging on it without success.

The Gurkha saw death in Kazakov's eyes and fell to the ground, exhausted by his wounds, drained by his exertions.

The SVT was useless as a rifle, so Kazakov repeatedly drove the butt into the face of the wounded man, smashing jaw, cheekbones, and cracking the skull, before throwing the rifle away, the bloodied kukri still lodged in its workings.

The shashka was in his hand before he moved away, deciding to avoid the melee in the trench, and investigate off towards the right.

Gurung recovered his own kukri and looked around him, immediately understanding the situation.

The Gurkhas were losing.

In such moments, men are born, and Company Havildar Major Gurung immediately determined to be a beacon and rallying point to his men.

Shouting the battle cry, he moved up and out of the depression he was in, exposing himself to friend and enemy alike.

The surviving Gurkhas took inspiration and fought back with renewed vigour, pressing the Cossacks hard, despite their inferiority in numbers.

Two Cossacks rushed at him, screaming, and slashing with their blades. Each received the same journey to Valhalla in short order.

A wounded Soviet officer emptied his Nagant revolver at the mad Gurkha, missing every shot, his fear growing as the whirling shape grew nearer.

A Cossack Sergeant, his hands pressed to a ruined face, staggered into kukri range and was dispatched, his blood splashing over the officer's hands as he fed more shells into his Nagant.

He started to scream in fear, his hands desperate to snap the revolver back together and kill the mad little man.

Fear leant him wings but also robbed him of the composure he needed, and Gurung's kukri bit deeply into his chest, spilling his life's blood.

A bullet tugged at Gurung's sleeve, and he wisely moved back into cover.

As he turned back, he saw another cavalryman, gleaming sabre in hand, stalk the position, occasionally hacking down through gaps in the flames, striking at a man in the trench below.

A pistol appeared in the man's hand, and more of Gurung's men died.

Despite his growing weariness, Gurung threw himself forward, shouting at the Cossack to distract him.

One bullet remained in the pistol and the trigger was pulled. It missed the charging Gurkha, so metal met metal, as shashka and kukri clashed again.

Kazakov felt the sting as the kukri slash slipped through his guard, opening his jacket side and slicing the flesh down the line of his ribs. However, Gurung had been falling away at the time, so the cut was not deep.

The Cossack replied in kind, using the extra length of his weapon, feinting a right handed slash and reversing, pushing the point into yielding flesh and dropping the Gurkha to his knees.

Gurung's thigh howled in protest as the blade bit deep. He struck out at the shashka, snapping it in two, the renewed surge of pain almost causing him to faint.

51

Kazakov was raging, his father's sabre broken by this small brown man, its blade now the same length as the strange knife the Gurkha wielded.

He slashed out with the broken sabre, missing his man and falling backwards as he lost his balance.

Throwing the destroyed sword to one side, he slipped his own knife from its scabbard and rose to his feet.

Taking advantage of the lull, he caught his breath as he watched Gurung try to pull the half-blade from his thigh.

His hand closed around the sharp steel and he gently pulled, slicing flesh on fingers and palm. The blade remained firmly embedded.

Kazakov used the moment to his advantage.

Sensing the Cossack's attack, Gurung pushed himself upright, the embedded blade slicing into muscle that was already struggling to support his weight.

The deadly knife missed its mark, swatted aside by the flat of the kukri.

A swipe similarly missed the Russian, splitting the air as the Cossack rocked backwards in avoidance.

Kazakov feinted with his knife and drew the expected defensive move from the Gurkha.

His foot lashed out and made contact with the protruding blade, catching the exposed metal and ripping it upwards.

Gurung wailed in pain and staggered backwards, thumping against a smouldering tree behind him.

He raised his kukri, but realised his strength was going, the extended wound in his thigh draining blood from his body at an alarming rate.

The Cossack lunged with his knife and the blade bit into Gurung's stomach, driving right through and into the wood beyond.

His kukri fell from his grasp, and he moaned loudly. The pain was unbearable, both that of the wound and in the knowledge of his failure.

Kazakov bent down and recovered the kukri that had slipped from Gurung's grasp. He weighed it in his right hand, nodding in acknowledgement of its deadly capabilities.

His adversary was dying, blood trickling from his mouth as well as from shoulder and thigh.

"You fought well, little man."

Gurung did not understand, and was past caring, his mind straying to family and the mountains of home.

The kukri sent the CHM to his ancestors, Kazakov slashing across his exposed throat in one economical movement.

The battle was won, and the defending Gurkhas were either killed at their posts or withdrew, the latter hotly pursued by fresh Guardsmen from the 2nd Battalion, eager for vengeance after suffering badly at the hands of the Indian Division's artillery.

One group of Cossacks, men from the 1st Battalion, moved northwards, bludgeoning into the right flank of 5th Platoon, as they struggled against the second wave of dismounted cavalry.

Elsewhere, the dying Rai was dispatched by a single sabre blow, and other Gurkhas, prisoners and wounded alike, were killed out of hand. 3rd Battalion was spent, over one hundred and sixty men having fallen, the Soviet dead and wounded littering the killing zone in front of the Allied position. The ground was shared with seventy-eight dead and dying Gurkhas.

The survivors rallied on the old German trench, trying hard to ignore the pistol shots as the special detail swept through the woods behind them, bringing merciful release to many a wounded beast.

Some cavalrymen sought out their own mounts, whether dead or dying, sharing a last quiet moment with a friend.

The Regimental Commander was in tears. Not open grief and crying, but the dignified weeping of a man grieving for comrades lost. Colonel Pugachev, who had spent his life in the saddle with many of the dead, watched in silence as the triumphant cavalrymen of 1st and 2nd Battalions moved on through the positions. They pushed the remnants of the Sirmoor Rifles back, the other Gurkha companies withdrawing slowly in an attempt to reform a shorter line, hingeing on the solid bastion of Vogt.

His horse snorted and stamped its front hooves, unsettled by the sudden whinny of pain from the woods behind. He turned to comfort the mare and a movement caught his eye.

"Comrade Serzhant Kazakov?"

The Colonel was unsure if the bloody apparition was that of the experienced but troublesome NCO.

"Comrade Polkovnik."

"A terrible day, Comrade Serzhant. So many of the old crowd are gone; so many."

A Cossack Lieutenant rode tentatively up, and dismounted to present a grim report.

Fresh tears ran down Pugachev's grimy face, his sorrow mixed with occasional joy, as a veteran officer was placed amongst the wounded, or an old comrade staggered into view as the 3rd gathered at the trench.

Acknowledging the report, Pugachev took a moment.

"Right. Thank you, Comrade Leytenant. Move up, and make sure the advance ends at the halt line. I'll be up shortly."

Salutes were exchanged and the junior man rode away.

"Comrade Kazakov, gather up the survivors and get them back to Wolfegg. Get the mounts and men fed and rested. We'll be passing over to the infantry soon enough. I'll bring the Regiment back to you."

Kazakov looked at the Colonel without comprehension.

Pugachev realised the man's lack of understanding.

"You're it, Comrade Starshina."

'Job tvoyu mat!'

That he had just been bumped to Starshina was lost on Kazakov.

Raising his voice, the Colonel spoke to the shattered men around him.

"Comrades! Well done! Well done! You broke the enemy. Now, go with Starshina Kazakov, and we will organise you somewhere dry and warm to rest. And some hot food too."

The men drifted in the direction of the still bemused Kazakov, the occasional attempt at 'Urrah' stifled by their recent experiences.

"Look after them, Comrade Starshina."

Kazakov nodded and led the survivors back towards Wolfegg.

Pugachev watched them go.

He spared a moment to look around the deserted position and then mounted up, moving forward to liaise with his battalion commanders.

A bird starting tweeting in the trees.

A tree cracked as fire reached a pocket of resin.

A distant gun discharged.

54

A flare thudded as it exploded into light.

The battlefield that had been so alive with sound fell into relative silence, the Soviet wounded removed, the Third's survivors on their walk to the rear.

Everyone was gone.

All except for 'B' Company, 1st/2nd [King Edward VII's Own] Gurkha Rifles.

Captain Lawrence Graham MC, Company Havildar Major Dhankumar Gurung, Naik Gajhang Rai, and their men, held the line, still.

2052hrs, Friday 7th September 1945, Airborne, east of Wolfegg, Germany.

The Beaufighter was a British bird, designed as a heavy fighter, and achieving the 'heavy' in spades. However, she was a beautiful aircraft to fly, and packed a punch, four 20mm cannon and six machine-guns ready for anyone who got in her way.

However, 'Gypsy Queen III', a Mark VI-F version in the air over Wolfegg, belonged to the 416th Night Fighter Squadron of the USAAF, and it wore a number of hats that evening.

The Mark VIII radar reported no contacts, which was no surprise, the Red Air Force having lost the night skies some time before.

Occasionally, some bigwig had risked a short hop on an aircraft, but Zhukov had now ordered his senior officers to avoid such stupidity, having lost three Army commanders in a week to night fighter attacks.

Soviet artillery spotting was their next purpose, the telltale trails of rockets or the muzzle flashes located and positions relayed back to waiting allied gunners.

When the 22nd Cossack Regiment finally sorted out its artillery support, the commander called down fire on the withdrawing Gurkhas, determined to press them and stop them from settling. More guns joined in as the self-propelled 122mm howitzers of the 1814th Gun regiment deployed, dropping their heavier shells to great effect.

Clark, 'Gypsy Queen III's' pilot, turned his Beaufighter gently, summoning the observer up to the cockpit.

"Sam, two o'clock low, muzzle flashes, say a battalion's worth at minimum."

"Yeah, I gottem, Cap'n," the statement was slightly lost, as a map was noisily jostled into position.

Without regard to the niceties of rank, Samuel J. King sought information.

"Any landmarks?"

"Yeah, Sam, Lakes." The water surface, now between them and the setting sun, proved an excellent point of reference, the shape of the lake prescribed in deep yellow.

"Reckon that one is due east of Wolfegg. The Stock?"

A further moment of intense map rustling followed, terminated by the observer's head reappearing.

'Yep, reckon so Cap'n."

King seemed slow to most people, but Clark understood his man well, and knew he was just methodical in his approach, and didn't rush into making mistakes.

"Flashes on the ground here," talking to himself he pencilled a cross, five hundred metres to the north-east of the lake.

"Happy, Sam?"

"I'm happy Cap'n", the monotone revealing no hint of excitement at what he was about to do.

"Call it in then."

Without another word, King dropped back into his position, checked the top-secret list he had been given earlier, and switched to the frequency of the nearest artillery unit, instigating an Arty/R mission.

Basically, Arty/R was a barrage called in by an airborne spotter, a procedure well tested in the German War. However, new security procedures were being tested in this sector after some problems with Soviet misdirections, interference that resulted in a few Allied casualties.

"Queen-five-seven-three, Queen-five-seven-three calling Omdurman-Six, receiving over."

A voice, clearly that of a man more at home in the east end of London, acknowledged receipt.

"Queen-five-seven-three to Omdurman-Six. Fire mission Baker, target..." he paused briefly, checking the coordinates again before delivering them.

"Omdurman-Six to Queen-five-seven-three, fire mission Baker received. Security check required."

The Beaufighter had a special list that gave it security access to men in the front line.

"Standby for check. Ready? Omdurman-six over."

The procedure was laid out precisely, and the artillery units along a fifty-mile front all possessed a copy of the same list. A word was issued that required a specific reply within three seconds or the orders would not be observed and further communications ignored. It could not be otherwise.

"Security check. Go. Troy."

"Achilles."

"Roger. Balloon."

"Otter."

"Roger. Sunburst."

"Victory."

"Roger, check complete, ranging shot on its way."

The Beaufighter continued on its lazy turn, Captain Clark ensuring that his aircraft was not going to get in the way of a stream of shells.

He was immediately impressed.

"Bang on the money, Sam. Give the Limeys the word."

The observer keyed his microphone, relaying the confirmation of 'on target', and quickly scrambling up to look out of the cockpit.

Seconds past with nothing, save the continued flashes of a few guns below, although the absence of the full count suggested that the Soviets were hitching up their guns, ready to relocate.

Sam King was disappointed for all of thirty-two seconds, at which time the 3rd Royal Horse Artillery put their shells 'bang on the money'.

A Baker mission was a strike against enemy wheeled artillery, and the gunners of the 4th Indian Division had mixed a barrage of high explosive and fragmentation rounds, creating a highly effective cocktail of death in the area of the 7th Guards Artillery's deployment.

The barrage of twelve rounds per tube caused casualties and destroyed guns, but the disciplined cavalry troopers worked to hitch up their guns and move away, calmly ignoring the men and horses that fell.

The sun finally retired and the night was lit by exploding shells.

The 7th Guards Artillery quit the field, relocating to another site and leaving the front troops unsupported.

The General commanding called the commander of the 1814th SP Gun Regiment, his deployed guns having been given orders to cease-fire and stay alert, ready for exploiting the breakthrough.

The displacement of the 7th Guards changed that once more, and the support role switched to them. The 122mm shells started to fall on the Indian second and third line positions, the intact battalions of Cossacks eagerly calling in fire, and accurately directing it, causing casualties amongst the enemy to their front.

Inside the 'Gypsy Queen III', the display on King's radar set informed him of a problem.

"Cap'n, two separate contacts bearing 110, height 15, distance to us roughly fifteen thousand yards, and closing."

The Arty/R mission went on the back burner as the Mk VI-F Beaufighter slipped into its more accustomed role as a hunter-killer in the night skies.

The Soviets, in an attempt to gain some sort of inroads into the Allied mastery of the night sky, had devised a simple solution.

During the German War, the Luftwaffe had inadvertently provided the Red Air Force with a lot of quality equipment, left behind by retreating forces or overrun when the red tide swamped the front.

The two blips that were the focus of King's attention were very dangerous beasts. No longer in their Luftwaffe markings, the two Heinkel 219 A-7's boasted the simple colour scheme of the Soviet Air force, and their sole purpose in life was to kill enemy night-fighters.

The Soviet aircrew had received a crash course on their new aircraft and were keen to test their skills against the despised Allied night fighter force.

Radars described the battlefield, painting the displays with light, each pinpoint signifying a target, the remainder of the screen dark and insignificant.

The three aircraft closed rapidly.

The lead Soviet pilot caught a movement against the last vestiges of the dying day, and flicked his aircraft into the right angle, sending a stream of 20mm cannon shells at whatever it was that had attracted his attention.

The majority missed, but his excellent reactions bore fruit as three 20mm shells hit the Beaufighter's starboard wing and engine hard, the final shell striking the propeller, causing one of the blades to immediately detach and spin away.

Clark suddenly had major problems to deal with. He shut the damaged engine down, the distorted propeller causing numerous handling issues until it was feathered.

The three aircraft swept past each other, with only the lead Heinkel engaging.

The Beaufighter was now down on speed, its single Bristol Hercules engine straining to the limit to provide as much assistance as possible for the coming fight.

King called in the enemy positions and Clark manoeuvred to get in a shot. Every time he tried, the faster Heinkel would move away, or the second aircraft would get in a position that threatened the Beaufighter.

The Soviet pilots had learned their lessons well, and the previously unblooded second Heinkel got in a long burst of cannon fire, ripping into the 'Gypsy Queen III' from nose to tail.

Shells ruined the radar equipment and much of the Beaufighter's necessary instrumentation. Other shells ripped open sections of the port wing, damaging the fuel tanks and sending the main aileron flying off like a piece of chaff.

The tail area, with its converted dihedral planes, received a lot of damage, but the control surfaces remained functional, a testament to the ruggedness of the design.

King was hit by two shells, explosive 20mm cannon shells, which transformed him into so much butcher's meat in the blink of an eye.

Clark was hit by only one, and it was one of three shells that did not explode on impact with the USAAF night fighter. Dud or not, the impact of it turned the pilot's left knee into mincemeat, the unexploded shell held in place by a few intact vestiges of gristle and bone.

The American pilot felt little pain. He had only survival on his mind now, and he struggled with the Beaufighter, expertly milking all the speed he could from the damaged bird.

Some sideslipping provided Clark with the comfort that he would not be an easy target, and he broadcast in clear, calling for help from his fellow nighthawks.

A Heinkel slid down the port side, easily outpacing the stricken Beaufighter.

Trained to be aggressive at all times, he considered attempting a shot, but the speed advantage of the ex-Luftwaffe aircraft was too great.

He could not see behind him, and his attempts to raise the observer had not borne fruit.

It would not have mattered.

A thousand pairs of eyes watching his tail would not have done the job.

One pair of eyes looking down might have.

In the German War, the Luftwaffe devised a weapons system that exploited the major weak spot of Allied heavy night bombers, namely the belly.

With the exception of the Flying Fortress and Liberators of the USAAF, Allied heavy bombers lacked an underside defensive position, or the ability to look below the aircraft with any certainty.

The two Soviet pilots were confident that they had their quarry, and so the leader ordered the concealed attack, treating the fight almost as a training exercise.

The flight leader watched as his second moved in underneath the stricken Allied airplane, the first hints of fire springing from the starboard engine.

The Heinkel 219 was fitted with an oblique firing cannon system, mounted behind the pilot, pointing up at an angle through the canopy.

Two 30mm MK 108 cannons were lined up on the belly of the Beaufighter, the Soviet aircraft throttling back and slipping underneath their quarry.

The pilot fired the Schräge Musik, named after the German nickname for 'Jazz'.

Shell after shell chewed up the metal framework and spent itself explosively in the destruction of the Beaufighter's integrity.

Clark was killed by multiple shells smashing through everything of note and turning the cockpit into a bloody Swiss cheese.

The Beaufighter came apart, the port wing folded, and the machine fell from the sky.

Underneath, the Heinkel pilot, elated by his kill, suddenly realised his predicament and rapidly jerked his aircraft to starboard, condemning him and his radar operator to death.

Luftwaffe pilots had learned to manoeuvre slowly in such situations, the high wing loading causing stalls if changes of direction were done too quickly.

The Soviet pilot did not have the benefit of a German's hard-won experience and the stall proved fatal, the Heinkel falling uselessly away, pursued by the fiery remains of its victim.

The radar operator in the leader's Heinkel shook his set, willing it to come back to life, his swift indoctrination in its finer points having failed to cover the obvious advice of 'not to slap it hard when celebrating a victory.'

His enthusiasm had knocked a vital connection loose, and the set plainly refused to fire up.

Had it done so, he might have spotted the approaching avenger. As it was, he had just sixteen seconds before death visited itself upon him and his commander.

'Warsaw's Revenge' opened fire, Radowski having hurried to the scene from his duty station, twenty-five miles to the south, responding to the call of the hapless Beaufighter, as well as the rescue orders of his controller.

The Hispano cannon shells smashed home, causing the tail plane of the Heinkel to lose its integrity and separate, the two sections coming to earth below, exactly three kilometres apart.

It was the Polish-American's eighth kill of the new war; a war he hoped would overcome the disappointments of the previous conflict and actually liberate his mother country.

His hate was very real, and directed at any group that occupied the lands of his fathers.

Sparing a disinterested gaze at the dark ground below, he noted the funeral pyres of the aircrew that had fought in the air space above that night, and then noticed something else besides.

Talking into the intercom, he kept his eyes firmly fixed on the second area of interest.

"Arty/R mission due north," he nodded towards where he thought Eintümen was, even though his radio operator, Sergeant Devaney Callister, could not see his gesture.

The efficient operator swung into action, grabbing his paperwork.

"Radio to Captain. Mission type, over."

Now there was no light to go by, but it was definitely artillery he was looking at.

'What type?'

Unbeknown to him, his attention was focussed on the self-propelled guns of the 1814th SP Artillery Regiment.

Making a decision, he called it back to the waiting Callister.

"Make it a Charlie mission."

He got his call right, opting for the 'Charlie' strike designed for hardened artillery.

"Radio to Captain. I have the position now."

"Send it now, Dev."

The Black Widow moved leisurely to a suitable safe distance, ready to observe an Arty/R Charlie strike on the SU-122's of the 1814th.

The whole procedure went like clockwork, and the guns of the Indian Division brought destruction down upon the Soviet SP's, wrecking nearly a quarter of the unit and, most spectacularly, sending much of its separate ammunition reserve into the night sky.

The 4th Indian Division reformed its line a mile and a half closer to Unterankenreute, without the missing 2nd Gurkha's 'B' Company, ready to start the killing and the dying all over again, once the morning sun was fresh upon the field of battle.

The Supply officer of the 1814th SP Artillery reported his unexpected difficulties to his commander. Refusing to accept the unbelievable statement, the Artillery Colonel made his own visit to the Lieutenant Colonel in charge of the Corps logistics.

Anger abated, transformed into concern, and then in turn was replaced by a resurgent anger. His situation was not helped when the second in command of the 7th Guards Horse Artillery Regiment rang through and secured all the replacement ammunition he needed over the phone.

Quite clearly, the harassed supply officer could not produce 122mm shells from his ass, as the stressed man had put it. However, the system had broken down for only the second time in the Colonel's considerable army service.

At this time, there were no more shells to be had, and his unit was combat ineffective because of it.

Determining to resolve the issue at the highest level, he took his GAZ off to the Corps headquarters, finding himself in a growing queue of concerned unit commanders, all waiting to lay their issues before an incensed Corps commander.

By 0230hrs, the rising wave of complaints had made their way to the Headquarters of the Red Banner Forces, and the night duty officer placed the bundle of reports on the top of the list for the morning.

Marshal Zhukov awoke to a very different day.

There was never a night or a problem that could defeat sunrise or hope.

Bern Williams

Chapter 79 - THE INSIDER

<u>0801hrs, Saturday, 8th September 1945. Headquarters, Red Banner Forces of Europe, Kohnstein, Nordhausen, Germany.</u>

The staff officers made themselves small, as the torrent of abuse flew in all directions.

Self-preservation dictated that they should not be noticed, lest they become a target for the wrath of a man recently apprised of a huge problem.

Even Malinin, upon whom had fallen the task of briefing the commander of the Red Banner Forces, retired from the private office as swiftly as possible.

The voice behind the closed door grew in pitch and volume, the unfortunate recipient of the tirade of oaths and threats, the Deputy Supply Officer of the 3rd Red Banner Front, afforded little opportunity to explain the position.

The 3rd's Chief Supply officer was apparently away in the Motherland on a mission of great importance in the spa resort of Yessentuki, an absence that had already condemned him in Zhukov's eyes, and guaranteed his execution in the near future.

Rokossovsky had already had his phone call, and was passing on the pain, wreaking his own brand of hell on his subordinates, angered as much by the problem as the fact that he had been apprised of it by his Commander, not his own staff.

Senior heads were beginning to roll throughout Soviet occupied Europe, as the unheralded logistical problem burst from its hidden location into the bright lights of close examination.

The sound of the telephone being rammed into its cradle sounded like a gunshot.

"Malinin!"

The normally cordial and professional relationship between the two men was very obviously on hold, the incensed Zhukov in no mood for niceties.

"Right now, I want Ferovan and Atalin here, right now."

64

Malinin made his note, unsurprised that the two colonels had been summoned.

"Immediately."

Understanding that his normal procedure was not suitable for the moment, the CoS opened the door and gave a clipped order to one of his Majors.

Beckoning to three other officers, he turned back into the office.

"Done, Comrade Marshal."

Zhukov heard but chose not to answer, his mind full of the necessaries of overcoming the supply issue.

"I want an immediate message to all senior commanders, requiring a full inventory of supplies, discrepancies against normal levels, consumption rates, replacement rates, and losses due to enemy action."

One of the officers, a young and very keen colonel was given the nod.

"I want the production and transportation reports from our Theatre Supply command".

Zhukov looked down at his list and saw the error, quickly scratching through one thing and scribbling something else.

"I have relieved the Theatre Supply Officer and he's on his way here to account for this fuck up."

Malinin made his own note.

"His deputy's in charge for now. Ferovan and Atalin will go to the Headquarters and report back to me just exactly what piggery has been taking place here. Organise the usual travel and authorisation documents for my signature."

Malinin cued a second officer who left with his urgent task.

"I want the latest GRU and NKVD transportation reports today. I want the latest GRU and NKVD reports on partisan attacks today. I want the latest GRU, NKVD, and Air Force reports on the effectiveness of the enemy air attacks on our logistical chain, here, today."

Uncharacteristically, Zhukov stabbed a finger at his CoS and friend.

"Get them here and get them analyzed, today."

The final officer, an overawed Captain, disappeared, trying hard to work out how he was to start the process his Marshal had ordered.

Zhukov fell back into his chair, his fury subsiding now that he had taken positive steps to discover what had happened.

He realised he had taken it out on his man.

Indicating the other chair, he encouraged Malinin to sit down.

"I'm sorry, Mikhail."

Malinin accepted the unexpected olive branch with good grace, understanding the new pressures on Zhukov.

Zhukov passed him the list he had been working on.

The CoS cast an eye over it, seeing the names of walking dead men upon it, some of whom were very good men indeed.

"Keep that safe until things are clear, Comrade."

Malinin nodded, happy that his commander was not acting so precipitously as to execute some seriously competent officers for guilt by association.

"Before today is done, I want to know the full position so that I can go to the GKO and offer up the correct heads, as well as correct our plans to cover any problems."

A knock on the door brought a calmer response from Zhukov, his face almost smiling as the tea was placed on the side table, the young orderly retreating at speed.

Malinin poured.

Holding their hot cups, both senior men pondered the problem in silence.

Taking a cultured sip from his vessel, Zhukov shook his head, expressing silent horror at the thought suddenly filling his mind.

"Mikhail, I want to know if we have been deliberately misled by our NKVD colleagues."

Malinin nodded his understanding of the delicacy of that order.

"Contact Alpine, Southern, and Balkan Fronts. Get me some shells moving in from them immediately."

That went into the notebook.

"Some figures on internal stocks such as Iran units, or anything that can be obtained from our Eastern forces, or our

66

Socialist brother Tito, although the time to transport them here may be a problem."

As did that.

"Most importantly, I need to know if we are sitting on a disaster here!"

That possibility had been only too apparent from the moment that the reports of a lack of 122mm ammunition made themselves so spectacularly known within 3rd Red Banner Front, and subsequent enquiries revealed a similar problem in its infancy within 1st Baltic.

"I intend to fly to Moscow on Tuesday, and I want to have answers for the General Secretary," the Marshal's face darkening slightly as he pondered the meeting ahead, "And some questions for our Comrade, Marshal Beria."

0917hrs, Saturday, 8th September 1945. North West Atlantic, 20 miles south of Cape Sable Island, Nova Scotia.

To the British and Canadians it was a Canso A. To the rest of the allies, and the Russians too, for that matter, it was a Catalina PBY flying boat. Built under licence, the Canso looked precisely like her American parent and was equally businesslike.

G for George of 162 Squadron RAF was on a rescue mission, as were a number of her sisters.

The weather was unfavourable, low cloud and squally showers, all driven along by high winds that were whipping the sea into white-tipped savagery.

None the less, G for George's twin Wasp engines drove her forward, fighting the resistance, keeping her at a steady 140 mph, eight hundred feet above the roiling water below.

As yet, there was no sign of the missing blimp, or her crew.

Radar had steered them onto a large contact, too large to be wreckage from the blimp.

Hawkins, the radio operator, reported to the pilot, presently circling the neutral vessel below.

"Skipper, Sparks. She's Swedish. Called Golden Quest. They are having some engine difficulties and are heading north to take shelter in the lee of one of the islands while they sort it out."

"Roger Sparks. Did you inform them?"

A short pause, either because the man had to put his mask back on, or because he was annoyed that his pilot felt he should ask. Or both.

"Yes, Skipper. He's seen nothing, but he has his own problems in any case. If he sees anything he'll sing out, over."

Flying Officer Joy didn't care for the man, recently arrived from training school to fill the place of his former radio operator, a competent man who had succumbed to some sort of heart problem and been taken off Ops.

"Skipper, Navigator, time to commence turn to port for next leg."

"Roger Navigator."

The Canso gently dropped its left wing and eased round ninety degrees to port, almost mirroring the intended course of the Swedish vessel.

The aircraft approached Blanche Island.

"Starboard Waist, Skipper. On the surface at two o'clock low. Huge slick and wreckage."

All eyes that had a chance to look strained but there was no need. The oily mark was immense.

"Pilot to crew. Going down for a closer look. Stay alert."

Turning to port, the Canso circled and bled of some height, coming back in over the site at two hundred feet.

"Anyone see anything other than rag and oil?"

There was no reply of note.

The aircraft turned again but this time to starboard, prescribing a figure of eight over the site of something that they suspected was the grave of a submarine.

Joy gave voice to his feelings.

"Pilot to crew. I believe that slick is confirmation that the Blimp killed the sub it was attacking. Anyone disagree?"

The crew, except Hawkins, were all experienced men who had their own U-Boat kill under their belts.

No one challenged Joy, and he determined to say as much in his report.

In any case, Hawkins was distracted by something else entirely.

"Skipper, Sparks. I've a radar reading here, heading 027. Picking up weak IFF, over."

Allied aircraft all carried 'Identification Friend or Foe' transponders that marked them as friendly when 'painted' by their own side's radar.

Joy acted immediately and the starboard wing dropped, as the Canso altered course to fly down the line of the signal.

"Pilot to navigator, now flying 027."

"Skipper, it's gone, over."

"Then find it man! I shall circle. Where are we, Nav?"

Squinting at the map, Flying Officer Parkinson thumbed his mike.

"Skipper, directly below us is Cape Negro Island and…"

"Got it, Skipper. It's back, same heading 027."

"Roger Sparks."

Joy's mind was already working the problem, and he thought he had the solution, especially when Hawkins lost the signal once more.

"Pilot to crew. I think it's on the island. Low sweep, keep your eyes skinned starboard side."

The Canso came slowly over the island, running south to north.

There were no sightings of anything of note, but, as per the standing instructions, the starboard waist gunner shot some film for development later.

"Skipper, Sparks. Signal has disappeared over."

On the island, the transponder, stimulated to reply by the radar signal, drained the last of the residual power and remained silent, the pod and envelope hidden under hastily cut greenery.

Joy made a decision.

'No wreckage of note, and if the blimp had come down on the island the site would be apparent. Must have been a phantom.'

"Pilot to crew, Log it, radio it in, but we continue with sweep. Navigator, give me a course, over."

On the ground, many eyes watched the large flying boat as she swept over the island, obviously searching for their now dead comrades.

In the small but functional sick bay, Sveinsvold heard the sounds of his expected rescue slowly fade into the distance, as G for George resumed her search elsewhere.

69

Smiling back at the rough but caring Russian sailor who was rebandaging his wound, he considered his options, which didn't take long.

At 1707hrs, a second Canso flying boat made a trip over Cape Negro Island, failing to locate any IFF transmission whatsoever.

Having fulfilled that part of its mission, N for November flew off to its allocated search area, already widening as the hunt for the USN blimp went on.

The presence of the previously reported Swedish steamship was recorded in the flight log.

2157hrs, Saturday, 8th September 1945. North West Atlantic, 20 miles south of Cape Sable Island, Nova Scotia.

Pulling smartly away from the small pier, the rowing boat headed for the steep sides of the merchant vessel.

Little of note was aboard for the return journey, the flow of stores and men being nearly all one-way.

Sveinsvold's wounded leg meant that he could not climb, but the sailors had swung out a rig, and he was swiftly hoisted aboard.

The second man took longer, requiring more careful handling as he was seriously wounded, having tripped and fallen onto sharp rusting machinery on the small dock, three days beforehand.

The delirious Soviet marine was carefully swung aboard and quickly spirited away to the ship's extensive medical facility.

On the island, the Russian Orthodox cross around Sveinsvold's neck had attracted some attention, especially as communism and religion were bad bedfellows.

As soon as he was swung aboard one of the Scandinavian crewmembers, all good communists, spotted the Norse amulet that shared his throat with the cross, the latter a gift from his good friend Vassily, in happier times.

Sveinsvold was not so good in Swedish, so he switched to Norwegian, the two men finally settling on Russian as a common language.

The old Swede helped the wounded 'submariner' below, as the 'Golden Quest' prepared for night to fully descend, before supplying the submarines that were waiting to surface with torpedoes

Her orders had also been changed, and fuel was also to be supplied, to cover the loss of the milchcow.

By morning, the ship was already fifty miles south south west of Cape Negro, an elektroboote in close, but concealed, company.

*We fight to great disadvantage when we fight with those who
have nothing to lose.*

Francesco Guicciardini

Chapter 80 - THE WEREWOLVES

1135hrs, Tuesday 11th September 1945, Skies over Hesse,
Germany.

Whilst the RAF's Bomber Command was licking its
considerable wounds, it fell to the USAAF performing daylight
missions to take the fight deep into Soviet controlled territory.

Reconnaissance missions were increasingly bearing
fruit, as the day skies started to become more friendly, or more
accurately, less murderous.

Today's target had been acquired by a Mosquito PR34
of the RAF's 540 Photo-Reconnaissance Squadron. The crew had
decided to take some extra frames after attracting a few unwanted
shots from a large wood, one mile north of Wolfhagen.

Excellent as the Soviet were with their camouflage, the
young WAAF's at 'Interpretation' quickly realised that not all
was as it seemed, and after more work they had identified four
hidden railway spurs from the main line which ran northwards,
adjacent to the western edge of the woods.

That the Soviets bothered to conceal them was proof
enough of their worthiness for further attention, and the belief
that it was likely a clandestine supply dump encouraged a prompt
visit.

Although the hilly wooded area would be less than ideal
for that purpose, photo interpreters had quickly learned that the
Soviet Army did things differently, and was less conventional
than their former opponents.

Therefore, the area of four square miles received the
bomb loads of three hundred and twenty-seven heavy bombers,
mostly B24 Liberators.

Soviet air defence scrambled numerous air regiments,
again an indication that they valued the target.

Casualties amongst the fighters of both sides were murderous, but the Mustangs and Spitfires kept the Soviets at bay, only one B24 lost to interception.

The bravery of the fighter pilots could not prevent the anti-aircraft guns from doing their work, and a score of bombers fell to high-altitude AA guns, mostly those liberated from their former German owners.

The wood was incinerated.

1801hrs, Saturday, 8th September 1945. Headquarters, Red Banner Forces of Europe, Kohnstein, Nordhausen, Germany.

Zhukov had been a different man ever since he had returned from Moscow on the Thursday night; late, tired and extremely frustrated.

A briefing from Nazarbayeva had done nothing to ease his growing anger at what seemed to be happening behind the lines, an area he had entrusted to others.

The GKO, more importantly Beria, had been prepared and had the answers to all his questions, something he had discussed with Malinin in the privacy of his office later.

They had concluded that one or all of the typists were NKVD spies, and promised to act accordingly in future.

The meat of the matter was simple.

Production was apparently at full tilt but there were difficulties with the increased distances involved in transporting the consumables of war. The reasons were as far apart as the gauge change in railways, from the Soviet Union's narrow gauge to European wider gauge, to the growing and increasingly successful attacks by partisans and cut-off allied military units.

General agreement was reached on how to address the matters, actions ranging from increased manpower for security or rail works, through to the normal Stalinist solutions of threats and executions.

The reports Zhukov had requested, prior to his Moscow flight, indicated a number of interesting things.

The Soviet Commander was already aware that consumption of everything from bullets to bridges was far higher than had been allowed for, and that casualties amongst his frontline troops were extreme.

73

That was balanced by a similar bloodletting inflicted upon the Western Allies.

It was the combination of production and transportation figures that troubled him the most, as the two figures seemed to marry up perfectly but not translate into adequate stocks where they were most needed; with the Red Army in the field.

Zhukov drank his tea quietly whilst he waited for Malinin to examine the NKVD figures he had brought back with him, setting them against the figures received from the Fronts.

The CoS leant back in his chair, wiping his face with his left hand, as if clearing his mind for what he was about to say.

"And these figures are the NKVD's official submission, Comrade Marshal?"

Replacing his cup in the matching saucer, the bald-headed commander of the Red Army responded with a shrug, heavy with his belief in the possibility that all was not how it seemed.

Seeing Malinin's furrowed brow, Zhukov added the same codicil he had received from Beria.

"Our Chekist comrades acknowledge a possibility of error up to 2% either way."

Malinin grunted as he brought his own cup to eager lips, sipped, and summarised some more.

"What are admitted in this document are considerable losses in the rear zone, some through air attack, some through partisan attack, and some through accident alone."

Malinin stood, wiping his wet lips with a handkerchief, moving to look at the map on the wall, not one of the intended advances into Western Europe, but one showing the heart of the USSR, and the lands westwards to Germany.

"Losses and expenditure, once the manpower and supplies are in the forward frontal zones, are heavy, this we know. And we have reliable reports to confirm losses well in excess of what we allowed."

Neither man needed to remind the other that new allowances were being complied, so that supply and manpower levels could be maintained.

'Provided...'

"Comrade Marshal, these figures simply do not add up to me."

It was nice to hear that another senior man also felt the wool was being pulled over the Army's eyes.

Malinin continued, finger quickly tapping out an indistinct rhythm on the map, marking the major manufacturing zones of the USSR.

"If the production figures are how they are stated, and traditionally, production figures are extremely reliable," Zhukov conceded that with a brusque nod, "Then what is being produced enters the transport system in the Rodina and only part of it comes out at our end."

His finger made a single sound as it contacted with the geographic representation of Germany.

"A part which, at first look, would seem to be about a quarter less than it should be."

The commander in chief took up the baton.

"With losses and expenditures way over expectations, and supplies less than anticipated, we have a serious problem, which is exactly what I told the General Secretary yesterday."

Part of Malinin marvelled that Zhukov was still here, given Stalin's propensity for head rolling.

"And how did the General-Secretary decide to resolve the issues."

Zhukov smiled at his CoS, understanding that the statement was couched in such delicate terms, just in case there was a recording in progress.

"The usual, as I have already said, plus he will be ordering some air assets from other areas, including the Far East, to increase our own ability to destroy Allied assets."

Both men knew that such an order would send many a mother's son to his early death, so dangerous was any excursion behind enemy lines at the moment.

"The Navy has been ordered to escalate its submarine attacks as much as possible, obviously making transports a priority to stifle supply."

"I'm sure the Navy will enjoy that."

The two shared a professional grin that was devoid of real humour, in the knowledge that the upped tempo would result in ships being lost and more men would die.

Pointing at the chair, indicating Malinin should resume his seat, Zhukov's voice dropped to a barely audible level.

"I cannot rely on what I am being told by Moscow, not at this time. I need to find out the truth."

A silent message passed between the two men, ending with both nodding as the senior man picked up the telephone.

"Polkovnik General Pekunin please."

Zhukov had time to finish his drink before the voice of the GRU commander resonated in his ear.

"Ah yes, and good day to you too, Comrade Polkovnik General. Yes, you may be of service, or rather, we both know someone who can."

2307hrs, Saturday, 8th September 1945, One kilometre south-west of Pörnbach, Germany.

The leader snorted quietly, soft enough to neither trouble any of the sleeping men some thirty metres to his front, nor for the sound to reach the ears of the handful of men patrolling the makeshift camp.

His men, well schooled in the arts of killing, watched as he made his hand signals, dispatching silent killers into the darkness, compromised only by the light of the moon and stars, and the small glow of a light in the single tent at the centre of the clearing.

Behind him, as well as to either side, MG42's silently waited, ready to turn the woods into a cemetery at a moment's notice.

Behind him were a handpicked group, twenty men who would be able to undertake the grisly work he had set aside for them, provided the first part went well.

That first part was in process, his experienced eye seeing the subtle change in shadows as his killers drew closer to the dead men walking.

Almost imperceptibly, the darkness around one sentry grew darker and the man disappeared for a second, seemingly reappearing, only slightly taller and thinner, and carrying a PPSh rather than the Mosin rifle he had been idly cradling a moment beforehand.

The nearest sentry decided to relieve himself, settling to unzip his fly at the moment that a dirty hand clapped itself hard to his mouth, pulling his head back, his surprise swiftly overtaken by the momentary pain of a blade severing everything of value in his neck.

Another sentry, spooked by something he couldn't exactly understand, dropped to one knee, looking back across the clearing.

As he watched his two other comrades, apparently patrolling without a care, he relaxed, deciding to drop into the bushes to sample one of the American cigarettes he had taken from the bloated corpse he had found outside of Regensburg, the night before.

His lighter flared, granting him flame for his cigarette and light to see the man who killed him.

The impact knocked the cigarette from his grasp and he fell to the ground, the full weight of his attacker on top of him.

Winded and unable to speak, he tried to stand but the weight increased, and a hand held his mouth tight as he struggled face down in the leaves of the newly arrived autumn.

The Werewolf Kommando rammed his pointed knife into the base of the Russian's skull, severing the spinal column.

SS-Hauptsturmfuhrer Lenz saw the last sentry go down and gestured his assault group forward, the score of killers swiftly passing by, the occasional muffled sound marking their progress until they halted, commencing the grisly work of the night.

SS-Kommando Lenz worked its way through the camp, dispatching the NKVD troopers of the 36th NKVD Convoy Forces Security Division silently and swiftly, employing blades for the most part.

Two of the men stood with silenced pistols, ready should a man awaken prematurely.

They were not needed.

The group spread through the camp, until only the tent had been left untouched, and fifty-seven young men had been brutally slain.

Artur Lenz strolled forward, his body once more accustomed to the rigours of war after weeks on the move avoiding Soviet security forces. Tonight he was making a statement, destroying one such force before swiftly relocating to another area.

There was also something he wanted to know.

As he assembled his men in the clearing, the MG42 teams relocated, providing external security now, the remainder of the Kommando adding to the ring around the camp, now facing outwards and ready for all comers.

Still no verbal commands had been issued; such was the expertise that SS-Kommando Lenz had developed since the start of the new war.

Readying his ST44, Lenz nodded at one of his men who spoke in casual Russian.

"Tovarich Kapitan, a word please."

The sound of movement inside indicated that the words had been received and the NKVD officer emerged sleepily, suddenly becoming wide-awake when he saw the muzzle of Lenz's assault rifle aimed at his chest.

Behind him came the unit's senior NCO, his PPSh useless in his hands, resistance so clearly futile.

Disarmed, the two men were moved into the centre of the clearing, more so that they could examine the work of the Kommando than for any other reason.

The Russian speaker set about his task, questions fired rapidly at the officer, a proud and haughty man, who remained silent, his contempt, and hatred plain for all to see.

After a third bout of unanswered questions, Lenz held up his hand.

The two NKVD soldiers stared at it, appreciating it had some significance well beyond the silencing of the interrogator.

The hand dropped and four men stood forward, grabbing the NCO, and dragging him towards one of the larger trees.

Lenz did not watch them; he watched the officer, the man's eyes changing, at first questioning and inquiring as he watched his Sergeant dragged away, then filled with fear, as he understood what was to come.

Most of Lenz's assassination party was plundering the dead for booty, cigarettes, and alcohol being the most prized.

The NKVD officer's attention moved to one group, the bodies of his dead men being tossed around like rag dolls as the commandos went in search of their trophies.

His attention refocused as the NCO groaned, his mouth full of oily cloth rammed home by unfeeling hands.

Lenz watched as the man's face went from fear to outrage to full blown horror in a microsecond.

The scream of pain was choked by the cloth.

The Serzhant was now suspended above the ground, his feet desperately trying to broach the gap from his boots to the earth below, the few inches being as good as a mile for a man who was being held up by knives rammed through his shoulders.

The first time that Lenz and his men had crucified a prisoner, they had made mistakes. Now, they ensured the flat of the blade was uppermost, supporting, rather than cutting.

The entry area was sufficiently low enough not to rip through the flesh, yet high enough to ensure no fatal wound was inflicted.

Extending the moaning man's arms, four more blades were rammed home, again supporting the weight.

Even through the rag, the man's agony could be heard.

Lenz watched the enemy officer's reaction.

'Two more will do it.'

He hadn't been wrong so far, but he was this time. The NKVD Captain did not crack as another two long blades were hammered into the sergeant's thighs, pinning him further against the cold trunk.

Nodding at his man, Lenz listened as the interrogation continued, the Russian clearly not talking despite ordeal of his soldier.

Those Kommandos at the tree waited for further instructions, receiving the signal from Lenz.

Bending the legs, slicing more flesh as the blade in the thigh resisted the movement, two of them rammed blades through feet held flat to the bark.

The muffled screams became animal-like, the extremes of pain being realised by the unfortunate man.

'Tough bastard.'

Lenz wondered for a moment which of the two men he was referring to.

Over at the tree, the Kommando torturers reasoned that they would soon need to be creative, as this was as far as they had gone previously.

The NKVD officer stood immobile, tears running down his face, his silence condemning his NCO to a painful death.

A simple nod from the Kommando leader followed, and the Russian closed his eyes, the increased sounds of extremis the only link to the brave man he was condemning by his silence.

The sound changed, an almost high-pitched whimpering, rhythmical in its nature, as a blade worked steadily and carefully.

Something struck the Soviet officer on the chest, falling to the ground, via his right toecap.

He opened his eyes.

Even in the low light, the sight of his NCO's testicles and scrotum were unmistakable.

He broke.

The answers quickly flowed, each one punctuated by a plea for mercy, a swift end to the tortured man's suffering.

Once Lenz had what he needed release was granted, a silenced pistol removing the temple of the crucified man.

Pointing at the broken NKVD officer, Lenz issued his last orders.

"Bind that piece of shit. We will put him with the others. Jensen, he is yours. Any trouble..." the Hauptsturmfuhrer drew a finger across his throat, ensuring that the Russian saw the universal sign and understood.

Turning away, he nodded to one of his NCO's.

"Leave our calling card, Weiss."

The young NCO extracted his Hitler Youth dagger and cut away at the crucified man's shirt, working quickly on the bare flesh below.

Watching the youth at work, Lenz lit a cigarette from a pack given to him.

"American," he said to no one in particular, as he drew the smoke deeply into greedy lungs.

Checking the clearing, and satisfying himself that all was in order, he gave the order to move.

"Emmering," the Senior NCO immediately attentive, "Pick up the other group, then north-west towards Neuburg."

The Kommando moved off, Lenz considering the recently gained information. Lenz was a cautious man, and had mentioned Neuburg openly, just in case.

As was their normal practice, two of his best men remained to, as Lenz called it, 'dress' the casualties for those who found them later.

Once they had all joined up with the rest of the Kommando, Emmering would steer them towards their real target, the newly formed Soviet supply base near Ingolstadt.

The reason that the United States Navy does so well in wartime, is that war is chaos, and the Americans practice chaos on a daily basis.

Karl Donitz

Chapter 81 - THE SWEDE

<u>1247hrs, Sunday, 9th September 1945, one kilometre south-west of Pörnbach, Germany.</u>

Using her binoculars, Captain Larisa Sverova surveyed the scene, trying hard not to focus on the disgusting sight that was screaming for her attention.

Her unit of twenty-one replacement mortar personnel had been moving up to the front, when their aged GAZ lorry had broken down.

Leaving the cursing driver to do his best, she and a few of her unit decided to explore the surrounding woods.

The discovery of a brand new Studebaker down a track was a matter of celebration, until one of her young girls spotted a pair of feet beside it, the blood purple and dried upon the exposed flesh.

Harrying the inexperienced women into some sort of organised group, Sverova moved forward carefully, her only combat-seasoned NCO moving amongst the female soldiers, advising here, pointing there.

As she approached the clearing, Sverova silently ordered the group to stay put, and beckoned her NCO forward.

It was then that she first saw the horrors of the new war up close.

Senior Sergeant Ponichenkarova silently dropped beside her officer, the PPD in her hands ready for action at a moment's notice.

"Govno!"

The almost male voice of the NCO spoke that which her inner voices screamed.

She had also seen the awful apparition that stood out from the slaughter.

81

Sverova's words interrupted Ponichenkarova's train of thought, bringing her attention back to the business in hand.

"I count at least thirty men here, Dina. NKVD uniforms."

A low-key 'uh-huh' confirmed her NCO's agreement.

"Pick two and move up to the right, there," Sverova indicated a denser patch of undergrowth, "Send me two, and I will work my way round to the tree," she had no need to say which one.

Checking around the position they were concealed in, it seemed fit for purpose.

"Get the rest of them lined up here. Put Astafieva in charge, with orders to cover us"

Sverova paused, looking around her.

"But leave two on each of the flanks for security."

This time Ponichenkarova managed a grunt by way of agreement, and the solid framed NCO was off, harrying the group behind into some sort of order.

Quickly, the women sorted themselves out. Astafieva, quietly efficient, organised her covering force and set the pairs on each side in position.

The two small flank groups moved off.

Ponichenkarova was first to her appointed spot, carefully examining the scene in front of her, the evidence of quiet massacre all too plain to her eyes.

Beyond the clearing, the horrified NCO could see the officer and her two soldiers moving up, approaching that unspeakably bloody something hanging from the tree directly opposite them.

Sverova nodded, a silent message across the divide, and both parties moved up and into the camp, picking their way over the horrors.

Both NCO and officer silently extended arms, directing their soldiers to move further apart.

The two met in the middle of the clearing, not even the tweet of a bird to break the tension.

"Killed while they slept, Dina, all except that one."

As if by common assent, they both turned to face the body that had been pinned to the tree with knives, the bloody swastika carved into the torso appearing the least of the apparent horrors.

82

"Werewolves."

Not a question, just a statement.

Sverova slipped her Tokarev pistol back into her holster.

An agreed hand signal summoned Astafieva's group.

"Check their lorry over. If it's fine, we will load the bodies aboard and take them to the nearest checkpoint."

The NCO moved off to inspect the lorry, the cover force emerging from the woods to start the grisly task of recovering the dead.

It took Ponichenkarova a few seconds to find the grenade booby-traps on the vehicle, and less than a minute to make them safe. She warned her soldiers to be vigilant, something that Sverova was also doing back at the clearing.

"Be careful, Comrades. Who knows what the SS bastards have left behind?"

Sverova and two of the older women removed the tortured man from the tree, placing him gently upon a blanket and rolling him up, as they would swaddle a baby.

The three of them carried the burden, moving gingerly across the clearing as others, similarly wrapped, started their own journey to the waiting Studebaker.

Most of the weapons had been damaged, the rifles and sub-machine guns bent, probably by smashing the metal against a tree trunk.

One PPSh sat propped against a pack, inviting attention.

"No, Olga!"

The female soldier who had been looking carefully at the vignette, nodded without moving her body, responding instantly to the voice of command, but keeping her eyes focussed on the threat.

Sverova knelt down gingerly and swept away the leaves with care, seeking the telltale signs of interference and hidden death.

There were none.

Both she and the soldier, Olga Matalinova, breathed out with relief.

The unit's youngest soldier was crying openly, her ginger hair matted with blood, saying a forbidden prayer over the men she was tending.

Her eyes fell on the German helmet and she snapped, a wail of anger escaping her lips.

Sverova screamed.

"NO!"

She lashed out viciously with her boot, sending the object of her hatred flying.

The moment the helmet moved, it activated a simple tilt switch, igniting a detonator.

Two-thirds of a second later the zinc-encased charge exploded.

A loud bang mixed with the high-pitched screams of the horribly injured.

Ponichenkarova rushed back to the clearing.

The pretty ginger girl was no longer intact, the pieces of her svelte body now spread around the clearing.

Other women soldiers were also amongst the dead, many dismembered and spread to the four corners of the open ground, the odd portion hanging from a branch like a macabre Christmas decoration. There were a handful of survivors, some hideously injured and yet still clinging to life.

Additional horrors had been wrought on the already dead bodies of the NKVD soldiers.

Sverova was propped against the torso of an NKVD soldier, looking across the clearing, the smoke of the explosion stinging her eyes and robbing her of her final clear memories.

She was silent, unable to speak, her lower body torn away from the hips down, her upper body naked and unblemished, save for some splashes of blood and other fluids from the unfortunate Matalinova.

The horrified NCO made it to her side in five huge steps. Sverova's destroyed body failed her before the third step was complete.

SS Werewolf Kommando Lenz had 'dressed' the site with a standard three-kilo explosive charge, and it had done its work well, twelve of the women soldiers joining their NKVD comrades in the after-life.

1328hrs Monday, 10th September 1945, Two miles south-west of Mother Owen's Rocks, Gulf of Maine.

The periscope hissed as it slid back up, breaking the surface above for the final time before the orders were given.

"Fire one."

A stopwatch clicked, four seconds passed.

"Fire two."

Both releases accompanied by the sounds of torpedoes in the water.

"Starboard twenty, both engines make revolutions for six knots."

The Elektroboote, B27, had found a fast mover, a single merchant vessel intent on crossing the Atlantic alone, relying on her speed to keep her safe.

The rumble of an explosion through the water, followed shortly by another, marked the folly of the attempt for the American steamship.

Manoeuvring to get away from the firing position, B27 relocated to the east of the sinking, the submarine's detection apparatus indicating that no allied vessels were in the vicinity.

The Captain raised the scope once more, focussing in the area the vessel went down, its bulkheads noisily surrendering to the inrush of water, tasting its final gasp of air just six minutes after being struck by the last torpedo.

As the commander quickly swivelled his periscope, he saw the lifeboats, two of them filled to the brim with survivors.

The flash of gold braid caught his eye, and he upped the lens setting immediately.

"What have we here, Comrades? Senior military personnel on the lifeboat ahead of us."

A moment's thought.

The First officer waited expectantly.

"Threats?"

Confirming with the sonar crew, he turned back to the commander.

"None detected, Comrade Kapitan."

As was his habit in times of deep thought, the Captain pinched at his nose, squeezing it to stimulate the process of decision-making.

"We will surface, and quickly, Gun crews on deck as soon as we are in air. Deck party armed. I intend to offer assistance to the senior military survivors."

A questioning look from the second in command was understood, and his concerns addressed.

"We will be up and gone before they have a chance to organise a search, even if she did get off a signal. Now, let us be quick, Leytenant."

The First Officer turned to organise the crew.

"Chief, I want you in your diving kit, just in case they lose something overboard, like a briefcase."

The ship's senior rating understood, acknowledged the order, and moved away quickly to get ready.

Eight minutes later, the ex-German elektroboote B-27 rose to the surface, thirty yards from the nearest lifeboat.

1337hrs, Monday, 10th September 1945, airborne over the Gulf of Maine.

"Enemy submarine, on the surface, bearing 035."

"Action stations, standby for bombing attack."

Other voices confirmed that it was one of the new submarines, which were unmistakeable and could not be confused with any Allied vessels.

New boy Hawkins had been in the cockpit passing out coffee, and it had been he that had spotted the sleek shape.

It was also he that spotted the lifeboats.

"No skipper, you can't attack. There are survivors there, in boats. Could be the Dawes Castle people."

Joy looked at the horrified man.

Momentarily confused, he alternated between examining the U-Boat and his crewmate.

With eyes suddenly heavy with duty and the responsibility of his decision, he opened his mike, directing his gaze at Hawkins.

"Stand by to attack," he said to the crew, seemingly cold and businesslike.

"To your station, Bob," was more softly spoken to the new airman.

The pain distorted the wireless operators face.

"You can't, you simply can't. Those are our people."

"To your station, Flight Sergeant! Send a contact report. Navigator, pass on the position."

The inexperienced man turned away, leaving Joy to line up the Canso.

86

Behind him, the sounds of argument between Hawkins and Parkinson grew in volume and ferocity.

The delay caused by Hawkins' outburst had caused the Canso to miss its prime approach, something that would guarantee Hawkins a court-martial once the aircraft returned to base.

The submarine had spotted them, and multi-coloured tracers leapt from her conning tower, indicative that the vessel intended to fight rather than dive.

'Perhaps they think the lifeboats are a shield?'

'Perhaps they should be!'

'That fucking sub could kill hundreds, no, thousands!'

'And you will kill how many of our own eh?'

The part of his mind that was screaming its objections was close to achieving supremacy, the thought of killing his own so abhorrent to the pilot.

Behind him, the fuselage had fallen quiet.

Parkinson appeared silently by his side, more stoney faced than usual.

"Is Bob alright, Nelly?"

Lionel Parkinson spoke in a matter of fact way.

"Had to clock him one, Skipper."

No more explanation was required.

Placing his hand on the pilot's shoulder, the navigator spoke softly, and with feeling.

"It's a shitty deal, Skipper, so let's get it done, or that bastard will sink more of our ships. I sent the contact message."

The Nav was gone before Joy could react, but his message of support remained, clear, and unequivocal.

The screaming in his brain subsided and the professional aviator was dominant once more.

'Thanks, Nelly.'

Some shells clipped the Canso, but nothing vital was hit, the flying boat inexorably bearing down on its prey.

A part of Joy spotted the frantic attempts by the boats, wasted effort to put life-saving yards between them and the bombs to come.

The Canso lifted, its full load dropped in a 'total release' attack.

Six Mark IX Depth Charges, with fuses set for twenty-two feet, left the aircraft and dropped inexorably towards B-27.

None struck her directly, but all were in the sea within fifteen yards of her, the right-hand charge actually clipped the nearest lifeboat on its way down to twenty-two feet.

Two charges continued to the bottom, never to explode.

Another faulty fuse activated two hundred feet down.

Three did the job they had been asked to do, propelling the elektroboote out of the water as they exploded either side of her.

The survivors in the lifeboats died instantly, the horrified waist gunners seeing bodies, and parts of bodies, propelled many feet into the air on a rising crest of white water.

B-27 slipped beneath the water, its integrity compromised, the surviving crew stunned and in shock.

In the sub's control room, the Commander tried to save his battered ship, but failed, the leak reports too numerous to deal with, overwhelming him.

B-27 struck the bottom, breaking into three pieces, two containing only the drowned.

The third compartment, the main control room, remained watertight. It contained men for whom there was no hope of salvation, and whose only expectation was a drawn out death in the dark.

Parkinson took over from the unconscious Hawkins, relaying news of their success to base, the first known sinking of one of the Russian Elektrobootes.

G for George was holed forward, and Joy decided to beach the aircraft, which was done skilfully.

In celebratory mood, the whole base lined the slipway as the tender brought the crew ashore, but the cheers turned to heavy silence when the red eyes and tear marked faces became apparent.

Joy saluted the base commander and reported, evenly and accurately, those gathered around all silent and straining to hear his words.

As the true horror of their mission was revealed, many turned away, appalled and ashamed, all thankful that it had not fallen to them to do the deed.

The base doctor and padre moved forward, their work about to begin.

<u>1645hrs, Wednesday, 12th September 1945, Mälsåker Castle, Strängnäs, Sweden.</u>

The first leg of the journey had been overt, a routine flight from France to London, the passengers dismounting to go to their various meetings in West End hotels.

The C-47 took to the air once its tanks were topped off, one of many transport aircraft that came and went in the course of a normal day.

Thirty-two uniforms had been observed getting onto the aircraft. The resident communist spy, a medium ranking French police officer, lazily counted them onboard, all from the comfort of his office. If his report was ever compared to that of a similar individual based at RAF Northolt, the numbers would have tallied.

None the less, the C-47 was still able to disgorge two more uniformed figures when it next set down, in bright sunshine, at the RAF Coastal Command base at Banff, Scotland.

Waiting there was a Mosquito Mark VI, in the markings of 235 Squadron RAF. However, Z for Zulu was no ordinary bird, her insides altered to take two passengers and the extra fuel load for long VIP journeys.

Within ten minutes of their arrival, the two officers had changed uniforms and were airborne for the next stop of their complicated journey.

Oslo, murky in a stormy afternoon, offered no respite, as the two were swiftly but quietly driven south, to meet up with their final aircraft of the day, a Northrop N-3PB of the Royal Norwegian Air Force.

The small floatplane launched itself eastwards, crossing into Swedish air space by prior agreement, and coming down to gently kiss the water of Lake Mälaren, before taxiing to the simple pier.

The two men were met informally, and took the brief walk up to the imposing baroque structure that was Mälsåker Castle.

Until recently, it had been leased to the Norwegians, and there were still some Norwegians present, hence the additional subterfuge of the marked aircraft and the uniforms both men had worn since Banff.

However, new ownership had made its mark, and the small party was challenged three times on the short walk to Swedish Military Intelligence's latest acquisition.

Waiting for them was a man who was, it was said, a myth; no more than a figment of overactive imaginations.

When his adversary was the German, Gehlen, Canaris, and the like would have given an arm to know what he looked like.

Colonel Per Törget was indescribably ordinary and inoffensive looking, which made him truly a dangerous adversary.

Törget was introduced to the other officer by the American. Shaking hands with the new arrivals and ushering them to comfortable seats, he waited expectantly to find out what exactly had brought the head of OSS so far so quickly, and, more importantly, so secretly.

A Swedish army orderly distributed drinks, giving Törget time to assess the German officer, unknown until two hours beforehand, when a personal dossier had been passed to him, with the man's exemplary service record plain for all to see.

'Exemplary if you were a Nazi that is,' had been his only private thought, for Törget was all business.

Rossiter opened his briefcase and passed over a simple folder, unblemished externally, save for the word 'Sycamore' in bold print.

Trannel, commander of the Luftwaffe's 40th Transportstaffel, was taken aback.

The contents of the 'Operation Sycamore' folder were known to him, and he was horrified that the entire plan was now in the possession of an unknown entity.

Colonel Törget took his time reading the file, asking a clarifying question here and there, until placing the file on the heavy pine table, left open at a schematic that he would revisit shortly.

"So, Sam. You need us to permit this purely on travel distance grounds?"

"No, but we are allowing for any possible enemy presence that could intercept the operation if it was run from Denmark."

Trannel shifted slightly, betraying his discomfort.

Yes, there were the fuel issues, but distance also greatly concerned him, despite the stated range of his aircraft.

Switching to perfect German, not textbook, but as it would have been spoken in a bar in Hamburg, Törget tackled the Luftwaffe officer, presently dressed as a Major in the Norwegian Air Force.

"You think otherwise, Herr Oberst? Perhaps you think that distance is also an issue?"

Trannel nodded, whilst Rossiter noted that the Swede had done his homework.

"Yes, Sir. We have been trying to work extra fuel aboard the aircraft, but we may have additional weight on the return journey. The situation is complicated by unknowns."

Looking at Rossiter, he received an indication to proceed.

"The 'objects' we are collecting," he employed the terminology that had been agreed upon, lest any hint of the plan escape, "Are unknown to us. The weight of fuel we will use en route is set to within 3%, depending on headwinds, which is an issue that could cause us additional problems, as my aircraft are highly affected by adverse wind conditions."

Törget permitted himself a swift look at the page he had left open before refocusing on the German.

"Our best guess is that the 'objects' will weigh in at more than the fuel, but only by a small amount. My unit is presently running tests to check fuel consumption under the weight conditions we anticipate."

He stopped, taking inboard some fluid, offering the two senior men a similar opportunity.

"At this time, the operation is not feasible from Denmark. It is feasible from Sweden, and time is not on our side."

The intelligence Colonel nodded, his reaction plainly one of understanding, rather than of agreement.

"My country has had a protocol in place with the Allies since 1944, regarding aircraft landings and routes of flight. What you propose is outside of that arrangement. A mission directly into Soviet territory that is likely to end up in a firefight, or worse. A mission based in a neutral country that has absolutely no wish to become involved in this latest abhorrence!"

Trannel looked away, whereas as Sam Rossiter held his ground.

"Why on earth are you coming to us...no...why on earth are you coming to me with this request? Go to the Government, I can do nothing here."

"This is why I have come directly to you, Per."

Rossiter opened his case again, removing a file with a picture of someone intimately known to the Commander of Swedish Military Intelligence. He handed it over and settled back to await the explosion.

Törget spent a moment looking at the photograph of a senior Swedish military figure. Opening the folder, he started to read about his compatriot's betrayal.

Rossiter revelled in the most overt display of emotion he had ever witnessed from his Swedish friend, small agitated body movements betraying his anger, until he placed the folder carefully on the table, lining it up perfectly with little movements, buying an extra moment to compose himself.

"Bastard."

Rossiter could only agree, and he knew that, it not only hurt that Sweden's Naval Commander was a communist spy, it trebly hurt the efficient spymaster, as he had no idea that Swedish High Command had been so massively penetrated.

"I will check all of this, of course, but the times you supply will undoubtedly match the records of meetings that my own service has on file."

Feeling unexpectedly awkward, Rossiter could only mumble agreement.

The Swede made miniscule adjustments to the folder's positioning once more

"Bastard."

Törget was already planning a cosy little chat with Admiral Søderling, a chat in which the pleasure would be all his.

"I understand, Sam. You need access to the military station on the south of Gotland. I can do this in the time frame you suggest, but I will want some of my people there to ensure things go smoothly."

He recited from memory.

"The refuelling station can easily be set up near Karlskrona; in fact there is a secure area that is perfect for our needs."

The use of the word 'our' was wasted on no one. Törget was fully onboard.

"I will provide medical facilities to welcome the 'objects'."

Graciously accepted, Sam Rossiter had expected the cunning spymaster to know exactly what the mission was bringing back.

He waited for the Swede's conditions, for he knew there would be some.

"This mission must be unattributable to Sweden in any way whatsoever. That is not negotiable. This folder will guarantee the compliance of my government."

He paused to look again on the face of the traitor staring up at him from the folder, the smiling face antagonising him.

"I insist that the personnel used wear German uniforms, and conduct this under the guise of the old Nazi regime. If it is attributable to the new republic, the Allies, or ourselves, there will be hell to pay."

"Agreed", the word slipped Rossiter's lips so fast that the Swede understood that was already in the planning, and had been omitted from the brief in front of him.

A third folder was placed before him, containing details of the small force of men that would carry out the mission, men who had once worn the hated uniform of the Waffen-SS.

Törget swiftly scanned the personnel details and set the folder aside, the uppermost picture being that of the mission leader, an ex-SS officer, Ukrainian by birth. According to his swift appraisal, the man had been given the Silver Star by Eisenhower shortly after the start of the war.

"He seems an interesting fellow."

Lassiter could only agree.

"I have great plans for him, Per."

The Swede retrieved a small silver bell, previously hidden behind the table's floral display.

Before the sound died, the door opened, and fresh coffee appeared, the orderly retreating before another word was spoken.

"Of course, I must know, the 'objects'. Who are they, Sam?"

"A family."

Rossiter answered reluctantly, knowing he was about to be pressed, and knowing that he would give in.

"Which family might that be, I wonder?"

The piercing blue eyes bored into the Marine, seeking clues, finding none.

"Some high-ranking Nazi? Some General?"

Rossiter fished in his case one final time, extracting a folder heavy with notations, keeping the nametag away from Törget's sight.

He removed two pictures, one recently acquired, and one copied from an original in the possession of a former enemy.

"I do not know these people."

He studied the new photograph closely.

"But I do know the Russian. NKVD Major Savitch. He has his hands dirty from Katyn onwards. Any special jobs, he is one of those who get the call."

Passing the photos back, the Swede shook his head.

"If that piece of rubbish is involved, you can rest assured he will have orders to kill them if there is any sign of trouble, and also know that he will do it."

Rossiter restored the photos to the file.

"So, whoever he is, is he worth the risk we are all taking?"

Strangely, for him, the Marine changed his mind, extracting the photo of a man in uniform.

"Ah! Now I understand."

The Swede returned the grainy photograph immediately.

"Colonel Knocke, a worthy adversary to you and the Russians, now fighting under the banner of the French, if my information is correct."

It was not often you got to score a point over Törget, so Rossiter savoured the moment.

"Indeed he is, but he outranks us both now, as he's a Brigadier-General in the Army of France."

Törget conceded the point graciously.

Sipping his coffee, he slipped easily to the next point, bringing Oberst Trannel back into the discussion.

"So, Herr Trannel, this," he twisted his head slightly to quote from the schematic of the unusual aircraft drawing, "This Achgelis. What sort of strange bird is he?"

Trannel, now in his comfort zone, leant forward and spoke confidently.

"The Focke-Achgelis is a helicopter, Herr Oberst."

The meeting continued for some hours, the operational capability of the Fa233 helicopter taking some time to explain, its specific needs at the landing stations laid out by the Luftwaffe officer.

Colonel Törget stood watching the Northrop from the pier, the small aircraft disappearing into the growing darkness for its return journey to Norwegian air space.

They had set a timescale, and a first possible date for the mission, if all went well. His orders were already flowing, carefully worded, restricted to a few trusted individuals.

His mind was full of SS Colonels, pretty little girls, and helicopters, the intended mission being a challenge for him personally, as well as risking much for his nation.

His mind cleared, focussing on the single folder that was still sitting on the table in the drawing room, and then it became once more absorbed, turning to how best employ the gift he had been given.

Admiral Søderling.

'Bastard'.

0957hrs, Friday, 14th September 1945, Langwedel Area, Germany.

The force holding Langwedel had been exterminated, Guardsmen from the Guards Armoured Division, stood and fought to the last man, desperate to permit their commanders to establish a strong defensive line on the Kiel Canal, some ten miles to the north-west.

The Soviets had stopped, the darkness preventing them from understanding the completeness of their victory.

Taking advantage of the opportunity, a scratch force was hastily assembled and rushed to fill the gap between the two lakes; Brahmsee to the south-west, and Manhagenersee to the north-east, the distance between the two bodies of water a mere twenty-two hundred feet.

Their orders were simple.

Hold at all costs.

The Soviet Lieutenant-Colonel understood his orders perfectly.

Attack and break the British position as quickly as possible, outflanking and turning the left flank of the solid position at Eisendorf. Open the road to the canal, permitting follow up forces to attack before the British had completed their fortification of the imposing obstacle.

He had been given units from the Army reserve, both of which were impressive on paper, but less so in the flesh.

The tanks of the 249th Tank Regiment had already been badly mauled by the 11th Armoured Division, and were now formed into two platoons equipped with both 76mm and 85mm T34's.

The 60th Guards Mortar's were reasonably intact, despite having sustained some casualties from accurate counter-battery fire, the bane of all Soviet artillery units since day one of the war.

His own regiment had lost its 1st Battalion in the meat grinder of Neumunster, and, even though the 19th Guards Rifle Corps had scarcely been involved, none of his fellow leader's commands had come away unscathed from the awful fighting there.

The surviving 2nd and 3rd Battalions had absorbed the few survivors of 1st, but both battalions were still significantly reduced in manpower and weaponry. Although their fighting spirit was not in question, Arsevin had requested more bodies. The request was swiftly answered, and a company of penal troops was sent to bolster his force.

A late adjustment was required when an extra company of engineers was also given to him for the attack.

As the command group broke up, he reflected upon the plan.

The initial bombardment from the 60th's Katyushas would blast the positions hugging the Manhagener See, entrenched infantry from what the hasty reconnaissance indicated.

The Penal Company and the engineers, each supported by a platoon of 76mm T34's, would demonstrate noisily against the position, hoping to pin the enemy force in place, as well as draw some reserves across.

2nd Battalion, already inserted into the southern edge of the woods, was ready to drive to the shores of the Brahmsee and secure the vital Mühlenstraße road. This would enable the bulk of Captain Volnhov's 34th Guards Tanks to push through, the remainder to move to the right with two companies of 3rd Battalion, and turn the flank of the forces fixed by the penal unit.

Fig #54 - 1000hrs, The Brahmsee Gap, Germany.

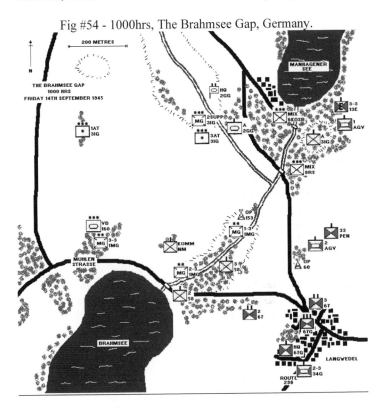

1000hrs, Friday, 14th September 1945, The Brahmsee Gap, Allied defensive positions, one mile north-west of Langwedel, Germany.

Allied Forces- 'A' Company, and Support Company [Reduced], both of 3rd Battalion Irish Guards of 32nd Guards Brigade, and 'A' Troop, 'C' Squadron of 2nd Battalion [Armoured] Grenadier Guards, and 'B' Battery of 153rd Field Regiment RA, and 3rd Platoon, 1st Independent Machine-gun Company, all of Guards Armoured Division, and 2nd & 3rd Kompagnies, 58th Reserve-Grenadiere-Regiment, and ZBV Panzer Kompagnie Von Besthausen, all of 160th Reserve Division, all of British VIII Corps, British Second Army, British 21st Army Group, and the remnants of Kommando Neumunster.

Soviet Forces - HQ Company, 2nd & 3rd Battalion, all of 67th Guards Rifle Regiment, of 22nd Guards Rifle Division, of 19th Guards Rifle Corps, and Armoured Combat Group Volnhov, of 249th [Separate] Tank Regiment, and 2nd Company, of 3rd Battalion, of 34th Guards Tank Brigade, and 3rd Company, 3rd Battalion, 13th Engineer-Sapper Brigade, and 60th Guards Mortar Regiment, all of 10th Guards Army, and 33rd Penal Company, all of 1st Baltic Front.

Circumstances dictated that the forces that opposed each other at the Brahmsee Gap were out of position and unready, even unsuited to the tasks required of them.

The British, after days of steady withdrawal, always holding on until the last moment, and then retiring, having given Uncle Joe's boys a bloody nose.

The Soviet forces had pushed hard either side of the Brahmsee, and met rock hard defences.

The route through between Brahmsee and Manhagener See was less than ideal, and the Soviets initially avoided it. The casualties sustained assaulting Ellerdorf to the south, and Route 255 to the north, were extreme, and forced the Soviet leadership to turn its gaze to the narrow Brahmsee Gap.

Determined to go quickly, to broach the Kiel Canal at the earliest moment, only the few units at hand were tasked with the initial breakthrough, others already moving to take advantage once the line was broken.

For the Allies, a handful of His Majesty's Guards were swiftly reinforced with some of the German Grenadiere units of the 160th Division, straight from their hard fighting around Ellerdorf.

The orders issued to the soldiers on both sides were straightforward, devoid of frills, brutal in their simplicity.

Red Army commanders exhorted their men to smash the capitalists and break through the line, regardless of losses. Sometimes encouraging their men with threats, sometimes with the sweet taste of vodka, the officers prepared to drive their soldiers into the narrow Brahmsee Gap.

Across the smallest divide, that was No Man's land, Allied and German officers made sure their men understood the simplest yet most feared of orders from above.

'Hold your positions at all costs!'

The Irish Guards had been fighting without a break for days on end, and the casualties had mounted.

The arrival of the Katyusha rockets on their positions caused havoc, killing and wounding indiscriminately, destroying trenches and foxholes, sometimes burying men alive to die in silent, indescribable horror.

'A' Company had been reinforced with men from the disbanded 15th Scottish Division, and platoons of 6th KOSB and 8th Royal Scots shared the suffering in the opening salvo.

The 60th Guards immediately commenced relocating, the new procedure adopted by the hard-pressed Soviet artillery and rocket troops, desperate to avoid the accurate counter-battery fire.

That fire came and, even though 60th Guards moved quickly, the mixture of high explosives and fragmentation shells still claimed lives and destroyed three launchers.

Men of the 13th Engineer Sapper Brigade moved up with the six T34/76's, slowly moving from cover to cover, approaching a small round wooded hillock occupied by a nest of enemy machine-guns, all of which were firing rapidly, claiming a engineer infantryman with every burst.

The T34's halted and started to put HE shells on the position, throwing up gouts of earth, occasionally stained with the blood of an allied soldier.

To the southeast of the Guards position, the second group of T34's, a mix of 76mm and 85mm gun versions, commenced their tentative advance, their route being more open and exposed. The supporting penal infantry knowing they had been handed a murderous mission.

Seven hundred yards away, Lance-Corporal Patterson was locked on his target, patiently waiting for the order to fire.

He adjusted as the enemy tank moved forward a few yards, angling for a better shot at the hillock. The lens also betrayed some of the Penal soldiers, scuttling into cover as the defensive fire grew in volume.

One soldier was struck in the head, his blood and brains splattering the side of the tank that he was moving past.

Automatically, Patterson screwed up his nose in disgust, as automatically as he discharged his 17pdr and sent its lethal APDS shell on its way.

The T34's armour yielded as the high-velocity dart penetrated with ease, the driver uncomprehending as it passed through him and into the body of the tank beyond.

Smashing into the breechblock, the APDS shell was deflected upwards, exiting through the rear upper plate in a blur of white sparks, taking the life of the Penal company commander. He had climbed up to liaise with the tank crew and was just leaning into the open hatch.

The gunner, only just realising he had lost both hands to the enemy shell, started to scream, his panic infectious. The commander and hull machine-gunner scrambled to escape, leaving the amputee to try and lever himself out on bloody stumps.

Neither escaping crewmember was hit by the bullets that spanged off the armour as they sought cover.

A second shell struck their tank, entering in at the front plate and burying itself in the engine block, starting a small but earnest fire.

As the gunner was a new man to the crew, neither of them was prepared to risk himself to save him, and those on the battlefield on both sides became aware of an animal-like howling as the fire spread.

The remaining T34's adjusted their positions, desperately seeking the powerful weapon that had already killed one of their number.

Screwing his eyes up, the Senior Lieutenant commanding the Second Section thought he saw something, his suspicions confirmed as the 'lump' lit up, betrayed by the muzzle spitting flame.

The shell sped across the battlefield, heading straight at him in tank 231.

Half a second of terror was ended by a simple clang, as the shell clipped the left side of the turret and went on its way, leaving a thin and gleaming silver stripe in the green painted metal.

"Driver, move right, now! Gunner, enemy tank at 11 o'clock, load armour piercing! You have it?"

"No, Comrade. Wait, I see it."

"Driver, halt."

Waiting for the rocking motion to cease, in order to give his gunner the best possible chance, Balianov judged the moment perfectly.

"Fire!"

The 76.2mm F32 spat its shell at the indistinct enemy vehicle, and the gunner showed why he was considered the best of his unit.

The armour-piercing shell hit the British tank on the glacis plate. It bounced off without penetrating, but wiped away most of the camouflage foliage that had been stacked around it to mask its presence.

Balianov had been studying his enemy silhouettes, but the vehicle he saw emerge from the ravaged greenery did not figure in the Soviet intelligence documents available to him.

"Driver, move left, into the gully!"

The experienced tank officer saw enough to know that it was a big tank with a big gun, and that his chances of survival had just got a lot worse.

231 slipped out of sight before Patterson could get off a shot, so he turned his attention to one of the other two T34's, 233, stationary, and believing itself concealed behind a large hedge.

The tank commander, Lance-Sergeant Charles, had already ordered a change to conventional rounds, the APDS shells far too good for the modest armour of the Tridsat Chetverka's.

A standard armour-piercing round crossed no man's land, eating up the yards in the blink of an eye, smashing into the nearside track and front sprocket of 233, destroying both before moving on and becoming lodged in the rear drive sprocket, jamming it in place.

The crew were made of stern stuff, and tried to fight their tank, sending a shell back almost immediately.

It missed, and buried itself in the ground, short of Route 36 to the north.

233 died dramatically, a solid shot penetrated and triggered an internal explosion that displaced the turret, causing it to flail away and come to rest, twenty yards from the burning hull.

The surviving anti-tank guns of Irish Guards opened up, scoring hits, but failing to kill any of the targets in front of them.

The penal troops had moved away from the tanks, conscious that they were not safe near them, pressing forward, not running upright, but hugging the ground or crawling.

Balianov had slipped out of his tank and moved up to the edge of the dip in which 231 had concealed itself, his binoculars studying the enemy tank, taking in its powerful lines.

To the north, the engineers had gone to ground, as the machine gun fire consumed their resolve. Most of their leadership was lying dead or wounded amongst the felled trunks and piles of severed foliage.

A PIAT shell had transformed the lead T34 into a torch, outdoing the sun in its illumination, before internal explosions eventually displaced the upper hull plates and ended the display.

The British anti-tank weapon and its crew lay in pieces, two HE rounds having exacted revenge.

The supporting T34's enjoyed a period of immunity, pumping shell after shell into the British positions and receiving no reply of note.

An engineer Lieutenant pushed his men forward, bringing them in a rush to the edge of the Guards positions, before he fell and the charge wilted. The badly wounded officer was carried back by willing hands, very happy to be moving away from the field of horrors.

Fires were burning everywhere now, grenades and the growing arrival of mortar shells from both sides, creating a desolate environment of destruction, often masked by smoke.

Occasionally, the screams of a wounded man reached by the spreading fires, assaulted the ears of men who could do no

102

more than block the sound, and hope that whoever it was died quickly.

Lieutenant Colonel Arsevin had ridden out from Langwedel, determined to observe the secondary assault, ready to order his main force into the attack.

His binoculars revealed a hellish scene, as the hillock and surrounding woods blazed, his eyes fixed on a moving figure, uniform streaming flame as he ran from the field, unrecognisable as friend or foe, so involved in fire was the screaming man.

Arsevin watched as tracers from both sides swept the ground on a mission of mercy, seeking the man out, finding him, and ending his misery.

Closer to his position, the Penal Company was having a hard time, their numbers thinned by machine guns and mortars, their tank support obviously in trouble against enemy guns of some power, judging by the ease with which the T34's were being killed.

For a moment, he considered calling off the diversion, the waste of men and vehicles appalling him.

The thought vanished as he dived into his scout car seeking safety, bullets striking his armoured vehicle, as a sharp-eyed enemy soldier saw an opportunity from the small hill to his left.

Another man, armed solely with a revolver, also saw the camouflaged scout car secrete itself behind a small farm building.

Consulting his map, he spoke into his radio. Receiving an acknowledgement, he returned to his observations to await the results.

The British battery fired one full salvo. He had decided to range one gun would scare the Soviet General away, assuming it was the enemy commander he was shooting at.

The first shell to arrive struck the floor of the lend-lease scout car seven inches to the right of Arsevin, exploding on contact.

Lieutenant Poulter, formerly of 662 AOP Sqdn, grunted in self-congratulation, as the enemy vehicle flew in all directions, the 4.5" shell dismantling it totally, and in the most brutal fashion.

Payback for his beloved Auster aircraft, long since smashed down by Soviet fighters. He had been lucky to escape that action, but was almost enjoying his time on the ground as an artillery observation officer attached to 153rd Field Regiment.

The five surviving 4.5" guns of the virtually destroyed 79th Medium Regiment RA had found a home with the 153rd, becoming an additional battery, and the one to which he had given the task of engaging the enemy command element.

It was some time before Major Dubestnyi realised his colonel was dead, and that he had command.

When he found himself in charge he immediately ordered the Siberian battalion's to assault down Muhlenstraβe.

The artillery observers had more targets than guns with which to fire.

Poulter's fellow officer called in a savage barrage, smashing into the enemy infantry that suddenly emerged from the woods to his south, stopping them in their tracks, as high-explosive dismembered and destroyed frail bodies.

Poulter himself selected an area in which he had seen enemy armour on the move, dropping his 4.5" shells on the northern outskirts of Langwedel.

Close by, a Vickers of the Independent Machine Gun Company opened up, its barrel streaming unwelcomed tracers, attracting attention on itself.

Disgusted with the stupidity of the infantry, the artillery OP team stripped down their radios and prepared to move away.

Captain Ganzin, commanding the mortars of the 67th, selected his own target and ordered a swift barrage, before moving his mortars to another position.

Soviet 81mm mortars dropped their lethal shells over a small area, silencing two of the IMGC's heavy weapons and killing their crews.

Relocating, Ganzin spared time to look through his binoculars and saw nothing but the dead.

On the hillock, Poulter struggled to get upright, his clearing vision informing him that his fellow officer was dead, decapitated, and eviscerated by high explosives.

The radios were smashed, the two operators beyond help.

The RA Bombardier who had kept all their spirits up with his jokes and lewd stories, was gently coughing his last few moments away, his lower jaw destroyed, and his throat laid open by shrapnel.

Surveying his own body, he counted his legs and came up one short.

"I say, that's rotten luck."

His comment was to no one in particular, the bombardier having crossed over into permanent darkness.

His battledress was blown open, revealing patches of disfigured flesh below, trophies of another dice with death.

Beyond the shrivelled old wounds, he saw a steady pulsing of blood coming from his crotch, indicating a severe bleed.

Momentarily panicking, he tried to reach in order to feel his treasured possession, realising that the act was beyond him.

A further check of his arms revealed his left hand all but severed, hanging by a few strips of skin and sinew.

His right arm seemed to be there, and seemed intact. It was just unresponsive, broken by the impact of his fellow officers binoculars, propelled by the explosion that claimed the man's head.

"Blast it. Well, that's bloody unfortunate, I must say."

Poulter bled to death within a minute.

1014hrs, Friday, 14th September 1945, MuhlStraβe, the Brahmsee Gap, Germany.

The experienced Siberians of the 2nd Battalion had gone head first into hell.

Their task was to cut a diagonal route, hitting the modest ridge above the main road, securing the flank for the 3rd Battalion to concentrate all its efforts on securing the small crossing.

The Allied artillery had wiped away many a veteran of years of fighting, pieces of men flying in all directions, as the unit attacked on a narrow front.

Urged on by the surviving officers, the soldiers of the 2nd Battalion charged forward, pressing closer to the defenders, where the artillery would fear to touch them.

Fig #55 - Soviet developing attack on the Brahmsee Gap, Germany.

105

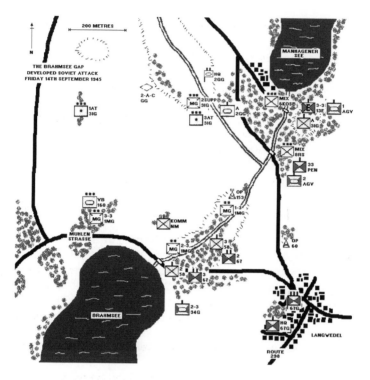

Their opponents, the German 58th Grenadieres, launched everything they had at the easy targets, dropping men to the ground with a mixture of modern MG42's to vintage Maxim's, taken from the Red Army in 1941.

Major Dubestnyi, slowly realising that he was out of his depth, ordered the Battalion commanders deputy to drive his men forward, failing to understand that another of the regiment's experienced officers had fallen.

Clearing his mind, he thought back to the plan, reliving the simple presentation.

The mortars.

'Yes of course'.

Then the tanks.

'Yes, Yes.'

Ordering his Gaz jeep to move off, he bore down on the OP of the mortar unit, intent on wiping the enemy off the ridge to his front.

The artillery that had claimed his commander had also dealt roughly with the observation team, his arrival unnoticed as the two bloodied survivors worked on the damaged radio.

Extracting his map, he spoke quickly with the senior survivor, a Lieutenant whose eardrums had been shattered by a close shell.

Writing out his orders for the deaf man, he succeeded in getting his message across.

It was even more of a fillip for him when the radio showed obvious signs of life.

Slapping both men on the shoulders, he moved off to his vehicle, secreted behind a small farm building, adjacent to a smouldering wrecked vehicle of a type that he couldn't recognise.

Behind the British lines, the battery commander, the incoming directions now dried up, took it upon himself to fire on the last location, sending his 4.5" shells southwards, one misfire earning his immediate attention.

The shells arrived on target.

Dubestnyi heard the scream of shells and threw himself into a hole.

The mortar OP survivors were obliterated by the first shell to strike the ground.

The second struck the building, blowing all four walls outwards perfectly, the flat brickwork lying symmetrically out from the solid, but cratered, base.

The third shell struck just behind the Gaz jeep, lifting it and its two occupants into a large tree some thirty metres away, the grisly package remaining stuck above ground level, flesh and metal swaying violently, defying the expectations of gravity.

The fourth shell landed close to the destroyed scout car, causing more insult to already slain men.

Back with the howitzers, standard operating procedure was applied and the gun re-fired.

Not that anyone expected the shell to fire off, but it did, a relief sweeping amongst the crew, now that they would not have to complete the misfire procedure.

Back at the target, Dubestnyi raised his head at the moment the shell landed, striking the fallen wall nearest the hole in which he had taken shelter.

A brick, perfect and undamaged, propelled by the force of the shell's violent end, struck him in the temple, staving in the front of his skull, and destroying much of the brain matter beyond.

The Soviet commander gurgled incoherently, dying alone and unseen in the bottom of his accidental grave, his death painless but protracted, the sound of fighting long ended before he took his last shallow breath.

On the Guards hillock, the fighting was desperate.

Command of the Irish soldiers lay firmly on the shoulders of the surviving officer, a recent arrival from the halls of Sandhurst, ill prepared for the realities of modern combat.

Despite his wounds, he moved position to position, bucking up his boys, doing what he was taught an officer should do, even though the officer in question had solely one good eye with which to find his way.

The Jocks of the Royal Scots had taken a fearful pounding and welcomed the young officer, their own leader having fallen in the first attack.

Every probe, every rush was bloodily repulsed, but every pile of Soviet dead came at a cost to the Irish and Scots.

An unseasonably hot sun broke through the cloud and started to bake the soldiers of both sides, adding to their discomfort.

An Irish Guards Lance-Sergeant sought out the new officer. Tumbling into the small log pile that now constituted the company headquarters, he gasped frantically for air, alternating between an upright and face down position as he struggled to get enough oxygen into his lungs. Face streaming blood from a nasty cheek wound, the NCO looked on his last legs.

"Sir, we can't hold the buggers. Me Brens have little ammo, and half the lads are down. We gotta pull back beyond the water there."

The bemused officer listened but did not hear, his shock taking over.

"O'Rourke, you're wounded."

"Sir, we gotta withdraw or me boys will all die here this day!"

"Someone fetch the medic, will you?"

O'Rourke spat as blood filled his mouth.

"For fuck's sake Lieutenant! Give the order or we'll all meet the Lord Almighty on this fucking hill!"

A flight of ground attack aircraft flew overhead, hugging the ground, as best they could, to avoid interception, intent on wreaking havoc somewhere to the north. The Irishman, distracted as he quickly checked the Soviet aircraft were not a threat, initially missed the movement of the mentally incapacitated Lieutenant.

The officer rose and headed off, his gait unsteady, his internal compass all wrong.

"Oh sweet Jesus! Sir, will you come back here now, for the love of God!"

Totally confused, the battered young man shouted constantly for medics to attend his NCO, even appealing to the Soviet engineers who closed in on him, before they battered his vulnerable frame to the ground.

His capture gave O'Rourke command of the company, a position he used immediately, shouting to nearby men, organising them to stand fast, whilst others were to slip away across the modest watercourse.

Seventy-nine sons of Ireland had pinned their colours to the hill. Exactly forty made their way back over the water to the north bank.

The Royal Scots did not get the order, but in any case could not have disengaged successfully, so close were they to the attackers. The Penal troopers stormed the Jock's positions, hand grenades and sub-machine guns doing awful work amongst the trees and foxholes.

The platoon was overrun, some men choosing death, some choosing life.

The prisoners were not all lucky, and more than one man was bayoneted in an act of vengeance, payback for a comrade lying dead or wounded in the hell the Russians had charged through.

The Soviet tank support had withered away, mainly destroyed by the accurate fire of the single tank that hugged the shallow slope, five hundred yards to the north-west.

Balianov had remained in his position, his tank concealed, whilst he tried to work out what to do about the unknown monster vehicle.

Charles made a decision.

"Driver, time to relocate. Reverse her up the way we came and we will pop round and up on top of the hillock."

In response, the Rolls-Royce Meteor engine increased its note from idle, and the Centurion reversed out of its firing position.

"Commander, gunner. Infantry target to front, range six hundred."

"I see it. Engaging."

The Centurion Mk I, of which the British Army presently boasted six pre-production trials vehicles, was equipped with a 20mm Polsten cannon.

The Polsten was a version of the Oerlikon, less parts, cheaper to build, but with no loss of performance.

Twenty-three explosive 20mm shells spat from the Polsten mount, transforming the target area into a mass of rising earth and dust.

Enough of them struck Balianov to remove everything from his armpits upwards.

Third Kompagnie of the 58th Grenadieres were enjoying the payback of a turkey shoot, their mixed machine-guns reaping a deadly harvest amongst the attacking Soviet infantry.

None the less, the Siberians of 2nd Battalion made it to the base of the hill, and the battle descended into a grenade exchange, small packets of death been thrown blind at suspected enemy positions, some resulting in silence, others bringing the screams of the injured and dying.

The 60th Mortar's observer brought down another barrage on the machine gunners, part of which caught the edge of the Grenadieres line, causing severe casualties to the platoon linking to the gunners.

3rd Battalion had an easier ride, enjoying direct tank support, driving hard into the positions of the 58th Grenadieres 2nd Company, although they lost both commander and second to the same tank shell.

An experienced Oberfeldwebel ordered his men to fall back, rallying them the other side of the watercourse, where the recently arrived platoon of Vickers machine-guns contributed to halting the Soviet rush.

The runner sent to 3rd Kompagnie did not deliver the message, and so the remaining grenadiers east of the watercourse were left vulnerable.

The Siberian Guardsmen were quick to notice the opportunity, and drove into the exposed right flank, rolling up nearly a hundred metres of the 3rd Kompagnie's position, halted only by an avalanche of MG42 fire from a small reserve unit the Kompagnie commander had hurriedly organised.

He now lay amongst the dead, although his men successfully retook the lost metres, throwing the stunned Siberians back down the slope.

An Acting Oberleutnant took command and reorganised the reserve, ready to meet any more threats.

Back closer to Brahmsee, the combined Soviet tank and infantry force broached the water defence.

A 6pdr anti-tank gun of the Irish Guards, stationed six hundred yards behind the bridge, took on the lead T34/85, scoring three hits without inflicting noticeable damage, before it was obliterated by the tank's second shell.

The gunners had succeeded solely in slowing the enemy advance, the tanks and infantry renewing the attack with the benefit of some mortar support. The 3rd Battalion's 82mm mortars put down an accurate mix of smoke and HE on the defending machine-gunners.

A platoon of Siberians tried to sneak around the lakeside of Brahmsee, keeping low to avoid being spotted. Failing to see the final platoon of the machine-gun company, half of them fell before they gave up the attempt and withdrew to cover further back.

Another anti-tank gun died.

It had been deliberately keeping quiet, waiting for an easier shot. The weapon's position was betrayed by a young gunner in the act of urination. The experienced tankers of the 34th Guards potted the movement and put HE shells into the woods, adjacent to their first kill.

Gun and gunners came apart under the hits.

The lead T34 committed to the bridge. The Siberians, conscious of their job to keep enemy AT weapons at bay, pushed

111

hard, shooting down a PIAT team that moved too soon from its concealed position.

A second tank, then a third, crossed the small bridge.

The fourth disintegrated as a solid shot took it under the turret, flinging the heavy mass of metal backwards and into the water.

The hull crew scrambled out, dazed and shocked, a Vickers machine-gun reaching out and touching both fatally.

The three tanks that had crossed already were in a funk, not knowing what had killed their comrade, but understanding that only movement would prevent them following their friends into Valhalla.

All decided to turn right, imagining the threat to be in the woods dead ahead, and seeing safety in the woods to the right.

The commander of the JagdPanzer IV needed no second invitation, his order sending a 75mm high-velocity shell into the side of the rearmost tank.

The T34 started to burn immediately.

A few Grenadieres on the reverse slope saw the fatal strike and played the game they loved to play with the Red Army tank men.

Their bullets beat upon the armour, keeping the tankers inside until the heat grew too much and they had to either bale out and risk being mown down, or stay, and burn to death.

There was no love lost between the infantry and the tanks at such times.

The men chose bullets rather than fire, and none made it to safety.

The tank platoon commander ordered his unit to advance over the bridge, relaying the news of something nasty in the vicinity, position unknown. He made the safety of the woods, putting solid green between him and the probable killer.

Behind him, the second tank took a hit, confirming the direction of the killer's location, something he immediately passed on to his men.

Spewing black fumes, the wounded T34/85 rallied, and made the safety of green mass.

The safety was an illusion.

Smoke trails erupted from the leafy shadows, panzerfausts aimed by vengeful men, two targeted on each tank.

112

The Commander's tank blew up, immolating the crew in seconds, both panzerfausts striking home and penetrating the armour.

Only one struck the labouring second tank, detonating on the mudguard.

In a panic, the driver slewed his tank to the right, heading for the north side, putting distance between him and the killer woods.

Exposing his tank to the Centurion.

"Target tank, one o'clock, range four-fifty!"

A short delay as the electrics moved the turret the required amount.

"Gunner, on!"

"Fire!"

Patterson was on a roll, a fourth T34 knocked out before his eyes.

"Gunner, it's still moving!"

Patterson had hit the damn thing, he knew he had, but there it was, still ploughing forward, kicking out more smoke than a rubber factory on fire.

"Gunner on!"

"Fire!"

A definite shower of sparks; another hit.

"Pats, are you firing fookin blanks, sunny Jim?"

Incredibly, the T34 was still rolling, its turret turning, seeking its assailant.

"Right ho, Gunner. Deep breaths. Get this one right or it's the cookhouse for yer. Line her up, Pats."

To Patterson, this was an affront to his professionalism.

Taking extra care, he slowly rotated, leading the tank in textbook fashion.

"Gunner on!"

"Fire!"

As unspectacular as the previous hits had been, the final shot brought about the catastrophic destruction of the third tank.

When the smoke had cleared sufficiently, all the crew could see was a useless lump of metal, already beginning to glow dark red.

Back at the bridge, the rest of the Guards tanks enjoyed little success, the JagdPanzer IV stripping the track off the second in command's vehicle.

Communications were virtually non-existent, any contact with supporting artillery impossible.

An enterprising infantry officer dispatched a runner with written coordinates, aiming him at the headquarters in the town behind them.

A grenadiere dropped the volunteer, knocking the life out of him with a Mauser rifle bullet, the message fluttering away on the breeze, never to be delivered.

Overhead came six IL-10 aircraft, rather less than the number that had distracted O'Rourke previously.

The survivors of the 118th Guards Assault Aviation Regiment were not alone, harried and hounded by the Spitfire Mk IX's of 308[Polish] Squadron RAF.

A Spitfire staggered in mid-air as its engine was flayed by the rear-gunner of the last Ilyushin.

At that height, there was little the pilot could do but try to control the crash.

The Spitfire smashed into houses in Langwedel, killing indiscriminately, German civilian and Soviet soldier alike.

The airborne melee disappeared from view, heading deep into Soviet territory.

In Langwedel, all was chaos.

Buildings were burning and the rescuers, soldiers of the headquarters submachine-gun company, found corpses and body parts spread throughout the scene, the Polish fighter having scythed through a kindergarten on the Rotdornweg, in use as a safe haven for the families of Langwedel.

It had been clearly marked so that it would not be attacked, something the already dead commander of the 67th Guards Rifle Regiment had found too attractive to ignore, moving his headquarters close by.

The staff of the 67th had also suffered. Although their building was missed by the impact, flammable aviation fuel first sprayed and then ignited, turning the large house into an inferno.

The Soviet attack was leaderless and uncontrolled, descending into a self-preservation exercise for the individual units.

Leaving a platoon of his men, the SMG company commander decided he could do little wrong if he headed to the sound of the guns.

Senior Lieutenant Yolkov ordered his remaining men forward, presenting a strange sight to the uninitiated.

His unit had been issued with steel plates as body armour, something they had baulked at using, until they had experienced its effectiveness.

Almost resembling knights of old, the eighty men doubled out of Langwedel, aiming to make contact with the 3rd Battalion and seek orders.

What Yolkov did not realise was that he was the senior surviving officer in the whole regiment, so the orders were his to give.

As Yolkov and his men moved up to 3rd Battalion, the sister unit displaced the Germans from the leading edge of the ridge.

3rd Grenadiere Kompagnie pulled back across the watercourse, dropping into hastily prepared positions on the north side, reliant on the small water obstacle to slow any charge.

Too many grenadieres did not fall back as ordered, incapable because of severe wounds, or uncaring because their lives had been terminated with extreme violence.

2nd Battalion's Siberians surged forward, but the watercourse did its job and, in conjunction with streams of 7.62mm bullets, the attack ran out of steam, the survivors falling back to the positions the grenadiers had recently evacuated.

They had hardly reached the positions before they were joined by a deadly hail of 8cm mortars shells, the swift barrage called in by the Acting/Oberleutnant, who was proving more than capable as a battle leader.

Back at the MuhlenStraβe Bridge, the 3rd Battalion's soldiers had pushed the grenadiers back over the watercourse, the ferocity of their attack causing panic in the German ranks.

In this area, there were no hasty positions to drop back on, and the danger to the whole position was clear, until the Vickers machine-guns of the 2nd Platoon 1MG discouraged the Siberians from pressing too hard, dropping enough to the earth to force the pursuers back into cover. Quickly recovering, 2nd Kompagnie formed a tentative line.

The situation was perilous, as much of the ammunition had been left behind. The senior NCO commanding the Kompagnie, Hauptfeldwebel Schränkel, radioed for ammunition and reinforcements, all the time praying to his god.

His efforts to contact the machine-gun platoon failed purely on language grounds, and the Hauptfeldwebel could only hope that the Britishers would stick like glue when the time came.

Yolkov determined otherwise, meeting up with the deafened mortar officer, and directing a strike upon the enemy beyond the MuhlenStraße Bridge.

The machine-gun platoon was not the direct target, but the Katyusha was a notoriously inaccurate weapon, fit for area strikes, not precision hits.

Seventeen rockets landed in an area of fifty metres by sixty metres.

2nd Platoon of the 1st Independent Machine Gun Battalion ceased to exist.

Many of the other rockets found themselves hitting water, either exploding on contact with the surface or disappearing beneath the lake, permanently consigned to the Brahmsee.

The remainder spent themselves in and around the positions of 2nd Kompagnie, rending the ground and the soft bodies of men equally.

Seeing the strike throw body parts in the air, Yolkov leapt up and screamed for his men to follow him, rushing the bridge.

The Vickers were all silent, a fact Hauptfeldwebel Schränkel noted through his extreme pain, two hot fragments of rocket casing lodged in his stomach.

Nonetheless, he served the gun.

Its gunner was dead, victim of the Katyusha strike, but the MG42 was intact, as was the white-faced loader.

The machine-gun started its work, lashing the bridge with small, controlled bursts. Men dropped, smashed to the ground by the impacts.

The body armour of the SMG troopers saved many a life, although exposed limbs received savage treatment at the hands of the MG42's intense fire.

Gritting his teeth as the recoil jarred his shoulder, agitating the shrapnel in his belly, the Hauptfeldwebel shouted at his number two.

"Ammunition, you idiot! Another belt!"

As he fired the last of his belt, the Soviets went to ground.

The young grenadiere showed the empty ammunition box by way of response.

"Go and get some, Hannermann! Raus!"

Bullets zipped around the position, one clipping the ammo box and sending it flying from the loader's hands.

Petrified, the young grenadiere hugged the earth, crying, urinating, defecating, and calling for his mother.

Schränkel looked at the boy with a mixture of pity and disgust. He hawked and spat fresh blood, before setting himself to locate more ammunition.

At the bridge, Yolkov had turned, his men rooted to the spot. Walking back and forth, screaming at the hiding soldiers, he threatened execution and reward in equal measure, but nothing he could do brought any response from those lying in the dubious cover of the side of the watercourse.

Furious, Yolkov gestured at the German positions, encouraged by the slackening fire, and the obvious damage wrought by the Katyusha strike.

One or two men started to rise, and the movement became infectious.

Satisfied, Yolkov turned back to face the enemy and ran, his armour clanking, as the metal panels clashed in time with his urgent movements.

Less than a hundred metres away, an MG42 hungrily received a new belt of cartridges and was brought to bear.

With a sound like tearing cloth, it spat out its bullets, and many found gaps in the metal protection, ripping Yolkov to shreds, and sending his bloodied corpse tumbling back amongst those who had started to follow.

117

A DP gunner, calmer than the rest, had set himself up beside a tree stump and returned fire accurately.

Five bullets struck the NCO.

Two took Schränkel in the shoulder, another added to the misery of damage inflicted upon his stomach, the final two striking symmetrically above and below his left elbow.

His screams pierced the mists enveloping the loader, the subsequent sight of his Hauptfeldwebel smashed and bleeding, proving more of a curiosity rather than tipping him over the edge.

Shuffling low to the wounded NCO's side, he started to pull at the bloodied tunic top.

Schränkel slapped his ministrations away with his good hand.

"There, Hannermann, there! Give them every bullet, boy. Keep the schwein away from our position!"

Like an automaton, the young grenadiere swept up the MG42, hefting its bulk in his right hand and feeding the belt with his left.

Russian soldiers fell regularly until he fired his last round. Somehow it kept firing, despite the risk of bullets jamming in the expanding red hot barrel. With no time for a barrel change, he dropped the weapon to the ground.

Hannermann pulled out his Walther and fired single shots, being occasionally rewarded with the obvious signs of a hit, and once, a red mist from a shattered head.

Again, a weapon was emptied and discarded, thrown with venom at the rapidly approaching avenging infantry.

The MP18 that Schränkel had been carrying lay where he had placed it, and the young grenadiere snatched it up, cocking it in one easy motion.

Stuffing the spare magazine in his belt, Hannermann quickly cast his eye around the battlefield.

A few of his comrades were returning fire, but 2nd Kompagnie was in danger of being overrun.

Incredibly, Hannermann attacked, screaming in a voice stimulated by his temporary lunacy.

The lead two Russians dropped, victims of fire from elsewhere in 2nd Kompagnie's positions.

Behind him, the JagdPanzer took a direct hit, found out by an 85mm on the south bank.

Framed perfectly by the sudden explosion, Hannermann looked almost demonic, stained by the blood of his wounded gunner, wide-eyed with a combination of terror and battle madness.

Through the mists of his pain, Schränkel watched the young man attack, one man against forty.

The forty retreated, the one pursued, putting a bullet in a running back here and there.

Those who watched on were incredulous, never to forget the sight.

Scrabbling back into the temporary bosom of the waters, a number of stouter Soviet hearts turned to resist.

T34's started to move up, encouraged by the fiery death of the tank killer opposite, giving heart to the Siberian infantrymen.

A Mosin rifle bullet punched into the grenadiere's groin, taking his breath away and dropping him onto the ground. Two more bullets found him there, both legs made useless by the hits.

Up on one elbow, he discarded the empty magazine and slipped in his only spare, the act of cocking the weapon proving difficult, as blood loss started to take its toll.

A Panzer III, its 50mm gun spitting defiance, manouevred to get position on the bridge, knowing that if the T34's crossed, its own existence would be short and spectacular.

Three direct hits were shrugged off, the superior armour of the Tridsat proving too much for the 50mm.

An 85mm shell ended the unequal fight, burrowing its way into the German's fighting compartment and starting a fire.

The crew bailed out, leaving their vehicle to burn unchecked.

The lead T34 crossed the bridge at speed, a grape of ten men from the 3rd Battalion clinging to its handholds, fearful of being thrown from the bucking vehicle.

Passing the prone Hannermann at speed, the Soviets failed to understand the threat until it was too late. Sub-machine gun bullets plucked them from their perches.

Two men remained in place, the rest lay in the wake of the vehicle, and only one of those showed any signs of life.

The young grenadiere swivelled to face the new threat, an approaching sound filling his senses.

119

The MP18 stuttered in defiance as a solid track supporting 32 tons of metal covered the distance from head to toe in under a second, squashing Hannermann into the Muhlen Straße, transforming him into an indescribable bloody mess, held together only by his clothing.

Across the battlefield, the Centurion MkI of Lance-Sergeant Charles, having dealt with all the tanks supporting the Penal Unit, had turned its attention elsewhere, and saw the end of the unequal struggle.

Witnessing the horrible end of the German soldier through his sight, Lance-Corporal Patterson growled his target acquisition, determined to avenge the brave man.

The order came, and a projectile leapt from the 17pdr, crossing the battlefield in the blink of an eye before carving a hole in the waters beyond.

"You missed, you tosser!"

Actually he hadn't, the APDS shell penetration was so extreme that it had gone straight through the second tank in line and out the other side.

The damaged vehicle slowed, its driver lacking clear instructions from the dead commander.

"I hit the bastard, Sarn't, its smoking!"

"Then hit him again, Pats!"

The main gun boomed again, and this time the T34 died, the shell wrecking the engine and starting a roaring fire.

The lead T34 was running amok over the German positions, repeatedly crushing men, its tracks red with the blood of its victims.

A shell from the last surviving vehicle of the 160th's Panzer unit dispatched the tank. The Marder III 139 mounted a captured Soviet 76.2mm weapon, more than capable of killing the Tridsat.

Another Soviet tank exploded, marking another kill for the Guards' Centurion, and the remaining tanks seemed to hesitate as one.

Perhaps inspired by Hannermann, the remaining grenadieres rose up and charged, screaming at the top of their voices, encouraged by the withdrawing Soviet armour.

The German Kommando rushed forward, urged on by their elderly commanders, who remembered the SturmTruppen assaults of another era.

120

And then, within seconds of each other...

The 3rd Battalion broke.

The SMG Company broke.

The Guards Tanks broke.

The Soviet left flank caved in completely.

The German 3rd Kompagnie, supported by the rampant Kommando, drove the Siberian 2nd Battalion survivors from the high ground, mercilessly hacking down the running men, wide backs proving inviting targets.

Next to be rolled up were the survivors of the penal unit, the kilted Scots of the 6th Battalion, King's Own Scottish Borderers, launching a swift attack around the Manhagenersee Bridge and testing frightened men who needed little encouragement to run, the more so as most of the NKVD security team lay dead upon the field.

The remainder of the Irish Guards and Royal Scots completed the rout, a screaming bayonet charge proving too much for the destroyed engineer unit.

Unfortunately, the Irish pushed too far and ran into the surviving tanks of the 1st Tank Group, whose machine-guns and high explosive killed many a son of Ireland in the moment of victory.

The two Cromwells, the only other surviving tanks from the Grenadier Guards, pushed up to the northernmost bridge, and helped the retreating Soviet troopers on their way.

The route between the two bodies of water, Brahmsee and Manhagenersee, had been an inviting route, seemingly a gap to be exploited, and the Soviets had hastily assaulted it in an effort to turn the Allied defences.

It was an unmitigated disaster for the Red Army, one that virtually destroyed every unit that the Red Army had committed, leaving many dead upon the field.

Not without cost to the Allies, the remnants of 58th's 2nd and 3rd Kompagnies joined together to form one under-strength unit. Barely one platoon of the MG company was still able to function.

Night brought an end to the sporadic shooting that had kept the fighting around the Manhagenersee alive.

The Royal Scots amounted to seven unwounded men

The King's Own mustered twenty fit for parade.

'A' Company, 3rd Battalion Irish Guards, consisted of forty-eight men under the command of a wounded Lance-Sergeant, with another thirty-nine wounded to varying degrees.

Perhaps the most remarkable result of the Brahmsee battle was the casualties inflicted upon the command structures, officers of all ranks seemingly culled across the range of formations on both sides.

The Soviet force withdrew in disarray, and, as was the habit, the higher authorities looked for scapegoats.

Only two Soviet officers survived the experience, both Junior Lieutenants, one from the Penal Company, the other from the Regimental staff.

To satisfy the baying of those desperate for scapegoats, the former was executed by the NKVD security troops before dawn rose, the stories of a monster enemy tank lost in the clamour for retribution.

On the Allied side, a late afternoon ground attack by a single Shturmovik robbed the Grenadier Guards of their surviving officer, his crew, and their Cromwell.

Apart from a wounded Lieutenant in the Independent Machine Gun Company, and a 2nd Lieutenant fresh from training and placed in charge of the 1st Anti-tank platoon, real authority within the British forces lay with two Lance-sergeants, one clad in a Centurion, the other a Bren gun toting Irish Guardsman.

Acting Oberleutnant Fischert found himself de facto commander command of very little, the small combined multi-national force exhausted by its efforts and its losses, but having achieved a great deal during the daylight hours of that awful Friday in September.

1214hrs, Saturday, 15th September 1945, Office of the Head of GRU Western Europe, the Mühlberg, Germany.

The new purpose-built facility was secreted in the woods that covered the Mühlberg, half a mile north-west of Niedersachswerfen.

Pekunin preferred to conduct the intelligence business close to, but not on top of, the main military headquarters, probably because headquarters attracted agents from their fellow agency and supposedly stalwart allies, the NKVD.

The facilities they had switched to inside the mountain were unsuitable, hence the priority given to quickly constructing the score of wooden huts that blended perfectly in with the trees and shadows of the German wood.

GRU personnel had finished transferring themselves and files from the underground facility, and the phone lines and radios necessary to conduct business were now fully functional.

Colonel General Pekunin was sampling the tea available in the new centre, and finding things much to his liking.

His staff was hard at work collating and interpreting the intelligence flowing in from every corner of Europe, desperate to avoid the errors that had plagued operations to date.

A knock on the door interrupted his pleasurable thought processes, causing an irritation that disappeared as soon as he saw Lieutenant General Kochetkov, or rather the look on his second's face.

"Ah, something tells me this is not good news, Mikhail Andreevich."

The report went from hand to hand, Pekunin showing his deputy the tea stand, before sitting down to read and absorb the information.

"Govno!"

Kochetkov had expected worse than that.

"We have confirmation?"

"Not yet Comrade, but it is an official government statement. It came in two hours ago, and is our sole source at this time. I have asked for further from our officer in the embassy."

Pekunin re-read the report, picturing the man in question, already working out how to replace his intelligence source.

A polite knock on the door, and a Lieutenant proffered a recently arrived communication.

Dismissing the messenger, the GRU officer opened the sealed report.

"And here it is, Comrade General. Polkovnik Keranin confirms the information is correct, although he has not yet seen the corpse. Death was as a result of a car accident. Apparently the vehicle burst into flames, killing all three occupants, including your man."

Handing the paper to his boss, Kochetkov seated himself, sampling the tea, and finding it as satisfactory as his boss.

Waiting until Pekunin had finished, he posed his question.

"Do you have someone else in place? According to our files, no-one senior enough from what I can see, Comrade General."

Pekunin gave a resigned shrug.

"We will not easily replace Comrade Vice-Amiral Søderling and his information."

Finishing his tea, the GRU head replaced his cup, almost knocking the saucer flying, his mind being elsewhere.

"There is a man, still relatively junior, but he is advancing well, and is highly thought of."

Pekunin moved to his personal filing cabinet and extracted a small folder marked with a numeric code.

"Not yet activated, but I have high hopes for this man."

Passing the folder, Pekunin revisited the tea stand and provided both of them with a second cup, whilst Kochetkov learned of the life and career of Överstelöjtnant Boris Lingström.

1335hrs, Saturday, 15th September 1945, Basement of Dybäck Castle, Sweden.

The rarely used door to the basement room of the Swedish Army's latest acquisition creaked in a monotone, as it was gently opened to permit entry to the uniformed man.

A guard entered with him, intent on cleaning away the lunch tray that had been provided at 1300hrs on the dot, as the new regime demanded.

The meal had not been touched, but it was removed, as per orders, the wooden cup of water removed and placed on the simple desk.

The soldier tidied up quickly and left the room.

A second guard closed the door behind him and took his station in the 'at ease' position, back to the door and facing the other army officer, avoiding eye contact with the fanatical looking soldier.

The uniformed man examined the surroundings, finding their sparseness highly suitable for the traitorous piece of filth in front of him.

The prisoner looked up and examined the new arrival with disdain, stiffening his back.

"What is the meaning of this, Colonel? You know who I am!"

Törget trumped the older man's look of disdain with one of real malice.

"I know who you are, Communist."

Søderling started to into a denial, but was cut short.

"You are dead already. The Government has announced your sad death in a car accident, something that your Soviet friends have already investigated."

The Head of Sweden's Military Intelligence Service passed his prey the wooden mug.

"I repeat, you are now dead, so anything that happens to you from now will not matter, will never matter."

Törget made a study of lighting an American cigarette, permitting the man time to understand the precarious position he was in.

Søderling was intelligent, so it did not take long.

"What do you want me to do?"

"Excellent. It is so much better to do things easily than to have to coerce."

Leaving the thinly veiled warning hanging, Törget moved to the door, slid the plate open, and whispered to the guard.

Returning to his seat opposite the broken Amiral, Törget waited until the second officer was stood by his side.

"Søderling, you will tell this officer everything he wishes to know, without fail."

A nod sufficed.

Törget rose and turned to his protégé, examining his watch.

"Take all the time you need Lingström. Return to Stockholm once you have answers to every one of your questions. Any lack of cooperation and he can drink the Baltic dry for all I care."

An exchange of immaculate salutes and Törget was gone.

125

Now Søderling permitted a mixed look of recognition and relief to cross his face.

"Thank God it's you, Lingström."

"Why is that, Amiral?"

"Because I know you are one of us, one of Pekunin's special projects."

"Do you? Do you really?"

"Yes, I was told to watch out for you, but keep my distance."

"Whereas I had no idea you existed, you fucking communist bastard."

The older man looked deep into the eyes of the younger, seeking some resonance of humour to excuse the words, some cunning disguising his outburst because of possible listeners, or some merest hint of sympathy.

All that stared back was ice-cold hatred.

And at that point, the naval man's defeat was complete. All hint of defiance gone, Överstelöjtnant Boris Lingström got answers to every question he posed.

You people are telling me what you think I want to know. I want to know what is actually happening.

Creighton Abrams

Chapter 82 - THE TRUTH

1000hrs, Monday, 17th September 1945, Headquarters, Red Banner Forces of Europe, Kohnstein, Nordhausen, Germany.

Nazarbayeva was late.

'Nazarbayeva is never late.'

Admittedly, a modest RAF night attack had struck the area around the Headquarters, and there had been a few casualties amongst the security force, but nothing and no one of significance had been affected. Many more deaths and injuries had been inflicted upon the remaining civilians and refugees in the old town, as well as the Allied prisoners of war, who were kept in some of the old camp buildings nearby.

Zhukov decided it would be wrong to enquire after the GRU officer, but Malinin had already taken the bull by the horns and got to the bottom of the issue.

According to the GRU duty officer, Colonel Nazarbayeva had been late leaving her office, a fact that had been rung through to the Headquarters at her request.

A quick check of the message log showed that indeed was the case. Malinin spent some time with the Communications Officer of the day, who had failed to forward the report, laying down standards and expectations.

The old Major understood his tenure was in question and that Siberia beckoned if he did not get his act together.

Malinin returned to the Marshal's office, arriving at the same time as the messenger left.

Zhukov was now refocused on the wall map, examining the situation, imagining how the day's attacks would carry the field and move the Red Banner Forces closer to their goal.

Sensing his CoS's presence the Marshal tapped the map.

"We must push them hard today Mikhail. They are close to breaking, I can feel it."

He turned to his confidante.

127

"However, the British are not as weak as we hoped. Perhaps it was a maskirova, eh?"

Malinovsky knew otherwise. So, for that matter, did Zhukov. Attlee's attempt had been genuine, and he had paid for it. The pugnacious old enemy Churchill was now installed at the head of a refocused coalition government, the belligerent rhetoric of the anti-communist Churchill indicating no lessening of the British war effort.

"The French? Perhaps it will be 3rd Red Banner Front that rips them open," his fingers caressed the south-west corner of Germany, focussing on the approaches to the Rhine and Switzerland.

"Many French units have been destroyed, Comrade Marshal, but the ones that are left are hard soldiers."

Zhukov nodded, both men leaving unsaid the thoughts of the newest Foreign Legion adversaries.

"So, it must be the Americans then, Mikhail, here, in the centre."

Zhukov took his hand away from the map, standing back to absorb the full picture.

'Every time we break through, they plug the gap. Every time. They are resilient, this Army from a Hundred Lands.'

The name had started as an illustration of a divided house, an army of disparate nations, and one easily toppled if pushed hard enough.

Now it was the name he used for his enemy, and one used in grudging respect for their worth.

"The third phase worries me," he digressed to the intended operations of 1st Southern European Front, 1st Alpine Front, and the forces in the Balkans, "Unless the supply situation is eased, I believe it is critical to maintain the pressure here before we open another arena and reduce the flow of supplies to us here."

The two had undertaken this discussion many times before, the end result being one of indecision. The commitment to the third phase required full and detailed knowledge of the supply problems to resolve.

However, the third phase was due to commence on the following Wednesday, so Tuesdays meeting in Moscow would be Zhukov's final chance to cancel the new attacks.

In the East, everything was going well according to Vassilevsky's reports, highlighting the increasing failure of his armies to reach their objectives.

"The updated report will be ready by midday, Comrade Marshal," Malinovsky's return to stiff formality indicating the impending presence of another.

Nazarbayeva entered, beckoned in by the CoS, stood at attention, and saluted formally.

"Welcome Comrade Polkovnik, welcome," Zhukov indicated the chair to one side of his desk, taking up a seated position in his own equally Spartan seat.

Whatever it was, it was wasted on neither general officer.

"Comrade Nazarbayeva, are you well?"

"I am well thank you, Comrade Polkovnik General," turning to face the senior of the two men she continued, "My apologies for being late, Comrade Marshal."

Zhukov liked that about the woman GRU officer. She was late, acknowledged it, apologised for it, no excuses.

However, he realised that something was not right but, again, resisted asking.

"Your report, Comrade Polkovnik?" deciding on a moment of formality.

"Yes, Sir," the document appearing as if by magic, placed before the commander in chief. A second copy was offered to Malinin.

"The figures are a day old, Comrades. If you require GRU to constantly update this file, it will be on a two day delay to be wholly accurate."

Most of that was lost on both men, as the true horror of the situation was laid out in black and white before them.

"Seventeen trains in one day!"

Zhukov swivelled immediately to his indignant CoS, the Colonel-General indicating the section on page two that dealt with the transport situation in the Ukraine last week.

That was the only outburst, the report consumed in a silence that grew steadily more oppressive, laden as it was with the stuff of defeat.

In a very un-Malinovsky like way, the CoS slammed his copy on the desk and paced the room.

"Are they mad? Are they totally fucking mad?"

129

Zhukov wanted to pace and swear too, but he simply let the enraged General do it for the both of them.

Nazarbayeva decided not to interrupt an angry senior officer in full flow.

"Fucking NKVD idiots, Chekist fools! Why did we not know this, Comrade?"

Tatiana suddenly realised that she was the focus of attention, and an answer was expected.

She cleared her throat.

"Comrades, in fairness to Marshal Beria, it appears that he was not informed of all matters. It has taken my units some time to discover what has been going on, and he would have relied upon reports and investigations from the very units and officers that were misleading him."

'An honest statement, Nazarbayeva, defending that sow.'

"The production figures are now all correct, the previous difficulties rectified."

Malinin sat down, his outburst over for now.

"It is the losses in transportation and misappropriation that are above the reported levels."

That required a comment.

"Misappropriation? Explain."

"Yes, Comrade Marshal. By example, one train load of engineering materials was sequestrated by the Party Committee in Kiev, to be used for rebuilding public bridges."

"You have names?"

"Yes, Comrade. GRU officers have already taken the whole committee into investigative custody."

Zhukov would take a keen interest in all of them, right up until the moment they were shot.

'My precious bridging equipment taken by fucking civilians!'

"The some of the new wave of infantry reinforcements have been organised into new divisions, and kept as a special reserve by STAVKA, presently numbering seventeen fully equipped and manned units, numbered 501 to 517 Motorised Infantry Divisions."

'There are new units available in reserve, and my Commanders haven't even told me?'

In honesty, that was less of a surprise to Zhukov than it had been to Nazarbayeva. Such was the lot of a Soviet Marshal.

130

"A munitions train disappeared from sidings in Rostov. It has since been found in Tbilisi, without any of its load of heavy calibre artillery shells."

'My own army stealing my shells!'

"A supply train with brand-new IS-III battle tanks was apparently diverted, with full and correct papers. I am awaiting confirmation that the tanks drove through Vladivostok last Thursday."

That was simply too much for Zhukov.

"Fucking Vladivostok? That swine Vassilevsky is stealing my armour! STAVKA steals my reinforcements and the Persian camel herders are taking my ammunition! It's no wonder we are stalling here."

A moment's silence enveloped the room, the previously unspoken now openly stated.

Malinin broke the awkward silence.

"GKO must be made aware of this immediately, Comrade Marshal. They and the others are sabotaging our effort, putting our victory in danger."

Zhukov nodded savagely, his blood coursing through his arteries, hot and angry, disbelieving, but also knowing that it was all true.

"Bring my trip to Moscow forward to tomorrow morning. You will accompany me, Comrade Polkovnik. I will need you."

Nazarbayeva had other plans, but that was of no import when the Commander in Chief gave you an order.

Theatrically, Zhukov set his folder aside, drawing a line under a document outlining some of the reasons that the Red Banner Army was running out of steam.

"Tea."

The drink arrived and was sampled before the GRU officer continued.

"We have lost our senior Swedish contact at a bad time. It was he who supplied the details of the British delegation's visit. The man in question was killed in an accident," Nazarbayeva passed a photo of a Swedish Admiral to Zhukov.

"We are trying to confirm the details, but it is proving difficult."

The need for good intelligence in the Scandinavian region was all-important. Søderling had been able to assure the

131

Soviet leadership that there were no plans for an Allied sally into the Baltic, and that there were no plans for any expansion of the war through Norway and into North Russia.

"Do you have a replacement, Comrade?"

"Comrade Polkovnik General Pekunin has someone, but he needs still more cultivation before he ascends to an appropriate rank and position."

"Thank you. Next."

"Allied losses. From what my staff are saying, the reporting of allied air losses is now correctly done, and that all enemy casualty reports should now properly reflect actual figures," she conceded generously, "This is in no small part due to the efforts of the NKVD units that have been energetically ensuring standards are being maintained."

Zhukov was well aware of the NKVD effort; his last business of the previous day had concerned a Chekist submission on two Corps commanders that had not observed the required niceties.

Nazarbayeva's statement was also a double-edged sword, as the accuracy of the new reporting system also betrayed the fact that allied air losses were much less than those of the Red Air force, and that ground losses were less than had been expected, and the attritional trade-off was not as hoped.

The GRU officer had stopped, glancing at her watch.

Both senior officers looked up at the wall clock, noting the preciseness of the hour.

"There is more, Comrade?"

Zhukov's enquiry was met with a stoney face.

"Yes, I believe there is, Comrade Marshal. This was partly why I was late. I need confirmation before I can present the information as fact. I had hoped that confirmation would be here by now."

"Tell me what you do have then, Comrade."

She took the plunge.

"All is not what it seems with Spain, Comrade Marshal."

Zhukov's eyes narrowed, a sense of foreboding suddenly filling him with a chill.

He nodded, inviting the full story.

"GRU lost touch with its main operatives after the attempted assassination of Franco; an operation that we know was run by the NKVD."

132

This was not news, but necessary groundwork for the two senior men. In truth, Nazarbayeva was buying time in the hope that the confirmation arrived.

It didn't.

"Our information now indicates that the operation failed because it was deliberately betrayed," she paused, making sure she delivered the next line perfectly, "By the NKVD itself."

Zhukov and Malinin remained silent, partly accepting that Beria and their political masters would do such a thing, and partly incredulous that they could do such a thing.

"Some of the agents were of German extraction, and this was used to demonstrate that it was the German government that made the attempt. The information given by the NKVD to Franco ensured that the agents were either killed or captured. Those taken alive used suicide pills."

"By this method, Spain was persuaded that the Rodina was her friend, and she reaffirmed her neutrality."

Zhukov remained immobile, Malinin nodding his understanding.

"Or so we thought, Comrades."

That got both men's full attention.

"This morning, we received three reports from Spain, and my staff are going through them now so that we can correlate them and confirm all of this."

Tatiana felt it necessary to remind both officers that her words were not yet set in stone.

"It appears that the Spanish understood that it was a Soviet operation all along, and merely went with it in order to create their own maskirova."

Consulting a sheet of paper she continued, "A maskirova that has kept vital information from all of us."

"Which is what exactly, Comrade Polkovnik?"

"That the Spanish are on the march."

Silence.

"We lost contact with agents in north-east Spain. One of the new reports indicates that at least eight Spanish divisions have been weapons training in the area, the whole region under martial law, known communist sympathisers rounded up and liquidated."

Nazarbayeva added a sour note for good measure.

"Preliminary indications are that GRU has lost eight good agents."

"On the march, you say. On the march. Where are they, Comrade Nazarbayeva?"

"We don't know at this time, but the unsubstantiated report I have seen tells me that the force left the region on Wednesday, so wherever one hundred thousand plus men could get to in five days."

It wasn't supposed to be flippant, but Zhukov flared quickly. Just as quickly, he subsided, understanding that the GRU officer was just speaking her mind.

"When you say unsubstantiated, how do you rate this information, Nazarbayeva?"

The softening of his tone was meant to reassure the woman as to her safety, and encourage her to speak freely.

Nazarbayeva needed no such encouragement.

"We will know soon enough, Comrade Marshal, but I believe that the Spanish Army is about to take the field, or more probably, relieve some experienced Allied units for duty in Germany."

That very statement opened a window of opportunity for both men, minds suddenly straying to Phase Three and the thought of inexperienced Spanish troops standing between them and the blue waters of the Mediterranean Sea.

The pleasant thought was quickly shelved, the nastier possibility of a flood of experienced troops arriving from Italy taking precedence.

Both senior officers looked at the map, making calculations on distances.

Malinin asked the question both needed an answer to.

"How are they moving, Comrade?"

"There are three units indentified that have their own integral motorisation."

Consulting her quickly pencilled notes, she continued.

"It seems likely that rail movement is restricted, most rolling stock having been drawn northwards. That is unconfirmed," careful not to exceed her knowledge, one of the GRU Colonel's qualities.

"An overheard conversation appears to indicate that at least four of the infantry units are foot and horse mobilised."

A knock on the door brought the anticipated file for Colonel Nazarbayeva.

Both men waited, sipping at their now warm tea, the growing anticipation overcoming the howls from their taste buds.

The GRU officer straightened her back and spoke matter of factly.

"Yes, Comrade Marshal. It is how I said. The three mechanised units are heading into Northern Italy, lead elements are identified as approaching Turin."

Checking the paper again, she continued.

"The foot and horse divisions, five in total, follow the same path but are some distance behind."

"The two divisions that were taken by train are now laagered on the Swiss border, south-east of Besancon."

A quick maths check brought Malinin into the discussion.

"Ten divisions then, Comrade Polkovnik?"

"No, Comrade Polkovnik General, twelve in total."

Again, checking the paperwork, she quickly backed up her maths.

"Two divisions, the two formed of veterans of the old Blue Division, sailed from Bilbao last Thursday, destination unknown."

Poking out of the bottom of the file was the corner of a photograph Nazarbayeva had deliberately left on her desk, and which had efficiently been included by Andrey Poboshkin, her staff Major.

"What are those, Comrade?"

Zhukov welcomed the diversion, as his mind processed the Spanish threat.

"Photographs of the NKVD operatives killed during the mission."

The Spanish had ensured that evidence existed as to the identities of the would-be assassins.

"Seven? There are seven photos here. I though you said there were six of them?"

Internally she was horrified, and Nazarbayeva avoided touching the top photograph, sliding the third into a clearer position.

Unlike the others Zhukov had quickly cast his eye over, this man was sat on some sort of bench, his face distorted, his tongue unduly extended.

"That man is Polkovnik Akin Igorevich Vaspatin, the GRU's senior man in Madrid. The device he is sitting in is a Garotte. He has been executed by strangulation."

"Blyad!"

"Undoubtedly, that picture is the Spanish Government sending us a message. Official photograph of a dead Soviet officer in uniform, executed on an official garrotte."

"Blyad! Have you informed the General Secretary of this?"

"Not yet, Comrade Marshal, but I suspect that Comrade Beria may have done so by now."

There was something in Nazarbayeva's voice that grabbed their attention, even more than the sight of a Soviet Colonel publically executed by a supposedly neutral power.

"Go on, Comrade Polkovnik."

"My prime source informs me that this man was the informant that blew the operation to assassinate the Spanish leader. He received no such orders from the GRU. We did not know of any mission."

She stopped, raising her hand to her mouth, stifling a cough that died as quickly as it appeared.

"Vaspatin was obviously involved in some way, but did not communicate any of it to us."

Pausing to ensure her words had the full effect, she waited for the echo of her voice to depart.

"The only conclusion is that Vaspatin was operating under orders from another Agency, a conclusion Comrade Pekunin is testing as we speak."

"Mudaks!"

Zhukov slammed the picture down, sending some of the others flying, pictures that showed young Soviet men lying dead, without dignity, openly paraded for cameras.

Nazarbayeva tenderly picked up the two photographs that had reached the floor.

"Brave men sacrificed to what end. No, betrayed to what purpose?"

Nazarbayeva touched a photo to her lips, an action that almost escaped notice.

Almost.

Zhukov spoke with unusual regret.

"What would their mother's say to that eh? Knowing that their sons died for nothing, at the express direction of our leadership."

Malinin interrupted, believing that his commander had unwittingly strayed into dangerous ground, needing to deflect him before he said something that could never be withdrawn, or apologised for..

It was he that had seen the woman's gesture, and he acted on his guess.

"What do you think that the mothers would say, Tatiana?"

Zhukov looked up, taken aback by the use of the woman's name, a break with formality he had not yet broached himself. He knew his man well enough to know that it was not done in error, but for a reason.

Malinin leant forward and picked up the top photograph, taking in the traumatised body, beaten and violated, even after death.

Marshal Zhukov watched as a lazy tear made its slow journey from the corner of Nazarbayeva's eye, dripping onto her tunic soaking into the coarse material just below her most treasured award.

"I think that all the mother's would say that the Motherland requires sacrifices from us all, Comrade Malinin."

Keeping his eyes on the red-eyed woman, Malinin checked the back of the photograph before showing the notation to his commander.

'Oleg Yurevich Nazarbayev.'

'Govno, you poor woman!'

"What would they say if they if they knew, Tatiana?"

Raising her head to look directly into Malinin's eyes, both senior officers watched as an internal battle was fought and won, and a face resolved to express a mother's true feelings.

"The mothers would say that there will be a day of reckoning, Comrade Malinin."

The eyes, normally so full of intelligence and life, carried only death and hatred, burning through Malinin and into the wall beyond, probably all the way to Moscow, and the office of the NKVD chairman.

Zhukov, being extremely unzhukov-like, took the GRU officer's arm gently.

"I am truly sorry, Tatiana."

That night, in a GRU officers billet on the Muhlberg, and a seedy bar in Lubeck, two parents mourned the loss of another their sons; many miles apart, and yet, somehow together, united in their grief.

We have been ordered to move off today; had our orders cancelled; warned for an alarm; had our passes stopped; had our foreign orders cancelled; had our passes and foreign orders renewed; and now have orders to move tomorrow. Great minds are at work.

Anon.
Diary entry of a soldier of the Great War.

Chapter 83 - THE DELAY

0911hrs, Tuesday, 18th September 1945, Les Hauts Bois, the Vosges, Alsace.

Looking through the sights, the target loomed large, its eyes betraying awareness and alertness, neither of which was going to save its life on this misty morning in the forest.

A hand reached out and touched the rifleman on the shoulder, giving a moment's pause.

The owner of the hand placed a finger to his lips in the universal sign for quiet, the finger then moving to point out a new problem.

There was no noise, save the sounds of the woods; trees creaking and swaying in the modest breeze, the low chatter of birds and other creatures, and the grunting of their prey.

The fully-grown male wild boar would have made a tasty meal, one they had been prepared to risk a shot for. That decision became history, as the finger pointed towards an indistinct shape in the shadows.

Raising its head high, the boar sensed the new presence, having failed to note the men in the trees above it.

The snout savoured the air, sampling the new scents on the breeze and finding them a threat, to not only him, but also to the female and two young he knew were nearby.

The litter was out of season, a rarity in the life of a wild boar, but one that gave the male a reason to act in defence, rather than move quietly away.

A foot set out of place broke a twig, not loudly, but enough to precipitate the animal's action. Tensing his large body, the boar defended in the only way it understood; all-out attack.

The owner of the foot, a Goumier scout, cursed his carelessness, quickly checking for signs of the Russian soldiers he and his unit were hunting.

His priorities quickly changed, as sounds of the approaching whirlwind reached his ears.

The boar came into view.

As the Goumier's eyes widened, the animal covered half the distance to his target.

"Ye elahi!"

Three hundred angry pounds of wild boar hammered into the petrified Moroccan, the impact snapping his legs below both knees instantly, the boar's lowered head tossed upwards, an automatic act that brought its sharp tusks into play.

Tusk met bone, as the boar opened the inner thighs, destroying the femoral arteries, his forward momentum carrying him beyond the dying man before the Goumier had even started to realise his death was approaching.

"Brothers! Help! Brothers!"

Even as he shouted for help, his voice grew noticeably weaker.

The boar turned and crashed back into the now-prone figure, the tusks destroying everything they hacked at, silencing the Moroccan when one tusk penetrated his eye socket.

A bullet took the boar in the side, passing through and into the undergrowth beyond, the pain only serving to enrage him further, increasing the frenzied attack on what was now rapidly becoming a lump of ripped flash.

Another bullet hit the beast, destroying his left hip, and spinning him away from the bloody mess.

Two more shots quickly followed, either of which could have been the one that extinguished its life.

A dozen anguished cries rose into the early morning air, the sight of their comrade causing great distress to the other members of the Goumier patrol. Three more shots were fired into the dead boar, more in anguish, than to serve a purpose.

A blanket was stretched out on the earth, and the remains were reverently covered up before being carried away for a burial in accordance with the man's faith.

In the trees, the four men had not dared to draw breathe, the staccato rattle of their beating hearts seemingly louder than that of the disturbed forest around them.

The Goumiers disappeared.

Nikitin relaxed his rifle, looking to his companion for guidance.

Starshy Serzhant Nakhimov was weighing up the pros and cons of the situation, and having difficulty finding any con.

A whispered order, and the NCO turned to the two men in the adjacent tree, simple hand gestures passing on his instructions.

When he reached the ground, Nakhimov waited for the other man, checking the two men above were covering as ordered.

"Right Vassily, tonight we dine on boar. Come on."

The two men moved gingerly to the location of the fight, the large quantity of blood and human detritus startling them.

The dead boar proved difficult to carry, but they managed to get it up and into a jury rig. Comprising two stout branches and weapon slings, the whole contraption more resembled something used on a safari in Africa

Struggling under the weight, they thanked their luck that the hiding place was close by.

2351hrs, Tuesday, 18th September 1945, Les Hauts Bois, the Vosges, Alsace.

Apart from the two men on watch, the whole contingent was present in the dry, warm cave. Waiting until dark spread its wings over the forest, the boar was cooked over a fire whose smoke disappeared into the cave system and, if it popped out in plain sight, would undoubtedly be lost in the increasing darkness.

The sounds filling the cave were those of contentment, as hungry mouths ripped at greasy meat, filling bellies that were contracting as every day passed.

Ivan Alekseevich Makarenko, commander of the last remnant of Zilant-4, chewed the sweet pork, happy that his men had been fed well for a change, but already planning to relocate, now that the hunters had come close again.

Nakhimov read the look on his General's face and, pausing to rip another hunk of meat from the carcass, he moved to his commander's side.

"You have orders, Comrade Mayor-General?"

Makarenko considered his thoughts, and made an instant decision.

"0200, Comrade Nakhimov. They can sleep for now, but we move out at 0200."

Producing his map, the firelight just sufficient for planning the march, he drew the NCO closer.

"We are here. This is where your forage party came across the Africans," he circled an area just east of Colroy-la-Roche.

"We will go north-west as quickly as we can, passing between," the officer screwed up his eyes, but was none the wiser.

Nakhimov took a burning stave from the fire, bringing sufficient light for Makarenko to read the small text.

"Thank you, Comrade. Between le Bambois and Waldersbach."

Testing the distance in his mind, he continued.

"I want us to be hidden away before first light in this area, southeast of Natzwiller. Clear, Starshy Serzhant?"

"As you order, Comrade Mayor General."

Neither man enjoyed the stiff formality, but both understood its necessity in the circumstances, ensuring military discipline was maintained under the extreme pressures of their circumstances.

"Get some sleep, Comrade. I will wake you at one."

Makarenko got no argument.

0917hrs, Tuesday, 18th September 1945, Tiste Bauernmoor, Germany.

Looking through the sights, the target loomed large, the eyes betraying awareness and alertness, neither of which was going to save its life on this sodden morning in the forest.

A hand reached out and touched the rifleman on the shoulder, giving a moment's pause.

The owner of the hand placed a finger to his lips in the universal sign for quiet, the finger then moving to point out the problem.

Other than the steady pitter-patter of rain, there was only the sound of spades at work, and the grunting sounds of the men using them.

142

The huge Russian overseer had erected a shelter from where he could watch his flock in relative comfort, prisoners who did not enjoy similar good fortune, being soaked to the skin as they toiled to dig the long holes.

The problem was the guard on the top edge of the site. He had moved, a relocation that had taken him away from the nemesis in the undergrowth.

The nemesis moved after his prey.

Both men watched as their comrade gently slid through the dense greenery, his progress betrayed by a gentle twitch of a stem here and there.

The four guards were positioned on the peripheries of the work area, making an approach easy enough for those tasked with the silent killing.

The overseer's shelter made a stealthy approach impossible, its position in the centre of the clearing ensuring that he would die last, at the hands of Schultz and Irma.

Satisfied that the killer was now back in prime location, Müller gave a warble, imitating some bird, in a signal that brought instant action.

The four guards died as one, their lives taken silently by whatever method their stealthy killers preferred.

The overseer, an NKVD Sergeant, was slow to act, his eyes seeing all, but his brain failing to understand the death scene he observed as his corporal had his throat cut.

Grabbing at his PPD, he intended to shoot down the murderer, but Irma spat a single bullet, dropping him into the dry interior of his shelter, as dead as his men.

The prisoners stopped working, some conscious only of the single gunshot that had rent the air, others aware that silent killers had taken the life of every guard.

"Good kill, I think, Feldwebel. Let's go and calm the nerves of our new allies."

Slapping Schultz on the shoulder, Müller dropped gently from their firing position on a huge fallen tree, finding his balance quickly, and walking off with the balance and speed of a man who possessed both his legs.

Schultz, wiping his beloved rifle down with an oily rag, watched his friend and commander, easily spotting the indistinct signs in Müller's gait.

143

The four killers moved out of the undergrowth, speaking in either English or French to the confused prisoners.

The Canadian prisoners were heartened to see men in their own uniforms, bearing weapons, and carrying the fight to the enemy, although the presence of the man in command, clad in the uniform of a Captain of the German 'Großdeutschland' Division, troubled more than one of them.

Müller moved to the shelter and took the item he coveted from the corpse, his professional side noting the entry wound in the left ear of the dead NKVD man. Picking up the PPD, and stripping away the two spare magazines, he moved to where his senior Canadian was talking with a dishevelled RSM.

The RSM followed his compatriot's lead, saluting the German officer.

"Müller, Kommando Bucholz."

He accompanied the words with his own salute, and followed them by proffering the Soviet sub-machine gun and magazines to the newly liberated RSM.

"Forbes, strip the dead, anything of use, distribute all weapons amongst the prisoners."

Tasked, Corporal Forbes led his men away.

MacMichaels was checking over his new weapon, clearing it, checking the magazines, his professionalism not dulled by his captivity.

Removing a cigarette from the pack he had just looted, Müller gasped in the pungent smoke, coughing as it stimulated his throat.

"RSM MacMichaels, Seaforth Highlanders of Canada, as are most of my boys here," the NCO indicating the silent men behind him, all waiting for some indication of what to do next.

The RSM's attention was taken by the approach of Schultz, similarly clad to Müller, but sporting a Soviet snipers rifle and wearing the Knight's Cross.

Having spent time with the small Canadian group they had stumbled upon after TostedtLand, Müller better understood the humour of his new allies.

"This is the tea boy, Feldwebel Schultz."

Deliberately ignoring the comment, Schultz too checked his handiwork in the shelter, his grunt indicating pleasure at the accuracy of his shot.

"Same in your army I suppose," addressing his comments to a bemused MacMichaels as he strolled past, nose in the air, ignoring the grinning Müller, "NCO's do all the work, officers get all the glory and girls."

Both men had profited from their time with the Canadian soldiers, their English much improved.

The RSM permitted himself a small smile, one that was not missed by either German.

"Now, I must ask that your men do some more digging for me," he looked around quickly, making a swift judgement.

"Over there, if you please, nothing fancy, just enough for five to stay out of sight."

The twenty-eight ex-prisoners quickly dug in the woods, creating a last resting place for the dead guards.

The final touches were made and it was difficult to believe that anything had been there, let alone dug holes and interred dead men.

"Attention men," Müller called the group to order, "We must move away before you are missed. Complete silence now. One, maybe two hours march, before we can rest up."

Turning to his own men, he nodded at the Canadian corporal, who understood and took the point, moving off towards their most recent base.

<u>1103hrs, Tuesday, 18th September 1945, Ekelmoor, Germany.</u>

Their hiding place was just under a kilometre north of Stemmen, a modest woodsman's hut, long since forgotten by its owner. It was not large enough to house the thirty-six men who now called it home, so small shelters sprung up quickly, providing a dry resting place for those wearied by their imprisonment.

The two men Müller had left in camp distributed some of their food stocks to the new arrivals, but supplies were short, so empty bellies with tantalised with a morsel, rather than a meal.

Bordered on three sides by streams, there was no shortage of fresh water, and everyone drunk their fill of the cool reviving liquid.

Most of the new arrivals took advantage of the security and fell asleep.

RSM MacMichaels observed the two Germans whilst drinking his third 'can' of water, careful not to cut himself on the rough edges of the tin that had once contained standard British bully beef.

The three, another Canadian Corporal was involved, were deciding the following nights activities.

He moved closer, expecting a rebuff at any second.

Far from it, as Müller realised the NCO was nearby, and beckoned him forward.

"Apologies, Sergeant-Maior, I had thought you would sleep."

Accepting the apology for what it was, MacMichaels took the proffered hand and found it firm.

"No problem, Sir. Now that I am back in the war, I don't want to miss out."

Turning to the other German, he nodded respectfully, understanding the requirements of the award that hung around the German NCO's neck.

"Sergeant Schultz, I believe?"

The two shook hands and both found strength there.

"Welcome Sergeant-Maior MacMichaels. And don't believe everything this one tells you," he indicated Müller, "Whilst I will grant you that he is reasonably competent at what he does, he forgets who gets things done around here."

Entering into the spirit of the exchange, the RSM challenged his counterpart.

"So you're not the tea boy then? Shame, I needed a brew."

That earned him a comradely slap on the back from Schultz.

"Corporal?" the word full of enquiry, aimed at the NCO wearing the Carlton and York uniform.

"Staunton, Lieutenant Staunton Sarnt-Maior, A Company, Carleton and York's."

Confused, MacMichaels awaited further explanation.

"I was knocked out by a shell outside Avensermoor. Came to wearing nothing but my pants and boots. This uniform belonged to my batman, poor fellow."

"I see, Sir," which he patently did not, but held his peace.

146

"I will do something about it, now you and your men are here."

Both the Germans had moved off to one side, seemingly fully occupied with arguing over how to smoke Russian cigarettes, so MacMichaels asked his question.

"What is happening here, Sir?"

Staunton deliberately misunderstood the question, and twisted the map towards the NCO.

"We are only a small group, but we carry the fight, Sarnt-Major, we carry the fight."

He tapped an area circled in charcoal, drawing the man into the plan.

"Now that we have your group, we have decided to go for a plum target. The airfield and supply centre at Lauenbrück."

"So we continue to fight the bastards then? But under a Jerry officer"

"Yes we do, Sarnt-Major, under the command of Captain Müller, who, incidentally, is the most competent officer I have ever served with, bar none."

His eyes challenged MacMichaels to comment further.

The RSM's prejudices died under their unblinking scrutiny.

"I want back into the fight, so that's good enough for me, Sir."

"Excellent, Sarnt-Major. Now, we gave this place the once-over a week back, just in case we ever had the opportunity to do some work there. Here's what we have."

And as he sketched the layout of the Soviet air base, Müller and Schultz drifted back into the impromptu briefing, aware that MacMichaels' issues had been addressed and that there would be no problems.

<u>1400hrs, Wednesday, 19th September 1945, Headquarters of 1209th Grenadiere Regiment, 159th Infanterie Division, Neuwied, Germany.</u>

Oberst Pömmering was furious, his wrath not confined to the lower ranks that strayed within range, but also heaped upon his closer officers, men who saw a new side to their quiet, laid back commander on this awful day.

147

Calling a meeting of his Regimental officers, the allotted hour had come and gone, and still Maior Gelben and Oberstleutnant Wilcke had not arrived.

Determined to get to the bottom of the sabotage, he waited for the two battalion commanders to put in an appearance, whilst hounding the Regimental Supply Officer, questioning him about the fire still raging in the ammunition compound.

He would wait long and hard for both missing officers.

Oberstleutnant Wilcke was dead, shot in the heart by his driver, the body and car dumped unceremoniously into the Rhine, leaving 2nd Battalion leaderless.

The communist soldier, a GRU operative slipped through the lines at the end of the war, walked steadily back to his unit, the story of their beloved commander's death at the hands of enemy aircraft already prepared in his mind.

Maior Gelben was actually at the regimental headquarters already, something that would give Pömmering the briefest moment of regret before he died.

Peter Gelben, or as he was known at school, Pjotr Gelben, was another agent who crossed over during the refugee influx into Western Europe.

Setting out his stall carefully, he rehearsed his actions, laying out his tools ready for the job that he was about to undertake. The other two occupants of the room were beyond help. One, a glassy-eyed Gefreiter, whose shattered forehead was gently dripping blood over the radio set. The second, a Hauptfeldwebel and the important piece of stage dressing, the tunic pocket containing some incriminating letters, already tainted with the blood from his chest wounds.

Gelben had removed the silencer, and ensured that he topped up his weapon, ready to catch three casings, equal to the number of holes in the dead Hauptfeldwebel's torso.

Quietly moving the desk to the door, Gelben readied himself.

The sound of raised voices in the main room encouraged him to act, and he pulled open the door, grabbing the grenades and pulling the cords, sending the first straight at the angry and surprised Pömmering, the second to the centre of the mass, the third to the closest edge of the nineteen assembled officers.

Ducking down, the sounds of men in panic were swiftly drowned out by the explosions, one after the other, the angry

148

frightened shouts were quickly replaced by screams and whimpers from those torn by high explosives.

A piece of something burst through the door, spurring him to move into phase two.

He followed the three grenades with two more, each phosphorous, designed to burn as much of the evidence as possible.

High-pitched screams indicated at least one wounded man caught by the unforgiving flames.

He grabbed the dead NCO's PPK pistol, and, without hesitation, fired into his right calf.

Anticipating pain is not quite the same as dealing with pain, and he grabbed at the desk as nausea washed over him.

Dropping the PPK by the Hauptfeldwebel's body, he aimed his own pistol out of the window and fired three times, making sure the casings flew inside the room, the ones from the bullets he had fired earlier already picked up.

Less than thirty seconds has past and he was done with all but the last phase of his plan.

Opening the door, a steadily building fire greeted him, the dead being consumed, and taking their secret with them.

He slipped off his tunic, using it to beat at some flames, trying to damage it and get himself as sweaty and dirty as possible in the short time he anticipated exposing himself to the danger.

Would-be rescuers found the wounded Maior, pistol in hand, struggling to escape the flames, his smoking tunic obvious testament to his narrow escape at the hands of whoever had committed this atrocity.

As he was helped from the scene, he ordered that the body of '*that traitorous bastard*' was recovered, also ensuring the preservation of his planted evidence.

As Maior Gelben had his wounds tended to, a written order, originating from the Divisional Commander, arrived for his personal attention.

As he read it, he understood the unexpected advantage that his actions now offered him.

He addressed the muddy motorcyclist formally.

149

"Confirm to GeneralMaior Bürcky that I have received this order, and that I acknowledge its contents. Dismissed."

The Private returned the salute and turned on his heel, anxious to return to his billet and away from the hospital that was now starting to receive the horribly burned corpses.

The Leutnant doctor stitching Gelben's calf finished his work with a flourish.

"Not quite as good as new, but look after it and there will be no lasting effects."

Nodding towards the message in the blackened hand of his patient, he enquired as casually as he could, more out of nosiness than any real quest for knowledge.

"Good news from our commander, Herr Maior?"

"Very good news, Herr Leutnant, and you may address me as Oberstleutnant."

And with that, the newly appointed commander of the 1209th Grenadiere Regiment rose to test his leg, walking out into the modest sunlight to consider the new opportunity he had been granted.

He spared no thought for the comrades he had killed, looking down only to pick his way safely through their dead bodies.

1005hrs, Wednesday, 19th September 1945, Headquarters, Red Banner Forces of Europe, Kohnstein, Nordhausen, Germany.

Summoned by an order from Zhukov, issued before the previous day's meeting with the GKO, most of the Red Army's senior European commanders were already gathered in the underground meeting room.

The Marshal sat there with his Chief of Staff, making final alterations to the presentation document, including details that had presented themselves after the overnight fighting.

The losses from a heavy bomber raid were still being assessed, but would undoubtedly illustrate one of the main points that Zhukov was about to make to his generals.

The Red Army did not have enough supplies.

The senior commanders were all engaged in their own conversations, discussing the military situation, and how their peers were coping with the extraordinary difficulties that were being experienced.

150

Zhukov rose and the room slowly became silent, as each group in turn realised that the meeting was about to begin.

"Comrades, the Red Army finds itself advancing, and winning battle after battle against the capitalist enemy. From the Baltic to the Alps, we are pushing them hard, and they give way before us."

No man in the room failed to recognise the dressing for what it was; the precursor to bad news.

"Our ground and air forces have done magnificently. Our naval comrades playing the part we have asked of them to the full."

He cleared his throat, preparing himself for the hard part.

"Comrades, it has not been enough, and we find ourselves in difficulty."

This was not news to the men present of course.

"Attacks are failing now, for the first time, because we do not have the means to push, and push hard."

Indicating Malinovsky, he cited an example.

"Forces of the 1st Red Banner Army were displaced by an enemy counter-attack, for no greater reason than the ammunition was not available to make a decent fight."

Some eyes swivelled towards Malinovsky and Zhukov decided to stop any negative thoughts developing immediately.

"Marshal Malinovsky was wholly correct to withdraw his units, given the circumstances. We cannot ask our soldiers to fight without giving them the tools to do the job."

Malinovsky inclined his head in acknowledgement of his superior's defence. Satisfied that he had done what was needed, Zhukov pressed on.

"This is not an isolated case, as many of you will know."

Nodding to Malinin, Zhukov consulted his papers as the CoS revealed a wall chart, laying bear the serious losses of trains and supplies, from the Motherland through to destinations in Germany.

Pointing out the most salient points, Zhukov moved on.

"The munitions, the equipment, and the vehicles are, for the most part, being produced. There were issues, but our efficient comrades in the NKVD have acted to ensure no repeats."

Everyone present understood his glowing praise was for the benefit of any report that reached Beria's ears.

"There are major issues with bridging, and I will come to that shortly."

Taking a sip of water, he shuffled his paper to the next page.

"Our losses are high, but so are theirs. None the less," he reluctantly conceded, "I have underestimated the resilience of the Capitalist forces."

They all had.

When the predictions had been made, none of them felt that the expectations of an Allied collapse were unrealistic. Nevertheless, the responsibility lay with the Commander-in-Chief, a fact that General Secretary Stalin had forcefully pointed out the previous day.

"The Third phase will not proceed as planned. It is postponed indefinitely, pending a resolution of the supply situation."

A message sent on the Monday had informed the commanders of 1st Alpine and 1st Southern to delay operations for 1 day, giving both men a chance to attend the meeting.

Neither of them had really believed it was anything other than that which had brought them to Nordhausen.

A chorus of disbelief rose from the room, the loudest voices easily recognisable as Chuikov and Yeremenko.

The bald Marshal held up his hand, asking for silence.

Chuikov was fit to bust, his face scarlet with the pressure of maintaining his silence.

"It is postponed only, Comrades. Phase Three is an integral part of our operations, but we simply do not have the resources available to conduct offensive operations on the broader front."

Making direct eye contact with the Commander of 1st Alpine, he tried to make light of the slap in the face for his old warhorse.

"There will be sufficient capitalists left for you, Vassily, honestly."

The humour was wasted on a man who faced more weeks of inactivity. He rose to protest and was cut off at the knees as Zhukov shouted at him, part in anger and frustration, and part to spare his old warhorse from saying something he might later regret.

"No, do not speak further. It is Comrade Generalissimo Stalin's personal order. Not for discussion or debate."

The display of emotion told everyone more about the Moscow meeting. It had obviously gone very badly for the 'Victory Bringer'.

Arriving in Moscow late on the Monday, the first meeting had gone on long into the night, breaking up in time for him to see the first faint rays of sunlight as he journeyed back to the quarters arranged for his personal use.

Tuesday was spent in the presence of Stalin and the GKO, fielding questions, often tinged with accusation and the allocation of blame, and receiving criticism and orders in equal measure.

Nazarbayeva was excluded, and gave no input during the two days, the GRU's written report considered sufficient at the time.

Zhukov's next words completed the picture.

"We are now directed to pursue the Five Point plan, concentrating as much of our resources as possible on breaking through, and permitting the Manoeuvre Groups to operate as outlined. Previous mistakes will be rectified, and will not be repeated. Anyone failing to discharge their orders to the full, will, without exception, be summoned back to Moscow for a full explanation."

Such explanations tended to end with a bullet in the head.

"So, the Five Point Plan."

Zhukov reminded each officer present by turning to the situation map on the wall, slapping each location in turn, reciting from memory.

"1st Baltic Front will contain Denmark and nothing more. Seal up the English and leave them to stew. The main thrust of 1st Baltic will be from Hamburg, through Bremen, aiming into the Netherlands, via the North German Plain."

Marshal Bagramyan understood his task perfectly, and was already holding a written request for more assets to balance his savaged order of battle.

Moving down the map, Zhukov turned, and caught the eyes of Malinovsky.

"1st Red Banner will focus its efforts on Osnabruck, pushing up to the Rhine and securing the southern flank of 1st Baltic. You will also drive south-west and threaten the Ruhr."

"Our main effort on the Ruhr will come from 2nd Red Banner," *'Konev again, why is it always that swine that gets the prime work?'*, "The main advance to come through Cologne, and into the southern edge."

Noting the grin on Konev's face, Zhukov decided on a word of caution.

"2nd Red Banner is also responsible for mounting the pinning assaults on the Saar, and west of Karlsruhe. Do not forget to give them the necessary support, Comrade Marshal."

Moving on before his nemesis could protest, Zhukov slapped the map for the final time.

"3rd Red Banner will aim towards Freiburg, and break into Southern France," he emphasised the next point by stating each word deliberately slowly, "And Swiss neutrality is to be respected without exception."

"To aid 2nd and 3rd, I have directed the Front Munitions Officers to liaise, with a view to 1st Southern and 1st Alpine supplying some of the needs of the two Red Banner armies."

Again, Chuikov and Yeremenko protested, having already helped with transfers of some munitions, the feeling of being second-class citizens completed by the ignominy of losing larger quantities of their carefully hoarded supplies.

"There is no choice here, Comrades," a reference to the directions he had been given during his frosty meeting with the GKO, "It will be done, and it will be done satisfactorily."

"There is to be no let-up in our pressure, all along the line, our soldiers must stay in close contact with the enemy. All commanders are to funnel their resources into the focussed attacks, using maskirova to conceal movements and intents."

Sweetening the bitter pill, Zhukov referred to a document recently received from the communications centre.

"I am having copies of this document made. It details additional resources that are being dispatched from STAVKA reserves, to help you in your successful execution of the plan."

Zhukov employed the 'execution' word that Stalin had used when discussing the depleted state of the Red Army and the need for fresh formations to complete the plan. The word had also been used another time that same meeting, but not in the same context.

"Now, Comrades, our air forces have suffered hideous casualties at the hands of the enemy, as you will know, but we have struck back, dealing a heavy blow to the bomber force of the RAF."

A few men mumbled, the sounds conveying neither satisfaction, nor discontent. Every man there knew more needed to be done.

"STAVKA have released more air assets. Chief Marshal of Aviation Alexander Novikov is here to tell you how they will be employed, and what new tactics he has developed to help wrest back the aerial advantage."

There were no illusions about the Air War. The night sky belonged to the Allies, the daylight hours seeing a rough parity constantly gained at the expense of large numbers of destroyed aircraft and dead pilots.

Novikov stepped forward and spoke briefly, outlining tactical changes in such a way as a simple soldier could grasp.

By the time he had finished, most in the room felt buoyed by his words, the emphasis on defending supplies and transport routes being welcome, although the pessimists amongst them assumed the extra vigilance in that regard would mean less direct support to forces in the field.

Vice-Admiral Vladimir Tributs, the commander of the Baltic Fleet, replaced the Air Force Commander, detailing the actions of the submarine war, and revealing just how much enemy materiel was not reaching European shores, thanks to the efforts of a few submarines and a lot of luck.

There was no need for Tributs to state that the luck could not last, had not lasted, as the Soviet navy had lost ten submarines in the North Atlantic in just the last six days.

Finally, Zhukov played his trump card, and an intelligence briefing from Colonel Nazarbayeva of the GRU proved informative, the confirmed neutralising of Italy being a high point, revelations of the Spanish commitment, a low.

She withdrew from the room, her task completed.

Without saying so directly, Zhukov had just ensured that his senior officers had their information from reliable sources, not just the sanitised NKVD reports.

Time to move on to other matters now.

155

"Comrades," the low chatter ceased as Zhukov brought them all back to matters in hand, "Permission to restore our released prisoners to the Red Army has been denied."

Most had heard the rumours, but it did not prevent the mutterings from starting once more.

"However," he practised the statement in his mind quickly, making sure he got it exactly right, "I see no reason why the lazy bastards should sit around doing nothing whilst they wait for transport back to the Rodina and justice."

'Perfect.'

"Your transport officers have rightly made them a low priority for return to the Motherland. I would not encourage a change to that, but I do suggest that you all put the traitors to use while they wait their turn. If they can chop down trees, then give them an axe. If they can carry something for the benefit of the Red Army, give them something to carry."

He need say no more, the meaning clear to every man that had the benefit of seeing his eyes and hearing the inflection in his voice. Any written report would not have the benefit of his presence or his tone, and would only serve to illustrate his clear agreement with General Secretary Stalin's stance.

None the less, Zhukov was taking a big chance, and they all knew it.

Unseen, Konev's eyes glinted maliciously.

None the less, assistance from qualified soldiers was most welcome to the assembled officers, and many minds had already turned to methods of employing them.

Zhukov looked to move on.

"I want complete revisions of your reinforcement and supply policies, in line with Comrade Marshal Novikov's air plan."

He put their fears into words.

"There will obviously be an effect upon direct support from the Red Air Force, but that cannot be helped. Our artillery and mortar losses have been murderous, but the relocation of units has been successful. Ensure your artillery forces can support your ground assaults, but follow the new doctrine to the letter."

In many ways, the Soviets had been guilty of underestimating the Allies, and that was most certainly the case in Artillery tactics. The waning power of the German Heer and

156

Luftwaffe might have lulled them into a sense of false security. Whatever the reason, Allied counter-battery fire was extremely effective, and the Allied ground-attack aircraft also exacted a high price on the supporting artillery and mortar units.

"Comrades, use your Air defence units wisely, and concentrate them to defend your key assets. Spread those assets out if you don't have the protection, but we are losing too much that is valuable to their bomber and ground attack regiments."

Uncharacteristically, he hammered his fist on the map table.

"Relocation, Comrades, we must do more of it, and do it much quicker!"

A staff officer slipped quietly into the room, bearing a message for one of the Marshals, his eyes moving from man to man until he saw the commander of the 3rd Red Banner Front.

Zhukov waited whilst the contents were consumed, the rest of the officers falling into whispered general discussion once more.

Rokossovsky finished reading the message and returned it to the Major, directing him to present it to the Commander in Chief.

Reading it for himself, Zhukov felt a moment of elation, before passing it to Malinin, and calling the room to order.

"Comrades, comrades."

The room came to order, and Zhukov indicated that Rokossovsky should deliver the news.

The Polish officer rose to his feet.

"Comrades, at 0820hrs this morning, elements of the 10th Guards Rifle Corps reached Lindau."

Suddenly realising that the momentousness of the news was lost on his fellows, Rokossovsky continued.

"Lindau is on the shores of Lake Constance, and looks across into Switzerland."

For the benefit of those who still did not fully grasp the significance, he went further.

"The Allied forces are now split in two pieces."

Whilst momentous in itself, the excursion of the 10th Guards was short-lived, a counter-attack by American tanks and

157

armored infantry restoring a narrow corridor between Germany and Northern Italy.

The meeting of the Soviet Commanders broke up just before 1800hrs, the senior officers making their way back to their commands, heads full of orders for the coming day.

You do not raise heroes, you raise sons. And if you treat them like sons, they will turn out to be heroes, even if it is just in your own eyes.

Walter M. Schirra Sr

Chapter 84 - THE TRAWLER

<u>1312hrs, Friday, 21st September 1945, nine miles due west of Fair Isle, North Sea.</u>

She was one hundred and sixty nondescript feet, rusted, and salt stained, but still a valuable part of His Majesty's Navy, purpose-built as an armed trawler by Smith's Dock Company Ltd of South Bank on Tees.

Launched in late 1939, HMT Sequoia had seen little of the war, other than the occasional brush with a floating mine or sight of a receding enemy Kondor reconnaissance aircraft.

Except for one horrendously stormy day, December 1st 1944, when she had risked all to rescue the crew of a crashed Catalina off Stronsay Island, plucking the crew from the water in time to save all but one life.

Today she was carrying out her orders in calmer seas, patrolling the gap between the Orkneys and Fair Isle to the north-west.

Or rather, she had been until the tortured sound of metal on metal had penetrated the whole ship, bringing on a period of enforced silence, as the engine room crew laboured to repair the damaged shaft bearing.

Even though helped by the millpond nature of the seas embracing the powerless craft, the engineers were finding the work heavy going, much to the annoyance of the ship's captain.

The previous day, an enemy submarine had sunk a small vessel to the west of Stromness, and Captain Boothroyd had the feeling that the Russian was coming his way.

So much so that he had his depth charge crews working hard, drilling, and drilling, getting the routine perfected, ready for the inevitable appearance of the underwater killer.

The killer was already there, watching, assessing the situation, before making the kill.

Shch307 had sunk the little steamer off the west coast of Orkney, and then run hell for leather for the open sea, intent on plying her lethal trade off the coast near Grimsby, where Soviet intelligence expected fat pickings.

Defects on the starboard lower tube gave the Captain much cause for concern. The inner cap had been hit by a reload swinging unexpectedly during an underwater surge.

The door and torpedo had been checked and found to be fine. As a precaution, the tube had been vented of air and the seals checked for leaks. There were none.

The torpedo had been loaded and it was this tube that fired the second weapon at the unfortunate steamer. The problems came thick and fast from that point, with the bow cap failing to close properly, and a leak around the seal of the inner door apparent from the moment the tube was fired. The decision was taken to weld the inner door shut as water leaked through the displaced joint at a higher rate with each advancing minute. Wooden shoring was used to press the cap home, and the Engineering officer undertook the welding work.

The submarine's commander had pronounced himself happy with the work, and added a dedicated watch on the weld, shoring, and leak, to reassure everyone onboard.

None the less, it was not just the torpedo room crew who felt uneasy that the cold sea was only kept at bay by one metal skin.

Kalinin was no longer in charge, ordered to take over the captaincy of B-29. His first officer, Senior Lieutenant Yanninin, was in command, and revelling in the new found freedom of operation.

Keen ears had detected the sounding of hammering, and Shch307 had slowly risen to periscope depth to take a look.

The most difficult decision had been whether the vessel was worth a torpedo.

Yanninin had decided it was not; neither was it worth the risk of surfacing and using the deck gun.

The fact that the enemy vessel was making no noise complicated the situation somewhat, so Yanninin decided to use minimum power on the engines, sufficient to maintain steerage, and drift slowly past the insignificant ship, before heading south to the rich pickings of Grimsby waters.

On the bridge, Boothroyd was enjoying his pipe, sucking greedily at the rich smoke, his eyes examining something indistinct off the port bow.

"Boy, get thee some glasses. See there," he pointed off to the left, "Port side there. What say thee, boy?"

The ship's boy did as he was bidden, seeking out the shape that had piqued Boothroyd's curiosity.

Holding up his hand, preventing the sweaty engineer from speaking, the Captain listened for the boy's report.

"Skipper, it's a mine. One of our'n, by the cut of her."

Boothroyd smiled, the boy's attempts at seafarer's talk understandable, but still funny.

"I thought as much. Go and find the Number One and tell him I asked for a rifle on the bridge. Explain why, and bring it here as soon as he issues it. Clear, boy?"

"Aye aye, Captain," the boy rushed off, charged with important matters.

"So, Obadiah, what news of my engine?"

Higginbotham, the engineer, hawked and spat in the brass spittoon set aside for the Captain's pleasure, for when smoking was difficult, but chewing tobacco fine.

"The engine is your'n now, Cap'n, but I won't guarantee her o'er six knot. The bearing's repaired, for the now, and I have Young Crouch refurbishing the broken section as we speak."

Higginbotham was an old woman when it came to his precious engine, so Boothroyd automatically added two knots. Sequoia could only steam at twelve knots at the best of times, so eight knots was a reasonable result, especially when the graunching sound had seemed so terminal.

"Thank ye, Chief, and pass that on to your crew there. There'll be an extra tot for your boys when the sun is over the yardarm."

The conversation was interrupted by the return of the excited boy, complete an old Lee-Metford rifle, closely followed by Lieutenant Clark, the ship's Number One. He had kept the ammunition tightly in his hand until he understood what exactly the breathless boy had been on about.

161

"Carry on, Chief," the friendly order about as formal as things got onboard Sequoia.

"Ah, Number One, give the boy some bullets there, and let him have a bash at yonder mine. But first, pass the word to the lads, let 'em know what's occuring. Don't want 'em wetting themsel when it goes bang, do we?"

Clark nodded and blew done some voice pipes, quickly announcing what was about to happen.

Gesturing at the port side, Boothroyd nudged the quartermaster.

"Ahead one third Jacko, steer," he paused for a second, checking out both the mine and the signs of the sea, "Steer 0-0-5,"

"Ahead one third, steer 0-0-5, aye aye Cap'n."

The ringing of the telegraph provided a backdrop to the sound of a magazine ramming home into the rifle. The boy, proud of the responsibility he had been given, scurried to the portside bridge to set himself to the task.

"What the hell was that?"

Yanninin asked the question, his ears glued to one side of the headphones.

"Sounded like a hammer hitting an anvil, Comrade Captain."

He had been there himself, heard the sound before, so he saw the surface vignette with the utmost clarity in the fraction of a second.

"Steer starboard 90, set speed for five knots."

The sonar operator silently sought an explanation from his commander.

"You use a rifle to shoot at a mine. I think they are trying to..."

The words became unnecessary, as a huge explosion rocked the boot, firing its sound straight into the left ear of the unfortunate sonar operator, the drum instantly ruptured.

'Mudaks, that's my fault', Yanninin chided himself, placing his hand to the mouth of the moaning man.

The shock waves of the explosion came next, jarring the boat.

In the torpedo room, the sound came as a surprise, as did the following shock wave.

One young seaman filled his pants, so complete was the surprise and savage the effect.

"Midships, set speed for three knots, silent running."

At the front of the boat, the torpedo room commander, a Chief Starshina on his twelfth patrol, braced himself quickly. Grabbing for solid support, he wedged himself between the starboard lower torpedo tube and the firing assembly, setting himself firmly in place.

The rocking subsided, the faint echoes of the explosion now gone.

Sighs of relief overcame the sounds of fear, the first comments about their unfortunate comrade starting.

The Chief was otherwise pre-occupied, examining his wet hand and the recently welded door, a metallic clicking sound noticeable with every rise and fall in the roiled water.

The experienced Warrant Officer drew a visual image of the area and quickly realised what had happened.

The errant outer door had come loose in the shock wave but, in the course of trying to close it earlier, the system had been strained, leaving a little play.

It was this play, twelve millimetres of movement in total, which was producing the clacking sound as the waters moved the door in a steady rhythm.

Without waiting for orders he grabbed the winding control, and commenced closing the outer door, an act that commenced smoothly, indicting his guess had been right.

The door came shut with a low sound as the two metal surfaces married around their rubber seals.

Checking he had completed the closing procedure, the Chief Starshina contacted the Control room, reporting the change.

Yanninin accepted the report from the Senior Midshipman, the most experienced Warrant officer on the 307, one of his problems solved by accident, although the welding of the tube meant that it would be unavailable until they had time to inspect it from inside and out.

Shch307 moved on silently.

A voice tube whistled, interrupting Boothroyd's congratulations, the boy openly proud that he had hit the target with every shot and that the third .303 had ignited the floating mine.

It was an incredible feat of marksmanship but one Boothroyd realised he could not overly publicise, lest the thirteen year old was removed from service on his ship.

He pulled the plug on the voice pipe, identifying himself brusquely.

"Captain Sir, I think there is something below us. I definitely heard clear metallic sounds but now they have gone."

The apparatus lost efficiency when dealing with targets immediately underneath the vessel.

Boothroyd considered the man on the other end of the pipe, putting his pipe to his lips, tapping his teeth in an indistinct rhythm.

Charles Maitland, very much a 'hostilities only' new navy man, a Sub-Lieutenant recently out of naval school system, trained up to run the 'garfangled box of tricks' and thrown aboard the Sequoia to learn his trade.

A trade he had mastered in spades by all standards the crew and himself applied.

None the less, he had to question further.

"Come on there, Subby, give me more than that."

"Sir, there was a low but regular metallic sound, which was then replaced by a single deeper sound, also metallic in nature. My belief is we are sitting on a submarine."

Boothroyd had not asked for his guess, but he accepted it in any case.

"Light it up, Subby, active search."

Turning to the bridge crew, he did what was necessary.

"Action stations depth charge, Number One."

The ship's bells rang immediately, the Lieutenant having readied himself, knowing what was coming.

"Full speed ahead, Jacko."

The bridge was suddenly filled with the sound of asdic returns, drowning out the quartermaster's response, bouncing back from something solid, something that should not be there.

Boothroyd already knew there were no friendly submarines in the area, his search area considered a weapons-free zone.

"Talk to me Sub."

"Contact dead ahead Skipper, range four hundred yards, depth one-fifty feet, identify as definite submarine."

Instant decision.

Moving to another pipe, he blew and received an immediate response, the depth charge crews still at their posts following the drill session.

"Thompson, get 'em set for one-fifty, and do it fast. We are almost on top of the bastard. Two and two, Sub, two and two."

"Aye aye, Skipper."

"Subby, the old lady can't make full speed. You understand, lad?"

The reply was slightly delayed, but none the less, firm.

"Understood, Skipper. Good luck, Sir."

'And to thee, young 'un.'

Sequoia's crew were top notch, despite the air of informality and relaxation that so exasperated the 'real' Navy men, marking her and her crew as a target for career naval officers ashore.

The Number One was now on the voice pipe, receiving information from Maitland, passing on the relevant parts as the excited young officer brought the trawler down on the unsuspecting submarine.

"Lost signal, Skipper!"

A sure sign that the undersea killer was beneath their keel.

"Very well, Number One."

Standing by the ship's horn, Boothroyd calculated all the factors in the equation.

'Wait.'

The tension on the bridge was extreme.

'Wait.'

The boy coughed, the strain apparent as he cradled the rifle to him, seeking its comfort and support.

'Now.'

He pulled the small handle, summoning a single blast of the ship's horn, spurring the depth charge crews into action. The system also had the advantage of giving the rest of the ship's company advance warning of what was about to happen.

Thompson, at the rear of the vessel, counted off the first depth charge, watching it roll down the metal frame and drop into the sea beneath the stern.

Not trusting his free counting, so watching his timepiece closely, he counted down, raising his hand on a count of six and dropping it on the nine.

The second depth charge followed suit.

In the water were four type D charges, each containing three hundred pounds of deadly amatol explosives.

On the bridge, Boothroyd decided to stay silent. No use in troubling the boy, and the others all knew that the depth charges were going to be too close at their reduced speed, and would probably mortally wound them too.

The Number One made the only possible comment.

"Brace yourselves!"

"Commander! Splashes in the water, close by!"

Yanninin acted immediately, trying to picture the surface vessel and its movements.

"Emergency speed, steer starboard 20, make depth one hundred."

It was a good effort, but ultimately, a wasted one.

Three of the charges exploded in as many seconds, the first two causing nothing but boiled water, either side of the 307.

The third charge detonated six feet behind the port propeller, bending the blades. The shockwave rammed the bent shaft back into the stuffing boxes and gears, causing catastrophic damage to the port engine.

Water started to pour in through ruined seals, immediately making the boat rear-heavy.

The secondary shock waves sprung the main air intake valve, adding to the inrush of the sea.

Yanninin knew his ship was dying.

"Blow all tanks, surface, gun action surface."

His words were punctuated by another huge explosion, this time the charge detonated off the port bow.

The remaining bulbs shattered, plunging the control room into temporary darkness, swiftly dispersed by torches.

The damaged bow cap gave way, not totally, but enough to permit an inrush of water.

166

The partially drained torpedo tube offered a space for the water to build momentum, the mass striking the welded tube door hard.

The Senior Starshina understood he was watching his doom unfold, the pinpoint high-pressure leaks springing around the failing door weld.

The following shock waves caused the door to fail and the tube was opened to the sea.

None of the torpedo room personnel had any time to do anything but scream as the cold water rushed over them.

In the control room, things went from bad to worse, the first officer virtually trepanned when he smashed into the periscope stand. Yanninin was trying to ignore his broken wrist, snapped in an instant as he had reached out to steady himself and missed.

Others also lay dead and bleeding, victims of the two charges.

Shch307 would not rise, the bow now heavier than the stern.

The depth gauge, functioning as it was designed, steadily altered, showing their accelerating fall into the depths.

The charts indicated a depth of roughly three hundred and thirty metres under their keel, a distance well past the crush depth of their hull.

Calls to the torpedo room were not answered, and the survivors started to understand that their deaths were but a few heartbeats away.

At two-hundred and ninety-eight metres, the damaged hull gave up the struggle.

Thompson was dying. The fourth and nearest shockwave displaced a ready-use depth charge, which rolled into him, crushing him against the ship's side and almost severing his legs.

Two members of his depth charge gang had already gone to meet their maker, dashed against unforgiving hard surfaces by the blasts. The rest were unconscious.

Sequoia would not long survive her vanquished foe, the leaks so severe in her propeller shaft and engine spaces that

Higginbotham had quit the boiler room without permission, saving most of his gang by the skin of their teeth.

The trawler was already down by the stern, and noticeably sinking deeper by the minute.

The boy was nearing the end of his journey, his injuries not obvious, his body broken on the inside. He had been thrown against the wheel, two handles driving hard into him, one catastrophically rupturing his liver, the other his spleen.

"Easy now, boy, easy. We'll get the doc to thee, and thou'll be right as rain in no time."

Boothroyd stroked the boy's hair, his tears betraying the lies.

"Did we get him, Skipper?"

"Aye, boy, we got him fair and square."

A cough brought forth a gout of crimson fluid.

"Rest easy, boy. Thy duty's done."

Seemingly drifting away, the teenager rallied one final time.

"Tell Mum it didn't hurt, and tell her I was a good sailor."

Boothroyd looked up as Higginbotham entered, the engineer's face betraying the horror of what he had stumbled upon.

"Oh Jesus Christ, George!"

He rushed forward, one hand on the dying child, the other on the man who had been his best friend since memories began.

Holding the boy's hand tight, the ship's captain made his pledge.

"That I will, boy, that I will. Now, rest easy, and know that I's proud of thee."

"Dad..."

The boy died.

The crew abandoned ship, pulling away in the undamaged boats, putting a little distance between themselves and the rapidly sinking trawler.

Higginbotham had tried, as had others, but all failed. So they obeyed the last order of their Captain, the man who now stood motionless on the port bridge of the Sequoia, sixty feet away.

The crews stopped rowing and watched, no one in the two boats turning away, all rigidly facing front as a mark of respect to their crewmates and their ship.

HMT Sequoia accelerated her descent, the rising water claiming her hull and superstructure in one violent, foaming minute, Captain Boothroyd disappearing from view in a whirl of white.

And then she was gone.

At one hundred and fifty feet, hydrostatic valves started to click, the depth charges doing what they had been asked to do by Thompson.

Eight of thirty charges had been armed and ready for use.

Eight charges exploded in short order.

HMT Sequoia and her crew became just a memory.

Forty men, plus one boy.

2109hrs, Friday, 21st September 1945, Headquarters, Red Banner Forces of Europe, Kohnstein, Nordhausen, Germany.

Colonels Ferovan and Atalin had been extremely busy, and their reports had enabled Malinin to supply the answers to Zhukov's direct questions.

"So, am I to believe that both of these considerable losses are as a result of coincidence and nothing more?"

The responsible Front Commanders had already supplied their own reports, but it was all so close to his briefing regarding the importance of their supplies that the reports were challenged and his own officers sent out into the field to check.

"Yes, Comrade Marshal."

Zhukov slid one of a stack of folders out of the pile and opened it.

"Start with Ingolstadt then, Comrade."

Ingolstadt had been the main deposit of supplies for the assault armies in Western Bavaria. From the initial reports, 'had' was apparently an excellent description.

169

"Comrade Marshal, the report you received has been confirmed. Colonel Atalin has inspected a number of bodies, two of which had blood group tattoos on their left arms, in accordance with the SS practice."

"Atalin's report details firm evidence of a considerable fire fight on the western edge of supply area, where the immediate guard force was wiped out to a man."

A grunt from Zhukov was all the recognition that the outnumbered guard force would get at this time.

"Reaction elements of the guarding infantry regiment acted swiftly, and prevented the partisans causing excessive damage.

The word 'excessive' drew a look from the Commander in Chief.

The CoS shrugged.

"Comrade Marshal, it could have been so much worse."

"Continue Mikhail", the olive branch offered up quickly.

"The arrival of another force, a motorized company of NKVD troops, forced the German saboteurs to call of their attack."

Turning the page, Malinin continued.

"The NKVD force acted in exemplary fashion, restricting the movement of the partisans, and it seems they are responsible for most of the casualties that were inflicted upon them."

The initial report had detailed twenty-seven enemy dead and three prisoners.

Malinin moved quickly into that area.

"Atalin confirms the numbers, and that GRU and NKVD interrogators are hard at work."

That statement carried a lot of meaning and needed no amplification.

"It would appear that the fires started by the partisans were responsible for attracting the attention of enemy aircraft."

Turning the page again, Malinin waited for his commander to follow suit, checking the original report against the Colonel's independent version.

"From the timings that Colonel Atalin has recorded during his interviews with survivors, the air attacks first started at 2342hrs, when there was still fighting on the ground. Further attacks come in, building in intensity. Atalin deduces, correctly in

170

my view, that enemy controllers became more organised and brought more aircraft in, encouraged by the secondary explosions on the ground."

Another grunt, not one of acknowledgement, but one of annoyance, did not discourage Malinin from continuing.

"It would appear that over two hundred Allied aircraft attacked the site."

Bending forward to closely study an item not so well printed, he struggled to make out the name.

"Mayor Stryabin? Skryabin? Shryabin? Whoever he is, he is the NKVD commander on the ground, and he reported the final air attack ending at 0459hrs. This differs from Pod-Polkovnik Zhuvashikin of the security regiment, who reports the final attack fully one hour earlier. Atalin suspects this discrepancy may have come about because of explosions on the ground."

He looked up at Zhukov.

"In any case, Atalin states that he highlights this as it is the only discrepancy he has discovered between his and the Front report we were given."

A loud resigned exhalation indicated Zhukov's opinion.

"So Comrade, do the losses marry up?"

Turning to the final page, Zhukov waited.

The Colonels report made its way over, and he placed them side by side.

"Really?"

"He was relying on figures given him by supply officers, but they had the benefit of some extra time to do their checks."

The losses were markedly less than those first feared, but still reflected nearly a third of the ammunition, and a quarter of other consumables.

With one exception.

"122mm shells again? Are the Allies psychic?"

Just under forty-six percent of the stock of 122mm shells had been damaged or destroyed.

"This will have an effect, Comrade Marshal, but it is not as bad as we feared, and my preliminary planning had already looked at reducing expenditures, so I believe we may be able to cope with this loss."

There was a silence, both men thinking along the same lines.

171

'Provided there are no more disasters!'

"Let us leave Ingolstadt for now. Your report will be ready when?"

Malinin thought swiftly.

"One hour from when we finish up here, Comrade Marshal."

"Excellent. Now, Lauenbruck."

"A different tale, Comrade Marshal."

Both men selected their reports, Zhukov again with the front Commanders submission alongside to identify any differences.

"A force of enemy soldiers, identified as Canadian troops, attacked the airfield and supply depot. We have a count of twenty-eight enemy dead and captured."

Flicking over the page, Malinin sneezed.

Zhukov watched in amusement as the Chief of Staff gathered himself for the traditional repeat.

It came, shaking Malinin to the core.

"Gesundheit," the German saying slipping badly from Zhukov's tongue.

"NKVD Polkovnik Cyrichov, the security force commander, reports his belief that the whole group of raiders was destroyed in the attempt. Ferovan is less forthright in his opinion, but does say that NKVD security forces have found no further trace of the partisans movements post-raid."

"Then we will leave it at that. Losses in equipment and munitions. Any discrepancies?"

There was none of note, the hastily prepared version tallying almost exactly with Colonel Ferovan's submission.

Losses in men, equipment and munitions were almost mirrored, the sole difference being in an extra two firefighters dead, both having succumbed to their injuries, one less Yakolev-9 fighter destroyed, and an additional four thousand hand grenades unusable, declared unstable by a senior munitions officer.

"The losses in engineer equipment are high, Mikhail. The Armenian already wails and asks for replacements."

That was something that needed no discussion. There were none to be had at the moment, despite the promises and protestations of those back in the Motherland.

172

"Ferovan makes an observation on the pre-disposition of Front Supply Officers for stockpiling. The reasons are sound normally, but the advantage of concentrating our supplies was, on this occasion lost. The secondary detonation of munitions on the ground seems to have caused more damage than the enemy attack itself. Even though some allied aircraft arrived, they spent more time and effort attacking the destroyed airfield and burning wrecks than the supply facility."

Zhukov wondered when a Commander might consider the loss of an elite fighter regiment and its crews an advantage to the loss of supposedly replaceable supplies.

'I will take that exchange every time until the damn problem is sorted.'

The thought did not make him uncaring; it just meant he was a General, with a General's problems.

"Your thoughts, Mikhail?"

Without a moment's hesitation, the reply, obviously already carefully considered, came tumbling out.

"Comrade Marshal, we have the manpower to guard our dumps effectively, and the AA capability to protect them from air attack no less than we did before."

That statement was a simple truth, although the Allied capability to interdict their supplies and transport routes was much higher than had been anticipated.

"Concentrating supplies is an accepted practice, but not one that can now stand, given recent events."

Zhukov nodded his agreement.

"Whilst our supply officers do not place munitions and non-munitions side by side, we clearly have a major issue with collateral damage. So, I suggest that we order Front Supply Officers to separate explosive and non-explosive stocks, to limit losses from secondary explosions, and set minimum distances between locations."

"Agreed. Prepare that order immediately, as a priority, Comrade."

Zhukov carefully laid the report back on the pile.

"And your report on this one?"

"Will exactly reflect that of Comrade Marshal Bagramyan in every way, Comrade."

Zhukov laughed, short but loud.

173

"He may be a bastard, and a wily old fox, but he is no fool, and certainly no liar. Sometimes I wish I didn't like him!"

Malinin smiled with his commander in chief.

Having second thoughts, Zhukov tapped the report with his fingertips.

"Have another look, Mikhail. Find me some bridging assets that I can give him as a present, eh?"

"I will do my best, Comrade Marshal."

Zhukov remained in the office as the door closed behind his CoS, interpreting the information in his mind, seeing the disadvantages grow as every day went past, and finding less in his pocket to produce to overcome them.

'We are still winning, and the necessary requirements will come, and they will allow us to end this stupidity within six months.'

'Do you really believe that you fool?'

'Of course I believe in our victory. Why else would I fight?'

'You fight because you are a soldier and your Motherland calls you. But can you still believe in the sweeping victory you spoke of two months ago?'

'Yes, I must!'

The other voice laughed deeply, in such a way as to show its contempt.

'Yes, Georgy Konstantinovich, the victory Bringer, you must!'

0907hrs, Saturday, 22nd September 1945, Headquarters of SHAEF, Trianon Palace Hotel, Versailles, France.

The previous evening it had been President Truman, the clipped tones stating the position of the country, the expectations of the country, the tolerance thresholds of the country, and in the doing, made Eisenhower aware that he was not indispensable.

'You think I care more for my career than I do for the lives of my soldiers?'

Truman has ended the call reiterating that the public appetite for the new war, and more so, the growing casualty lists caused by it, was disappearing fast.

Ike had lit a cigarette as the President had approached his verbal zenith, and then, afforded an opportunity to put over

174

his view of the future, firmed up the military operations he had roughly outlined sometime beforehand.

Roused at 0700 precisely, abruptly awoken by a concerned voice, as the flustered orderly thrust the telephone receiver into his hand.

The voice on the end of the phone had finished the job of drawing him from his slumbers. Quite clearly, his political masters had a plan to impress upon him their displeasure at the losses suffered by the Allied Armies.

His president the last evening.

The British Prime Minister in the morning.

Churchill, starting with yet another apology for Attlee's antics, soon turned predator, stating a national position identical to that of Truman's, the night before.

Eisenhower found his plans sat easier with the British Leader, perhaps because of his personal military experiences. Truman had served as an artillery officer in the Great War, but never quite seemed, certainly not to Ike, to demonstrate the military understanding that Winston brought to discussions.

The Prime Minister had wholeheartedly approved of Eisenhower's intentions, and promised that the British and Dominion forces would be fully committed when the time came.

The last part of the conversation was less comfortable for both men.

The Attlee issue was a source of great embarrassment to His Majesty's Government, and Churchill returned to it, and spent much of his time reassuring Eisenhower as to the strength of the British commitment.

So, two hours later, Eisenhower was listening to the report from his senior intelligence officer, hearing the confirmation he needed to hear to feel secure in his relationship with the Brits.

Major General Kenneth Strong, SHAEF's G2 Intelligence Chief, was passing on the official report from Winston's office, detailing everything that was known about the Attlee fiasco, which report confirmed that it was simply the failed nerve of one man that had caused such problems for the Allies.

Ike was only just realising how many problems, as McCreery's weekly report was also fresh on his desk, illustrating the heavy casualties taken by the United Kingdom and her colonies.

The policy of inserting suitably recovered POW's was working, but still the levels of manpower had fallen noticeably.

The attritional losses of equipment were heavy, by both wear and accident, as well as combat.

Of note were the losses of Churchill tanks, far and away higher than those of the other British types.

A cough made him realise that he had become unfocussed.

The report had finished.

"I am sorry, Kenneth. Anyway, thank you, and that all seems to be a done deal now, so let's move on. What else do you have for me?"

"I have received intelligence suggesting that the number of active armed groups behind the lines is much larger than we thought, Sir."

Lighting another cigarette, Eisenhower looked puzzled.

"I thought you had limited assets the other side of the line, Kenneth?"

"True, but not so our German Allies. Their General Gehlen has been extremely obliging, providing us with information that his network has obtained throughout Eastern Europe, including Russia herself, Sir."

Bedell-Smith had made his acquaintance with the shadowy Gehlen an hour beforehand, exchanging brief pleasantries before the German spymaster disappeared into the private office of Lieutenant Colonel Rossiter USMC.

His first impressions were not good.

'Handshake like a wet fish.'

None the less, it was impossible not to give him credit for what his organisation was achieving for the Allied cause.

"Sir, according to Gehlen's reports, the Red Army is losing upwards of a dozen train loads of supplies a day. Losses that are starting in the Ukraine, where there is considerable discontent, through to Poland and Czechoslovakia, where partisans are being extremely successful."

This was music to Eisenhower's ears, and the modest, savoured draw on his cigarette was a sure sign of his approval.

"Gehlen also draws attention to the Werewolf network, which is functioning so much better against the Soviets than it ever did against us."

'That isn't difficult, Kenneth.'

176

"Preliminary indications are that it was a Werewolf unit that was responsible for the ground attack on the large supply site near Ingolstadt, an attack that we subsequently exploited to great effect, judging by the air-recon I have seen."

Ike nodded, partially in pleasure, and partially to encourage the Brit to get on with it.

"The similar event at Lauenbruch was not Werewolves. The Soviets have reported that it was British soldiers caught behind the lines and making mischief. That's unconfirmed Sir."

"Bottom line, General?"

"Sir, there seems to be an awful lot more going on behind their lines than we suspected, much of it aimed at their logistical tail. I believe it may account for the changes in tactics we have been encountering."

"Walt?"

"I concur, Sir."

Eisenhower became pensive, his mind working the numbers.

"OK, so we may have an opportunity here, is that what you are saying?"

Both officers looked at each other, seeking support and reassurance.

Bedell-Smith took the plunge.

"Sir, we need to work on this a hell of a lot more. But, if the situation is as we believe, well, then the Reds are having a whole lotta trouble with their supplies."

Encouraged, Eisenhower drew his cigarette virtually down to the filter.

"Firm it all up, Generals, firm it all up."

Business in USMC Colonel's office had concluded some twenty minutes beforehand, and Sam Rossiter was sat waiting for his call to French First Army headquarters to come through.

He could not discuss the new knowledge he had acquired over the telephones, but he could certainly advise De Walle that he was on his way. He had no doubt that the shrewd Deuxieme Bureau man would work out why.

A handwritten message was already in the possession of a courier, whose orders took him to a sleepy little hollow called Camp 5A, on the shores of Lough Neagh, Northern Ireland.

177

Another such victory over the Romans, and we are
undone.

Pyrrhus

Chapter 85 - THE FLAMES

<u>2058hrs, Sunday, 23rd September 1945, Scientist's Residential
Block, Los Alamos, New Mexico, USA.</u>

Since her arrest and interrogation, Beatrice Perlo had
been watched every second of her day.

The insistence that there be no change to her normal life
practices meant that even her liaisons were closely scrutinised, a
fact she found strangely invigorating. Far from affecting her, it
enhanced her passion, and her lovers became more and more
anxious for repeats.

Da Silva, left in charge of the everyday surveillance and
running of the turned agent, gathered information on the
indiscretions and preferences of a number of senior members of
the Manhattan project, information that would become an
embarrassment should they be confronted with it in the future.

Given their obvious errors with Perlo, the FBI went
through everything with a fine toothcomb, finding a few
interesting facts that had previously gone unnoticed.

A lucky break brought an American citizen, one Harold
Gold, to their attention.

Observing him highlighted others, and soon a list of
other possible problems brought a reasoned response.

Suspected agents were placed under arm's length
scrutiny and moved to areas where they could be less effective in
gathering secret information.

Klaus Fuchs, codename Gamayun, found himself back
in England. His constant arguing that the secrets of the Atomic
Age should not be for nation states, but should be shared across
the world, had given a number of people cause to wonder, his
association with Harry Gold seen as the final straw.

The FBI intended to remove all possible Soviet assets
within the project, leaving Perlo as the sole supplier of

information, and therefore, in Soviet eyes, both more valuable and less disputable.

In Washington, the Calderon's surveillance was watertight, agents having carefully sown the house and surroundings with listening devices.

Teams of watchers followed both women, and anyone who came into contact with them.

Michael Green received more attention, but still he did nothing overtly to draw suspicion.

The programme was controlled from FBI Headquarters in Washington, and from there came a carefully worded instruction.

The knock on the door was not unexpected.

Da Silva always arrived just ahead of schedule, every Sunday evening being set aside for his review of her week and planning for the week ahead.

Emilia opened the door, her breasts deliberately exposed, tantalising the Colonel from Military Intelligence.

"Good evening, Emilia."

""Karl, do come in."

She stood aside in such a way as to ensure he could not enter without pressing himself against her.

Karl Da Silva stood his ground, indicating that she should move into the room first.

"I do wish you would stop this game, Emilia."

Perlo moved to the table, tying up her robe, sweeping up her Chesterfields, and lighting up, all in the same easy movement.

"I know you like to see them, Karl."

He could not think of a suitable reply that was truthful, so he remained uncomfortably silent.

"So, I take it you have something for me to send," she indicated the brown secure message envelope clipped to the folder, previously present when the higher controllers wished her to write to Cousin Victoria.

"Yes indeed, Emilia," holding up his hand to refuse the offer of bourbon, "It is time for you to start earning your luxurious lifestyle."

Perlo snorted and raised the glass to her lips, savouring the rich taste.

"Hardly luxurious, Colonel Da Silva," dropping tetchily into using his rank, as she always did when annoyed.

"Certainly more luxurious than it would have been, had you not chosen to work for the right side, Miss Perlo."

Da Silva caught the flash of anger in the woman's eyes.

"And also remember that your continued presence here, working for us, ensures that your Aunt and Cousin continue their safe little existence."

The anger burned less brightly in her eyes, as proper thought replaced her momentary indignance.

"Oh well, at least I get plenty of cock."

Da Silva was unready for the sea change and snorted in amusement, but quickly regaining his professional poise.

He returned to the matter in hand, noting the amused triumphant look in Emilia's eyes.

'Did you just set me up Emilia?'

'Gotcha Karl.'

Perlo produced her textbook noting that, as expected, Da Silva took possession of the Bourbon until she had finished composing her letter to Cousin Victoria.

The envelope became the focus of attention as it made its way into Perlo's hands.

She read it slowly, in the manner of the brilliant mathematician she was, analysing, understanding, ensuring no misinterpretation.

'Que? You gotta be kidding me!'

Looking up at the Intelligence Officer, she saw only serious eyes.

"You're kidding, right?"

"Word for word, Emilia."

"Three years?"

"Three years."

"Lavincompái!"

Da Silva was taken aback by the profanity.

"Three years, Miss Perlo. We can sell it, and they will buy it."

"They won't buy that at all, Karl."

"They will, for one simple reason, Emilia."

180

The spy took a last drag on her cigarette before stubbing it out theatrically.

"And that is what?"

Da Silva repeated a phrase he had heard from the lips of a three-star General, no more than forty minutes previously.

"Because they will want to."

1107hrs, Monday, 24th September 1945, Headquarters of SHAEF, Trianon Palace Hotel, Versailles, France.

"Brad, it's so good to see you."

The handshake was warm, the friendly relationship between the two men genuine and tested.

Eisenhower looked up, first at the man who stood hovering with coffee, and secondly at Bedell-Smith.

The three Generals slipped into a small alcove, followed by the staff corporal with the fresh and steaming coffee.

Drinks poured, the orderly withdrew, leaving the senior officers to discuss the momentous news.

Ike ceded the moment to Bedell-Smith, who slowly went through the preliminary report on Soviet supply difficulties.

It took just under ten minutes, by which time the change in Bradley's demeanour was noticeable.

When he had arrived, the burden of his command and the nature of his task were both obviously heavy upon his shoulders.

With the latest intelligence report, a new hope was awoken, and the fire in Omar Bradley's eyes burned bright and fierce.

"Well I'll be. So what's the plan, General?"

Eisenhower smiled softly, but his eyes also reflected a new steel.

"We do what we said we were going to do. Move back to the Rhine. Their engineering issue has not improved."

Bradley moved to remonstrate.

"Hold on, Brad. Hear me out here."

It could have been an order but, between friends, it was a reasonable request.

"If the situation is how it seems they are perilously close to having a logistical breakdown. I do not want to do anything to dissuade them from sticking their necks out, understand?"

Bradley did 'kind of' understand, but that understanding brought visions of continued retreat, stand, retreat, all the way back to the Rhine.

"The further we move them westwards, the worse it will get for them. Our air power will only grow now. Stateside factories are now fully online. Even Boeing is back to full production despite the sabotage."

The previous week, a number of Soviet special troops, probably six of them, had blown up part of the Boeing's Plant 2 facility in Seattle. None of the saboteurs had survived the attack.

"Our training schools are working full-time, and new pilots are coming into play all the time, no loss of standards."

"We have new units arriving, either from stateside or created in country, adding to our order of battle on a daily basis."

Eisenhower understood Bradley's silence.

"Brad, I will make sure you have the resources to conduct a proper fighting withdrawal, but I want that withdrawal, and I want the Soviets to see our weakness, and continue to exploit it."

Eisenhower nodded at Bedell-Smith.

"This is something we have yet to firm up, but it is a start, General Bradley."

Bedell-Smith and Bradley tended to be formal in their exchanges.

The document listed units and resources.

It did not list times or dates.

Clearly marked were names of Generals and Armies, his own being top of the pile.

There was no indication of location or direction.

The paper was relatively innocuous.

However, despite that, Bradley knew he was holding a document that, even in its infant stage, represented the planning of a major Allied counter-offensive.

Heading off Bradley's most obvious questions, Eisenhower paused in the act of lighting his cigarette.

"This has not yet been discussed with our Allies, Brad. I just wanted you to see it, so you would understand better why I need you to keep going at the moment."

Bradley nodded his understanding.

"I want the commies extended, their supplies exhausted, their men exhausted, and then I'm gonna hit them the hell back to Moscow."

Eisenhower's normally calm exterior had cracked ever so slightly.

Bradley felt suddenly enthused by his commander's confidence.

With controlled humour, he made the obvious enquiry

"Can you tell me where we will undertake this miracle of modern warfare, General?"

Eisenhower flicked his lighter.

"Walt."

Bedell-Smith produced a map that, so far, had only seen the light of day in his and Eisenhower's presence.

Unrolling the paper gently, he set it before Bradley, placing a fountain pen to hold down one curled edge, as Eisenhower used the weight of his lighter on the other.

What they were unprepared for was the laughter, uncontrolled, deep, unforced, genuine laughter.

"Hot dog, but you have a sense of history, Sir."

Eisenhower could not help but smile back.

"It's going to be on your turf, and will be yours to command."

"Yessir," the smile was welded to Bradley's face.

Rechecking the document, looking at the map, returning to the document, more and more questions formed in Bradley's mind.

"Some of these assets presently belong to 6th Army Group."

The notable arrival in Bradley's order of battle was US Third Army.

"Keep that under your hat for now, Brad. General Devers is due here this evening, and I will discuss it with him then. In any case, he will get a lot of extra bodies to keep him happy."

The rest of the questions were stowed away. They would keep for now.

Eisenhower stubbed out his cigarette and recovered his lighter, the rolling up of the map drawing a line under their collective thought processes.

The senior man could not resist one final moment of fun.

183

"Got anyone in mind to lead it, Brad?"

'So that's why you are giving me the Third, is it?'

"I have just the man in mind, Ike. He's been on Jake's back for some time now, and he hates being hogtied."

"A fine choice, General Bradley," Eisenhower rose and led the others back into the main room, where they could look at more current matters, although each man took some time to erase the mental picture of the hogtied man on General Devers' back.

A certain pistol-toting General George Smith Patton.

As was often the case with Patton, US Third Army was doing all it could to exceed the orders it was given.

It was elements of 4th Armored and 90th Infantry that had kicked the 10th Guards Rifle Corps out of Lindau, on the shores of Lake Constance.

It was not tank country, and the American armour started to suffer casualties at the hands of valiant Red Army soldiers armed with every variant of anti-armour weapon that the infantryman had in his arsenal.

The 4th was withdrawn, leaving the infantry to hold the ground alone.

Meanwhile, the commander of 10th Guards Rifle Corps, stung by his reverse, directed his units to the west, smashing elements of the 90th Infantry out of their positions at Laimnau, and driving them towards Route 333, where another force from 5th Shock smashed into them and threw them back to the outskirts of Tettnang.

US 17th Corps' commander had earlier responded to a Soviet thrust on Ravensburg, creaming off units, and sending them north to bolster the vital defence. An order was misinterpreted, and the entire force guarding the Argen crossing on Route 7776 headed to the sound of the guns, leaving a hole in the line.

Major General McBride commanding the beleaguered 80th US Infantry Division, a tested and competent officer, realised the error swiftly. He dispatched a small ad hoc infantry force to block the open Route 7776, with orders to hold on the River Argen until the situation was properly assessed. He also contacted the 4th US Armored to get some extra beef in the line.

Nikolai Berzarin, commanding the 5th Shock Army, had been confused.

At first, the orders were to hold position. Then more arrived, encouraging him to expand his position on the shores of Lake Constance.

Even more instructions followed, concerns from above about ammunition stocks, seemingly woven into woolly orders that could be interpreted in many ways.

Seeking clarification, Berzarin had flown to 3rd Red Banner's Headquarters at Haunstetten and spoken directly with Marshal Rokossovsky.

The trip had been worth it, and Berzarin returned to his own headquarters at Leutkirch im Allgau with clear instructions.

Fresh orders cascaded down through 5th Shock Army, and the whole force went over to the attack, part of which displaced the American defences at Laimnau.

The commander of the 60th Guards Rifle Division, a number of his units pressing the retreating force northwards, sought and received permission to test other defences, and took the opportunity to also exceed his orders by sending a large group westwards down Route 7709.

1349hrs, Tuesday, 25th September 1945, Route 7776 Bridge
over the River Argen, Germany.

Allied forces - Task Force Butcher [remnants of L and H coys of 359th Infantry Regiment and a composite reinforced Platoon from 305th Engineer Combat Battalion], all of 90th Infantry Division, and Task Force Hardegen [elements of 37th Tank Battalion, 53rd Armored Infantry Battalion and 25th Cavalry Squadron], and Composite Battery, 66th Armored Field Artillery Battalion, all of 4th US Armored Division, all of US 17th Corps, of US Third Army, of US 6th Army Group.

Soviet forces - 1st Battalion, 185th Guards Rifle Regiment, of 60th Guards Rifle Division, of 32nd Rifle Corps, and 2nd & 3rd Companies of 116th Independent Engineer Sapper Battalion, and 379th Guards Rocket Mortar Battalion, and 2nd Company, 1504th Self-Propelled Gun Regiment, and Armoured Group 'Antonov' [112th Guards Tank Battalion, 67th Guards

Reconnaissance Platoon, 67th Guards SMG Company & 1st Company, 92nd Engineer Tank Battalion], all of 5th Shock Army, of 3rd Red Banner Central European Front.

Fig #56 - The Argen River Crossings, Germany.

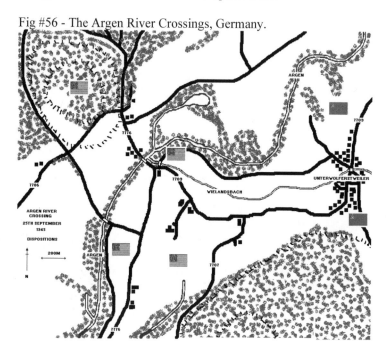

Major Butcher was in command, and he let everyone know it.

A recent arrival in the 'Tough 'Ombres', he had seen some combat time with the 8th Division in the Hürtgenwald before being wounded. Other non-combat assignments followed, until the Army could no longer spare him, and he found himself placed at the head of a composite infantry group and rushed to block the Argen river crossings.

The Armored Force Major was not going to get into a pissing contest with the obnoxious man, so deferred to his command, especially as the dispositions that had been set seemed reasonable.

Major John Johannes Hardegen was not to know that the acceptable efforts of Task Force Butcher had little to do with their namesake, and were more due to the efforts of a slight

186

Captain from L Company, and a wizened Master Sergeant in H Company.

Given the dubious honour of point duty, Sergeant Fusilov tentatively ordered his T-70 light tank to advance.

The '70 was a two-man reconnaissance tank, in which the driver drove, and the commander did everything else from serve the gun to use the radio.

At the moment, Fusilov was concerned with only one matter; that of survival

With binoculars seemingly glued in place, his head swept left to right and back, halting while his eyes examined a clump of bushes here, a stand of trees there.

Others from the recon unit moved warily on the flanks.

Fig #57 - Soviet assault on the Argen River, Germany.

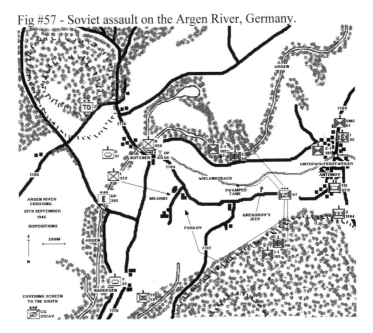

A flash of static warned Fusilov and he ordered his driver forward at the same moment that Lieutenant Gregorov got on his case.

187

"Push up, Fusilov, push up quicker. Don't be an old woman."

Removing his eyes from the binoculars for the briefest of moments, the experienced reconnaissance NCO hawked and spat off to one side, his crewman judging it a suitable reply to that asshole of an officer.

Gregorov was new and keen to impress, regardless of the effect he had on the men around him. He cared solely for the next rank and glory.

Recon Platoon had already lost two tanks due to his pushing too hard, something that he seemed to neither regret nor remember.

Emerging from behind a building on the edge of UnterWolfhertsweiler, the T70 moved swiftly around a long right-hand bend.

Fusilov suddenly tensed.

"Driver, hard left into the woods."

Needing no second invitation, the tank slipped down the gears and did a 90° left, heading up a rough track, and into the apparent safety of thick woods.

The radio hissed again.

"What now, Fusilov? I need you pushing forward, not hiding."

Keying the microphone, Fusilov spoke in the soft tones of men used to spending their time in close proximity to the enemy.

"Comrade Leytenant. The fields on the right show signs of recent vehicle movement. I have taken cover to assess before reporting. Over and out."

Not quite proper radio procedure, but good enough for the moment.

Fusilov had an itch he couldn't scratch, and it wasn't just the bent grass and damaged hedges.

The binoculars swept the ground, seeking further clues to his unease.

The remainder of the recon platoon had gone to ground, with the exception of Lieutenant Gregorov, who felt the eyes of Berzarin himself upon him, and acted accordingly.

Spitting again, the incredulous NCO watched as his commander's jeep bounced up the road and moved left, onto the same track he had followed. It slid to a halt next to his T70.

188

"Serzhant Fusilov, what the fuck do you think you are doing?"

Discarding his first thoughts, Fusilov prepared a properly respectful response.

Unnecessarily, as it happened.

"Serzhant, get your fucking vehicle up that road now. You're supposed to fucking scout! So fucking scout, not lie around in the shade while better men do the work!"

Not trusting himself to speak, the NCO saluted and dropped into the turret, ordering the driver to take the light tank forward as slowly as he could manage, staying within the apron of the wood.

The jeep raced away, taking Gregorov off to harangue another of his tank commanders. Just south of the river, the T70 he had been similarly encouraging, had slipped into a small stand of trees on the riverbank.

By chance, Fusilov cast a glance at the jeep at the moment of detonation.

The yellow light came first, swiftly followed by the hard crump of an explosion.

'Mines!'

The jeep was flipped onto its top, and was already well alight. The driver, at least Fusilov thought it was the driver, was struggling to escape, pinned under the weight of the wrecked vehicle.

Dropping his glasses to his chest, he used his wider vision to detect the other body, even now struggling to its feet, some yards away from the site of the mine's detonation.

'Gregorov. You damn fool!'

The screams of the trapped driver reached the Sergeant's ears, and he sought some kind of recognition in his officer's face; some sign that he would respond to the petrified man.

There was none.

Nor could there have been.

Gregorov was deaf and blind, the former temporary, the latter permanent.

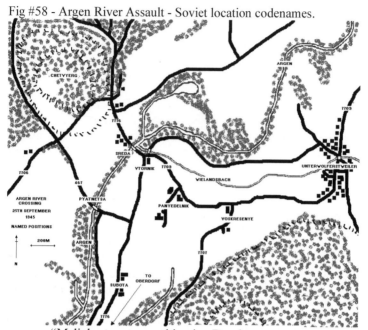

Fig #58 - Argen River Assault - Soviet location codenames.

"Malinky-two-two, this is Drook-one-zero, report, over."

The deep voice of Antonov, the 112th Guards Tank Battalion commander, was unmistakable. He had seen the event from his position in UnterWolfhertsweiler.

"Drook-one-zero, Malinky-two-zero has struck a mine and is out of action. Two-two now in command. Mines to north of main road. Signs of enemy movement in same area, over."

"Is 'Voskrenseny' occupied?"

Both Antonov and Fusilov looked at the ruined old farm, considered indefensible in their planning. It had also been disregarded by the US defenders.

"Drook-one-zero, Malinky-two-two, no sign of any defenders. Position is open from my position, over."

"Received two-two. Is the road clear, over?"

Guards Lieutenant Colonel Antonov was not standing on ceremony.

"Drook-one-zero, Malinky-two-two. Unknown," from memory Fusilov summoned the correct map code, "Am moving

190

up to point 'Panyedelnik' immediately. Will report, over and out."

Knowing the rest of the recon unit had heard, Fusilov concentrated on fighting his own vehicle.

Addressing the driver, the NCO talked through his intended route.

"Right then Comrade, bring her forward, stay in the woods until that hedge line, then hard right at speed and tuck in behind the buildings on that junction there," he indicated the red brick farm buildings at the junction of the 7709 and 7707, despite the fact that the driver could not see him.

The light tank surged forward before the driver brought his charge under full control, nervous of taking the thinly armoured tank into what he considered harm's way.

The radio crackled into life.

"All units, Drook-one-zero. Strike called on 'Vtornik'. Do not approach. Out."

Antonov had decided to flush the game, his heavily armoured IS-II's already shaking out on the outskirts of UnterWolfhertsweiler.

In under a minute, 120mm mortar shells were falling in and around point 'Vtornik'.

1412hrs, Tuesday, 25th September 1945, US defensive position at point 'Panyedelnik', west of UnterWolfhertsweiler, Germany.

The building shook all around them, waterfalls of dust cascading over frightened men.

"Steady guys, steady. They're just chucking shells. They don't know we're here. Just keep your heads down."

H Company's senior non-com was one of the oldest in the US Army, having served with Pershing in World War One and now, with Patton, in World War Two and again in...

'Whatever the goddamn hell this goddamn latest fuck up is called!'

Winchester Mearns did not have a spare ounce of fat on his five foot ten body, but he had more wrinkles than was considered acceptable for any three men.

His eyes seemed permanently closed, his facial skin collapsed in around them.

Even when using his beloved BAR, there was barely a crack between the flesh through which to see.

Nevertheless, he rarely missed, and there was little that evaded his gaze.

"Bazooka team, front and centre!"

The T70 seemed intent on closing his position, and Mearns was intent on ensuring its silence.

Slapping the bazooka man on the shoulder, Mearns picked out a position.

"Haul your ass over the road to the pile," he indicated a stand of felled trunks, some creative infantryman already having constructed an all-round position much like a frontiersman's cabin without the roof.

"Take him as soon as, but make sure you get the sonofabitch. First shot ok?"

A nod was all he got, the two-man team already steeling themselves to run the gauntlet of mortar shells.

Mearns clicked his fingers at two riflemen.

"Stand ready as back up if I holler."

Again, Mearns received no reply, his men trained up to the hilt and confident in their senior man.

Checking on the T70, and noting it had slowed, he gave the word.

"Move out."

The bazooka team slipped swiftly out of the ruined front door, and was safely hidden in the wooden redoubt within seconds.

The tank moved from right to left as Mearns watched, turning just a few yards short of the road, and facing the red brick farmhouse in which the US troops were posted.

"All units, Druck-zero-one, cease fire on 'Panyedelnik'. Out."

'I swear I saw movement.'

"Do you see anything?"

The driver's response was immediate.

"No, Comrade Serzhant, nothing."

Not satisfied, Fusilov considered sending a couple of shells into the ruined farmhouse.

The radio blared loudly in his ear, a stiff reminder of his mission from Antonov dissuading him.

The T70 moved slowly forward.

A slap on the gunner's back indicated that the loader had connected up the rocket grenade, and the bazooka was ready to fire.

The M9 fired a 2.39" diameter M6A3 hollow-charge shell, capable of penetrating anything up to 102mm of armour.

The front armour of the T70 was 60mm at best, and that on the front of the turret only.

Coolly following the track of his target, the gunner aimed for the spot immediately below the driver's hatch, where the armour was thinner.

The driver died instantly.

Fusilov felt the wave of pain as pieces of the tank and driver were propelled into him, bone and metal fragments penetrating his lower limbs in a hundred places.

He keyed the radio as he triggered the machine-gun, his tracers reaching out and into the little pile of wood he had so stupidly failed to spot.

Both men and bazooka were struck, the DT machine-gun fatally defeating the cover as the two men hugged the earth.

"Malinky-two-two, enemy infantry in 'Voskresenye', strength unknown. Am knocked out and abandoning. Out."

As if to emphasise his words, flames started to lick out of the drivers hatch, blown open by the blast. The heat build up inside the stricken light tank gave Fusilov all the encouragement he needed.

Fusilov grabbed the edge of the turret and pulled, but his legs were unable to push upwards.

Panic started to seize him, and small animal like sounds accompanied each exertion, sounds that grew in their intensity, urgency, and pitch. His strength left him, as each effort drained him of more of his reserves, and the blood flowed freely from ruined legs.

"Poor commie bastard."

193

Master Sergeant Mearns spoke to no one in particular, the sight of the hands urgent scrabbling at the turret ring betraying the struggle going on out of sight.

The sounds of terror reached their ears, Fusilov breaking down from professional soldier to terrified animal, as horrible death stalked him within the confines of the small tank.

"Fuck it."

The ancient BAR was placed against the wall.

"Corporal, you're in charge til I get back, ok son?"

And without waiting for a reply, Mearns was gone.

Fusilov had been wounded before. Indeed, he had received burns before, when his T-60 had been knocked out by a mine in the winter of '43.

That had been child's play compared to the pain of being slowly roasted alive.

He gathered himself for a final effort, willing his legs to bend and find some purchase to aid his escape.

Squealing with the pain, his left knee moved and found something, he knew not what, but sufficient to give him a small extra lift upwards.

He repositioned his right arm, the weight of his body perilously supported by his knee.

His arm took the weight, and he levered himself upwards, bringing his face into the afternoon light, partly brought by the rich sunshine, but also contributed to by the flames from his vehicle.

The fire surged, licking at his bleeding leg wounds, causing agony at new levels.

He pushed upwards again, but found no strength and no more leverage, his damaged limbs refusing to function.

Head above the rim, he could see a soldier, an enemy soldier at that, running in the crouch of a veteran, speeding towards the tank.

He screamed, waving his hand in joy, dislodging his tenuous hold and slipping back down inside the tank.

Gratefully, he looked up as the American mounted the burning tank. Holding up his right hand, Fusilov waited to be pulled out.

Two .45 bullets blew his head apart.

194

Mearns, sucking air greedily after his exertions, slid two replacement rounds into his Colt's magazine, holstered it, and picked up his BAR.

He looked into the face of the young soldier, whose wide-eyes silently questioned what the Master Sergeant had just done.

"No-one deserves to die like that, son, no-one, y'hear?"

The boy said nothing, but his face said everything.

A shout from the far window cut short the exchange.

"Sarge, here they come. Lots of infantry, and some fucking big tanks."

"Ok people, let's get ready to bug out. Corporal," the younger man looked at him, awaiting the direction, "Call it in, and give them some numbers. You have a minute."

Whilst the corporal made the radio report, Mearns slapped the angry teenage soldier on the shoulder.

"Stow it for later, Reynolds. We'll talk. For now, we gotta get the fuck out of here."

1420hrs, Tuesday, 25th September 1945, Soviet mobile command point, Unterwolfertsweiler, Germany.

On Colonel Antonov's orders, Soviet mortars had recommenced hitting 'Panyedelnik', taking down three of the Master Sergeant's men.

Eager hands grabbed the wounded, dragging them painfully clear, as the short platoon withdrew to the main line position.

Antonov was an experienced and capable no-nonsense officer, and he didn't like his orders one bit.

Reading the ground, he tried to put himself in the position of the defending commander.

A quick conversation with the officers commanding the infantry and support elements, and a change of plan was set in motion.

Swift notations were made on maps, codenames checked, questions answered, and the command group broke up.

The orders cascaded down to unit level, and 1st Company, 185th Guards immediately deployed to the left,

195

pushing up through the woods as quietly as possible. 2nd Company of the sappers followed fifty metres behind, ready to assist or exploit, as the situation demanded.

One light tank had tried to use the Weilandsbach stream as a cover, but found the modest watercourse to be deeper than expected. The recon tankers sat in the water, their engine swamped and useless.

Another T70 had already penetrated some way into the woods adjacent to the Argen, escaping the potential open killing ground either side of Route 7709.

The Guards infantry of 3rd Company were soon level with the stationary reconnaissance tank, and the combined force moved slowly forward, intent on reaching their first designated line on the 7707.

Smoke from the burning farm buildings, recently vacated by Mearns and his troopers, mingled with the richer, sweeter smoke of the burning T70, flowing gently south in the modest breeze, stinging eyes and tickling throats, as the infantry took their positions in the woods.

As the 3rd Company had been advancing, so too had the 3rd Company of the Engineers, hugging the edge of the river in single file, crawling slowly through the trees and undergrowth that marked the banks of the Argen River.

Antonov judged the moment.

Waiting, …waiting, …waiting.

A final check of his binoculars, quickly sweeping the open area all the way to his target.

Decision.

"All units, all units, Drook-one-zero, execute Adin, repeat, execute Adin."

1430hrs, Tuesday, 25th September 1945, Soviet assault force, Unterwolfertsweiler, Germany.

On receipt of the codeword 'Adin', the Soviet attack began in earnest.

Leading off in four columns, the armour of the 92nd Engineer Tanks emerged from UnterWolfhertsweiler, the strange apparatus they pushed creating loud metallic sounds that could not fail to attract the attention of any would-be defender.

Fig #59 - Soviet developed attack, the Argen River, Germany.

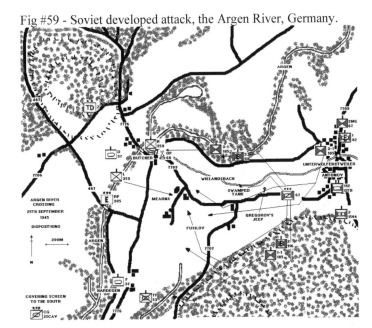

Two of the PT34 tanks were kept back, ready to move up if one of their comrades was knocked out.

The PT34's were 76mm gun T34's with a difference. A metal jib protruded from the bow of each tank, pushing a heavy metal spoked wheel assembly, designed to sink into and chew up the ground ahead of the tank. It was called the Mugalev system, and it killed mines.

Behind each PT tank came a line of four IS-II's, their 122mm guns sweeping the area ahead, ready to lash out at any threat. Each IS-II had a grape of infantry from the SMG Company, each man steeled ready to throw himself off and into combat with the enemy.

Five more IS-II's, including Antonov's own vehicle, lay waiting in UnterWolfhertsweiler.

1431hrs, Tuesday, 25th September 1945, US defensive position at point 'Vtornik', west of UnterWolfhertsweiler, Germany.

Butcher panicked.
"Hit them, open fire, open fire now!"

197

The experienced men around the Major did not react, knowing full well that he had lost it.

Only Travers followed the order, the young Artillery liaison officer sending the fire order to the waiting 105mm's of the 66th Artillery.

Again, Butcher repeated his order, incredulous that no hive of activity had followed, no rumbling thunder, as the guns of his command engaged the enemy.

"You idiot, Butcher. You fired off too soon. Now we're for it!"

Captain Towers, commander of H Company, was furious, the hard work and planning sold down the river in a moment of panic by the inexperienced commander.

Lieutenant Travers, understanding little, tried to make amends by stopping the 66th's guns.

Towers tried to make the best of the bad situation.

"Keep 'em going now, goddamnit, keep 'em going."

Grabbing the radio from the operator, Towers brought himself up to his full five foot seven inches and threw a contemptuous look at Butcher as he got through to Hardegen.

Understandably, the tank man was extremely pissed off.

Towers nodded as he listened, alternating between a look at the battlefield and a contemptuous glare at Butcher.

"Yes, I know that! You can imagine what happened here. Over"

Clearly, the tank officer was spot on in his guess.

"You got it, Major."

Pausing as another flight of 105mm shells landed in front of the oncoming enemy, Towers risked a look out of the window.

Shouting at Travers, Towers focussed the inexperienced officer on getting his shells on target.

"Advance your fire, Lieutenant, you're falling short."

Turning back to the main radio, he returned to his exchange with Hardegen.

"I'm keeping the arty on the go. No one else fired, thank god. The enemy infantry in the woods on the right seem static for now."

Hardegen clearly interrupted, Towers taking the opportunity to gesture for a canteen.

The water was cool and refreshing.

198

Wiping his lips with the back of his hand, he responded.

"Roger that. Has to be best. Can you deal with those monsters? Over."

The tanker's reply clearly hit the mark, and the small man laughed a big laugh.

"I hear that, Major. Good luck to you. Over and ou..."

Butcher snatched the radio from his hand.

"Hardegen, this is Butcher, I am in command. You will open fire immediately. Over."

Onlookers were unclear whether it was the collision with the doorpost that knocked Butcher senseless, or whether it was the flashing impact of Towers' rock hard fist.

Either way, the man was down and out for the count.

The radio was back in competent hands.

"Small problem, now resolved. We will execute as agreed, Over and out."

Hardegen was grinning from ear to ear.

"I was right. Sounds like Butcher panicked, but Towers has it under control."

His gunner grunted, focusing on the job in hand.

Hardegen's mind slipped back to his first meeting with Towers, a misnomer for one of such short stature.

The man clearly knew his business.

Which was very much an asset for the hairy minutes ahead.

Mearns burst into the command point.

"Who in the name of all that is fucking round and sacred ordered that fire?"

Enough eyes swiveled to an insensible lump in the corner for him to get the full picture in an instant.

Snorting in disgust, Mearns moved to Towers and threw up a salute.

"Captain, we bugged out as you see, three wounded, one dead. Took a light tank out before we left. I've slotted my platoon in at the end of the track there."

Towers nodded, rubbing his bruised right hand, for no other reason than it hurt like hell.

199

"OK, Win, you get them settled in there. Just spoke to tanks, and they are still sitting on plan."

Towers jerked a thumb at the inert form.

"That prick lost it and called fire. Now we have to go with that."

Another volley of artillery shells punctuated the statement, closer this time, walked forward by Travers.

Both men checked the approaching enemy, largely obscured by the smoke and flames of the farm buildings, as mortars and tank guns reduced it to rubble.

"Keep your eyes skinned for the flares, and when they come, move like grease lightning clear?"

"You got it, Captain."

Mearns knew the plan, they all did, but he understood that Towers was going to reinforce the message all he could.

They exchanged salutes and Mearns left the CP, pausing only to chuckle over the unconscious officer.

1435hrs, Tuesday, 25th September 1945, Soviet assault force, west of Wolfertsweiler, Germany.

Antonov had lost two tanks, one of the PT's and an IS-II, both from the same group, both to direct artillery strikes.

The enemy artillery started to walk back, dropping just in front of his vehicles.

Ordering his men to move slowly he found his attack force approaching the first objective behind a curtain of smoke and earth kindly created by the Allied artillery.

"Time to move forward, I think. Driver!"

The IS-II moved smoothly through the gears.

The explosion blew off the track.

The young Lieutenant, already a veteran of a score of battles, cursed his driver.

Eager to push forward, the IS-II had slipped outside the area disturbed by the passage of the Mugalev, and found a mine.

Needing no second invitation, the infantrymen had already dismounted, three of them working to save the life of their Corporal, desperately wounded in the mine's blast.

Although sympathetic, the Lieutenant had no choice.

200

"Get him out of the way now. We need room to work here, Comrades."

The infantry gently removed the heavily bleeding NCO, permitting the tank crew to set to work repairing the track, removing spare links from the rack on the front of the tank.

As they worked quickly, removing the bent and twisted links, replacing them with spares, a voice called for help.

Two of the infantrymen went to investigate, and returned leading the blinded Gregorov, his uniform more red than brown, the destroyed and empty eye sockets horrifying to all who beheld him.

One of the 67th's recovery vehicles arrived to assist in the track work, closely followed by an ambulance, which whisked both Gregorov and the dying Corporal away.

Antonov was pleased, but knew that things could change in an instant.

His lead elements were now up with 'Vtornik' and the enemy artillery had stopped.

Reports from the sappers on the riverbank indicated nothing, save a few enemy soldiers having run from 'Vtornik' some while ago.

It all seemed too good to be true, and being an officer who had survived many encounters with the Germans, Antonov suspected it was.

Nevertheless, he determined to push it as far as it would go.

"All units, Drook-one-zero, execute Dva, execute Dva."

On his order, Katyushas of the 379th opened up, plastering the area to the west of the river, paying particular attention to the high ground that dominated both bridges.

His 120mm mortars, more precise in their targeting, brought every tube to bear on Route 7776 and the buildings to the east.

The 1504th's SU76's dropped their HE shells in the woods surrounding the river, south of the Route 467 road bridge, codenamed 'Pyatnetsa'.

The IS-II's pushed forward slowly, but with purpose, and the infantry advanced across the whole frontage of the assault.

Crossing the 7707, the 1st Company emerged from the woods, crossed a small brook and advanced to cut Route 7776, and drive into the flank of the defending force in and around Subota. The 2nd Engineers cut across open land, rounding the small stream, focusing on their objective of the 467 bridge, light fire plucking the life from a man here and there. Defending fire was light, rifles and machine-guns in the main, all originating from the area being flayed by the infantry's mortars.

3rd Company of the 185th charged from their hiding place, and was on top of the Weilandbach bridge in an instant.

The Sappers on the river line, 3rd Company, pushed up, staying tight to the river. They ran straight into booby traps and mines, stopping them in their tracks.

2nd Company of Soviet infantry pushing up behind the advancing tanks, half ran, half walked, moving up the tracks left by the Mugalevs.

1431hrs, Tuesday, 25th September 1945, US defensive position at point 'Vtornik', west of UnterWolfhertsweiler, Germany.

"Do it."

Towers gave a Pfc the word, and a flare soared lazily into the autumn sky.

His men had brought down fire on the attackers, both the infantry to the south and the tank force to their front, the purpose of which was to announce their presence.

"Don't forget to bring the Major!"

US infantrymen bolted from their positions, each believing another had undertaken the task, racing back the two hundred yards to the positions set out on the banks of the river.

The Soviet mortars continued to bring down fire, and men were killed and injured as they withdrew.

In the barn that had been the CP, Major Butcher slid himself upright, his vision blurry, his brain not functioning as it should.

Rubbing his face, trying to bring life to his vital senses, he sensed that all was not well.

As his vision slowly returned, he was greeted neither by the sight of friendly faces, nor by the smell of fresh coffee, nor the sound of American voices.

He was alone.

A shell crashed into the building, producing a red hot wave of tortured air and dust, shifting the already delicate structure from impending collapse to full blown disintegration.

Quickly trying to lever himself up, he found himself overtaken by a deluge of material as the upper storey folded in, compromising the first floor loading and bringing it and the ceiling down in dramatic fashion.

Butcher screamed in agony.

One large joist fell flat, striking both his knees simultaneously, shattering both, and pinning his legs to the stone floor, Part of a floorboard still attached to the joist, splintered and pointed where it had been ripped away as the heavier piece fell, was driven through his left thigh, smashing the femur into fragments.

He screamed as burning material fell around him, his hands beating ineffectively at the growing flames.

He screamed as the joist shifted, pinning him down harder, dragging the splintered section through his thigh muscle.

He screamed as his hands blistered and his hair caught on fire.

'Not like this, I don't want to die like this!'

"Jesus!"

And then he screamed no more.

1439hrs, Tuesday, 25th September 1945, US defensive position at Point 'Sreda', Argen River, Germany.

Towers was furious.

Not with the plan, that was working well, so it seemed. The Soviets were doing what had been hoped, and committing forward.

The Gods of War had finally seen fit to give him a painful token of battle.

The last few yards to the river positions had been a nightmare for him, a lump of mortar shell embedded in his left buttock.

Mearns slipped easily into the small hollow and took in the sight of the Captain, his trousers round his ankles, the medic probing in a small bloody hole in the man's backside.

Towers had a sense of humour failure.

"One word out of you, Win, and I will shoot you myself, clear?"

"My lips are sealed Captain."

One look at the Master Sergeant's face was enough.

"Yes, it hurts OK?"

"Don't they all Captain, don't they all."

"Are your boys ready for this now?"

A nod was sufficient.

"Casualties seem light."

It was posed as a statement, but had all the hallmarks of a question.

"Reckon so, Captain. One of the 57's is down, hit over the river, crew all dead. Some doughs gone too, but light, really light, considering."

"Goddamnit Doc!"

The medic mumbled an apology and dropped the small fragment into the empty cigarette packet that he had provided for the purpose.

"Here you go, Sir. Souvenir for ya. Just gonna fix it up now, and it'll be good as new."

Towers slipped the packet into his pocket, very much doubting his ass would be 'good as new' for some time to come.

Mearns had slipped up to take a look at the field, and dropped back into the hollow again.

"Soon, Captain."

Unable to resist a parting shot, Mearns made much play of checking the magazine in his BAR.

"Avoid the can 'til after the battle, Captain. With two assholes to choose from, an officer type, such as yourself, could be in there all day, deciding which to shit from."

The laughter was universal, a light moment in a sea of hurt.

The moment passed as high-velocity guns started their deadly work.

<u>1441hrs, Tuesday, 25th September 1945, concealed US defensive positions astride Route7776, Argen River, Germany.</u>

The Soviets had codenamed the area 'Subota', as it was important, sitting on the left flank of their main advance.

Although it was apparently unoccupied, Antonov had ordered the 1st Infantry to move forward quickly and form a block.

The experienced Soviet Colonel returned to pushing the main assault forward, unaware that two problems were about to surface.

Firstly, the infantry fell foul of a small stream, the boggy ground slowing their forward momentum to a crawl.

Secondly, the defenders had recognized the significance of 'Subota', and it was occupied by an officer who knew his trade.

They ran straight into the waiting armored-infantry of the 53rd, set for precisely such a threat.

1st Company dropped into the marshy ground, their advance halted.

"Mohawk-Six, all Fox units, on my command," he tapped the gunner and received a low uh-huh to indicate he was on target, "Fire!"

Positioned in camouflaged positions either side of Route 7776, the six M4A3E8 Shermans engaged the flanks of the lead IS-II's.

In three incidences, the results were spectacular, a trio of the leviathans exploding in bright orange flame as vehicle and crew died together.

Two other ground to a halt, penetrating rounds wreaking havoc.

One heavy tank shrugged off the strike and turned to place its thicker frontal armour to the enemy.

Three shells hit it simultaneously, smashing wheels and tracks from its offside, the 57mm anti-tank guns of the 359th Infantry positioned across the river hitting in unison.

A PT76 suddenly realized it was a small fish in a big fish world, and jettisoned its Mugalev, turning in towards the farm buildings, seeking cover. It died instantly, transformed into an oily hearse by a high velocity 76mm shell.

"Nice shot, DeMarco."

205

The gunner, light on words as ever, merely grunted and went about his business.

Antonov responded immediately.

He ordered the 1st Infantry to close up and distract whatever it was that was killing his tanks, ignoring the excuses and protestation of the commander on the ground, reporting the wet ground and new contact with dug-in infantry on the left flank of his position.

"Just get your men up there, Comrade Kapitan. Unless you want to command a penal mine detail!"

He shifted his heavy mortars to the river line, bringing down smoke to protect his flank, and swung part of his armour south towards the 7776 to take the enemy head-on.

The remainder of his force he halted level with the same route, with orders to engage any target to their front.

He moved his own reserve group up to the junction of the 7709 and 7707.

The 379th was held back, their next salvo saved until he knew exactly what was happening. The SU-76's of the 1504th were given orders to move up closer to the action.

One of the defending M4's took a hit. The 122mm shell was not a precision instrument like the scalpel of a surgeon; more the blunt sledgehammer of the labourer.

This sledgehammer removed the turret with ease, propelling it backwards over one hundred yards.

Hardegen, angry at the loss of one of his senior NCO's, put one right on the money, but the shell speared into the sky, bouncing off the thick armour of the IS tank.

The Soviet vehicle moved forward and disappeared behind a small rise in the ground.

The radio crackled, and the high-pitched voice of Captain Clayton penetrated the sounds of battle.

"All Dog units, on my order... fire!"

From behind the rise came a flash. Instantly, black oily smoke marked the spot the IS had died.

206

Nine IS-II's now lay immobile on the field of battle, over half of those committed, all for the loss of an anti-tank gun and a Sherman.

The 1st Company, 185th Guards Rifle Regiment had run into big trouble, barbed wire, booby traps, mines, the whole area swept with fire from US armored-infantry and tanks, all well hidden in trenches, tank pits, or in the woods by the river.

Casualties were murderous, and made worse when the US infantry commander brought his mortars into play, tree bursts wreaking their own special brand of horror on the unfortunate soldiers.

Antonov received the reports impassively, his Armoured Group desperately fighting back.

He got through on the radio to Corps commander.

The situation was grave, but not unsalvageable. Nonetheless, he broached the possibility of withdrawing and going around the stubborn defence. The reply virtually mirrored that he had given to the infantry officer a few minutes beforehand, so he concentrated on the task in hand, splitting the efforts of his tanks between the two main sources of enemy fire.

Across the river, an enemy vehicle blossomed into an orange ball, as two 122mm's simultaneously struck its turret and hull, causing the Sherman to disintegrate. A huge solid metal lump cartwheeled skywards, as if carried on the wall of flame.

Encouraged by this, and other reports of more success to the south, Antonov brought his reserve up, focusing on the prize of the 7776 bridge at 'Sreda'.

<u>1447hrs, Tuesday, 25th September 1945, in and around Position 'Sreda', Argen River, Germany.</u>

The radio exchange had terminated abruptly, D Company's commanders situation report cut short by the arrival of the two heavy tank shells.

The second in command took over.

207

Hardegen received the report of Clayton's death impassively, setting aside the loss of another old comrade to fight his tank, and command his unit.

"Mohawk-Six, Zebra in position. Waiting orders."

Hardegen's ace, held back from the obvious artillery target of the dominating high ground, had moved up and was now in position.

Normally, the 37th Tanks didn't have the 'Zebras' on its TOE, but in times of war, things change. Hardegen had welcomed the three vehicles into his unit, their own parent formation long since gutted north of Munich.

The 'Zebras' had earned their spurs against Hitler's Panzers, and put their skills to good use all through the bitter days in August 1945.

To the crews of the M36B2 tank destroyers, this was going to be payback time.

"Zebra, this is Mohawk-Six, engage, over."

The three shells ate up the four hundred and fifty yards to their targets.

One missed.

Two did not.

The 90mm's had fired the deadly HVAP rounds, more than enough to penetrate the IS-II's frontal armour at a thousand yards.

One shell each punched through the side armour of two of the heavy tanks engaging Hardegen's force.

Apart from the death of its gunner, the first tank experienced no difficulties, the shell passing through and out the far side without causing major damage.

The second IS-II was knocked out when the HVAP shell penetrated and struck the breech of the gun, twisting the turret, and transforming the shell and parts of the main gun into deadly whirling fragments from which there was no escape.

The Russian Colonel knew he had a disaster on his hands.

'Mudaks! This is murder!'

Antonov did what he could, directing fire against the high ground once more, bringing forward the infantry to assault the bridges direct whilst his beloved tanks soaked up the pressure.

Almost unbelievably, one of the PT76's had got off a shot and killed something on the hill.

The Tank Officer had no idea what they were, except that they were deadly and now there was one less.

The PT slipped back behind its protective wall, only for two vengeful shells to punch through the brickwork, and reduce the medium tank to scrap.

Infantry from 2nd Company swarmed past his command tank, sensing that survival lay with closing to the enemy fast, as mortars and artillery started to fall around their positions.

Hardegen watched the surge and went to contact the artillery. The artillery contacted him first.

"Mohawk-six, this is Rainman. We are out in three, Have to keep some. Sorry, over."

Hardegen had known that the artillery had very little ammunition, something that he had factored into his plans. However, now, faced with reality and prime targets, the loss of the 105's was important.

"Roger Rainman, and thanks."

Soviet infantry were dropping now, some in search of cover from which to fight back cover, others put there by bullets or fear.

Antonov gripped the cupola in his anxiety.

'I must have that fucking bridge, or my men will have died for nothing!'

The Lieutenant Colonel ordered forward every man he had left to him, sending the Su76M's of the 1504th forward to act as direct support, focusing all efforts on the 7776 bridge over the Argen.

"Mohawk-six, this is Apache-six, we are bugging out now."

Hardegen acknowledged the expected message, the obvious wave of Soviet infantry inexorably pushing towards the river.

"Mohawk-six, all Fox units, standby to execute Plan Delta", the tank commander swiftly checking his rear to ensure that the withdrawal manouevre 'Delta' was safe.

His supporting infantry had beaten the 1st Company back, and they would slip away on the execution of his order.

"Mohawk-six, all Fox units, execute Delta."

His surviving four Shermans reversed away, swiftly disengaging, following the plan to cross the river to the south at Kressbronner Straße, intermixed with the handful of halftracks that bore part of the armored-infantry.

The rest of the armored-infantry force slipped into the various boats they had acquired, and quickly made the relative safety of the other bank.

Antonov recalled some of his tanks, already moving off to the south, intent on pursuing the withdrawing US armour.

"Drook-one-zero, all units, execute Pyat, execute Pyat, concentrate on the bridge comrades, support the infantry, but we must secure that bridge."

The Soviet force neared its objective.

<u>1453hrs, Tuesday, 25th September 1945, US defensive position at Point 'Sreda', Argen River, Germany.</u>

"Goddamnit but that hurts."

The position was empty, much like his BAR.

The platoon had slipped over the river in the dinghies supplied by the 305th Engineers, his own dinghy ripped to shreds by shrapnel from the same shell that had killed his two men and removed his left foot.

Ramming home his last magazine, the Master Sergeant slid away from the water's edge, propping himself up against a shattered tree trunk, and slipping a lucky strike into his mouth.

As he lit it, he heard the rush of footsteps as three enemy soldiers rushed forward and threw themselves down behind the wall of ammo boxes at the back, unaware of his presence.

The heavy BAR hammered out and the three lost interest in anything but the pain of their hideous wounds.

Another sound filled his ears, taking precedence over the screams of the three wounded men.

'Oh shit!'

It was a tank, and it was coming his way.

Antonov pushed himself hard, all the time aware that his men were bleeding, all the time believing the bridge to be more precious with every extra drop of spilt Soviet blood.

"Driver, halt."

The tank swayed even though the tracks had stopped turning.

"I have him in my sights, Comrade Podpolkovnik!"

The gunner's voice betrayed his fears, but the man had stuck to his task thus far, and Antonov knew he would not fail him.

"Fire!"

An American tank blew up, his shell bludgeoning through the frontal armour and into the bodies beyond.

"Excellent Comrades! Driver, forward!"

A hideous metallic clang robbed him of his hearing, the smell of burning and spent explosive informing him that his tank had been badly hit.

The IS-II was still moving forward, the dead driver's hands on the controls, the gradual right turn taking the heavy tank away from the water, further exposing its side to the enemy across the river.

Mearns saw it coming and dragged himself out of its path, his leg leaving a bloody smear behind him.

Another two Soviet infantrymen dropped inside the hollow.

This time, the American was spotted.

The BAR was slow to deploy, and one of the Russians got a shot off with his rifle as the Master Sergeant sent them both to hell.

The impact of the bullet knocked the breath out of Mearns, punching into his right breast and out his back in a millisecond.

The pain followed quickly.

He discharged his final round as his body surrendered to the wounds. In its weakened state, it refused point-blank to hold the Browning any longer.

He coughed violently, sending gobbets of blood over the earth around him.

'Goddamnit, if the bastards haven't done for me!'

Two of the three wounded Soviet soldiers had either died or lapsed into unconsciousness. The third lay immobile, looking straight at Mearns, his eyes full of hate for his killer, but also laced with triumph that his killer would not long survive him.

In the IS-II, still moving slowly forward, Antonov started to feel the pain of his stomach wound. Deeply sliced by a whirling piece of hinge, mashed from the driver's hatch and transformed into a flying razor.

The tank lurched, sending the dazed gunner cannoning into him.

Antonov screamed, his wound split and permitted some of his entrails to escape.

Within seconds, he was alone with the dead driver, the other two tankers scrabbling up and out of the vehicle.

Across the river, soldiers from H Company, already enraged by the wounding of their NCO, and their inability to get back over the water to help him, discharged their angst with violence, pouring heavy fire into the two crewmen.

Bullets found them with ease, and both dropped lifelessly to the ground.

There were external fuel tanks mounted on the rear sides of the IS-II, metal containers that Antonov had insisted were topped up, given the rumours about supply problems.

These were struck many times by the fusillade, and diesel fuel started to leak. The engine decking became awash, and fuel spilled down the sides of the tank.

Still the metal leviathan crawled forward.

Mearns dragged himself in behind a tree root, trying to extract his pistol, something he could not accomplish with his chest wound.

In H Company's position, it seemed clear that the tank intended to run down their Sergeant, and the bazooka team risked themselves in order to prevent that.

The shell missed, and then it hit.

At first, the rocket passed between the 2nd and 3rd rollers, touching nothing on the way through.

Three feet beyond it kissed the ground and flipped upwards, striking the 4th roller on the other side of the tank, wrecking its axle, the roller itself, and fracturing the heavy track.

The impact did not dislodge the dead driver, who continued to discharge his duty. The offside track parted, and within seconds, all drive came from the nearside, slewing the tank into a broken tree stump, sending rivers of fuel across its hull plate and onto the earth all around.

The IS-II stalled.

Over the water, the disconsolate bazooka crew saw that they had another opportunity and took the shot.

Inside the heavy tank, Antonov was in agony, his efforts totally focused on keeping his stomach inside his body.

Outside, Mearns was counting his blessings, although the now leaning tree stump had trapped his good leg, leaving him stuck close to the front of the knocked-out tank.

The second rocket struck, penetrating the hull side adjacent to the huge twelve-cylinder diesel engine.

The IS-II caught fire.

The flames spread, feasting on the free fuel vapour from the two ruptured tanks, greedily moving on to find welcoming diesel fuel in all directions.

Burning fuel dropped around the tree stump.

"What the hell?"

Mearns pushed and scrabbled, his limited strength of no use against the inexorable downward pressure of the tank on the tree truck.

He exerted his strength, dug with his good hand, pushed with his good leg, all to no avail, all the time growing weaker.

More burning fuel dropped around him, catching his trousers alight

In a moment of clarity, he had a last rational thought.

'I don't deserve to die like this!'

And then the moment was gone, and Master Sergeant Winchester Mearns became a mental wreck, howling and screaming his last few moments away.

Inside the tank, Antonov knew what lay in store.

As he reached around to his side, his thoughts turned to his wife and his three fine sons.

The heat was unbearable and he did not prolong the moment unnecessarily.

The barrel of the Tokarev was against the side of his forehead, the act of pulling the trigger granting him one final second of life.

'I don't want to die like this!'

The sound of the shot was lost on Mearns, his legs engulfed in flames, his animal panic having robbed him of every vestige of humanity.

The sounds of his screams were truly awful, and rose above most sounds of the battle.

Across the river, a young man's mind found resolve and his Garand put a bullet into the suffering man.

Pfc Oberon Reynolds dropped the rifle from his shoulder.

'You were right Sarge, you were right. No-one deserves to die like that.'

1459hrs, Tuesday, 25th September 1945, US defensive position at Point 'Chetvyerg', Argen River, Germany.

The M36 tank destroyers died within a second of each other, their tender rears fatally exposed to the new arrivals.

To the north, Allied forces had repulsed a Soviet attack aimed at Tettnang, so Berzarin had sent a considerable force southwards to help out on the Argen River, ready to turn westwards and undercut Tettnang.

It was this battlegroup, elements of the 11th Tank Corps, which now took to the field, surprising the US defenders on the hillock, codenamed 'Chetvyerg' by the now-dead Antonov.

Communications between the two attacking groups was non-existent, but both exhibited excellent control and restraint, with no friendly casualties resulting in their coming together on the west bank of the Argen.

T34's of the 65th Tank Brigade supported by motorized infantry from the 12th [Motorized] Rifle Brigade hammered into the rear of the US positions, sweeping all before them.

From the height, they were able to control all of the area west of the Argen through which the American forces had to withdraw.

The Soviet tanks knocked out vehicle after vehicle, aided by the survivors of Antonov's force.

One anti-tank gun was repositioned, and managed single shot before it was trashed by a wave of HE from the 65th's armour.

214

On the Argen, the Soviet engineers finally managed to push through the booby-traps and barbed wire, achieving the 7776 bridge.

The assault elements of the 2nd Company 185th Guards pushed over the other bridge at the same time.

The final phase of the US defensive plan was to destroy both of these bridges, and the surviving NCO of the 305th US Engineers discharged his responsibilities, electronically detonating first the nearest bridge carrying Route 467, then that carrying Route 7776 to the north.

The lead platoon of the 185th Guards was killed outright. First, the soldiers were thrown skywards, as the huge charge propelled body and the 467 bridge into the air. The jumbled mass of men and concrete fell back, either to earth or water, and none survived.

The shock wave claimed more casualties from both sides, the US troops unable to fall back as planned because of the arrival of the northern force.

The delay in switching to the second bridge circuit gave the Soviet sappers hope for survival, hope that died with them, as a second huge charge brought about a repeat performance.

The 116th Engineers did have inflatable boats at the rear, but command and control was shot to pieces, so they remained there, unused.

Soviet mortars, freed by the loss of the bridges, brought down a furious attack on the defensive positions, pinning the US infantrymen in their shallow scrapes in the ground, or killing them with blast and shrapnel.

Some men tried to move away down the river line, but they were seen by the survivors of Antonov's tank unit, who enjoyed the turkey shoot, mowing down the defenceless men as they struggled in the water.

There was no escape, and hands started to rise, as first, individuals, and then groups, surrendered.

Hardegen's unit pulled back successfully, crossing over the Argen at Oberdorf, and marrying up with their covering infantry force from the 53rd.

The military situation dictated that they had to withdraw again, and the composite unit withdrew further back to Eriskirch, but not before Hardegen had called in a priority mission on the intact bridges around Oberdorf.

215

As he settled into the new line at Eriskirch, fighter-bombers of the USAAF took out both bridges, losing three aircraft in the process.

Positioning his tanks to defend the river crossing, west of Eriskirch, Major John Hardegen was frustrated to find no supply vehicles waiting to replenish his low stocks of ammunition and fuel.

Taking time out to eat the rations cooked up by his crew, Hardegen reflected on the day.

'Some damn good boys died today.'

Task Force Hardegen had certainly lost some good men, but it was intact, although depleted. The 53rd Infantry had lost a handful of doughs, the 37th Tanks left four of their vehicles on the field, whereas 25th Cavalry had escaped casualties. Their positions, covering the rear of Hardegen's force, had not been tested. The relatively fresh unit was presently out providing a security screen, whilst the rest of his task force rested.

Task Force Butcher was a different story.

There was none of it left as far as he could see, not a single GI had yet reported in; a single half-track or gun found its way to safety.

'Poor bastards.'

Sure, the Soviet infantry had been given a good hammering, and their armour, particularly the heavy tank unit, had been heavily worked over.

But the enemy held the field, the unsuspected arrivals from the north clinching the victory for them.

A particularly hot piece of beef burnt his tongue, causing him to breathe furiously, bringing cool air to the afflicted area.

The pain brought a new line of thought.

'I wonder how old Knocke would see today?'

He determined to test the next piece of beef before committing to its consumption.

It was fine, and he chewed as he contemplated his own question.

'I daresay he would say you're alive, tomorrow is another day and you will do better next time.'

Hardegen laughed loudly, amused by his own reply.

DeMarco toyed with his meal, the appetite drained from him by the loss of some of his friends. Hardegen's laugh seemed so out of place to a man grieving for close comrades.

'Merda! How can you laugh, you heartless bastardo?'

Hardegen caught the gunner's look, and immediately knew what the Italian-American was thinking.

Picking up his coffee, he moved over and dropped down beside DeMarco.

They ate together, drank together, smoked together, and spoke of friends they would never see again.

You people are telling me what you think I want to know. I want to know what is actually happening.

Creighton Abrams

Chapter 86 - THE BRIEFING

Nazarbayeva had timed everything very deliberately, ensuring that she had sufficient time to visit St Basil's Cathedral, a long cherished ambition.

Never particularly religious, but also not anti, like good communists were supposed to be, the splendour of the domes gripped her, and the incredible interior transported her with its beauty.

The fact that she was in the uniform of Soviet Military Intelligence guaranteed that she would enjoy it in peace.

After having her fill of the grandeur, the GRU Colonel strode purposefully across Red Square, through security, and into the hallowed halls, for her 10am meeting with the GKO.

She sat outside the conference room, her eyes drawn to the huge ornate clock, ticking away with a steady and heavy beat, just as the radio propaganda clock did at Stalingrad. Her mind was suddenly transported back to those desperate times, *'tick-tock, tick-tock, another German dead.'*

10:23.

It was unusual for all meeting times not to run to order.

'Is there something wrong?'

The door opened, and a stern-faced NKVD Major-General she did not recognize, demanded her presence.

On entering the room, she was momentarily surprised to find the entire GKO seated around the huge table, all expectantly looking directly at her.

The door closed noisily behind her, stiffening her resolve.

Stalin rose from a small separate desk and moved to the prime position, sat between Bulganin and Molotov.

218

"Comrade Polkovnik Nazarbayeva, our apologies, but other matters have had to take precedence this morning. May I offer you my condolences for the loss of your son."

Beria remained transfixed by the report in front of him, a small curl in his lip the only sign of his inner thoughts.

"Thank you, Comrade General Secretary."

More than one pair of eyes swiveled to examine their leader's face, desperate to find some reason for his uncharacteristic apology and concern.

They found none.

Extending his hand, Stalin invited the GRU Colonel to begin.

Nazarbayeva had been kept waiting because the GKO had been looking at a report from the Far East, in which Vasilevsky detailed reverses, both to his own and Japanese forces, in northern and southern China respectively.

They were already chastened, and had no need for more bad news.

Which was unfortunate.

"Comrade General Secretary, Comrades, a GRU asset within the Royal Air Force has informed us that the targeting of Allied airpower resources has now firmly changed to our support and supply assets, based on their interpretation and intelligence gained, regarding a definite supply issue for the Red Army."

More than one of the old men slumped in his chair.

"This has been the case for a few days now, and the results are wiping out the improvements made since the issues of supply were first highlighted."

Nazarbayeva handed over a report containing estimates on losses in reinforcements and supplies.

Stalin slid it across to Bulganin, who deftly deposited it in front of Beria.

The rest of the GKO watched the balding NKVD supremo closely as he quickly scanned the figures and gave the briefest of nods.

'They knew?'

"Your figures tally with those supplied by Comrades Beria and Kaganovich. However, the reason behind this has now become clearer. Continue Comrade."

"Comrades, the situation will not improve and GRU expects the attacks to grow in frequency and strength."

There was an expectant silence, and one that also carried all the dangers of telling great men that their plans were failing.

"Allied air power is growing. Their factories are producing at full capacity. Efforts, such as the NKVD sabotage mission at Boeing in Seattle have had no effect."

Their silence invited her to continue, but had she looked at Beria, she would have noted something unpleasant in his eyes.

"Our Red Navy has performed magnificently, but recent losses in the Atlantic submarine force have reduced their effectiveness, and no sinkings of note have been made for some time now."

All in the room understood that the Soviet Navy would try to get more submarines into the deep waters of the Atlantic, and those who were not foolish enough to believe the assurances of the Admirals understood that the attempts would almost certainly end in failure. After all, the Allied navies had defeated the most powerful submarine force in history, a force designed to be ocean-going, and their combat efficiency in anti-submarine warfare was now back to German war levels.

"Our Air Force makes accurate claims now that the system for reporting has been adjusted."

Sliding free a page from one report, Nazarbayeva quickly reminded herself of some figures.

"Our own air regiments have suffered crippling losses, and we have been unable to make good the gaps in our order of battle, especially as we have started to lose machines from mechanical failure, caused by an absence of spares. By example, two regiments equipped with Capitalist Aircobra aircraft can now muster eight aircraft between them, the others having been cannibalized to keep the remainder flying."

Malenkov, whose portfolio was primarily concerned with aircraft production, started coughing and spluttering, so much so that all attention focused on him, until a helpful but overzealous thump on the back from Molotov brought an end to the interlude.

"Losses in air force personnel have been huge, both in the air and on the ground, the allied attacks on our airfields killing many qualified ground staff."

Another file was opened.

"The loss of the train transport shipment T#7979831A, as sustained on Sunday 23rd September, outside of Gniezno, was of huge importance."

Beria shifted uncomfortably, his own NKVD troopers having suffered grievously at the hands of the Polish brigands.

"A special action train, containing an NKVD battalion, and sent ahead of 831A, was derailed and destroyed."

Beria did not care for his shortcomings to be aired in such a fashion. The Special Action Units went ahead of important trains, intending to draw fire or set off any ambush, the well-armed NKVD battalions thought sufficient to deal with any partisans.

"831A was forced to halt, and was brought under fire from heavily armed partisans. The NKVD party travelling with 831A performed valiantly, and saved many of the personnel from being killed."

'You offer me an olive branch do you, bitch? Fucking bitch?'

Nazarbayeva meant no such thing, her briefing being concerned solely with the facts.

"As a result of that attack, three hundred and one newly trained aircrew were killed, and another three hundred and sixty-three wounded, removing them from immediate flying duty."

Some had been aware that the train's personnel had been badly hit, some had even been aware that they were precious aviators. None had been aware of the numbers, except for one man, who had managed the delivery of the bad news in the first place.

Beria removed his handkerchief and cleaned his glasses, conscious of the fact that he was under the unwavering eye of Stalin.

Nazarbayeva saved him, drawing the Soviet leader's attention back to her.

"Comrade General Secretary, many of our air regiments are operating at below 50% strength, and the loss of 831A ensures that our air power will remain weakened for the foreseeable future."

Taking a moment to control her delivery, she pressed on.

"On the 19th September, Marshal Novikov informed the European commanders of the new air plan, a plan that is now endangered by these losses in personnel and which, according to

221

Air Force projections, may now only be possible if all other offensive air operations are ceased immediately."

Stalin crushed his cigarette, doing so noisily, and making himself the focus of the room.

"So, Comrade Polkovnik, you always tell us the facts, and give us your honest interpretation. Do so now."

There was no dressing it up, but Nazarbayeva tried to let the GKO down as lightly as possible.

"At this moment, we are barely holding our own in the air. We have some successes, but overall we lose more crews and machines than they do. The Air Force plan to limit excursions over enemy lines, as much as possible, may save a few pilots from captivity, but such efforts pale into insignificance alongside the losses sustained by events such as the attack on 831A."

Stalin struck a match, lighting his next cigarette, the flare of the phosphorus highlighting the fact that his eyes were locked firmly on the GRU Colonel.

"That being said, the Allies are recovering from the huge destruction wrought on the RAF bomber force, and seem to be growing stronger across the spectrum of their regiments."

She caught Beria's eye by chance, and something flared inside, removing some of her caution in the delivery of the bad news.

"Comrades, unless new aircraft reach the regiments in large numbers, complete with properly trained flight crew, the Red Air Force will be beaten, and with that the skies will belong to the Allies, day and night."

The atmosphere changed, so unused were the powerful men to such stark and direct delivery, all save Stalin and Beria, who had experienced Nazarbayeva's honesty before.

The change in atmosphere did not stop her from continuing.

"Without air cover over the assault formations and supply centres, the Allies will destroy the Red Army's capability to fight, and destroy many of the ground assets, removing the advantage we enjoy in numbers."

Kaganovich, Bulganin, and Molotov stayed silent, their white faces indicative of the fact that they had heard something new and worrying.

222

Malenkov and Voznesensky spoke in shocked whispers, the invincibility of the Red Army suddenly not as assured as they had been led to believe.

Beria and Stalin, both with more information than the rest, did nothing.

"Carry on, Comrade Polkovnik, you have come this far, you should finish your delivery. What do you foresee here?"

Stalin's voice, unusually soft, encouraged the GRU officer.

"Comrade General Secretary, unless we can give the Army and Air Force the necessary means, there will be great difficulties ahead."

A hubbub grew as great men whispered with those sat alongside them.

It ceased as quickly as it started, as Stalin rose from his seat and walked briskly round to his small desk. Sampling the drink he had left upon it, he turned to Nazarbayeva and pounced.

"So Comrade Polkovnik, the GRU's official position is that we are going to lose the war because of a few difficulties with our supplies, and the loss of a handful of pilots. Is that right?"

Many men had paled and shriveled under such an assault. They were not Nazarbayeva.

"No, Comrade General Secretary, that is not the official position of the GRU, neither is it my own view."

Stalin moved closer, intimidatingly close.

"So what is the view of GRU Polkovnik Tatiana Nazarbayeva in these testing times eh? Come on, Comrade, don't be shy!"

"Comrade General Secretary, we cannot lose the war militarily. Over the centuries, powerful armies have tried and failed, and the reasons they failed will stand Mother Russia in good stead, if she is tested again. But, I believe that if we do not resolve these present issues then we will not win the war, and that amounts to the same as losing it, as far as Mother Russia will be concerned."

The silence was thick with risk, heavy with danger.

Stalin's eyes bored into her own, but she stood her ground.

His eyes dropped to the Gold Star on her chest.

His face relaxed, a gentle nodding indicating the escape of tension.

Switching his cigarette into his left hand, Stalin extended his right hand and tapped the bravery award with his index finger, the touch seemingly a switch that made his face split into a grin.

The Generalissimo turned to the rest of the GKO.

"So you can see, Comrade Nazarbayeva did not get this in the ration packs, or because of her political affiliations."

Inside, the GRU Colonel let the relief wash through her.

"I agree with your assessment, Comrade Polkovnik."

Stalin walked round to his seat and dropped into it smoothly.

"Continue, Comrade."

Nazarbayeva shifted her weight, the injured foot beginning to protest.

"Comrades, my information is that the Allied Commanders have not yet understood the Italian position, and they continue to bleed experienced units away from their own Italian armies to send into Germany."

Stalin leant back in his chair and permitted others to speak, low rumbles seizing upon the positive offered to them.

Nazarbayeva decided that she could not let them continue.

"Comrades, if I may. The balance of forces is not as great in our favour as you may think. GRU can now confirm that twelve division of the Spanish Army, fully manned and equipped, with a mix of German and Allied weapons, have crossed the frontier into Northern Italy."

The silence was deafening.

"Allied planning seems to be to permit these divisions to take over in the line from the experienced Allied divisions, which are then sent northwards."

The low conversations broke out again, but were quickly stopped by Beria, tapping his pen on the table, eager to demonstrate his abilities to Nazarbayeva.

"So, Comrade Polkovnik, what did Marshal Zhukov see in this latest development?"

Momentarily thrown by the question, Nazarbayeva realized that the NKVD chief probably knew only too well what had been said the day before, when she had briefed Zhukov and Malinin.

"Comrade Marshal, I believe that the Commander of the Red Army in Europe sees this as a big opportunity, provided the supply situation is resolved."

Tatiana relayed the official position, assuming that Beria had a report on everything that had been said.

In the deeper recesses of her mind, a voice she recognised as her own asked a simple question.

'Have you just made an error, Chekist?'

"So, Marshal Zhukov believes that these Spanish troops might, in the main, be more vulnerable, and therefore the way into Southern France could be opened more easily than planned."

The voice inside laughed.

'Yes, you have, you arrogant little prick!'

"Yes, Comrade Marshal, that is precisely what Marshal Zhukov believes."

This was the truth, as Beria had quoted the conversation word for word.

Stalin came back into the discussion.

"That is a matter for another time, Comrade Polkovnik. Proceed."

Nazarbayeva's sharp mind suddenly sensed the danger of another part of the conversation and acted swiftly, thinking only to reduce the danger to Zhukov.

"Comrade General Secretary, the Allies have been particularly successful in integrating their returned prisoners of war back into their combat forces, bolstering their numbers across the board, replacing losses in existing units, as well as creating whole new divisions and squadrons, all of which consist of men with skills and experience. My sources inform me, unequivocally, that these units are all well motivated and the equal of the existing formations."

Stalin and Beria had seen the verbatim record of the conversation, and recalled what Zhukov's response had been to that information.

"We have similar assets that are not taken advantage of, and the Motherland's forces are suffering as a result."

The penalization of those taken prisoner was a basic tenet of the way Stalin conducted the war, and to criticize it was to commit suicide.

More than one in the room could see a mental picture of Nazarbayeva swinging from a rope before the day's end.

"GRU understands the need to pursue sanctions against those who were weak and permitted themselves to be captured, depriving the Motherland of their skills at a time of great need. There can be no suggestion of permitting these 'people' to retain the rights of citizenship, such as those who have fought throughout, enjoy."

In the minds of those present, the hangman paused in his work, curious to hear more.

"Many of these soldiers are unfit, the deprivations of German captivity too much, and yet they can be of use."

The hangman relaxed, and set the rope aside, just for the moment.

"Supply officers already have placed the repatriation of these men at the lowest possible priority, which means that the majority still remain in or close to the combat zone."

Both Beria and Stalin knew of Zhukov's comments on that score.

"GRU believes that those who are unfit for combat could serve a purpose, and even release some normal troops to other duties. Those fit enough to serve could be formed into special units, established without frills or favours, and given over to the harshest tasks, such as our existing shtrafbats."

The hangman looked pensive.

Stalin spoke in a very measured fashion.

"Comrade Nazarbayeva, it is accepted that those soldiers of the Red Army that permitted themselves to be taken prisoner are not afforded the status of soldier, and are lost in the eyes of the state. This you understand?"

"Yes, Comrade General Secretary, this is understood."

"And yet, you presume to stand in front of this group and put forward a recommendation that undermines that which is wholly accepted by the people and the state?"

The hangman was back preparing his noose.

"Comrade General Secretary, if I may. I have lost two sons to the great patriotic enterprise on which the Motherland has presently embarked. As a mother, and as a soldier, the thought that some others, who are quite capable of serving the Motherland, are excluded from risk, because they have failed before, is curious to say the least."

226

The hangman smiled, shook his head, and advanced with the noose ready.

There was no sound from the assembly.

Nazarbayeva continued.

"Comrades, as a mother and a soldier, I would welcome the possibility that these failures could be offered a chance of redemption, placing them open to the same risks faced by my remaining sons, and my husband, rather than some warm and cosy Gulag in the heart of the Motherland."

Silence.

The hangman disappeared instantly, and was replaced by silent debate, as each man looked again at the issue.

'We can't let this happen.'

'She has a point.'

'We need the manpower.'

'Why not let the Allies shoot the bastards for us?'

'This will undermine our authority.'

'Why not?'

'Why can we not do this?'

Despite the result of their own thought processes, everyone took their cue from Stalin.

"Comrade Polkovnik, you understand the effect that this reversal could have upon the credibility of the State, and the effectiveness of the Red Army?"

"Comrade General Secretary, I understand that the Red Army, Air Force and Navy are exhibiting the highest courage and skill in beating the Western Allies. I also understand that will not continue unless solutions are found. GRU recommends this as one solution to one problem. Clearly, this is a momentous decision, and one that rightfully belongs with this present company. I can only place the information before you all, and hope that I have done enough to permit you to make a properly informed judgment."

Stalin considered his response carefully, sparing a look at his senior men, reading a raised eyebrow here, a furrowed brow there.

"Quite so, Comrade Polkovnik. You have given us your briefing, and we will consider its contents. Have you concluded your briefing?"

"Yes, Comrade General Secretary."

"Thank you, Comrade Polkovnik. I see no need to detain you further."

<u>1203hrs, Friday, 28th September 1945, Headquarters, Red Banner Forces of Europe, Kohnstein, Nordhausen, Germany.</u>

"Read that again. Did I misunderstand?"

Malinin, as taken aback as Zhukov, reread the passage aloud.

It was the same second time around.

"Mudaks!"

Malinin grinned at his superior's choice expression.

"How long before we can implement this? I'm thinking immediately for integrating, say four days for stand alone units, as a minimum."

"I would agree up to a point, Comrade Marshal, but we must remember the poor physical state of some of these men."

"Yes, yes, I know."

The order before them removed the objections to utilizing the released prisoners of the German War, but specified their lack of privileges and status, and encouraged Zhukov to place them at the points of highest danger.

Nonetheless, the Red Army and Air Force had just been handed a new reserve from which to cherry pick the best and most qualified men.

More to the point, the document granted Zhukov full authority to integrate the prisoners as he saw fit, ensuring the best possible advantage to the Red Army.

The previous evening, Nazarbayeva had relayed the content of her meeting with the GKO, and passed on the knowledge she had gained from Beria's mistake.

Here was evidence of that she had been able to influence the GKO on an extremely important matter, one on which even Zhukov himself had not been able to get movement.

The Marshal looked at his CoS and laughed.

Zhukov's laugh was infectious, and so Malinin joined in.

"Balls of steel, Mikhail. I swear it, that woman has balls of steel."

A knock on the door brought the pair back to earth, their serious side emerging, as the newly promoted Major Viktor

228

Serebryakov strode in and sprang to the attention position in front of Zhukov's desk.

An immaculate salute started proceedings.

"Comrade Marshal. Thank you for this great honour, and it has been a privilege to serve under you. With your permission, I will leave now."

"You may, and thank you for your service, Comrade Mayor. You deserve this. I wish you good luck."

The door closed behind the Major, ensuring he did not hear Malinin's snort of derision.

"Chekist bastard."

The then-Captain Serebryakov had been present during the discussion between the two senior officers and Colonel of GRU Nazarbayeva, and was the obvious source of Beria's knowledge.

His transfer to command a rifle battalion in one of the 1st Baltic's rifle corps placed him in harm's way and, more importantly, where he could do no more damage with his reports to the NKVD.

"Now then, Comrade, let us get this windfall sorted before they change their minds!"

Another knock on the door, timed to the second, gave each man a moment of thought that just such a thing had happened.

The messenger left.

The new directive from the GKO dealt with Phase Three.

Zhukov acted decisively.

"Get this sorted out immediately," he indicated the order regarding the integration of POW's, "Inform Novikov, Tolbukhin, Chuikov and Yeremenko that I wish them to present themselves here by 1300hrs tomorrow."

Malinin made his customary notes.

"Ask General Pekunin to be here for 1800hrs today."

Removing a hand-written note from his drawer, Zhukov grinned mischievously.

"Please ensure that this is forwarded, 'eyes-only', to Mayor General Kudryashev, Chief of Staff of the 4th Shock Army."

Unusually for Malinin, he was slow to grasp the matter.

Sensing his CoS's confusion, Zhukov spoke softly.

229

"Just letting Comrade Kudryashev know what he is getting."

Malinin immediately understood.

'Serebryakov, the treacherous shit.'

"Right, Comrade, let us get to work!"

*Unfortunately, this earth is not a fairyland, but a struggle for life,
perfectly natural and therefore extremely harsh.*

Martin Bormann

Chapter 87 - THE PAST

<u>1147hrs, Sunday, 30th September 1945, Legion Command
Group 'Normandie' Headquarters, Hotel Stephanie, Baden-
Baden, Germany.</u>

General Molyneux had moved the Corps Headquarters
back to Strasbourg the previous week, releasing the Hotel
Stephanie to Group Normandie. With only the Group Staff, the
hotel was spacious and uncrowded, more than suitable for
purpose.

The Soviet assaults had outflanked some legion units,
forcing withdrawals or minor adjustments to the line, but mainly
there had been little advance on the Legion front, the two larger
assaults being dealt with bloodily by Camerone and 16th US
Armored Group respectively.

Despite the successes, the group present in General
Lavalle's office was subdued.

Lavalle, Knocke and Pierce had sat impassively,
listening to Bittrich, as he read aloud an official document that
had been handed to him by the last occupant of the room, a
French Army Major from the Military Police.

Bittrich finished, and carefully folded the document,
proffering it to Lavalle.

A shake of the head refused the damning paperwork,
and it was offered back to the Major who had presented it.

Lavalle waited whilst the man returned it to his tunic
pocket, and then addressed him directly.

"Of course, we will comply with the requirements of
that order, Commandant. If it is as stated, then he will get what
he deserves. If not, then a fair trial will establish his innocence.
We can do nothing now; it is out of our hands."

The reaction of Knocke was all-important here, and
Lavalle watched him carefully.

"I agree, Sir."

231

Clearly, Lavalle need not have been concerned.

He shifted his gaze to the next man in line.

Pierce was unequivocal.

"General Lavalle, if he did this, then I will shoot him myself, Sir."

He had already canvassed Bittrich's opinion, as the police Major had arrived some time beforehand.

"Then let's get it over with. Commandant, if you please."

The Military Policeman nodded, immediately opening the door.

"Colonel Lange?"

Karl-Gunther Lange strode in, recovered from his injuries, and recently promoted to full Colonel.

Lavalle sat stiffly in his chair and accepted Lange's formal salute.

"Colonel Lange, with regret, I am relieving you of your command, effective immediately."

Lange went from curious to furious in an instant.

"What? Why? What have I done? You can't do that!"

Knocke silently sought, and received, permission to act.

He sprang out of his chair.

"Achtung! Stillgestanden!"

Lange automatically snapped to the attention.

"Standartenfuhrer Lange. You will surrender your pistol to me, now."

The hand was imperious, demanding immediate compliance.

Lange's Walther was handed over in an instant.

"Stand at ease. Now, please listen to the Sturmbannfuhrer."

Knocke deferred to the French officer, who opened the document and read aloud in perfect German.

"Colonel Karl-Gunther Lange, you are under arrest for your alleged part in the murder of two French citizens, Father Leblastier and Father Lebarbanchon, and the killing of nine wounded United States paratroopers of the 82nd US Airborne Division at Graignes, Normandy, France, on or about the 11th June 1944, whilst you were serving with the 17th SS Division."

There was more, much more, but the military policeman wished to be on his way with his prisoner.

Lange looked at Bittrich, then Knocke, seeking their understanding and support.

Both men had fought a fair war, without excesses, and their support was not forthcoming.

Although, perhaps, they did both understand.

"These things happen in war, the heat of the moment, it happens," he appealed to Bittrich, "You know that, you know that!"

Bittrich responded with uncharacteristic contempt.

"No, actually, Lange, I don't."

Lavalle encouraged the MP with a wave of his hand, and Lange was taken away.

The four officers sat in uncomfortable silence, Pierce being the most uneasy, as he had come to respect the quality of his former enemy, and had suddenly been reminded that some of them may have a past for which they should be held accountable.

Lavalle tried to break the moment.

"Regrettable, gentlemen, highly regrettable."

Pierce responded.

"Why, General Lavalle? That he's been arrested here? Now? Or that the whole damn business happened in the first place?"

Christophe Lavalle went to speak but held himself in check, noticing Knocke turn to the American officer.

"Everything is regrettable, General Pierce. The war, the deaths, the injuries, everything. But if Lange has done this thing, then he must stand accountable for it, for without such cleansing, Germany will not stand tall and proud again."

Knocke shook his head.

"Is it regrettable that Alma now has to find a new commander? You might say yes, for it could cause us problems. But I would say no, because both this Corps and the new Germany cannot entertain those who have baggage from the past, or we will all be tainted for generations to come."

Pierce nodded his head in understanding.

Knocke fell into silence.

"So, who is next in line for 'Alma'?"

Lavalle posed the question, and each of them understood perfectly that it was rhetorical, the issue already settled in the Legion officer's mind.

Even Pierce, who had no input on the matter, understood whom Lavalle was thinking about.

There was silent agreement.

Lavalle picked up the phone.

"Ah, Georges, please contact Colonel St.Clair, and ask him to report to me immediately. Thank you."

Replacing the ornate receiver in its cradle, Lavalle smiled mischievously.

"I will inform Génèral Molyneux in due course."

Which everyone understood to mean once it was too late for the commander of the Legion Corps to interfere.

1219hrs, Sunday, 30th September 1945, Weiβenburg in Bayern, Germany.

Weiβenburg airfield, home of 19th, 20th and 21st Guards Bomber Air Regiments, suddenly became a hive of activity. It was the sort of activity that an experienced observer might have suspected to be the standard pandemonium associated with panicking officers and NCO's confronted with the unexpected appearance of a senior commander.

In this instance, the experienced observer would have been totally correct.

Colonel General Aleksandr Repin, Deputy Commander in Chief of the Red Air Force, had arrived unannounced, and he was on a mission. He and his entourage swept in through the main entrance, swiftly carrying him all the way to the Regimental Headquarters before the guard officer had an opportunity to warn the 21st's commander.

Nikishkin, Colonel of the 21st, heard the growing kerfuffle that risked interrupting his lunch. Looking up from his plate of bread and ham in indignation, he moved from annoyance to concern for his life in a single heartbeat. The Colonel General, backed up by the commander of 9th Guards Bomber Corps, Major General Georgiev, stood over him in silence, awaiting his report.

Trying not to spray the senior men with his lunch, Nikishkin, now at the attention, delivered the necessary details on the state of his command.

"Comrade Polkovnik Nikishkin, how is it that you are not prepared for my visit? My staff sent you the details yesterday."

"Sir, I regret that no such notification was received."

Technically, Nikishkin was telling the truth, although it is possible that such a notification had been received, and that it might have become a victim to the regimental mascot's playful approach to all things paper.

He recalled the trashing of the communications office the previous day.

Eyes flitted to the basket in the corner, and Nikishkin shot the hound a crushing look, which was returned by one combining complete indifference with disdain for those who had interrupted its slumber.

Repin decided to accept things at face value, do what he needed to do, and get back to his headquarters.

"Oh well. I'm only here briefly, and not to see you either, Comrade. Direct me to where I may find your hero pilot."

"I will escort you myself, Comrade Polkovnik General."

Jamming his cap on his head, he made a silent vow to pass the mascot on to the 19th Regiment in the near future, and acquire something less destructive.

The albino Weimaraner opened an eye as Nikishkin hurried past, unaware that its days were numbered.

The entourage swelled with extra staff and hangers-on, so that a party approaching twenty entered the relaxation room of the 21st Regiment.

The sole occupant was inappropriately dressed for the occasion, boots off, and his uniform jacket spread over him like a small blanket.

As the officer's orderly fled, he had thrown a cloth at the reclining pilot in an attempt to wake the man, which cloth was now hanging off his dangling foot like a flag of surrender.

The group strode in and gathered close to the armchair.

The silence was punctuated by an explosion of bodily gases.

"Comrade Kapitan."

There was no reaction, so Nikishkin raised his voice and leant forward further.

"Comrade Kapitan."

Georgiev stepped forward and ended the sleeping officer's dream.

"Comrade Kapitan Istomin, attention-shun!"

Instantly awake, Istomin swung his legs, sending the cloth flying, coming to the attention with his jacket wrapped round his feet.

His eyes took in the gold braid surrounding him, each extra strand and rank marking he looked at, bringing the expectation of increased trouble.

Georgiev looked him up and down, ending back looking into Istomin's wide eyes.

"Put your jacket on, man!"

Ceding the prime position to Repin, Georgiev stepped to one side.

The Deputy Commander of the Air force moved in front of the now wide-awake pilot, and nodded to a bespectacled Colonel from his staff, who cleared his throat and commenced reading from a small document.

"Comrade Kapitan Sacha Burianevich Istomin, 21st Guards Bomber Air Regiment, 9th Guards Bomber Corps. The citation reads that, on the 14th September 1945, Starshy Leytenant Istomin took command of his unit, following the death of his commander, and gave orders that saved many lives and aircraft. During the course of the air combat over Birkenfeld and points eastwards, Starshy Leytenant Istomin displayed great personal bravery and heroism, shooting down two enemy fighter aircraft, despite severe damage to his own bomber and personal wounds.

Comrade Istomin subsequently undertook and completed a difficult landing, bringing his aircraft back to a Soviet airbase.

For his bravery, leadership and heroism, Comrade Kapitan Sacha Burianevich Istomin deserves the conferring of the title 'Hero of the Soviet Union'.

Repin, on cue, slid the pin in place, the red ribbon and gold star standing out proudly on Istomin's disheveled jacket.

Grabbing the newly appointed 'Hero' by the shoulders, Repin planted a kiss on each cheek.

Stepping back, the Colonel General breathed in cleaner air, and decided that any further talk would be wasted.

236

"Congratulations, Comrade," his words were echoed by most of the others in the room.

Within a minute, Istomin found himself alone once more, gazing down at the shiny star and already planning his excuses for his changed afternoon, which now commenced at 1400hrs, in Colonel Nikishkin's office.

'Properly dressed', as the Colonel had put it with his final shot.

2132hrs, Sunday, 30th September 1945, the Kremlin, Moscow.

The small report lay on the table between the three men, silent, unobtrusive, but none the less dynamite. In their troubled minds, the very presence of it threatened to collapse the heavy wooden structure, so weighty was its content.

Stalin ate heartily of bread, sausage, and pickles, his attention very obviously on his NKVD chief.

Malenkov was working the finest Beluga onto his bread, his eyes fixed on the report, his ears focused on the NKVD Chief.

Beria sipped daintily at his tea, trying to ignore the scrutiny, working through the questions that Stalin had posed to him.

He recited the message in his mind.

'[priority code] HHH
[agent] Alkonost
[date code] 230945c
[personal code as an authenticator] FB21162285
[distribution1] route x-eyes only
[distribution1] AalphaA [Comrade Chairman Beria].
[message] Major setback to project. A+ direct contact. Errors in Baratol explosive lens maths, and in initiation. The Baratol 32 ELM is perfect on paper, but is somehow flawed. ELM project restarted from scratch. EBW initiation scraped and restarted. Aim-Eve.
[message ends]
Message authenticates. Codes for non-compromisation valid.
Attention is drawn to spelling error, in last sentence. Check has been done with accepted distress indicators, and this error does NOT indicate distress.
RECEIVED 09:19 21/7/45-B.V.LEMSKY'

"Comrade General Secretary, firstly to explain the terms. ELM is the explosive lens maths, a complicated set of equations that dictate the shape of the thirty two identical charges, ensuring equal focus when they explode."

Beria had had an extended phonecall with Igor Kurchatov, head of the USSR's Atomic Research programme, trying to understand the scientist's interpretation of the message, and deciphering it all into non-technical language, suitable for Stalin's consumption.

"EBW is a type of detonator, extremely precise, by all accounts, which is necessary for the exact ignitions required to compress the core material."

"I understand this, Lavrentiy. Now, Kurchatov's interpretation?"

"Comrade Kuchatov believes it is definitely possible that our own programme may well be affected. Both EBW and ELM have progressed, not as far as he had hoped, by his own account. Given our limited suitable material, he believes it is advisable to commence our own review of the maths, prior to conducting tests."

"What sort of review?"

"Mirroring those of the Amerikanski, Comrade. The message is quite specific. It is perfect on paper, but flawed. The Capitalists have missed something, and Kurchatov wants us to find it before we test."

Beria loosened his collar.

"I should also say that Alkonost is a mathematician, and a specialist in Geometry. Undoubtedly, our agent will have worked in this area, although there is no claim to having sabotaged the calculations. My understanding is that all such calculations are doubled-teamed, to ensure consistency and accuracy."

Stalin grunted and leant back in his chair, filling his pipe, and digesting that instalment of Beria's report.

Stalin brought Malenkov into the firing line without warning.

"What delay does Comrade Kurchatov anticipate if the check goes ahead?"

Malenkov hadn't thought up a way to sweeten the pill, so he was committed to baring the facts and hoping the tirade wouldn't come.

238

"Anything up to eight months, Comrade General Secretary."

Silence.

Striking a match, Stalin drew the orange flame down into the bowl of his pipe, drawing noisily on it, until rich smoke started to fill his mouth.

He shook the match out, placing its charred remnant carefully in the ashtray.

"Eight months? Eight months, to do a set of sums? Is he mad?"

The questions lacked much of Stalin's normal bite, and both men sensed it was just for show, and that the Soviet Union's leader was resigned to the delay.

They stayed silent, just in case, leaving Stalin to continue after a few furious puffs.

"And the detonators? What of them?"

Malenkov deferred to Beria.

"Kurchatov is less clear, but it should be less time than the maths. Even less, if one of our agents is successful in obtaining better information on the EBW. He only has a hand sketch by Alkonost to go on as the basis for our own devices."

The rapid puffing continued.

"So, Comrade Marshal, we come to the spelling error. What do you make of that?"

Back on safe ground, Beria could speak more easily.

"Alkonost has never made an operational spelling mistake before, and only once during training."

He shuffled through a report originating from the Agent in charge of her American training programme, and read the relevant line.

"In a speed typing test, the word 'Goebbels' was misspelt, omitting one 'B'. Operative confirmed it to be a simple error."

Stalin clearly drew on a dead pipe, and coughed his way through the relighting process, whilst Beria waited, ready to continue.

"The available means of informing us of duress are unused. There are a number of ways that could be done, although," he conceded, "If the Americanski controlled our agent, some, not all, might prove difficult to conceal."

He shied away from Stalin's unwavering gaze, pretending to read a few more lines of the report.

"I see nothing here to throw doubt on the information. However, I do feel some unease here, Comrade General Secretary."

Stalin's eyes sparkled, enthused by the discomfort of his Chief of Spies.

"Calm yourself, Lavrenty, calm yourself. If this message was an attempt to mislead us, would it say that their own project was disabled by errors? No, I think not. It would speak of their progress and readiness."

Beria could not argue against that.

Turning to Malenkov, the Soviet leader silently sought a response.

"I think you are right, Comrade General Secretary. Comrade Beria's assurance and your logic is enough for me."

There had been great debate over what, if anything, should be fed back to the NKVD. A number of important participants felt that it would be far better to do nothing, and that utilising the Soviet agent to send disinformation was playing with fire on a grander scale than the world had ever known.

A decision had to be made.

Either abandon the opportunity or use it. If the decision was to use it, then something had to be done quickly, or the turned agent would be out of touch for too long to maintain usefulness, and her absence could have been seen as suspect.

The eventual decision was to allay the USSR's fears about Allied progress, and introduce the geometric and ignition failures, with the secondary hope that Soviet scientists might commence their own review, causing further delay to their project. Further lines of disinformation would be cultivated and fed into the exchange at a later date.

0817hrs, Monday, 1st October 1945. Office of Lieutenant Colonel Rossiter USMC, Headquarters of SHAEF, Trianon Palace Hotel, Versailles, France.

"So, what brings you to my door so early, General?"

240

As was his normal style, Gehlen said nothing as he sorted through his small briefcase, extracting the set of photos that were the subject of his visit.

Rossiter took in the details of the first shot.

"Ah, Major Savitch, we meet again."

The picture showed the NKVD officer presiding over the hanging of some unfortunate individual.

The rest of the pictures were of the remains of the village of Fischausen, shots apparently taken of ruined buildings, and a handful of complete dwellings, which just happened to also illustrate the defensive positions and other things of interest to anyone planning to visit the area.

"Excellent work, General. I hope your agent is ok?"

Gehlen nodded.

"I assume there is something else?"

"My agent informs me that, according to Savitch, discussions are underway to bring all family members of known serving German officers into one camp."

That would be bad news for Operation Sycamore.

"Our attempt to provide advance evidence of Werewolf activity may have backfired on us, Oberstleutnant Rossiter. Some additional units have been sent to the area, which we anticipated of course, but…"

That had been a calculated risk, but creating a 'history' of partisan activity would help satisfy the Swedish need for the operation to appear German in origin.

Leaving the last word hanging in the air, Gehlen produced another three photographs from the set.

The armoured cars in two of the pictures started the bad news rolling, a post with two quadruple Maxims AA mounts completing the recent arrivals at Fischafen.

"My agent also took these two pictures. I suggest they stay between us."

Rossiter looked at the first, and then the second, incredulous. In the initial shot, the identity of the man was unclear, although certainly a man in Soviet uniform. What was without question was the identity of the woman performing the sexual act.

The second was more revealing, taken from further back and bringing the window frame into view. Precise, in focus and unequivocal, the agent had perfectly captured Frau Greta Knocke's act of oral sex on Major Savitch of the NKVD.

"Jesus."

"My agent observed for a while," Gehlen could imagine that the photographer observed for as long as possible, and also retained copies of the shots for his own enjoyment, "And states that Frau Knocke appeared to be a willing participant."

"Jesus."

Gehlen remained silent, waiting for Rossiter to deal with the discovery.

"OK, we bury these," he waved the pornographic shots, "And we say no more about it. Things may not be as we see here, and we cannot judge. Leave it to Knocke and her to sort out in time. Agreed?"

"Most certainly, Oberstleutnant Rossiter."

'Do you keep mentioning my rank because you're a General, eh?'

"So, we have new forces in situ, but now we have excellent information of their set-up. Combine these with the photo-recce shots and we should be able to put a good plan together, and put it together quickly."

Speed was obviously now essential.

The photo-recce mission had been a thing of beauty, a squadron of RAF Mosquitoes being tasked to attack the Kaliningrad harbours, a mission that they did not press home with their normal vigour.

The retreating aircraft flew straight back home, well almost, passing directly over the village of Fischafen, where the photo-recce aircraft that had hidden in plain sight within the larger formation did its vital work, without giving away its presence and alerting the Soviets.

"I will get the rest of these to our assault force, and to Trannel. What help can we hope for from your agent on the night? Can he or she get involved?"

Gehlen had the answer at his fingertips.

"Yes indeed."

Seeking out one of the photos, he handed it to Rossiter, who was annoyed to see a marking he had missed on first sight.

Sorting out the appropriate recon photo, Gehlen made a similar marking.

242

"This house is on the edge of the village as you can see. This area here," Gehlen tapped the open ground, "Is considered suitable for the Achgelis to land. The lights will be on in this building."

Rossiter looked at the two photos, one in each hand.

"Blackout? Won't the police be all over them for showing light?"

Gehlen managed not to smile too triumphantly.

"That building is the temporary Police Station. My agent is the local Police Officer."

Rossiter considered that for a moment.

'That's why he could move about freely. Or She obviously?'

"A man?"

"Yes, just so. Recently retired, but reactivated by his sense of duty to the Fatherland, and his association with Savitch.."

'And my knowledge of his shady past.'

"OK. 'Sycamore' is live, and the clock is running."

There was no more to be said, and so much more to be done.

0857hrs, Wednesday, 3rd October 1945. Headquarters of US Third Army, Albert Ludwig University, Freiburg, Germany.

"Well that's the bare bones, George, but we can't possibly start thinking about it until we have sorted out the mess we find ourselves in right now."

Eisenhower had travelled to Patton's headquarters to give him the heads-up on the future assault tasking, as well as delivering encouragement to continue in the defence.

He decided to ignore recent events in Southern Germany, where the Third had counter-attacked to mixed results.

"Well, that's fine, Ike, but still I think the best way to sort out this cluster-fuck is to pull me outta the line completely now, gimme time to sort my formation out, and then slot me back in when I'm ready to kick ass."

This was typical Patton.

"We are moving units up from Alexander's command, round Switzerland and into the line here. When I can spare you, the Third will be withdrawn and made ready, ok George?"

243

He hadn't meant it to sound like a question, but it did.

Before Patton could take advantage of the slip, the phone on the General's desk erupted into urgent clamouring.

"Patton.... Kenneth...yes he is...one moment."

Handing the receiver to his superior, Patton waited for his moment.

It never came.

"I see."

Eisenhower's face was like thunder.

"And that is confirmed?"

His free hand became occupied with the extraction and lighting of a cigarette, a pleasure he normally avoided in Patton's headquarters.

"And when will they deign to make the official announcement?"

The reply was obviously unsatisfactory.

"We'll find out very quickly, General Strong."

Inhaling the smoke deeply, Eisenhower nodded unconsciously.

"I would think that is a possibility, wouldn't you? Get on that, and get some Intel firmed up very quickly Kenneth."

Taking a final deep draw, the Supreme Commander of the Allied Forces in Europe made his parting shot.

"Thank you Kenneth. I'm with General Patton, so I'll brief him personally, but pass that to all other commands immediately. I will contact Alexander myself. Now get me that information, before we find ourselves with a disaster on our hands."

Replacing the receiver with the utmost care, Eisenhower took a draw on his new cigarette before apprising the Third Army commander.

"George, it seems our Italian Allies are about to go neutral on us. Restricted movements, no over flights, territorial waters et cetera."

"Yellow sons of bitches, and always have been, Ike."

"My guess is the Soviets know, or are even party to this."

Patton lapsed into uncharacteristic silence.

Eisenhower, unused to the lack of fighting talk, concentrated on his cigarette, whilst Patton completed his mental reasoning.

"You think the Commies are coming through Northern Italy sometime soon?"

Exhaling deeply, a light coughing prevented him from answering immediately, during which time Patton rummaged around and pulled out a map of Italy, a relic from his days in Sicily, pinning it to the wall with overly dramatic hand actions.

"George, they have two large formations just sat there", Ike circled the areas containing the 1st Alpine and 1st South European Fronts.

"We thought they were for screening should the Yugoslavians start playing up, or as feeder formations to replace their losses in Europe. There's even another, smaller formation here." He accurately placed Tolbukhin's small 1st Balkan Front.

"We have been removing formations from the 15th Army Group, feeding them into the line north of Switzerland."

Patton knew this. Indeed, he had received one of the formations himself.

"15th is down by nearly 40%, and now definitely minus the Italian manpower."

"They counted for diddly squat anyhow, Ike."

Patton had met the Italian soldier in Sicily, and immediately developed contempt for his capabilities in the field.

"The Germans are not yet deployed, but I daresay Alexander has them spoken for in some way. All we have new are the Spanish units moving through North Italy, mainly inexperienced, and training on the march."

Both men dropped into silence, poring over the old map, desperately trying to unlock its secrets.

"Where exactly is the line in the Alps, Ike?"

A marking was made from memory.

Patton thought out loud.

"Plain as day when you look at it right. Sons of bitches have kept this one close since day one, I'll bet."

Running his finger along the marking Eisenhower had just made, Patton put into words each man's thoughts, or more precisely, fears.

"They have pushed through Southern Germany, never turning south. Our Alpine line is secure, we think, as they display no interest. Here, in Austria, they have pinned our units in place, and we have congratulated ourselves for our successful defence."

Picking up a pencil, Patton drew a cross on the map, his actions leaving no doubt that he had just sorted the problem of where the Russians would come.

"Here is where they will focus, and here is where they will aim at," the pencil drawing a thick arrow all the way to the sea.

Eisenhower leant forward, his eyes taking in the simple pencil line, his mind already hearing the base sounds of battle, the screams of the dying, and the screams of the living.

"Can you get Alexander on the horn please, George?"

Patton was on the phone in a second, brusquely ordering a connection through to Field Marshal Alexander's headquarters.

Eisenhower took the proffered receiver.

"Harry, it's Ike."

Clearly, Alexander had heard a buzz.

"Yes, I can confirm that to you now. General Strong has just informed me."

Eisenhower listened politely, not caring to interrupt the Englishman in full flow, using the moment to get another cigarette going, oblivious to Patton's displeasure.

"I agree. Try this one on for size, Harry. The Soviet reinforcements that have been spotted in Bavaria aren't reinforcements for the German Front. They are new units with a different purpose."

Patton opened another two windows, whilst Alexander said his piece.

Eisenhower patiently let the British Field Marshal finish.

"Well, it makes perfect sense to me. They move the new Army up, shaping like a wave of reinforcements, until they are ready. One swift oblique movement, and they fall on the Alps to the south."

"Just think about it, Harry. We have weakened your forces in favour of Germany, and now the Italians have done an about turn. They will hit you on a broad front, and find a weakness, but our best guess", he acknowledged Patton with an inclination of the head, "Is that their main axis of advance will be from Innsbruck, Trento, Brescia, aimed at the Mediterranean at Genoa."

Eisenhower stubbed his cigarette out furiously, unusually irritated by the Field Marshal's reply.

"Yes, I do know that, Harry, and they are good troops too. But no matter what, that enemy force in Bavaria can turn and descend on Innsbruck before we have a chance to reinforce."

Alexander clearly wanted his units back.

"No, that's not possible, Harry. They're either in harm's way, or needed. None will be coming back to you. Use the Spanish and the Germans to thicken up your force."

The conversation was drawing to a natural close until the line went dead, the silence enforced by a sneak air raid on Alexander's headquarters, one bomb knocking out the telephone communications centre on which 15th Army Group heavily relied.

Eisenhower returned the receiver to its cradle.

"Air raid in progress. Lost the line."

Eisenhower took another look at the map, almost reminding himself of the precarious nature of the position.

"Ok George, I gotta get back to manage this thing. I will get your men disengaged when I can so that you can sort them out."

"General, my boys are spoiling for a fight. Hell, so am I. We are sick and tired of running, so just give us a chance to fight back and kick some Commie ass soon!"

The two exchanged formal salutes and Eisenhower returned to his vehicle for the drive back to the airfield, where his aircraft waited to take him back to Versailles.

If you prick us, do we not bleed?
If you tickle us, do we not laugh?
If you poison us, do we not die?
And if you wrong us, shall we not revenge?

William Shakespeare

Chapter 88 - THE RESCUE

<u>1732hrs, Thursday, 4th October 1945, with 616 Squadron RAF,
Airborne over Bremen, Northern Germany.</u>

616 Squadron RAF, or rather, what was left of it, was airborne on an interception mission. Soviet bombers had been spotted by a returning flight of ground attack aircraft, and the Meteors had been quickly redirected onto an interception course.

Flight Lieutenant de Villiers, the de facto Squadron commander, led his six jet fighters forward into yet another air battle.

His war so far had been exhausting, mission after mission stacking up, sleep and relaxation becoming rarer beasts by the day.

Like the rest of his flight crews, he was tired, but he understood that every Allied pilot was the same. Every Allied flyer also understood that they had to be in the air, because air power was all that was presently holding the Soviets back.

Baines, as usual, spotted the enemy aircraft, flying in close formation at roughly twenty-five thousand feet, some five thousand feet below the rapidly closing Meteors.

"Gamekeeper, Gamekeeper, nine bandits at ten o'clock low, four engine bombers, type Polikarpov Eight's."

Six pairs of eyes took in the unusual sight of a group of the Soviet Union's only four engine bombers.

The PE-8's had been retired before the end of the German War, but the Russians never threw anything away, and so the venerable old birds were brought out to play the greatest game once again.

"Gamekeeper, Gamekeeper, Blue-One calling, line astern formation, rear approach. Starboard turn, then port wheel. Attacking now."

The Meteor responded as de Villiers applied more power, the twin jet engines pushing him in a fast turn to starboard until he reversed stick, and started to haul the fighter round to port. His turn was timed to bring him perfectly in line behind the rear bomber.

"Gamekeeper, Gamekeeper, Blue-two. Escort fighters down low. Our Spits are all over them."

The Meteor's cannon pumped out their shells as De Villiers pressed the button, every single 20mm missing its target.

The Polikarpov was travelling at less than half the speed of the Meteor.

"Gamekeeper, Gamekeeper, second pass, throttle back, speed 300."

The line of jets circled again, the sky inky and smudged from the smoke of the sole victim of the first pass, still in formation, but full of men who knew they were on borrowed time.

De Villiers lined up on a different aircraft, and was rewarded with pieces of its wing flying off, as the cannon shells exploded on contact.

Circling for a third run, the South African checked the enemy formation, immediately spotting that nine had become seven, three of which were smoking badly.

The Soviet bombers turned, staying tight, but bleeding off height, desperately calling for assistance, as scared pilots tried to find some way of staying alive for another minute.

De Villiers selected the nearest aircraft, smoking badly and clearly in great difficulty.

Enough of his cannon shells hit the lumbering bomber to ensure its death, port wing and engines flying into pieces.

1749hrs, Thursday, 4th October 1945, With 25th Long-Range Guards Aviation Regiment, Airborne over Luneberg Heath, Northern Germany.

"Crew, bail out!"

Voitsev, the pilot, shouted the order, unsure who was still alive, or who was like his co-pilot, so recently transformed into a lump of warm and bloody meat.

The PE-8 had a crew of eleven, and he was determined to hold the dying bird steady long enough for them all to escape.

He knew his own fate was already sealed.

The Flight Engineer had rushed into the rear of the aircraft, and Mladshy Leytenant Voitsev could hear him shouting at the crew above the rush of air through the increasingly numerous holes.

Another attack silenced all sounds of the man, as more 20mm shells hammered through the fuselage, killing and wounding a number of the escaping crew.

Three managed to get out, their white canopies marking their escape. The rest lay dead or incapacitated inside the PE-8.

All except Borlovski, the dwarf, an airman so small that his Comrades had to give him a lift up to get in the large bomber, a fact they kept to themselves for fear of losing their talismanic gunner.

Borlovski knew the Polikarpov was dying, but he was determined to get one last shot off before jumping to safety.

The wheel of jet fighters came round again.

Borlovski was a fine gunner, one of the best in the 25th, and he had learned from his previous misses.

The 20mm ShVAK cannon rattled as he took on the lead Meteor.

1751hrs, Thursday, 4th October 1945, With 616 Squadron RAF, Airborne over Luneberg Heath, Northern Germany.

Everything started to go wrong in the same second.

The noise was instant and loud.

Gauges went bad, airspeed fell away, and controls went sluggish.

De Villiers knew his aircraft was doomed, his peripheral vision registering the surge of yellow on his starboard side, where 20mm cannon shells had smashed into the turbines in the starboard engine, transforming it into shrapnel. Flying metal that, in turn, smashed through more of the engine and escaped the nacelle, only for much of the sharp metal to find a home in the fuselage beyond.

The South African didn't even feel the two pieces that buried themselves in his right thigh, the white hot metal cauterizing the wounds as they lay in his flesh.

Escaping fuel enlarged the fire in the ruined engine, and the Meteor fell lazily away to starboard, the controls barely giving De Villiers a response, let alone any vestige of control.

Ditching the canopy, the heat from the fire was immediately apparent, and the wounded pilot did not hesitate to part company with the dying plane.

The silk blossomed, and the South African watched with fascination as the rest of his Squadron avenged him, knocking the surviving PE's from the sky in two more passes.

De Villiers examined the ground beneath his feet, realising very quickly that it teemed with life, ants moving all over, until, the lower he got, the ants transformed themselves into uniformed men with guns; and lots of them.

1800hrs, Thursday, 4th October 1945, With 25th Long-Range Guards Aviation Regiment, Airborne over Luneberg Heath, Northern Germany.

The damaged aircraft still managed to fly, almost kept in the air by the will of Voitsev and Borlovski.

The gunner had made his way through the fuselage, reaching the cockpit, where he was able to confirm that he and Voitsev were the last living occupants of Silniy-Two-Two.

Responding to the pilot's request, Borlovski plugged up the holes, stopping the wind whistling in.

In so doing, he ensured his pilot could start to feel his hands again.

He also killed them both.

The ventilation had constantly purged the fuselage of fumes, the fuel tanks being amongst the casualties of the Meteor attacks.

A small fire had been extinguished, but, beneath the grey exterior, smouldering continued.

The fumes from the aviation spirit built up slowly, until the balance of vapours and oxygen was perfect, and all that was needed was a source of ignition.

As the Polikarpov flew low, it occasionally encountered obstructions.

Voitsev did not see the church steeple until very late, and he hauled urgently on the stick, causing the used fire extinguisher to drop off the map table where Borlovski had placed it. It struck the smouldering area, uncovering it, disturbing it, and sending a small, but concentrated, plume of sparks upwards, where the perfect mix of fuel vapour and oxygen waited hungrily for a source of ignition.

The PE-8, Silniy-Two-Two, exploded violently and catastrophically, transforming itself into small pieces of metal in the blink of an eye. The largest pieces, the engines, raced each other to the ground, pursued by a myriad of smaller bits.

On the ground below, closely packed and moving swiftly, part of the supply train of the 6th Guards Army was deluged in life-taking metal and burning fuel.

Scores of horses were killed and maimed, their handlers equally ravaged.

Part of the bomber's port wing came to ground on a spot occupied by the Colonel commanding of the 6th's Supply units, where he was deep in conversation with a communist party member of the Army's Political Council.

It was some days before the bloody mulch was recovered. The two men buried together, for fear of putting the wrong headstone over the wrong pieces.

De Villiers hit the ground hard, the jarring contact bringing his thigh wounds to the forefront, causing him to yelp aloud.

All around him, guardsmen from the 2nd Guards Rifle Corps gathered, some with curiosity as their motivation, others with more sinister intent.

A young Major strode into the group and spoke loudly, causing the majority to lose interest in the new arrival.

The four men he had detailed scooped up their prisoner, and marched him swiftly to the rear.

0030hrs, Friday, 5th October 1945, Swedish covert military installation, Gotland.

According to plan, and to the second, the five Achgelis took off and immediately turned towards their target, intent on

252

describing a straight line above the cold waters of the Baltic, all the way to their destination on mainland Europe.

Törget and Rossiter watched them go, silently and without excitement, both men wholly aware of the risks involved, and the possibility that none of the men they had just watched fly away would ever return.

The fuel issue had been resolved satisfactorily, so much so that the point of take-off had nearly been changed.

However, Rossiter had introduced some nasty, but necessary, changes to the plan, and that still meant Gotland as the nearest point.

<u>0158hrs, Friday, 5th October 1945, Fischausen, Soviet Occupied Prussia.</u>

The impending move to centralise the 'guest' families had knocked Savitch back. He immediately understood that his days with Greta were numbered.

So he made the most of the time her had, spending his evenings and nights in her company, sometimes not returning to his billet until the dawn was already spreading itself across the dewy ground.

Tonight, he was indulging in his favourite 'Troika', and Greta Knocke was performing with all her normal enthusiasm and flair.

He had already taken her once, orgasming noisily, fantasising about fertilising the woman, as he spent himself in her moist depths.

The second party of the troika was recently completed, his hands gripping her head as she moved her mouth around him, accepting his gift.

The third section of the Troika gave him so much pleasure; its significance, the domination, the subservience, all being much to his liking.

Greta, face down over the dressing table, moaned. He knew not whether it was pleasure or pain, and cared not a jot either, as he slid himself into her anus and commenced a deep and rhythmic thrusting, his large penis, hard and unforgiving with her soft female flesh.

253

Each Achgelis had been adapted quickly, converting to the specific needs of the mission.

Three men onboard each, rather than two. On three of the Achgelis were women, or more correctly, a woman and two girls, making the one-way trip from Sweden to the mainland.

The pilots, now over land, throttled back, and looked for the sign.

The Police Station was illuminated as promised and a small bonfire pointed the way to the selected landing zone, where the agent had placed four metal buckets, the contents of which burned brightly enough to describe a square inside which the five helicopters could safely land.

The helicopters touched down and men dressed in familiar uniforms moved quickly away, three carrying burdens, three with strange backpacks, the others empty-handed, for now.

As had been planned, each Achgelis pointed in a different direction, enabling the pilots to take up the MG15 defensive machine-guns, ready to defend the landing site if necessary.

A swift discussion took place as the twelve men gathered on the fringes of the open area, their police officer contact gesticulating quickly but carefully. The group disappeared into the dark, swallowed up as they moved off towards the village.

Karl-Lothar Pohlmann waited until they were out of sight and then hefted the two small drums he had 'appropriated', keen to discover whether his new air force comrades would appreciate his efforts in finding a modest amount of petrol for their return journey.

Four of the Achgelis shared the extra litres greedily, their gauges not registering the modest addition.

As Savitch plunged ever deeper inside Greta Knocke, his other senses encouraged him to become more alert.

'Engine sounds? This time of night? What's that about? Surprise inspection?'

254

The yelp of pain as he drove hard brought him back to the matter in hand, the delicious thought that he had hurt the bitch arousing him even more.

'If there's a problem, Honin will deal with it and let me know.'

He became more vigorous.

0210hrs, Friday, 5th October 1945, adjacent to Route 192, Fischausen, Soviet occupied Prussia.

The planning had been rushed, but thorough, the photo-recce work proving a real bonus to the Kommando unit.

In silence, they went to ground, permitting their commander to survey the ground up to, and the other side of, Route 192.

He tapped two of the men on the shoulders, and they immediately set to work on two others, each man carrying one of the heavy backpacks.

Both men also carried the Sturmgewehr-44 assault rifle, although theirs were different from the norm, being equipped with the Vampir infrared system.

The two soldiers stepped back having secured the packs, both sets of batteries now online.

Having seen the order from the Kommando leader, the machine-gunners had set to work powering up their own Vampir, this one attached to an MG42.

The work completed swiftly, the raiding party moved off on cue, crossing the road one at a time, each movement covered by one of the infrared weapons.

Moonlight started breaking through the high clouds and, just occasionally, enough light filtered down to earth to pick out the insignia of the Waffen-SS on the collars of the twelve men.

Moving slowly westwards, the two ST44 Vampirs led the way, carefully sweeping back and forth, until suddenly one froze and gave the signal to halt.

Shandruk moved carefully forward, the point man's hand indicating the direction of the sentry.

Another one of the Ukrainians responded to Shandruk's silent order, placing his Gewehr43 on the ground and drawing a long blade. In a second, the man had melted into the darkness, only seen by those with the infrared equipment.

The point Vampir grunted at Shandruk, the only recognition that a man had died in the silence of the autumn Baltic night.

The group moved forward, one man pausing to retrieve the Gewehr, ready to return it to its waiting owner.

Buildings recognisable from their photos came into view, as the moon made greater efforts to cast its light on Fischausen.

Without instruction, the group became three separate entities, the two ST44 Vampir soldiers moving to the rear of the NKVD barracks, the MG42 team slipping past them, and into the rubble of a large house to the south of the T-junction.

The larger group stole towards the Gasthaus, pausing only to attach something to each of the three BA-10 armoured cars parked on the road.

Shandruk risked a look through the shuttered window, a crack of light enticing him to make the effort. He was rewarded by the sight of two men drinking, whilst two more lay gently snoozing in front of an inviting fire.

Silently, he passed the information to the assault party of five, the three females and their escorts not needed at this time.

The group rose up and slipped around to the rear entrance, easing the door open, and entering the old Gasthaus.

Ignoring the sound of carnal pleasures that faintly drifted down from the upper floor, the five men prepared for the kill.

Kuibida, one of Shandruk's old pioneer company, stood ready, hand on the knob, testing the action without turning it.

The signal came and the handle was turned, silently, the door pulled open to permit Shandruk to see the sleepers.

They still slept, and soon would sleep forever. However, for now, his priority was the two men mumbling over their cups.

A glance around the door brought him eye contact with one of the two drunks, contact that instantly sobered the NKVD soldier.

He went for his rifle.

The clack-clack-clack of the silenced Sten was lost in the sound of a dead body striking the wooden floor.

256

The other drunk turned, knowing he was already dead, but needing to see his nemesis.

The SS officer sent a burst into him and he knew no more.

Kuibida had quickly moved in, and was pushing his knife into the throat of the second sleeper before the last drunk slipped to the floor.

The front door opened, and in strode Kapitan Honin, still sampling a bottle, his eyes glazed with the alcohol so recently liberated from a nearby farm. He had been drinking from the moment they strung old Lerner up, to the moment he walked into his last second on earth.

A shout died in his throat, as Shandruk ripped him from crotch to breast with a ten round burst.

The sounds from upstairs became more urgent, the familiar rhythmic sounds of a man approaching the moment of release.

Shandruk slid a replacement magazine into his silenced Sten, and whispered an order to a soldier, who disappeared back out of the room to order the outside party into the house.

The three soldiers brought the females into the house now, setting them down as best they could, ready to perform their vital role.

The pace picked up.

Shandruk, Kuibida, and two others, mounted the stairs, the rest moved through the ground floor.

A door, invitingly ajar, permitted a look inside and silent entrance, where Kuibida's knife found more work, the female guard slaughtered as she sat dreaming. He left the two young girls asleep for now, but let Shandruk know that he had found them.

The second bedroom had yielded nothing at all, except the uniform of an NKVD Major hung neatly on the wardrobe door.

Again, Kuibida tested the third door as Shandruk readied his submachine gun.

The door opened slowly, silently, revealing a scene of depravity, the soft, rounded curves of a woman's buttocks being pounded heavily by a wiry naked male.

Immediately deciding that he could not shoot, Shandruk gestured to Kuibida, who almost leapt across the small space.

257

Savitch groaned and squealed, his orgasm complete and intense, his semen pumping inside the compliant woman.

Savitch groaned, but he could no longer squeal as a sharp blade penetrated his windpipe and sliced his jugular.

He fell to the ground, blood spilling everywhere, his eyes wide with the horror of his approaching death, his hands desperately sealing the cut in an effort to stave off the inevitable.

Greta Knocke, naked, dirty, and sweaty, turned to look at the dying NKVD officer.

There was something there that made the man very afraid, and his panic intensified.

Sparing a thankful look at the two SS soldiers in the room, she held out her hand, silently demanding the knife from Kuibida.

He passed it over without a word, both soldiers silently accepting what was about to happen.

She knelt beside Savitch, his eyes wide and pleading, his mind resigned to what was to come.

"I have endured you to protect my girls, you fucking bastard."

His eyes followed the bloody blade as she slowly waved it in front of him.

"Every time your cock defiled me, I promised myself I would have my revenge!"

The knife dropped low and made a decisive movement. The blood pulsed as his penis was separated from his body.

Savitch screamed, despite the neck wound, the act causing his blood to flow around his desperate fingers.

"I will feed this to the dogs," she held up his manhood.

The knife worked swiftly again.

The pain almost caused him to pass out, but his brain fought back, seeking to remain alert for as long as possible.

His testicles were dropped onto his chest.

"These will feed the pigs at Lerner's farm."

The blood loss was now becoming critical, and Savitch started to drift off.

Greta Knocke spoke into his ear.

"And now, for every time your cock has penetrated me, I penetrate you."

The tip of the blade probed the awful wound between his legs, the pain stimulating him into consciousness once more.

258

The next time it entered his body was through his navel, the penetration limited to no more than a centimetre, not enough to kill in its own right, but sufficient to cause extreme pain.

Shandruk and Kuibida watched as the naked woman worked the blade all over the Russian's body, shocked, but aware enough to know that the woman needed the few moments to do what she had to do.

Greta slid the knife into Savitch's left armpit, not noticing that the eyes had glazed, and the blood no longer flowed.

Shandruk took hold of her hand firmly, and removed the blade, passing it back to his NCO in silence.

Greta Knocke stood, unashamed of her nakedness, looking down on the piece of dirt that had threatened to rape her two daughters unless she became his mistress.

She spat venomously, missing the corpse, but discharging more of her angst.

Shandruk held out some clothes and turned around as Greta put them on.

A shot made all three jump.

Downstairs, an unseen sentry had been drawn back to the Gasthaus by the scream from the dying Savitch. On seeing the hated SS in the downstairs room, he had fired through the window, killing one of the SS men instantly.

Shandruk clicked his fingers at Kuibida, sending him down to investigate, the sound being sufficient to mask the clack-clack as a Sten gun put the sentry down.

"Frau Knocke, we have no time to lose. Please give me that," he indicated the opal necklace she always wore, a treasured wedding present from her parents, "Now, please go with this man, and bring your children downstairs. We must leave very soon."

The woman took it in her stride, something that he was not surprised about, given her pedigree.

A firefight erupted outside, the covering sections becoming swiftly engaged.

Three rapid explosions marked the end of the venerable armoured cars. Although old and out of place on a modern battlefield, they had been considered a threat to the raiding force.

Spurred by the closeness of the combat, Shandruk moved swiftly, shouting his encouragement to the two men organising the girls.

259

Once downstairs, he set the subterfuge in motion.

The three female bodies were taken upstairs and placed in the correct rooms, the two girls, recently carefree Swedish school children, had died because they ate the wrong sort of mushrooms. They were to replace Knocke's daughters and Shandruk's team set them in place with suitable reverence.

In the next room the adult corpse was put in place; a librarian, who had just dropped dead next to the classics section at her place of work.

A change of plan was necessary, requiring a more creative 'set'. A knife was slipped into the hand of Elisabet Hägglund, spinster, former employee of the Gothenburg University Library.

The necklace followed, garish against the milky white and lifeless skin.

The substitutions complete, the group moved off, their dead comrade dragged clear, in order to preserve the evidence of his uniform and corpse. They had all understood the risks. Uniform scraps had been prepared, had there been no casualties. However, a comrade had fallen, and they were prepared to leave him behind; a necessary evil that they had planned for, and reluctantly accepted.

The last three soldiers, now relieved of their dead female burdens, set fire to the old Gasthaus, before joining the rear of the group.

Kuibida, breathing heavily, slid in beside Shandruk.

"The '42 has butchered the bastards. They came out straight into the line of fire. All down, from what I can see. Be careful, in case any are just wounded. The Vampirs have been firing round the back too."

"Our route out?"

"Clear, as far as I can see, Sturmbannfuhrer."

The Major's rank was an acknowledgement of Shandruk's worth to OSS, a personal recommendation by Rossiter himself.

The Ukrainian officer slapped his senior NCO heartily.

"Move them up then, Oberscharfuhrer. Back to the spinning tops as quickly as we can."

It was as good a name as any for the strange machines that had brought them to Fischafen.

The rescue party rose up and moved off, each of the Knocke females having a personal escort, either to steer them, support them, calm them, or to get their bodies between the rescued and the bullets, whichever was needed.

The MG42 team remained vigilant, as the main group slipped across their line of fire, the loader commencing the countdown for their own withdrawal.

The Vampir gunners saw the group first, and watched for signs of pursuit. There were none, as they and the machine-gun team had been extremely effective in subduing the NKVD guard unit.

There was no sign of the tanks, nor of the Maxim machine-guns.

Gehlen had managed to organise a demonstration at Baltiysk to the south, and all four T34's had been sent to assist the local forces.

One of the Maxim mounts lay to the north, covering the most obvious approach. The second was situated to the south-west, its dual purpose to guard the air approach from that direction as well as to serve as a guard post on the shoreline.

The third was thirty feet in front of the main body of Ukrainians.

"Stoi!"

A frightened voice screamed the order, immediately freezing the Ukrainian veterans.

Shandruk thought quickly, and acted.

"Silence, you fucking fool! Do you want the German bastards to know where we are?"

A moment's pause indicated swift thought on the part of the owner of the voice in the dark.

Quieter this time.

"Password!"

"I'll give you fucking password, you idiot. Now shut your fucking mouth or Savitch will have your ass!"

The use of the Major's name did the trick, and the sullen soldier dropped back into the sandbagged position again, happy that he had done his duty, unhappy that the loudmouth officer had embarrassed him in front of the female loader.

The clacking sound reached his ears as the young girl sprouted red stars all over her body, his own blood joining hers as Shandruk's Sten switched targets.

Moving quickly past the AA position, Pöllman loomed out of the darkness.

"All clear through to the landing zone."

"Danke, mein freund."

Shandruk surrendered a precious moment to shake the hand of the elderly man who had risked so much to make the mission a success.

No more was said, Pöllman stepping aside to let the group move on quickly.

As they approached the nearest Achgelis, those with German Army torches switched them on, the red lenses identifying them as friends.

Greta Knocke insisted on seeing both her daughters aboard their craft, partly to reassure them, and partly to reassure herself.

Behind them, things started to go wrong.

For once, Shandruk had not been the efficient killer.

Regaining consciousness, the wounded Soviet gunner pulled himself up, using the Maxim mount for handholds, the pain causing him to nearly pass out.

Crucially, he made no sound.

In the clearing beyond, the Achgelis helicopters started up, warming their engines ready for the flight home.

Red torchlight flitted through the bushes and undergrowth, as the wounded gunner squinted in the direction of the noise.

Pöllman moved, revealing his position.

Startled, the wounded gunner pressed his triggers, and the Maxims burst into life.

The retired police officer was killed immediately, his upper chest, shoulders, and head struck numerous times by the 7.62mm bullets.

Through the bushes, one red light went spinning away as it was struck by more lead, the impacts sending it into the air, and throwing its dying owner to the earth.

One more burst was fired into the clearing, a few bullets striking one of the Achgelis, but causing no great damage.

Three bullets hit flesh.

The MG42 gunner acted quickly. The grenade was in his hand almost as swiftly as the thought spurred him into action. Retiring late, along with the Vampir gunners, he heard the sound of the AA gun, and knew it had to be stopped quickly.

The stick grenade struck the nearest water-cooled barrel, and dropped into the lap of the dead female loader.

It exploded, the blast throwing up a crimson spray, noticeable, even in the darkness.

Again, the gunner escaped death, but it was purely temporary.

His spine was severed, and he dropped lifelessly into the gun pit, his pain gone. He had no understanding that his lifeblood was draining from his shattered legs and ruptured buttocks.

The last four SS raiders moved into the clearing.

Shandruk's wrist was on fire, a single bullet having nicked it on its way through the clearing.

It was just a scratch, but one that reminded him of its presence every second.

But, for now, he had other serious concerns.

Greta Knocke lay at his feet, her lifeless eyes slowly being obscured by blood seeping from the horrendous facial wound. The unforgiving bullet had then blown the back of her head off.

A second bullet had struck her in the abdomen, but she was already dead by the time it had exited from the small of her back.

"Blyad!"

No time for remorse or ceremony, Shandruk and one of the Vampirs grabbed the corpse, and bundled it into the waiting Achgelis, following Greta Knocke into the interior as the helicopter took off, the third to rise from the field,

Below them, Fischausen was awake and petrified, the remaining civilians, woken by gunfire, aware that buildings were burning and that men had died in the night.

The last of the Achgelis' touched down and switched off, plunging the base into an uncanny silence, punctuated only by the sobs of young girls coming to terms with the death of their mother.

Törget was there to meet the special force, and to welcome the Knocke's to Sweden.

Confronted by the grief of two inconsolable girls, Per Törget found himself out of his depth for the first time in his life. His decision to bring a female doctor and nurse rescued him, and the two girls were gently lead away by the two medics.

Quickly discussing the mission with Shandruk, he discovered that it was the finger of fate that had reached out and touched Greta Knocke that night, and that nothing could have been done.

Moving away, and leaving Shandruk to tend to his men, Törget entered the communications centre, where the operator sat ready to send his pre-arranged signal, seemingly a routine military base report.

He accepted the change to the signal without thought, not understanding that those who received his transmission would see the report of a generator problem as a mission failure.

"SS bastards?"

"It seems so, Comrade Polkovnik."

The Army Major beckoned forward three of his men carrying a blanket, heavy with some inert load.

They spilled the contents at the feet of NKVD Colonel Bakhatin, roused from the comfort of his lodgings in Königsberg to travel to Fischausen and investigate the disaster.

GRU Colonel Witte had travelled the same road, only minutes behind, similarly tasked.

Both men examined the corpse of a man clad in SS camouflage uniform, a single gunshot wound in the throat, the cause of his death, now mainly obscured by the beating his

264

corpse had sustained at the hands of vengeful NKVD security troops.

Another blanket arrived, bearing the shattered body of the local police officer.

"It seems that he wandered into the firing line of one of the AA mounts. However, we have found police fire buckets set out in a pattern on the field to the east of the village, so it is possible he is not the innocent that we believed him to be."

Another line of thought to explore later, the two Colonels looked at each other and agreed on the point.

Another body arrived, this time dragged from the landing area. The SS soldier had been struck by four, possibly five bullets.

Looking up at the Major, the two senior officers waited for him to continue.

"It seems that they had a machine-gun set up there," he indicated a ruined building at the T-junction.

The dead bodies of the NKVD security squad had been cleared away and laid out, ready for burial.

"We have found numerous German casings there."

He turned, catching the two Colonels off-guard.

"There we have found signs of other groups waiting at the rear of the barracks building, and at least four of the NKVD unit died there."

The GRU officer was there for something completely different, but could not show his main interest. Perversely, Bakhatin was not privy to the true nature of matters at Fischausen, as he was a recent arrival in Königsberg

Witte took the lead. Rather than force the Major's hand, he tried to gently steer him in the direction he needed.

"So, two buildings caught fire. The NKVD barracks and that one there. What is that?"

"Good question, Comrade Polkovnik. I had assumed it was the officer's quarters, but that was here," he indicated the building directly opposite the smoking ruin, which had once housed the NKVD security force.

"Why did you assume that, Comrade Mayor?"

"Because that is where we found both officers. The fire was very intense, Comrades."

There was no need to be more forthcoming, each man there had seen his fair share of death.

"The bodies of the military personnel have been recovered, and placed ready for burial."

Witte looked back at the line of covered Soviet corpses, his mind totally alive and waiting for the next words.

"We assumed the women were German whores, so we quickly buried them over there."

He indicated a freshly turned patch of soil beside the destroyed gasthaus.

"Women, you say Mayor? Why assume they were whores?"

"Apologies, Comrade Polkovnik, the NKVD unit here did not have female soldiers, so there seemed little alternative."

The GRU officer hesitated, then took the plunge.

"I will need to see the female bodies, Comrade Mayor," the NKVD Colonel's head swivelled at lightning speed.

The Army Major contemplated asking why, but quickly decided that he was better off doing the job' and getting the two Colonels off his back.

He shouted at a Yefreytor commanding a small work detail, who ran to his side and sprang to attention.

"Get your men to uncover the female bodies immediately, Comrade Istlov. The Colonel wishes to inspect the corpses."

Yefreytor Istlov harried his men into position, and shovels made short work of disinterring the dead.

'I hope the Chekist bastard has a strong stomach.'

The thought brought the slightest of smiles to the NCO's face.

The NKVD officer sauntered over, the GRU Colonel moved swiftly, betraying his anxiety.

More than one mind noticed, and logged the information for another time.

The two smaller corpses were badly charred, no distinguishing features of note, save the few strands of blonde hair on one skull, preserved by contact with something that didn't burn.

Witte moved his attention to the adult corpse, almost destroyed by the fire.

"That one held a knife, Comrade Polkovnik."

Witte held the Major's gaze for a moment, partly to press him to continue, and partly to give him time for what was to come.

"It seems likely that she and Mayor Savitch had a fight, during which the Mayor was killed."

The army officer threw a casual hand at the line of uniformed corpses.

"His throat had been cut, and it also seemed he had lost vital parts. We counted over fifty small stab wounds to the front of his torso."

Both colonels immediately wondered why the Major had not informed them of this as a priority, and the NKVD officer promised himself to ensure a black mark was recorded against the infantryman.

Witte stoically accepted the man's inexperience with investigative matters.

In any case, the swine Savitch was no loss.

Pulling out his pocketknife, he extended the blade and went to work on the eyelids, both fused by the extreme heat.

Faint hints of blue-grey greeted his enquiry, and he mentally ticked a box.

He examined the woman's right breast, but was unable to find the childhood scar, so obvious during her initial NKVD examination.

Something caught his eye, a sliver of gold, and he pushed at the blackened skull, tilting it sufficiently to uncover a chain around her neck.

Slipping his blade underneath it, he teased it out millimetre by horrible millimetre, until the opal cluster came into view, relatively untouched by the attention of the flames.

Satisfied, Witte stood back, permitting Bakhatin his own opportunity to see the body of Greta Knocke.

The two Colonels moved patiently through the affected area, gradually picking up a picture of a Werewolf attack against the hated NKVD, an attack that had inadvertently claimed the lives of the three Knocke's.

Later that evening, when both men were back in their warm and cosy billets, the report writing began, sheets of paper to satisfy the higher authorities and to be filed for posterity.

267

At the end of his submission, Colonel Witte considered the matter very carefully, and only after twenty-five minutes of solid reasoning did he commit himself to paper.

When the report fell under General Pekunin's gaze later the following day, the GRU head weighed the suggestion of the investigating officer

'...it would seem reasonable to assume that this was a random act by an isolated group, leftover from the German War, stimulated into action by the latest fighting. As such, there is no record of the action happening, and no record of the casualties.

With that in mind, it would seem reasonable to assume that the German officer Knocke cannot reasonably develop knowledge of the loss of his family, and, therefore, can continue to be employed under threat..."

Pekunin waited whilst his deputy read the report through, infuriatingly slowly for a quick-witted man.

"Well?"

Kochetov returned the report to the desk.

"I agree, Comrade General. I think Witte is right. The operation is still ongoing."

Pekunin's thoughts exactly, and he dictated a report for the personal consumption of Beria and Zhukov, supporting the submission by Colonel Witte.

Pekunin signed the finished documents with a flourish, unaware that he was contributing to his own downfall.

Man never made any material as resilient as the human spirit.

Bern Williams

Chapter 89 – THE WOUNDED

1057hrs, Sunday, 7th October 1945, Legion Command Group 'Normandie' Headquarters, Hotel Stephanie, Baden-Baden, Germany.

Her employment in the residence of Oberst Christian Adolf Löwe had terminated abruptly.

It had not been the plan, but natural reactions meant that her departure from Baden-Baden was immediate and irrevocable.

It had been an error obviously, and she should have found some other way to remove his wandering hands, but no one was prepared to challenge Valois on the matter. De Walle started to, but decided against pushing it, the flashing anger in his subordinate's eyes telling him silence was a wiser course of action.

Her replacement, another female 'Deux' agent, reported that the elderly Löwe still carried the evidence of his failed sexual assault on Anne-Marie Valois. Perhaps the physical damage she had wrought on the retired German Colonel had also served another purpose, for Löwe had become withdrawn, and no longer pestered his female staff.

Maybe he would revert to type, once the plaster came off, although the scar on his face would probably never disappear.

Released back to her duties within the Legion Intelligence set-up, she had been with De Walle and De Montgomerie when the awful news had arrived.

She broke the strained silence.

"I will do it."

Neither man argued in favour of an alternative, and neither man wanted the duty.

Knocke was due to arrive at the headquarters within the hour, and would receive a very different reception to that he was anticipating.

269

De Walle went off in search of Lavalle, so he could be informed, and know why Camerone's commander would not be at the Senior Officers meeting that lunchtime.

De Montgomerie remained in his office, pondering the ramifications of the horrible news, not envying his friend the task she had taken upon herself.

Valois took herself off to prepare for delivering the bad news to a former enemy, a man she had come to admire and respect, and to whom she owed her life.

1127hrs, Sunday, 7th October 1945, Headquarters of US Third Army, Albert Ludwig University, Freiburg, Germany.

He knew he wasn't popular with his peer group, but it was just their envy of his natural ability, as far as Patton was concerned.

That holding such a belief was possibly why he wasn't popular with his peer group did not even occur to George Smith Patton.

He had just completed a difficult telephone discussion with Devers, the Army Group commander.

Patton snorted to himself as he recalled the verbal confrontation.

'Jake Devers Nil, George Patton One.'

Notwithstanding some admitted minor character issues, Patton knew he was not the mad egotist that he was considered to be. However, that was something he mainly kept to himself.

Easing himself into his campaign chair, the white-haired General commenced mapping out his new orders to Third Army.

In 1943, George S. Patton, then a three-star in command of Seventh Army, had given his normal fiery pep talks to some of his units prior to the invasion of Sicily, using phrases like, 'the only good German is a dead German', de facto verbal orders that cost many a Axis prisoner their life. In particular, the 45th US Infantry Division had taken his words literally, and shot many prisoners out of hand. Although the notorious slapping incident was blamed for his loss of the Seventh Army, the prisoner 'order' to his soldiers also contributed greatly.

270

Patton had little doubt that it would all come back and haunt him in his later days.

He had no idea that it would visit itself upon him this very day.

Sabine Faber knew this was her moment, and she acted decisively.

She had harboured and nurtured her inner feelings, keeping them safely hidden, earning trust, and becoming a familiar figure around the Third Army Headquarters.

Fraulein Faber was an intelligence-cleared cleaner and, in that capacity, had been entrusted with tending more sensitive areas, especially as she was the daughter of a German officer serving in one of the new Republican units.

Intelligence had missed one vital matter.

She was also the sister of the dead Oberleutnant Maximillian Faber, late of the 1st Fallschirm-Panzer Division 'Hermann Goering'.

Max Faber had been taken prisoner in Sicily, at the Biscari Airfield, on the 14th July 1943. He had been summarily executed by men of the 45th US Infantry Division, some of whom were tried for the offence.

Had they not been brought before the military court, then Sabine would never have learnt of the circumstances of her brother's death, and would not have built up a hatred for the man responsible.

The man in the room, outside of which, she now prepared herself.

Picking up the tools of her trade, she knocked on the dark wood doors.

"Enter."

Pushing open both doors, Sabine slid into the room, receiving a cordial welcome from the man she had come to kill.

"Good morning, Sabine. How are you today?"

"Much better thank you, Herr General."

She had tried the day before, but the arrival of some Ranger officers had prevented her, and she had feigned a sudden sickness to excuse herself from the room, in case anyone noticed the contents of her bucket.

271

She moved quickly around the room, tidying and dusting, the map stands covered with their light linen covers to ensure prying eyes saw nothing of value.

She swept, moving around the room with barely concealed haste, Patton so engrossed in his writing that he failed to notice that she did not clean around the desk.

Moving the bucket to the window, Sabine pulled out the mop. Any casual glance at the implement would have betrayed its dry state. The bucket contained a Walther PPK, now in the hand of the vengeful Faber.

The sudden silence associated with lack of movement broke into Patton's consciousness, the sole sound he recognised being the heavy breathing of Sabine Faber.

He turned.

'What the...'

"Say nothing, you murdering swine. Say nothing at all. Keep your hands in front of you, and sit still. Just listen."

The General nodded his understanding, and leant back in his chair, displaying a calmness he did not feel inside. He forced himself to focus on the woman, knowing that she had something she wanted him to hear, or he would already be dead.

"In Sicily, you ordered your men to kill prisoners. One of them was my brother. Your men killed him at the Biscari airfield."

She snarled, her words almost hissing through her teeth in the increasing anger.

"He pleaded for his life, and they shot him in the head."

She took half a step closer, and gestured with the small automatic.

"I want to hear you plead for your life, you bastard."

Patton's face became thoughtful, almost as if he were debating his response. But no words came. He just maintained eye contact.

"Plead for your life, General, or I will shoot you down now, like the dog you are."

Sabine moved closer, the muzzle of the PPK now three feet from her target.

Raising her voice, she lashed out with her foot, catching Patton on the shin.

"Scream for your miserable life, get on your knees. GET ON YOUR KNEES!"

Her raised voice blotted out the sound of the opening door, as the cleaner who had actually been detailed to clean the room, entered to investigate.

The PPK erupted, the first bullet aimed at Patton.

Swivelling quickly, the next bullet took the new cleaner in the chest, and dropped her to the tiles, where her head smashed into the solid floor and knocked her out.

It took Sabine Faber less than three seconds to fire both shots and return the weapon to cover Patton.

It took General George Scott Patton just over two seconds to snatch up the paper opener and ram it through the assassin's solar plexus.

The pain was so total and debilitating.

Faber tried to bring the pistol up again, but the strength was not there.

Suddenly, she was flung against the far wall, as a .45 slug smashed into her. She was dead before her corpse had finished its bloody slide down the Mediterranean mural.

"Sonofabitch!"

The Captain who had shot Sabine down could not better that. Others rushed into the room, keen to confirm that their General was alive.

Her shot had missed, passing through the gap between his epaulette and shoulder, and clipping away some of the woodwork beyond.

The area was quickly secured, the Lieutenant Colonel in charge of security acting swiftly, conscious of the fact that there had been a grave error, and that they had been very lucky that day.

Still unconscious, the wounded cleaner was stabilised and whisked away to the medical facility, where later Patton would visit her and thank her for saving his life.

The body of Sabine Faber was removed from the room, drawing a cursory look from Patton as he spread the word through other Allied commands.

Whilst the woman had spoken of her own reasons, it did not pay to take chances, and so the alert went out to all commands in Allied Europe.

Knocke was pleased to see Anne-Marie Valois waiting on the steps.

It had previously been agreed that he would not be told when the OSS operation to rescue his family would take place.

That had been for sound operational and personal reasons.

But he sensed something was in the air, and the presence of the 'Deux' agent confirmed it in his mind.

He alighted from the jeep, smiling at the pretty agent.

His smile was not returned, and his heart twisted in agony.

"Mademoiselle Valois? Are you well?"

"Yes, perfectly, thank you, Général Knocke."

Which she very obviously was not.

His body cold, Knocke did not know what to say or do.

"Shall we walk together, Général?"

Side by side, the two strode around the Hotel and into the garden, the area where it had been agreed that Anne Marie de Valois would break the news.

Sitting down in a small arbour, Valois invited Knocke to sit.

'Mein Gott!'

"I shall stand, if that's alright with you?"

"Please, Ernst, please sit."

That did it, and as he sat down, his resolve started to disintegrate.

A hand found his, and he looked up into the moist eyes and knew that he had lost them all.

'Nein! Nein! Nein!'

"Ernst...I..."

Instinctively, her other hand moved to comfort the grieving man.

The timing went astray, the minder misunderstood the signals from Valois, and he set the pair loose ahead of schedule.

Running for all they were worth, Greta and Magda Knocke sprinted from the hotel, and threw themselves upon their father.

274

Tears of joy spilled down his face as he swept them up, hugging them, and kissing them in his happiness.

As he held them close, his brain connected one vital piece of information.

He mouthed the words to the watching Valois.

"My wife?"

Anne-Marie did not need to reply, her face spoke for her.

More tears ran down his face, as he took solace in the presence of his girls.

Later, he listened to the events of that night on the Baltic; the rescue, the substitutions, and how his wife had died.

Or at least, the version that they chose to tell him.

<u>0953hrs, Tuesday, 9th October 1945, 20th US Field Hospital,</u>
<u>Soissons, France.</u>

All the senior medical staff had protested, but it was to no avail.

The infantry Colonel was there under orders, and he was not prepared to take no for an answer.

Major Swift and Captain Montoya had secured the man's agreement that they would be able to veto those who simply were too sick to go, so they accompanied the emotionless officer into the prime recovery ward of the hospital, a room containing thirty-four cots.

"Attenshun!"

Those that could, in the main, did. Those that couldn't, didn't. And there were those that could, but chose not to.

"Men, I appreciate that you are here because you have already paid a price in action, but the situation is grave, and I have to ask more of you all."

There was a general hubbub, and the keen ear could pick out some uncomplimentary words, and some that would have made a vicar blush.

"Uncle Sam needs volunteers, and we are going through the hospitals to find men who are nearly recovered, to sign up to lighter duties, releasing fit men into the fighting zone."

No one could fail to hear the general reply of 'bullshit'.

Colonel Stoltzfus let the sound die away, and went to start again.

275

A low rumble in the nearby bed preceded a vile smell that pervaded the entire unit, invading the respiratory passages of everyone present.

The wounded man had been on liquids only until the day before, when the bandages were taken off his facial wound, and his wind had been known to clear the building.

"Shorry, Colonel, but I was shoth in the assh."

The obvious damage to his face made his voice slurred, although they all knew he was emphasising his speech problem for comic effect; all except the Colonel of course.

Corporal Rosenberg had been badly wounded, but his backside had actually escaped damage.

"That will be all the kosher crap you eat, you yiddisher bastard," and a pillow sailed across the space in front of the Colonel, landing precisely on target.

"Oh Nursh, Nursh, the bad man attacked me again! Oi Vay, but can't an honesth man get reshpite from the Genthiles!"

The only one there who was not privy to the relationship between the two men was Stoltzfus, and as a god-fearing son of an Amish Rabbi, he took exception to the NCO's tone.

"Now you can cut that out, Master-Sergeant. We leave that sort of crap to the Germans!"

A look of innocence crossed the NCO's face, the sort of innocence that a certain type of officer could see as a challenge.

Colonel Stoltzfus was such an officer.

"Attention! Name and rank?"

The NCO made an upward body movement that more paid lip service to the order, rather than obeyed it.

He fixed the officer with a neutral eye and spoke, using as much of the tone of his second language as was possible.

"Hässler, Friedrich, Master Sergeant, Sir."

Rosenberg giggled uncontrollably.

So did Nurse Captain Montoya.

So did most of the men, who were being thoroughly entertained.

Hässler dropped back onto his bed, maintaining his deadpan face.

The Colonel wisely decided to cut his losses.

"We need men, combat veterans, to insert into units presently reforming. Men who can pass on their knowledge, and

276

let the greenhorns know what to expect in battle with the Commies."

The medical Major interrupted.

"That means, no combat, just instructor stuff for you men. Nowhere near the front lines."

The reaction from the wounded men was universal.

"Bullshit."

"Bullshit!"

"Bullshith."

The Major retreated behind Belinda Montoya.

Stoltzfus welcomed the medical man's distraction, and spoke up again, playing his trump card.

"Your country needs you this one last time. Once it is over, it's Stateside for every man of you."

A man-mountain rose from the bed next to Hässler.

"I will go, Colonel, but not stateside. My duty is here."

Hässler looked at Bluebear as if he was a rabid dog.

"Pardon the Chief, Colonel. He's a little loopy after a shindig a'ways back. He don't know what he's saying."

Rosenberg followed behind quickly, the two statements almost blending together.

"He'sh fucking mad ashtually, Colonel. No-one wantsh a mad Commanshee, do they now?"

Waiting for a sign from Montoya, Colonel Stoltfus welcomed the nod, and turned back to the huge Indian.

"Uncle Sam will gladly take you, son. What's your name and rank?"

"Sergeant Charley Bluebear, Sir."

"Oh shit!"

"Oh shith!"

Hässler and Rosenberg made their decision, confirming it to each other with a swift nod.

"Well, if the chief's going, best I go too. Someone's gotta look after him."

Hässler stretched and swung his feet out of the bed, the aching in his body apparent on his face.

Montoya shook her head.

"I think not, Master Sergeant," the Colonel understanding that the man was not yet healed.

"Well, I think so, Sir. We here've bin through a lot together, and reckon we'll be sticking together. Eh boys?"

277

A chorus of agreement went up from thirty-two of the men.

"You speak for yourshelf, you German shith."

Hässler grinned widely.

"You're coming, and that's an order. Any crap, and I'll finish the job on your pecker."

"Ben Zonah! If I didn't like you, I'd kick your assh, Shergeant!"

"I'd have to put a block there for you to stand on, you Alter Kocker!"

The Colonel interrupted, and earned himself disdainful looks from the two friends.

"Thank you all for your service. I will have an officer report here at 1200hrs to take you on to the correct camp. Good luck to you all, and give the Commies hell."

Turning on his heel, he swept past the shocked Montoya and out of the hospital, intent on visiting the next base on his list, and escaping the two idiots who had baited him.

Belinda Montoya managed to speak.

"Are you totally mad, Sergeant Hässler?"

"Yesh, he fucking ish!"

She shot a look at Rosenberg.

"Shorry Captain, pardon my frensh."

The Master Sergeant looked up, his face, for once, clear of humour, with seriousness prevailing.

"Captain, I'm here because my own buddies put me here. Hell, I ain't even seen a commie yet! I did my bit in the last war, so I guess I'll do my bit in this war, and then go home with my head held high."

She nodded her understanding.

A pillow flew back across the room striking Hässler on the head.

"Oi vay! What bollocksh! Whatsh a hero, whatsh a mensh, whatsh a Chochem, I'm sho privileged!"

Hässler disappeared under an avalanche of pillows from all corners of the room, the sound of the soft strikes mingling with genuine laughter.

Captain Montoya left the room, unsure of her emotions.

'I will never understand these boys, but God bless them.'

278

Bedell-Smith waited for his cue to commence the morning briefing. Both he and Eisenhower had been summoned from their beds earlier than they had intended, the increased pressure on the Allied front requiring their immediate attention.

As more and more information came through, the jigsaw came together.

"Proceed, Walter."

"Sir, we have reports of general attacks up and down the line, from the Baltic to the border with Switzerland."

'And not the Alps or Italy' went unsaid, but was fully understood.

"Most of these attacks seem mainly intent on pinning our forces in place, and we are seeing the largest concentrations of Soviet artillery since the second wave of assaults on August 13th."

Colonel Hood started to cough uncontrollably, causing the briefing to come to an abrupt halt, the fresh blood apparent on the handkerchief he had pressed to his mouth.

Eisenhower felt great sympathy for the man.

"Aww, Thomas. Get yourself down to the medics now. Your deputy can take over."

Hood did not protest.

His ulcers had flared up, and the pain was excruciating.

As Hood was helped away Eisenhower reflected on the workload and strain upon his staff, and for the first time he really noticed the haggard and drawn faces of those whose day consisted of work and work, punctuated by a few hours sleep, if they were lucky.

'Didn't Thomas warn me about that? Must do something about it.'

Bedell-Smith interrupted his thoughts.

"Sir?"

"Continue, Walt."

"At this time, four main thrusts have been highlighted."

Using the pointer, the CoS started from the top.

"Here, in the area of their First Baltic Front, we have extreme pressure on the British. The attack is already into the outskirts of Bremen. Information just in from intelligence

279

indicates that the Soviets have greatly reinforced here specifically, and 1st Baltic in general."

The pointer described a line that extended beyond the Allied front line.

"Our expectation is that the general attacks will stop soon, and that their resources will be channelled into these four assaults. Firstly this one, through Bremen, heading south-west, and into the Netherlands, via the North German plain."

Reports from McCreery already indicated that his front was buckling.

"Secondly, the First Red Banner Front seems to be threatening a drive into the Ruhr, from the direction of Osnabruck."

A quick sip of water and Bedell-Smith continued, moving the pointer expansively over a key area.

"Their Second Red Banner Front seems also to have been heavily reinforced, and they are shaping to attack to the south of the Ruhr."

The pointer did a rapid circular movement, describing a military situation that was a nightmare for all Commanders.

"It is possibly an attempt at an encirclement manoeuvre, combined with the First Red Banner, aimed at creating another Ruhr pocket."

Bedell-Smith referred to the Allies' own encirclement of the German Army earlier in the year, which resulted in vast numbers of men being made prisoner, and huge stocks of equipment being captured.

"General Bradley is expecting that the fall-back to the Rhine will now be forced upon us, despite the order to hold as much German soil as possible."

Von Vietinghoff looked pale and tired, the ramifications of this latest Soviet offensive obviously extreme for his country.

The German Army was paying a high price in the defence of what was left, and that was shrinking on an hourly basis.

"Finally here, where we think the Third Red Banner Front will strike for the Rhine, and attempt to force its way into France, either through Freiburg or Strasbourg. We are a little hazy on that one at the moment Sir."

Eisenhower nodded his understanding.

"In each of these areas, our intelligence assets have identified units previously held in the general reserve or high command reserve, the latter of which tend to be committed only to important missions."

The question had to be asked.

"The Alps and Italy?"

"Not at this time, Sir. Although, as we recently discovered, there is a large grouping of enemy units in Bavaria presently untasked."

Since Patton had made the suggestion, the enemy units had not moved an inch.

"Their supply situation?"

"That seems to have improved a little, Sir. They have tightened up on rear-line security, and have had some increased success against the irregular German forces, and other partisan groups."

"How are they on equipment now?"

"Intelligence still suggests that they are light in a number of key areas. Signals and engineering equipment being the main two, although latest contact reports indicate more of the older T34 tanks in combat than expected."

Eisenhower lit a cigarette from a dying butt, declining Tedder's offer of a lighter.

He took a deep draw before posing his final question.

"Manpower?"

"On that point, there is an element of uncertainty, Sir. General?"

Bedell-Smith stepped aside, ceding the briefing position to Kenneth Strong, the intelligence chief.

"Sir, I have received reports that there has been a reversal in the Soviet's policy regarding their POW's."

A door slammed, snatched from the grasp of an orderly, provoked by a sudden gust of autumnal wind rushing through the room. The unfortunate sergeant who was deemed responsible, suddenly found himself under the direct gaze of a number of annoyed generals.

He beat a hasty retreat, careful not to repeat his error.

"Go on, Sir Kenneth."

"Sir, it seems that the Soviet High Command has relented, and has now started to integrate the qualified personnel into existing units, or form new ones in their own right. Other prisoners are being employed in the most dangerous areas, mainly as infantry, or mine clearing details."

Everyone present started to process the information, but it was Eisenhower who spoke first.

'Why they didn't do this before beats me, but then the commies play by their own rules.'

"Sir, I believe this decision will increase the combat efficiency of their qualified units across the board, in the same way that using our own released POW's has bolstered our capability."

The telephone rang.

A staff Major picked it up.

"Yes, Sir."

He offered the receiver to Eisenhower.

"General Bradley, Sir."

Ike took the receiver, exchanging a serious look with his Chief of Staff.

"Eisenhower."

He was silent, listening, assessing, and realising the weight of the news.

The horror was apparent on his face, causing both Bedell-Smith and Strong to strain their ears towards the telephone receiver, its buzzing distinctly illustrating the concerns of the 12th Army Group Commander.

'Dear God.'

"Are you positive, Brad?"

Ike took a deep drag of calming smoke.

"I'll send what I can, but you must hold. I repeat, you must hold, Brad."

Eisenhower closed his eyes, imagining the horrors being visited upon Bradley's command, the voice in his ear reinforcing the mental images.

Ike shook his head at the distant Bradley.

"No, no, no. We're not ready yet, General."

To the listeners, it was clear that the commander of 12th Army Group pushed even harder.

Eisenhower shook his head once more, this time at Bedell-Smith

"No, I will not give that order, General. We need the fighting room, and the Rhine is not yet ready. Plus, General

Strong has come up with Intel that suggests their engineers may no longer be as weak as we hoped."

Very obviously, that statement was not well received.

Eisenhower's voice and approach softened back to its normal level, having momentarily risen in the face of Bradley's insistent pleas.

"Yes, Brad, I know how close that is, but I will not yet give that order."

Ike rarely had to repeat himself to Bradley, and listeners took it as a sign of the extreme nature of the problem.

"Yes, Air will be prioritised to you for now. Round the clock ground support."

Eisenhower failed to notice Tedder blanche at the prospect of the exhausted pilots being called upon in such a fashion.

"Ok Brad. I will get Walter to contact you with a list of those units we can cut to you. In the meantime, hold those sons of bitches, or we are in deep trouble."

There was little Bradley could say to that so he acknowledged the instructions.

"And good luck to you too, Brad."

Handing the phone back to the Major, Eisenhower took a moment to compose himself before looking up into a number of expectant faces.

He walked to the situation map and placed his finger on a specific point.

All eyes strained to see.

"Cologne, gentlemen, Cologne. The front has folded in here, and the Soviet lead elements are five miles from Cologne."

A thoughtful silence overtook the assembly, each man searching his own mind for the full ramifications of that statement.

Eisenhower saved everyone the bother.

"Five miles from the Rhine."

The briefing had been completed, and the new problems were being addressed, Bedell-Smith hard at work implementing Eisenhower's orders.

Sat back, drinking coffee, and consuming the first cigarette of a second pack that day, the SHAEF Commander watched the map develop unfavourably, as the focussed Soviet attacks bore fruit.

Kenneth Strong approached, accompanied by Rossiter, and an unknown French officer, all looking fit to burst.

"Gentlemen, something tells me you bear good news for a change."

Strong deferred to Rossiter, who introduced General de Walle of French Intelligence.

De Walle then outlined the intelligence situation within the French First Army area, and made a bold suggestion on how to capitalise on recent events.

The idea was sound but risky, the benefits potentially huge. By the end of the discussion, the suggestion was approved, and the wheels set in motion to organise a massive setback to the Soviet plan in Southern Germany.

1207hrs, Friday, 12th October 1945, Headquarters of SHAEF, Trianon Palace Hotel, Versailles, France.

Eisenhower sat watching, liberal use of coffee and cigarettes failing to overcome the concern and tiredness brought about by the present disaster.

His emotions were in turmoil, his belief in Allied victory stretched to breaking point.

The Red Army had achieved a breakthrough and crossed the Rhine, the best efforts of Bradley's soldiers, and the close attention of the air forces, not enough to stop the inexorable tidal wave that had gathered momentum at Cologne.

Efforts were being made to contain the breakthrough, and USAAF bombers were already being briefed to attack the crossing points as a matter of priority.

Nevertheless, the long cherished plan of an impenetrable line on the Rhine had become an illusion overnight.

Colonel Hood, back on duty, and with medicines to calm his ulcers, brought a message to Eisenhower.

It was from McCreery, and it was stark in nature.

Bremen was about to fall.

Bedell-Smith approached, face flushed.

Eisenhower passed him the message from the British commander, wrongly assuming that it was the source of his CoS's angst.

284

It was not, and the report Ike proffered was replaced by another, originating from the defenders of Baden-Württemberg, the German state bordering France and Alsace.

He didn't read it, inviting his CoS to get whatever it was off his chest.

"Sir, Karlsruhe has fallen. Mannheim will follow within the hour."

The double shock hit Eisenhower like a left-right combination from a heavyweight boxer.

1210hrs, Friday, 12th October 1945, Headquarters, Red Banner Forces of Europe, Kohnstein, Nordhausen, Germany.

Zhukov sat watching the developing situation, the map being updated second by second by an army of personnel, fed information from the front line. His hand occasionally strayed to the table by his side, alternating between a plate of his favourite sweetbreads, and a cup of fresh tea, constantly refilled by an attentive orderly.

Inside, he was ecstatic, the map openly screamed at him, announcing the triumph of his armies.

Cologne had fallen, and the 2nd Red Banner was already spreading outwards on the west side of the mighty river.

'Why is it always that ass Konev?'

He dismissed the irritation he felt, and focussed on the success.

Bagramyan's reports indicated that the fighting in Bremen would soon be over, and that 1st Baltic would be able to push forward into the North German plain.

The latest news from 3rd Red Banner was hugely significant.

Their imminent successes meant that the angled thrust into Southern France could go ahead as planned, and it could even be that an alternative of greater value might present itself.

'Don't get ahead of yourself, Comrade!'

'I'm not, but I would be a fool not to consider the possibility, would I not?'

'True enough, but you would be a wiser man if you focussed on the plan, Georgy. Stick with the plan for now.'

'But...'

285

"No buts, it's working and we are defeating the Allied armies.'

Malinin's face betrayed the fact that Zhukov had been mumbling his 'conversation'.

'Enough for now then. Stick with the plan.'

"Comrade Marshal, the Allied air force is making heavy attacks all over the Cologne area, and we are taking huge casualties."

Zhukov's eyes inadvertently swivelled to the area where Novikov was working furiously.

"Our own air force is fighting magnificently, Comrade Marshal. There is no more they can do that is not already in hand."

Zhukov accepted Malinin's defence of Novikov.

"The situation in Bremen is less clear. Marshal Bagramyan has had a setback. Their Polish Armoured Division reappeared, and drove into the flank of the 11th Guards Army. Apparently, it caused havoc amongst the artillery elements and losses have been heavy. The Armenian states there will be a delay, but no more than that."

"And the Poles?"

"Have been driven off, Comrade Marshal. Kuzma Nikitovich personally organised an armoured force, and pushed the vipers back, causing heavy casualties."

Zhukov grunted, content that Major General Kuzma Galitsky, a soldier very highly thought of by both men, was on hand to sort the problem.

"Sir, the situation at Karlsruhe and Mannheim. Have you considered a change in the plan?"

"Yes, I have considered a change. No, I will not make such a change, Mikhail."

Malinin could not hide his disappointment.

"Not at this time anyway, Comrade," Zhukov conceded.

"Moving south-west down the Rhine line is still risky, Comrade Marshal. Moving directly westwards does offer appealing opportunities..."

Zhukov interrupted.

"This I know, Mikhail, but there are also possibilities that we have discussed before, the same possibilities that made the drive south-west to the Belfort Gap so attractive."

Zhukov stood and beckoned his CoS to follow. Once in his private office, Zhukov gesticulated at the wall map.

"We have a chance to isolate a large enemy force to the east of the Rhine. The possibility to drive around Switzerland and into the rear of the Northern Italy defences remains a distinct possibility, even with the presence of the Spanish."

Malinin, always expected to speak freely in private, tapped the map in three places.

"Bordeaux? Paris? The Channel?"

Zhukov couldn't help himself, and his eyes lapped up the possibilities.

'No!'

He punched a fist into his cupped left hand to frighten away the part of him that agreed.

"Once we get there," his finger shot out, aiming specifically at Belfort and Mulhouse, "Then we can explore the options."

Malinin has stated his objections before, but felt the need to cover them again.

"Comrade Marshal, I still believe that committing on a narrow front, one flank to the Rhine, the other to the mountains, is a risky strategy. We will be confined."

Zhukov sighed the sigh of a teacher trying to explain an easy problem to a difficult child.

"As will they, Mikhail, as will they."

Pausing to look at the map, a thought occurred.

"Mind you, Comrade, there is nothing to stop us expanding westwards from either point, if circumstances permit it. When we first planned, we did not possess the extra manpower. Have another look at it please."

Malinin felt more comfortable with that, and moved to start his work.

He opened the door as Nazarbayeva was about to knock.

"Ah, Comrade Polkovnik. Please come in."

Salutes were exchanged and business commenced.

"Comrade Marshal, General Pekunin has received a full report on the events in Fischausen, and has asked me to pass it on to you."

Puzzled that such an insignificant matter should be brought directly to him by the head of the GRU, Zhukov skimmed the file.

287

"Ah yes, the blackmail of the German Knocke."

He remembered the simple briefing, but had not expected any worthwhile advantage to come of it, and merely acknowledged it, permitting the Chekists and the GRU to play their games.

"Comrade Marshal, the investigating officer believes that the attack was undertaken by rogue SS elements, who had no idea who or what they were attacking."

Zhukov had just read that section as she spoke it.

"Further to that, the investigating officer also concludes that no knowledge of the fate of the Knocke family has leaked out; all three confirmed dead, of course. General Pekunin endorses this view, and believes that Knocke can still be controlled."

"And the other projects?"

"Are all in place, Comrade Marshal. We have direct influence over some very senior commanders in the new German army."

"Excellent."

There was a silence; one that Zhukov decided needed further investigation.

"And what are your views on the Knocke situation, Comrade Polkovnik?"

"Something is not right, Sir. It is not clear to me, but something is not right."

Malinin's interested perked up.

"How so, Comrade Nazarbayeva?"

"Comrade General, I find myself asking about this SS unit. Where have they been, and what have they been doing all this time? There have been a few recorded attacks in the area, mainly in the last three weeks, so have they been somewhere else? Hiding? I don't know what, but I have a problem with it, Sir."

"And Comrade Pekunin? What is his view?"

"He sees no issue here, and illustrated his point with examples of other groups that have only recently started to cause trouble."

"And yet, you disagree?"

"Comrade Polkovnik General Pekunin made an excellent case."

Malinin looked to Zhukov for further input.

288

"Comrade Nazarbayeva, thank you for your opinion, honest as ever. In this instance, the overall matter is of little importance I think, but we will bear in mind your concerns, if Knocke becomes involved again."

Nazarbayeva accepted that without rancour.

"Proceed, Comrade Polkovnik."

"Comrades, the Italian government have still not declared their neutrality, as you know. That is on hold until you signal a start for phase three."

That was a bugbear to both men, the supply situation putting 'Three' on hold indefinitely.

"However, I have a report that indicates that the Italian's situation is known to the Allied High Command."

No surprises there; such a thing was difficult to conceal.

'Next?'

"There has been a failed attempt on General Patton's life."

"When?"

"Last Sunday, Comrade Marshal. We have not learned of it until today. GRU's agent was shot during the attempt, and has only recently managed to communicate with us. She was attempting to remove Patton, but was shot before she could act."

"Shot before she could act? I don't understand, Comrade."

"Our agent was shot by someone trying to assassinate Patton, before she could act, which is why her cover remains intact, Comrade Marshal."

"That all sounds very complicated, Comrade Polkovnik. Who was the other assassin?"

Nazarbayeva nearly shrugged.

"Not known at this time, but definitely not one of ours, or of the NKVD."

"Anything else, Comrade Nazarbayeva?"

"No, Sir."

"Thank you for your report as always."

The female officer saluted and withdrew, leaving the two men to their thoughts of Italy.

<u>2302hrs, Friday, 12th October 1945, Headquarters of SHAEF,
Trianon Palace Hotel, Versailles, France.</u>

Eisenhower replaced the receiver, and took a moment to compose himself.

Bedell-Smith, Hood, Foster, in fact, pretty much every man and woman in the close staff was stood watching him, his reaction, his anguish.

Gathering himself, the Supreme Commander reflected on the day's events.

One hour beforehand, to the minute, McCreery had called in with the bad news about Bremen and its loss, compounded by the destruction of some fine Allied formations, such as the 51st Highland Division, gutted and decimated in the hard city fighting.

Mannheim had fallen that afternoon, and the situation across the board was dire.

The front had ruptured, and Soviet forces were pouring through, headed west into the Saar towards Luxembourg and south-west towards Strasbourg and the Alsace.

And now Bradley.

Eisenhower stood.

"I have just been informed by General Bradley that 78th Infantry has collapsed under extreme Soviet pressure, and that, as a result, enemy units have seized the vital junction at Sindorf-Kerpen. He also reports contact at Wanlo, three kilometres south of Mönchengladbach."

There was no sound to speak of from the listeners, but a tangible feeling of horror was easily discernable as many eyes turned to take in the situation map, its servant clerks already logging the third major break in the Allied line that day.

"There is nothing I can say that will disguise the seriousness of our position. Nothing at all."

A few faces grew dark, those affected by doubt and the foreboding of defeat.

A wave of defiance swept over Eisenhower.

'Not on my watch!'

"What I can say to you all is this." Ike's voice grew unusually large, impressing everyone with its strength and belief.

"We will stop them, of that, there is no question. Very soon, I will tell you how we will do it. What I do know is that we

290

will not achieve this unless we are all focussed, and all fully committed to achieving victory."

Eisenhower set his face and played hardball with his staff. He was a different General to the one they were used to; he needed to be.

"Anyone who doesn't feel that they can sign up to that, regardless of rank, submit your request for reassignment by midnight. Now is not the time to have doubts. Now is the time for the best of us to produce the best we can."

Ike looked down, his eyes feasting on the cigarette pack that was calling him so urgently.

"To that end, we are going to give our Armies the resources to patch this up, and then they can start driving the Commies back."

Casting a deliberate look at Tedder, he continued.

"We are going to make sure the boys in the field get the best support we can possibly give them."

Arthur Tedder's jaw was very deliberately set, and Eisenhower knew the man was resolved.

"We are going to pull every trick in the book, and many that haven't yet been thought of yet, to get back to an even keel."

A low murmur greeted his declaration.

"Tonight, right now, we are going to start this work anew. I want every gun, every bullet, every man, brought up to the field. We will get units moving tonight, supplies moving tonight, we will give our Generals the means to stop this...tonight."

The murmur became a rumble of voices signing up to the task ahead.

Searching out Von Vietinghoff, Eisenhower specifically appealed to the German Liaison Officer.

"We will speed up the organisation and deployment of the German Republican forces."

It was a statement, but was undoubtedly a question too, a question that received a firm nod from the German General.

Eisenhower returned the nod, knowing that the Germans would come up with more resources.

"By the morning, we will have a workable plan to stop them cold, and by the evening, a plan to roll them back. Are we clear?"

The replies were mixed, from firm and committed to doubtful and concerned.

"OK. First things first. I need Air immediately. Get them in the battle and hurting these three attacks immediately."

"Secondly, I want the special reserve kept out of the planning for now. It is not to be sent forward, no matter what. Clear?"

That was universally understood.

"Thirdly, if it's at sea, training in England, or resting in France, I want it, and I want it right now."

The staff was more focussed and inspired by an Eisenhower gaining in firmness as he went further on.

"I want our old units reinforced. Comb the services again, comb the hospitals again, comb anything you want, but get manpower in the line."

'God but I need a cigarette!'

"I want to create new units, and I don't care how. I want the Soviets to find new divisions, new corps, and new armies in our order of battle. If you can't do it for real then do it like we did with First Army Group, when we fooled the Germans in '44!"

He avoided looking at Von Vietinghoff.

"I want the Russian to feel he is opposed by a steel wall; a line of bayonets from the top to bottom of Europe."

Now there were smiles, enough to let him know he had made a difference to his people.

"I want you all to be positive, speak positive, do positive, inspiring those you deal with, making them understand that we, here, believe. Don't say 'no', say 'will do', and then get it done.

'Maybe this was long overdue?'

"OK then. Let's get to work."

A general hubbub broke out as solutions were discussed and orders formed.

The cigarette was in his mouth and lit within seconds, the comforting nicotine calming his insides, bringing them to a level to match his calm exterior.

The recently promoted GeneralOberst Von Vietinghoff stepped forward.

"My apologies, Heinrich."

"Not necessary, Herr General."

There was no side there, nothing to make Eisenhower think that he had offended the man.

"Can you get your government to speed up the process of mobilisation from the released POW's?"

"We are already doing it as fast as we can, Herr General, but the urgency of the situation will make us find ways."

"See what you can do, please?"

"I will try, Sir. Now, this is bad timing, but there it is."

He handed over a message sheet, recently in from Guderian's command.

"Langenfeld?"

"Yes, Sir. It is about six kilometres south of Dusseldorf."

'Oh Lord!'

"Can the Field Marshal hold?"

Guderian had also been bumped up the ranks, receiving his country's highest military post.

"He thinks so. The Soviets seem to have stopped, and unconfirmed reports have them digging in, Sir."

"Digging in?"

"Perhaps they have learned the lesson of the Ruhr encirclement, Herr General, but I do wonder if they have learned the lesson of the First Army Group, Sir?"

Bedell-Smith stood waiting his turn, almost willing the two men to finish.

"I wonder that too, Colonel General Vietinghoff, I wonder that too."

The German saluted impeccably, as always, and departed to throw the wheels of mobilisation into a swifter gear.

Bedell-Smith approached, as Eisenhower lit another cigarette.

"Walter, what do you have for me?"

"McCreery's idea on hitting back Sir. What do you want to do with it? The resources are there, or close at hand. No effect on the main action, unless you were considering transferring assets from there to here?"

Eisenhower considered it for the briefest of moments.

"I think we are going to need everybody on the mainland, Walter. Cut orders to bring the units that we cut out for the Danish operation over to Europe soonest."

293

Whilst he understood, Bedell-Smith found himself feeling disappointed that a genuine opportunity to successfully hit back was lost.

'Would I do any different? Really?'

The Chief of Staff disappeared to set the ball rolling on transferring British and German units from Norway to mainland Europe.

A message arrived from Field-Marshal Alexander, a reply to Eisenhower's urgent request for information.

"Ask General Smith to come over please."

Anne-Marie Foster doubled away and returned with the CoS.

"From Alexander."

Ike handed over the brief report, watching the furrows on his CoS' brow deepen.

"Nothing?"

"So it seems. Nothing at all. Should we be worried or grateful, I wonder?"

Bedell-Smith didn't hesitate.

"I'll take it at the moment, Sir. We've enough on our plate, but we can't forget the possibility. On that note, I assume you have not rescinded the stop order on Italian forces?"

Such a question deserved a considered reply, which gave Eisenhower an opportunity to indulge himself in his habit.

"I think not, Walter. We can't take the risk by weakening him too much. We've already cleaned a lot of his top assets out. No, we will leave him be."

Turning to the female officer, Ike continued seamlessly.

"Anne-Marie, return a message to the Field-Marshal please. Tell him we will not be removing any further assets from his command. Also, request that he contacts this headquarters immediately there is a change in Soviet activity on his front line."

"Yes, Sir."

"Thank you."

Now alone, the two senior men pondered the map.

"This is really serious, Walter."

Eisenhower got no argument on that score.

Discussing some of the finer points of the Soviet threat, both men became aware of a drenched Marine officer heading their way.

"Judging by the look on Rossiter's face, he has a story to tell, Sir.'"

'God, please let it be good news.'

Both men uttered the silent plea to higher authority.

"Sam, you're soaked. Go and get changed, and we can talk about whatever has you so fired up shortly."

The dripping Marine shook his head, spots of water reaching the table and beyond.

"I don't think it can wait, Sir."

Eisenhower poured the cold, wet man a hot coffee, and made him drink some before he continued.

"Sir, it's the Poles."

Bedell-Smith nodded his understanding.

"Yes, we know. They've been badly hit and are out of the line reforming."

"No, Sir. You don't understand. I mean the Polish Army."

Eisenhower caught on immediately.

"You mean the Polish Army, in Poland."

"Yes, Sir. I have a Polish officer in protective custody outside. If I may have him shown in?"

A nod was enough, and Rossiter moved quickly.

Eisenhower flipped a quick look at the Marine's holster. It was empty, as was the holster of the US officer accompanying the Pole.

Standing orders had been changed since the attack on Patton, and any visitor not from the parent unit, regardless of rank or status, had their weapons secured by the guard detail on arrival.

The Polish Cavalry officer, complete with the trademark Rogatywka pointed cap, snapped to attention and saluted.

'Something about the Poles. Always so damn smart.'

Rossiter introduced the newcomer.

"PodPulkownik Zajac, General Eisenhower."

The Pole became even more rigid at the mention of his name.

The Marine officer continued.

"Lieutenant Colonel Zajac is from the headquarters of the First Polish Army, and here at the direction of the Army Commander, General Berling..."

'Where is this going?'

"...And with the agreement and knowledge of General Świerczewski, commander of the 2nd Polish Army."

'OK, impeccable credentials, now get to the point.'

The Marine took a deep breath.

"Sir, the Polish Army is ready to fight on our side."

'Thank you God!'

"Tell me more, Sam."

"Sir, the Colonel is here to make this offer to you, and to take back your reply to his Commanders."

Eisenhower noted the faint spread of a smile on Bedell-Smith's face. He resisted joining him.

"Your view, Sam?"

"Kosher, Sir. One hundred percent. Our contacts have implied an increased feeling of rebellion amongst the Polish Army. I believe this is a genuine offer, but," he conceded, "Both us and the Brits will quietly knock on some doors and learn more."

'You said to your people 'tonight, right now', didn't you? So, why not?'

Eisenhower extended his right hand, taking the Pole's hand in a firm grip.

"We will welcome you with open arms, Colonel, when the time is right," Lassiter translated, "You will understand that we must check some things first."

The Pole nodded in acceptance, Lassiter's swift translation no less than had been anticipated.

"When you return to your Commander, you can give him my personal assurance that, if his offer is genuine, and his forces wish to fight, en masse, against the Soviet Union, then the offer will be accepted, and we will fight them together, as full military allies."

Eisenhower felt that would not be an issue for his political masters, as the Poles were already de facto Allies. In any case, he would sell them on it, if there was a problem.

"Thank you Sam, now will you and Colonel Zajac get cleaned up and rested. We will talk further about this in the morning."

Both men saluted and went in search of a hot shower and a comfortable bed.

The American had been away in Ireland de-briefing a mission, the Pole had been tossed about on the Baltic, before finally getting an aircraft from Denmark to Versailles.

As he watched the two men disappear, his mind immediately flagged an issue.

"Walter, scrub that order about Norway. We prepare planning for McCreery's operation as soon as is practicable. This new development, if it is 'kosher', presents us with a massive opportunity.'"

Bedell-Smith nodded, and went to turn away.

"Plus," he turned back and refocused on his Commander, "Get Sir Roger Dalziel over here, as quickly as possible."

There was obviously more.

"Also, I need Admiral Somerville here today, straight away."

The CoS immediately understood where the energized Eisenhower was coming from, and smiled.

The Allies were going to hit back in a big and unexpected way.

Suddenly Eisenhower found himself alone.

He relaxed into one of the comfortable chairs and savoured his latest cigarette, alternating tobacco and drink, enjoying some of the newly arrived coffee.

The front line in Europe drew his main attention, working his mind to the limit.

However, there was a part of him, the rarely surfaced gambler and adventurer part, which snuck an occasional look at Denmark and the Baltic Sea to the east, naturally drawing his eye further to the Northern Coast of Germany and, beyond it, Poland.

A thing of orchestrated hell - a terrible symphony of light and flame.

Ed Murrow, radio broadcast about his Lancaster bombing mission over Berlin in 1943.

Chapter 90 - THE RAIDS

<u>0917hrs, Saturday, 13th October 1945, Headquarters, 2nd Red Banner Central European Front, Schloss Rauischholzhausen, Ebsdorfergrund, Germany.</u>

Konev was a man on a mission.

His orders were clear.

2nd Red Banner Central European Front was to bypass the Ruhr to the south and strike up into Eastern Holland to isolate the enemy forces in a pocket from Dortmund to Dusseldorf, whilst 1st Baltic, similarly reinforced, pushed to the south-west, intending to meet up with 2nd Red Banner somewhere on the Rhine.

However, Konev also sensed that Zhukov was deliberately hamstringing him, keeping him almost confined, in favour of 3rd Red Banner to the south, and that damned Armenian in 1st Baltic.

Both of those commanders had unlimited powers to advance, whereas he, and only he, was to remain this side of the Rhine and concentrate on the encirclement of the Ruhr.

Well, he would see just how far he could stretch his orders. Success always brought with it understanding for those who had exceeded their instructions, and he simply couldn't ignore the possibility that the map threw up at him.

His Chief of Staff understood the bald Marshal, or more importantly, understood the ambition that drove him.

It was no surprise that the Marshal started to look at things beyond the orders from Zhukov, and the CoS was so unsurprised that he didn't query the procedure, merely recorded Konev's instructions for translating into movement orders as soon as possible.

Working with a set of dividers, looking at distances and travel times, logistics and the terrain, Konev quietly made his plan.

Satisfied with its feasibility, he threw the dividers down and looked up at Petrov, stood with pad at the ready for his commanders orders.

"Good. Now then, we will proceed with the orders as received. Our forces will focus on this area," he indicated the ground behind the Ruhr, "But we must also obey our orders, specifically the section about ensuring we have secure flanks."

He drew his Chief of Staff into the conspiracy with an inviting gesture.

Bending over the map, Petrov continued to make his notes.

"We will send the 5th Guards and 6th Guards Tank Armies this way. I want to secure these bridges on our flanks, just to make sure there is no threat of a counter-attack on our left flank."

Two of the bridges sat on main routes into Holland, the first at Maasbracht, the second to the south at Stein.

The final bridge was in the middle, a small village called Berg an der Maas, three kilometres behind Sittard, home of the 101st US Airborne Division.

Konev was going for the Maas and intended to cross it in force, regardless of the restraint Zhukov had placed upon him.

1702hrs, Saturday, 13th October 1945. Airborne over the Caspian Sea, approaching Baku, USSR.

The mission had been looked at previously, and set aside for a number of reasons.

The biggest one was the strength of Soviet air defences, a strength that had been eroded over time, as the demands of the European Front called fighter unit after fighter unit to the German front.

Secondly, the limited strength of the Allied air forces that could carry out the mission.

Thirdly, the situation regarding Soviet supply had not been fully appreciated until recently.

In 1940, the British and French had considered bombing Baku and Grozny, to strangle the fuel supply to Nazi Germany, such supply being a by-product of the Molotov-Ribbentrop Pact.

The groundwork done at that time, Operation Pike, was looked at and used to plan the newest attempt to knock out a major part of the USSR's oil production.

Three of the India-based RAF squadron's were tasked, flown from the sub-continent to a hastily refurbished facility at Shiraz in Iran. From there, 99 Squadron's Liberator Bombers, supported by 211 Squadron's Mosquitoes, both covered by the Beaufighter Mk X's and XI's of 177 Squadron, were sent northwards to damage the oil production facilities at Baku on the Caspian Sea.

They appeared high on the eastern horizon and caught the Soviet air defences on the hop.

Nothing was in the air.

No flak, no aircraft, no balloons, just a scoop of Pelicans, and a mated pair of Whooper swans to interrupt the rich blueness of the perfect late afternoon sky.

Once the defences appreciated that the growing dots were enemy aircraft, the warning went out, and the civilian populace scurried for cover, as the gunners prepared their weapons, and the fighter pilots ran to waiting machines.

From the airfield considered home by the 57th Guards Fighter Aviation Regiment, the surviving six P-63 KingCobras rose to meet the threat.

On the other side of Baku, the 773rd Fighter Aviation Regiment responded by putting eight P-39 Aircobras in the air. From the same field, three Spitfire Mk V's of the Baku District Pilot Training Unit added their venerable strength.

The Fighter Regiments had both been transferred back from the Western Front, returned to safer airspace to recover and bring themselves back up to strength, before going back to Germany.

As the Soviet planes went up, the Allied bombs came down, the Liberators dropping from a comfortable height of twenty-two thousand feet.

Five hundred pound bombs fell amongst the storage tanks and wellheads, the refineries and the chemical plants.

300

The target was so densely packed that it was difficult for the bomb-aimers of 99 Squadron to miss.

211 Squadron came in lower, with more precise intent, pressing hard behind the torrent of descending bombs, their mission to ensure that the prime refining and chemical facilities received direct attention.

The training unit Spitfires flogged themselves to death, seeking valuable height, as they pursued the Liberators.

The Aircobras and Kingcobras latched onto the Mosquitoes of 211 Squadron, spoiling many a bomb-run, causing misses, or even preventing release.

Above the whirling mass came the Beaufighters, plunging down to take the pressure off the unarmed Mk XVI Mosquitoes.

Too late for one RAF crew, their aircraft coming apart around them, as the heavy 37mm cannon shells of a Kingcobra ripped the plywood wonder apart.

The firepower of the Kingcobra was impressive, adding four .50cal Brownings to the heavy cannon that fired through the propeller boss.

The Beaufighter brought a lot more to the aerial combat, its standard four 20mm Hispano cannons supplemented by six extra .303 machine guns on the wings.

Three of the cobras were hacked down on the first sweep, the weight of metal defeating the Bell's robust airframe.

None of the pilots escaped and all five aircrew, British and Soviet, were dead before their aircraft hit the ground.

The Wing Commander in the lead Mosquito was hopping mad.

"Sinbad Leader calling Sabre leader, get them off our backs. Now! You just cost us an aircraft. Now do your jobs!"

Squadron Leader Arkwright grimaced at the open remarks, made more uncomfortable by the fact that the WingCo was right. 177 Squadron, no, he had been slow to respond to the enemy fighters.

"Sinbad Leader, roger."

The Beaufighters roared in again, keeping themselves between the interceptors and the regrouping Mossies.

In the sky beyond, smokey, fiery trails marked the death dives of two of the training unit's Spitfires, victims of the defensive armament of the withdrawing Liberators.

The Kingcobras flew off to one flank, the Aircobras diving to ground level, in an attempt to split 177 Squadron's defence.

Arkwright nodded in acknowledgement.

'These boys know their job;' a professional's opinion on the swift reaction of the Soviet pilots.

"Sabre leader to all Sabre. Blue Flight come to port and stick with the yellow tails," the unofficial marking recently adopted by the 57th Guards helping him in his description, "Red Flight take the flight at ground level. Green flight return to protect the bombers. Execute."

Three distinct groups of Beaufighters formed, Blue flight scoring a swift success, downing another of the Kingcobras. Red Flight pursued the Soviet 773rd Regiment, and came under fire from light AA weapons, one of the heavy RAF fighters losing an engine as bullets smashed home.

Green Flight, complete with the Squadron Leader, ran straight into a barrage of fire from heavier weapons, guns that had been waiting for the moment that they no longer risked hitting their own.

One Beau received a direct hit in the observer's position, severing the fuselage in two. The rear portion fell away like a piece of garbage, its descent irregular and uncontrolled.

The front section, still powered by two brutish Bristol Hercules engines, flew on unsteadily, the horrendously wounded pilot trying hard to make his aircraft stay in the air.

He failed, and the front section fell away, arrowing into the water of the Caspian Sea.

Three more Beaufighters took hits.

One lost an engine and part of its wing, but a magnificent piece of flying brought the aircraft safely down, landing heavily on one of the wider local roads.

The pilot brought his damaged aircraft to a halt and immediately set about destroying everything of value. He need not have bothered, as the gunners in two venerable BA-11 armoured cars smashed the Beaufighter and her crew to pieces, happy to be doing something to protect the Rodina from the terrorist flyers.

The second fighter lost four foot of its port wing and, more importantly, the fuel cell in the wing was punctured, spilling precious fuel.

302

None the less, it remained airborne and limped off in the direction of its home base.

The third aircraft hit belonged to Arkwright.

The 37mm shell had failed to explode, which, for Arkwright, was just as well.

It had entered the aircraft just behind the control column, travelled between his arms without touching uniform or flesh, and exited the canopy, smashing everything in its path and ventilating the cockpit.

Face cut by shards of perspex from the damaged cockpit, Arkwright struggled to see, the blood dripping into his eyes.

None the less, he was still called upon to fly the aircraft and make decisions, the first of which was reacting to Red Flight's failure to interdict the Aircobras.

Green flight were best positioned now, and so he sent them in, staying back as his lack of proper vision could be more of a liability in the close quarter fight.

Blue flight was directed to recover their station on the Mosquito squadron, which unit was holding briefly, whilst the Aircobra situation was resolved.

Green Flight attacked and scored immediately, sending the enemy commander spinning spectacularly into a burning oil tank and driving the Aircobras away, opening up the attack run to the Mosquitoes of 211 Squadron.

"Sinbad Leader calling all Sinbad aircraft. Commence your run, commence your run. Execute."

The twelve bombers swept over the target area, the main refining facility a priority target, as was the rest facility of knowledgeable technicians and engineers who kept the whole of Baku running.

Mixed loads of five hundred, two fifty, and incendiaries left their bomb bays, adding to the damage that had already been wrought by the Liberators.

The cracking towers, previously unscathed, were transformed into useless metal, high explosive commencing the job of destruction, greedy flames fuelled by widely available hydrocarbons completing the job.

One Mosquito staggered as it was struck by 12.7mm bullets, rolling over and adding itself and its hapless crew to the inferno at the distribution head, killing over thirty fire-fighters as they battled the flames.

One Aircobra had slipped Green Flight, and it bored in on the bombers.

Arkwright, lazily circling and directing his squadron, saw it in a brief moment of clarity.

"Sabre leader to Sinbad aircraft. One bandit eleven o'clock low, closing fast. Am attacking."

Bringing the Beaufighter around in as tight a turn as he dared, Arkwright drove his aircraft straight at the gap between the hunter and the hunted.

The Mosquitoes were fast aircraft, but bombing at low-level did not afford them this advantage, and they were going to be in harm's way unless Arkwright could interpose himself.

Beaufighter, Aircobra, and Mosquitoes converged inexorably.

Had he been able to translate his thoughts for the benefit of the casual onlooker, then the reasons for his manouevre would have been made clear.

But he didn't, or rather couldn't, so he just rose lazily into the air, leaving his partner still scrabbling on the ground.

Rapidly gaining height, he decided to avoid the strange goings-on to his left and move away, bringing him straight into a line of convergence with a number of aircraft unaware of his presence.

Another easy and powerful surge gained him extra height, and he became aware of something closing rapidly on his left side.

A swift angling of the neck told him it was worth avoiding, so he dropped his right wing and came round in a tight turn.

To the children of Khojahasan he was 'Old White', an object of affection, and to the smallest, one of some fear.

He had lived on Khojahasan Lake for years, returning every year with his mate, for 'Old White' was a C.cygnus; a Whooper Swan.

Fifteen kilos of solid male swan crashed into the shattered cockpit of the Beaufighter, and transformed both Old White and Squadron Leader Arkwright into an unidentifiable mess, spreading through the cockpit and the fuselage beyond, and in 'Old White's' case, only after his solid body had demolished the pilots seat and smashed the observer beyond.

The young pilot of the Aircobra had watched, both horrified and fascinated, as the huge white swan had flown into the Beaufighter. His inexperience cost him his life. The uncontrolled enemy aircraft spiralled away and he reacted late, the heavy aircraft clipping his Aircobra's tail plane, sending him into a death dive.

Both aircraft crashed in the oil storage area, the Aircobra igniting a full storage tank previously spared from damage.

The huge blossom of fire marked the end to the raid, and the air combat, both sides drawing off to head for home and mourn comrades lost.

On the ground, the dying continued into the night, as the fire brigade and civilian volunteers strove in vain to control spreading fuel fires, more facilities falling victim as every minute passed.

Timed to coincide with the Baku attack, units of the USAAF took off from the fields in Northern Italy, and headed for the Ploiesti area, the oil-rich heartland of Roumania.

In 1943, a mission had been flown from Libya with the same purpose, generally considered a costly failure.

The 1945 version had one advantage.

The lead bombers belonged to the RAF's 9 Squadron, and had a special capacity that had not been available during the previous 'Operation Tidal Wave'.

9 Squadron had flown from their base in France to Northern Italy, where they were loaded with the Tallboy 12000lbs earthquake bombs. Along with 617 Squadron, the famous Dambusters, 9 Squadron was equipped and trained to deliver the huge bombs with precision.

The theory was simple.

Hit or miss the target, the bombs would penetrate the earth and create shock waves that would affect the facilities integrity by disrupting pipes and services, affecting the solid bases of the storage facilities and the refineries, and generally disturb everything, making the target vulnerable to the mix of

305

high-explosives and incendiaries that the USAAF aircraft would drop immediately afterwards.

In this instance, the Soviet air defences had not been unduly weakened, and covering fighters rose early to meet the approaching bomber force.

Escorting Mustangs interposed themselves, but the Lavochkin's and Mig's smashed their way through and downed four of the RAF heavy bombers.

The remaining ten Lancasters dropped on the main targets.

Two bombs plunged into the Concordia Vega refinery; another four shared themselves equally between the Asta Romana and Columbia Aquila refining facilities.

Of the remaining four Tallboys, only one went wide of the mark, plunging into the Ploiesti sewage works, its three companions expending their considerable power in and around the storage facilities at Româno-Americană and Unirea Speranta.

The first bomb to land on the latter site could not have been bettered. It penetrated straight through the largest tank, burying itself deep in the ground, before exploding with spectacular results.

The pressure fired thousands of gallons of petroleum spirit skywards in a huge orange wall that rose, curved over, and then plunged back to earth, igniting everything in its path.

Any USAAF bombers depositing their loads on Speranta would waste their time, as the entire facility started to consume itself, further failures in pipe work and storage tanks adding more products to the expanding fires.

In 1943, five Bombardment Groups of the Eighth and Ninth US Air Forces had attacked and, in most estimations, failed to permanently affect the production from Ploiesti.

In October 1945, three Bombardment Groups of the Twelfth US Air Force caused more widespread and deep-seated damage than previously thought possible, and at a much lower cost.

Whilst the heavy bombers had been harried all the way, in their flight over Southern Europe, Mustangs from all European commands had accompanied them, and inflicted heavy casualties on the defending Soviet air force, although not without significant losses themselves.

306

The difference this time was the lower defensive capacity of the Soviet air force combined with the spectacular deployment of the Tallboy bombs.

Ploiesti had its production capacity reduced by over 60% in as many minutes.

2309hrs, Saturday, 13th October 1945, Headquarters, Red Banner Forces of Europe, Kohnstein, Nordhausen, Germany.

The image of the scantily clad young peasant girl started to fade, the sound of her inviting voice being replaced with the urgent sounds of knocking on his door.

Marshal Zhukov had taken to his bed early, well satisfied with a day during which his armies had sundered the Allied line in three places.

The knocking grew more urgent, and he shook off the last vestiges of deep sleep and shouted at whomever it was to enter.

Malinin, his tunic undone and clearly also roused from his slumbers, burst into the room clutching message slips.

"What's got you so rattled, Mikhail?"

The Marshal reached across for his own tunic, and he stood, unsteadily at first, as his hand detoured to the proffered reports instead.

"Talk to me," his eyes not yet clear, the paperwork a jumble of meaningless symbols.

"The Allies have hit Ploesti and Baku in simultaneous raids. Proper damage reports are not yet available but first indications are that the facilities in Baku are badly damaged, those in Roumania even worse."

No report was needed to make Zhukov aware of the consequences of the raids.

"If this is true, we will lose some mobility, some supply ability, and some air capacity."

The tunic was slipped on and buttons fastened as he paused for further thought.

"We need firm figures and projections from the Minister for Fuel before we can assess the impact, but I think we should immediately put in place something to prioritise fuel for our frontline and air forces."

Sitting down again, Zhukov posed a question.

307

"How did the enemy get at these two prime facilities?"

"It would appear that the Air Force weakened the defences in favour of sending units to the Western Front. Some under strength units were at Baku, and they were overwhelmed. The response over Ploesti was more structured, but the defensive fighter formations were too numerous for our own forces to have much effect."

Pulling on his boots, Zhukov stood and stamped down hard.

"I assume Moscow has been informed?"

"Yes, Comrade Marshal. This report indicates that NKVD teams are already at the relevant headquarters making enquiries."

Both men understood that others would die that night, their decisions condemning them to the righteous indignation of others armed with 20/20 hindsight.

"Right, Comrade Malinin, let us go and sort this mess out!"

Both men moved quickly towards the main command centre, both sharing the thoughts about how quickly situations can change in warfare.

Author's note on 'Stalemate' from this point forward.

Stalemate will now divide into three sections, and each will be taken to its conclusion before starting on the next.

Each section will deal with a major Soviet attack and the areas affected by it, as well as the occasional general matter. In general, these attacks are within the area of responsibility of a Soviet Front, so I have labelled each chapter according to which Front is involved.

This will result in the time line extending for one Front's chapters, and then returning to an earlier time for the next.

This has been done to limit the amount of chopping and changing between areas so that the reader may get a better feel for each individual area.

The order in which they are addressed is purely one of my own selection. I indicate nothing by my choices.

Historians, examining each of the three major encounters at their leisure, have argued for decades over which was the most important victory or defeat for the protagonists of World War Three.

I will leave the resolution of those arguments in the hands of the reader.

2ND RED BANNER ARMY OF SOVIET EUROPE - MARSHAL KONEV

Pride goeth before destruction, and a haughty spirit before a fall.

Proverbs 16:18.

Chapter 91 - THE COLOSSUS

<u>0800hrs, Sunday, 14th October 1945, Western Germany.</u>

Throughout the central area, every Allied unit had a mission, whether it was to rush to the front, hold a valuable position, or fall back in good order.

Except the 18th Airborne Corps, it seemed, left untouched by Eisenhower's express order. Removed from Bradley's direct command, the paratrooper formations were recuperating and rejuvenating in their bases through Belgium and Holland.

Perversely, the 101st was in the best shape, despite its excursion into Bavaria. Swiftly recovered, losses were made up by the disbandment of the 13th US Airborne Division, whose personnel filled out the vacant spots in both 101st and 17th Airborne Divisions, the latter formation having ventured into the fighting in Central Europe, where it suffered badly.

The 17th, on paper, was up to full strength, but there were questions about its morale and ability in combat, following its heavy losses.

The British 6th Airborne Division was up to its full TOE, but many of its personnel were recently liberated POW's, who needed more time to regain the top fitness required of a paratrooper.

Another welcome addition to the 18th Corps was a German jump-qualified Regiment, ex-POW Fallschirmjager that had earned their spurs in Holland, Crete, and North Africa, mixed with a handful of hardened veterans who had fought through to the end on the Western Front.

310

Their commander had been released from British captivity and installed as head of the newly formed 'Fallschirm Regiment Von der Heydte'. It was a unit that had existed in the previous war, and that had fought directly against the troopers of the 101st at Carentan, Normandy.

FallschirmRegiment VDH was encamped at Venlo, twenty-five miles north of the Eagles division, which was centred on Sittard-Geleen.

The British airborne concentrated around Eindhoven, with the 17th spread thinly from Maastricht through Genk to Hasselt, and beyond.

<u>0812hrs, Sunday, 14th October 1945, Headquarters, 2nd Red Banner Central European Front, Schloss Rauischholzhausen, Ebsdorfergrund, Germany.</u>

Konev pored over the map with his CoS, making small notations with a pencil here and there, occasionally scribing a wider appreciation of the situation.

He had already decided to exceed his orders and not be unduly confined by Zhukov, whom he was convinced held him back, because of his success at Berlin a few months before.

Allocating sufficient forces to the stated task of sealing up the south and south-west of the Ruhr, Konev had gathered the 6th Guards Tank Army, a newly allocated formation, ready to send it down a path towards his own personal target; a crossing of the Maas River.

5th Guards Army, recently removed from frontline duties, was committed back to the action in support of 6th Guards Tanks, having been bolstered with some of the prisoners of war, so recently made available by the change in policy in Moscow.

Whilst he waited for the right moment to make the key decision, he employed the two formations, in harness, west of Cologne, hammering into the thin screens that had been hastily formed in front of them, brushing most aside without too much difficulty.

But it was always the aircraft, the ground attack squadrons, or the bombers of the USAAF and RAF that halted the columns.

311

Throughout his command, casualties were heavy. The list of dead and wounded mounted up on both sides, but it was the Soviets that sustained the worst of it so far.

"Comrade General," he didn't bother looking up, knowing that Petrov would be attentive, "I want to open things up here."

Petrov looked down at the markings indicated and started to recall the formations, both enemy and Soviet, that would soon become involved in and around Kerpen and Bergheim.

"We must keep up the pressure to the north, but we are in position there, and so we can switch our resources to pushing out to the west."

This was no surprise, of course, but as each hour passed, Konev put more meat on the bones of his overall plan."

"This difficulty at Wanlo must be resolved soon."

Consulting a list of units not yet assigned, Konev selected two within reasonable distance of the troublesome spot.

"Pass orders to 6th Rifle, 40th Rifle and..." he considered the list further, "Also, 3rd Guards Rocket-Barrage, to move up and place themselves under 31st Army at Grevenbroich. Contact Comrade General Glagolev and inform him that these new resources are his, and he will take Wanlo within eighteen hours."

Petrov made the appropriate note quickly, only too aware that Konev didn't pause for long when he was on a roll.

"4th Guards Tank Army. Resources?"

"At this time, sufficient to undertake the mission assigned, Comrade Marshal. As normal, that could change, but the new supply procedures seem to be helping preserve quantities near to appropriate levels."

Konev nodded, factoring in some additional losses in vital supplies.

"I see no reason why the 4th should not push a little harder here," he indicated the area immediately south of Dusseldorf, "And even develop westwards towards Mönchengladbach..."

Konev searched his list once more.

"Send them them orders to hold the north front at Neuss, but develop the area to the west with a view to capturing Mönchengladbach, and opening the routes to Roermond and

Venlo. Send them the remaining assets from 13th Army as a bolster, plus 112th Rifle Corps."

Petrov had hardly finished before Konev made his important decision.

"6th Guards Tanks and 5th Guards will move up to," the bald officer strained his eyes to see the finer detail of the map, "Titz and Immerath, and no further. And not at the rush either, I want little attention drawn to their forward movement, by comparison to Mönchengladbach and Düren. There, I need our forces to demonstrate heavily, encouraging the Allies to respond against them and ignore the centre."

That meant a change to the instructions already noted, which Petrov swiftly made.

"As soon as 31st Army has secured Wanlo, 6th Guards Tank and 5th Guards will move through it and turn westwards and drive hard and fast towards the water."

Again, he stooped to take in the relevant names.

"Hucklehoven, Geilenkirchen, Gangelt, Brunssum, Sittard-Geleen, and make a bridgehead across the Canal and River Maas at..." Konev double-checked, "Stein, and Berg."

Waiting on Petrov's furious scribbling, Konev took a deep breath, having finally committed himself to a course of action in excess of his orders.

Nodding to himself, he cast a look further down the map and circled a large green area.

"I want 60th Army to move to the south-west, and block against Aachen, and secure this forest to provide our forces with a secure flank."

Petrov oriented himself, and frowned.

"Yes, I know. The Amerikanski learned a lesson there, did they not? So, we shall teach them some more."

Petrov finished his notes, and removed his glasses, producing a handkerchief to clean them. As he carefully rubbed the lenses free of grease, he wondered if Kurochkin and Goncharov, commander and Chief of Staff of 60th Army respectively, would recognise the Hurtgenwald by name before they reconnoitred, and discovered it for what it was; a hellhole that had already made over sixty thousand soldiers casualties in the German War.

"I have the report from 31st Army, Comrade Marshal."

Anyone hearing Petrov's voice would recognise the strain in it. Lack of sleep was the main culprit, but there was also anxiety, mainly for his part in exceeding the instructions from Zhukov.

Konev extended his hand, his eyes assessing his Chief of Staff.

"Thank you, Comrade. Now," he theatrically examined his watch before continuing, "You will take yourself to your quarters, and not return to the command centre until 0600hrs at the earliest."

As the CoS drew breath, the commander shook his head.

"No. That is my order. I will make sure that no one disturbs you. Now, Comrade, go and rest."

Petrov looked both pained and grateful.

"I need you fresh for what is to come."

"Thank you, Comrade Marshal."

Petrov was asleep in his quarters before the clock could strike nine.

The report guaranteed Konev wouldn't rest, as it described, in precise military terms, how 31st Army had been halted at Wanlo and Erkelenz.

Opening the door to his office, he witnessed increased agitation amongst one section of his staff.

Wandering over as inconspicuously as is possible when you are a Marshal of the Soviet Union in his own headquarters, Konev managed to arrive at the group of four officers without them seeing his approach, whilst the rest of the staff had seen him coming and moved to safety.

Konev singled out the senior man, whose words he had just overheard.

"Comrade Polkovnik, what is the problem?"

The four jerked to the attention, ramrod stiff, the three eyeing the fourth sympathetically.

"Comrade Marshal, we have just received two reports of some significance."

314

"Significant enough for you to mention defeat, Comrade Polkovnik?"

The Colonel knew he was a dead man walking, so chose to remain silent.

"And what do these reports say?"

Clearing his throat, the Colonel summarised the contents.

"This is from the acting Commander of the 90th Tank Regiment."

Konev recognised the unit as one he had set aside for important support work.

"The report states that the 90th has been wiped out in an Allied air raid outside of Frankeshofen."

"And?"

"The second report comes from the commander of the 3rd Guards Rocket-Barrage Division. It states the division has taken modest casualties from counter-battery fire and air strikes. His main concern is the absence of supply since he moved up under 31st Army command. His fuel and ammunition status is critical, his medical and food situation is," the Colonel passed the report to Konev, "Well, they have none, Comrade Marshal."

Konev read every word, digesting the meaning and the implications in one angry sweep of the paper.

Looking around the headquarters, he spotted the man he was looking for, the eye contact sufficient to bring the NKVD officer across the room in short order.

"Comrade Leytenant General Grebbenik, arrest this man and transfer him immediately into one of your shtrafbats. Please provide him with an early opportunity to redeem himself."

It was a reasonable bargain for ex-Colonel Amanin, who had expected to be shot.

Both men, officer and former officer, saluted and walked smartly away.

One of the remaining three, a Major, attracted Konev's attention.

"Speak, Comrade Mayor, speak."

"Sir, Comrade Polkovnik Amanin stated that it was his view that if the supply situation was not sorted out quickly, then we might have to face the possibility of some short term defeats, Sir."

Fully aware that he had just signed his own transfer order, the Major contented himself with the fact that he had acted in honour, and to hell with the consequences.

Konev's eyes narrowed.

"And what do you think, Comrade Mayor?"

He was a proud man, and had never backed away from anything in his life.

"I believe that Comrade Amanin is wholly correct, Comrade Marshal. Unless we can supply our soldiers with the means, their bravery and skill will count for little, if all they have to use is sticks and stones."

A hush had fallen over the headquarters, a silence that deepened tangibly, with what had amounted to a speech by the junior man.

Most there braced themselves for a storm.

Konev's gaze bored deeply into the man's eyes, but the junior man stood his ground under the pressure.

The gaze relaxed.

"You are quite correct, Comrade Major. The situation is unacceptable. Your name?"

"Mayor Kristian Borisovich Tarasov, Comrade Marshal."

Konev grinned, finding the man's resilience strangely invigorating.

"As of now, you are Polkovnik Tarasov, and attached to my personal staff."

The Marshal turned on his heel and disappeared into his office, the slam of the door a signal for the room to relax and wonder at the survival of the sweating Major, now a bemused full Colonel.

<u>0942hrs, Friday, 19th October 1945, Headquarters, 2nd Red Banner Central European Front, Schloss Rauischholzhausen, Ebsdorfergrund, Germany.</u>

The sirens had long since hushed themselves, the all clear now in full swing.

Here and there, casualties were taken up, and swiftly delivered to medical stations.

Other bodies, less fortunate, were removed for suitable disposal later.

The early morning raid had not gone unpunished, the Red Air Force's Area Commander had anticipated such a move from the Allied medium bombers, and had put assets in the air to stop them.

For the first time since hostilities had begun, he was able to honestly report more losses on the Allied side than his own, a very satisfactory state of affairs for a General with one foot in the Gulag already.

Little real damage had been caused to the military targets. Yet again, the German civilians seemed to have suffered most.

Konev observed the work of the rescuers whilst he drank tea, completely oblivious to the rapidly approaching Petrov.

"Comrade Marshal."

Despite the quiet tone, Konev, deep in thought, jumped noticeably.

"Apologies, Comrade Marshal. I knew you would want to know immediately."

Konev licked the tea from his hand, where it had splashed when he started.

"Go on then, Petrov, and make it good."

The sound of a man in pain gave both men pause, and they watched as the hideously wounded soldier was lifted from the ruins and spirited away.

"31st Army have taken Wanlo. General Glagolev reports his troops exhausted, but capable of holding their ground. Your orders, Comrade?"

"Contact both major units immediately, implement..." he cut off short, reflecting on the possibilities open to him.

Narrowing the choices down to two, he went for the safer option.

"Implement Plan Blue-Two at oh-seven hundred on 20th October."

Petrov looked quizzically at the Commander.

"You disagree, Comrade?"

"No, Comrade Marshal, just surprised. I always thought you intended a quicker advance."

Konev laughed.

"I did, of course, but the logistics do not permit me that luxury at the moment, Comrade."

'Soon, I hope! By Mother Russia, let it be soon!'

"Now, Comrade General, whilst our Air Force comrades are still jubilant, let us go and extract a little more help from them."

The two senior men entered the main building, intent on pressurising the Air Force General into providing more air cover for their assault force.

0759hrs, Saturday, 20th October 1945, Headquarters, Special Grouping Kravchenko, Schloss Bedburg, Bedburg, Germany.

The commander of the 6th Guards Tank Army checked his watch for the final time, his eyes watching as the second hand swept upwards, inexorably moving to the upright position.

And beyond?

Colonel General Andrei Kravchenko frowned, the second hand continuing on its endless journey, but without the audio backdrop he had anticipated.

It had reached eleven seconds past the allotted time when the sounds of war reached the General's ears.

A huge artillery barrage was initiated, the artillery of the two Guards Armies, joined with extra formations taken from sister units, or released by Konev from the Front reserve, expending considerable amounts of the stocks each commander had hoarded since the supply difficulties made themselves known.

He exchanged looks with Major General Zhadov, the commander of 5th Guards Army, the other major formation in Konev's special plan.

With additional assets, such as artillery, anti-aircraft, and engineers, Special Grouping Kravchenko was a powerful force, albeit one that had already suffered at the hands of Allied aircraft and artillery.

5th Guards Army was oriented to the north of the central point, its assets focussed on rounding Mönchen-Gladbach and taking the towns of Roermond and Venlo.

6th Guards Tank Army intended to take west and south-west routes, broaching the Maas, west of Sittard-Geleen, whilst driving to Maastricht with the intent of isolating Aachen.

Between Roermond and Maastricht, only the bridges at Stein and Berg were intact enough to permit passage for the

318

armour of SG 'Kravchenko', both protected by the small Dutch towns of Sittard and Geleen.

The radio crackled in Zhadov's ear, the static still awful, as it had been since the attack commenced.

He tried again.

"Viktor-zero-zero, Viktor-zero-zero, can you hear me, Nozh-zero-zero over?"

The voice was unrecognisable, but just understandable, Kravchenko's distinctive tones lost in the disruption.

"Viktor-zero-zero receiving, I can just hear you, General, Viktor-zero-zero over."

Zhadov, sat in the back of his M3 scout car, quickly checked the details before speaking.

"Viktor-zero-zero, confirm Objective Akula taken. Nozh-five forces heavily engaged at Akula-three, request more Vol..." the radio clearly failed, the message lost once more.

The operator tuned the apparatus, keen to keep his commander happy, nodding and smiling as the signal was restored.

"...ay again. Understood Akula taken. Say after, Viktor-zero-zero over."

Desperate to get the message off before the signal let him down again, Major General Zhadov spoke quickly.

"Nozh-zero-zero, Nozh-five heavily engaged at Wegberg. Request more Volga, repeat request more Volga, over."

At the other end of the exchange, understanding Zhadov's need for more tanks, Colonel General Kravchenko consulted his map. He ignored the lapse in radio procedure, and assessed the situation at Akula-three before replying.

"Viktor-zero-zero to Nozh-zero-zero, I am unable to help you. Use Nozh-One, out."

He used the codename of 31st Tank Corps, 5th Guards Army's armoured unit, which Zhadov was clearly trying to preserve for the bigger battles to come, some of its units having already been savaged in the fighting in Wurtemburg.

The Commander of 5th Guards Army tossed the handset in the general direction of the operator, who deftly caught it, and placed it in its proper position. Her eyes then stayed fixed on the set in front of her.

Zhadov had expected nothing, and so was not disappointed, although he was annoyed with himself for his small lapse in radio procedure.

Shaking out the map that recorded his intended advance, he started to dictate orders for the commander of 31st Tanks, the now-moving scout car rocking him gently as he worked.

0953hrs, Sunday, 21st October 1945, Station X, Bletchley Park, England.

Happy that the conversation had now ended, Harriet Fraser-Brown completed her notes and called the supervisor.

The Naval commander, a veteran of the Atlantic convoys, moved forward in that strange 'dirty pants' gait that all the listening room staff secretly mocked. Or they had, until the moment that they discovered the man had left his right leg inside his last command, which escort destroyer was lying at the bottom of the Western Approaches, with half its crew still listed as missing.

"So, what do you have for me today, Harry? Comrade Zhukov's dining arrangements by chance?"

"No Sir, but I can fill in another of the blanks on the enemy Westphalia operation."

Fraser-Brown rarely attracted a second look from men who were hungry for female company, but she understood that her asset was hidden away, a powerful brain secreted behind a plain face.

As did her contemporaries and overseers, who understood the beauty of an incisive mind.

Lieutenant-Commander Trelawny read the rough text of the conversation and grunted by way of thanks, moving over to a board where the 'listeners' and those who interpreted the conversations posted their suspicions.

Encouraging the visitor forward, Trelawny handed him the message and then examined the board.

"We know that only one important location has been lost this morning, and that is Erkelenz, so that confirms our belief," he tapped the chalk notation indicating the codeword 'Akula'.

His guest passed back the form without comment.

"Clearly, Akula-Three is within the same district, and the speaker mentions Wegburg, which fits the bill quite nicely I think."

The 'Westphalia' board was nestled in the middle of a set of nine such displays, each carrying its own set of definites and possibles, all products of the intelligence game.

Four of the boards had red areas, inside which were items of information that the Allies' pet spies had told Moscow were known to Allied Intelligence.

That side operation was one of the main reasons that Sir Roger Marais Dalziel was present in Station X, checking that the game was still being played according to his rules, and those who had been caught still observed the niceties of their position, niceties that kept them from the hangman's noose.

One board, that of the group of enemy units suspected of planning to attack southwards into Northern Italy, remained virtually blank.

That also told them something, as that much military hardware never stays silent without good reason.

The 'what's and where's' caused the Allied Intelligence community a great deal of angst.

None the less, Rear Admiral Dalziel was still buoyed by his previous meeting with the code breakers.

Operation Venona, based mainly in the States, had presented Bletchley Park with a morsel of information, a snippet of enemy code that was recognisable, and on which the machines had worked incessantly.

Today, in the breaking dawn, the Colossus machines had presented the Allies with the ability to read much of the new NKVD code.

As soon as he had completed his business in Bletchley, Dalziel had a date with a transport aircraft for a ride to Versailles.

<u>1002hrs, Monday, 22nd October 1945, Headquarters of SHAEF, Trianon Palace Hotel, Versailles, France.</u>

"You come at a bad time, Sir Roger."

Even to a man more used to naval engagements, that fact had been obvious from the moment he alighted from his staff car.

SHAEF staff were running in all directions, some obviously charged with important business, others seemingly milling in panic.

Eisenhower turned back to the map, not waiting for a response, exchanging urgent whispers with Bedell-Smith.

The situation map reflected a Soviet surge, the front spectacularly sundered in four places and folding badly in two others.

Bedell-Smith hurried away, ready to carry out the decisions that Eisenhower had just passed on.

Ike resorted to his standard psychological prop, the smoke stinging the eyes of the non-smoking Englishman.

"Is it as bad as it looks, Sir?" the question came from a man who had witnessed the first days on 'The Bulge', so he had seen chaos recorded on a map before.

"Actually, I don't think so, Sir Roger. Sure, they have hurt us, and we will be going back some, but we have new formations, experienced men, formed ready to go. They still have a supply problem, and you can bet your hat that the Air force will mess that up some more."

Dalziel nodded his understanding.

"So, I can give you a few minutes. What brings you here, Sir Roger?"

"This, Sir."

The Naval Intelligence Officer handed over a report heavy with the symbolism of extreme secrecy, some of which Eisenhower had seen only a handful of times previously.

"What sort of dynamite have you got here, Sir Roger?"

"The extremely useful kind, Sir."

Opening the folder, Eisenhower's first impression was one of disorganisation, the Cyrillic text made more meaningless by being clumped in groups of three to five letters.

The next page was better presented, the same Cyrillics overmarked and grouped, with roman text bracketed above each code set.

"Damn. Is this for real, Sir Roger?"

"Absolutely, Sir, the machines made the breakthrough yesterday. We have back-checked, and our decryption works across the board."

322

Leaning forward and lowering his voice, the British Admiral's sense of the dramatic lent weight to the document in Ike's hands.

"Sir, we now possess the means to read all NKVD radio messages across the range of their departments. Specifically, the reports in that folder cover many of the Railroad protection units in the Ukraine, complete with schedules and provisions for defence."

No further information was needed; Eisenhower understood perfectly.

"Sir, if I may," Dalziel fished in the back of the folder and produced a double-sided sheet of paper.

"Sir, this is a message from the Senior NKVD officer in the 2nd Red Banner Army, firstly detailing the assignment of the prisoner Amanin to a penal unit."

The enthusiastic nodding spurred Dalziel on.

"It then details the security units that will protect the extremely important shipment for 2nd Red Banner Army," Dalziel paused as Eisenhower's eyes rose to the situation board, his memory confirmed by the large sign on the map.

"Damn!"

"Anne-Marie!", the nearby Major moved quickly to her commander's side.

"Please get Marshal Tedder, Generals Vietinghoff, Bedell-Smith, and Robertson. Tell them I want to see them immediately in my office."

The Canadian Women's Army Corps officer saluted and sped away on her mission.

"Can this information be consistently presented in time for us to act on it?"

"Sir, we can set up a radio system at best. Failing that, messages can be on your desk less than two hours from when the Soviets sent it."

Eisenhower held out a steady hand, directing the Naval officer to somewhere quieter.

"Shall we, Sir Roger?"

The two disappeared into the private office, joined, within four minutes, by the chosen men.

The value of the new intelligence was grasped quickly, and the group broke up, each man understanding that the Allies had been handed an excellent opportunity to hurt the enemy, and how much depended on their ability to use it quickly and effectively.

*Our greatest glory is not in never failing, but in rising up every
time we fail.*

Ralph Waldo Emerson

Chapter 92 - THE EAGLES

2ND RED BANNER ARMY OF SOVIET EUROPE - MARSHAL KONEV

<u>1119hrs, Tuesday, 23rd October 1945, 18th US Airborne Corps
Headquarters, Bree, Holland.</u>

Around him, the headquarters buzzed with low voices,
but the Corps Commander's attention was elsewhere.

Lieutenant General Matthew Ridgeway examined the
situation map, his battered corps reflected in the coloured
markings spread across eastern Holland.

The only formation available to plug the gap had been
the 18th Airborne Corps, so, though it pained him beyond
measure, Eisenhower had sent the Paratroopers into the fight,
immersing them in a battle for which they were not designed.

Ridgeway ran his fingers over the maps contours, the
rivers, the roads, and the villages, his face steady as his mind
worked the problems raised by the Soviet breakthroughs.

All three major formations had suffered heavy losses as
they struggled, and failed, to hold back the advance of Konev's
soldiers.

17th US Airborne Division had been knocked back
towards the Maas, and was hanging onto a line from Margraten,
through Valkenburg to Beek, whilst also managing to maintain
contact with the neighbouring 101st Airborne at Spaubeek.

The 'Screaming Eagles' troopers had fought hard, but
even they had given ground under the huge stream-rolling
assaults.

The battered division held a front of nearly twenty
miles, from their tenuous contact with the 17th at Beek, curving
eastwards through Hegge, Merkelbeek and Gangelt, before

turning back west through Saeffelen and terminating at Sint Odilienberg, secured on the banks of the River Rur.

North from the Rur River, the defences of the 6th Airborne Division, bolstered by numerous smaller armoured and anti-tank units, held the line firmly against firm, but substantially less pressure.

The 35th British Armoured Brigade, assigned from 21st Army Group, was reformed enough to provide armoured support to the Red Berets, new tanks and crewmen filling out its ranks to nearly three-quarters strength.

Early on, 'Fallschirm Regiment Von der Heydte' had been transferred into the rear of the 101st, to act as a reserve, and more small independent units, some of them fully armoured, were sent forward to bolster the lightly-armed airborne soldiers,.

Four Belgian Fusilier Battalions were sent to pad out the 17th Airborne's front line, a fifth dispatched to the 101st's area.

Elements of the 31st US AAA Brigade were at Ridgeway's disposal, the light flak guns perfect for dealing with infantry attacks, the heavier weapons tasked with keeping the Red tanks at bay.

The 4th US Infantry Division had recently arrived from the States, and was slated for his command, once it had disembarked, a task made more difficult by the fact that Antwerp was still not fully functional since the Germans had damaged it. Occasional acts of sabotage there testified to the continued presence of communist sympathisers, but did little to affect the steady flow of troops, equipment, and supplies.

A heavy rumble of thunder drew his attention.

'Or is it artillery?'

Standing upright and easing his back, Ridgeway looked out of the window, watching with interest, as a smoke cloud developed in the driving rain, a downpour that was keeping aircraft on the ground, both sides of the front line.

'Not thunder then. Artillery.'

He pulled himself away from the sight and returned to the map, sparing a quick thought for whatever asset he had just lost.

A startled voice cut through the general hubbub.

"Are you sure? That can't be right!"

Ridgeway ran his hand carefully over his shoulder, conscious of the wounds still healing, a German grenade coming close to terminating his life during Operation Varsity in March 1945.

"Well, you goddamn better firm that up, Lieutenant."

Tossing the handset down, the staff Captain suddenly became aware that he was the centre of attention in a silent room.

Ridgeway raised a questioning eyebrow.

The Captain moved swiftly to the map, drawing Ridgeway's eyes to the location in question.

"Sir, confused reports from one of our units on Route 56. Positioned just outside Süsterseel, they report seeing Soviet tanks and infantry on a broad front ranging from the north-east to south-east, coming from Gangelt."

"Gangelt?"

"Yessir, so he says."

"Which unit are you talking about, Captain?"

"Divisional Band, Sir."

Ridgeway silenced the sniggers from a number of junior officers with an unwavering glare.

"The Divisional Band?"

"Yessir, Captain Jarrold commanding, although I just spoke with a Lieutenant Jones, as Jarrold has gone missing."

"Get that firmed up right now," Ridgeway jerked a finger at the staff captain.

Another swift appreciation of the map and the commander asked, of no one in particular, "Who do we got at Gangelt?"

"George Company, 2nd of the 327th, 101st, Sir."

The glider boys.'

"Get them on the horn immediately!"

Another Captain stepped forward.

"Sir, we can't get hold of them, Sir."

Realising his voice had displayed the stress of the moment, the officer took a deep breath and spoke in a lower more controlled tone.

"Sir, Colonel Harper's been trying to get them for twenty minutes now."

'Bud is on the case already.'

The command phone rang, its noisy jangling all invasive, seemingly louder than the sound of the other phones that started to ring, or the radios that started to burst into frantic life around the headquarters.

"Ridgeway."

It wasn't necessary to listen in to what was being said to know that it was bad news.

Ridgeway's face went suddenly dark.

The man at the other end stopped to receive another report, before updating his Corps commander.

Adjusting the map on his desk, Ridgeway married the spoken word to the printed paper, developing more understanding of the precarious position that was unfolding.

"What can you do about it, Max?"

Ridgeway grimaced, partially at the reply he received from the commander of the 101st, and partially at the growing number of officers waiting to relay information.

"I agree. Look Max, all hell seems to have broken loose at the moment, and I need time to see the whole picture. For now, stop them before the river, but get the bridges ready, understand?"

The commander's eyes narrowed and he looked more closely at the map.

"Süsterseel? Apparently you have your damn band there, Max?"

A cough from one of his officers drew Ridgeway's attention.

"One moment, Max."

"Sir, I can't get Lieutenant Jones back on the radio."

'Spit it out man!'

"And what else?"

"There are reports from the 907th Artillery, placing Russian tanks at Tüddern, Sir."

Acknowledging with the slightest of nods, Ridgeway remembered that Tüddern was west of Süsterseel. Taking a deep breath, he faced the inevitability of the situation head-on.

"Ok then, Max. Süsterseel is probably gone already and the Commies are at Tüddern, according to unconfirmed reports. You will hold Sittard-Geleen at all costs. I want those bridges ready to blow, but you must retain control of the roads. Hold them there at all costs. I will get everything that I have that's spare to you, as soon as I can get it in the saddle."

Ridgeway started shaking his head.

"No. You must stand, Max."

The momentary flash of anger that crossed Ridgeway's face went undetected.

"Yes, Max, and if it becomes another Bastogne then so be it. The 101st will hold until relieved."

The moment passed.

"Good luck to you, Max."

Replacing the receiver, Ridgeway could understand Maxwell Taylor's reluctance to risk his division having to endure another encirclement, particularly when the Allies did not possess the ready resources that were available in the winter of 1944.

Part of him offered the observation that, at least, the Eagle's commander would be involved this time, as General Taylor had missed the deployment of the Screaming Eagles during 'The Bulge'.

Officers waited expectantly for orders, orders that immediately started to flow.

"Get the Heydte unit up there pronto."

The staff officer looked at the point indicated and went off to get the German paratrooper unit on the road.

As each order came, staff officers took it onboard and actioned their General's commands.

It did not take long, as 18th Corps was spread pretty thin, but at least Ridgeway had reacted quickly to the threat to the Maas.

It was some time before he realised that he was already too late.

1152hrs, Tuesday, 23rd October 1945, Oligstraße, Broeksittard, Holland.

Randolph Black was wide-eyed, despite the rivers of water than ran off him.

"What the fuck was that?"

"Fucked if I know, Sarge, but now it's dead, ain't it?"

That could not be denied, as the unknown light tank was wreathed in flames, two bazooka hits having stopped it dead on the road, just before the junction with Aan het Broek.

The hissing of water turning to steam on the super-heated metal rose above the sound of the torrential rain.

The Soviet Union had stopped producing light tanks in 1943, but they kept everything, and the T-80 that was presently incinerating its dead crew was a prime example of their habit of using everything they had, and never throwing anything away.

"Call it in, Cowboy."

The corporal radio operator got through to his company headquarters with the contact report.

The Sergeant doubled back through the undergrowth, finding the mortar platoon, alert and ready for action.

Slipping into the small bivouac, Black enjoyed a moment out of the driving rain.

"Milletti, stand by now. They're coming down the north road from Tüddern. Gimme your map."

The junior Sergeant handed it over, and Black satisfied himself that the information tallied with his own.

"Set up on 'Philadelphia' right now. That seems most likely, Milletti."

"Roger that, Sarge."

"And if we have to skedaddle, then haul ass fast, and get set up here," Black extended the map, marking the new location with his finger, "As quickly as possible, ready to support us when we fall back, kapische?"

"Capisco, Sergente."

Satisfied that the mortars would do their job, Black headed back towards a frontline that suddenly erupted in explosions.

'Commie artillery. Jesus!'

The journey back to his modest platoon headquarters took much longer, as he constantly dropped into cover, as shell after shell pounded the northeastern area of Sittard.

He also battled against the increasing mud, sucking at his boots, and clinging to his clothing, as he slipped and slid towards the front positions.

He didn't recognise the headquarters when he got there, so transformed was it by the two direct hits.

Cowboy Morris, the whinging Texan, had disappeared, probably evaporated by high-explosive force.

Gillman, the bazooka king, was still there, or at least the two-thirds of him that still bloodily spluttered away the last few moments of life.

There had been six men in the position when he had left, and Gillman represented the largest piece of meat that Black could recognise.

330

Forward of the mangled site, a .30 cal machine-gun started pumping bullets into the tree line. Black's eyes focussed on indistinct movement there, the details hidden by a haze, partially smoke, partially small particles of earth and other matter being tossed around by explosive force, the whole vision being through a wall of water coming from the heavens.

'Commie infantry!'

Momentarily forgetting that the radio and its operator had disappeared, Black looked to send a message to the mortars.

'Goddamnit!'

He looked behind him to where the Soviet barrage had advanced, gauging his chances of getting through to the mortars on foot.

'Fuck that!'

He took another look at the wood line. The Soviet infantry had stalled there, as the remaining paratroopers hit them with accurate small arms fire.

He spotted the unfamiliar men in US combat uniform, appreciating the shape of the walkie-talkie instantly.

Launching himself forward, he dropped into the shell crater beside the petrified OP team from the 907th Artillery.

The Lieutenant had taken a shell splinter in the face, the right side packed with blood soaked bandages, masking the hole where his jaw, teeth, and tongue used to be. The man's stare looked all the way back to America, and Black knew the man was in shock.

The other two Glider artillerymen were firing their carbines at nothing in particular, clearly unhinged by their experiences.

"Hey! Knock it off, you guys!"

To his surprise, both privates stopped immediately, and slid down the slight bank back into cover, dropping their lower bodies into the water that was filling the hole.

Easing the walkie-talkie from the glassy-eyed officer, he tasked the two soldiers to evacuate the man.

With orders that spelt safety, both artillerymen moved at speed, sweeping up the wounded officer, and heading to the rear.

Dialling the radio in to the right channel, Black tried the set.

"Diamond-one-niner, Diamond-one-niner, this is Diamond-one-four over."

331

"One-four from one-niner, I got you, Blackie. Talk to me."

"Put it on 'Chicago', all you got Milletti, over."

Screams brought his attention back to the escaping artillerymen, all three struck by a single shell burst. Whichever one of them it was that hung from the tree, briefly screamed a second time before dying. The other two were already dead.

There was no time for the horror of the sight to affect him, as a grenade exploded a few feet away.

The Russians had pushed forward, the mortar barrage landing uselessly amongst their dead and wounded in the woods, on the area designated 'Chicago'.

Black went to roll away, but he had no strength in his right arm, the muscle ripped and flayed by shrapnel. Similarly, his right thigh was opened to the bone by a large piece of stone, thrown in his direction when the Soviet grenade exploded.

The tears flowed involuntarily, his pain extreme.

None the less, Black grabbed up his carbine just in time, shooting the first man who dropped into the hole.

The wounded man dropped close by him and the sergeant squinted for a better look.

"Oh fuck! Oh god, I'm sorry Clancy. Oh Jesus!"

Clancy Mann had been with the 101st since week one, day one. Black's bullet had taken him in the right side, breaking a rib and driving the broken bone into his liver.

None the less, Mann put two bullets from his Garand into a Soviet infantryman, who loomed large over the edge of the hole.

The next Russian received the same treatment, even as Black dragged himself painfully over to the paratrooper he had wounded, pulling out a field dressing from Mann's pouch.

Another enemy infantryman fired blindly into the shell hole, his arms waving the PPSh around, sending bullets everywhere.

Mann was hit seven more times, none immediately fatal, but the combination sufficient to bleed him out in minutes.

Black was hit twice; the first carrying away his left little finger, the second striking him in the head, and bringing instant darkness.

Seven hours later, Sergeant Randolph Black opened his eyes, taking in the sights in silence, his ability to hear taken away by the head wound.

His arm and finger stump had both been bandaged, the pure white linen standing out against his naturally dark flesh. His leg, presently held aloft by a set of wires, was encased in plaster.

His head was pounding, and generally, he hurt like hell.

However, he was alive.

The nurse eyed him suspiciously, but gently held his head up, so she could administer an oral dose of pain relief.

Black thanked her, and detected a faint buzzing in his jawbone as he spoke.

Her reply was mumbled and unintelligible, so he gave her his best smile.

Without returning the gesture, the nurse moved away from the bed, no longer obscuring the young soldier on guard duty.

'Oh shit!'

The man wore the uniform of the NKVD.

1332hrs, Tuesday, 23rd October 1945, Sittard, Holland.

Within the environs of Sittard, a desperate fight for survival was in full swing, soldiers standing toe to toe, neither side willing to give ground.

It was the recipe for a bloodbath.

For the Soviets, the situation was advantageous.

They had broken through the 101st's lines at a number of points, breaking up the division into manageable pieces, each of which would be either bypassed and cleared up later, or, as in the case of the defenders of Sittard, reduced by weight of shot and attrition.

The only black mark was the destruction of the Born Bridge over the canal, an error that the commander of the 34th Guards Rifle Corps artillery had paid for swiftly, his body displayed with the normal placard suggesting treachery and sabotage, as it swung from the balcony of the unit headquarters on LindenStraβe, Saeffelen.

For the Allied forces, the situation was dire.

Elements of the 501st Parachute Infantry and Fallschirm Regiment 'Von der Heydte' provided the main manpower for the defence. Stragglers from the decimated 327th Glider Infantry continued to work their way back into the Dutch town, each soldier a welcome addition to its defence.

Add the remnants of a few smaller units and almost two thousand five hundred men stood in defence, against the might of the relatively intact 5th Soviet Guards Mechanised Corps, still boasting over twelve thousand men and women.

The main Soviet effort seemed to be to the south of town, undoubtedly aimed at passing on to the Maas beyond, but enough of the Mechanised unit was pressing Sittard directly, for the risk of being surrounded to be very real.

The Soviet command had also recognised that the assault aimed towards Venlo was failing in the face of heavy resistance, and had redirected some of the 5th Guards Army to a more southerly advance, bringing the 34th Guards Rifle Corps and 40th Rifle Corps into the northern edge of Sittard, adding their battle-weary seven thousand men to the unequal struggle.

At 1332hrs, the worst fears of those in Sittard, and those in the headquarters of the 18th Airborne Corps, were realised.

The 101st was surrounded again, and this time, there was no Patton to come to the rescue.

<u>1400hrs, Tuesday, 23rd October 1945, Hotel Limbourg, Markt, Sittard, Holland.</u>

Brigadier General Joseph Higgins, the 101st's Chief of Staff, waited for the assembly to come to order.

He had come to Sittard for an 'eyes-on' sit-rep, only to become its de facto commander, as the Soviet forces encircled the Dutch town.

Slowly, the noise died away, as the unit commanders he had summoned realised that Higgins was ready to speak. The pervading sound of the heavy rain, combined with the constant crash of incoming artillery, and now thunder, combined to provide a suitably Wagnerian backdrop for the military disaster that was unfolding in Eastern Holland.

334

Fig #60 - The situation at 1400hrs, Sittard-Geleen, Holland.

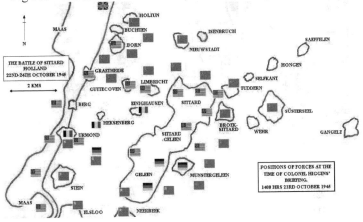

"Ok, now listen in."

The officers stiffened.

"We have a Bastogne all over again, and we got ourselves out of that then, without the Third Army, I might add."

That wasn't totally true as it happened, but it served Higgins' purpose.

"This storm will pass, and then we will have Air, but until then, we stand, and we fight."

More than one of the experienced men in front of him had the thought that there was nowhere to run to in any case.

"We have plenty of supplies, and our men are in top shape, with good morale; very good morale."

On the bench in front of them was a map of the town, blocks of wood marking the position of each defensive unit.

Deliberately, Higgins started with the section to the south.

"Colonel Heydte, your men are holding well at this time?"

Although the Germans were welcome, few in the 101st could forget that it was the 6th Fallschirmjager Regiment 'Von der Heydte' that had fought them to a bloody standstill in Normandy, in hard battles around Carentan.

"Yes, Herr General. A panzer-grenadiere attack on Munstergeleen was driven off with heavy casualties. We are well

335

provisioned with Panzerfaust, and stopped the first panzer assault here," his finger pointed out the leading edge of Geleen.

"However, the enemy force shifted to our right flank, and moved on through Neerbeek, before turning back behind us, and coming to a stop at Urmond."

Roughly one kilometre south of Berg, Urmond marked the high-water mark of the Mechanised Corps' advance.

"We stopped them there, with the help of your Flak gunners, and our Belgian friends."

The German's understated report did not fool any of the experienced men present. The Fallschirmjager had paid in blood for successfully halting the enemy drive.

"I am fully committed, except for an alarm Kompagnie, equipped with a few half-tracks, in the centre of Geleen."

"Thank you, Oberstleutnant," Higgins deliberately used the German rank.

"And you, Colonel?"

Verier, the commander of the 5th Belgian Fusiliers, knew he was in esteemed company, but did not falter, knowing his inexperienced men would have a full part to play in the battle ahead.

"Mon Général, two of my companies are on the river at Urmond. I have one at Heksenberg, adjacent to Route 294, behind the Von der Heydte positions."

Wiping an imaginary speck of dust off the map in front of him, Verier concluded.

"My remaining unit is around Einighausen, guarding the medical and supply facilities, Sir."

When the Fusiliers had first been assigned, not one officer in the 101st felt they could be trusted, despite their previous good efforts during 'The Bulge', but Verier's unit had shown fighting spirit and, with the addition of some heavy machine-guns and bazookas, was proving to be stubborn in defence.

"Thank you, Colonel. Lieutenant Colonel?"

The recently promoted Marion Crisp stepped forward and adjusted the position of two of the wooden blocks.

"I pulled back from this position outside of Wehr. Soviet infantry had taken Broeksittard and had some of my units outflanked."

336

No criticism was forthcoming, as it was the only possible move.

"That actually freed up Fox Company, and we put in a counter-attack, pushing up the Tüddernderweg, and we halted the advance here," he moved the Fox marker to a position one kilometre short of Tüddern.

"Easy Company is here. Lieutenant Colonel Heydte's defence of Munstergeleen deflected the Soviets our way, but Easy stopped them dead, and we hold this zone solidly."

"The rest of 2nd Battalion is strung out to the north of Munstergeleen to the Wehr road. 1st Battalion takes over on the road, and round to Limbricht," he indicated a small hamlet to the north-west of Sittard.

"3rd Battalion has suffered badly."

He picked up the marker for King Company and, respectfully, placed it off to one side.

The whole company had fallen in the defence of Nieuwstadt and Isenbruch in the early stages, the extent of the loss only recently apparent to the temporary commander of the 501st Regiment.

"Part of the 3rd is outside the pocket, here at Born, and they are holding. I suspect the commies ain't interested in it any more, since they took the bridge down themselves yesterday."

To the others, that seemed a fair conclusion.

"I've managed to form a group from the remnants of 3rd, and they are holding from the canal here, at Graetheide," his finger ran southeast, one and a bit kilometres to Guttecoven, "To here, where they link up with 1st Battalion."

"The route over the canal at Berg is still open, but the Soviets are constantly artillerying the approaches, although they are careful not to drop near the bridges themselves."

As an after-though, he added.

"My frontline is sound, but I have no real reserve until I recover Fox. At this time, I have a group of approximately sixty men, postmen, bakers, musicians, and signallers uncommitted. They have tracks and the Chaffee," he referred to an M24 light tank, which had mysteriously come into the possession of George Company, the day beforehand.

Marion Crisp stepped back.

"Thank you. And now, the Air Force. Major?"

The USAAF officer looked dejected, his contribution to the proceedings little more than confirming the obvious.

"Sir, Air is unavailable until this storm moves on."

The statement was punctuated emphatically by the smash of a lightning bolt striking nearby.

"According to met reports, this could be set in all day. Some indications are that we may also have problems tomorrow, Sir."

Above the sound of the storm, the screech of a vehicle was heard outside. The door flew open, permitting a disgruntled and extremely wet Colonel to enter.

"Hot damn, but you're a sight for sore eyes, Bud!"

Joseph H. Harper, Colonel of the 327th Glider Infantry, was not pleasantly disposed, but still managed a dry comment.

"Well don't get too excited, Joe, it's pretty much only me that's here."

The Colonel threw off his wet jacket, and accepted a towel offered by one of the staff officers hovering on the fringes of the briefing.

Higgins quickly brought Harper up to speed.

"So, where are you, and what have you got Bud?"

Moving around to the northern edge of the map, Harper dripped water as he illustrated his words with movements over the map.

"I've brought two companies and some heavy weapons platoons with me, presently inside the 501st's lines, here at the woods," the position was west of Tüddern, and on the flank of the area attacked by Fox Company earlier.

"The rest of my Regiment is either at Born, Holtum, or Echt, outside the encirclement."

"Thank you, Bud. What sort of shape you in?"

"Mad as hell, General. The boys are spoiling for a brawl, and that's no error."

Higgins pondered for a moment, and then went with his gut decision.

"OK, Colonel Harper, your companies will take over responsibility for this northern area from," he squinted at the writing, "Guttecoven into North Sittard here."

Harper nodded, understanding and already working on the movement.

"Crisp, that means you can use your relieved units as a reserve. Added to Fox, that should give you three companies in total."

Fig #61 - Soviet Assault developments, Sittard-Geleen, Holland.

Crisp did not bother to remind the General that a company was only a company in name, as battle had taken its toll on the numbers.

"I want one of these under my command as my personal reserve, as soon as possible."

"Yes Sir," Crisp's eyes already transmitting his order to the commander of Able Company. The man nodded his understanding.

"Right then, Gentlemen. We can do nothing fancy, but that doesn't mean that we can't take advantage when the opportunity presents itself. Be aggressive when you can, try and keep them on guard and worrying about what we are going to do."

He accepted the general low mumbling as agreement and understanding.

"We have no room to trade here, so we must stand where we are now. Every man that can hold a gun, or throw a grenade, must be in the field."

Almost as if suddenly realising the predicament the force was in, Higgins wearily ran his hand over his forehead, taking a moment's pause.

339

"The Dutch authorities have already offered to help where they can. I have agreed that their people can help move our supplies where they can, and take our seriously wounded back to the aid stations."

"Some have military experience and will even fight."

Von der Heydte sneezed.

"Gesundheit!"

"Danke, Herr Oberst."

Crisp returned the German's grin, although part of him felt he shouldn't.

'Carentan.'

"Return to your units, and get the changes done immediately, Report in constantly. I want no surprises like we had at Gangelt ok? No retreat. Questions?"

There were none.

In the end, it was quite straightforward.

They would hold at all costs, or they would go under.

1529hrs, Tuesday, 23rd October 1945, Allied frontline positions at Urmond, Holland.

"Mon dieu!"

The artillery barrage swept up and over the defenders, transforming the already battered Dutch village into a moonscape of holes and rubble, shattered wood and piled earth, all liberally decorated with the body parts of the Belgian and German defenders, and their civilian Dutch helpers.

Captain Alain Cirisse, the commander of the Belgian Battalion's 3rd Compagnie, was an interested observer, undistracted by his present predicament. His men worked swiftly in the area around him, not realising that he still lived. Some recovered and repositioned the machine gun, knocked over by the force of the shell that had demolished the building, dropping tons of brick and cement on top of the position in which Cirisse sheltered.

Attempting to escape the collapse, the Belgian Army officer, and former resistance fighter, had nearly made it, until a large chunk of wall smashed him down, crushing his legs, and pinning him to the roadway.

His Sten gun lay next to him, pristine, untouched by the passage of tons of building.

340

The damaged machine-gun opened up again, its tracers probing the sodden air, the downpour the same, if not slightly increasing.

Soviet tanks moved carefully forward, wary of the Panzerfaust that had already claimed a number of their comrades.

Stopping to fire at a safe distance, they put shell after shell into the defending positions.

A 90mm anti-aircraft gun, emplaced across the canal in Urmond, took up the challenge, smashing one of the T34's with its first shot.

The tanks moved forward, into the lee of a large building, from where they continued to put accurate rounds into the Allied lines, whilst their flank was protected from the fire of the big American gun.

A German paratrooper took his chance and popped out of a manhole, putting his Panzerfaust on target, knocking the Soviet tank battalion's commander out of the fight, along with the entire crew.

A hull machine-gun lashed out at the tank killer, bullets striking home and sending him tumbling down into the sewer below.

Cirisse felt nothing below the waist now, his legs completely crushed and numb, the anaesthetic nature of the cold rain helping to kill the pain.

The machine-gun crew next to him were taken out by a mortar shell, the three men badly wounded and out of the fight.

Soviet mortars increased their rate of fire as the infantry moved in front of the T34's, pushing forward to protect their armoured colleagues from the deadly anti-tank weapons.

The mix of Belgian fusiliers and German paratroopers stood their ground, pouring fire into the advancing Russians.

The guardsmen crouched lower, and continued to move forward, the downpour helping to obscure much of their movement, although many of their number were shot down.

Again, the T34's moved forward, tucking in behind the knots of infantry.

The mortars halted their fire, fearing friendly casualties, pushing the barrage up to concentrate on preventing enemy reinforcements from getting forward.

Cirisse now started to feel the pain again, the numbing effect of the cool water overcome by the severity of his injuries.

Gritting his teeth, he tried to pull himself from under the wreckage, almost screaming as his exertions produced some forward movement, and he felt his flesh tear on the rough edges.

A Soviet guardsman, wounded and scared, saw the struggling Belgian officer and went for the easy kill.

The bullet struck the road in front of Cirisse and clipped his ear on its way past.

Despite his pain, Cirisse swept up his Sten and was more accurate in returning fire. The wounded Russian was thrown back into a deep puddle, the escaping blood creating a swirl of colour in the brown water.

He quickly drowned.

The front line was a mess of orange and red, brown and black, as sub-machine guns and grenades threw up mud and blood, the Russians trying their best to close with the defenders, the Belgians and Germans trying equally hard to keep the enemy at arm's length.

A DP team dropped to the road, oblivious to the presence of the wounded Cirisse, so intent were they on firing into the flank of the defenders.

Again, the Sten gun chattered away, and the two men were hit. The machine-gunner died face down in the gutter, the single bullet having smashed into the back of his neck.

The loader, howling with pain, his ankle shattered, got off a hasty shot with his Mosin rifle.

Cirisse emptied the Sten gun into the man, who fell back against his comrade, his eyes wide open in horror and fear, full of disbelief that his life's blood was escaping from the holes across his chest and abdomen.

It was beyond the now exhausted Cirisse to reload the Sten, and he painfully eased the Browning Hi-Power out of its holster.

With a magazine holding thirteen rounds of 9mm, the Hi-Power was a serious handgun, capable of putting an enemy down at fifty metres.

Unfortunately, in this instance, the enemy was encased in Soviet steel. The killing of the DP crew had been witnessed by the commander of T34 3882 of the 5th Guards Mechanised Corps.

Bouncing over the scattered bricks on the road, 3882 completed the work started by the collapsed building, and

Captain Cirisse became a red smear on the track of the Soviet vehicle.

The Soviet attack surged forward, and the Belgians and Germans had no choice but to withdraw, their position now outflanked on both sides.

1703hrs, Tuesday, 23rd October 1945, Allied frontline positions at Guttecoven, Holland.

The remaining 327th Glider boys had taken over, relieving the 501st's 1st Battalion, and they had immediately faced an onslaught.

The attacking Soviet infantry had been flayed and sent packing, the high water mark of their failed assault clearly marked by numerous still forms.

Soviet artillery, enjoying the liberty offered by the awful weather, pounded the small village, and neighbouring Limbricht, causing more casualties amongst the exhausted glider troops.

Colonel Harper toured the positions, encouraging his men, checking on their welfare, all the time with an eye to the north, and the enemy lines.

1707hrs, Tuesday, 23rd October 1945, Soviet frontline positions north of Guttecoven, Holland.

"Govno! Govno! Govno!"

Colonel Artem'yev had seen some serious fighting in this new war but this was the first time he stared defeat in the face.

His regiment, the 179th Guards, had started the campaign at a good strength, over eighteen hundred sons of Russia, all soldiers with experience gained in the harshest combat.

After the severe battles on the road to Wurzburg, an advance that had culminated in the encounter with the American Armored Command at Rauschenberg, the 179th was on its last legs, less than a third of its men still standing, the rest spread evenly between aid stations and cold graves.

The first attack on Guttecoven had been a hasty affair, ordered by a Divisional Commander under pressure from above.

Another hundred of Artem'yev's men had paid the price of the General's folly, some fifty-nine now lay bleeding in the aid stations to the rear, forty-one left inert on the Dutch soil.

The field telephone rang.

Eyes blazing, the angry commander snatched the receiver up.

"Artem'yev."

Those standing nearby could hear every word.

"Polkovnik, if you want to keep your fucking head, stir those fucking girls of yours into action, and take that fucking village. I want no excuses. Understand?"

Artem'yev's knuckles went white around the receiver.

"General Karamyshev. I just lost one hundred men for nothing. Another frontal attack like that is nothing short of stupidity. I need time to ..."

"You need no such fucking thing, Polkovnik. The Amerikanski are collapsing. I'm ordering you to make another attack. By 1800, you will be in possession of Guttecoven. Am I clear?"

A deep breath controlled Artem'yev's rage sufficiently for him to reply, although it failed to hide his anger from the commander of 59th Guards Rifle Division.

"Comrade General, I will send my men forward, but not in some foolish gesture, ordered by someone sat at a comfortable desk. I need artillery support and I need armour. Without them, I will lose what's left of my regiment in front of that Dutch village."

The silence was electric.

Slowly, in measured angry tones, the commanding General replied.

"Comrade Artem'yev. The 179th Regiment will attack, and will take Guttecoven, completing its capture by 1800hrs at the latest. Acknowledge that order."

"Give me the tanks and guns, Comrade General."

"Do it with what you have, Artem'yev, or I'll find someone who will, and you will answer for your fucking failures."

Artem'yev laughed, a laugh without humour, the sort that the mad emit just before they go berserk.

344

"One hundred of men have already answered for my failures, Comrade General. I owe it to them not to fail again. Now, I need tanks and artillery."

"Pass the telephone to PodPolkovnik Fyokhlachev immediately."

Extending the hand holding the telephone, Artem'yev looked at his second in command with a forced smile.

"The General wishes to speak to you."

Taking the receiver in his good hand, Fyokhlachev took his time before speaking.

"PodPolkovnik Fyokhlachev here, Comrade General."

"Ah Fyokhlachev. You are now regimental commander and temporary Polkovnik. You will attack Guttecoven as soon as possible, and be in possession of the village by 1800 latest. You will first arrest that imbecile there, and place him under guard until the NKVD come for him. Have you understood your orders, Polkovnik Fyokhlachev?"

"I have understood your instructions quite clearly, Comrade General."

"Excellent, Fyokhlachev. Now..."

Standing slightly more upright, the Lieutenant Colonel looked directly into his commander's eyes as he spoke to the man on the other end of the line.

"I have understood your instructions, but I am unable to carry them out, Comrade General. Comrade Polkovnik Artem'yev is absolutely correct. An attack without tanks and artillery would be suicidal."

"This is fucking mutiny! Obey my orders, Fyokhlachev!"

Very deliberately, the phone was passed back to the signalman who, like the rest of the staff in the 179th's headquarters, sat wide-eyed and speechless at what had just happened.

"Thank you, Nikita, although I fear you may just have signed your own death warrant."

2010hrs, Tuesday, 23rd October 1945, Allied frontline positions at Geleen, Holland.

Von der Heydte knew the Fallschirmjager were on borrowed time; the pressure on his regiment was building, as his ability to deal with it reduced, the casualties mounting by the minute.

His positions in the rail yards had shrunk, drawing closer in towards the centre of Geleen, but they still held the Soviet infantry and tanks at bay, although the supply of Panzerfaust was nearly exhausted.

One of his best friends had led a counter-attack, restoring the positions lost when the Belgian fusiliers had been overrun at Urmond. His friend had died, along with many men from the old days.

Picking up his MP40 and pulling his white peaked cap more tightly onto his head, he moved quickly out of the Hotel Normandie, the building in which he had set his headquarters.

The sound of increased firing greeted him as he emerged into the driving rain, the water immediately making him feel cold. He spared a moment to look up at the sign, the irony not wasted on him.

"Head toward the sound of the guns, Kameraden."

The small group of staff and lightly wounded men took off after their commander, jogging steadily northeast, to where a serious fight was taking place.

Von der Heydte's last reserve was committed to the fight.

Soviet artillery had just taken a big hit.

Eisenhower had grabbed units from all over the frontline, and sent them to the threatened area, gradually forming some sort of defensive line on the Maas.

Part of that defence was the 309th Field Artillery Battalion; a 155m equipped artillery unit that still retained enough of the deadly 'Long Toms' to bring down a world of hurt on the artillery of the 5th Guards Mechanised Corps.

The 122mm Howitzers of the 355th Guards Artillery Regiment were busy pounding Geleen, preparing the way for a huge assault aimed between the two Dutch towns.

Using the methods developed and refined over the past two months, the 309th put a mix of high explosive and air burst on top of the Soviet artillery regiment.

Each of the nine 155's put eight shells into the area occupied by the twenty-four 122mm, two full batteries of the Soviet heavy howitzers.

355th Guards ceased to be an effective force, the destruction widespread, the survivors mentally shattered by such accurate fire.

Switching their fire to a likely supply route, the 309th put more shells into the air.

Their first target was clear of enemy forces, the only casualties being four Dutch civilians in Vaesrade.

Their second choice fell amongst a horsed supply column of the 25th Guards Mechanised Brigade, wreaking havoc on the unfortunate beasts, and killing many of the supply troops.

Men from the 3rd Battalion rushed back to help, tending the wounded, and shooting the maimed horses.

The 1st and 2nd Battalions attacked Geleen, smashing into Von der Heydte's exhausted paratroopers.

The Fallschirmjager Commander threw himself behind the body of a dead Dutch civilian.

"Mein Gott!"

The experienced German paratroopers all dropped into cover immediately, disappearing to ground, at the very moment that the squad of Soviet Guardsmen had burst around the corner.

Bullets flew, the majority striking Russian flesh, as Von der Heydte's group tackled the small breakthrough efficiently.

The Russian survivors turned and ran.

Moving forward quickly, the paratroopers made the same corner, checking around it carefully, expecting more trouble.

As they moved over those they had shot down, their battle experience made them check the bodies for signs of life.

Two of the Russians were still in the land of the living, so a pitiless Gefreiter killed each with a single shot to the forehead.

Around the corner, the Russians that had escaped were stood with their hands up, five men desperate to live.

They had run straight into a small German force that had been sent back to hunt them down.

Von der Heydte motioned his group forward, his eyes away from the surrendering Soviet guardsmen, therefore only hearing the telltale sound of a PPSh firing.

He snapped his head back to find the prisoners falling dead to the road, the PPSh still spitting bullets as they hit the paving.

"NO!"

It was too late.

The Lieutenant Colonel strode forward.

The killer, a senior NCO, clicked to attention to report.

"Herr Oberstleutnant, I beg to report that the prisoners tried to escape, and were shot."

Both men knew that was not true.

"Oberfeldwebel Bosicki, never again, clear?"

More heavy firing drew a line under the matter, and the two groups of paratroopers moved back to the frontline positions.

The fighting became more desperate.

The blood obscured his vision.

The wounds, although nothing much, bled profusely, and the blood ran down his face, soaking into the neck of his tunic.

A PTRD anti-tank rifle bullet had struck the corner of the wall behind which Von der Heydte had been hiding, missing him, but creating enough projectile stone fragments to transform the paratrooper's face into a mask of red.

The Mechanised soldiers had drawn off once more, the second attack having been made on foot, their lend-lease universal carriers proving particularly vulnerable to the defensive combination of Panzerfaust and Molotov cocktails.

Many Guardsmen had sprung screaming from the small British and Canadian built carriers, their hair and clothing alight, flesh starting to split and fall away.

This time the killing of unarmed men had been a merciful release.

The Fallschirmjager had held, but only just.

Artem'yev cradled the bloody body as the hideously wounded man screamed and kicked his life away.

As the 179th had swept into Limbricht, a last act of defiance from a 101st trooper had sent a burst from a BAR into the command group, catching the group as it moved up behind the assault force.

One bullet had tugged at Artem'yev's sleeve, nicking the flesh, painfully reminding him of the fine margins between survival and death with each small movement.

Nikita Fyokhlachev was a mess, one eye rolling around on his cheek, as he thrashed around in agony.

Other heavy bullets had taken him in the chest, stomach, groin, thigh, and both calves.

"No! I can't die! Don't want to die! Fuck no! Not here! Oh Please, not like this!"

Artem'yev held him tighter.

"Arrrrggghhhhh!"

His scream seemed to reflect more his fear of death than the pain that was wracking his body.

The medical orderly, himself a victim of the BAR gunner, worked swiftly, trying to stop the flow of blood from the wreckage called Fyokhlachev.

The wounded man vomited, a combination of lunch and blood projecting itself over the orderly.

"Arrrggghhhhhhh No!"

The pain gave him immense strength, and Fyokhlachev broke Artem'yev's grip, arching his back like a longbow under strain.

A calm settled upon his face.

Fyokhlachev was dead.

Gently easing the body to a position of rest, Artem'yev stood, and took a moment to honour his long-time comrade.

Limbricht had been gained only with the expenditure of valuable blood, and, even though Fyokhlachev's death hit him hard, the Colonel understood the need to exploit the costly gain.

Approaching the signaller, Artem'yev checked his PPS magazine, using the distraction to steady his thoughts.

"Inform division. Limbricht taken, advancing into the centre of Sittard, need reinforcements."

Artem'yev peered into the gathering gloom, his eyes straining to identify the vehicles so neatly parked, now beyond the use of their former owners.

'Why not?'

2303hrs, Tuesday, 23rd October 1945, Soviet breakthrough, Markt, Sittard, Holland.

The rain had finally stopped.

Crisp took a moment in the entrance to the church. He ached from head to toe, the strain caused by weeks of combat was beginning to take its toll, and carrying the wounded Pfc had eaten into his dwindling reserves.

"Light 'em if you got 'em."

He took in the views around him.

Saint Michael's Church, across the Oude Markt from the 101st's headquarters, housed in the Hotel de Limbourg, had been set aside as a hospital, a fact easily deduced from the liberal blood trails that marked the route taken by the stretcher cases.

Crisp, and a number of his officers, had brought more wounded troopers with them, depositing the damaged bodies with the overworked staff of 326th Medical Company.

Both St Michael's and the 'Limbourg' fronted on to the main square, an open space that thronged with more medical facilities, triaging many of the new arrivals, as well as military vehicles and stores in equal measure.

The Soviet threat to Einighausen had been too great, and the facilities there had been hauled into the centre of Sittard at record speed, leaving only the Belgians behind.

His officers waited, taking advantage of the delay, drinking whatever was in their canteens and smoking their cigarettes.

Crisp was too tired to even get his packet out, a fact realised by Reeves. The G Coy commander lit up an extra Chesterfield and passed it to his boss.

Crisp nodded his gratitude.

"Damn, but if this isn't one hell of a goddamn mess."

He got no argument.

Suddenly the veterans hunched automatically, the response of their combat sense to an approaching shell.

350

The sound, almost like a sudden deep intake of breath, was followed by a moment's silence.

Then the five-storey building across the square exploded outwards, a 152mm shell exploding at second floor level and turning the upper floors to a collection of wood and brick moving at high speed.

The cries of 'medic' rang through the failing sound of the explosion, men hit by the debris screaming in pain at their awful wounds.

By comparison, the mortar shell that followed it did next to no damage, creating a modest hole in the square itself.

Bits of shell and road flew out from the epicentre, striking indiscriminately.

Reeves shielded Crisp from the blast, his body taking the fragments that would have hit the Regimental commander.

He sank to his knees, blood spilling from his mouth, coughing as the warm liquid filled his lungs.

Galkin, Fox Company's CO, dropped heavily to the road, his left leg knocked away from under him by the impact of a lump of stone.

Others in the square lay silent, or rolled noisily in pain.

Two medical staff that had emerged for their own tobacco break, crossed themselves in acknowledgement that their God have saved them from death, and carried the moaning Reeves into St Michael's for immediate treatment.

The Russian-born Galkin held up his hand, seeking support, and pulled himself upright with the help of Crisps' firm grip.

"How is it, Con?"

The Captain tested the leg, ignoring the pain, seeking to find out if the damage was more than just flesh.

"Hurts like hell, of course. Do I get leave?"

Crisp snorted, appreciating the man's efforts, despite the obvious pain he was in.

"Not a snowflake's."

Sizing up the injury, and satisfying himself that Galkin could walk, Crisp was happy that he hadn't lost another company commander

"Get yourself seen to, Con, I want you back on line a-sap."

"Roger that, Colonel."

"And check up on Josh when you are through, please."

Galkin was already hobbling away to the nearest triage point.

Making his way across the narrow lane, Crisp and the rest of the men entered the Hotel Limbourg.

Opposite the main entrance was a sunken beer cellar, cleared out, and filled with the artefacts of command, now the combat headquarters of the 101st US Airborne Division.

Brigadier General 'Joe' Higgins broke off his animated discussion with Bud Harper, commander of the 327th Glider Infantry.

"Lieutenant Colonel Crisp, thanks for coming. Take the weight off."

He gestured at one of his array of NCO's, and a coffee magically appeared in front of the weary Crisp.

"So how goes it with the 501st?"

"We are holding, Sir, but each time there are less of us to fight back. We may have to concede some ground, shorten our lines some, but we will hold."

Raised voices at the main door interrupted the conversation, and a bloodied Von der Heydte moved quickly through and into the headquarters.

"Apologies, Herr General. There is a problem. We have lost our radios, so I am here."

Harper produced a lily-white handkerchief, extending it to the German so he could remove the blood from his eyes.

"Danke, Herr Oberst."

Moving to the map table, Von der Heydte drew everyone to view the problem.

Problem was an understatement.

"The Communists have penetrated deeply here, and split my command."

Experienced military brains worked the problem, the collapse of part of the Fallschirmjager's front at Munstergeleen, permitting a deep incursion almost to the railway line.

The edges of both Sittard and Geleen had held firm, but the Soviets had developed a penetration five hundred metres wide, and it threatened to cut the defence in two.

The sound of small arms fire started to develop, coming nearer, and growing in intensity, so much so that the fire fight drew the attention of all present.

Higgins was about to direct one of his officers, but spotted Crisp's signal to a nearby NCO, who quickly slipped out the door in response.

As quickly as it took the group to refocus on the map, Rocky Baldwin crashed back through the door.

"Russians! Just down the road here. Platoon strength, coming in fast!"

Weapons were grabbed and cocked, the headquarters staff shocked that they should suddenly find themselves close to the action, but unaware that the worst day of their lives was about to begin.

The St Petrus school building was burning brightly, illuminating the corpses of both sides, victims of Artem'yev's swift assault.

The subterfuge of using the captured transport had worked well, and a little play acting with some of his own men firing at the vehicles but wide of the mark, ensured that the airborne troopers let the lorries through with no checks.

Bailing out from the 6x6 Dodge's, the Guardsmen of the 179th Regiment fell upon the American airborne from behind.

The frontline was overwhelmed in minutes.

A smaller, but equally effective repetition got the Soviet infantrymen into the outskirts of Sittard, where they slowly moved forward, the only casualty being a Dutch civilian whose curiosity proved terminal.

Until they moved into Walramstraat.

A roadblock at the junction with Overhovenerstraat looked unoccupied.

It wasn't, and the .30cal machine-gun posted there knocked down the lead squad of Soviet infantry, the rest taking cover, either behind the rubble and wreckage in the road, or by kicking in doors on either side of the killing zone.

More Dutch civilians died, some for no reason other than they got in the way, others for protesting at the intrusion of armed men in their homes.

Making their way through the gardens, a determined group of soldiers flanked the roadblock, and rushed the defenders.

353

Four MP's from the 101st's police unit fell, two dead, two wounded. The only man untouched by the Soviet volley got off a shot with his Garand, putting down the NCO leading the group, a destroyed knee bringing screams of agony.

Hands were raised, but ignored, and all seven MP's were dead in a heartbeat.

The main Soviet force swept on, pushing hard, brushing aside the occasional modest resistance, until reaching St Petruskapittel.

In the church and the academic building, night was turned into day by grenades and gun flashes, fires growing throughout the two separate buildings. Street fighting developed, often of the closest kind, and death came to the soldiers of both sides in every bestial way imaginable.

Inside the church, the US airborne troopers ceded ground, and were driven into the tower, holding the stairs against all rushes, killing a score of Guardsmen.

A small stock of gasoline nearby provided the inspiration for an act that stood out in a night of extreme barbarism.

Screaming and laughing maniacally, the Guardsmen sloshed the petroleum all round the base of the tower, setting it alight, and screaming with pleasure as the flames took hold and rose higher with every second.

Somewhere inside, men grabbed at the bell ropes, and the whole scene was accompanied by indiscriminate maniacal tolling.

Those outside watched as men jumped from the side openings onto the main building roof, some slipping and falling to their death below, others being shot off by the maddened Russians.

Still others chose to die by falling, rather than the alternative of death by burning. They hurled themselves out into the darkness and fell to the ground. Two managed to drop on top of an enemy, each Soviet soldier killed in turn.

Yet others had no choice over their end, and fiery living plumes started to descend, each screaming meteor ending in an awful mound at the base of the tower. Each pitiful pile burned, marking the body of a paratrooper, the area around the church scattered with such piles, burning like candles set around an altar.

Artem'yev did not interfere, leaving the mopping up to others, and pushing his units forward towards his goal; the Markt.

It was the lead group of the 179th's 3rd Battalion that Master-Sergeant Hawkins had seen in the Oulde Markt, approaching the Hotel Limbourg.

Men went down on both sides as the two groups clashed on the Oude Markt.

The Americans had the advantage of cover, vehicles and crates providing excellent firing positions, the Guardsmen had numbers on their side.

Cover won, and the depleted guardsmen withdrew around the corner, some of their number investing the houses at the junction of Oude Markt and Kloosterplein, quickly setting up their DP's and rifles, to put fire into the paratroopers.

Artem'yev took over from the dead battalion commander, switching the 3rd's advance, a tourist map now his most useful tool in organising the assault.

Leaving some men to cover Kloosterplein, he focussed one company on a rapid assault up the Gats, a road that reduced to a narrow lane, winding through the buildings before terminating in the Markt itself.

The other intact company moved past the church, intent on securing Limbrichterstraat, and entering the Markt beyond.

The telephone was answered by his commanding officer, and so Higgins wasted no time.

"Sir, Higgins. We are in danger of being overrun here!"

Higgins waited with a patience of a saint, whilst Maxwell Taylor delivered the standard rhetoric about standing fast, and the expectation that all his command would do likewise.

The opportunity to talk came eventually.

"I don't think that's possible, Sir"

"Joe, I need more time, and you are going to give me it, goddamnit! Hold that town for two more hours. That's all, just two goddamn hours, Joe!"

"Sir, I seriously doubt we can give you that. The commie bastards are on top of my HQ as we speak."

As if to emphasise the point, a grenade detonated alongside the Hotel Limbourg, bringing screams from injured men.

"Joe, I will do what I can, but you must hold. I'm sorry, but that's it, General. I will put a burr up the ass of the engineers, but you gotta hold!"

Two Russians ran into the headquarters, trying to escape from the slaughter spreading slowly into the square, straight into a burst from a Thompson sub-machine gun.

Both men collapsed, side by side, reflecting each other, with arms and legs in a star pattern.

One was dead, his face and chest destroyed by .45 bullets.

The other lay silent, unmoving, save for his eyes that flicked in all directions, trying to comprehend why he could not move, unable to see that his spine had been severed by the heavy Thompson round.

"I will hold, General."

Joe Higgins waited whilst one of his Lieutenants put a bullet into the wounded Russian.

"Unless there's anything else, Sir, I gotta go."

"Good luck to you and your men, General."

"I think we'll need it, Sir. Goodbye."

Handing the receiver back to the operator, Higgins pondered for a moment.

"Ok, listen in! Pack it up, and get ready to move. Get the latest reports in from the units, and get that updated", he gestured at the situation map, "We will stand until ordered out, if anyone asks. I will be back in three minutes. You have three minutes."

Higgins grabbed his carbine, its folded stock wet with blood from an unknown source, and moved to the main entrance to start his own assessment.

Only friendlies were in sight, but the Soviets were obviously still near.

The rush that had almost carried to the Markt had been thrown back by a surge of men from the reserve, the bakers and postmen fighting with unexpected ferocity. The Chafee tank had long since lost its battle for survival.

Some of the Soviets had got to the entrance of St Michaels. The grenades they threw inside wounded the already

356

wounded, and added doctors and medics to the growing list of battle casualties.

Higgins saw that Crisp had already organised a withdrawal of the wounded, and grunted his approval.

Turning around, the barricade obstructing the route coming from the Gats was silent, the men there hunched ready but, as yet, untested.

Beyond that, the Limbrichtstraat entrance on to the Markt was more animated, the defenders active in their defence but, as yet, no sign of what they were firing at.

The Markt itself had emptied of the living, its sole occupants a handful of dead, some laid out in organised rows by caring medics, others thrown into bloodied heaps by whatever high-explosive shell had ended their lives.

Crisp's voice cut through the sounds of battle, detailing men to find usable transport from amongst the thirty or so vehicles in the Markt.

The Gats suddenly burst into life, followed almost immediately by a flurry in the Oude Markt behind him.

Almost in slow-motion viewing, he had a grandstand view of the Gats defenders rising up as an assault force of Guardsmen overran them, PPSh's lashing out, opposed by Carbines and Garands, momentum alone carrying the assault force to the barricade.

One Russian left the melee and moved towards the 101st's commander, screaming like a Viking Berserker.

Higgins let fly from the hip, four bullets whistling past the unhinged Soviet soldier.

The Carbine jammed.

Scrabbling for his pistol, Higgins was about to lose the most important race of his life, the advancing soldier slapping his new drum magazine to make sure it was properly home.

Unable to get his automatic out, Brigadier General Higgins faced death with stoicism, until the Guardsman's throat blossomed like a huge scarlet rose, and he was thrown backwards, the impact of other bullets killing him three times over.

"Thank you, Sergeant."

"No problem, Sir."

Montgomery Hawkes swiftly moved past the relieved General, ordered by Crisp to back up the defenders of the Gats.

357

Another group of paratrooper reinforcements followed, and the situation was restored, the surviving Russians withdrawing to think again.

Artem'yev ordered them forward once more, but this time, his platoons moved through the buildings, manufacturing holes in the brickwork with explosives, spades and bayonets.

As many of the houses had been damaged, and there were small ways through between the houses in any case, the new Soviet attack made good progress.

The headquarters personnel, ready and waiting for their General to return, suddenly realised that the firing was in their own building, a small but determined group of Russians at first floor level, battling to take the stairwell.

Three of the officers moved to investigate, and found a solitary trooper using his BAR to good effect, holding back the enemy force.

Two fragmentation grenades added to the defence, and drove the Soviet infantrymen further back.

Outside, Higgins was tossed against the wall of the hotel, a medium artillery shell exploding nearby, the blast picking him up like a piece of chaff.

Artem'yev was incensed; the order to cease fire on the Markt had been clear and unequivocal, the latest barrage endangering his own men.

Snatching up the radio, he discovered that his orders had actually been followed to the letter.

The artillery was American.

Winded, and bleeding from a broken nose, Higgins had just reached the same conclusion.

One shell landed squarely in a 6x6 full of wounded, tossing the bodies and bits of bodies over a wide area.

Higgins strode purposefully back into the headquarters.

"Find out which fuck is firing at us, and tell him I am going to pull his fucking ass up over his shoulders if he is lucky enough to survive this shit!"

The normally cool Higgins was clearly raging inside, the combined effects of seeing his men killed by friendly fire, and his own injuries, taking their toll on his mental resilience.

Even as he stood silently, listening to his officers searching for the guilty US artillery unit, the darkness that was

358

spreading around his eyes, as the bruising made itself known, was shared by the darkness spreading in his mind.

'Pull yourself together, man!'

He shook his head, and with that, his momentary melancholy departed.

"Anything from Corps?"

"No, Sir."

'Much more of this and there will be nothing left to save General,' he wondered if he was rehearsing pleading to Maxwell-Taylor, or asking himself if he should make a more difficult decision.

The answer was not forthcoming, Von der Heydte's return destroying any chance of resolution.

"Herr General, we must withdraw. My men cannot hold. Tanks and infantry have cut my force in two."

He grabbed the map.

"Here, Herr General, here they are now."

'Sweet Jesus!'

A rough calculation put the mixed enemy force less than a kilometre from Einighausen.

'If you don't go soon, you ain't going at all, General.'

"How long can you hold, Herr Oberstleutnant?"

Von der Heydte considered his reply.

"If they come with all their might, then about as long as it takes to smoke a last cigarette, Herr General."

"Do your best please, Herr Oberstleutnant. I will try and get you some more men, but it is imperative that we have a corridor of escape for when that order is given."

This was clearly understood by the experienced German officer, who saluted, and left without ceremony.

Before Von der Heydte had returned to his unit, or the handful of reinforcements Higgins had found to give the German were on the move forwards, the Soviet forces came together at Einighausen, totally surrounding the Screaming Eagles.

<u>0047hrs, Wednesday, 24th October 1945, 18th US Airborne Corps Headquarters, Bree, Holland.</u>

The two senior officers pored over the map.

They had been in each in each other's company for ten minutes, and the last two of them had been spent checking that their decision would work.

The German was the first to stand back.

"Ja, Herr General, it is the best way."

Maxwell Taylor stole another look back at the basic and risky plan, and concurred.

"Then it's a go, Field Marshal Guderian. 0200hrs?"

"Ja."

The order was given.

The 101st was to be rescued.

0214hrs, Wednesday, 24th October 1945, Soviet positions, Markt, Sittard, Holland.

Not for the first time that day, Artem'yev was beside himself with rage.

His guardsmen had achieved miracles, eventually displacing the tough American paratroopers from the north-west edge of the Markt, seizing all the buildings, including the enemy hospital set up in the next-door church. Soviet and American medical personnel worked side by side, keeping alive 'Boris' or 'Chuck', without any discrimination.

Despite the sacrifices of his men, the attack had stopped dead, for no other reason than a lack of munitions.

He had no grenades. Literally. The whole surviving assault force of two hundred or so men did not have one grenade between them, and lightly wounded soldiers were presently scavenging the battlefield for anything of use.

Many of his men possessed only one magazine, or a partial one, still fixed to their weapon.

As the Colonel toured his positions, glad that the rain had gone once more, he found many of his men with American weapons, and laden with spare enemy ammunition.

His guardsmen had already acquired respect for the Garand rifle. It was a prized possession, and one that was rarely traded or given up, once a soldier had 'liberated' one of his own.

The pride that Artem'yev felt in his men's courage and skill was challenged by the anger that churned him up, as the advantage of their efforts was gradually lost waiting on resupply.

360

The 179th's supply train was not responding to calls, and he promised its commander a hard time when they met.

The row of trucks was burning fiercely, occasionally illuminated more dramatically by a secondary explosion, a box of grenades here, a stock of mortar shells there.

The supply column was utterly destroyed, man, horse and vehicle smashed by the lightning surprise attack.

The Lieutenant Colonel commanding the 59th Guards Rifle Division's supply column fought against the pain, his moans low, as his mind raced.

'Where did they come from? Where are they going?'

Through glazed eyes, he saw a strange vehicle illuminated by the fires, its single large 'eye' sweeping the area.

'What is that?'

The question died with him, as the Panzers rolled past towards their first objective.

<u>0237hrs, Wednesday, 24th October 1945, Berg an der Maas, Holland.</u>

"Yessir, we are ready."

Finally, the engineers had prepared the main bridge at Berg.

"Not before time, Major, not before time. Standby to drop that sucker, but hold until the 101st gets back over it, clear?"

"Yessir!"

"But, if the Soviets arrive in force, you drop that bridge, or there will be hell to pay, clear?"

"Yes, Sir, that is clear."

It was silent in the 18th Corps headquarters, no translation necessary.

Guderian was enjoying the fresh coffee, and raised his mug in acknowledgement of what he had heard.

The plan had been communicated to the Eagles, and they were ready to go.

So now, the two officers just needed to wait.

361

The Soviet tank commander was confused; how could the enemy tank reach out in the darkness and kill them with one shot?

Dropping off the side of his smoking tank, he managed to lean up against the wheels, the darkness of the night hiding the loss of most of the flesh below his left knee.

The Junior Lieutenant watched with interest, as the column of German vehicles swept by, the Panthers and Panzer IV's recognisable for the old adversaries they were, the halftracks mounting the large searchlight-like structures unknown to him.

"Here they come!"

The cry went up from the paratroopers, who could hear the sound of approaching armour.

The 101st's perimeter had shrunk, still holding fast on the eastern edge of the Markt, but spread in an odd 'in and out' shape, centred mainly on the precincts of Stadbroek, Lahrhof, and Overhoven.

It was those in Ophoven, sat astride the road coming from Nieuwstadt, who had first sight of their saviours, although those veterans of the German War felt mixed emotions at the sight of Panzers.

Preceded by two eight-wheel armoured cars, the German tanks moved quickly through the paratroopers lines, closely followed by a range of other vehicles, numerous M4 Kangaroos, once of the disbanded 49th Armoured Personnel Carrier Regiment, eight LVT4's of the 1st Northamptonshire Yeomanry, all shepherded by the newly formed, but under strength, 52nd Royal Tank Regiment. The British unit combined qualified volunteers from amongst the returned POW's, and Sherman tanks relinquished by the Czech Armoured Brigade before they were repatriated.

Artem'yev first knew of the recent arrivals when HE shells started hammering into his positions in Markt.

There was no future in his units staying put, so he ordered the bulk of his men to move back fifty yards, leaving a few brave souls to observe, and warn of any counter-attack.

The glider infantry and paratroopers were ready, and started to move units back to the relief force, preparing to collapse their defensive perimeter faster than the enemy would be able to react.

The German officer leading the armoured force dismounted from his Panther tank, and approached the small command group of American officers, gathered to oversee the hastily arranged withdrawal.

Crisp recognised the man instantly.

Oberstleutnant Kuno Von Hardegen, late of Symposium Biarritz, now commander of the tank battalion in Panzer Brigaden 'Europa', paused to issue a quiet order to an enquiring subordinate.

"Colonel Von Hardegen."

Hands were extended and clasped, the recognition mutual.

To save on time, Crisp did the introductions, the nod exchanged between Von der Heydte and the Panzer officer understandably warmer, the two having fought side by side on other occasions.

Von Hardegen got straight down to business, producing an annotated map.

Fig #62 - Sittard-Geleen. The Breakout.

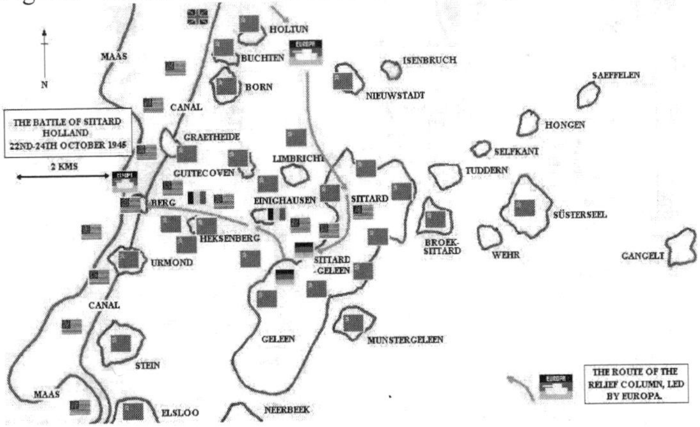

"Meine Herren, when I last checked in, the Deutsche Fallschirmjager were still holding here," he indicated the northern edge of Geleen.

"That is so, Kuno. There are enemy tanks, T34's mainly, and lots of infantry, but they have halted their attack for the moment."

"Sehr gut, Friedrich. Herr General, now is the time I think. Berg is ready, and won't wait for long."

Higgins made his calculations, looking around at his men, either loading up into Kangaroos, or finding a niche onboard one of Hardegen's panzers.

Out of sight, the LVT's received the wounded, the open deck space more suitable for stretchers.

Artem'yev had requested artillery but, surprisingly, none was forthcoming. Instead, he turned to his regimental support units, and soon Soviet mortar shells started to fall, not on the Markt, but beyond it, where the relief force was gathered.

Men started to fall instantly.

Higgins made his decision.

"We go now. Send it."

The headquarters radio operator had already been primed for the task, and his voice spoke rapidly on the open net, passing on the codeword inspired by the US army camp where the 101st was activated in 1942.

"All units, all units, Claiborne, all units, Claiborne."

The hastily conceived plan envisaged each of the units withdrawing their manpower quickly, but maintaining a presence in the front line, until it was safe to pull out the rearguard out as well.

It required skill, and some units lacked the leaders with the necessary tools. Platoons of both the glider and airborne troops got it wrong, and the guardsmen, sensing something was happening, pressed home and overran a few squads.

But, as a testament to the professionalism and skills of most of the soldiers, the column started to move off within six minutes, tanks protecting the core of transport containing the 101st and Von der Heydte's Fallschirmjager.

Moreover, the enemy mortar fire slackened, radar sets from the 31st AAA Brigade seeking out the point of origin and passing the details to waiting gunners, who brought down swift retribution.

At the point of the column was Von Hardegen's 1st Kompagnie, its Panthers especially suited for the night combat to come.

Alongside them came the specially equipped halftracks, their huge infra red lights sweeping the battlefield. Used with success during his defence of the Kustrin Road, at the end of the German War, Von Hardegen understood well how to use his infrared night fighting capability to best advantage.

Russian tanks, immobile and vulnerable, highlighted to the commanders of the specially equipped Panthers, the cupola fitted with an infra-red sighting system that turned night into day and betrayed the position of virtually every Soviet soldier and vehicle.

'Europa's' crews started to kill; clinically and professionally.

Behind them came the 'UHU's', the SDKFZ 251's equipped with 60cm Infra-red searchlights that illuminated the battlefield, solely for Europa's benefit.

Soviet soldiers started to die, their nemesis unseen in the dark, reaching out with incredible accuracy.

2nd Kompagnie, partially equipped with the same FG1250 sights, peeled off on cue, smashing into a Soviet infantry unit at rest, sending it flying in a whirl of bullets and unforgiving tracks.

Von der Heydte, riding on the back of the company commander's Panther G, watched fascinated as the infrared equipment gave the armoured group total command of the battlefield.

Behind the Panthers and Uhu's came four Falke, half-tracks carrying support troops equipped with Vampir ST44's, and behind them more Kangaroos, empty this time.

The Vampir panzer-grenadieres debussed, quickly clearing a channel through the dazed Soviets, permitting the small column to press on unmolested, and into the survivors of the other part of Von der Heydte's command.

The Paratrooper officer watched with pride as his men swiftly mounted the unfamiliar Kangaroos, his pride tinged with sadness at their greatly reduced numbers.

A single Buffalo waited in vain for the stretcher cases and followed on empty, the last but one vehicle to exit Geleen's northern suburb.

Having drained most of his tanks dry, Colonel Danskin, the 25th Guards Mechanised Brigade's commander, had filled six tanks with enough fuel to support the night attack on the bridges at Berg.

As his wristwatch clicked inexorably to the 0400 deadline, the sound of fighting increased to his rear.

The radio had been full of sounds of consternation, of reports of phantoms, even German tanks with red eyes.

For all he cared, it could be Lucifer himself behind him. If he failed to reach the Maas today, he would never see another sunrise.

The Soviet attack commenced, or rather, it tried to, but failed immediately.

From out of the eastern darkness emerged death, dark undecipherable shapes spitting out shells and bullets in all directions.

Danskin watched helplessly as his immobilised armour fought back, the vital factor of manoeuvre absent, and contributing to the slaughter that ensued.

Two enemy vehicles moved past a burning shop, the fire providing sufficient illumination for Danskin to recognise the hated Panthers.

Ahead, confused by contradictory orders, the infantry of the 25th's 2nd Battalion pushed ahead, running forward, the six supporting tanks turning about, and coming back towards Geleen to help their comrades.

The axis of advance for both T34's and Panthers was the Bergerweg, a modest avenue, running straight for the three kilometres between Berg and the edge of Geleen.

'Europa' filled the three kilometres with corpses, their IR sights giving them so much advantage over the Soviet tanks that no hits were received in return, all six running T34's killed with their crews.

As the relief column gathered itself in the area south of Einighausen, American artillery started to drop behind the rearguard, formed by Sherman tanks of the inexperienced 52nd RTR.

The plan now required the Panzers to turn back eastwards, forming the sides of a defensive corridor, through which the rest could pass.

'Europa' accomplished this tricky manoeuvre well, the Panzer IV's of 3rd Kompagnie taking the lead.

Soviet anti-tank guns, the standard Zis-3 76.2mm type, deployed at Heksenberg, south of the Bergerweg, waited patiently for their chance and took it at the first opportunity.

Two Panzer IV's were struck, the lead tank fatally, the surrounding area rapidly transformed from night into day by the ferocity of the blaze.

The IR Panthers sought out their foe, and killed each in turn, but not without cost.

2nd Kompagnie's commander died, exposed outside the turret hatch, whilst using the IR equipment.

A Soviet maxim machine gun lashed out, normally useless against such leviathans, the burst fired more in anger than expectation of success.

The dead Hauptmann slithered onto the floor of the Panther's turret like a rag doll, face and chest destroyed by Russian bullets.

The machine-gunners escaped retribution, the German tanks sticking to plan and folding back on the end of the column.

A Sherman tank was struck, its engine belching black smoke as it struggled against the damage.

For a moment, it seemed like the tank would escape, the driver deliberately accelerating hard to make a small but steep incline ahead.

The incline won, and the damaged engine gave up the unequal struggle, a small orange glow escaping from the rear compartment.

By the time the crew had safely climbed aboard a Kangaroo, the Sherman was the brightest light on the battlefield, burning merrily, the shells starting to 'cook off' as the temperature inside rose.

At Berg, the Engineer Major was more than happy to be relieved of overall command, and withdrew to his sandbagged position to take charge of the detonating circuit.

Thirty minutes before the Eagles were due to escape, a sour-faced bird Colonel had arrived, complete with two companies of armored-infantry, men of the experienced 4th US Infantry Division.

Three minutes from the moment the first fully-laden M3 half-track started to disgorge fresh troops, a further surprise occurred, this more dramatic, as a number of German self-propelled guns arrived, taking up positions on the western bank of the canal.

4th Kompagnie of Europa's Panzer Abteilung had been tasked to provide overwatch on the Berg bridges.

Unteroffizier Jablinski was not a popular man, despite his impeccable credentials, service with the Fuhrer-Begleit-Brigaden amongst his glittering resume.

His skills did not seem to measure up to his record, and his performance in training bordered on the inept at times.

The commander of 4th Kompagnie placed him with a good crew, and the JagdPanther started to do better in unit exercises.

None the less, the Unteroffizier's personal performance was still well below that expected of a senior NCO.

Perhaps unsurprising, as Jablinski really wasn't Jablinski at all, the present incumbent being a Soviet plant with precious little experience of combat, but with the ideals of communism as his driving force.

Manoeuvring his tank destroyer into a forward position, Jablinski satisfied himself that his moment of destiny was upon him, and composed himself for the task ahead.

Across the river, the sounds of combat got nearer and nearer, the relief column clearly closing on the Berg Bridge.

Mentally rehearsing the short journey and his actions when he arrived, 'Jablinksi' ensured his crew were otherwise engaged, quietly watching them as he slipped two hand-grenades from the rack.

Muttering to the gunner to take charge, he levered himself out of the cupola and onto the cool steel roof.

As he unscrewed the caps of the stick grenades, he re-checked the distance to the sandbagged position, satisfying himself that he would make it.

Both grenades rattled on the deck of the fighting compartment of vehicle 414, the silence suddenly punctuated with yells of alarm.

Jablinski was already halfway across the road as the first head appeared in the hatch.

When he was four feet from the sandbags, the first grenade exploded, the screams of the injured almost immediately cut short by the second explosion.

"Partisans!," he screamed, as he rolled over the top of the position, the US soldiers in it taken by surprise, both by his sudden appearance, and the obvious destruction of one of the German AFV's.

The Engineer Major quickly composed himself, and ordered two of his men to post themselves on the same side, eyes peeled for any saboteurs.

He had other things on his mind, and waited for the order to drop the Berg Bridge, once the airborne column had gone through.

He strained his eyes to see anything, but was only rewarded with the occasional flash as a large weapon fired.

Jablinski's knife slammed into the base of his skull, penetrating his brain, and severing his spinal cord, killing him instantly.

Holding the cadaver up in an embrace, the Soviet agent moved to one side, placing the dead officer against the sandbags and withdrew the knife, clamping his hand over the mouth of the radio operator, and opening his throat with one vicious and deep cut.

His eyes were fixed on the other two men as he held the dying radioman upright.

He needn't have worried, as the developing fire in the JagdPanther was providing adequate distraction for the two engineers.

Jablinski slid the radioman's bayonet from its sheath and, a blade in each hand, he moved quietly to the two men.

Repeating the proven method of an instant kill, he rammed his knife home, killing the first man, and then repeated the execution with the bayonet, the force of the blow carrying the longer blade through the victim's head, the point emerging in glossy scarlet from the forehead of the dead man.

Jablinski was the only living man in the position, the only other object of note being the plunger for the demolition charges on the bridge.

'Europa' blew the remaining armour of the 25th Guards Mechanised to pieces; the stationary tanks no match for the experienced Panzer gunners.

The Soviet infantry melted away in the face of huge casualties.

As dictated by the plan, the Panzer elements that approached the bridge peeled either side, turning back to provide a funnel down which the transports could move in safety, channelling them over the bridge, and into the waiting arms of their comrades.

Jablinski briefly toyed with the idea of detonating the charges and then disappearing, but his sense of duty made him stay, the opportunity that fate had presented to him worthy of full exploitation.

Dawn's first light gave him enough vision to start seeing distinct shapes, darker shapes in a vista of darkness.

The first vehicle that he could identify was a large amphibian, the sort capable of carrying a full platoon of men.

Soon four were in view, driving hard down the road, heading straight for the bridge.

"What the name of fucking Davy Crockett's balls is going on here?"

Jablinski wheeled, his immediate instinct to attack halted by the menacing barrel of the grease gun.

Momentarily panicking that his sacrifice might now come to nothing, the Soviet agent checked the advancing column, the lead vehicle of which was already on the apron of the bridge.

Shouting in excited German, he waved desperately at the bodies, slowly edging his way nearer the electronic detonator.

The moment came, as the American NCO noticed the bayonet sticking out of the back of the dead man's head.

A punch knocked the American to the ground, and he threw himself forward.

The wire was not connected.

"Govno!"

His fingers, trembling with excess energy and fear in equal measure, twisted the wire, and made the connection.

The stunned NCO pushed himself up on his elbows, shaking his head.

The Soviet agent snatched up the radioman's Garand and fired twice, both bullets hitting the groggy American.

Jablinski checked again, the Buffaloes perfectly positioned on the Berg Bridge.

He twisted the arming lever, and sent a charge of electrical energy to the detonators in the demolition charges.

Every head in the relief column swivelled in an instant, the huge explosion unmistakeably marking the end of the bridge.

Those close enough watched fascinated as two fireballs described golden arches in the sky, each one consisting of approximately sixteen and a half tons of metal and containing thirty souls.

The two Buffaloes crashed to the ground, one on the edge of the canal, the other onto the roof of the house nearest the bridge, killing and burning some of the 4th's infantrymen stationed there.

Two other Buffaloes were wrecked, both flipped over on the sides by the shock wave.

Over one hundred Americans had died in a fraction of a second.

Jablinski spared himself a moment of celebration before slipping away unseen.

On the eastern bank of the canal, Oberstleutnant Von Hardegen ripped his eyes away from the bloody mess and consulted his map.

Despite the excellence of his IR weapons, the day was nearly upon them, and daylight would be a great leveller, as would the sheer numbers of the enemy.

A decision was needed, and quickly.

Such a decision was made and communicated, again the training and expertise of 'Europa' showing as the armoured pocket moved southwards.

Soviet guardsmen in Urmond stood and fought back, one of the Falke halftracks dying messily with its crew.

Securing their flank on Heksenberg, the relief column moved towards the new crossing point, south of Stein, where one damaged bridge stood waiting for them, also wired for demolition, but, Von Hardegen hoped, not placed in the hands of some lunatic, like at Berg.

The 3rd Kompagnie, pushing along the western edge of the rail yards, barrelled into an unsuspecting Soviet unit, sat waiting, ready to move up to Stein when summoned.

The 6th Pontoon Bridge Brigade, a brigade in name only since the USAAF attack on Limburg, lay waiting to back up the advance. If the enemy blew the crossing, the plan was to rapidly deploy its engineer bridge, once the enemy had been pushed away from the river, to permit the heavy tanks of the 2nd Red Banner Central European Front to cross the Maas.

Despite an influx of manpower, mainly former POW's, the 6th was still only at two-thirds strength. The engineer unit had received some new equipment straight from the Motherland, but lacked much of the heavy bridging equipment it needed, and was low on transport.

3rd Kompagnie swept through the engineer's deployment area, the Panzer IV crews enjoying the opportunity to slaughter lined up vehicles and machine-gun helpless men in the open expanse of the large rail yard.

The eight-minute action saw the 6th sustain 60% casualties, lose the vast majority of their best equipment, and all of their remaining barges.

As Von Hardegen had ordered, the two Puma armoured cars pressed ahead and crossed the Stein Bridge, accompanied by a jeep containing Bud Harper and four of his men.

With little explanation, the Glider Colonel and his boys took post with the Engineer officer, backed up by the impressive looking Puma's, their sole purpose to ensure that there was no repeat of the Berg debacle.

Again leading the way, the Buffaloes of the Northamptonshire Yeomanry, blazed over the bridge, this time achieving the relative safety of the west bank, and Belgian soil.

A German Pioniere officer, attached to 'Europa', had arrived at Stein shortly after Harper, his experienced eye there to examine the damaged structure and report the problems back to Von Hardegen.

372

A quick discussion with the British liaison officer from the 52nd RTR established the weights of the different vehicles in the relief column, and the kangaroos were halted, to permit the lighter vehicles to cross first.

After each crossing, the Pioniere officer gave an update on the bridge condition.

A small force of IS-II's appeared, pushing up from Beek, and it clashed with the Panthers of 2nd Kompagnie.

This time, the Soviet tankers were on a more even footing, and they left three destroyed German tanks behind them before withdrawing from the field, an equal number of their own now smoking and quiet.

The 'Europa's' sole recovery tank, an original field conversion from a Panther D, moved forward to recover the one vehicle that had not been smashed apart by the heavy 122mm shells. The BergePanther crew worked quickly, connecting towropes, dragging the heavily damaged vehicle with them, and into the relative safety of the buildings of Elsloo.

Soviet artillery started to fall, lending speed to the evacuation efforts.

The fact that the bursts stayed well clear of the Stein bridges was not wasted on the Allied troopers, so vehicles and men pressed closer to the river, avoiding most of the high-explosive.

The last 6x6 lorry had crossed, and the Kangaroos were now moving, carrying the exhausted 101st troopers to safety.

A Soviet infantry assault struck Elsloo, threatening the southern flank.

Marion Crisp had not yet crossed the canal, and organised a rapid counter-attack, a mixed force of German and US paratroopers throwing the Russian Guardsmen back, and away from the bridge.

In Stein itself, the 52nd RTR had little problem bringing up the rear, as the Soviet forces seemingly lacked the will to pursue the relief force.

Suddenly, the situation changed, as an M4 Sherman was wreathed in flames from numerous Molotov cocktails.

The British unit stalled as more petrol bombs were launched from the surrounding buildings, Guardsmen from the 25th Mechanised's Engineer company surrounding the main route of escape.

Again, the Vampir troopers, supported by some Fallschirmjager and Belgian fusiliers, counter-attacked.

In the early morning light, made brighter by the flames of buildings and tanks, the Belgians were halted by fierce resistance based around two DP's firing from a bakery.

A platoon of the Vampir troopers moved right, flanking the bakery, but were held up by another similar block of engineers.

Von der Heydte moved his force to the left, and drove into the flank of the Soviet engineers, opening up an alternate route down Bosweg, avoiding the danger zone.

Not without cost, as a dozen more of his Fallschirmjager fell in the action.

Running beside the paratrooper officer, Bosicki gasped as the rifle bullet slammed into him, sending him flying into a shell hole on the junction of Daggeweide and Bosweg.

Von der Heydte stopped to check the NCO.

The man had something he needed to say.

"Sorry, Herr Oberstleutnant."

Pressing a field dressing to the probably fatal wound, Von der Heydte shrugged his shoulders.

"It is done, Oberfeldwebel. It should not have been," he grunted with the effort of tying off the ends, "But it is done."

"My brothers. Both of them. Executed by those red bastards," the pain started to affect the wounded man's speech.

"I am sorry, Oberfeldwebel. Now, stay still. I'll be back when I can."

Touching the NCO on the shoulder, Von der Heydte emerged from the shell hole, straight into the blast from a stick grenade, dispatched from the hand of one of his own.

The blast knocked the Fallschirmjager commander unconscious, and he was carried from the field on the shoulders of the horrified grenadier.

Bosicki lay in the hole, unseen, and unmissed.

The British rearguard moved out of Stein, leaving behind a vacuum swiftly filled by Soviet troops.

The surviving Engineers from the 25th emerged from their hiding places, their company shattered by the joint efforts of the British Shermans, the Vampir soldiers, and the Fallschirmjager.

374

One shocked Soviet Corporal stood over a shell hole, its single occupant wearing the uniform of the enemy that had just killed both his cousin and best friend.

He locked eyes with the wounded German, understanding the man's fear.

The corporal lit his cigarette, rough cut Russian tobacco rolled in the page of a book he had 'liberated' some days ago, flicking open his lighter, also liberated, this time from the dead body of a US paratrooper.

The flame remained, the petrol lighter steady in the hands of a man resolved to revenge.

Lighting the Molotov cocktail, he enjoyed the look of panic on the German's face, and grinned as the man tried to move out of the hole.

He tossed the bottle, and was rewarded with the sound of breaking glass, immediately followed by animal-like screaming.

Standing on the edge of the hole, he watched, enjoying the immolation of the German soldier, taking it all in, as if he was watching a silent movie in the theatre.

Except it wasn't silent, the hideous screaming rising above every sound of battle.

The petrol burned away, leaving small flames where a piece of clothing had yet to totally yield, or where flesh was still capable of sustaining fire.

Yet the man still lived, and the screams went on.

On and on.

The Corporal watched as the sounds of suffering started to curtail and shock set in. He felt satisfied that the man had paid for the deaths of his cousin and friend.

The Engineer company regrouped and moved away.

Bosicki was dead before the rats started to gnaw on his burnt flesh.

1100hrs, Wednesday, 24th October 1945, Stein, Holland.

At approximately the same time that Colonel Danskin, late of the 25th Guards Mechanised Brigade, was shot by the NKVD, a group of weary officers assembled in a large tent on the outskirts of Dilsen, Belgium.

Even Von der Heydte was there, groggy, and sporting his own black eyes, brought on by his contact with the road when he was felled by the grenade.

He and Higgins went together like bookends, and the pair earned more than one grin from their comrades.

Crisp and Harper were holding their own miniature debriefing, both poring over the map of their last battles, trying to find out what could have been done better, or been done differently.

It would be some time before the full situation was clarified, but it seemed likely that the 101st had less than 50% of its manpower on the right side of the Maas, and that officially put the division out of the war for some time to come.

Maxwell-Taylor was on the phone, dealing with the plethora of matters that accompany such a defeat, or, as some called it, a victory.

'That will be left to the historians to sort out.'

The Corps commander's lips curled at that thought, safe in the knowledge that his men had done all they could, regardless of what history would reflect from the comfort of its armchair when the firing had stopped.

The last man to arrive, did so with a flourish, two SDKFZ 251 halftrack's rattling up at full speed and sliding to a halt, adjacent to the tent.

Von Hardegen, his face like thunder, alighted, followed by a group of men who were with him for a very specific purpose.

Maxwell-Taylor had rehearsed the moment in his mind, but was beaten to it by the swift movement of Higgins, who reached out for the hand of the Panzer officer.

"Lieutenant Colonel Von Hardegen, thank you, from myself, and my men. Without you, we would have been lost. Thank you, Sir."

Von Hardegen could not deny that it was true, but was tactful enough to not confirm it.

"We were all lucky, Herr General, and we all played our part today."

That was undoubtedly true.

The others pressed forward, slapping shoulders, shaking hands, relieved to still be alive, and attributing it all to this man and his tankers.

Modest as ever, Von Hardegen just shrugged and smiled through the barrage of praise. As it subsided, he interrupted, for he had an important matter to address.

"Now, meine Herren, I have some business to attend to, and ask if you will be my witnesses."

He turned on his heel and walked out.

Off to the left, a German panzer NCO stood, his hands tied behind his back, placed against a tree on the edge of a cinder track.

In front of him stood a line of his peers, grim-faced men, there to perform a duty and salvage some pride for their unit.

The eight men, all members of Europa's 3rd Kompagnie, stood ready, Kar98k rifles held in the attention position.

To one side stood the 3rd's commanding Captain, his face still like thunder, the way it had set ever since the destruction of the Berg Bridge.

Turning to the Allied officers behind him, Von Hardegen enlightened them, their eyes narrowing, focussing on the prisoner before them.

Turning back to face his men again, Von Hardegen clicked to attention.

"Proceed, Herr Hauptmann."

Out of the corner of his eye, the 'Europa' commander watched as two men painfully exited the second halftrack.

The first, a heavily bandaged German, the gunner of JagdPanther 414, had been blown out through the rear hatch, his survival unseen by Jablinski. The second man was an American, with both arms in plaster, because Garand bullets had smashed his bones. He was the 4th US Infantry NCO, who had stumbled upon the scene in the sandbagged position.

Their evidence had been damning and unequivocal.

Jablinski had been confident enough to try to slip back into the unit, as if nothing had happened, and, for the most part, had been successful. That is until a burned and angry Panzerkanonier spoke to the 3rd Kompagnie commander.

The same officer now spoke, listing the charges, and the verdict of the field courts-martial, as chaired by Von Hardegen.

There were no frills attached, no last words, or final cigarette.

With a nod from Von Hardegen, the firing squad commander got on with business, the time from first order to weapon discharge just under seven seconds.

Despite the obvious demise of the man, the Panzer Hauptmann still added to the injuries suffered by the Russian spy. He put a bullet in the corpse's brain, solely for his own satisfaction, rather than ensuring life was extinct.

1145hrs, Wednesday, 24th October, 1945, Headquarters, 2nd Red Banner Central European Front, Schloss Rauischholzhausen,

Petrov finished his briefing, the headquarters of 2nd Red Banner so quiet, that the sound of a circling aircraft almost filled the room.

Apart from the destruction wrought upon the 5th Guards Mechanised Corps and 34th Guards Rifle Corps, there was the not insignificant matter of the destruction of the 6th Pontoon Bridge Brigade.

Three full artillery regiments added to the list of losses, along with numerous smaller units, mortar battalions, tank companies, and the like.

North of Sittard, 40th Rifle Corps had been badly handled by the British Red Devils, soldiers that lived up to their name and fought with incredible ferocity.

Gradually, the staff officers started work on reassembling their shattered units, to make them ready for another day.

Two of Konev's armies were badly knocked about, perversely, the two that had formed the spear point of his plan to cross the Maas, which plan now lay in tatters. In addition, the failure of his effort meant that the overall operation had been jeopardised, without the balance of tangible success, something that Zhukov would use against him when he found out.

'If he finds out?,' Konev mused.

Worse was the supply situation, some of his units having been incapable of properly defending or attacking, for want of bullets and shells.

And worst of all, the situation had no resolution in sight, the consumption rates higher than predicted, the losses due to partisans the same, the only thing lower than predicted being the amounts arriving from the Motherland, after the losses sustained by enemy air attacks and armed groups on the ground.

'How can it get any worse?'

Again, the room filled with heavy silence, the low hubbub abating instantly.

Konev became aware that Petrov looked decidedly uncomfortable, eyes widening as he took in the new arrival.

The commander of 2nd Red Banner understood immediately.

"Greetings, Comrade Marshal Zhukov."

"Greetings, Comrade Marshal Konev."

"Tea, Comrade?"

"Later, thank you. First let us deal with what the fuck you have done here, and your answers better be damn good."

The two NKVD Generals and their accompanying men filled Konev's vision.

"Your office, Comrade?"

The two moved off into the separate private office.

The staff worked on through the tirade, as the constant shouting, all by Zhukov, escaped through the glazed door.

Wishing to keep their heads, they worked diligently under the close and unwelcome scrutiny of the implacable NKVD officers, even Tarasov, who had kept Zhukov supplied with the minutiae of Konev's plans from start to finish.

One thought puzzled him.

Had Zhukov permitted the attack to go ahead in case of success, or had he turned a blind eye, in the hope that Konev would fail, and so fall?

No matter what happened in the next few minutes, and the hours ahead, one thing was certain.

2nd Red Banner had been stopped in its tracks.

3RD RED BANNER CENTRAL EUROPEAN FRONT - MARSHAL ROKOSSOVSKY

All warfare is based on deception. Hence, when able to attack, we must seem unable to; when using our forces, we must seem inactive; when we are near, we must make the enemy believe we are far away; when far away, we must make him believe we are near. Hold out bait to entice the enemy. Pretend disorder, and crush him.

Sun Tzu

Chapter 93 - THE TURNCOAT

1112hrs, Sunday, 14th October 1945, Headquarters, 1st Legion Chars D'Assault Brigade 'Camerone', Baden-Baden, Germany.

"You've done well so far, Knocke. My generals are pleased, although you did get very close to the Enz, did you not?"

Kowalski looked smug.

Ernst-August Knocke pursed his lips, failing to hide his contempt for the man opposite.

"It was not easy."

That was actually completely untrue, as rumours of the Legion's movement north of the River Enz had been unfounded in any case, but, none the less, the apparent act of compliance was welcome.

"Not easy, but you managed it, Knocke. Good boy."

Kowalski was deliberately provocative, all the time assessing how well Knocke was controlled by the possession of his family.

"We have another task for you, one that requires you to move backwards at the right time. Even you should be able to manage that."

Knocke had his own agenda to follow.

"And my family? They are still safe with you?"

380

As Kowalski had no idea of the events on the Baltic Coast at Fischausen, he answered easily.

"Your family are quite well; and quite safe."

Opening his blouse, the Soviet intelligence officer extracted an envelope.

"And to make sure they stay that way, we need you to ensure that this goes smoothly."

He dropped the item on the desk in front of the Legion officer. Knocke neither eyed it, nor picked it up, sensing that the man opposite had his own agenda.

"I am told that this will be the last thing to be asked of you, Knocke."

Kowalski produced another photo of the whole family, albeit tainted by the ever-present NKVD officer.

"Then, they will be free to go, and you can join them, if you surrender and identify yourself to one of our units."

The Russian gestured at the envelope.

"There is a safe passage note inside."

Knocke nodded gently.

"And where would we go, Major?"

"By the time you need to choose, the Soviet Union will include most of Europe, so the choice would be considerable."

Knocke grunted, mentally removing one item from his list of things to do to keep up appearances.

Kowalski grunted, mentally removing one item from his list of things to do to confirm Knocke's continued subservience.

"Your side is losing in any case, Knocke, and this," he casually gestured at the envelope, "Ensures less will die, before our victory is complete."

Biting back his first response, Knocke merely shrugged, trying to convey some sort of agreement.

"So, Herr Maior, what would you have me do?"

Kowalski indicated the envelope.

"We want you to make a hole."

<u>1232hrs, Friday, 19th October, 1945, Headquarters, Command Group 'Normandie', 1st Legion Chars D'Assault Brigade 'Camerone', Railway Station, Lipsheim, Alsace.</u>

The Legion Corps had tasted its first defeat, albeit one that was expected, given the circumstances.

Successful actions at Gaggenau and Rastatt had come to nought, as Soviet forces in the Saar broke the American lines and drove southwards, forcing the Legion to retreat at speed, for fear of being cut off on the east bank of the Rhine.

Two rearguard groups, one at Achern, and a larger one at Appenweier, had been overrun and destroyed.

The blame for that lay fairly and squarely on the shoulders of Molyneux, and his previously unsuspected ability to withdraw more swiftly than was necessary.

Thanks to his interference, neither group had been left with artillery cover or dedicated air support, and both, in turn, were eliminated.

Knocke had been furious, even though neither group belonged to 'Camerone', as the ineptitude of it all spelt out future danger to every man in the Corps.

There were even moments when those in 'the know' wondered if Molyneux had any family under the protection of the NKVD, so complete was his ability to withdraw and undermine well-laid plans.

In any case, much of what was planned for the Legion Corps was kept from Molyneux. De Gaulle's strange continued insistence, in the face of growing pressure, that the General remain in charge of the Legion, was difficult for anyone in French First Army to grasp. However, it was offset by De Lattre's insistence that, for the sensitive operation ahead, Molyneux knew as little as possible.

The loss of Strasbourg was imminent, and was not down to Molyneux's incompetence, rather the unsanctioned withdrawal of a neighbouring American unit, which permitted the old city's flank to be turned, rendering her defence nothing short of suicidal.

Lavalle had some good news for the small group that knew 'everything'.

"The preparation is complete, Gentlemen. Once Général De Lattre approves the operational planning, then we can commence, immediately our Russian friend gives the word."

The battleground had been of the Soviet's own choosing, fit for them to penetrate to the heart of the Allied defence, reaching the Swiss border, and opening up the possibilities of a drive into the French interior.

It was flat, reasonably dry, and almost perfect for a precise deep attack in strength, such as the Legion anticipated the enemy plan to be.

It was also a perfect killing ground.

"Ernst."

Lavalle ceded the floor to the man who had conceived the plan.

"Gentlemen, once we know the timetable, and the timing of the enemy attack, we will initiate the withdrawal, as outlined in the Soviet document, falling back in front of their advance towards Colmar."

Listening in was the cream of the Corps' officers, Legionnaires and Americans, men who understood they were just about to be given an opportunity to inflict a huge defeat upon the communist forces.

"The valleys will be sealed with mines and other works, and defended sufficiently enough to discourage their reconnaissance. It will be a fine balance, meine herren, but they must not appear overly defended, or important. Nothing to encourage their interest, for obvious reasons."

A chorus of assent encouraged Knocke to continue.

"Whilst we are openly falling back, we must not lose opportunities to hurt the Russian. In the opening stages, if we stick occasionally and bloody their noses, we will discourage too close a pursuit. That will help our withdrawal at the start."

He grinned at the men around him.

"Don't stick too well though, we want them kept hungry!"

The laughter showed that his experienced commanders were confident and at ease.

"Seriously, Kameraden," Knocke occasionally lapsed back into the language of another time, "If you do stick, don't lose the flank of the adjacent unit. We cannot afford gaps."

Knocke tapped the map.

"Unless opportunities present themselves. We will hold for a while. The Aubach is where 'Camerone' and 'Alma' will first stand, and then we will invite them on to us, give them time to stack up before we move away, this time keeping them close if we can, as we give more ground."

He moved past Selestat.

"We will cede Selestat to them. The capture of a major city will encourage them to believe."

His finger drew a line between two points further to the south.

"Here, this line between Guémar and Elsenheim, this is where we will stand and hold them."

He looked around the ensemble, his eyes dwelling on those whose units would eventually occupy the indicated defensive line.

"Your officers have already inspected the prepared positions. Any issues?"

St.Clair spoke.

"Sir, there was an issue with some badly sited secondary positions that has now been resolved."

Von Arnesen followed.

"That was also an issue for us, Sir. Distances were wrong, and often they were too obviously placed. New alternatives have been prepared."

Knocke accepted that his officers had resolved the issues, and continued the brief.

He cupped his hands around the area north of that defence line, embracing Selestat to the banks of the Rhine.

"We will halt them south of Selestat, and their next echelons will push forward, because we will have conditioned them to expect our withdrawal."

With little movements of his hands, Knocke began to sweep the imaginary Soviet units into a pocket.

"They will press together in this area."

Each man present could see it clearly, the hands holding Soviet mechanised units, bunched together, and ripe for the plucking.

"And, on the command, we will visit hell upon them."

One American voice rose above the hubbub of excitement.

"Amen to that, Général Knocke."

Brigadier General Pierce's newly designated 16th US Armored Brigade had a pivotal role to play, partially because it was relatively fresh, partially because it possessed some of the USA's newest tools of warfare, and partially because Pierce had sought the honour, and the opportunity to expunge the sad memories of August that it represented.

384

In harness with the detached Panzer regiment from 'Camerone', the 16th had a vital part to play in executing Plan Thermopylae.

The plan required the strength of 'Camerone', 'Alma', 'Tannenberg', and the 16th US, a force representing the cream of the Legion Corps' units.

However, unknown to those in the briefing, the inclusion of 'Tannenberg', not part of the 'Normandie' Group, had resulted in a leak of information, one that brought an unwelcome visitor to their door, in the shape of General Molyneux, commander of the Legion Corps D'Assault.

The convoy screeched to a halt outside the station building, the sounds of doors slamming and imperious shouts rose as the entourage deployed.

Those present in the waiting room that served as the temporary headquarters for 'Normandie', resigned themselves to a haranguing at the very least. After all, much of what had been planned had been done without Molyneux's knowledge.

Only De Walle seemed unfazed by the sound of marching boots, growing louder, as the man himself arrived at the door and entered with a flourish.

The assembly sprang to attention, and saluted.

As was Molyneux's custom, he touched his cane to his cap in return.

Lavalle stepped forward.

"Welcome, mon Général. We did not know you were coming. Some coffee before I update you on our situation?"

"You were not informed of my arrival for a particular reason, Lavalle."

He looked the immaculate soldier up and down, as if he was inspecting some dog mess in the street.

"You were not informed of my arrival, so that I could catch you and your little group in the act."

For the first time, Lavalle and the others became aware of the two caporal's, armed with Thompsons, innocuous at first, but now so obviously out of place, and present for a single purpose.

"I am here to arrest you all for treachery, for your intended betrayal of France!"

"There is no betrayal here, mon Général!"

"Really, Lavalle? Really?"

385

Molyneux lunged at the map, sweeping it up and inspecting it closely.

Finding nothing to support the information he had received anonymously, the infuriated General went at it head on.

"This map shows me nothing. No mark for a line of defence, no line for holding the enemy up, no plans for offense; nothing!"

Knocke went to speak.

The cane shot out like a rapier, falling just short of the German's chest,

"You shut your mouth, you German bastard!"

For once in his life, Knocke was at a loss.

"So, have any of you traitors got anything to say, before I have you all court-martialled and shot?"

De Walle pushed his way through the tight-lipped men, emerging directly in front of Molyneux. His appearance caused the caporal's to stiffen, their fingers shifting to triggers, ready to defend the man who had promised them promotions and leave.

"Général Molyneux, permit me to introduce myself. I am Général de Brigade De Walle, of 'La Service de Documentation Extérieure et de Contre-espionage'", extending his identity card, De Walle used the full formal title of his organisation, thinking that it added gravity to his status.

"You have arrived in excellent time. I have been monitoring these men and it is as you say, but, not how you believe, Sir."

Molyneux quickly moved from relief that a senior officer of France's security service was present, to confusion, as the man suddenly cast doubt on his information.

"How do I know that you are not in league with these traitors, De Walle, eh?"

The 'Deux' man's sage nodding gave weight to Molyneux's thought that he was on top of the situation.

"If I could speak to you in private, then that is a matter than can be easily resolved, Sir."

"I am not an idiot, De Walle. That will not happen."

As he was ten steps ahead of Molyneux, the next line slipped easily from De Walle's tongue.

"Then might I suggest that your aide, Colonel Plummer, stays with us, and covers me with his pistol, Sir?"

The matter was quickly considered.

"Yes, I suppose I can do that. Colonel, your pistol please, and shoot him if he does anything at all."

Plummer withdrew his Browning automatic and mumbled his compliance.

"Shall we go next door, whilst your men stand watch over these officers, mon Général?"

Molyneux followed De Walle, with Plummer bringing up the rear.

Once ensconced in the small ticket office, De Walle transformed himself.

"Molyneux, you are a total cretin."

"What?"

"Those men are not traitors to anyone, let alone France. They are soldiers, planning to hurt the enemy in a way that he may not recover for some time, and part of that is an operation with which I am closely involved. You have already placed that operation in peril by your actions and, by rights, I could shoot you myself, here, now!"

"Colonel Plummer!"

Molyneux turned to his man, only to find that 'his' man was not 'his' man at all.

"I suggest that you listen to what Monsieur De Walle has to say, mon Général."

Stunned into silence, Molyneux did just that.

"Some very important people have sanctioned this operation, and it cannot be risked, am I clear on that point, Molyneux?"

"But I command the Corps, and have a right to know what my soldiers are used for, what my officers are doing..."

The confused man tailed off, his eyes again seeking some sort of clarification from Plummer.

None was forthcoming.

"Understand me, Molyneux..."

The man rallied as best he could.

"Général Molyneux, if you please!"

De Walle extracted a piece of paper, and held it under the Corps commander's nose.

"You are Général Molyneux, until I employ this piece of paper, signed by Général de Lattre himself. At that time, you become Private Molyneux. Understand?"

387

The mouth worked, but no sound came out, such was the impact of De Walle's words.

The 'Deux' man nodded at the aide, who extracted a similar piece of paper.

"Colonel Plummer has his own letter, empowering him to remove you from your command. Do I need to say more, Molyneux?"

Stunned, the Corps Commander remained silent as his mind sought a way forward.

He suddenly brightened.

"De Gaulle will hear of this outrage, De Walle!"

Nodding in acceptance, De Walle made a study of folding the document, before replacing it inside his tunic.

"That is correct, Général Molyneux. I shall be briefing him this very afternoon."

This time the mouth also failed to function, hanging open, as the General realised he had no saviours.

"Now, shall we return to the main room and announce that an error has been made, before you return to your own headquarters and leave the fighting to real soldiers?"

"Yes."

Molyneux turned on his heel and moved back towards the briefing area, completely missing the grins of his two tormentors.

Within ten minutes, the entourage had departed, Molyneux sharing a car with someone for whom he had a newfound respect, hand in hand with a newfound deep hatred.

De Walle watched the convoy leave, musing as to whether Molyneux would contact De Gaulle about the situation, and how that conversation might go, especially as De Gaulle had no idea of 'Deux's' activities in partnership with SOE in general, and the Knocke affair in particular.

A swift conversation with Plummer had focussed the Colonel's mind on the requirements of the situation, and the lengths that he could go to in order to ensure that secrecy was maintained.

That problem now removed, it now fell to the troopers of the Legion Corps to carry out the plan.

To betray, you must be trusted, so who's to blame? You, for doing what you needed to do, or them, for believing you in the first place?

Samuel Rossiter, Lieutenant General [Ret'd], USMC.

Chapter 94 - THE MEETINGS

3RD RED BANNER CENTRAL EUROPEAN FRONT - MARSHAL ROKOSSOVSKY

1112hrs, Sunday, 21st October 1945, Headquarters, Group 'Normandie', Unterlinden Museum Building, Colmar, Alsace.

The exhibits had long since disappeared, the building no longer a cultural focus.

In the thirteenth century, the building housed a Dominican convent, the nuns finally leaving during the French Revolution.

Open as a museum for nearly one hundred years, the Unterlinden boasted some of the finest works of European art.

Until the shadows of approaching conflict spread across the continent.

Some artefacts were removed by the authorities, prior to the sound of approaching jackboots in 1940, others afterwards, now somewhere in Germany, having been released from the Nazi's 'safekeeping'.

The empty rooms made for an excellent headquarters, and 'Normandie' had made its home there, ready for the upcoming operation.

Knocke had received another visit from Soviet agent Kowalski, and the timetable of Soviet expectations had been set, the Legion plan changed accordingly, actually withdrawing slower in some places than had been originally planned.

Lavalle and Knocke had taken a last quiet stroll through the thirteenth century cloisters, enjoying the sights and sounds of the old convent in silence.

Soviet aircraft had hit 'Alma' hard at last light the previous evening, seventy-six troopers killed, and half as many again wounded, and out of the coming fight.

389

The adjustments had been made and the gaps closed.

Now all that was needed was one small piece of information.

H-hour?

Kowalski was equally elated and scared; the effects of both emotions making his body feel more alive with every breath.

His meeting with the airbase commander had been brief, the man more interested in his own problems, than the arrival and swift departure of one aircraft.

Some hours beforehand, his visit with Knocke had been even more satisfying; the defeat he could sense in the man had started the boost that his body was still thriving on.

Whilst Kowalski would have preferred to be alone, the drivers that he and the other liaison officers had now been assigned, took the strain of the journey, and the Soviet agent had made the most of the extra time to examine the SS bastard's plan.

It was simple, and should be effective, provided that the German stuck to it.

His sense of the man today was that he just wanted to get it all over with, and Kowalski annotated his summary report with his solid belief that Knocke would stick to his side of the bargain.

'After all, when he had showed the man the latest picture of his wife in prime health, had he not shed a tear of joy'

He leant against the jeep, parked in the middle of the airfield adjacent to the ground controller's cabin, enjoying the bracing air, and watching the morning mist slowly clear. The American aircraft had left just under an hour beforehand, off to do mischief somewhere unknown to him.

His senses lit off, the indistinct hum on the edge of his consciousness developing into the sound of a single engine, bringing a small observation aircraft in to land.

The Westland Lysander kissed the grass runway, a perfect landing that even Kowalski appreciated.

The RAF aircraft, sporting Polish identity markings, rolled across the field, closing on his jeep.

390

"Feel free to take the jeep, and find some way to amuse yourself, Corporal."

He checked his watch, calculating for the umpteenth time, confirming the flight time there and back, plus his time with the General.

"1900 hrs. Back here on the minute, Corporal."

Salutes were exchanged, and Kowalski walked towards the waiting aircraft.

The female NCO jumped back into the little 4x4 and started the engine.

As the Lysander took to the air, she drove to the small house that constituted the USAAF headquarters building, parked, and entered.

Finding the appropriate door, her knocks brought an invitation.

"Thank you for your cooperation, Colonel. Our man will be back at 1900hrs precisely. If you can repeat the charade, we can get him away without any further inconvenience to yourself."

Her precise English belied her German ancestry. Whilst not, by any standards, a beauty, Gisela Jourdan had classical features, the likes of which had graced art and literature since man developed the ability to draw a likeness.

"May I use your phone please, Colonel?"

Knowing that she wasn't the dumb ass corporal her uniform suggested, and not knowing what to call an agent bearing impeccable credentials from the OSS, the man fell back on his lifelong method of address to a woman.

"Certainly, ma'am," and he offered up the receiver.

She slid her thigh onto the desk, and worked her way through the operators until she got to the required phone.

"Hello Max? This is Rita."

Jourdan slipped into the coded exchange easily.

"Yes please. Can you tell Captain Logan that I won't be able to honour our date tonight?"

She smiled disarmingly at the USAAF officer, who was starting to appreciate her other, more physical charms.

"Yes, I'm really sorry, but I'm stuck here until nineteen hundred hours, and then I have to drive back."

Seeing the Colonel greedily eyeing the obvious outline of a suspender through the tightness of her skirt, she provocatively stroked her own leg through the material.

391

"That's alright, Max," she looked directly into the USAAF officers eyes, "I will find something nice to do while I wait. You know me."

As Gisela had heard that retort before, the call came to a premature end, and within fifteen minutes, so did the Colonel.

For the first time, at least.

0847hrs, Monday, 22nd October 1945, Böblingen Airfield, Böblingen, Germany.

The Lysander came in low, as it had flown from Bischoffsheim, over the lines, and into Soviet territory.

Again, the pilot executed a perfect landing, and the monoplane taxied towards the waiting vehicles.

Switching off the engine, the airman stayed in his seat, knowing that his passenger had priority.

Stretching himself into some sort of shape, Kowalski dismounted, coming to the attention as the figure of GRU Colonel General Pekunin approached him.

"Comrade Kovelskin, welcome, welcome."

The agent found himself grabbed in an unceremonious hug, his cheeks kissed passionately by the senior man.

"Your flight was satisfactory, I hope? A stroke of good fortune presented us with this fine machine," he indicated the Lysander, on which Kowalski now noted the presence of tell-tale patches, where battle damage had been hastily repaired.

"It was good, thank you, Comrade Polkovnik General. The pilot is highly skilled."

Steering the younger man towards the waiting Mercedes, Pekunin could wait no longer.

"So, I hope that what you have is worth the risk we take here, Sergey Andreeyevich?"

"That is not for me to judge, Comrade Polkovnik General, but I believe you will not be disappointed."

Pekunin wasn't, and neither was the man waiting in the Mercedes, for Konstantin Ksawerovicz Rokossovsky, the commander of the 3rd Red Banner Central European Front, was handed the means by which to split the Allied lines and enter France.

392

1907hrs, Monday, 22nd October 1945, USAAF temporary airfield, Bischoffsheim, Alsace.

The aircraft didn't stop moving, Kowalski alighting after a brief exchange with the pilot.

It was already airborne before the jeep drew up.

"Good evening, Corporal."

"Sir."

"I hope you were not too bored waiting?"

Inadvertently looking at the headquarters building, Jourdan kept a straight face, despite the waving from one figure, with whom she had spent a less than boring day.

"No, Sir. I found something to occupy myself with."

The 4x4 accelerated away into the gathering gloom of the autumn evening.

1001hrs, Tuesday, 23rd October 1945, Headquarters, 3rd Red Banner Central European Front, Hotel Stephanie, Baden-Baden, Germany.

Rokossovsky and his closest advisors had listened to the briefing from the 19th Army Chief of Staff, Lieutenant General Liapin.

The operation had already been in place, but the latest information, provided by the GRU agent, had meant that some changes were desirable.

Overall, Rokossovsky was satisfied with the plan conceived by Liapin, and the 19th's commander, Lieutenant General Romanowsky.

However, he wasn't a Marshal of the Soviet Union for nothing, so ventured his own orders, couched as suggestions that could not be ignored.

"I think you might increase the artillery strikes on these points, Comrade Liapin."

The Marshal indicated the valley entrances that threatened the right flank of the advance.

"Our pet German may well assure us that they contain purely defensive forces, but we will have no surprises from them, Comrades."

Acknowledging the 19th's planning effort, Rokossovsky continued.

393

"You are quite right to assign good forces to blocking these routes, but I suggest more air regiments set aside, just in case, Comrades."

He tapped two points on the Rhine that had been circled in pencil, and annotated with markings that clearly represented bridges.

"This I like. An excellent move, just in case, Comrades." He moved on quickly.

"Overall, the plan is approved, but it must be done quicker and push deeper."

Drawing both Generals in closer, Rokossovsky dragged his finger down below Colmar, through Mulhouse, and obliquely left to Belfort.

"I cannot risk the Front with its flank exposed to the Vosges for very long."

That was understandable, and one of the reasons why the valleys leading from it had come in for special attention.

"This whole area is like a funnel. It attracts our advance because of what it offers, but it holds dangers, Comrades, dangers we cannot negate, so we must minimise them."

They both nodded their agreement.

"Speed will protect us here, keeping them on the move, so they have no time to organise. Our pet German should keep his units rolling back, but keep close to them, just in case someone develops balls and stands without orders. Keep pushing hard, sealing up the valleys as you go, and I will feed you units, from Front reserve, to keep the momentum up."

Standing back from the table, Rokossovsky produced a handkerchief, and cleared his nose noisily.

"I see no reason to limit your advance through this 'funnel', Comrades. Beyond it lies the open heartland of France, from where we can turn north and into Belgium, behind the bulk of the Allied forces."

This they knew, of course, but Rokossovsky was on a mission.

"Turn to the south, and our units can open up the route into Italy."

The 3rd Red Banner's commander revealed himself in his next exhortation.

"Or, we can open them up totally, and we can drive on, on to the Atlantic, or the Channel, and cut the Allies in half.

Stavka would give us the assets we needed to do the job, and the war would be over."

The room fell silent, each man seeing an end to the fighting, but only after more death and destruction.

"So, when do we attack, Comrades?"

Neither General spoke, understanding that their opinion was not being sought.

"How long to organise the changes, Comrade Liapin?"

"Six hours maximum, probably less, Comrade Marshal."

Adding a little as a safety margin to cover the unexpected, Rokossovsky announced his decision, exchanging nods with Lieutenant Generals Trubnikov and Bogolyubov, his Deputy Commander and Chief of Staff respectively.

"We go at 2100hrs, Comrades."

The five exchanged salutes and four filed out. Rokossovsky found himself alone with the map that carried out Operation Berkut.

Unconsciously checking off some of its content, Rokossovsky picked up the telephone. He spoke a few clipped words and waited, running his fingers over the markings, before getting through to his chosen recipient.

"Ah, Comrade Malinin. I hope all is well with the higher echelons of command?"

The two men liked each other, both personally and professionally, and the CoS clearly responded warmly.

"Berkut is a go at the agreed time. I will have the changes sent to you by messenger as soon as possible..."

He waited as the voice on the other end asked a question.

"No Comrade, nothing major in the ground plan, artillery re-tasking, and some extra air, that's all, Comrade."

Rokossovsky laughed.

"But of course, Mikhail Sergeyevich, but of course. I will contact you beforehand if anything else comes up. Goodbye Comrade."

The die was cast.

*My centre is giving way, my right is in retreat; situation
excellent. I shall attack.*

Ferdinand Foch

Chapter 95 - THE FUNNEL

3RD RED BANNER CENTRAL EUROPEAN
FRONT - MARSHAL ROKOSSOVSKY

2050hrs, Tuesday, 23rd October, 1945, Front line positions,
Assault formation of 19th Army, 3rd Red Banner Central
European Front, Lingolsheim, Alsace.

The artillery, the rockets, the air strikes, all had been
merciless and unceasing, the last two hours filled with the
orchestral sounds of an Army stirring itself for the advance.

The Allied front had been bathed in high explosives,
rear positions carpeted with Katyusha rockets; huge quantities of
munitions were expended to break the ex-SS soldiers that faced
the 19th Soviet Army.

On the receiving end, the legionnaires of 'Alma' and
'Camerone' took their punishment like the veterans they were,
some dying in a flash of white light, others just hugging the
welcoming earth more closely, guardian angels and gods called
upon in equal measure.

True to the latest policy, the Red Air Force was
operating mainly above friendly soil, either protecting against
Allied incursion, or standing ready to swoop to the relief support
of a ground formation in difficulty. Only if conditions proved
favourable, would the ground attack regiments venture outside
the protective comfort of ground anti-aircraft cover.

At 2100hrs precisely, the Red Army steamroller moved
forward and crashed into the front positions, bunkers and
trenches, which had contained units of the Legion Corps up to
three hours beforehand, when most were withdrawn to a line
further south.

Soviet infantry swept through the first allied positions,
some riding on tanks, others enthusiastically charging forward on

foot, all arriving with the expectation of close combat, but finding only the dead.

Men, both civilians and soldiers, who had died of wounds, had been placed in the front line, relieving the living.

Finding only corpses, the Soviet forces praised the effectiveness of their artillery, and charged forward again, running into a hidden defensive line bristling with machine-guns and anti-tank weapons, unbowed by the extensive barrage.

Artillery was switched and mortars deployed, their shells descending on the defenders, killing and maiming with each passing minute.

The assault started again and, yet again, the defence melted away, both legion units moving back quickly to the next defensive position.

Three USAAF Thunderbolts arrived, intent on halting the enemy drive.

Both sides had a grandstand view as the evening turned into day. A Soviet Katyusha round struck the rearmost Thunderbolt, transforming the aircraft into ten thousand pieces of nothingness, all surrounded by a huge orange fireball that slowly burned itself out.

The ground attack was totally ineffective and the two survivors left the field, the leader smoking badly, his engine knocked about by machine-gun fire from the ground.

The two legion units continued to gradually fold back, giving ground, but staying ahead of the enemy advance. The ex-SS soldiers did not give battle, but also ensured the Soviets did not fall out of contact either. It was a skilled withdrawal, designed for a higher purpose.

By the time that midnight brought the new day, 19th Army had been able to report success, already through and beyond the Illkirch-Graffenstaden line, and fighting inside Molsheim.

Other forces were secure on the banks of the Rhine, mirroring the advance southwards, but with next to no opposition.

There was a party atmosphere in 3rd Red Banner's Headquarters, the supposedly mighty ex-SS units so obviously badly hurt by Plan Berkut. The euphoric mood had quickly found its way to Zhukov's own headquarters, where a map of Alsace reflected 3rd Red Banner's breathtaking advance into Alsace.

2159hrs, Tuesday, 23rd October 1945, Overlooking Route 1420, Bruderthal, the Vosges, Alsace.

They had heard the rumbles, instinctively knowing what was causing it. Their leader remembered the soldier's age-old maxim.

'Head towards the sound of the guns.'

So they had done so, all of a sudden inspired by the possibility of release from the burden of their circumstances.

The handful of men, survivors of the Zilant assault on the Chateau du Haut-Kœnigsbourg, had stopped for the night, slipping into a hollow covered with fallen tree trunks on the Holzplatz, a piece of higher ground some three hundred metres south of Route 854, and the adjacent watercourse, Le Kirnech.

A double watch had been set, as the small party had been aware of the sounds of an army on the march throughout the Vosges.

Indeed, on their journey to their present hiding place, a number of patrols had forced them to take cover, slowing their progress.

Makarenko, his uniform unrecognisable as that of a Soviet Paratrooper General, took first watch with Nikitin, their eyes enjoying the site of explosives illuminating the undersides of the clouds, and understanding how it meant that salvation was close at hand.

He stretched and yawned quietly, and then froze.

A match flared, probably over a hundred metres away, but none the less, Makarenko realised he had chosen a spot dangerously close to a concealed enemy position.

He debated for a moment, and then chose to withdraw.

Makarenko threw a small piece of wood at Nikitin, gaining the soldier's attention, and using rapid hand movements to inform him of the threat.

The young sniper moved quickly through the mass of bodies, waking them up, before dropping by Makarenko's side.

398

"Everyone is awake and ready, Comrade General."

Even though Nikitin's whispered words would not have woken a light sleeper next to him, the words seemed intolerably loud to Makarenko, a man who had brought his unit a long way, too far to see them fail at the final hour.

Makarenko led his men away, moving to the northwest, putting distance between them and the unknown sentry.

Nakhimov led the way, the small column moving in single file, until a raised clenched fist brought them all to an immediate halt.

Senior Sergeant Egon Nakhimov did not recognise the gaudy emblem on the wet metal, but he certainly understood that, but for the flash of Soviet artillery, he would have walked the entire group into the perimeter of a parked Tiger tank unit.

The paratroopers moved backwards slowly, moving away from the Panzers, not knowing that they had found part of 'Tannenberg' secreted in the valley, waiting to implement Operation Thermopylae.

0415hrs, Wednesday, 24th October 1945, Benfeld, Alsace.

Fig #63 - The Locations of Operation Thermopylae, Alsace.

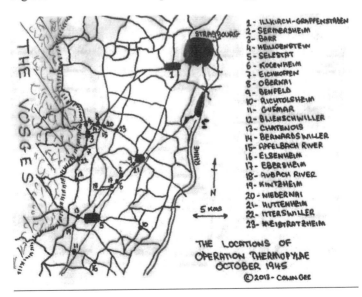

Lieutenant Colonel Blagoslavov was not impressed, despite the gains his unit was making.

It was too expensive, both in consumables, and in manpower, seven of his tanks already lying behind him, five of the crews awaiting recovery by those who dealt with the menial task of extracting the shattered bodies and performing the subsequent burial.

Enemy artillery fire was ineffective, surprisingly so, an indication that his own artillery and rocket batteries had been successful above expectations.

However, as always, the German mortars made up for it. No matter what uniforms they wore, these men were Germans, and they were masters of the mortar.

Thirty minutes ago, Blagoslavov had been listening to the bitter complaints of a Starshy Lieutenant, the new senior officer in his SMG Company. The previous commander, an experienced Captain, lay bleeding in an aid post on the side of the Route de Sélestat, south of Sand, his body sundered by mortar shrapnel.

Now, that same Lieutenant was waiting for the arrival of a burial detail, his life taken by the same damned mortars that had claimed nearly half of the company he led.

Blagoslavov's 110th Tank Regiment, of the 38th Guards Heavy Tank Brigade, was presently halted within Benfeld, whilst their comrades of the 18th Rifle Division ousted the defenders of Huttenheim ahead.

132nd Rifle Corps had the lead at this stage, supported by Blagoslavov's 38th Brigade, and was making good going, despite the occasional solid pocket of resistance, such as was being offered in the small village of Huttenheim.

They had been promised that the defence would not stick, and, so far, the promises had held.

The radio next to him burst into life, the Brigade commander informing all his sub-units that Huttenheim had been cleared, and that the advance was to continue.

Engines roared as the T34's and IS-II's moved forward once more, eating up the kilometre between them and the new front line.

The 38th was, by the simple factor of availability, mixed medium and heavy tanks, the supply of replacements limited by factors beyond Blagoslavov's control. His protests on the additional complication to his logistics were swiftly dismissed by senior officers, who clearly knew something he didn't.

The Soviet tanks approached Huttenheim.

The signs of a swift and desperate fight were everywhere. Buildings and vehicles burned, their flames illuminating the bodies of comrades and enemy alike, lying where they fell, the whole hellish scene mixed with the cries of those in the extremes of pain.

The deputy commander of the 424th Rifle Regiment waved the tanks through, the survivors of Blagoslavov's SMG Company clinging to their sides, as they rattled on towards Sermersheim.

Behind them came the mobile companies of the 424th's 1st Battalion, ready to debus, and put in an infantry assault on any obstacle.

Encountering no resistance, the column moved on through Sermersheim, and on to Kogenheim.

The night slowly gave way to the day.

Blagoslavov halted his lead tank battalion on the outskirts of Kogenheim, permitting his SMG infantry to move through the village. His second battalion shook out to the right flank, protecting the whole force. The 3rd Battalion stayed back, ready to act as a reserve force if things started to come alive again. While his men carried out their orders, the Colonel's own gaze fell upon the shattered bridge over the Ill River, yet another example of the destruction of anything useful, carried out as the enemy force retreated.

Overhead, a flight of Shturmoviks headed south, a sign that the sky did not belong to the Allied air force that day.

His orders required him to wait in Kogenheim, allowing other units to arrive and deploy westwards, using Route 203 to protect the flank of the assault force. Their objective was the village of Blienschwiller, at the mouth of one of the passes into the Vosges.

All along the route of advance, other units were similarly tasked and some, if not all, had encountered resistance from dug-in enemy guns and infantry, supported by mines and artillery.

The Tank Colonel chose to question his orders, conscious that a delay in following the retreating enemy might permit them time to re-establish themselves.

Major General Konovalov, commander of the 38th, agreed, and sanctioned the premature advance.

110th Guards Heavy Tank Regiment moved forward again.

0701hrs, Thursday, 25th October, 1945, overlooking Legion frontline position on the Aubach River, Alsace.

Fig #64 - The Aubach River, south of Ebersheim, Alsace.

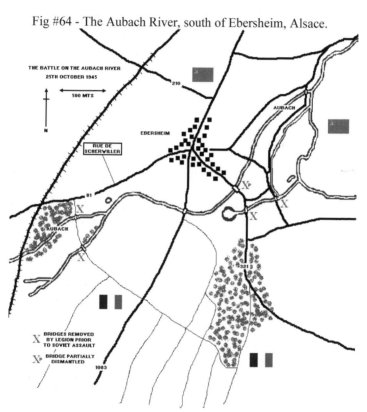

"Steady, mes amis, steady."

Some of the infantry force covering the anti-tank guns seemed disturbed, and Colonel St.Clair moved among them calmly, doing what good officers do.

'Alma' had suffered over the weeks since the division had first been committed, but the unit had shown it was

402

dependable, which was why Lavalle and Knocke had chosen it for the first major defensive action.

Reduced in size by losing the 5th RdM to 'Camerone', 'Alma' was more of a large brigade than a division, but had been punching above its weight since the start of the Soviet offensive.

The Alma's new commander, Celestin St.Clair, stood with the commander of the special anti-tank company, upon whom, much depended.

The anti-tank guns were positioned one and a half kilometres behind the River Aubach, silently awaiting the order to fire.

A stand was called for in the plan, and Alma was about to make it.

0711hrs, Thursday, 25th October 1945, Ebersheim, Alsace.

Lieutenant Colonel Blagoslavov groggily dismounted from his tank, blood pouring from his mouth.

A young girl had run out from her hiding place in Ebersheim, causing the driver to brake suddenly.

As Blagoslavov hit the cupola, face first, one of the SMG troopers had shot the child down, for fear that she had a grenade in her hand.

The crew of the command tank rallied to their officer, sitting him down, and pressing a dressing to his face.

One of the infantry unit's medics appeared and took command, the elderly man deftly removing some shattered teeth, before preparing to stitch the nasty wound.

The needle worked quickly, pulling together the split flesh. Blagoslovov winced, but held firm, the pain almost unbearable.

Major Svir, commander of the 1st Tank Battalion, quickly assumed temporary command whilst Blagoslovov was being attended to, extending the infantry cordon to the edge of the village, and pushing his tanks beyond it to the banks of the Aubach.

0712hrs, Thursday, 25th October, 1945, overlooking Legion frontline position on the Aubach River, Alsace.

This place had been chosen for a number of reasons; the river, the terrain, the open killing ground. The positioning of the guns had been decided days beforehand, but still, to the Legion Officer, the distance seemed too great.

"Are you sure you can kill then from here, Capitan Bäcker?"

"Ja, these are no ordinary guns, Colonel."

And they weren't, certainly not to look at, if nothing else.

Despite their low profile, the four weapons were still larger than any anti-tank gun St.Clair had ever seen, and he quietly thanked his maker that he had not chosen tanks as an Army career.

"Standby, Capitan."

"All guns, standby," the anti-tank officer spoke softly into the mouthpiece, even though the nearest enemy was nearly two kilometres away.

"You think, when the rear one is level with that tree, Capitan Bäcker? This is your business, after all."

The former SS Hauptsturmfuhrer grunted in response, waiting calmly, assessing ranges and angles, like the veteran he was. Bäcker was an anti-tank specialist; a brilliant training officer from the Beneschau SS-Panzer-Jäger Schule, a man who had earned his spurs on the Russian steppes in charge of a 50mm Pak 38 outside of Moscow.

For this battle, he had a very different weapon at his disposal.

There were four of the monsters, two either side of Route 1083, defending the approaches to Selestat.

St.Clair almost forgot himself, the rearmost IS-II slipping past the marker tree.

"Tirez!"

The experienced Foreign Legion officer wasn't sure what he had expected, but he was sure he didn't expect the huge explosion that followed, as the adjacent anti-tank gun sent its heavy shell down range.

Representing the last of Germany's anti-tank weapon development, the 128mm PAK K44 was a beast. Huge and unmaneuverable though it was, the punch it possessed ruled the

404

battlefield, and it could reach out to nearly three kilometres, killing with relative impunity.

Three of the four shells struck home, each of the heavy IS-II's succumbing to the irresistible force of the PAK's huge shell.

Fig #65 - Trap on the Aubach River, south of Ebersheim, Alsace.

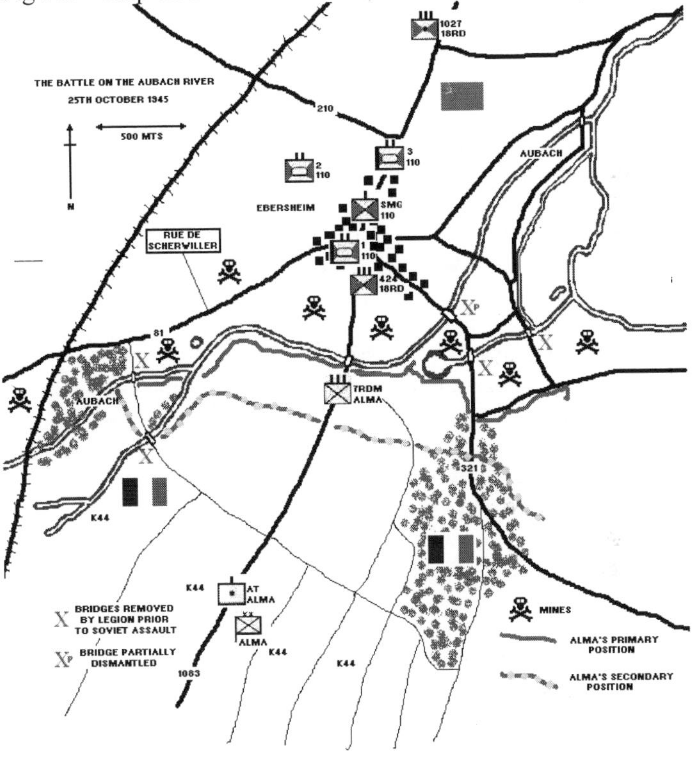

THE BATTLE ON THE AUBACH RIVER
25TH OCTOBER 1945
500 MTS
N
1027
18RD
210
3
110
2
110
EBERSHEIM
SMG
110
RUE DE
SCHERWILLER
1
110
424
18RD
AUBACH
81
7RDM
ALMA
AUBACH
321
K44
K44
AT
ALMA
ALMA
K44
K44
1083
BRIDGES REMOVED
BY LEGION PRIOR
TO SOVIET ASSAULT
BRIDGE PARTIALLY
DISMANTLED
MINES
ALMA'S PRIMARY
POSITION
ALMA'S SECONDARY
POSITION

<u>0715hrs, Thursday, 25th October 1945, Ebersheim, Alsace.</u>

A low moan escaped Blagoslavov, slightly muffled by his bandaging.

All eyes had swivelled at the sound of explosions, the heavy crack of a supremely dangerous weapon arriving sometime after the tanks had been struck and killed.

Major Svir was dead, his IS-II sat turretless, already wreathed in flames. The turret had struck the building behind, demolishing it, bringing down a cascade of brick and wood to engulf the hot metal and its softer human contents.

Another IS-II sat smoking gently, its surviving crew staggering around behind it, badly concussed, and shocked by the heavy strike.

A third heavy tank showed no outward sign of damage, but its loss was betrayed by the bloodied figure emerging from the turret, his one good arm working in unison with the stump of the other, desperate to escape the horrors of the interior.

The remaining tanks were moving at top speed, their commanders desperately trying to find some cover; any place to hide from the lethal killers.

Two failed spectacularly.

The first exploded in a fireball, a shell taking it through the side just below the turret ring.

The second did not burn, neither did it explode, but it was no less spectacular watching a tank of some forty-five tons simply come apart at the seams, as two 128mm shells struck simultaneously.

Climbing onto his command tank, Blagoslavov tried to broadcast to his unit commanders, the tightness of the bandaging preventing the attempt.

He ripped away at the linen, exposing his wounds to the air again, desperate to call in orders to stop the destruction of his command.

The second circuit was alive with requests for information, requests that became more strident with each extra Legion volley.

His voice failed him, his split tongue swollen in his mouth, the bruising to his face and mouth preventing the clarity he so needed.

One of 1st Battalion's IS-II's had made it to safety.

Just one.

Of the rest, all fourteen were destroyed, and not one shot had been fired at their killers, wherever they were.

Lacking orders, 2nd and 3rd Battalions moved up to assist their comrades, and immediately, the lighter T34's of 2nd Battalion started to be smashed apart.

Pointing, and making urgent sounds, Blagoslavov managed to make the gunner understand that he needed the tank to move over to the 2nd's position.

The IS-II moved off, the driver choosing the route that placed a row of buildings between him and whatever they were out there.

The command tank halted behind a pretty bungalow, totally concealed and safe, the agitated Blagoslavov immediately dismounting and running to the 2nd Battalion commander's tank.

0720hrs, Thursday, 25th October, 1945, overlooking Legion frontline position on the Aubach River, Alsace.

Captain Bäcker chuckled to himself.

"Watch this, Colonel. A party trick."

Turning to the nearest gun, he shouted at the commander.

"Wagner, heavy charge."

Moving to the gun layer's position, Bäcker slapped the Corporal on the shoulder and replaced him, leaning out from behind the gun shield to quickly check his bearings.

The gun was cleared ready, and Bäcker sighted the weapon on the quaint bungalow.

Careful to remove his face from the sight mount, he fired the weapon, leaning out once more to watch his handiwork.

The building stood, apparently undamaged.

Beyond it, the 128mm shell had slammed into Blagoslavov's tank.

The Soviet tank Colonel turned, watching the flames engulf his vehicle, the combination of shell and fire leaving him the only survivor.

Observed from the Pak position, the column of smoke indicated Bäcker's success.

Relinquishing the seat to the gun layer, the Panzer-Jäger commander resumed his previous position, surveying his handiwork more closely with his Zeiss binoculars.

"Impressive, Capitan Bäcker, very impressive."

The officer nodded thoughtfully.

"And now we must relocate, Sir. I don't think they've seen us yet, but I want to move anyway."

Turning back to the anti-tank crew, he yelled his order.

"Achtung! Relocate to position Bruno immediately."

The order was relayed to the other three guns, and the line fell silent as they prepared to move off. The accompanying mortar section put down their smoke, as arranged.

<u>0724hrs, Thursday, 25th October 1945, Ebersheim, Alsace.</u>

The dismounted infantry of the 424th moved quickly forward, believing they were charging whatever it was that had destroyed the tank battalion.

The waiting legionnaires of 'Alma' let them come on, waiting silently in their prepared positions, luring their enemy into the killing ground on the banks of the Aubach.

The low cracks started, the Soviet infantry setting off mines as they ran. Men went down, holding shattered legs and feet, the small mines doing no more than maiming, but doing so in numbers.

Then the defensive line opened fire, machine-guns and rifles filling the air with buzzing metal, angry wasps with a deadly sting.

Still they came on, growing smaller in number every second, until the order was given and they dropped to the ground, hugging Mother Earth for all they were worth.

Two batteries of the Legion Group D'Artillerie then brought down a barrage upon both emasculated companies, one battery firing the standard LeFH 105mm, the other the more spectacular Nebelwerfer.

It proved too much for the 424th, and the survivors retreated, ending up back where they had started, but with over a hundred casualties.

Other companies from the 424th started to arrive, and another infantry assault was put in over the Route 321 Bridge, shaping to turn the flank of the defending legionnaires.

It had been partially dismantled by legion engineers, prior to the arrival of the Soviet forces, but still the guardsmen threw themselves at the standing piles and remaining cross-members, swinging across as best they could.

The six-barrelled Nebelwerfers, reloaded after Soviet counter-battery fire from the 1027th Artillery Regiment had caused casualties amongst the crews, brought down a full strike on the assault force, and the arrival of accurate Legion heavy mortar fire again caused the 424th to falter.

Blagoslavov, his misery added to by a painful cut from a piece of flying glass, commandeered the tank belonging to the 2nd Tank Battalion's third officer.

2nd Tank Battalion drove hard up the Route de Scherwiller, angling away from the Aubach defences, looking for an advantage against the 'Alma's' left flank.

One of his leading tanks stopped, and he watched as the turret swung.

Assessing the aiming point, the covering smoke screen opened up by a sudden stiff breeze, Blagoslavov finally got a look at one of his tormentor's, the huge anti-tank gun bouncing along behind a German half-track as it tried to relocate.

With difficulty, he communicated his orders to the gunner, the turret eventually turning to engage the distant vehicle.

A number of shells had already been fired at the beast, but none had come close to scoring a hit, so far away and fast was it moving.

The Artillery liaison officer with the 110th Tanks calmly called it in, knowing he needed to state the coordinates of where the PAK would be, not where it was now.

His efforts were rewarded, and the 122mm's of the 1027th Artillery smashed both the gun and prime mover in their second volley.

Enemy artillery was now dropping smoke rounds between their lines and the infantry of the 424th.

'The bastards are going to withdraw!'

Blagoslavov halted his tank again, concealed in a small stand of trees, and quickly scribbled on a pad, communicating his orders to the loader.

Fiddling with the radio, the man contacted 3rd Battalion, and ordered them forward immediately.

From his position on the flank, Blagoslavov could see the enemy infantrymen moving backwards, unmolested by fire from Ebersheim, their escape concealed by the smoke barrage.

However, the smoke did not prevent 2nd Battalion's tanks from seeing the movement, and a number of vehicles started to engage the legionnaires with high explosives and machine-guns.

The mass of men suddenly went to ground.

3rd Battalion's tanks, sporting grapes of infantry, rushed forward into the smoke, intent on running down the retreating men.

Emerging from the smokescreen, they were puzzled to find an empty landscape, not the target-rich environment that they had anticipated.

Beneath the metal tracks, the small anti-personnel mines started to detonate, with no effect.

The mass of tanks converged on the two bridges over the Aubach.

0742hrs, Thursday, 25th October, 1945, overlooking Legion secondary position 'Bruno', the Aubach River, Alsace.

"Right about now."

St.Clair judged the moment almost perfectly, the flash of exploding mines filling his binoculars less than two seconds after his words.

He watched as the trap was sprung, enemy heavy and medium tanks rolling over anti-tank mines, shattering tracks and bogies, and coming to an enforced halt in an extremely dangerous environment.

"Wait."

Grudgingly, he recognised the courage of the enemy soldiers, watching as the infantry grapes dismounted and rushed forward, intent on securing the bridges, as well as covering the tankers while they worked on repairs.

Men were bowled over as the deadly anti-personnel mines in the third layer started their harvest, linked combinations, and strings of all shapes and sizes of mine inflicting heavy casualties on the running men.

"Fire!"

Behind Colonel St.Clair, two radiomen spoke into their mouthpieces, passing his order to the waiting units.

Legion mortarmen filled the sky with bombs, intent on smashing the infantry force.

The heavy anti-tank guns, now in their secondary positions, started working the crippled vehicles, enjoying the turkey shoot.

Soldiers from 'Alma', whose feigned 'retreat' had started the planned trap, rose up out of their second line positions, and ripped more holes in the ranks of the advancing Soviet infantry.

St.Clair watched the destruction of the Soviet assault force with a professional eye, revelling in his contribution to the plan that had delivered the enemy up, although a small part of him felt sympathy for the men who were being destroyed in front of his eyes.

As a soldier of France, most of him enjoyed the sight of the invaders being vanquished so totally. As an officer, and commander, he felt immense pride in the discipline and expertise of his men, regardless of its lineage.

The crack of high-velocity weapons to the west drew him momentarily, but the sight of two T34's starting to burn confirmed that his left flank was secure.

0744hrs, Thursday, 25th October, 1945, Route de Scherwiller, Ebersheim, Alsace.

Blagoslavov ripped off his bandages, tearing his stitches, his anger driving him through the pain, just as if it was not there.

Ordering his own artillery to set down smoke, he attempted to extricate what was left of his command.

3rd Battalion was in real trouble, with its leadership gone, and its vehicles mainly immobilised, either by mines or by fear.

2nd Battalion had been stopped by enemy tanks, positioned west of the Route de Scherwiller. In any case, moving further up that route was pointless, with the main body being butchered behind him on the outskirts of Ebersheim.

The men of the 424th were dying in droves as mines, mortars and machine-guns gave them a working over, an examination the like of which none of the Soviet veterans had experienced before.

Lieutenant Colonel Blagoslavov ordered his unit to fall back, knowing that he was condemning some of those lying immobilised, but knowing that he needed to save as many of his men as he could.

Acknowledging an incoming message from Major General Konovalov, and warning the 38th's commander not to proceed too far forward, Blagoslavov prepared to move his own tank to safety.

The 2nd Battalion had enjoyed a success against their tormentors, and one of the enemy vehicles on their flank had been set alight by direct hits.

The mix of T34's and IS-II's pulled back, making the edge of Ebersheim with only one more loss.

Smoke from the Soviet barrage had drifted on the wind, helping to mask 2nd Battalion's withdrawal, and Blagoslavov also used it to cover his own drive back to the relative safety of the German village.

The survivors of the main thrust started to appear, a man here, three there, a tank moving at high speed, jinking from side to side to escape the enemy guns that still fired across the smoky divide.

Returning his borrowed tank to the normal commander, Blagoslavov started the job of reassembling his shattered regiment.

2nd Battalion was still relatively intact, fifteen vehicles ready to move on orders. 1st Battalion now had three tanks up and running, testament to the skill of his mechanical engineers.

3rd Battalion had seven tanks back in the village, probably more still marooned in the minefield beyond.

By any standards, he had suffered a defeat, the loss of over thirty tanks in one engagement only surpassed by the horrendous casualties inflicted upon his SMG troops, and the infantry of the 424th.

In return, he could claim one enemy armoured vehicle and one anti-tank gun, as well as numerous infantry.

Setting up a headquarters at the Mairie, Blagoslavov liaised with the senior officer of the 424th, the wounded Major seemingly still in shock from the losses inflicted upon his battalions.

The infantry could do nothing more than hold in place for now, so shattered were they, and the tank officer doubted that they would manage that, if pressed hard by the enemy.

The pain was starting to return, his jaw working overtime issuing orders to hard-pressed tank officers, trying to pull his unit back into some kind of order.

A small column of vehicles drew up in the Rue Principale, and an irate Konovalov emerged, determined to salvage the situation.

There were no niceties or formalities.

412

"What the fuck has happened here, PodPolkovnik?"

Expecting nothing less from his commander, Blagoslavov started drawing on the map, showing enemy lines, routes of advance, describing the attack in sufficient detail for Konovalov to understand exactly 'what the fuck' had happened.

"And your Regiment? How much is left?"

"At this time, I have twenty-five vehicles, Comrade General, fourteen IS and eleven Tridsat's, with maybe another five to come after repair."

"And the infantry?"

"I've no longer an SMG company of note. Perhaps a platoon of men left standing, but I don't think they're fit to fight at the moment, Comrade General."

Konovalov understood.

"The 424th is reorganising for defence at this time. Mayor Din informs me that he can muster three companies of men in total, Comrade General."

The commander of the 38th Tanks winced, understanding that each supporting battalion had been reduced to a company, and that such news represented appalling casualties.

"What else have you done?"

"The artillery is hitting the last known enemy positions. I have requested release of the mortar brigade to my control, and await the answer."

"I have your answer, and we must do without them, for now."

The men exchanged looks, the Lieutenant Colonel because he was disgusted not to get the support he needed, the General because he understood the man's disgust, and also because he understood that Blagoslavov had done the best he could, in the circumstances.

"Go on, Panteleimon Tarasovich, what else?"

The use of the patronymic was not wasted on Blagoslavov, and he knew he was no longer in danger.

"All units are being reorganised as we speak, and I've ordered up supplies and more medical personnel to deal with the large number of wounded."

Words were obviously becoming more difficult, the swelling more pronounced, the pain increasing.

"Comrade PodPolkovnik, I am moving the 108th up to take over the van. Our comrades from the 419th Rifles will take over from Din's men."

Grabbing the map, and twisting it round to face him, Konovalov showed the wounded tanker his next assignment.

"Once they pass through your positions, I want you to move back here, to Barr and Eichhoffen. Get your units rested, Comrade. We need a security screen on our flanks. The valley entrances are heavily mined, and Army engineers will be coming up to open them up ready. There are light enemy defences, some guns and infantry, but nothing major in place. You shouldn't have any problems, Comrade."

"Yes, Sir."

In a softer voice, Konovalov offered his support.

"This was obviously prepared, and you were the unfortunate one that walked into it, Comrade Blagoslavov. You saved half your unit from the SS bastards, remember?"

'I lost half, you mean!'

"Now, get your men ready for the move. The Rifle Corps has detached 424th to your command until further notice. Make sure your tank repair unit is ready to salvage what it can, after we have pushed the Germanski Legion back."

Slapping Blagoslavov on the shoulder, Konovalov ended the meeting.

"Now, go and get your own wounds seen to, Comrade PodPolkovnik."

Konovalov took personal charge of the next assault. A handful of men were lost to mines, a few more when the damaged bridges disintegrated within seconds of each other, command detonated by some Legion demolition engineers.

Rokossovsky had dedicated some of his precious bridging engineers to the assault, and they made short work of erecting something to carry the IS-II's of the 108th Guards Heavy Tank Regiment.

Launching an attack over the Aubach, the Soviet force met with no resistance.

The Legion had withdrawn again.

414

Unfortunately, this earth is not a fairyland, but a struggle for life, perfectly natural and therefore extremely harsh.

Martin Bormann

Chapter 96 - THE TIGERS

3RD RED BANNER CENTRAL EUROPEAN FRONT - MARSHAL ROKOSSOVSKY

1307hrs, Thursday, 25th October, 1945, Headquarters of Mobile Group Blagoslavov, Hotel le Manoir, Barr, Alsace.

Rather surprisingly, the pain in his face had subsided to a constant dull ache.

The proper dressing, completed in a less pressurised environment, may well have helped. Certainly the painkillers pressed into his hand by the medics did, although Blagoslavov himself suspected that the vodka had been the greater measure.

The move north-west had been done quickly and efficiently, the ravaged units settling in at Barr and Eichoffen in record time, both villages relatively untouched by the two wars that had rolled over them.

Quickly, he directed his units into rough defensive positions, and set his officers to the task of reorganising the shattered regiment.

His second in command returned to the small square, the smug look betraying the man, and that his search for somewhere appropriate to house the regimental headquarters had been more than successful.

Le Manoir was an imposing manor house set in its own grounds, and the splendour and sophistication of the interior was the precise opposite of everything that the tank officer had experienced over the last two and a bit months.

Within two minutes, the exhausted Blagoslavov was snoring louder than one of his tanks at maximum revs.

Infantry from the 409th Rifle Regiment had cleared much of the woods, three kilometres north of Guémar, a handful of snipers lashing out, particularly at the officers, before melting away into the greenery and, all save one, escaping unharmed.

That one had received over two hundred puncture wounds, as the distraught platoon members avenged their dead Lieutenant, shot by the sniper they subsequently wounded, captured and bayoneted to death.

Moving up Route D1083 behind them came the 108th Guards Tank's, confident and self-assured, their fight so different to that of the 110th.

Elements of the 109th Tanks moved towards Heidolsheim to the east, one battalion moved westwards to secure Châtenois and Kintzheim.

132nd Rifle Corps provided the infantry strength, closely backed up by the 134th Rifle Corps, its fresh divisions being kept in hand, ready for the assault on Colmar. Behind that came the most powerful unit of the 19th Army, namely the 3rd Guards Tank Corps.

The 3rd GTC had already seen some action, and had acquitted itself well. Now, or at least that was how it seemed to the jubilant tankers, the enemy line was nearly broken, and one more push would be enough for the whole front to open up before them.

The reports had been filtering through to the command centre of 'Normandie', some routine, some not, and yet more providing vital ticks on the battle plan called 'Thermopylae'.

Lavalle silently enjoyed his coffee.

It was not yet time.

The sleep had only been brief, and Blagoslavov felt groggy. He pulled his tunic on, doing up the buttons, the aches

416

and pains of such simple tasks making him feel old before his time.

Once he was presentable, he permitted the regimental clerk to bring in the papers for his signature.

Coffee was presented to him as he worked, and that also helped to bring him more into a land of consciousness.

The paperwork complete, Blagoslavov decided to visit his positions facing the Vosges, just to make sure there was no possibility of his command catching a cold.

Plus, as he had just learned, two full companies of engineers from the 12th Engineer-Sapper Brigade had been assigned to sweep the entrances of the passes under his responsibility.

Climbing gingerly out of the Gaz 4x4 he had scrounged for his command vehicle, Blagoslavov took in the sights.

Some of his T34's and IS-II's were in hull-down positions, not easily spotted, even from his perspective.

Others were even harder to spot, the only betraying factor being a gun barrel here, a small plume of engine exhaust there.

He made his way over to an engineer officer. The man was using an oil drum as his work desk, recording details of his engineer's surveys.

He was startled by the appearance of the tank unit's commanding officer, springing to attention and dropping his pencils in the same rapid movement.

"No ceremony here, Comrade Kapitan. Blagoslavov, 110th Guards Tanks. How is your progress?"

"Comrade PodPolkovnik, Kapitan Esher, 12th Sapper Brigade. We are mapping the enemy minefields now. I have two platoons already working," he turned the map to share the information, "On the Altenburg road here. The main road is heavily mined; very nasty."

"Nasty, Comrade Kapitan?"

"Yes Sir. They have booby-trapped mines, placing grenades under them, linking chains of them, mixing types."

Clearly, the Engineer officer was not content.

"There are mine types there that my men haven't seen before. It's all very nasty, Comrade PodPolkovnik."

417

Blagoslavov was certainly glad that his normal enemy was a large lump of self-propelled metal, and did not envy the engineer his problems.

"Are you in contact with your unit at Eichoffen, Comrade Kapitan?"

"Yes, Comrade. It is the same for them. They have lost three men on the booby traps already."

A muddy Lieutenant arrived and saluted both officers casually, his mind clearly on other matters.

"So what have you established, Georgi?"

Junior Lieutenant Georgi Harazan spread his own map out, next to his commanders.

"Very strange, Comrade Kapitan. As you can see, the enemy has sown everything up tight. Lots of problems throughout, until you come to here."

Blagoslavov leant forward to see what the problem was.

'Rue D'Altenberg?'

"There are no problems here, Comrade Kapitan."

"None?"

"That road is open, and there is a free zone at least six metres either side of the roadway, Comrade Kapitan."

Esher and Blagoslavov exchanged knowing looks.

The tank officer took up the running.

"Comrade Mladshy Leytenant. Are you positive that this road has been left clear by the enemy?"

"Yes Sir, positive. There are no mines, devices, nothing."

Esher and Blagoslavov spoke at the same time.

"Job tvoyu mat!"

"Mudaks!"

The young Lieutenant was surprised at the reaction his news provoked.

"Get your men ready, Comrade Kapitan. We'll stop them here," he tapped the Engineer's map, "Or there'll be hell for us all!"

The tank officer ran to his command vehicle and it raced away, the senior officer already shouting into the radio set.

Harazan was confused.

A clipped order brought the radio into life, the Captain issuing brief instructions to his platoon commanders.

Esher had his binoculars out as he spoke, quickly sweeping the Vosges, seeing threat in every shadow.

"Comrade Kapitan. What's happening?"

The radio dispensed with, Esher spared the junior man a moment.

"Georgi Illiych, if the enemy's left a gap, it's not by accident."

The look on Harazan's face showed his failure to comprehend the problem.

"The gap is there for a reason, and that can only mean something very bad."

Now the young officer understood.

"Get back to your men and organise them with the infantry for now. If you can, get some of the lifted mines down on that route. Stay on the net, Comrade."

The Lieutenant's reply went unheard.

At the same time as Esher had explained to the confused young man, the final piece of the jigsaw puzzle slotted into place in the 'Normandie' headquarters.

Lavalle took a moment's pause before issuing the expected order to the waiting signallers.

"All units, Spartan, repeat Spartan."

1501hrs, Thursday, 25th October 1945, the Alsatian Plain.

Unlike Blagoslavov, the Legion observers on the High Vosges above Barr had noted precisely where the tanks had secreted themselves, and the information had already been passed to the waiting artillery, and other units.

On receipt of the codeword 'Spartan', Operation Thermopylae swung into action, and the destruction of the 19th Army commenced.

'Thermopylae' was a thing of simple beauty, enabled by the Soviet attempt to control Knocke, and the GRU's belief in his continued support.

That condemned 19th Army to drive on a small frontage into a funnel, one side lined by the Rhine and her tributaries, the other by the imposing Vosges.

419

Knocke's information tailored perfectly with Soviet expectations, or so it seemed.

The valleys would be mined, and that proved to be the case.

The valleys would be defended by infantry and anti-tank guns with artillery support, which Soviet patrolling had confirmed.

The Legion units would fall back in front of 19th Army, all the way to Colmar, and had done so at first, the blip at Ebersheim designed to bunch the Soviet formations up and ensure that sufficient time was available to prepare the welcome south of Selestat.

And then, it all went wrong for 19th Army.

Fig #66 - The ambush of Soviet 19th Army, Operation Thermopylae, Alsace.

Mortars flayed the Soviet infantry in the woods, north of Guémar, high explosive filling the air with metal fragments and wood splinters, as airbursts cut down scores of men.

Tanks waiting on Route 1083 found themselves under attack from special tank-hunting teams. Men from 'Alma' and

Kommando Alsace, experienced with panzerfausts and anti-tank mine, caused huge casualties amongst the waiting 108th Guards Tank Regiment.

Artillery, targeted by observers that had sat patiently on the hill tops, sought out, and neutralised, many of the defensive positions that had been set up to protect the Vosges valleys.

Small groups of volunteers from the 'Lorraine' and 'Aquitaine' Command Groups had remained within Selestat and other places on the main road network, emerging on receipt of the codeword, causing havoc amongst the units that were bunched up on the plain.

Most Allied tanks had lain silent, engines off, the need for secrecy overcoming normal routine. The Legion commanders accepted the risk, balancing cold engines, and the accompanying issues, with the excellent maintenance routine that was put in place as the force lay in wait for the enemy.

The 16th US Armored Brigade flooded out from the Aubach River Valley, and that at Blienschwiller, and overwhelmed the few units posted there.

Pierce was in his element, and he intended to pay the Commies back for the ignominy visited upon his division in the early days of the conflict.

Above the 16th Armored, at Itterswiller and Eichoffen, the larger grouping of 'Camerone' hammered into the Soviet screen, overrunning Eichoffen in a matter of minutes.

The bulk of 'Tannenberg' emerged from the Lauterbach, and made immediate inroads into the columns of Soviet rear-line troops, laid out before the advancing legionnaires, who found the logistical support units nose to tail on the Alsatian roads.

And then, there was Barr.

1501hrs, Thursday, 25th October 1945, Mobile Group
Blagoslavov, Barr, Alsace.

A mix of 75mm and 105mm shells fell around the defenders of Barr, killing and maiming indiscriminately.

Soviet tank crews in their hull down positions, supposedly hidden from the enemy, died in their steel coffins, as superbly targeted artillery shells crashed through tender top armour.

Some tanks were not struck directly, but the constant hammers of concussion were sufficient to kill or incapacitate the crew, and remove the vehicle from the battle.

Kapitan Esher lay silent, unable to speak or move, shock and blood loss already prevailing, the combination condemning him to a lonely death in an Alsatian shell hole.

Junior Lieutenant Harazan had two pieces of shrapnel in his buttocks, but hardly noticed, as he ran back to command his engineer platoon on the road out of the Vosges.

Major Din was screaming into a silent radio, trying to contact anyone, not realising that the fragments that had killed the operator had also destroyed the vital parts of his communications equipment.

Lieutenant Colonel Blagoslavov had alerted his command, and was now calling for reinforcements, unaware that he was not alone in his situation, and that all along the Alsatian Plain, Soviet units were in big trouble.

As with all the valley exits, it was essential to Legion planning, that the counter-attack force secured the non-mined lanes and broke out quickly.

It was only at Barr that this did not go according to plan.

One of the 424th's surviving anti-tank guns could sight on the exit on the Altenberg, a gun that had not been identified by the spotters on the heights.

The lead Allied tank took a hit that fractured the nearside track, the heavy metal spilling uselessly off its runners. The vehicle, a Tiger I that had once accompanied Wittman into the field in Normandy, attempted to manoeuvre on one track, the expert driver working wonders, gaining room for the following vehicles to pass.

The 88mm gun swivelled, seeking out its tormentor, before the crew realised that death was closer at hand.

Two engineers from Harazan's platoon leapt up to attack the Tiger, each holding a Haft-Hohlladung magnetic mine, of German origin.

The first man looked in vain for a patch of armour without the anti-magnetic zimmerit paste applied. He circled the stationary leviathan and found a bare patch on the rear engine compartment, but was cut down by machine-gun fire before he could stick it to the Tiger.

422

The second man circled the other way and struck lucky, a suitable scab of zimmerit missing on the hull side.

Slamming the mine in place, he tripped the igniter and dove for cover.

As often happened in late war German devices, faulty or deliberately sabotaged equipment went wrong, and, although the mine exploded, the premature blast killed the Soviet engineer too. The tank remained undamaged, and the crew, now aware of the local danger, turned the main turret and hull machine guns, using both to flay likely hiding positions.

A PTRD gunner produced a fluke shot, destroying the barrel of the hull machine-gun, rendering it inoperable.

Four more Tiger tanks moved past their companion, the leader receiving two hits from the 76.2mm anti-tank gun, hits that it shrugged off, the two scars gleaming testament to the ineffectiveness of the Soviet shells.

The next shell to hit the Tiger knocked it out, an IS-II's 122mm penetrating the thickest armour plate adjacent to the driver's position.

As the Legion tank did not burn, the IS-II slammed another huge shell into it, this time with more spectacular results. The 122mm hit the same frontal plate, but two foot to the left, causing the plate section between the two areas to disappear into the tank. It did not matter to the crew, who had all perished with the first shot.

The IS-II relocated, before enemy observers hunted it down.

Harazan leapt from his position, intent on retrieving the unused charge, two of his men leaping and running the other way as a distraction.

It worked, and the turret rotated, the gunner ready to fire as soon as the sights came to bear. Both men were seen by other eyes, and they were forced into cover by fire from the armoured infantry that accompanied the Tigers and Panzer IV's of 5th Legion Regiment du Chars Spéciale.

Junior Lieutenant Harazan dropped out of sight into a gully by the roadside, cover that he now used, scurrying along on all fours, approaching the disabled Tiger unseen.

The 76.2mm anti-tank gun spoke again, its slow rate of fire the result of high-explosive effects upon its crew.

The gun was intact, but the men that served it were the opposite, dead and injured to a man, with only two capable of loading and laying the weapon.

Wiping away the tears of pain, the wounded gunlayer took deliberate aim on the third tank and fired, another track hit disabling the Tiger, reducing further the width of the mine-free trail, down which the 5th and 'Camerone' intended to flow.

Back up the road, one Panzer IV breasted a small ridge, and gained a position on the anti-tank weapon, only to be hammered into submission by the 110th's surviving T34.

The attack was failing, the mines now constricting the Legion force.

The fourth Tiger spotted the IS-II and lashed out, striking the turret, but not penetrating, the huge Soviet tank.

However, the commander dashed his head as the tank rocked, and now lay unconscious on the turret floor. His crew took the opportunity to carry out a hasty withdrawal, in self-reservation, opening up the defence.

The fifth Tiger I had been captured in perfect condition when the Ruhr Pocket surrendered, and had never fired an angry shot. It contained an experienced crew, men once comrades in the 102nd SS Schwere Panzer Abteilung, all captured during the Battle for Hill 112 in Normandy.

The 88m gun cracked, and the Tiger, known as 'Lohengrin', began compiling its legend.

An HE shell struck the gun shield of the anti-tank gun, just to the left of where the layer was deliberating on his next shot. He and his comrade died instantly.

'Lohengrin' moved forward, the sound of tortured metal reaching the ears of Russian and German alike, as it pushed its way between the dead and disabled tanks to its front.

Blagoslavov found the IS-II backed into a wall and stalled, the crew dragging their insensible commander out of the tank to tend his head wound.

Ensuring the wounded old comrade was placed in the hands of some nearby infantry, the 110th's commander mounted the IS-II, and ordered it back into battle.

Approaching a blind corner, Blagoslavov dismounted quickly and ran to check.

Hugging the stonework, he risked a quick look, and was horrified to see a Legion Tiger tank bearing down on his position at speed.

He yelled a warning at his own tank, knowing he had no time to get back onboard, a yell that was understood by the gunner.

'Lohengrin' rattled across the junction, moving from right to left at full speed. The IS-II gunner fired at a range of forty metres, and missed by nearly as much.

The Tiger kept going, and Blagoslavov watched it move on at least two hundred metres, before it turned left, and into the built-up area.

More noise attracted him, and he turned, immediately spotting a number of enemy tanks following the same route.

This time he could remount and fight the IS-II properly.

Climbing aboard, he ordered the driver to round the corner and cut left, using a wall to mask the hull.

The gunner had recovered from his jitters and destroyed the lead Panzer IV with his second shot.

Shells were returned, but none struck the IS-II, missing by metres in all cases.

The Panzer IV's scattered.

Harazan shook his head, trying to overcome the blackness that had overtaken him.

One of his own men had thrown a grenade at the Tiger, not knowing his platoon officer was within the burst.

Temporarily stunned, Harazan found his hearing had also been affected; every sound was muffled.

Rising up from the gully, he nearly lost his balance scaling the side, but he persevered, and found himself less than five metres from the abandoned magnetic mine.

He slid quickly over the ground and picked it up, the growling engine of the disabled tank the only thing he could hear in all the cacophony around him.

Enemy soldiers were twenty metres away, but none had spotted him, so he pushed himself upwards and rammed the magnets onto the rear of the tank, rolling away, and dropping back into the ditch.

The mine exploded, stopping the huge Maybach engines in a second, and starting a modest fire in the engine compartment.

In the rear of the Tiger's turret was a circular hatch, and this opened slowly as the turret turned, enabling those inside to check on the problems with their tank.

The tank commander obviously felt that enough was enough, and the hatch dropped fully open, as the turret rear rotated away from the Soviet line of fire.

Even the hull crew wormed their way through the inside of the Tiger, so all five men escaped through the same circular hatch.

As the last of the Tiger's crew dropped to the ground, Harazan made it back to his own platoon's positions, his wounded buttocks now howling their displeasure at every movement.

Two more Panzer IV's had been knocked out of the fight, although only one had been destroyed, the second one abandoned when its gearbox failed.

Blagoslavov skilfully manoeuvred the IS-II, spotting an eight-wheeled armoured car moving tentatively through the gardens.

Having fired off an AP shell at a large shape the other side of the roadblock of Tiger tanks, the tank officer redirected the loader.

"Load HE for this one. That will be enough for the bastard."

Calling the gunner in on target, Blagoslavov watched in annoyance as the HE shell clipped the angled front cowling, and ploughed into a fairytale house beyond, the explosion instantly transforming it into flying pieces.

"Take it steady, and get it right, Comrade Gunner."

The calm words helped, but the SDKFZ 234 did not intend to remain around to be shot at a second time, and it surged forward, disappearing down an alley. The crew had succeeded in gaining an extra twenty seconds of life, as their vehicle was hunted down quickly. Its end came at the hands of vengeful infantry from Din's 424th, improvising with petrol bombs, which proved very efficient on the open hulled armoured car.

The IS-II did not have a complete shell, rather a warhead and propellant, which had to be loaded separately, thus slowing down the reloading process.

Sensing rather than seeing, Blagoslavov ordered a reverse move, backing the Soviet heavy tank through a ruined house and into the road beyond.

A few seconds later, Legion artillery burst around the former position, testament to the skill of the artillery observers.

The IS-II found itself reversing alongside 'Lohengrin', the two crews only just becoming aware of each other.

"Job tvoyu mat! Germanski tank alongside, right. Driver, halt!"

The IS-II jerked immediately to a rocking halt, and Blagoslavov ordered the driver to rotate on the spot, turning the hull towards the Tiger performing a similar manoeuvre.

It was a race, and one the IS-II won.

The shell misfired, failing to send the warhead at the enemy tank.

Blagoslavov looked from the silent breech to his sights and back, conscious that he was about to die.

'Lohengrin's' 88mm spouted a gout of flame, and a shell was sent on its way, striking the IS-II on the angled front plate and ricocheting upwards, hammering into the barrel from underneath.

Inside the turret, there was mayhem. The impact threw the breech downwards, driving the weapon beyond its design parameters, destroying the trunnions, and causing the misfire to ignite within the now-displaced main gun.

The loose weapon recoiled into the rear wall of the turret, passing through the area that was occupied by the loader, transforming him into indistinct pieces, stuck to the deformed metal of breech and turret.

Horrified, Blagoslavov ordered the driver to put his foot through the floor, and the IS-II sped behind a low building to safety.

The impact had obviously affected the engine, and thick smoke started to mark their movements around the village.

'Lohengrin' hunted them down eventually, but had to content itself with destroying the abandoned tank, as Blagoslavov had ordered them out when the engine gave up.

The IS-II burned spectacularly, setting fire to a number of buildings around it, the fire eventually filling the whole area with acrid smoke suitable for any purpose, be it escape or stealthy approach.

Whilst the 5th Legion Tank Regiment had been badly handled, it had achieved its goals, and the way was opened up.

The 110th Guards Tank Regiment had ceased to exist in all but name, not a single tank on its roster, its strength now lying with the forty men crammed aboard a single GAZ lorry heading north on Route 1422.

The Legion and 16th Armored cut the main highways, isolating the 19th Army units, cutting them into small digestible portions, each of which was overcome in turn, and for little loss.

A momentary rally by the 3rd Guards Tanks, at Obernai and Bernardswiller, enabled much of their Corps to escape, but the resistance was overcome, and 'Tannenberg' cut straight across the Alsatian Plain, securing Obernai, Niedernai and Meistratzheim. Further stout defence by an AA unit attached to 3rd Guards, kept the spearheads at bay long enough for a number of rag-tag units to escape up Route 1083, amongst the last of which was the lorry carrying the survivors of the 110th Guards Tank Regiment.

16th US Armored Brigade had discovered that its Pershings were still vulnerable to the massive 122mm guns of the enemy heavy tanks, and some had also been lost to the deadly 100mm anti-tank gun, a handful of which had been hastily dug in north of Selestat.

But, on the whole, the mixed force of Pershings and 76mm Shermans performed extremely well, the combination of their tank gunnery and supporting artillery, proving too much for the 109th Guards Tank Regiment and its supporting units.

Whilst still in possession of a number of vehicles, the 109th was vacating the field as fast as it could, occasionally lashing out at its pursuers.

US Infantry linked up with Legionnaires of the 'Alma' and the German irregulars of Kommando Alsace in Selestat, the three forces coming together at the base of the neo-medieval water tower.

St Clair's 7th RDM, flank secured on the Rhine, had rolled northwards, supported by 4th Kompagnie of Uhlmann's Tank Regiment, and the 128mm guns of Bäcker's special anti-tank unit.

The Soviet forces had formed a defensive position between Schwobstein and Richtolsheim, centred on the Route 209 Bridge over the Rhone-Rhein Canal.

Over two hundred of the 7th RDM's men had been killed or wounded overwhelming the position, along with the loss of two precious JagdPanzers and a Sturmgeschutz.

It was also here that the smiling and slightly mad Captain Friedrich Bäcker fell, a wayward mortar shell falling close enough to take his life with the smallest piece of metal.

Caught between two fires, 134th Rifle Corps was battered into submission, marking the largest surrender of Soviet manpower in the war thus far, some five and a half thousand men moving off into captivity.

132nd Rifle Corps was savaged, although some units, such as Major Din's, made their way back northwards to more stable positions, None the less, the 132nd was finished as a formation.

The spearheads that launched themselves out of the Vosges sliced the 3rd Guards Tank Corps into manageable pieces, often catching units between two fires, and grinding the experienced Guards Corps into a mass of dead and wounded. A further harvest of prisoners brought the total to just less than ten thousand.

Support elements from 19th Army suffered horrendously, particularly at the hands of 'Tannenberg', and the roving ground attack squadrons, whose planes, tanks, and armoured infantry swept the Alsatian plain, destroying or capturing valuable supplies, killing rear-echelon troops, including overrunning the headquarters of 3rd Guards Tanks itself.

By mid-afternoon on the 26th, the Allied frontline was as far forward as Illkirch-Graffenstaden, the flight of 19th Army affecting others units that might have stood tall in defence. Only a need to rearm and refuel prevented the lead units from 'Tannenberg' entering the city.

Over two thousand legionnaires were casualties, over a third the sort that never rise again.

Five hundred and seventy-two casualties were sustained by the 16th Armored, a strangely high proportion of those were dead upon the field.

The Kommando Alsace had also suffered badly, over two hundred of its four hundred and forty men lost to wounds or worse.

However, the Red Army had suffered worse still. Counting prisoners, wounded and dead, over thirty-two thousand men had been lost, and whole formations removed from the Soviet order of battle.

Operation Thermopylae was a brilliant success.

1816hrs, Friday, 26th October 1945, on the banks of the Apfelbach, north of Heiligenstein, Alsace.

Indeed, Operation Thermopylae was a brilliant success, but the price had been high.

A gathering of men, large in number, but nowhere near as many as would have liked to have been there, stood on the banks of the Apfelbach, on the Rue de Stade, next to a line of recently planted poplars.

Leading the group were the senior men of the Legion Corps, all save Molyneux, who was at French first Army headquarters, basking in the reflected glory, and busy ensuring he received as much credit as possible for the efforts of his legionnaires.

Lavalle, Knocke, Plummer, and Uhlmann stood in silence, the heaviness of the occasion given more weight by the steady trickle of light rain across the whole of the Alsace.

Behind the senior officers were others of varying status, such as Aloysius Fischer and Heinz-Sebastian Pöll, Ulrich Weiss and Oscar Durand, Haefeli and Rettlinger, bandaged arm and all, and even an old Irish legionnaire who remembered the man they were there to honour.

A grave had been prepared, fit for the nineteen men who were to be its permanent residents.

Nineteen men of the legion, but once of the Waffen-SS, all of whom had died in the ambush of a small column, leading a legion battalion in the rush to join the battles further north.

The names of the dead were read aloud, each receiving a small personal eulogy provided by a close comrade. Every man

430

there stood at the attention, officers saluting smartly, arms rigid in remembrance of a friend or loyal comrade lost, listening to the soft tones of the speaker.

Faces were wet, and not all because of the rain, for old comrades were being laid to rest in the rich Alsatian soil.

The Legion Padre, perhaps a curious choice to talk over the graves of former SS members, arrived at the last name; a man he had met, and who had impressed him with his character, his knowledge of European history, and of life itself. A learned man, and someone greatly admired by his comrades, many of whom were here this day.

Pausing, the Padre gathered himself, suddenly finding it all very heavy going.

"And lastly, we place our good comrade and friend, Colonel Jurgen Fabian Von Arnesen, into the care of the Lord, and we give thanks that we were blessed to have him as our friend and comrade."

The Padre swallowed noisily, gaining a moment to gather himself.

"Jurgen Von Arnesen was, by my own observations, and by all accounts, a man and a soldier of the finest quality. That being said, when one of his men has spoken to me about him, I must say that he was held in the highest regard by everyone who served with him," he stole a look at the silent man to his left and detected the slightest of nods.

"And I know that he was so proud of his comradeship with all of you, and with those that went before and fell."

Selecting some appropriate words to conclude the simple service, he gestured to the men who had volunteered to interr their dead comrades, and soon the only sounds were the working of spades and the constant rain and wind.

Many of the ensemble waited until the end, and some even helped the grave detail complete their task.

Some lingered long, but eventually all walked on into the future, leaving solely Ernst-August Knocke beside the newly turned soil.

The rain grew heavier, the sound of its drops rising with the wind that drove it.

And quietly, in his own way, Knocke said goodbye to the man who had been his best friend.

1ST BALTIC FRONT - MARSHAL BAGRAMYAN

All we know is that, at times, fighting the Russians, we had to remove the piles of enemy bodies from before our trenches, so as to get a clear field of fire against new waves of assault.

Paul von Hindenburg

Chapter 97 - THE DIVERSION

<u>1230hrs, Saturday, 20th October 1945, Headquarters of the 1st Baltic Front, Schloss Holdenstadt, near Uelzen, Germany.</u>

Marshal of the Soviet Union Hovhannes Bagramyan had the floor, the rest of the room quiet as he outlined the plan to punch through the Allied armies and enter Holland.

Bagramyan was not a fool. The silence from his senior officers was not just attentiveness; it was also concern that they and their men were to be pitched into further horrors.

The German War had its own special brand of violence, fought with a shared national hatred, and that inspiration had carried the soldiers of the Red Army through situations when they could easily have floundered.

Fighting the Western Allies was different, but no less bloody; in fact, with the air attacks that wrought havoc on a daily basis, many of his men thought the new war was worse.

'Perhaps they need to hate again?'

The commander of the 1st Baltic Front halted for a moment, dealing with that thought.

He moved on quickly.

"With those diversions in place, it is my intention to launch a series of sequential attacks on this river line, the Hunte, moving progressively south."

The Colonels and Majors now understood that this was where they would be employed.

Zagrebin of the 77th Engineers exchanged a rueful look with the commander of the 4th Guards Tank Brigade, Arkady Yarishlov.

432

"Starting at Pfennigstedterfeld, 11th Guards Army," he acknowledged Galitsky and Semenov, commander and CoS respectively, "You will launch attacks designed to commit the enemy reserves forward or force them to change position."

"At these points," Bagramyan tapped the map to punctuate each name as he went, "Wildeshausen, Hölingen, Colnrade, Goldenstedt, Barnstorf, Rechtern, Dreeke, Drebber, and finally Heede, and Hengemühle."

"11th Guards will take 3rd Guards Mechanised Corps and 22nd Guards Rifle Corps under orders, to be employed only as blocking formations once an attack is halted. Clear, Comrades?"

"Yes, Comrade Marshal."

Although, in truth, neither man understood exactly why they were being given two prime formations, and then being restricted on how to employ them.

"The timetable for your attacks is to reflect the need to draw the enemy reserves southwards all the time. I need 11th Guards to create a timetable in the minds of the Allies, one to which we will conform, until we strike and open them up like a ripe peach."

"Comrade General Christyakov," the commander of 6th Guards Army came to attention, "Your Army is my breakthrough formation, ready to exploit the gap once it is made."

Outlining a different area of the front, Bagramyan continued.

"Here, you will follow the descending frontline with some assault formations; openly, not hidden in any way. I want the Allies to know of them."

He stopped at two large wooded areas.

"Here, this is where I want you to hide the rest of your units. My plan is in the process of approval with the Stavka, and I have requested a Tank Corps to be assigned to you as an essential part of the breakthrough."

Christyakov beamed at Rybko, his CoS, having just been handed his largest and most important command since he had taken to soldiering.

"Also hidden in these two woods," he checked the names, "Wietingsmoor and Freistattermoor, will be Special Group Obinin."

Major General Obinin, the temporary commander of 2nd Guards Tank Corps, had already been briefed on his part, so he was not fazed by the announcement. In truth, the man was bordering on total mental exhaustion, but the front he presented gave no indication on how close he was to breaking.

Bagramyan paused to sip some water before continuing.

"Special Group Obinin will be responsible for breaching the Hunte River defences, and capturing intact the rail bridge here," the group leant forward as one, "At Barnstorf."

Each man could mentally envisage the sights, and smell the smoke, that would envelop the small German township, whose only crime was to possess an undamaged rail bridge capable of sustaining the weight of heavy armour.

In each man's mind's eye, the Soviet forces swept over the defenders in a glorious wave.

Then the euphoria of the moment was gone, replaced with the fatalism of the experienced soldier,

More than one in the room looked at the map with a jaundiced eye.

'Barnstorf.'

"Comrade Obinin has already submitted a plan of attack based upon the best intelligence available, and it may be that we will obtain three bridges over the Hunte as a result of this assault."

Returning his attention to Christyakov, the cunning Armenian Marshal smiled encouragingly.

"6th Guards will commence deploying its concealed forces as soon as the forcing of the Hunte seems likely, timed to cross as soon as the river line is ours, keeping up the pressure, and forcing the Allies to keep moving westwards. You will concentrate your Army as soon as possible, passing them over the river immediately the opportunity presents itself."

It was Zagrebin's turn to receive attention.

"Our comrades from the 77th Engineer Bridge Brigade will commence their work as soon as you give them the signal, either repairing the existing, or laying new bridges, whichever will give us the most benefit at the time."

Bagramyan's voice took a sterner tone.

"I don't need to remind you how valuable the 77th is, and its preservation is to be considered a priority over all others, Comrades."

434

Simply put, there were few bridging unit left, and even fewer with the resources to actually construct a viable bridge; 77th was one such rarity, albeit one missing its 3rd Battalion, and of reduced strength across the board.

It was Galitsky who broached subject number one.

"Comrade Marshal, our supply situation seems to have eased at the moment, but are we guaranteed sufficient for our needs in this operation, and beyond?"

Galitsky had already suffered because of a lack of vital munitions and fuels, and had been bound to raise the matter.

Bagramyan was ready with his reply.

"Comrade Marshal Zhukov assures me the extra resources are on their way, and will be distributed within the next two days. They will also be protected by additional assets from our brothers in the NKVD."

"Comrade Marshal, Special Group Obinin," Christyakov took the floor, "What is its strength? Is it enough to do the job, or will I need to reinforce it?"

Bagramyan was momentarily irritated, as that information was in the operational plan in each man's possession.

Then a thought overtook him.

'He's an excellent soldier, so why hasn't he looked at the document first?'

He looked around the ensemble, and now saw something dangerous in all their faces.

'They are tired. Blyad, but they are all tired!'

Nonetheless, 1st Baltic had a job to do, so he continued.

"Comrade General, Group Obinin is an all-arms formation made up of sections from 2nd Guards Tanks, 36th Guards Rifles, 6th Guards Heavy Tanks, and the 77th Engineers. Assign one of your Guards Rifles Corps to be prepared to lend modest assistance, by all means, but I want you to preserve your Army to fight west of the Hunte. You will **not** get embroiled in the fighting at Barnstorf."

That was clear.

For the benefit of all, but focussing on Obinin and the two Colonels flanking him, Bagramyan spoke forcefully.

"Group Obinin has the strength, and the quality, to take Barnstorf, and to permit the 77th Engineers to do their job. If they expend their last bullet and last tank," he deliberately avoided saying 'last man', "In doing it, then they will have succeeded in their mission, Comrades. Is **that** clear?"

Undeniably, it was crystal clear.

Special Group Obinin would take Barnstorf, or be wiped out in the attempt.

"Comrade Marshal," all eyes swivelled on the Guards Colonel of Tanks who dared to speak. His awards were impressive, and spoke volumes for his experience, as well as his experiences.

"Comrade Polkovnik Yarishlov?"

"Sir, you have outlined excellent provisions by our comrades in the Red Air Force, but how effective can they be, given the grievous losses they have sustained in beating back the Allied regiments?"

More than one listener smiled, understanding that, Colonel or not, the man understood how to speak without incriminating himself in defeatist talk. They all understood that the Red Air Force had been crucified by the capitalist squadrons, and was bordering on ineffective, unless real efforts were made to focus resources on limited operations.

"Comrade Polkovnik, I am assured by our frontal aviation commander, General Mayor Buianskiy, that all our forces involved in this operation will receive the maximum fighter cover possible, and that tactical air support will also be widely available to units on the ground."

'Very carefully answered Comrade Marshal.'

"Thank you, Comrade Marshal."

An unseen signal from Bagramyan had brought fresh tea into the meeting, a break that the wily Armenian had instigated for his own purposes.

Standing alone, he assessed each officer in turn, reading their gestures, the tone of voice, all to decide on how each man was taking his role in the operation.

Only one man drew extra attention.

Catching Yarishlov's eye, he silently invited the Colonel of Tanks to come closer.

"You are still troubled, Comrade Polkovnik?"

Arkady Yarishlov was not known for hiding his light. Tactfully avoiding mentioning the air force losses was one thing, but lying to a direct question from his Front Commander was another.

"Yes, Sir, I am."

Bagramyan licked his lips, removing the sweet tea residue.

"You are right to be, Comrade Yarishlov."

Yarishlov was surprised at such candour from the senior man.

"We are old soldiers, you and I, Comrade Yarishlov. Let us enjoy some straight talking."

"Yes Comrade Marshal."

"The Air Force is on its last legs. The Allies have dealt very harshly with our Air Regiments, and I doubt that Comrade Buianskiy will be able to honour his promise to us, even in skies directly above our air gunners"

Wisely, Yarishlov just nodded, leaving the older man to continue.

"Despite the fact that they suffer every time they take to the air, they still go. They do their duty for the Motherland in the same way as we ground soldiers, Comrade Yarishlov."

Turning around to the larger map pinned to the wall, Bagramyan waved his hand over the 1st Baltic Front's area of responsibility.

"My area has grown, as we have gained our victories. All of this now lies under my responsibility, and I have less manpower than ever to protect it with."

Lowering his voice, the Armenian Marshal spoke directly to Yarishlov.

"My air force is operating at about 30% of the strength we had when we started this war, Comrade Yarishlov, 30%."

'I had no idea it was that bad!'

"And yet they still go up and face terrible odds. So, how can I ask them to do that, if we mud crawlers doubt them before they even start?"

Yarishlov winced, made to feel that he had dishonoured his Air Force comrades for even thinking that they were not up to the job.

"They may well not be able to do all that Comrade Buianskiy has promised, but it will not be for lack of effort and commitment to the Motherland, Comrade Yarishlov. And if we ground soldiers have to take more risks because of their poor state then, so be it; we will do so."

"Yes, Comrade Marshal."

"Good. I'm glad you understand, Comrade Polkovnik."

Bagramyan drew a line under the temporary intimacy by the use of Arkady's rank and his sterner tone.

Neither man had realised that the entire room had fallen silent and the senior officers were engrossed in the exchange.

Bagramyan took the initiative.

"Comrades, unless you have further pressing business within my headquarters, you are dismissed, and I will expect your preliminary plans by 1400hrs tomorrow."

The meeting broke up immediately, each commander heading off to develop his plans, some with the euphoria of an organised attack against weakened opposition, others burdened with the uncertainties of command in a vital operation.

Back in his own base, Yarishlov sat on his bed, studying the map.

He fell into a troubled sleep, unable to explain or justify the sense of foreboding that filled him.

'Barnstorf.'

1450hrs, Sunday, 21st October 1945, Allied Holding Camp,
Baggersee am Berg, south of Hagen, Germany.

'Oi vay! What a dump! Are you shure thish is for us, Shergeant?"

Hässler mimicked the wounded man's affected speech.

"Mashter Shergeant to you. I'm important and don't you forget it, Corporal."

The diminutive Jew looked the Senior Non-com up and down with disdain.

"Most shertainly, it ish difficult to remember shometimes."

Grinning from ear to ear, the tall NCO went to playfully cuff his sidekick.

Rosenberg ducked away, and formed his lips into a kiss.

"Mein liebshen."

The two sniggered and returned to assess their surroundings.

It was certainly pretty enough, nestled on the shores of a modest sized lake, the Baggersee.

However, the accommodation looked like it had seen better days, the signs of age and swift repairs presented easily to their experienced eyes.

Men of all nations moved around, some in organised parties, off to drill or undertake work details, others strolled in a leisurely fashion, enjoying some time at rest.

The officer had travelled in the front of the lorry, and now announced his arrival at the tailgate, standing back as two soldiers opened up the rear of the Ford 6x6.

"Master Sergeant, get your men lined up to the left, two ranks. Move."

The greenhorn pointed imperiously at a point some ten yards distant, the mud and puddles that filled the chosen spot more than obvious to everyone, except him.

Hässler cut the boy some slack, and jumped down from the lorry, helping down the Jewish corporal, both of them moving gingerly because of their wounds.

He exchanged looks with another NCO, a man the Lieutenant either failed to notice, which was unlikely, given his size, or ignored, more likely, because of the colour of his skin.

They shared a shrug.

"You heard the officer, now dismount and get fell in. Hustle up there! Raus, Raus!"

Rosenberg fell in as marker, deliberately in front of the muddy ground, and the rest of the group formed on him.

Most of the men were former hospital patients, a few were new recruits, for whom this would be the first time in a combat formation.

The squeaky clean 2nd Lieutenant fell into that category, and it showed.

Unfortunately, he did not have the sense to understand that he had good men who would help him, if he did but unwind for a moment.

"Detail, detail, atten-shun!"

The men eventually organised their bodies into the appropriate position, and then 2nd Lieutenant James R. Yorke commenced inspecting his men.

Across from the line of GI's, Major John Ramsey of His Majesty's Black Watch, finished his discussions with the base commander, a sour-faced American Colonel of Artillery.

Whilst the man was unpleasant, he had agreed to Ramsey's request, and the extra blankets would be shortly be forthcoming.

Emerging from the Colonel's office, Ramsey nodded at his waiting men, the gesture bringing smiles of relief. Passing over the signed document, he sent them off to the US camp's supply section to obtain the blankets, for which he had just negotiated away two cases of Glenfoyle malt whisky.

Lighting a cigarette, the Englishman took in the amusing vignette across the parade ground.

The difference between combat veterans and new troops was totally obvious.

There was also something huge in the line, looking extremely out of place; wide, muscular, a foot taller than the others, looking like a grizzly bear, and just as dangerous, except for the smile that spilt the man's face.

Ramsey was intrigued, and suddenly he found himself edging across the intervening ground, closing on the inspection.

Yorke saw the man approach, half wondering if the soldier with the red feathers in his strange hat was a circus act or a serious soldier, but erring on the side of safety and saluting in any case.

Ramsey replied in kind.

"Good day, Lieutenant. Fine group of men you have here, I must say. That fellow is particularly striking," he gestured at the man-mountain in the centre of the rear line.

"Thank you, Sir, but I can't agree. Bunch of no-hopers and cripples, some from the repple-depple, the rest straight out of the hospital. Normally, I wouldn't wanna go into combat with them, but the Colonel has given me no choice."

The American spat to punctuate his disgust at being given such a worthless command.

"Leastways, I've got a little time to train them up."

Ramsey had made his assessment quickly, and he was on the money as usual.

"What unit are you, Lieutenant?"

"I was assigned to Able Company, 116th Infantry Regiment of the 29th Division, Sir. My platoon was wiped out

440

before I could take up my command. I have received orders from the Regimental Commander himself, and I am to organise these men into a fighting company."

Ramsey smiled disarmingly.

"The 29th, you say? Fine unit. Fought with them around Bremen for a few days. Were you there, Lieutenant?"

Yorke coloured noticeably.

"I have not yet had the honour of combat, Sir."

The smirks from some of the older faces on parade were not wasted on either man.

"My apologies. I suspect you will get your chance very soon, Lieutenant."

Ramsey and Yorke exchanged salutes, the US infantry officer turning back towards his parade, and standing them at ease.

Ramsey made brief eye contact with one battered-looking NCO, enough to recognise the man's mettle.

Sparing a final glance at the huge man, he returned to his two trucks, now boasting enough spare blankets to keep the survivors of B Company warm.

Yorke went in search of the billeting officer.

"Very pwetty, washn't he?"

Rosenberg grinned wide enough for Hassler to see his teeth out of the corner of his eye.

"Sure was, but he's a fighting man, and that's a fact."

"You think? Sheems a little too balebetishen to me."

Hässler spared a momentary glance at the smaller man.

"Will you cut that yiddisher crap and talk properly!"

"And there wash me thinking I could enlighten you with shome more of my culture. Oi vay! I mean he sheems a little too reshpectable to be a fighting man."

The Master Sergeant snorted in derision.

"Not every fighting soldier has to look like a bag of shit, something you would do well to remember, Corporal."

"I choose to, sho as not to make you look bad, Yutzi."

"Stop with the yiddisher crap, or I will find a shit shovelling detail that has your name on it."

"Yutzi is a term of endearment for a closh friend, my Shergeant."

441

Rosenberg's grin told Hässler otherwise.

"Mein liebchen, if you were paying attention, you might have noticed the man's salad bar."

"Pah, we get medal ribbonsh for trapping a finger in a typewriter."

The Master Sergeant could not argue that point.

"OK, wise guy, that may be true, but that pretty soldier had the limey equivalent of the Medal of Honor, and a whole lot of other important shit, so I rather suspect he's our sort of people, and more than handy in a brawl."

Rosenberg hadn't noticed any such thing.

In any case, other matters took precedence as Yorke returned.

"Master Sergeant Hässler, take command of the detail. Get them bunked down in Hut 9," the officer gestured to the dingiest looking of the many dingy huts, "Get them all squared away, and muster on the parade ground at 1600, full pack, for drill."

"Yes, Sir."

Yorke departed again, having discovered a passable Officers Mess in his travels. He had a date with a pot of fresh coffee, before he marched his men around for an hour or two.

Hässler stood at the front of the detail, sharing his gaze equally between the largest soldier and the door to hut 9.

"You gonna fit through that teeny hole, Sergeant?"

Charley Bluebear grinned widely.

"If not the first time, then surely the second, Master Sergeant."

Bluebear was a popular comrade, and the laughter was unforced.

"Good answer, well presented, Sergeant. Ok then. Detail, detail shun. Fall out. Now, go and get that shit heap into some order before our squeaky has a fit. Move it."

He gave extra attention to his best friend.

"And, as it isn't the fucking Sabbath, that means you too, Corporal Rosenberg."

As the group streamed towards the unknown delights of Hut 9, heavy drops of rain started to fall, a rain that threatened to be ever-present in the days to come.

442

One of the serious problems in planning the fight against American doctrine is that the Americans do not read their own manuals, nor do they feel any obligation to follow their own doctrine.

Entry in a Soviet Mladshy Leytenant's Notebook

Chapter 98 - THE INTELLIGENCE

1ST BALTIC FRONT - MARSHAL BAGRAMYAN

<u>1734hrs, Tuesday, 23rd October 1945, Headquarters of SHAEF, Trianon Palace Hotel, Versailles, France.</u>

"So, what's the bottom line, Walter?"

Eisenhower had his own views, but wanted the input from his Chief of Staff. The report, thus far, had been factual, covering Soviet attacks along a wide front, some of which seemed designed as distractions, others almost bursting with energy and power.

"Our special information seems reasonably accurate, Sir."

Bedell-Smith was referring to the intercept intelligence supplied by Station X, the latest of which had been personally handed over by Dalziel that afternoon.

"Reasonably accurate, General?"

Bradley had been a late arrival, still wet from the rain and carrying a fair share of German mud on his boots, and he was not in a mood to mince words.

"Yes Sir. We have two major attacks in progress. Here, south of the Ruhr," something Bradley was only too aware of, "And here, in Alsace."

Returning to the top of the map, Bedell-Smith continued.

"Here, there is supposed to be another major attack, but all we are presently experiencing is a grazing assault, moving down our front line, starting just south of Bremen."

Again, Bedell-Smith moved his pointer around the map.

"These are all points of assault, but the intelligence is such that we are discounting them as serious threats, Sir."

Turning to Eisenhower, Bradley aired his concerns.

443

"Is that wise, Sir? Can we afford not to take these other attacks seriously?"

Eisenhower had already had the same discussion with a number of his senior commanders, and so was able to reply quickly.

"Brad, it all fits. The Intel is good, and we are acting on it. We do not have the resources to go chasing after all these other attacks, and if we do, we risk not having enough in place to stop the main thrusts."

Ike pulled at another map, and stood slightly aside so that the commander of his 12th Army Group could see.

"We are concentrating our forces, but I do not want to commit them yet. If we can stop the Communists with what we have online, then we have our reserves with which to counter-attack. We need to start taking back the initiative here."

Bradley could understand that, and the list of units that SHAEF was keeping back was growing in number and capability.

'But...'

He never got to say it.

"But, if the Soviets do breakthrough, I will employ some of these assets to stop their advance. Either way round, we will be counter-attacking, according to the plan we discussed with George a while back, timetable to be decided."

Bradley could not help but stare at the Supreme Commander, the change in him so marked since the last time the two had met.

There was a confidence there, not previously seen since the Bulge had been eradicated and the Allied divisions had flooded into Germany.

Ike was drawing on a newly lit cigarette, so Bradley took advantage of the coffee that had been given to him on his arrival.

He missed the signal from Eisenhower.

Von Vietinghoff closed the door, sealing off the office from the outside world.

Bradley understood that the sudden change in atmosphere represented a new imposition of secrecy; something special was in the air.

Eisenhower remained smoking his cigarette, now joined by the German liaison officer.

444

Bedell-Smith remained silent also, the quiet inviting the final member of the ensemble onto the stage to deliver his information.

Sir David Petrie, Commander of MI5, took his cue.

"Sirs, there will be no paper record of this conversation, and none of you is to mention it outside these four walls."

Such an edict could ruffle a feather or two, but for the obviously serious nature of what was to come, information which had only been whispered into Eisenhower's ear an hour beforehand.

"MI5 has a source," he corrected himself, "A brand new source, within the Soviet Red Army command structure."

That, in itself, was a shock. But they had heard nothing yet.

"Our source is highly placed, and in a position to supply information across the range of military matters. The agent's identity will be kept secret at all costs, as is the fact that such an agent exists."

That was obvious, but Petrie was determined to press the point.

"This agent has supplied us with information that was verified by other means initially, but the latest receipt brings with it staggering news."

The silence was electric, almost unbearable.

"According to the report, the Red Army will shortly attack into Northern Italy, via the Alps and Southern Austria."

"We knew that would come, General Petrie. That's old news. In fact, it seems to have been a stop-start thing for weeks now."

Bedell-Smith was right, but that was an aperitif only, and Petrie followed it up with starter, main course, and dessert in succession.

"Indeed, General Smith. His reports inform us that there is a personal rift between Zhukov, and one of his front commanders, Konev."

Clearly, it was nothing of great note to Generals who had their own difficulties with colleagues, so Petrie felt the need to go further.

"This is probably something that could be exploited, with the acquisition of more intelligence. I will know more in the fullness of time, but it appears their relationship is so bad that military judgement is being affected."

Interest perked a little, but Petrie moved on.

"Secondly, Stalin has relented on his policy on their POW's, and they are using them to fill in gaps in their formations."

Eisenhower frowned.

"Excuse me? They refused to do that during the German War. Have we really hurt them that badly?"

Petrie kept a straight face.

"I have people working on the figures at the moment, but, if the report is accurate, we can add at least 25% to their casualty figures."

The gathering exploded into life.

"25%!"

Petrie remained silent, permitting the men to trade looks and words of astonishment.

As the hubbub subsided, Eisenhower noted the expression on the face of MI5's senior man, and realised that there was something even more staggering to come.

He firstly calmed the crowd, before encouraging the performer.

"Gentlemen, please. Sir David, you're dying to tell us, so please do."

"And finally, the Red Army is running short on supplies."

Faces cleared quickly, eyes asking question after question, all silently directed at the head of MI5.

"Gentlemen, my source informs me that stocks of everything from ammunition to hay for the horses, are at an unacceptable low, and that the Red Army is gambling much on this attack, so that they may focus their dwindling resources on the three main axis of attack. Very soon they will lack the resources for offence."

Bradley saw a problem immediately.

"But General Petrie. If that is so, how come they are going to open up Italy? How can they have the resources for that?"

"The Italian slated formations have passed on some of their supplies to the main front, which has helped provide enough for them to come up with the triple prong attack."

Petrie paused, ready to bring the proverbial 'coffee and mints' to the discussion.

446

"The Yugoslav authorities are still rather upset with their communist allies, but have relented sufficiently to offer some assistance."

More than one brow furrowed, even Eisenhower's, who had already heard that snippet.

"The Yugoslav's have huge stocks of equipment and supplies, and have agreed to release large quantities to the nearby Soviet formations. According to the agreement, these formations will be employed in the liberation of Italy, and only in the liberation of Italy, which I believe the Yugoslavs feel will then remove any direct pressure on them."

Von Vietinghoff spoke for every man there.

"So, they gain advantage, at no risk to themselves, by giving the Communists back what they gave them in the first place, and get the Red Army to do their work for them."

That about summed it all up nicely.

"Tito, die scheisskerl!"

Petrie found his German language skills up to the mark.

"I think that puts it rather well, Herr GeneralOberst."

Eisenhower summed up.

"So, the Italian offensive will happen, mainly because the supplies are coming from Yugoslavia, and they insist that the Russians do something to relieve the pressure on their country. Meanwhile, in the main theatre, the Red Army is steadily running out of everything it needs, despite an influx from the Alpine formations that have just be resupplied by Tito. Is that correct, General Petrie?"

A moment's pause occurred, as if by comment assent; a moment in which the immense ramifications were fully understood by all those present.

The silence went on, no man prepared to break it, for fear of ruining the images that were springing up in the mind's eye.

A knock on the door broke the moment forever.

"Sir, urgent call from General Ridgeway," the flustered Captain indicated the silent phone on Eisenhower's desk.

"Thank you, gentlemen, but I must take this call."

The senior men filed quickly out, leaving Ike alone with his thoughts and the apparatus.

"Eisenhower."

The news was not good.

"Yes indeed, General Ridgeway."

The news did not get any better.

"Matthew, all I can offer you is what is already on the road."

The Paratrooper General's pleas fell on deaf ears, but Eisenhower was aware that the harassed commander needed something to pin his hopes on.

"I am sorry, General. Look, Matthew, understand this. Your stand is vital, absolutely vital, or I would not be asking you to make it. Hold the communists on that side of the line, and we will gain the initiative."

Ike stopped, listening to the man's reply.

"Yes, I mean just that. We will start driving them back."

Eisenhower smiled, a genuine pleasure at hearing one of his favourites buoyed by a few simple words.

"And to you, General Ridgeway. Goodbye."

Another cigarette magically went from pack to mouth in an instant, the smoke giving his lungs the boost he sought.

'So, if they can't advance, have we won the war.'

The Supreme commander laughed aloud.

'If you believe that, you are a fool!'

He laughed again.

'But we will win the war, that was never in doubt.'

Ike pursed his lips before delivering his reply.

'I don't doubt it now, but there were times when...'

'Times? Times when what? Times when you thought we would lose?'

Eisenhower shook his head wearily.

'Times when I believed that we could all lose.'

The other inner voice took a moment to think that through.

'Ah, you mean the bomb, don't you?'

There was a momentary silence, in recognition of the enormity of the thought.

'As well you know, General, as well you know.'

'It so often happens that, when men are convinced that they have to die, a desire to bear themselves well and to leave life's stage with dignity, conquers all other sensations.'

Winston Spencer Churchill

Chapter 99 - THE CAMPFIRE

1ST BALTIC FRONT - MARSHAL BAGRAMYAN

2330hrs, Tuesday, 23rd October 1945, Headquarters of the 1st Baltic Front, Schloss Holdenstadt, near Uelzen, Germany.

"The attacks have succeeded so far, Comrade Marshal. It appears that the Allied reserve is keeping pace with our forces, all moving south as we hoped."

Bagramyan was pleased, and motioned for his CoS to continue.

"Allied air power is negated by the heavy rain, as we expected."

Without that piece of luck, the situation would be more 'fluid'.

"The first attack on Barnstorf is due to commence this morning, the exact timing was left to the local commander."

Checking his notes, the Chief of Staff made the important announcement.

"If everything goes to schedule, the main thrust by Special Group Obinin will commence at 1000hrs on the 25th."

As was his nature, the CoS added a note of caution.

"Our meteorologists predict that there could be some clearing of the weather during the afternoon of the 25th, possibly as much as four hours, Comrade Marshal."

There was nothing that could be usefully said, or done. If it did not happen, then the spearhead would breakthrough, and release the follow-up forces. If it did happen, then it was possible that the enemy ground-attack squadrons would have a small window of opportunity to attack the ground forces.

Bagramyan decided to look positively upon the matter.

"Then we must ensure that our own air regiments and anti-aircraft units are ready to do their duty, Comrade."

Outside, the rain lashed the window, drawing attention to itself.

Once again, it was Bagramyan's friend.

Fig #67 - The Battleground, Barnstorf, Germany.

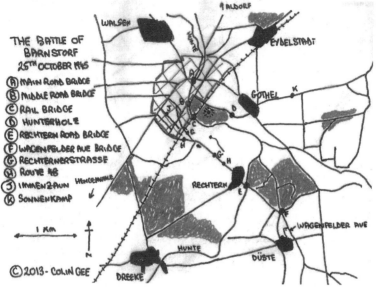

0057hrs, Thursday, 25th October 1945, Barnstorf, Germany.

Using the cover of the rain, both its power to obscure vision, and the noise of its contact with the ground, the Soviet infantry had got in too close for comfort.

The scratch force at Barnstorf came from US, British and German units, although the Germans were made up of Kommando soldiers from a number of local forces.

Kommando Regiment Friedrich, named for its former regular Army commander, comprised some 350 men, many of them veterans of the Western or Russian fronts, men invalided out, or used in the rear line. The others were either old men or boys, of varying skills and uses.

The battered 116th Regiment of the 29th US Infantry Division formed the bulk of the defences, supplemented by a few tanks in an ad hoc company. The US Army also contributed artillery and mortars to the defence.

It had not been a powerful lunge by the Soviets, but it had still been a close run thing as far as Lieutenant Colonel Willoughby, the 116th's commander, had been concerned. The evidence of dead Russians, some a hundred yards from the main road bridge, was sufficient for him to seek for reinforcements in Barnstorf itself.

Fortunately, there were some close at hand.

Behind the Hunte River, elements of the destroyed 51st Highland Division had been gathered up and formed into a small brigade, the 154th; a brigade in name, certainly not in numbers.

Companies that had survived the attritional battles in Northern Germany were pulled together into the new infantry brigade. All were placed under the command of the elderly Brigadier Philip Blake, a career soldier, who had done his main soldiering on the South-African veldt, in Picardy, or the sands of Palestine and, for whom, the greatest battle was the daily struggle with haemorrhoids, and the constant presence of malaria.

There were enough Seaforths to make up a full battalion, by far the healthiest unit in the Brigade, especially as it possessed a machine-gun company from the Northumberland Fusiliers.

A second battalion was formed, consisting of three short companies of Gordon Highlanders and the Argyll and Sutherland Highlanders, the two extremely clannish groups tolerating each other in a good-natured way, whilst despising the other two brigades for their inclusions of some sassenachs.

A third battalion was formed around two ravaged companies of the Black Watch. Ramsey's B Company from 7th Battalion, bolstered by thirty men from the Queen's Own Cameron Highlanders, men who had been through hell outside of Bremen. A mishmash of survivors from 1st Battalion, The Black Watch, made up two companies that were well down in numbers, and also poorly equipped. There were also two men from 5th Battalion, the rest of the unit cut off somewhere to the north. Two platoons of Royal Engineers made up the numbers, bereft of equipment, to be employed as infantry if needed.

For artillery support, the 154th Brigade was fortunate to call upon the veterans of the 127th Field Artillery, a 51st Division regiment that had survived reasonably intact.

A handful of armoured cars from 2nd Derbyshire Yeomanry, and anti-tank guns from 61st Royal Artillery completed the Brigade's order of battle.

Willoughby waited for the British unit to arrive, still hopping mad from the latest supply clusterfuck, when valuable space had been taken up with a large supply of divisional cloth badges and stationery, and the requested maps for his defensive position had not arrived.

He had men working on hand copying from the few maps he possessed, something that grated on him.

'At least I got the ammo, or I would have been throwing badges and pencils at the commie bastards!'

He snorted at that thought, drawing looks from the surviving officers of the 116th's headquarters.

Like a number of allied divisions, the 29th had been hit very hard, and Willoughby rose to command the 116th Regiment by filling dead men's shoes.

The 29th had landed on Omaha, and had stayed in combat throughout the German War, and the price, for them, had been extremely high. The new war was no kinder.

At the last count, the whole division mustered at about seven thousand five hundred men, just over a half of its full strength, and it had been one of the few units that were at peak strength on 6th August.

It was rare that a rear line medical facility did not contain at least one wounded soldier from the 'Blue and Grey' Division.

Blake arrived with his second in command, assumed overall command, and immediately set to work on a plan to integrate the two forces as best as possible.

Between the two staffs, it was decided to split the forces in two, allowing Willoughby to form a reasonable reserve behind his front line. This entailed handing over responsibility for the main road and rail bridges to the British, integrating the new arrivals in between the 116th US Infantry and the 3rd British Infantry Division, holding the Hunte river line to the north.

The 116th would then join onto the 154th at the rail bridge, covering southwards through Rechtern and Düste. The main advantage for Willoughby was that he could now find a formation to place in Dreeke, a spot previously only lightly defended.

Kommando Friedrich, it had been decided to retain the name of its now dead commander, was withdrawn, and split into two alarm companies, one positioned at Walsen, the other on the Nagelskamp, to the south-west of Barnstorf.

As the staff officers worked out the details of the defences, Soviet artillery continued to harass the rear line positions, in line with Bagramyan's plan of reducing the efficiency of the shadowing Allied reserve force, which continued to move steadily southwards, in line with the Red Army assaults.

The defenders expected two assaults on the 25th, as had happened at each of the attack points earlier. These had been interpreted as a genuine attempt to cross the River, followed by a second, less powerful thrust, more designed to fix some of the reserves in place.

The pattern had been noticed, and was catered for.

The rain relented at two o'clock, to the second, and the sky cleared shortly afterwards, permitting the stars to illuminate the soldiers below.

<u>0300hrs, Thursday, 25th October 1945, Junction of Nagelskamp and Osnabrucker Straβe, Barnstorf.</u>

The old farmhouse had started as the headquarters of the 3rd Battalion, 154th Infantry Brigade, as designated by its present senior officer, Major John Ramsey.

However, it soon became apparent that the position was not suitable, and the headquarters was moved one hundred yards further forward.

One thing the old farmhouse did possess was a walled courtyard, partially roofed, fully intact, and integral, providing a safe location for the soldiers to light a fire, and dry out themselves and their kit.

Unofficially, it became the area to which off-duty personnel migrated for peace and quiet, or what counted for peace and quiet in an active war zone.

The American contingent had set up an area intended to provide as many of the creature comforts as possible, and it was inevitable that their British and German counterparts would be attracted to the courtyard and its promise of real fresh coffee, amongst other pleasures.

Gathered around a modest fire, many of the hierarchy of the Barnstorf defences took their leisure.

There was something different about this campfire, different from all those that night, and from those from countless nights before.

Each and every man there had a sense of foreboding; a real feeling that something truly awful was waiting in the wings, ready to descend upon them.

Each kept his own counsel, or maybe shared his feelings with his closest friend, but, none the less, they could sense it in each other.

The latest round of scalding hot Columbian was doing the rounds, and the ten officers and NCO's drank quietly, the hubbub of conversation coming from the other ranks gathered around similar small fires throughout the large courtyard area.

It fell to the commander of the German 2nd Reserve Company to break the moment.

"Tis are gut cafe, meine Herren. Welly gut."

Captain Strecher had enough English to manage to make himself understood, but was not actually as proficient as he thought he was, which made for some moments when his fellow officers had to work hard to keep a straight face.

"Aye, that it is, Sir."

Murdo Robertson, the RSM of the 7th Black Watch, recently returned from hospital, could only agree, draining the last dregs and looking around for more.

Ramsey sat quiet, still enjoying his coffee, slowly sipping, not possessing the asbestos throat with which some of the party were obviously equipped. Continuing his silent observations, he moved his gaze from the obviously competent Master-Sergeant Hässler and his shadow Rosenberg, and on to the mountain sat next to them; the man he had seen that very morning.

At that time, Charley Bluebear had been a sergeant. Now he was sporting the insignia of a Warrant Officer, reward for something achieved on a far-flung field.

Of particular interest to Ramsey were the tomahawk and battle knife; the stuff of legend to a man whose childhood was littered with tales of the Seventh Cavalry and Apache Indians.

Much as he was keen to ask, he kept his own council, hoping to find out more at another time.

He had heard of the confrontation between Bluebear and the idiot Yorke. That exchange was the talk of the town, the few men who had witnessed it spreading the story like wildfire, the men all eager to hear something that could put a smile on their faces.

Ramsey laughed to himself, the recollection of Robertson's version making him smile.

Yorke had rounded on the Indian, demanding that he relinquish the non-standard weapons of his ancestors.

Robertson's version had contained a lot more choice language, and was done in the style of an old story-teller. Through the skill and clarity of the RSM's style, Ramsey had mentally conjured up the scene, seeing quite clearly just how stupid the American officer would have looked, as he hung on grimly to the tomahawk, his feet kicking, some three feet off the ground.

Apparently, Bluebear had quietly informed Yorke that he could not have them, and that he had express written permission to carry them.

Argument followed examination of the paperwork, Yorke stating that it was applicable only to the 12th US Armored, which, he sneered, *'chicken-shit Armored outfit bugged out, and is probably half way to the Atlantic and still running.'*

Bluebear held out the tomahawk, and Yorke had grasped it with both hands, He clearly expected it to be surrendered, and yet had found himself suddenly pulled off his feet, until his face was level with the Red Indian.

According to observers, the officer dangled there for at least two minutes, looking directly at the Cherokee, their faces merely inches apart.

No one actually heard the brief conversation. Given the small movements in Bluebear's jaw, and Yorke's statue-like immobility, onlookers suspected that it was mainly a one-sided affair.

The witnesses certainly agreed that Yorke was not put down until he had given a discernable nod to Bluebear.

When the officer was returned to ground level, he saluted smartly, spun on his heel, and strode off as fast as he could.

There had been no further comments made about Bluebear's private arsenal, and the only witnessed exchange between the two men, since the encounter, had been without problems.

Quite clearly, the young Indian had made a good impression upon Robertson, a man who suffered fools lightly.

The two were involved in a soft conversation, punctuated by a few hand gestures, and culminating in the RSM's examination of Bluebear's tomahawk, as the Indian took in the feel and balance of Murdo's dirk.

'Murdo will fill me in on our Indian friend's story tomorrow.'

Moving on again, Finlay and Green of the 1st Black Watch were sat together, silently, the strain apparent on both men's faces.

1st Black Watch had been very badly handled, culminating in an attack by Soviet flamethrower tanks.

Captain Finlay and CSM Green were the only two known survivors from the 1st's A Company. The former, a public schoolboy from an old Scottish family. The latter of full Irish blood, his presence in a Scottish regiment explained by affiliations made in the trenches of the First War, when his father had fought alongside a member of the Scottish nobility, and had moved to Scotland to become his Gillie after the conflict had ended.

They, and Aitcherson, were of concern to Ramsey, for all three were almost at the end of their tethers with the strain of command and combat against a competent enemy.

The Right Honourable Iain Alisdair Aitcherson was actually the worst of the three, the Queen's Own Cameron Highlander sporting a permanent bandage around his head, there to protect a nasty head wound sustained in the defence of Bremen.

He also possessed the ingrained distant look of a man who had been pushed to the limits of endurance.

'I must watch him closely.'

Returning to the first two characters, he found the German 2IC, Oberleutnant Dieckhoff, in animated conversation with the newest arrival, 1st Lt Fielding of the US Engineers. Apparently, both men hailed from the same birthplace, and they conversed rapidly in German, bringing forth memory after memory.

Rosenberg, after some disagreement with Hässler, renewed the contents of each mug there, the new pot seemingly containing something other than coffee.

Whatever it was, it was welcome, and created a more relaxed atmosphere amongst the group.

Interrupting Robertson in mid-swipe, Ramsey sought an answer to a vital question.

"So, how are your legendary powers? Will it rain today, Sarnt-Major?"

Returning the Tomahawk to Bluebear, impressing the Cherokee with the reverence he displayed towards the ancient weapon, Robertson sniffed the air, taking in the night sky, biding his time before replying.

"Aye Sir. Not as much rain as yesterday. Only Angels tears, Sir. Enough for us to know that heaven cares about the men that will die here this day."

Ramsey nodded, aware of Robertson's folk status amongst the men, be it for his weather predictions, or his ability to create poetry in an instant, words that could impress even the roughest of soldier's minds.

"That's rather poetic, Sarnt-Major. Time for one of your creations, I think."

The group was made more affable by the inclusion of some fiery spirit in the coffee, and they all encouraged the RSM to speak.

"Go on, man, give us one of your poems."

Robertson rose to his feet, the very act attracting everyone's full attention.

"Aye, that I will, Sir. But I'll no be alone tonight. There are more here than me as can bend their minds to the craft, of that I'm sure."

He grasped Bluebear's shoulder, indicating that at least his new friend should be able to contribute.

They shared a grin.

"Anyways, I'll tender ye something appropriate, but not just the now; I will have a moment to mysel first, Sah."

Loud enough to be heard, Rosenberg could not resist a comment to his friend.

"I thought theesh limeysh all talked English. What the fuck wash that he wash shpeaking?"

Those in earshot laughed, knowing the statement for the baiting it was.

Robertson duly retaliated.

"Listen, ye colonial bas. I'm nay English. I'm Scots born and bred, and my daddy's daddy's daddy were at Waterloo, with Ewart and the Greys, snatching the Eagle from the Frogs!"

Rosenberg feigned shock and horror.

"Oi Vey Shergeant Major! Eaglesh? Frogsh? Did your family run a zoo?"

Robertson set his jaw and bent over, bringing his face level with the diminutive Jew.

"It's called tradition, ye mouthy dwarf, something of which ye know little, unless ye are talking docking your cocks."

The little soldier looked mournful.

"I had mine done for medical reasons, Shergeant Major."

Hässler snorted.

Robertson waited, grinning widely.

Rosenberg continued.

"Parshially because the docsh shaid that the extra shtrain on my heart was too much of a rishk," laughter erupted from the group, "And Parshially becaush the Rabbi ordered me to shpare the female of the shpecies and redushe it to more of a normal shize."

Robertson's retort was lost in loud and uncontrolled baying, amusement that doubled when Dieckhoff tried to translate the lines for Strecher, and failed to finish the job, coming apart long before he had made sense.

Honours roughly even, Robertson sat himself down and produced a small pad, his pencil quickly going to work.

As he completed his work, small raindrops started to fall, complying with his earlier prediction.

He nodded at Ramsey who rose to his feet.

"Gentlemen, I pray silence for the Bard of Black Watch, Murdo Robertson."

Ramsey's gentle call brought a stillness to the group.

The RSM adopted the mournful Scots style of delivery.

"Aye well, here is ma wee offering to the day ahead."

The start was delayed by a small flash in the night sky, a brief light that rallied and grew, marking the return to earth of an aircraft that had died violently in the darkness above.

458

Robertson read his poem.

"Is that rain upon my face this day?
Or angels tears from heaven, to say,
We feel for ye, Oh sons of men,
Prepared to do your work again.
Though such a price was ne'er fore asked,
Or so brave a group, so heavy tasked,
So feel our tears upon your face, and know,
We care about you, down below. "

A gentle clapping commenced, the words so quickly penned making an impact upon those who had listened.

Rosenberg took his time and spoke as clearly as he could.

"For shertain, you ain't English, Shergeant-Major. Ain't one of 'em could shtring together wordsh like that," he caught Ramsey's eye, "Preshent company exshcluded of coursh!"

Bluebear rose, silently encouraged by Robertson. His voice was soft and firm, and he made no attempt at rhyme or balance, but his words seemed to take poetic form naturally.

"I am a warrior of my people, of a warrior race,
Traced back through the line of our ancestors.
I am Tsali Sagonegi Yona of the Aniyunwiya,
Brought forth upon this land to kill,
And if I am worthy, then tomorrow,
And for a thousand years to come,
The Aniyunwiya will know of my name.
I am Tsali Sagonegi Yona,
And tomorrow, and for the days to come,
I will fight alongside fellow braves. "

The Indian resumed his seat to the sound of approving voices, shaking the extended hands of both Robertson and Hässler.

"Excellent, excellent."

Ramsey's approval was genuine.

Checking his watch, he was about to announce his departure, when he noticed Aitcherson standing quietly, just waiting to be recognised.

459

"Gentlemen, gentlemen. I'm afraid that I must depart, time is pressing now, but, before I go, I believe our comrade from the Cameron Highlanders wishes to contribute."

"Aye, that I do, Sir. If I may."

Silence fell on the group, not even the sound of a distant barrage or a waking bird, even the remainder of the courtyard was silent, men either asleep or withdrawn into their own thoughts.

Aitcherson rehearsed his presentation, his lips moving silently before he spoke.

"The old folk speak of glory and honour,
Won on the bloody fields of yore,
Names that have long since passed into legend,
Such as Balaclava, Plassey, Quebec, Agincourt.
A thousand years, and a thousand battles,
Yet mainly the olds boast of Waterloo,
But after this day, a legend'll be born,
For they'll all speak of Bloody Barnstorf too."

The Cameron's officer spoke the words with great meaning, his voice of perfect tone for the delivery.

"Bravo old chap, bravo. However, I do hope that you are incorrect, Aitcherson. To be frank, I rather hope that no-one will remember the name of Barnstorf in a week!"

He got no disagreement, and whilst the ensemble appreciated Aitcherson's efforts, they all preferred to hope that battle would pass them by that day.

Strecher received the last of the translation, and nodded his approval.

Patrick Green decided to throw in his two-penneth.

"Right, well here's mine, with no bloody apologies."

He coughed to clear his throat and then ran the words out in record time.

"I'm here fighting for the fookin English,
As my dadda did afore me.
When we will ever learn,
To leave it to the fookin English,
To fight their own fookin wars."

460

Green's skills were probably better adapted to the battlefield, but his contribution brought polite responses none the less.

"And something more from our American cousins?"

Ramsey laid down the gauntlet, and Hässler picked it up immediately.

"I'm American, so I guess my style is more direct and to the point than you old world types, Sir."

"You have the floor, Master Sergeant."

"OK, well, here goes."

He winked at Rosenberg.

"Barnstorf, a boil on the arse of humanity. Fuck it!"

Even Strecher laughed, without the need of translation from Dieckhoff.

Ramsey choked lightly, regaining his poise before speaking.

"Thank you for that pearl of wisdom, Master Sergeant, and I daresay we all agree with you!"

A bout of rapid exchange in German followed, preventing the group from breaking up.

Dieckhoff stood to explain.

"Herr Hauptmann Strecher has ask me to quote something for him as his contribution, Kameraden. Before the war, Strecher is scholar of Ancient Greece, and he has ask me to speak his words at you."

Unusually, Strecher had, for once, decided that his English was not up to the job.

Strecher took his cue and spoke slowly, permitting Dieckhoff to deliver his words precisely.

"In 480BC, a small number of Greeks fights a huge army of Persia, using the ground to help resist the invasion. A small force, only few thousand Greeks, from a number of States, held back the power of," Dieckhoff confirmed the pronunciation before continuing, "Xerxes, a king with an army totalling a million men."

Strecher finished speaking his next portion and leant back to savour his coffee.

"At the end of the battle, monuments are erected in their honour, and this words comes from one such monument."

461

Dieckhoff listened as his Captain repeated the text twice, fixing it in his mind.

"Go tell the Spartans, stranger who passes by, that here, obedient to their laws, we lie."

A modest ripple of acknowledging applause rose briefly, the occasional mug tilted to toast the words from ancient times.

As one, they rose. Handshakes were exchanged, and they went forth to whatever the day held.

Back in their position, Hässler was unusually quiet.

"They might not attack ush. It might all be bullshith."

The mumbled reply told Rosenberg that his friend was troubled.

"Hey Rish, it'll be fine. What'sh got you sho blue?"

"Gotta bad feeling about this battle, Rosie, a real bad feeling."

Rosenberg stayed silent, and an awkwardness filled the foxhole.

Hässler shook himself out of the melancholy, and sought to brighten the moment.

"So, brain box, that Spartan thing. What happened to them?"

"Shergeant, are you telling me that you Gentilesh weren't taught hishtory?"

"What I'm telling you is that this fucking soldier wasn't taught that bit of history, ok?"

"Whoa, Mashter Shergeant," Rosenberg realising quickly that there was no humour in his friend's words.

"OK, OK, Isaac. I just wanna know, that's all."

The use of his first name indicated just how rattled Hässler was.

"They were killed to a man, Mashter Shergeant."

"Well, that's just fucking dandy!"

462

'We few, we happy few, we band of brothers. For he today that sheds his blood with me, shall be my brother; be he ne'er so vile, this day shall gentle his condition. And gentlemen in England now abed, shall think themselves accursed they were not here, and hold their manhood's cheap while any speaks, that fought with us upon Saint Crispin's day.'

Henry V's speech to the English Army before the Battle of Agincourt.

William Shakespeare

The Battle of Agincourt was fought on St Crispen's Day, Friday, 25th October 1415.

Chapter 100 - THE HELL [BLOODY BARNSTORF]

1ST BALTIC FRONT - MARSHAL BAGRAMYAN

0430hrs, Thursday, 25th October 1945, the Hunte River, Barnstorf.

'Can there be any more bloody water in the heavens?'

It seemed a very reasonable question to Ramsey, as he was drenched yet again, the cold water penetrating to every part of his body.

There was no time to change.

There was no point in changing, even if there had been time.

"My other uniform is probably just as bloody wet."

Exchanging looks with McEwan, Ramsey could only grin at the man, who looked more miserable than the rest put together.

The first attack came in hard, direct, and with power behind it.

Fig #68 - The start, Bloody Barnstorf.

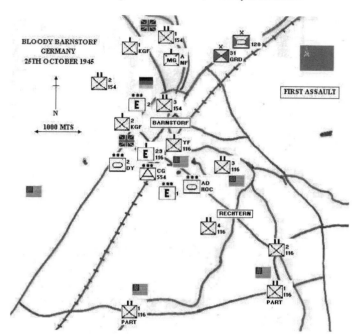

The Allied forward forces positioned in Eydelstedt were pushed out quickly. In truth, they ran, for there was no sense in the sacrifice of their lives when the Soviet attack was so large.

Waves of infantry, fresh troops from the veteran 31st Guards Rifle Division, supported by tanks from the 128th Tank Brigade, all under the umbrella of fire support from the elite 9th Guards Mortar Brigade and elements of the 4th Breakthrough Artillery Division.

The Katyusha rockets of the 9th Guards fell to the rear of Walsen and Barnstorf, giving the reserve elements a very torrid time, 4th Artillery hounding the shadowing Allied response force, occasionally scratching a tank here or an APC vehicle there.

Lighter mortars from the Guards infantry were deployed, also adding their weight of shot to the barrage endured by the defenders of the Hunte River, and all the time the assault waves drew closer.

The Battalion comprising the Seaforths had it easy enough, as no fire was directed at the front line troops, sat in sodden foxholes between Walsen and the river.

Linking between the Seaforths and 7th Black Watch were some MG troops from the Northumberland Fusiliers.

Ramsey's Battalion, and in particular, B Company, had been allocated the prize position, or at least that was how Blake had put it.

It was the prize, in as much as it was Barnstorf itself, and for B Company, the main Osnabruck road bridge, which even in its damaged state, seemed still usable for tanks.

Some explosives would put it down permanently, but there were none to be had. In any case, the rail bridge, as the most intact structure, would get priority attention when they did arrive. For now, the rail bridge was a problem, but there were mines covering the approaches, and Allied eyes were more firmly fixed at Ramsey's position and the bridge to the south.

That second structure, on Friedrich-Platte-Straβe, was also damaged but, in the view of the 116th's present hierarchy, was likely to fall down 'if so much as an ant farted near it.'

None the less, it was covered by a short company of men from the 1st Black Watch.

The rail bridge itself formed the junction between the British and American defenders, the other 1st Black Watch company defending up to the rails, the bridge and south from that point was the responsibility of the newly designated 'Yorke Force', the recent arrivals thickened out with stragglers and the reorganised engineers of the 29th Composite Engineer Company.

The other four units of the 116th Infantry either held the Hunte, sat close by ready to respond, or in the case of the 1st Battalion, waited silently in Dreeke and Duste.

The 116th Regiment had absorbed the survivors of the 175th, and was unique in having four reasonable sized battalions, plus Yorke Force.

They would all be needed.

The human wave approached the Hunte, and defending commanders gave the order to fire.

Much of Barnstorf was in ruins already, but the use of defensive artillery, mortars and grenades, did little for the remaining architecture.

The assaulting troops ducked down low, using the rubble and ruins to mask their approach, but the bursts of high explosive often grabbed the running soldiers, tossing men skywards, grim indicators of the progress of the attack.

7th Black Watch was pouring fire down the channels, hacking down any soldiers brave enough to try and form for a direct assault on the bridge.

The Soviets were already seeking a solution, working their way through the wrecked houses and shops, getting closer in safety, if not in sufficient numbers.

Such a group inadvertently betrayed themselves, a helmeted head popping up directly opposite Ramsey's position.

Two Mills bombs removed the threat quickly and permanently.

Bullets clipped off the road surface around the Black Watch position, as some distant Maxim machine-gun tried to give support, its crew oblivious to the friendly casualties they caused amongst another group, previously enjoying a measure of safety behind the rubble from a collapsed building.

The infantry attack in the town ground to a halt, and the Soviet commander screamed for tank support.

A gaggle of T34's pressed forward, confined to the roads, and vulnerable, but none the less answering the call.

Behind the bridge was a piece of high ground, not lofty, but sufficiently raised for an anti-tank gun to be able to work efficiently from its crest.

One of the 61st's six-pounders barked, the high-velocity shell burning white-hot as it roared down Osnabrücker Straße, crossing above the bridge and striking the turret of the lead tank, two hundred metres beyond.

Sparks flew, but no great harm was done, the medium tank advancing slowly over the rubble, its machine-guns lashing out at the defending Scots.

Again, the six-pounder fired, this time missing altogether, the gunner almost beside himself with fear.

A steadying hand was placed on his shoulder, the gun commander, a young subaltern, himself a boy of twenty years, calming the frightened youth with his presence and soft words.

The T34 fired at its tormentor, decapitating the anti-tank officer. The torso stood rigidly in place for a full two seconds, which was long enough for the gunner to put his own shot on target, penetrating the hull and the driver. The shell travelled at high speed through the fighting compartment and exited the rear wall, before the engine block put up enough resistance to prevent further travel.

Thick black smoke filled the street within seconds, enabling the surviving tank crew to get clear unhindered.

The tank behind commenced pushing its damaged compatriot forward, offsetting the risk of track damage for the bonus of extra protection that the smoking hulk offered.

A scream startled Ramsey. The veteran Lance Corporal next to him sank to the ground, clutching what had been his shoulder.

A large chunk had disappeared, leaving ivory bone on open display.

The medic sprang forward, dropping into cover, and immediately setting to work to stem the flow of blood.

The medical orderly didn't scream when the bullet hit him, his death instantaneous, as the metal passed through the back of his head.

"Stay down, stay down. Sniper has us, Lads."

"I canna see him, Boss."

McEwan had his own weapon ready, a beautiful precision engineered Lee-Enfield.

"Well, he has us bang to bloody rights, Corporal!"

Another bullet ended the life of the wounded Lance Corporal.

McEwan whispered in self-congratulation.

"I see ye."

The muzzle of the Enfield shifted almost imperceptibly and fired, the muzzle flash greatly reduced by the special flashless ammunition McEwan always seemed to have access to.

In less than half a second, the Scot was squealing in pain, as the rifle was hammered from his grasp. A bullet tore away the telescopic sight and struck the body of the rifle, just in front of the redundant rear sight.

His right index finger protruded at a funny angle, dislocated by the impact of the rifle as it was knocked aside.

"Ah jings, but yon man is good!"

"Is good or was good, McEwan?"

"Oh, the bas is still there, Boss. Make nae error on that."

Staying in cover, Ramsey made a quick assessment. The positions to either side were firing as normal, clearly unseen by the enemy marksman. The assault forces were still not grouped enough to attack successfully, so he estimated he had time to do what was needed.

"Right-ho McEwan. Is that bundook still working?"

The Scot had retrieved the Enfield, showing his open horror at the abuse caused by a Soviet rifle bullet.

"Well, the sights and mounts are fecked." Almost as if examining the grazes on the knee of a beloved child, McEwan continued his inspection.

"Damage is nae so bad. Rear sight is fine, so I can fire, but I canna vouch for the accuracy n'more, Boss."

"Will it do the job?"

"Aye, it will do the job for the now, but the bas will have shifted his sen, Boss."

"Sort your bundook out man, and I will find a way to flush the quarry."

McEwan's interest peaked, the opportunity of revenge overtaking common sense.

Patiently, Ramsey alternated between glimpses of the fighting either side of him, and the slow deliberate actions of McEwan reassembling his pride and joy.

He knew better than to rush the man.

A bullet pinged off the brickwork, forcing him back into cover.

Sitting against the wall, with his back to the enemy, the Black Watch Major slid his canteen out and washed away the accumulated smoke and brick dust, his throat welcoming the clear, cool liquid.

'Dear God, a bloody mirror!'

As he raised his mouth up to drink, his eyes had followed, and there it was. A previously unseen mirror hanging in the hole between floors, perfectly angled for him to see the road to the bridge and beyond.

He watched closely.

Nothing, save two burning T34's, the second one having fallen victim to something unseen as it pushed forward.

468

Robertson scurried through the door, momentarily exposed.

"Get down, Sarnt-Major!"

The bullet must have missed the NCO by no more than an inch.

"Got him. McEwan?" Ramsey looked over to his number one marksman, receiving a businesslike shake of the head, "Junction about two hundred metres up from the bridge. House on the left as you look. Three holes in the roof. Have a careful look at the middle one."

Slipping his middle finger into the trigger guard, the Corporal edged the rifle carefully into position. McEwan stopped as a barrage of rockets hammered the area behind them, the Guards Mortars firing as fast as they could in support of their infantry comrades.

The rifle moved forward again.

The whine of artillery shells interrupted McEwan's concentration once more, but this time it was friendly 4.5" shells from the 127th Field Artillery.

The Enfield slipped into position and McEwan took sight on the damaged roof, in time to see the first of two impacts.

The initial explosion blasted the whole of the roof skywards, the top floor accompanying it, as the blast split the upper storey into fragments.

The Soviet sharpshooter was ripped apart, all shape or form lost in the unforgiving process.

As the pieces started to descend, another 4.5" shell plunged through the building, exploding on the fifth step of the basement stairs.

Nine members of the Bergmann family, taking shelter there, evaporated in a split second, never to be seen again.

The whole building imploded, collapsing spectacularly, and killing a dozen Soviet guardsmen as it came to ground around their ears.

Ramsey's position could now respond, free from the threat of the Soviet marksman, and they added their weight to the defence once more, the stalled attack becoming even more bogged down, as dead bodies and vehicles started to clog the streets.

At the middle bridge, the story was different, there being less cover to mask the Soviet approach, and less cover to grant them some scant refuge from the storm of bullets.

The men of the 1st Black Watch had a score to settle, and they did so, ably supported by two venerable Vickers machine-guns.

Both weapons fired continuously, their water jackets hissing, as the heat generated steam, and steadily consumed the coolant.

Men brought water from the river, or urinated into buckets, anything to keep the guns firing.

The constant rain of bullets matched the driving storm for ferocity, hacking down scores of Soviet infantry as they tried to advance.

It was the nearest thing to murder possible in war, but not one Jock tear was shed, for the 1st had been on the receiving end themselves, and this was payback time.

At the rail bridge, the situation was again different, those attackers to the north of the tracks vulnerable; those to the south better off, gaining cover from the woods and embankment.

The US defenders enjoyed almost limitless supplies of ammunition, and flayed the woods with bursts of .50 and .30 cal from machine-guns spread all along the Hunte.

Again, huge gaps were torn in the Soviet ranks.

T34's rushed through, intent on getting into a firing position, and ripping up the defences whilst their infantry comrades formed for another assault.

Equipped with a number of bazookas, the 116th's doughboys smashed T34 after T34, leaving seven dead on the field before the tanks drew off again.

Not without cost, as the bazooka teams themselves took heavy casualties in order to keep the tanks at bay.

The courage of the attacking Russians was impressive, the infantry rising up again, shouting their 'Urrahs', and throwing themselves forward, the human wave coming to a high water mark only four yards from the end of the bridge. Its terminus was marked by a pile of bloody bodies, men smashed into the ground by the soldiers of Yorke Force.

As the surviving Soviet guardsmen started to give ground, Yorke stood up and called to his men.

"Up and at 'em, men! Charge!"

Some of the younger soldiers started to rise, only to be dragged back into cover by older hands.

Yorke charged forward, his Thompson spitting at the backs of distant men.

Not one soldier followed.

Each man kept his own thoughts on the fool who disappeared into the rain to their front.

0620hrs, Thursday, 25th October 1945, the Hunte River, Barnstorf.

Brigadier Blake was in good form, doing the rounds of his battered, but unbowed, infantry, the sights of the enemy dead in front of the river impressing him greatly.

Ever the stickler for the military niceties, he formally saluted the hallowed piece of ribbon.

Major John Ramsey, 7th Black Watch, returned the salute, and reported on the state of his unit.

"Jolly good work, Ramsey. Tell your boys, a big well done from me.

Old though he may be, with his best soldiering years behind him, you could not help but like the affable old man.

"That I will, Sir. Now, may I offer you tea?"

Again, Blake was impressed, the seemingly empty position suddenly yielding strong hot tea, just as he liked it.

"Thank you, Corporal," he grinned at the NCO who thrust the mug into his hands, the look fading slightly as he took in the strange angle of the man's index finger.

Ramsey beat him to it.

"I will get it sorted directly, Sir. Just leaving him be for the moment, but I will sort it."

The tea was divine, and Blake hated to spoil the moment, but he had made a decision.

"Ramsey, we have about an hour or so before the next phase, if they play the game according to form."

Plucking a tatty map from his pouch, Blake showed the infantry officer his intentions.

"I want you to wait here until relieved by the Argyles,"

471

'That is music to my ears,'
"And set your company up here, at Nagelskamp."
'Couldn't be more perfect,'
"And be ready to act as my reserve force when I call,"
'Sod it!'
"Just the job for you, eh Ramsey?"
The slight delay was deliberate.
"Delighted, Sir, really."
"That's the spirit, old chap!"

"Now, I have arranged for the Argyles to leave enough of their transport there," he indicated the agreed position, "So you can have mobility in your role."

"Thank you, Sir."

"Command of the 3rd Battalion will now pass to Major Cound of the Argyles, who I have detached from 2nd Battalion, so all you need to worry about is being in the right place at the right time."

"Now," he drained the last of his tea, returning the mug to the magically reappeared Corporal, who had clearly been listening from a concealed position, "Get yourself and your men back into reserve, and be ready when I call, and not before I call if you please, there's a good fellow."

Throwing up a magnificent salute, Blake was gone in the blink of an eye.

Robertson emerged from the same hidey-hole that had spat out McEwan a moment before.

"Och! Oot of the fucking frying pan, intae the fucking fire, Sah."

"I think that puts it rather well, Sarnt-Major!"

Ramsey finished his own tea, pressing the mug into McEwan's reluctant hand.

"Get the men ready to move, once the Argyle's get here, if you please, Sarnt-Major."

"Sah!"

0755hrs, Thursday, 25th October 1945, the Hunte River, Barnstorf.

Despite the fact that intelligence had briefed them on the probability of a follow-up attack, the defenders were nearly taken off-guard.

472

The Argyle's CO, Beattie, an old Major, whose experience, it was humorously rumoured, went back to Balaclava and beyond, had a sudden seizure.

The sight of their commander thrashing around on the floor, frothing at the mouth, eyes rolling in his head, unnerved some, and distracted all.

Inadvertently, the Soviet commander had put in his attack five minutes before schedule, for no other reason than the Artillery's need to move on with the main body quickly.

Attention strayed from the fitting man to the eastern approaches, once again full of charging enemy infantry.

The Argyles rose to the challenge, and put up a terrific defence, stopping the assault cold, forcing the enemy to again seek the advantage of shelter in the ruins of Barnstorf.

Despite being without a head, the 2nd Battalion still functioned well.

In the flooded fields, west of Gothel, bogged down tanks from the first attack lent their firepower to the second assault, but to no avail, the defences proving too strong. The American and British soldiers recognised the difference between the second half-hearted attack, and the all-out assault of the first wave.

None the less, the action cost the 116th Infantry two of its company commanders, one dead, the other wishing he were, his triple amputation promising a mundane life of care, above the few functions he would be able to perform with his remaining leg.

0945hrs, Thursday, 25th October 1945, Scharrel, Germany.

The plan seemed to be working, although the heavy rain made verification more difficult.

Best information put the enemy shadowing force off to the south, following the units of the 11th Guards, as they rolled the attack further away from Barnstorf.

The heavy rain was a double-edged sword, providing good cover for the ground operations, and keeping the potent enemy air force out of the sky, offsetting the loss of visibility, the reduced effectiveness of his artillery support, and the restriction of movement caused by flooding.

Major General Obinin decided, on balance, to accept its presence as a positive.

"All units, attack. Artillery, standby."

The order was relayed, and the assault group moved forward as one, intent on forcing the Hunte, and opening the way for the 6th Guards Army.

Silently, the lead units moved forward, the rain, if anything, growing in its strength and fury, visibility at a hundred and fifty yards at best.

'Perfect! Keep raining!'

0953hrs, Thursday, 25th October 1945, the Hunte River, Barnstorf.

Blake was drinking more tea, wishing his batman had the skills of the unknown Scottish corporal who had conjured such delights from god knows where.

None the less, he was determined to enjoy the brew.

'Warm and wet, that's all a man ever needs.'

Blake had never heard of atheroma.

He stifled a belch.

'Indigestion.'

He rubbed his chest, convinced the stewed tea had affected him adversely.

Another piece of atheroma, this one larger, joined the first, starting on its own short journey.

The first piece lodged in a coronary artery, diameter reduced by the build-up of fatty material, complimented by years of bodily abuse, the effects moving quickly beyond simple indigestion in a blink of an eye.

His left arm suddenly became incapable of holding the mug, and it dropped to the ground, smashing noisily. His jaw set firmly, the pain in it causing him to freeze all movement therein.

The second piece of atheroma, a detached piece of fatty deposit from the inside of an artery, came up against the first blockage, and caused a near-perfect seal, resistant to the pressure of blood trying to go on its way.

The pain was intense, cutting through every sensation, every sense, until it was all-pervasive.

Blake slid to the floor, his arms heavy and useless.

Behind the blockage, a long-standing weakness in the coronary artery decided that its time had come, and the artery gave way under the pressure build-up caused by the pumping of the heart itself.

The commander of the 154th Brigade was dead before he could blink.

0955hrs, Thursday, 25th October, 1945, Main road bridge, the Hunte River, Barnstorf.

"Stand to! Stand to! 'Undreds of the bas!'"

The Argyle and Sutherland Highlanders were caught unawares, but quickly recovered, although the Soviet rush had made it to within one hundred yards, the volume of fire quickly stopped them in their tracks, dropping men to the sodden roads and pavements, never to rise again.

The Argyle's Major was on the way to the rear, destined never to fight again, command of the ad hoc company now in the hands of a young Captain, whose heaviest responsibility before this bloody day had been organising the battalion boxing competition.

None the less, Brian Jesmond came from soldier stock, and was up to the task.

Within seconds, he had organised a mortar barrage on the lead elements, and a minute after that, artillery started to fall on the echelons behind.

As dictated by the Soviet battle plan, contact meant that their own artillery and mortars commenced firing, falling behind the river, restricting the movement of the local reserves.

To the north, Soviet forces were rushing the river line from Eydelstadt, the survivors of the 31st Guards Rifle Division, intent on pinning the defenders in place at least, although men of the 77th Engineers followed closely behind, in case opportunity arose.

The British 154th Brigade was under greater pressure than before, as much by the surprise of the assault, as its severity.

Back at the courtyard on the Nagelskamp, Ramsey heard the growing sounds of fighting and, along with his men, grew restless, not knowing that Brigadier Blake was unable to issue instructions.

Blake's 2IC was struggling to control the battle already, thoughts of self-preservation more paramount in his mind.

Without thinking, he had dispatched one of the reserve companies of his 2nd Battalion, directing the men of the 5th/7th Gordon Highlanders to the defences at Walsen, passing them through the local reserve force of the reduced C Company, 2nd Seaforths.

Whilst the fight at Walsen was intense, the commander on the ground was content that he could hold, the assaulting troops being kept at a suitable distance from the water.

All of a sudden, he had an embarrassment of riches, and was able to report confidently that the line would hold.

Kommando Friedrich's 1st Alarm Kompagnie had shifted north, mirroring a Soviet move, pushing up to a line between Rödenbeck and Aldorf, slotting in beside the other Seaforths, mainly members of the old 2nd Battalion.

Spurred on by the example of some Red Army NCO's and officers, a handful of brave men tried to swim across and were machine-gunned in the water, Brens, Stens, and Enfields turning the water maroon with blood.

There was no room for mercy on the Hunte that day.

However, there was opportunity for error, and the petrified acting Brigade commander made more gaffs, as he struggled with his inner demons.

The remaining company of 2nd Battalion, more Gordon Highlanders, was sent forward into the mill, at the main road bridge, compacting the defenders, bringing problems as enemy mortar fire started to yield three or four casualties a shell, rather than the one or two had the units been properly spaced.

Junior officers and NCO's tried to sort out the problems, some of them joining the ranks of the fallen, as they bravely exposed themselves in the effort.

At the bridge itself, Soviet infantry swarmed forward, accepting terrible losses for speed of advance, a brave rush bringing the survivors to the ruins next to the east bank.

Grenades flew one way, and then the other, casualties screaming as flesh was sliced by hot metal.

As if to try and mask the sounds of suffering, the rain redoubled its efforts, the noise drowning out screams and gunfire to all those but those closest.

Five hundred yards upstream, the fight for the middle bridge was intense, the assault force being backed up by some tanks, including those still bogged down from earlier attacks.

1st Black Watch were exhausted, but still fighting, their casualties higher than other units, as the Soviet mortars proved more effective, causing many casualties with tree bursts.

The commander urgently called for assistance, knowing that his position was dire.

A Soviet mortar shell had landed alongside one of the old Vickers, tossing it forcefully into the air.

It dangled from the tree still, accompanied by the detritus of its gunner.

Two men had been wounded trying to knock it back down to earth before the attempt at recovery was abandoned.

The other machine-gun continued to wreak havoc with the advancing Soviet infantry, although they had taken to crawling forward, their bellies deep in the mud and puddles, edging closer to the river line.

Captain Finlay lay in peaceful repose, his quiet form not betraying the horrors of the shrapnel wounds that had ripped his back to shreds and stilled his heart.

Kampfgruppe Friedrich's 2nd Kompagnie answered the call for help, moving up without orders, integrating themselves with the Jocks and stiffening the line.

The first German casualty was Dieckhoff, shot in the groin and ankle as he ran forward.

A number of the Kommandos fell, but the position was soon restored.

Hauptmann Strecher moved gingerly around the frontline, encouraging a soldier here and there. Despite the pain from a sprained ankle, he brought his brand of cheerfulness and encouragement to his men.

A renewed bout of firing marked the start of another Soviet probe, lead by tanks, and Strecher moved quickly to the nearby anti-tank gun, another of the 61st's six-pounders.

The crew were all experienced men, and the evidence of that was the five T34's already lying smashed from the first attacks.

Strecher was satisfied that the men knew their craft, and moved away.

Suddenly he was lifted, a silent force propelling him into a tree, chest first, knocking the wind from his lungs and stunning him.

Groggily, he knelt on the soaked ground, shaking his head to clear his vision, drawing hard on the cold air.

His eyes started to focus on the six-pounder, lying on its side, one wheel pointing towards the gods.

An HE shell had landed next to the gun, the blast tipping it over and ripping through the crew.

One man, probably the gun layer, was trapped under the gun, the wheel pressing him into the ground.

The gun commander, who had been nearest to the explosion, lay on the ground adjacent to the new shell hole, no injury apparent, but none the less dead.

Three other crewmembers had died, coming apart under the force of the shell.

One man survived, unconscious, knocked out when the unpinned trail of the gun had struck him in the face as it flipped over.

The ex-Luftwaffe officer hesitated for a moment, his eyes alternating between the horrors around the gun to the gathering force of enemy tanks.

Calling to no one in particular, but none the less calling for all he was worth, Stracher leapt forward, the pain of his ankle and broken ribs, lost in the adrenalin of battle.

Three men answered his call, and together they rolled the gun back onto its wheels, releasing the gun layer, and dragging him clear.

He did not survive the move.

The rain stopped, going from downpour to nothing in a few seconds.

"Kameraden, how is to fire this gun?"

CSM Green spoke up.

"No idea, Sir. Seen them a few times, but never fired one."

"I can do it, Sir. Easy enough. My cousin is in the gunners, so I've seen it done."

Private Johnson grinned as he slipped into the gun layers seat.

"Sarnt-Major, grab that lever," he indicated the breech handle, "That way to open it, a shell goes in," Johnson leant back and adopted a serious tone, "Make sure it's in now, ok?" Green considered a reply, but held his tongue. The private was looking through the gun sight, playing with the gun laying controls, almost pre-occupied in thought before he remembered he was only halfway through his brief.

"And then push the lever back round. Step out of the fucking way tout-fucking-suite like, and tell me the shell is loaded, OK?"

"OK, I got you."

Turning back from his minor adjustments, Johnson adopted a serious tone.

"Keep out of the way of that breech, Sarnt-Major."

"OK, I got it."

"Achtung!"

Strecher yelled a warning, as one of the T34's pushed forward, furthest forward of a wedge of seven metal beetles, angling towards the bridge.

"Enemy tank to front, Kameraden. Engage the one on the road!"

The other soldier, MacPherson, another of the 1st Black Watch, slipped a shell out of its box and passed it across to Green, who in turn fed the breech, drawing the lever across and sealing it. Stepping back, he yelled at Johnson.

"Clear!"

The breech leapt back and the new crew were all surprised to see a spectacular direct hit, the front of the T34 disappearing in a blossom of red and orange.

The tank moved on through the fire.

Green was fit to burst.

"You fucking tosser! That's explosive! Gimme armour piercing, quick!"

Stretcher mouthed some unsavoury German words, although unsure if he would have known himself.

"Clear!"

Johnson's second shot struck the road underneath the advancing tank and carried on, rising as it went, just missing the rear plate of the tank, before it carved its way through the knot of infantry at the rear of the vehicle.

The carnage was awful, the solid shot smashing aside five men before continuing on its path.

"C'mon man! Hit the fucking thing!"

The breech closed once more.

"Clear!"

Again, the six-pounder fired, and again the shell missed, this time by a clearer margin, as the vehicle had increased speed.

A smoke trail reached out from the riverbank and struck the Soviet tank on the glacis plate.

The tank crew died, some instantly, the rest when they tried to bail out of the stricken vehicle, as vengeful German and Scottish infantry cut them down within seconds.

An old German Kommando soldier, once a member of the Volksturm, had swum across the Hunte to get a better shot, his Panzerfaust easily disposing of the tank.

He joined the number of floating bodies in the slow-moving river, a tossed grenade killing him as he struck out for the friendly west bank.

"Clear!"

This time Johnson scored a kill, a more difficult shot by far, but one that gave spectacular results.

Strecher, with the benefit of his binoculars, had directed the gun's fire onto a T34, positioned more towards the rear, drawn as he was by the telltale flapping aerials.

The tank contained the company commander and radio, both now being incinerated as the vehicle brewed up dramatically.

A shell exploded, followed by another, and then many more, vengeful observers bringing down mortar fire on the anti-tank gun position.

Green yelped as piece of shrapnel buried itself in his left buttock, and then again as a larger piece of metal opened the back of his left hand.

The temporary crew sought cover as best they could, only Macpherson escaping injury, although his decision to hide within the ammo compound was debateable at best.

Seeing the gun silent, and mindful of the ammunition issues, the Senior Lieutenant in control of the mortars ordered the fire stopped.

Strecher, the tip of his nose altered by a stone thrown up from a blast, was first to sit up.

Spitting away the blood and earth, he called to the rest of his crew.

"Kameraden, back to the pak!"

Green, angry as hell, the pain motivating him, picked up the shell he had been about to load, cleaned the earth and leaves from its glistening casing with his hands, before sliding it home.

"Clear. More ammo, man!"

Macpherson was slowest to respond to the call, but quickly produced a pristine shell from the nearest box.

Again, the gun thundered its defiance, and again it hit home, this time catching one of the T34's as it turned, penetrating the lower hull, removing the back idler and last road wheel, causing unknown but probably terminal damage to the engine.

The crew made a quick escape, and were luckier than their comrades were, all five making it to cover without injury.

Strecher searched for more targets, conscious that the only live tanks he could see were backing up, moving away as their guns hammered out to cover the withdrawal.

The defensive fire of the Highlanders also started to slacken, the men tired of firing, refusing even the easy targets of retreating men's backs, as the Soviet infantry moved away from the field.

Soviet mortars again opened up, this time dropping a mix of HE and smoke, trying to cover the withdrawal.

Green's backside was hurting like hell, and he could not find a position that was comfortable.

Arching his back, he became aware of one of nature's glories, the spectacular phenomenon curving across the autumn sky, its colours rich and vibrant, as the sun gave full vent to its powers.

As is the want of every observer of such things, many an eye followed the rainbow's curves to establish where it came to ground.

Green and Strecher looked at the rainbow, and then looked at each other.

It terminated at the rail bridge, from whence came the sounds of extreme violence, punctuated by the flashes of guns and shells, as the Soviet main assault charged forward.

<u>0956hrs, Thursday, 25th October, 1945, Main rail bridge, the Hunte River, Barnstorf.</u>

"Next bridge up river's under attack too."

"You don't shay."

481

Hässler slithered in beside Rosenberg, and ignored the usual provocation.

"Well, we have problemsh of our own, Mashter-Shergeant."

To their front, occasionally obscured by the renewed downpour, but visible enough to see their intention, Soviet infantry were sneaking forward through the sparse wood.

Soviet mortars had been falling for a few minutes now, to their rear, and to little effect, as far as Hässler was concerned.

US artillery was zeroed in on the area either side of the rail track, and 105mm shells were ripping gaps in the loose Soviet formation.

From the direction of Rechtern came crashes, this time recognisable as tank and anti-tank guns, as more bad news visited itself upon the Allied defences.

A recent arrival to the field was a composite group of survivors from the 554th AAA Battalion, now boasting eight SP weapons, and just about enough men to make them function.

The two surviving radars were set up, and immediately went to work mapping out the Soviet mortar positions.

The Red Army had learned the hard way, and now repositioned constantly, in order to avoid the Allies extremely effective counter-battery fire.

The Guards Mortar men of the 36th Rifle Corps had been in constant combat since 6th August, and they knew to relocate, doing so after a standard four shells were launched from their 82mm mortars.

Major Deniken waited in cover with his soldiers, the tired units not yet committed.

His binoculars swept the immediate battlefield, but the spectacle of the full-scale assault was ruined by the downpour.

To the right, mortar men from his own regiment redeployed, moving uncomfortably close to the overgrown hill on which his force was concealed, just east of HülsmeyerStraße, and a full kilometre from the rail bridge.

He watched as the mortars quickly set up and fired four rounds, relocating again, and becoming lost in the rain as they moved forward into the outskirts of Gothel.

The rain was a huge problem for the tankers, not the least of whom was Arkady Yarishlov, his ability to effectively command virtually lost in the deluge.

The ground to the west of Gothel was sodden, and had already claimed some unwary tankers.

The track known as Hunteholz was suitable, but single file only. Another similar track, Stichweg could be used, but clashed with those forces assaulting the middle bridge.

Yarishlov had made a decision to risk some of his tanks in an attempt to gain good firing positions and the best cover for his infantry support, and so he had committed two companies of T34's in column, straight up the railway line. This gained advantage from the harder going, and the height, but at the cost of risking their vulnerable sides to anti-tank weapons, and placing them in a position where they could be more easily seen.

'Such decisions are the privilege of rank.'

The thought was not a happy one, and he strained through his binoculars to observe how the exposed group was doing.

He had ordered it to advance at good speed, accepting the loss of immediate infantry support for the bonus of kilometres per hour.

The lead tank blossomed into a fireball, and he gripped his binoculars tightly, relief sweeping over him as he realised it was just a mine, and only a track had been lost.

Relief quickly gave way to concern, as the tank seemed to be blocking the route, slewed as it was, almost sideways across the rails.

Relief came again as the second tank pushed past, risking more mines to follow the orders and keep the advance going.

Combat engineers from the 36th Guards Rifle Corps moved up, intent on removing as much of the hidden menace as possible.

Yarishlov switched his attention to the Hunteholz, the combination of rain and trees doing an excellent job at hiding his tankers.

The infantry were pushing on through the woods, and were clearly involved in a heavy fire fight with the enemy soldiers across the river. The frequent flashes illuminated the grey damp world he was trying so hard to decipher.

He had chosen to be here, at the rail bridge assault, because of its key nature. However, the assault through Duste and Rechtern could prove to be the battle winner, and a huge part of him wished to be there too.

That force was led by his 1st Battalion Commander, backed up by a good portion of the 36th Guards Rifle Corps.

Turning in his turret, Yarishlov checked the squat shapes of the four IS-III's he had positioned in between two small hillocks, either side of a track known as Sonnenkamp.

He had been disappointed when the 'Regiment' of heavy tanks he had been promised materialised as four battered tanks, commanded by a young Lieutenant, who barely seemed old enough to drink, let alone command the Soviet Union's best battle tank.

Still, Kriks had chatted to some of the old lags in the 6th Heavy Tanks, and it seemed their faith in the young man was unshakeable.

Yarishlov was broken from his reverie by the crash of artillery, US 155mm's hammering the road from Brockmannshausen, hoping to catch support and supply elements in the open.

The shells destroyed grass and wood; nothing more.

He looked back to the railway line again, and was encouraged by what he saw. His tanks had moved on, and none seemed affected by the defensive fire, which increased in volume as he watched.

Ramsey replaced the receiver, puzzled, but none the less in receipt of a direct order.

Blake was nowhere to be seen, believed dead, and the 2IC sounded like he was coming apart at the seams.

None the less, he had ordered Ramsey's Highlanders to go to the support of the rail bridge defence, an area that he was not supposed to be involved with in any of the discussed defence options.

None the less, the order was there, and had to be obeyed.

"Sarnt-Major, get them up and ready to move immediately. We are off to the railway bridge."

Robertson was on the case immediately.

"Iain, I want you to take fourth platoon, and bring up all the ammunition you can manage, clear?"

Aitcherson seemed fine, his melancholy shaken off by the presence of the enemy.

"Absolutely, Sir. Shall I take some of the half-tracks?"

Ramsey thought about that.

"Yes, do, but do not bring them up into the combat zone. Load them up, by all means. Drive them forward, but stop short. Move the ammo in by hand, as it will be too risky otherwise."

A swift look at the map provided him with firmer thoughts.

"Here, Iain, bring your tracks in here," his finger ran down the length of 'Immenzaun', terminating in some railway land, some three hundred metres from the bridge.

"Make the dump there. I want you and Fourth Platoon to be my mobile reserve. Stand ready, keep on the radio, and move when I call, clear?"

"Perfectly, Sir."

The QOCH officer saluted and went to leave.

Ramsey added one other thing.

"The RSM will accompany you, Iain. He can organise and supervise an ammo chain, leaving you free to command the essentials. Take good care of him, will you?"

Aitcherson understood that Robertson was there to watch him, and stand in if he was not up to the job, and Ramsey knew that he knew it. However, the younger man welcomed the support, as much as he welcomed the sensitive way the Black Watch officer had provided it.

Two minutes later, 7th Black Watch was on its way to the rail bridge.

<u>1023hrs, Thursday, 25th October 1945, the Rail Bridge, Hunte River, Barnstorf.</u>

The rain stopped abruptly, the grey gloom almost immediately lost in sunshine.

The colours were magnificent, and men from both sides wondered at the rainbow in all its glory, the end seeming to terminate on the eastern side of the bridge.

However, the combatants did not permit one of nature's finest displays to restrict the battle, and dozens of men died, or were wounded, under its wondrous arch.

Hässler was under pressure, now the de facto commander of the ad hoc infantry unit called Yorke Force, and he was no longer had time to fire his weapon, his method of destruction being the radio.

His latest messages had called the Yeomanry reserve forward, three Staghound Mk III Armoured cars, and a Comet tank, soon to add their firepower to a growing fight.

Two of the Allies' 3" anti-tank guns were destroyed in short order, their shells seemingly ineffective against the angled hull armour of the T34's, whereas the Soviet HE shells were more than up to the job of subduing the AT defence, allowing the Soviet tanks to move closer all the time.

The ad hoc company was firing at a phenomenal rate, encouraged to expend ammunition, now that more and more targets appeared in the clear autumn morning.

The lead T34 was on the approach now, moving inexorably towards the bridge, some fifty metres to its front.

A small smoke trail reached out, hit, and the rocket projectile bounced off, failing to explode.

Accompanying Soviet guardsmen hacked down the bazooka crew before they could get off a second shot, a grenade finishing both men off and wrecking the weapon for good measure.

A Staghound swept forward, the odd looking armoured car a hybrid, the lower half all T17 Chevrolet Armoured Car, the upper half, a Crusader III gun turret sporting a six-pounder gun.

The armoured car came apart as two 85mm shells struck simultaneously, both HE, and both possessing sufficient power to utterly destroy the vehicle.

The third T34 in line stopped abruptly, a large mine, having been narrowly missed by the lead two tanks, claiming its offside track.

Ramsey's Black Watch arrived just as the Comet deployed and got off its first shot, a solid AP shell, which deflected off the mantlet of the lead Soviet medium tank.

Neville Griffiths had joined the Derbyshire Yeomanry in an age of horses, but armoured warfare had come as second nature to him.

During the advances in 1944-45, he had been credited with no less than seventeen Panzer kills, including three Panthers in one hectic day, the previous February.

Thrice mentioned in dispatches, sporting the Military Medal and Bar, Sergeant Griffiths should have been an officer, except for his quick temper and fists to match.

He had been up and down the NCO ratings more often than, in his own words, 'a busy whore's knickers', and his recent step up to Sergeant had been opposed by Captain 'Knobber' Lensh, the squadron adjutant. The officer had once felt Griffiths' fist on his nose, but now felt nothing at all, as most of him was buried outside of Bremen.

He was sober and angry, a combination that transformed him into an excellent tank commander, and he relocated just before a flurry of rifle grenades landed where the Comet had fired from.

Popping back up, the British tank missed its second shot completely, staying put, and relying on its faster rate of fire to give it the edge.

The 77mm gun spat out a sabot round before the Soviet tank crew had even found the enemy tank.

The fast-moving core penetrated the hull of the tank, precisely at the ball mount of the hull machine gun.

Smaller in diameter than the gun it had been fired from, the projectile was more of a dart, the increased power of penetration pushing it rapidly through everything in its path.

In this instance, it first traversed the machine-gunner before finding the shell in the hands of the loader.

The effect was immediate and catastrophic, the turret and hull parting company in the blink of an eye, as the internal explosion destroyed the tank, one of those recently acquired from the Poles.

Two shells streaked past the retreating Comet, testimony to the fighting spirit of the 4th Guards Tank Brigade.

The battle was getting desperate.

At Rechtern, matters were even worse, the 116th's infantry having taken heavy casualties, as a result of a Soviet error of judgement.

The support artillery had been accidentally dropped on the defence line, risking the bridge's integrity, but catching the men exposed, so used were they to the Soviets avoiding strikes on bridges.

For the Red Army assault force, it could not have worked out better. There was no damage to the bridge and dozens of US infantry were out the fight.

Only one serviceable 3" anti-tank gun remained, and it got off one telling shot before it was swept aside by a direct hit, as the T34's closed in.

Lieutenant Colonel Willoughby, desperately trying to piece together what was happening to his command, and without decent information from the temporary commander of the 154th Brigade, did all he could, as well as he could.

Orders went to the Adhoc tank unit, seven vehicles of varying types and battle worthiness, sending them down Route 48 to stiffen the defence of Rechtern, the position he saw as most under threat.

With them went one platoon of the Royal Engineers, hanging on tight, as the venerable tanks moved off at speed.

The 3rd Battalion, more of a short company in reality, sent two of its platoons down the river line to bolster the northern edge of Rechtern, removing half the firepower from a point directly opposite the few Soviet engineer inflatables.

His last but one act withdrew half of the mortar support allocated to the rail bridge, sending that south in the wake of the tanks.

By the time that Willoughby had all the information he needed, it was too late, and the rail bridge was left vulnerable.

Willoughby's final act was to ensure his signals troops screamed for assistance to any Allied unit that had ears, pleading with them to come to Barnstorf, where a disaster was in the making.

<u>1029hrs, Thursday, 25th October 1945, The Hunte River rail bridge, Barnstorf.</u>

Major Ramsey had arrived into a scene from Armageddon itself, the now bright sunlight picking out death and destruction on a grand scale.

Two Staghounds were burning, the survivor manoeuvring as best it could on three wheels, trying to find somewhere safe to lick its wounds.

The US infantry holding the rail bridge were under pressure, two Soviet tanks on the bridge, their turrets sweeping from side to side, scouring the defensive positions, claiming a life here and there, and effectively keeping Allied heads down along the line.

Behind them, Soviet infantry were running, converging on the structure that would get them across the river and onto dry land.

"Quickly lads, quickly."

Directing a Vickers gun into position, he made sure the crew understood his purpose.

"Not one of those bloody swine crosses that bridge, Hamilton, not one. Clear?"

The man grinned at the unusually colourful language of their beloved officer, revealing an absence of teeth, not suffered in combat, but caused by his love of the barley sugar sticks made by his confectioner father.

"Not one bloody swine, aye Sir!"

A slap on the man's back and Ramsey was gone.

Next, the PIAT section got their orders, the two weapons directed to the task of destroying the lead T34's on the bridge.

The task became easier as somewhere to the Black Watch's front, a bazooka put a shell into the side of one of the tanks, knocking the vehicle out of the fight as the crew bolted for safety.

More firing erupted as the defending GI's took advantage of the slackened fire to mow down their tormentors. The whole crew were killed or wounded within seconds, the open bridge providing no cover as they ran.

The surviving Black Watch Officers and NCO's were shaking the Jocks out, forming a firing line, ready for the Soviet infantry.

Cupping his hands around his mouth, Ramsey yelled a warning.

"Watch for friendlies to the front, boys! There's still some cousins there, watch out for them!"

As he spoke, another T34 nosed onto the bridge, intent on maintaining the advance.

The Comet had manoeuvred slyly and popped out in prime position, the woods just to the south of the rail bridge giving it quality cover until it was too late for the Russian tank.

Another APDS shot sped across the water and hit down low, passing through the tank and out the other side.

A serious disadvantage of the APDS was that its high penetration often took it through targets, and the modest explosive power of the smaller shell was sometimes insufficient to kill the tank, even if it exploded inside.

This shell lost on all counts.

Griffiths put his head out to check the target, and was surprised to find his immediate location more smokey since his arrival. The smoke was from the Comet's engine, and it should not have been there.

As he ducked inside, a heavy bullet pinged off his cupola, an AT rifleman on the far bank chancing his arm, and coming close to ending the Sergeant's life.

"Check the engine, Drives. It's bollockin out smoke!"

Trooper Droves, or 'Drives' to his mates, swept his eyes over the gauges, although he knew everything felt right with 'Lady Hamilton'. The tank had been named by the previous tank commander, Herbert Nelson, now in hospital in Blighty, where they were hopeful his sight could be saved.

"All's tickety-boo, Sarge."

"No it fucking ain't, Drives. Check again."

Droves did the full routine again and spotted that the oil reading had changed from a few seconds before.

"Oil levels dropping, Sarge. Must be a leak. Not serious at the moment."

Griffiths pondered that for a second.

"Massage the engine for a while and keep the revs down. Once the bastards have buggered off, we can have a gander and sort it."

To some, it would be enough reason to fall back, but Griffiths was made of sterner stuff, and 'Lady Hamilton's' crew accepted his decision without quibble.

Beside the Sergeant, the telephone squawked, announcing some infantry type outside. Fixed to the rear of the Comet was a handset for use by supporting troops.

"Room Service?"

"Maybe later. Major Ramsey of the Black Watch here. To whom do I speak?"

"Sergeant Griffiths, 2nd Derbyshires, Sir."

"Hot day, Sergeant, and likely to get hotter. Can you see tanks at your one o'clock, through the trees there?"

A pause as the tank commander strained his eyes in that direction.

"No, Sir. All I can see is greenery, and infantry."

"Well never mind. I assure you they are there, about a dozen of them, from what we can make out. They will make a surge shortly, so stand ready. We and the Yanks have AT weapons on this side of the bridge, but we need you to even the odds quickly. Keep them at bay if you can. You ok for ammunition?"

"Yes, Sir, provided they only send the one tank battalion, we should be fine."

Ramsey was unsure whether that was humour, bravado, or pessimism, but decided he would let the man be, as his job was a difficult one.

"Bottom line, Sergeant. We hold where we are. There is no alternative plan. They do not cross the river, or we are sunk. Clear?"

"Yes, Sir."

"I'm leaving a squad here to provide you with close protection. They will keep their eyes skinned for tank-hunters. The rest is down to you. Good luck, Griffiths."

"Thanks, Sir, You too."

Replacing the receiver, Griffiths took a swift look through the vision block, but could not see the officer.

"Well, you'll be glad to know that our Jock friends have found a dozen Soviet tanks for us to play with."

He ignored the groans.

"We are it, the only tank. Those Red shitehawks don't get close to the bridge, and that's the bloody short of it. The Major seems to know his business, and he's left us some friends to watch our back."

Droves summed it up quite nicely.

"Bollocks!"

Bullets kicked up at his heels, but the Black Watch officer made it safely to the forward defensive position, as did McEwan, although the latter sported a painful nick to his left calf.

"Master Sergeant Hässler reporting, Sir."

"One moment..., Sergeant."

Ramsey wheezed. The rush over open ground, the acrid smoke coming from the Comet and other sources, all combined to make breathing difficult.

"Let me... get my... breath."

Producing a pack of Lucky Strike's, Hässler took one and passed them on, Rosenberg and another GI took one a piece. The other US soldier declined the offer.

McEwan eyed the cigarettes with longing.

"Want one, Jock?"

"Aye, that I do, Sarnt. Thank ye."

A hand signal to the soldier who did not smoke sent the man to the edge of the position, eyes firmly fixed on the approaches.

Breathing now stable, Ramsey grabbed one of his own cigarettes, raising a hand to stop the Sergeant's apology.

"What's your situation, Sergeant?"

"I'm down to half my doughs from forty-eight starters. Managed to evacuate the wounded during the last lull, but that was awhile ago, and the commies ain't taking time outs anymore."

Ramsey could never get used to the American way of speaking.

"How about ammunition?"

"Plenty of it, of all shapes and sizes, but I am down to two bazookas now, Sir."

Hässler pointed down a small off shoot from his position, the beginnings of a veritable arsenal in view.

"Splendid. Good work, Sergeant. I've got my chaps spread in a line behind you at the moment. Fields of fire seem fine, so long as you chaps keep your head down. I've also jollied up the tank boys."

Hässler could never get used to the British way of speaking.

492

For once, Rosenberg stayed silent, a painfully bruised elbow keeping his mind occupied.

The Master Sergeant stubbed his cigarette out and grabbed his canteen.

"So, Sir, what happens next? We have stopped the big red machine, but it ain't broke yet."

"True enough, Sergeant. If I'm any judge, our Red friends are gathering themselves for something more complicated."

He took the offered canteen, and was surprised to find it contained water.

A quizzical look drew a response.

"We lost our supply of quality booze when we were sent to hospital. Haven't managed to find time to replace it yet, Major."

Ramsey could not help but like the man, so he nodded to McEwan, whose hand was suddenly filled with a full canteen.

"Have a wee dram of that, Sarnt. That'll put hairs on ye chest, so it will."

The brandy was the very best quality, found amongst the abandoned vehicles of some unknown Allied General's headquarters.

"Wow!"

McEwan waved the canteen on, and it was passed to the unhappy Rosenberg.

A sudden burst of firing made everyone instinctively duck, and a body came tumbling into the position.

"Oi vay, Chief! Don't you Shergeants ever knock?"

Charley Bluebear unrolled himself and brushed his uniform into place, experienced enough not to salute in the front line, despite Ramsey's seniority.

"I am Warrant Officer, Corporal Rosenberg."

The Jew smiled disarmingly, testing his painful elbow by extending the canteen to the big man.

"Thank you, Corporal Rosenberg."

A quick swig and the canteen found its way back to the rightful owner, the dour Scot looking somewhat overwrought at the reduced contents.

"So what's cooking, Chief?"

Hässler and Bluebear had come to an accommodation over the nickname. If the Master Sergeant used it sparingly, and

493

not in a derogatory fashion, then Bluebear wouldn't break all his fingers.

So far, the agreement was holding.

"Lots of men crawling up as close as they can get over there. Over two companies, maybe even a battalion. Good cover if they stay down low, Master Sergeant."

Hässler hummed a response, his mind working the problem.

Ramsey wondered why the senior man, Bluebear, was deferring to Hässler, a lower rank. He decided that they must have made another accommodation, and it wasn't his place to interfere.

The American-German NCO thought aloud.

"We've got a good position, and they still have to come the one way."

Looking at Ramsey, he went on.

"Yeah, they've got armor, but we can mess that up enough to hold them."

The Black Watch Major pursed his lips, his mind also caught up in matters other than those directly in front of him.

Bluebear, conscious that minds were working, posed a simple question.

"So?"

Hässler remained quiet, looking at the English officer.

Ramsey believed he knew what the NCO was thinking, and nodded his agreement to the Master Sergeant.

"So, they are not coming here. This is a diversion."

He liberated the map from his pouch, and opened it up, placing it on the ammo box that Bluebear slid into place with ease.

The answer was as clear as day.

"Here, at Rechtern and Düste."

Even Rosenberg nodded, despite the fact that such matters were beyond his comprehension.

"Sho they will be past ush then. Should we bug out?"

The three faces looked at Rosenberg, as if he had been caught with his hand in the poor box.

"Nope. The fuckers will be coming here after that, my little friend."

"Why? They don't need thish town do they? They are past ush!"

494

Ramsey prepared to explain diplomatically, but was beaten to it by the slightly less sensitive Indian.

"It's the bridge, you stupid corporal."

Rosenberg looked from face to face, seeking further explanation.

Ramsey supplied it.

"It's a rail bridge. Heavy load. Stands to reason the Soviets want it, and I will warrant that there is no other such bridge for miles in either direction."

In that, Ramsey was absolutely correct.

"Sho why haven't we blown the fucking thing up...err...pardon me... Shir?"

Hässler supplied the answer this time.

"No explosives, you dumb fuck! Are all your people so stupid?"

Unusually, Rosenberg bristled at the comment.

"Only thosh of ush who have to put up with you fucking Krauts."

Ramsey went on, eyeing both men as he spoke.

"So, we need to reorganise a little."

The resources were thin, but Hässler and Bluebear could jiggle things a little.

"You gonna dial it in to the man, Major?"

Quickly decoding the Master Sergeant's words, Ramsey nodded.

"You first, Sergeant. Get him in the picture now. I will nip off back to my boys, get them reoriented to the south, and then give my report to the Colonel."

Without standing on ceremony, Ramsey quickly checked the lie of the land, and then was up and gone, McEwan following in his wake, determined never to bring best brandy near the Yanks again.

Willoughby was already making some changes, but the additional call from the competent sounding limey had made him tweak them some more.

"Get me Ramirez at 2nd."

The handset made its way over as the Commanding Officer of the grandly named 2nd Battalion came on line.

"Major, I just got off the line with a British officer who has firmed up the Intel. Best guess is the commies will definitely come straight at you with everything they got. You must hold, Oscar."

Quite clearly, Major Oscar Ramirez was unhappy with that decision.

"If they get through you, they will have options, Major. But we think they are after the rail bridge, so I am trying to locate some explosives, to at least drop the bridge at Rechtern as quickly as possible."

Willoughby had enough time to drink half a cup of coffee as the Spanish-American officer vented his spleen down the field telephone.

"Now hold on there, Oscar! You will hold, and that is a goddamn order, son! I'm sending up some assets. Armor, and extra bodies from 3rd Battalion."

Clearly, that had little effect upon the Major's tirade.

"Well, Major Ramirez. You will goddamn hold that position, or I will goddamn find someone who will, and I will make it my goddamn mission in life to visit myself upon your fucking sorry ass for the rest of your days. Am we clear, Major?"

Clearly, the response from Ramirez was unsatisfactory.

"Major, you are relieved immediately. Put your second in command on the horn immediately, and consider yourself under arrest."

1051hrs, Thursday, 25th October 1945, Command Post, 3rd Composite Battalion, on the Wagenfelder Aue River.

"He wants to speak to you, Phil."

"Jesus, Oscar. You told him to fuck off!"

"He is hanging our asses out to dry for a hunch. Pinning us here with no manoeuvre, all on a fucking guess from some limey."

The telephone changed hands.

"Captain Oakley."

He listened, sparing an occasional horrified glance at his friend.

"Are you sure of that situation, Colonel?"

The Captain almost jumped as the storm broke quickly in his ear.

"No, Sir, I am not questioning you, as such."

Oakley winced.

496

"Well, Sir, that's unfortunate. But to fix this unit in position on that basis is just wrong, Sir."

Suddenly, the jaw grew tenser, teeth set hard against each other in response to some direct words.

"Let me be frank, Colonel. We can give you some time, for sure, and maybe enough time for the engineers to do their job. But if the Red Army comes down that road in force, we haven't got a hope in hell of stopping a full scale attack, and to stand here and let it roll over us would be suicide, Sir."

His decision made, Oakley grinned at his ex-commanding officer.

"Well, if that's the case, Colonel, I believe that you'll be down to the corporals in no time, cos your order is a cluster fuck."

He replaced the phone on its cradle.

"So, what now, Oscar?"

The handset flew across the tent.

"Cowards! Fucking useless fucking cowards!"

Pulling out his Colt automatic and dramatically chambering a round, Willoughby rounded on his staff.

"Get my goddamn vehicle out front, now! Macey, with me. I'm going to visit myself upon them yellow sonsofbitches!"

1059hrs, Thursday, 25th October 1945, Route 344, east of Rechtern.

He waited.

The Colonel, his face betraying the strain of command, concentrated on his watch, the steady growl of the T-44's engine hardly a distraction.

The second hand swept with agonising slowness, finally reaching its zenith.

Patiently, Yarishlov waited, again, time not his friend.

However, when the expected fire arrived, the results were spectacular. No matter how often you saw a Katyusha Regiment put down a barrage, the sight was still an awesome one.

"All units advance! Driver, forward."

The T-44 moved gently off, Sergeant Lunin's skills easing the thirty-five ton beast into motion without so much as a sway.

Ahead of Yarishlov, the entire strength of his 1st Battalion was already edging forward, intent on overrunning the Allied defences on the nearby tributary of the Hunte, along with men from two of the 16th Guards Rifle Division's shattered regiments, banded together to make a special unit, charged with a single purpose; to cross the Wagenfelder Aue river.

He had switched his own position from the Rail Bridge, expecting his presence would ensure that the 1st Battalion pressed as hard as it could.

Accompanying Yarishlov's tanks were all the surviving Guardsmen of the recently reinforced 49th Guards Rifle Regiment, under the command of the newly promoted Lieutenant Colonel Deniken, and a full battalion of the 77th Engineers waiting to rush forward if things went wrong.

The 49th had taken a hammering over the previous two months, but had been bolstered by the arrival of men from units that were disbanded after receiving heavy casualties, bringing the regiment up to about 75% strength, all being veteran soldiers.

Ahead, the first wave engaged, and the radio waves were filled with the sound of orders and calls for assistance.

1104hrs, Thursday, 25th October 1945, Wagenfelder Aue Bridge, southeast of Rechtern, Germany.

The red brick timber mill sat adjacent to the west end of the bridge, its windows sandbagged, indicating its nature as a strongpoint, and the centre of the US bridge defence.

From each window, at least one weapon was being fired, sometimes as many as four. Carbines to heavy machine-guns, the whole range of automatic weapons available to the defenders of the 116th Infantry was on display.

All along the riverbank, foxholes and hastily dug trenches held more men, all of which were up and pouring fire into the advancing Soviet infantry and tanks.

The position was completed by wooden strongpoints, created from interlocked tree trunks, four such positions holding heavy machine guns, two containing anti-tank guns, all at the front line and, further back, another eight providing cover for the mortar support.

The Soviet soldiers were knocked over in great numbers, an individual man often struck by four or five bullets at a time, the defending Americans profligate with ammunition to balance their lack of numbers.

One of the anti-tank guns revealed itself, seeking out a T34, but the shell went wide of its intended target, wiping through a command group from one of the infantry companies. It left only the senior officer unwounded.

The experienced tankers of the 1st Battalion did not miss in their turn, the wooden structure, and the gun and men it held, disappearing as five HE shells struck home.

A mine claimed the lead tank's track, an unavoidable problem for the Soviet armour, given the sodden nature of the surrounding fields that confined them to a narrow approach.

The second vehicle immediately moved up and commenced nudging the disable T34 forward.

Almost immediately, another mine exploded, on the same side as before, sending a pair of heavy road wheels flying.

The tank's commander emerged from the hatch and waved off the pushing tank.

Once the shoving had stopped, the tank crew attempted to evacuate, the driver's broken leg fatally slowing him down, his body left hanging from the hatchway. The defending machine-guns switched their attention elsewhere.

The shoving started again when another vehicle moved up, and two more mines exploded as the advance picked up pace.

The second anti-tank gun joined the fight, its solid shot bouncing off the glacis of the abandoned T34.

A volley of tank shells missed the gun position, but the crew, unnerved and already worn down by weeks of fighting, abandoned their gun, and ran from the field.

From his own command bunker, Ramirez observed the slow but inexorable advance of the tanks.

He motioned to Oakley, knowing that he could be sending his friend to his death.

"Captain Oakley, I need that gun in action a-sap. Take three men from the Reserve platoon; get it up and running yesterday. Clear?"

His delivery was matter-of-fact, cold, impersonal, all designed to hide his anguish.

"You got it, Major."

Returning to his binoculars, Ramirez could hear the Captain sorting out a small group from the reserve, shaking out men with some AT experience. Then it was quieter again, the would-be gun crew moving off at speed.

To his front, the tanks had crawled to within one hundred yards of the bridge, their main guns starting to inflict casualties upon the defenders. High explosives shells proved particularly useful in pummelling the red brick timber mill, occasionally blasting men out of windows, as another point of resistance was silenced.

As the T34's drew closer, they spread out in a fan shape, following their orders, and readying to commence the infantry assault.

A bazooka shell smoked its way over the water, the shot speculative and ill advised.

Ramirez gripped his binoculars tighter as another of his precious AT weapons was lost, a single HE shell blotting out the gunner and loader in the blink of an eye.

The mortar officer, three yards to his left, redirected the fire, bringing his unit into action against the concentration of tanks at the end of the bridge.

Success was immediate, and one of the tanks started to burn, a direct hit on the engine deck causing a fire, disabling the tank.

The crew decided there was no future in their staying put, and attempted to retreat. Emerging into a hail of bullets, they quickly reassessed that, for now, remaining within the cast metal was the safer option.

The infantry attack rolled over the top of the T34's, the US mortars ripping holes in the mass of men, holes that were further widened by the heavy defensive fire.

But still they came, pushing on at the running crouch, the famous 'Urrah!' accompanying their advance.

The attack floundered halfway over the bridge, the new wall of bloodied bodies providing some cover for those whose courage failed them in the face of extreme fire.

A young Lieutenant stood and screamed at his men, most of them old enough to be his father, exhorting them to greater efforts for the Motherland.

He sprang towards the mill building, advancing only two yards before being struck down by numerous bullets.

Inspired, the survivors rallied and surged forward again, many suffering the same fate, but a few made it over and broke into the ground floor of the mill, clashing with the defenders there, as the upper floors received the undivided attention of the supporting tanks.

The Soviet infantry commander launched his second wave immediately and, although many were cut down from positions on the riverbanks, the bulk of his men made it across, fanning out and pushing the 3rd Battalion's doughboys away from the bridge.

A T34 nosed onto the bridge and quickly rushed across, no thought for the mangled meat it left in its wake, as it crushed dead and wounded alike.

Immediately turning sharp left, the tank was engulfed in a shower of sparks, and fire erupted from the turret hatches.

Oakley's gun crew had scored a direct hit with their first shot.

Other tanks moved over the bridge and spread out as soon as they touched the west bank.

The fourth tank across was struck as it rammed into the mill house, its engine immediately dying, as a solid shot smashed through the compartment.

The crew were cut down by a .50cal in one of the second line tree trunk positions.

Ramirez jerked his head in the direction of the nearby sound, his eyes catching the aftermath of the direct hit on the anti-tank gun.

Almost lazily, the screaming body tumbled through the air and smashed down across one of the disturbed tree trunks, destroying the unfortunate's spine in an instant.

The Major knew who it was and turned away, eyes filled with tears, fed by grief and anger in equal quantities.

Ramirez stayed silent, his eyes taking in the immolation of his battalion, with part of his brain screaming at him to make the decision to save what was left, and to hell with Willoughby.

The decision was reinforced immediately, as a flight of four Soviet aircraft swept over the bridge, immediately attacking the US troops at Rechtern.

"Fucking hell! I thought there was no air!"

It wasn't said to anyone particular, except maybe to himself, to reinforce his decision to retreat.

Brave men on the Red side of the divide had taken to the air, and the four Shturmoviks were the first to arrive over the crucial battlefield.

Although the air support was haphazard and uncoordinated, it was highly welcome, especially at a time when the Red Army suffered on a daily basis from the Allied superiority in the air.

Yarishlov, in contact with the commander of 1st Battalion, grunted in satisfaction as he received the man's report.

Looking at his watch, he calculated how long it would take for 1st Battalion to complete its deployment, before issuing his orders.

"Comrade Major, make sure your tanks are in position within seven minutes, and no later. The enemy force in Duste is engaged, but post men and tanks to watch for a counter-attack. Orient south-west, west, and north-west. I will be passing through your positions to Rechtern. Clear, Comrade?"

Satisfied with the response, Yarishlov watched the young Engineer officer checking the bridge structure. The Captain's orders were simple. Signal either 'yes' or 'no'; there were to be no 'maybes' on this day. Either Yarishlov could drive his whole force over it, or he couldn't.

The specialist gave the 'yes' signal, having paid particular attention to the large crack across the roadway and, on receiving an acknowledging wave from Yarishlov, set his men to work putting strengtheners in place, just in case.

Yarishlov turned his attention and radio frequency to Major General Obinin, the Special Group Commander, who had eagerly pushed his command group up to Brockmannshausen.

The early pleasantries over and done with, Yarishlov made his report.

"Comrade General, our first attack has taken the Wagenfelder Bridge, and the old mill buildings. Enemy infantry are still in the area in numbers, but I intend to pass through them with my 2nd Battalion, and the Guards Infantry, to get to Rechtern as quickly as possible. Over."

"Excellent work, Comrade Polkovnik. I can sense another Star in this for you! Now, Duste is still a problem, clear? Over."

"Yes, Comrade General. I have my 1st Battalion orienting against any threat from there as we speak. Over."

"Excellent again, Comrade Yarishlov. We have been stopped at the other bridges, so we must proceed with Plan Four at high speed. Acknowledge your orders, Comrade Polkovnik."

"Plan Four. Order received and acknowledged, Comrade General. Out."

Obinin's message of good luck was spoken to a dead mike, Yarishlov already consulting his map, preparing to direct his units into the rear of the defenders at the rail bridge.

At the appointed second, his force moved forward, crossing the Wagenfelder Aue, and turning north-west to Rechtern.

The bridge protested, but held.

In the command bunker of the 116th's 2nd Composite Battalion, Major Ramirez still held the field telephone, the order to retreat not given.

Partially because a mortar shell had severed the main phone line at the entrance to the position, and partially because the same shell had decapitated the US officer.

2nd Battalion was put to the sword, and the reinforcements from the 1st Battalion in Duste ran head long into Soviet tanks and infantry placed there for just the purpose.

1136hrs, Thursday, 25th October 1945, Rechtern Bridge, Barnstorf, Germany.

Colonel Willoughby was also dead, his command vehicle too tempting a target for the Shturmoviks to ignore.

Using their cluster bomb ammunition, they transformed it, and five of the US tank force, into scrap metal in the first pass.

Despite the attentions of a 40mm Bofors AA gun, lineage unknown, the Soviet attack craft swept in again, but failed to increase their tally of kills on the second run.

The defence force assigned to the Rechtern Bridge had been halved by the air attack, and had no chance to recover, before Yarishlov's 2nd Battalion barrelled into them at full speed.

None the less, the tank attack was halted by a combination of mines, and fire from the two M10 Wolverines, sited to the right flank of the defence.

Yarishlov gathered his thoughts and changed tack.

He sent a company of his infantry through the woods to the northeast of the bridge with simple orders.

Most of his tanks and the majority of the remaining infantry were kept back to limit the danger, disappearing onto the woods north of Rechterner Straβe, feinting noisily to the north.

However, the wily Tank Colonel kept a small number still on view, to keep up the pressure, and ensure that the defenders understood they had some enemy still to their front.

The detached company of Guardsmen, supported by mortars pulled from all the companies, made a noisy demonstration against the river line, bringing the handful of stretched out defenders under heavy fire, and causing them to scream for reinforcements.

A small Allied force moved northwards, weakening the bridge defences, accompanied by one more of the ad hoc tank company, an elderly M4A2 that had seen better days.

Enemy artillery fire started to arrive on the woods, prompting Yarishlov to move up his schedule, and he ordered the new assault to go in immediately.

The tanks of 2nd Battalion swept out of the woods en masse, moving wide to the left of the bridge, risking fire on their rear from Duste, the infantry stayed on a more narrow front, more focussed on the approach that was wooded and the cover it afforded them.

The lead squads ran into hastily planted mines, barely concealed, but no less lethal.

The advance slowed, and two more of the T34's succumbed to fire, one to an M-10 tank destroyer, and one to a bigger brother.

However, the latter vehicle, a deadly M36 with a 90mm gun, fell victim to three consecutive strikes from Soviet shells, its inexperienced crew failing to relocate in time.

Large calibre shells, probably 155mm, started to churn up the soil around the advancing Soviet tanks.

A message from Deniken indicated that the infantry could not advance, and so Yarishlov brought his tanks back again.

Once the Soviet troops were all back at their start positions, the two forces commenced an exchange, whose purpose seemed more to be about reminding the enemy of their presence, than to actually hit anything.

The American heavy artillery stopped, and had Yarishlov and his commanders known that the guns were permanently out of action, then they might have considered a different course of action.

Seven Il-10's of the 118th Guards Assault Aviation Regiment had stumbled across the M40 guns as they were redeploying, smashing the already depleted US Artillery Battalion to a meaningless group of shattered survivors, before finding themselves on the receiving end of an attack from a group of vengeful NF30 Mosquitoes. The RAF's 29 Squadron, normally tasked with night-fighting operations, was aloft this day on the back of simple courage, and with no small help from their onboard radar sets.

One IL-10 escaped, one Mosquito was lost, and the 118th Guards were stricken from the Red Air Forces' order of battle.

As the NF30's quit the airspace over the battle, more rain began to fall upon the combatants below, lightly at first, but gathering in its weight and intensity.

The Allied defence was relatively leaderless, but, worse, the officers in the front line did not know it.

Worst of all, there was a force at work that destroyed much of the cohesion.

Lieutenant Colonel Cameron Dunn, his unexpected prominence the result of the loss of so many senior ranks, was now the senior officer in 154th Brigade's headquarters. Feigning competence, he issued orders to units, sending reserve companies of Gordon Highlanders in all directions.

Contact from the now leaderless 116th brought more disaster, and his orders pushed the 1st Battalion northeast from Dreete.

They ran into Yarishlov's 1st Tank Battalion and lost the unequal struggle, retreating in disorder, and leaving a third of their men on the field.

Back at Rechtern, matters were taking a bad turn for the Allies, as the detached Soviet Guards infantry found that some fallen trees had made the crossing of the Hunte a possibility.

Quickly, a platoon was pushed over and established itself. It was rapidly reinforced by a second platoon, and Yarishlov informed of the development.

Deniken was ordered forward again, but timed to strike after the two platoons had announced their presence on the north bank, a noisy diversion to draw the defenders attention at a critical moment.

With perfect timing, the ancient M4A2 was turned into a fireball, an AP shell reaching across the river from the east bank. The US tank exploded almost immediately, providing a distraction greater than the attacking forces could have dreamed of.

Taking advantage of the unexpected lack of Allied artillery, Deniken harried his men into a full-scale leg race for the bridge, the enemy fire slackening as allied casualties mounted, the supporting fire from the mortars and the supporting T34's becoming increasingly effective.

The surviving M10 decided that discretion was called for, beating a hasty retreat to a position further back.

Yarishlov urged his armour forward, prepared to accept the disadvantages of the boggy field for the closer support he could offer Deniken's guardsmen.

The US mortar platoon increased its rate of fire, self-preservation lending speed to the process of reloading, but to no avail.

The first of the Guards infantry crossed the bridge over the Hunte, and dropped into the trenches and foxholes beyond, some occupied, some not.

Vicious disputes for ownership erupted, and the GI's were rapidly thrown out of the positions.

Two of the 2nd Battalion's T34's were badly bogged down, their thrashing tracks doing no more than digging the metal monsters deeper in the quagmire.

Aware that bullets were still pinging off their armour, the crews wisely decided to stay put until such times as the field

506

was in friendly hands. Both continued to provide the best close support they could, despite the nervousness caused by their immobility.

The nearest T34 to the river, enjoying a stable firing position, planted an 85mm shell in the surviving M10 as it moved away in the distance.

Damaged, its main gun useless, and its crew badly knocked about, the tank destroyer moved away to the west, in no condition to take any further part in the battle.

Three Soviet tanks, two 76mm T34's and a later model with the larger weapon, rolled over the bridge in close column, fanning out immediately.

The remaining allied infantry decided enough was enough, and the defence crumbled.

Yarishlov watched through his binoculars as the retreat gathered pace, becoming a rout, more and more Allied troops adding to the flow.

Running men swept through the US mortar positions, urging their comrades to come with them.

At first the mortar men started to dismantle their weapons but, as the tide grew stronger and the voices more panicky, most left their tubes behind and fled the field.

A short company of the 154th's 1st Battalion, all Gordon Highlanders, mistakenly, but fortuitously ordered forward by Dunn, ploughed headlong into the retreating US troops, sweeping many of them up, and adding to their numbers as they moved forward.

The Jocks stopped at the mortar positions, and swiftly dug in on the edge of the woods, just to the east of the rail line, defending the southern flank of Barnstorf.

Other men had run in the direction of Dreeke, and were similarly met by men from the 116th's 1st Composite Battalion.

Again, the running men were taken onboard and a strong position established in the wood line, either side of the west running Rechterner Straβe.

A tentative probe by one Soviet platoon was swiftly repulsed by this blocking force, but the Gordon's were, for now, left alone.

1140hrs, Thursday, 25th October 1945, Allied defensive position on Barnstorf Rail Bridge, Germany.

The lone Mustang fighter left a smoky trail behind it, product of a close encounter with Soviet AA fire.

None the less, the pilot circled the position for two minutes before closing the ground and dropping his speed.

An object was seen to fall from the aircraft, dropping onto the rail line directly where Route 48 crossed the metal tracks.

The P51 increased speed steadily and flew off to the south-west, disappearing into a sky once again become grey before its time.

One of Aitcherson's men retrieved the bundle. The white silk aviator's scarf continued a notebook, held open by a rubber band on the appropriate page.

The Cameron Highlander officer consulted with Robertson, the RSM in no doubt as to the significance of the message.

With Aitcherson's blessing, RSM Robertson and two men doubled away to find Ramsey, and give him the bad news.

Ramsey was found in strained discussion with the US Engineer officer, Fielding.

"It's not enough, Major. Simply put, if I try bringing it down with what I have, I may as well goof off, Sir."

"Is there nothing that you can do, Fielding?"

"Unless you have about a thousand pounds more Composition C, then I reckon not, all save wreck the tracks, Major."

Hässler, witnessing the conversation, whispered to Robertson, bringing the Senior NCO up to date on events.

"Some douche bag in supply sent up crates of 'C' for the engineer boys. Wrong goddamn size, half pound blocks, instead of full pounds, and then only a part of what was asked for."

Shaking his head, Ramsey brought up his binoculars, the landscape to his front devoid of any Russians, save the dead and dying, his focus upon the stout rail bridge.

"Sah, I have bad news the now."

Although he said nothing, the Black Watch Major's face spoke volumes.

He accepted the notebook.

508

"A Yank pilot dropped it tae us, Sah."

Ramsey read the brief message, his face turning to thunder by the time he had finished.

"Gentlemen, our flyer friend informs us that about three miles to the east is a large concentration of enemy forces, oriented this way, estimated at over divisional strength."

The silence was deafening.

"He also insists that there are two armoured trains sat with them, ready to move."

1st Lt Fielding snorted in derision.

"Well, anyone who has read the reports knows the Soviet track gauge is different, so that's a non-starter."

Ramsey inclined his head and, yet again, was beaten to it by Bluebear, who went for the less sensitive option.

"The German had them, so maybe the Russian has the German one's, Lieutenant."

He spoke the words in his monotone way, and not as a question.

Fielding ceded the point with his silence.

"So, we can stop the trains by smashing up the rails some, Major, but the Commies will repair the track quick enough, and in this weather, a rapid advance with them could do us no end of hurt."

Ramsey's mind hit upon a solution.

He gathered the assembly close around the map he held, fingering a specific point on the east bank.

"This here looks like an underpass of some sort? Anyone seen it at all?"

No takers.

Ramsey continued.

"If it is, then you have to be able to drop it with what you have available. An underpass won't be so easy for the Soviets to repair."

There was a general nod of agreement, but most noticeably, not from Fielding.

"There is an issue for you, Lieutenant?"

"You betchyer goddamn ass there's a fucking issue, Major."

Robertson grimaced at the remark, but held his peace.

"You want my boys to wander over onto the commie side of the river and lay a load of charges? Sure sounds like a suicide mission to me, Sir."

"If you were alone, then possibly so, Lieutenant. However, you won't be."

Making his mind up, Ramsey snapped into action.

"Can you carry the explosives with just your unit, Lieutenant?"

"I guess so, Sir," replied Fielding, tentatively, in case the Limey had not got the message.

"I will move my lads over the water, to here," his finger picked out a small raised area to the south of the supposed underpass.

He drew Hässler and Bluebear in tighter.

"This railway embankment is a natural divide for us, so you will take the left flank."

They nodded.

"I want your boys to position here," he indicated a wooded area diametrically opposite the intended Black Watch position.

"How long do you think you'll need to drop the underpass, Lieutenant?"

Fielding grabbed his chin in thought, happier now he knew that others were exposing themselves too.

"Based upon what I've seen of these things before, I reckon half an hour at the rush, forty minutes to be comfy, Major."

Others may have dithered, but not Ramsey, and the move was set in motion immediately.

"Right then, gentlemen. Get your troops up and moving immediately. Robertson, you take the first platoon over and secure the other side straight away. We'll cross on your signal. Clear?"

It was.

"Lieutenant, as soon as the covering force has moved forward, bring your men and equipment over, come up whichever side, but get cracking on that underpass. Clear?"

"Will do, Major."

The Captain commanding the recently arrived Gordons was last of all.

510

"Grayson, your men will filter into the positions we vacate as soon as we move off. Be careful who you fire at. We may not have time for the niceties when we return. Make sure your lads are clear on that point."

"Sah."

Addressing the whole group, Ramsey concluded his brief.

"We'll stay, no retreat, as long as the engineers have a job to do. Once their job is done, we'll retire to a safe distance, on the east bank, for detonation. I assume the end of the bridge will be a suitable firing point, Lieutenant?"

Fielding cast a quick eye at the map scale and nodded.

"Once successful, we'll fall back over the river, you 116th lads first, my men last. There are no further orders. Any questions?"

It was simple enough in concept, but had all the makings of a hard battle ahead.

"RSM, as soon as you're ready. We will work off the RSM for our timings. Up and at 'em, Gentlemen."

1145hrs, Thursday, 25th October 1945, The Rechtern Bridge area, Barnstorf, Germany.

Deniken had no need of any relay from Yarishlov, Obinin's voice carried very clearly over the radio net.

Obinin had just received a verbal lashing from those above, and, as usual, the threats cascaded downwards.

"Get your men moving now or you'll be counting trees, Polkovnik. Now!"

Yarishlov smiled half-heartedly to himself, recalling a conversation not so long ago, when the same officer had feted him as a hero.

'The line between success and failure is thin indeed.'

"Moving now, Comrade General. Out."

Deniken received a whispered verbal report from one of his officers and nodded in response, dismissing the man with a pat on the back.

"Bad, Comrade Deniken?"

"It could've been much worse, but I've lost many good men, Comrade Yarishlov."

511

"It's up to us to make sure our men haven't died uselessly, so we'll move forward immediately, as the General demands."

Deniken's map was to hand, so the two pored quickly over the terrain they were about to traverse.

Yarsihlov spoke with conviction.

"Your platoons that crossed the river downstream; they can advance along the river to here?"

Deniken nodded his agreement.

"Good," and quickly moving across the map, Yarishlov found Route 48.

"We have a single road, and I will use it wisely. Get some of your men on board my tanks, and we will drive like hell into their rear, here."

He indicated the west end of the rail bridge position.

Pressing his finger against the area to the west and south-west, Yarishlov was less forceful.

"I have ordered most of the remaining forces of the 128th Tanks and 31st Guards Infantry up to here, providing us with a secure base, and sparing them any more suffering for now."

He indicated the area to the west of the Wagenfelder Bridge.

"That will release my first battalion and SMG Company to probe westwards here, where your men ran into that little hornet's nest."

He referred to the Dreeke road positions, recently stiffened by the 1st Composite Battalion, 116th Infantry.

As if to reinforce his next point, sounds of sawing and hammering reached both men's ears.

"Our comrades from the 77th are working to make good the damage to this bridge, but I intend to take as many of them with us, in case the Amerikanski damage our prime objective."

Deniken's eyes were drawn to the map, despite his full knowledge of what the tank colonel was pointing at.

Yarishlov continued.

"Our comrades of the 3rd Guards Mechanised Corps and 22nd Guards Rifle Corps are already preparing to move up, the two armoured trains will do so, the moment we report contact to the rear of the Allied positions, and that the track is clear."

512

Yarishlov folded his map quickly, finishing the brief in a conspiratorial tone.

"At the same time, we will order our surprise package forward, against the eastern end of the bridge."

Deniken understood, and made a final notation on his pad.

"Comrade PodPolkovnik."

Yarishlov extended his hand.

"Comrade Polkovnik."

The two shook hands and went their separate ways.

<u>1145hrs, Thursday, 25th October 1945, Soesterberg Airbase, Holland.</u>

Before the Second World War, Soesterberg had been a military airfield for the Dutch Air Force. During their time as residence, the Luftwaffe had created a much larger facility, but it was still very tight for the squadrons from all arms of the RAF that found themselves shoehorned in, as the Soviets advanced, and airfields were lost.

Blue Flight, 182 Squadron RAF, gathered around the door to the Wing Commander's office, straining to hear the conversation above the panting, all three out of breath having sprinted from the main radio room, once they understood Hall's purpose.

"Absolutely not, John. They'd have my guts for garters if I let you go!"

"Sir, I respectfully request permission to try."

"No, John, that's final."

"Sir, we have to give it a try, we simply have to. Those boys need us."

"No, John, no, no and thrice, no."

"Sir, the weather has a window, a small one. Old Runes says so," he referred to the Station Meteorological Officer by his nickname, "And he's never wrong, is he? Never wrong."

The Wing Commander stood up abruptly, eyes flashing with anger, controlled, but only just.

"Flight Lieutenant Hall, you will not, repeat, not be given permission to fly. I have my orders, so there it is."

The silence that followed was an opportunity for both men's frustrations to become apparent.

Hall's, because he wanted to get his aircraft up and into the battle. The Wingco's because he did too, for he had been a pilot. He understood what made such men tick, but rank and responsibility made him take a different course.

Hall tried one last time.

"Sir?"

The one word carried much in it, the tone, the inflection, the absolute dejection of a man who saw his duty clearly.

The pilot in him struggled with the leader, and won.

'Fuck it!'

The thought occurred, and the expression on the Wing Commander's face changed almost imperceptibly.

Almost.

"John, understand me clearly. I cannot, and will not, grant you permission to fly. If I see you on the apron, I will have you confined to quarters. If I see you near an aircraft without my express permission, I will have you thrown in the guardhouse. Is that clear enough?"

"Yes, Sir."

'Understand me, son, please, understand me!'

"Now, let's hear no more of it. I'm off to my quarters for some well-deserved kip, and I do not intend to rouse myself before dinner. Flight Lieutenant."

The salute was returned and Hall found himself staring at an open door. Wing Commander Smith, the notoriously heavy sleeper, was already on his way to his quarters, some distance from the runway apron, having knowingly cast an eye over the three men who seem too preoccupied with a poster outside the office to bother with a salute.

Hall's grin was genuine.

'Well, you slippery old bastard!'

"Boys, we're on!"

Wing Commander Smith lay on his bunk, wide-awake, his ears straining at every sound, his tension increasing at the noise of Sabre engines dragging aircraft into the watery skies, rose above the sound of the rain on the tin roof of his hut.

Looking at the greyness outside his window, he spoke quietly, sincerely, longingly.

"I wish I could be with you, boys."

1145hrs, Thursday, 25th October 1945, the Underpass, Barnstorf, Germany.

Fielding was excited, and out of breath.

Ramsey waited, taking the extra time to survey the hastily scraped positions that his Highlanders were occupying on the small wooded mound.

"Major, we can do it; we can blow that motherfucking rail bridge sky high!"

"Go on, Lieutenant," exchanging a swift look with the newly arrived Robertson, his attention drawn by the US engineer's noisy dash.

"It's full of artillery shells, hundreds of them."

"Pardon?"

"Major, the underpass was secured and marked with unexploded munitions signs. Seems to me like the Krauts used it as an ammo store. It's wall to wall with HE shells, Sir."

"And you can use them?"

"Sure thing, Major. I can do both, underpass and bridge, if we have enough time to stack them on the middle of the fucker."

He waved a finger at the solid structure, already imagining the trek of three hundred yards, staggering with a heavy artillery shell.

"How many do you need on the bridge?"

"A hundred would make a pretty mess, Sir."

"And you have enough left to drop the underpass too?"

Fielding was extremely enthusiastic.

"More'n enough, Sir."

"Then we shall get it done."

He quickly checked to see if the field telephone was ready; it wasn't.

"Corporal McEwan!", he shouted, and the man magically appeared from the next hole.

"McEwan, my compliments to Captain Grayson. I need him to send forward a work party of twenty-five men immediately, reporting to Lieutenant Fielding in the underpass.

515

He can have them back in twenty minutes. Off you go, and be smart about it, man."

McEwan was gone as quickly as he appeared.

Turning to Fielding, Ramsey continued.

"We will hold and give you your time, Lieutenant, but make it as quick as you can, if you please."

The engineer threw up a hasty salute, and departed as quickly as he had arrived, armed with renewed purpose.

Robertson stayed silent, waiting, his face set.

"Yes, RSM, I know."

Looking to the sky, Ramsey jumped automatically, as a large raindrop hit him in the eye.

"Angel's tears, Sah, angel's tears."

Ramsey nodded, knowing in his heart that there would be a heavy price to pay this day.

"Nae room for jessies and bairns here, Sah, not today."

"Quite so, Murdo."

The shock of hearing Ramsey use his first name was only superceded by the Major's offered hand.

"Good luck to you."

Murdo Robertson took the hand of the man he admired most in the world.

"And the same to yersel, Sah."

Ramsey smiled, knowing that the RSM had crossed a huge boundary with the handshake, and accepting that Robertson could not go so far as to call him by his name.

"Pass the new plan onto our American cousins, if you please, Sarnt Major."

Along the Allied rear positions, a few extra units arrived and slid in beside the exhausted men of the 116th and 154th Infantry. Some 4x4's with AT mounts, the occasional platoon of infantry rounded up by MP's at the rear.

There were no more tanks to be had.

Droves had found the problem, and fixed it. The loose connection had been squirting a mist of oil over a hot manifold, leading to the smoke problem.

516

Meanwhile, Griffiths had consulted with the first officer he found, namely Aitcherson, and established what was happening.

Deciding to relocate, just in case any surprises appeared from Rechtern, the Comet tank snuggled in behind a protective wall, near the junction of Route 48 and Rechterner Straße. A small mound offered a dominating position, whichever route the Soviets selected.

The first inkling of possible disaster for those at the rail bridge was the sharp crack of the Comet's 77mm weapon, closely followed by Griffith's urgent message over the radio waves.

"All stations, all stations, enemy tank and infantry force on Route 48... FIRE! TARGET LEFT 15! ENGAGE! ...approaching positions from Rechtern, in Regimental strength... FIRE! ...over."

In his excitement, the tank commander forgot to unkey his mike, sending his local instructions over the radio to all listeners.

The Soviet attack fanned out, two of their tanks already smoking after receiving fatal attention from the British tank.

"I'm down to ten AP shells, Sarnt, the rest's all HE."

Butler, the normally unflappable gunner, expressed his alarm in his own special way.

"Ten fucking AP ain't e-bastard-nough. We're fighting a fucking army out there, Sarnt."

There were nine tanks to the front.

"Well, don't fucking miss then, you pillock. Show me you're as good as you reckon you are, eh?"

"ON!"

Butler's automatic call was responded to equally automatically.

"FIRE!"

Another T34 shuddered under a hammer blow, the engine compartment immediately spouting a firm candle of fire.

"Apparently, you tell everyone you're the fucking bees fucking knees, so prove it!"

A shell struck the wall, sending pieces of stone smashing against the armour plate.

"Five degrees, left gunner! Target tank."

The turret rotated effortlessly.

"ON!"

"FIRE!"

The shell struck, deflecting off through the frightened men clinging to the back of the T34, sending a deluge of pieces in all directions.

"You tosser! You missed!"

"I hit it, Sarnt.

"Well then, hit the bastard again!"

"ON!"

"FIRE!"

The shell punched through the turret ring, transforming the interior into a charnel house.

"Right, Bert, shake it up, man! Reverse up behind the building, then right across the street. Move it, will you!

The Comet moved back, as two more shells struck the stonewall.

Ramsey did not have a radio with him; that remained in the western defensive positions.

However, he now had a field telephone in position, a working EE9 US Army model, which now screeched at him in an urgent fashion.

"Ramsey."

As he could see the other position, code and formality was unnecessary.

"Major, the Reds have tanks and infantry in our rear, coming from Rechtern in Regimental strength."

Thought and deed were very different

'Jesus Christ!'

"Righty ho, Captain. Orient yourself mainly on that axis. I assume that racket is our lads from the Derbyshires?"

"Yes, Sir."

"Fine, make sure you support them with some infantry. I'm relying on you to hold them back for as long as you can, clear?"

The reply was lost in a whirl of thought.

'This bridge is suddenly very important. I'm missing something.'

Back in the now, Ramsey issued further instructions.

518

"I think the next bridge up had extra reserves. 1st Black Watch lads. Send a runner. Get them up here, as quickly as possible."

Soviet mortar shells started to fall, to the second that the rain stopped once again, and sunlight burst through the clouds.

"Once that's done, get onto Brigade and tell them the situation. I am going to destroy the bridge within the next forty-five minutes. You...," he summoned up a mental image of the pale face of the modest blonde officer, "We...We must hold for an hour. That is an order, Captain."

"Yes, Sir. Good luck, Sir."

Ramsey looked automatically towards the bridge defences, and caught the end of Grayson's salute.

He returned it across the divide, and prepared to live his last few minutes on earth in a manner befitting an English Officer.

"Stand to! Stand to!"

The shout, once voice at first, then repeated around the whole Black Watch position, as other voices took up the warning.

On the extreme corner of the hillock, one Corporal gave an order to fire, and the Vickers started its deadly work.

Through the trees to their front came a horde of Soviet infantry, driven forward by their NCO's and officers, their losses growing as more weapons joined in the defence.

Ramsey spared a look towards the underpass, from where men emerged carrying the artillery shells, two men to each, bodies hunched in fear and anticipation.

On the other side of the railway embankment, more firing erupted, proof that the Americans had troubles of their own.

"Mac."

The corporal raised his head.

"Aye, Boss?"

"I want you and your pair to watch the top of the embankment. Kill anything on it, and keep me informed please."

"Right enough, Boss."

As the volume of offensive fire increased, more and more Soviet bullets whipped through the trees and undergrowth, removing pieces of the greenery in large clumps. A smaller fir tree fell to the earth, its trunk sawn in half by hot lead.

Sparing a swift look at the bridge, Ramsey was encouraged to see that the pile of artillery shells had grown.

A nearby Bren gunner screamed as the top of his head was removed by fast travelling metal, his weapon falling silent.

The loader looked on in shock, immobilised by the sight of his friend and the spray of blood that had lashed his face.

Ramsey shouted from his position.

"Private Fraser!"

Nothing.

Ramsey repeated himself, drawing the same blank.

Shouldering his Sten gun, he propelled himself up and over the edge of the position, rolling and slithering into the Bren pit, beside the petrified Fraser.

"Come on now, Fraser. There's work to do, lad."

The nineteen year old looked at his commanding officer through watery, uncomprehending eyes.

"Come on lad, come on now! What will you think of yourself in the morning?"

The tears continued, but the soldier started the process of composing himself.

Ramsey grasped the boy's neck and gently shook him.

"Come on now, laddie, show the Reds how the clans make war eh?"

A Lance Corporal, keen to know why the Bren was silent, rushed to the pit, and threw himself on top of Ramsey.

"Jings, ah'm sorrah, Boss!"

Although winded, Ramsey managed a response.

"Don't make a habit of it, McClendon, especially as we haven't been formally introduced."

"Aye, Major. We'll no be daeing it tomorrah anyways, and that's fer sure."

The Major grinned and slapped the NCO on the shoulder.

"Stay with young Fraser for a bit, just until you can get back safely to your own position."

That was not what Ramsey meant, and both McLinden and Fraser knew it, but it sufficed to save the young lad's blushes.

Ramsey was up and out of the hole in an instant, fighting the new pains in his chest and stomach, and making the distance to his own position in short order.

He collapsed into cover, conscious that McLinden's unexpected arrival had probably sprung a couple of ribs.

McEwan waited for the officer to recover.

"The bas tried the top like ye said, Boss. They're all doon."

A swift look was enough to confirm the presence of nearly a dozen bodies, some wearing the tell tale cylinders of flamethrower troops.

"Well done, Mac."

"Oh, there's more, Sah.

The finger pointed down a path that afforded a restricted view of the top of part of the embankment, almost certainly some seven hundred metres away.

"I dinna know what they are, but for sure, they're big bas, Sah."

Searching his memory, the briefing document he sought came clearly into view.

"Stalin tanks, look like mark three's, Mac. Very nasty."

'Well that's us up shit creek without a paddle!'

"RSM!"

Robertson heard the call and stopped bandaging his wrist, laid open to the bone by a wood splinter.

He sprinted to the HQ hole.

"RSM, the enemy is pushing heavy tanks up the rail line, on top of the embankment."

Ramsey extended his arm down the same line that Mac had indicated. They both looked, but the monsters were now not apparent, a cloudburst obscuring them.

"They're there for sure. The Yanks have got two Bazookas. Get a runner over to them, and let them know the Stalins are their problem for now."

'Until they become our problem!'

"I need you to hold here, and keep the boys at it. I'm off to see the engineers and chivvy them along with the good news."

They shared a laugh, unforced, two professionals doing their jobs as best they could.

"Let Grayson know about the Stalin's. He might persuade our Derbyshire friends to have a crack at them."

"Aye, that I will, Sah. But they'll run in the other direction if they have any sense!"

Ramsey was up and out of the trench once more.

521

Bullets lashed the ground around his feet, and he realised that the fire came from three Soviet infantrymen who were nearly at the underpass, having crawled on their bellies, unobserved.

His run had taken him directly at them, and they fired instinctively, believing that he had spotted them.

Throwing himself behind a fallen tree truck, he landed heavily, increasing his chest and stomach pain.

'Grenade? No, too close to the Yanks.'

In confirmation of his decision, one of the US Engineers risked a peek around the corner, and was shot dead immediately.

'Too close.'

One of the Russians flopped lifelessly, as others noticed the small group.

The two survivors rose up, intent on finding sanctuary in the underpass.

More of the engineers emerged, stooping low with their heavy burden.

'Oh my lord!'

Reacting instantly, Ramsey charged and yelled, his lunacy bearing fruit, the two Soviet survivors drawn to him, rather than the struggling engineers.

Firing a burst from his Sten, the Black Watch Major was amazed to see both men go down, blood flying from numerous wounds.

Ramsey was unaware that RSM Robertson had seen his plight, and chopped both men down, his own burst having buried itself uselessly in the embankment.

Struggling for breath, Ramsey placed his hands on his knees, trying to conquer the achy chest pain that was all encompassing.

The cane, slid between his webbing, proved obstructive, and Ramsey slid it out, quickly massaging his bruised torso.

Fielding emerged from the underpass and found the Black Watch officer in some discomfort. He had seen the cane before, but never expected the stuffy Englishman to actually carry it in combat.

"Major, you ok, Sir?"

"Tanks... Lieutenant... Stalin tanks... on top of... the embankment... half a mile off... need this... blown now."

522

Checking the work behind him, Fielding replied confidently.

"This is ready to go when you give the order, Major. We just need to ship out more shells for the bridge."

"How many... more?"

"Twenty, Major, no more'n twenty."

"Speed it up... please... we're running... out of time."

Hässler appeared.

"Hey, LT. I was coming to tell you we have enemy armour coming," he looked at the dishevelled Black Watch officer, "But I guess you've got the dope already?"

"Yes, I got the dope, Master-Sergeant. What's happening out there?"

Wiping his nose with the back of his hand, Hassler reached for his canteen, pouring some water over his face to clean away the muck of combat.

"The commie infantry are held, LT, for now anyways. They got up real close, but they fell back after Bluebear ripped them up some."

He spat at the memory of what he had seen.

"The Chief is sure something else when he gets up fighting close, and that's a fact."

He had no wish to go further than that, but he now had more understanding of the horrors that the legendary US Cavalry must have experienced.

Fielding had an idea.

"Maybe we can speed things up, if some of your boys fall back through here, and grab a shell between pairs?"

Ramsey liked it slightly more than Hässler, but the Master Sergeant saw the sense of it, although not the desirability of carrying a lump of metal filled with high explosive in a close-quarter fight.

Unable to speak, Ramsey nodded his agreement to Hässler, who took it as an order.

"I'll drop a squad back through here right now, LT."

Something that passed for a salute quickly followed, and the NCO disappeared back from where he had come.

"So, what's the situation, Major?"

Taking a deep breath, Ramsey tried speaking normally.

"Not good, I'm afraid Lieutenant."

523

Grasping the man by the arm to move him out of the way of two men struggling with a larger shell, Ramsey lowered his voice.

"The Reds are coming at us... from both sides now. A Regiment's worth of tanks and infantry from Rechtern. Heavy tanks across the embankment... infantry on both sides. Mortars only at the moment... for reasons known only to themselves."

That was a lot for a Lieutenant of Engineers to take in.

Ramsey laughed, the act increasing the stomach and chest pain.

'Only when I laugh. Yeah, right!'

Fielding look at Ramsey as if he had just arrived from another planet.

"What's so funny, Major?"

"I was just remembering another Lieutenant of Engineers, faced with a similar situation, Fielding."

The memory of one Lieutenant Chard RE, commander of Rourke's Drift, kicked his mind down another path, and he quickly wondered how Llewellyn was doing in these dark times, before switching back to the present.

"We have no time, By hook or by crook, get what you need piled on that bridge in five minutes. Clear?

"Yes, Sir!"

Turning away, Fielding saw something that displeased him.

"Private, set that det cord out properly, knucklehead!"

Ramsey returned to his positions, ready to ensure that Fielding would get his five minutes.

He dropped into the headquarters pit, finding Robertson in complete control of a hopeless situation.

"Sah, the buggers rushed us agin, but we stopped them the now. They've dropped back into the trees awa's back there."

The RSM spoke more softly.

"The bas had flamethrowers, Sah. They dinna get within range, thank God."

A bullet passing through the tree overhead severed a small branch, the lump descending and striking the RSM on the shoulder.

"Perhaps you should wear your tin helmet, RSM?"

Ramsey often spoke of his RSM's preference for the Tam-o-shanter in combat, never pushing, only cajoling.

524

"Where would I be wi out ma tam, Sah? The bhoys demand it of me you know."

Soviet mortars brought a pause to their discussion, their suddenly increased rate of fire, coinciding with growing sounds of battle from the west bank.

"The engineers are nearly done; just a few more shells on the bridge, then they'll blow the underpass."

The noise of battle grew in an instant, the 'Urrah's' of the Soviet infantry rising as they launched themselves forward.

"We must give them enough time, Sarnt-Major!"

The men of the Black Watch needed no orders on who to put down first. The Soviet soldiers carrying the deadly cylinders were singled out, and fear lent them accuracy, as all six of the Soviet operators were shot down. One cylinder exploded, the deadly yellow flames grabbing out for more victims, engulfing men for yards around.

The screams were hideous, but the Scots spared the writhing figures no thought.

This was not a day for pity.

Now within grenade range, the leading Guardsmen threw a number of devices into the British positions, some explosive, some smoke.

The surviving Black Watch Vickers stopped firing immediately, water flowing from its ravaged cooling jacket, as blood dripped from its dead crew.

Ramsey prepared himself, knowing that the enemy could not be stopped before they closed on his positions.

He became aware of some screaming and shouting, feet running past his hole, heading to his front.

Some soldiers fell, men clad in the uniform of the 1st Battalion, Black Watch, but others, led by the mad Irish CSM, charged headlong into the Guards infantry, putting them to flight with a combination of rifle butt and bayonet.

Recalling his men, CSM Green spread them out to fill the gaps in the depleted B Company positions, and then went in search of Ramsey.

"Close call that, Sarnt-Major. Thank you."

"Think nothing of it, Sir. But if you'll take my advice, I'd get the feck out of here, soonest."

Turning back to point across the river, Green did a double take.

"You sneaky fucking bastards you! Major!"

Soviet infantry were moving slowly up the riverbank, intent on making a surprise rush on the bridge.

Ramsey kept his eye on them, assessing the risk. He shouted at Robertson, and he pointed in the direction of the river.

"RSM!"

Robertson saw them immediately, and shouted in his best parade ground voice.

"Second platoon, with me, action to the rear!"

A handful of men rose up and followed Robertson to the back of the mound, flopping into loose cover, waiting on the word.

Ramsey was already on the field telephone to Grayson.

"Captain Grayson, there's at least a company of reds moving up tight to the river to your south; some in the water, some on the bank. The RSM is about to engage, but you might like to make arrangements yourself."

On cue, Enfield rifles and 2nd Platoon's surviving Bren gun began their deadly harvest, the wading men horribly exposed and vulnerable.

Within seconds, the gently flowing waters were tinted red, bodies floating, wounded men floundering and drowning.

Fielding dropped in beside Ramsey, his cheek laid open by a mortar splinter.

"We're all ready, Major. Ignition point is just to the left of the entrance there. Two minutes of fuse. Safe point is this end of the bridge and no closer."

"Two minutes? I wanted the position at the end of the bridge, Lieutenant!"

"We couldn't do it in the time, plus we had problems, bad det cord, Sir."

He could not decide if that was good or bad.

"But we're set, yes?"

"Yep, we sure are, Major. Some of the cord was unusable, but we done the best with it we could, and I guarantee it'll do the job. Plus," conscious of the fire fights that raged in all directions, Fielding added unnecessarily, "Two minutes seems like all we're gonna get."

"Fair enough. Well done, Lieutenant."

"We'll save that for when the fucker blows, I think, Major. Now, I'll do it, but we have to get your boys well back. The 29th boys are already moving."

"What?"

"The 29th boys are already moving, Major."

"Too soon, they're falling back too soon!"

"But your commander ordered it. The Kraut top kick took orders from a runner, direct from your man Dunne."

Ramsey knew that could not be the case, as the last information he had was that Dunne was totally incapacitated with shock.

Ramsey did not know that a GRU agent within Kommando Friedrich had acted on instinct, and interfered with the defence in a dramatic and terminal fashion.

That the man was killed by his own mortars was just the fortunes of war, his sacrifice forever unknown to his family, peers, and Motherland.

<u>1218hrs, Thursday, 25th October 1945, astride Route 48,</u>
<u>Barnstorf.</u>

Six of Yarishlov's tanks were knocked out, the others either hidden away from the demon tank, or scurrying at top speed for anything that could provide safety.

The infantry had pushed up, and it had seemed that they would carry the position, until innocuous bushes exploded into life, and whole lines of men were swept away.

From his rear position, he was able to spot some of the vehicles responsible, and destroyed two, but the others continued to flay Deniken's men as they milled around, thrown into total disarray.

"What the fuck are they firing? I want some, Sarnt!"

Griffiths was also in awe of what they were witnessing.

A number of different weapon systems had come together to halt Deniken's men.

Gun mounts from the 554th AAA, quadruple .50 cals in Maxson turrets, mounted on M20 trailers, did great damage. However, they were vulnerable to counter fire, as the crews exposed themselves when re-ammunitioning the weapons.

Similarly, the three 40mm Bofors that hammered the approaching masses with HE shells were vulnerable, their servants all exposed to the lightest of fire.

The weapons which drew the admiration of 'Lady Hamilton's' crew were T33 Motor Gun Carriages, sporting 37mm guns, weapons more effective in the previous decade but thrown into the fight here, instead of languishing in a run-down depot on Salisbury Plain.

As anti-tank guns they were obsolete, but in the role needed that the day, they ruled supreme.

At short range, the 37mm's M2 canister shells were like shotguns, producing a widening stream of 122 steel balls, each one capable of taking a man's life.

Whole squads were wiped away, chopped to pieces by streams of metal, all reminiscent of a battlefield, another continent, and century away, when a place called Cemetery Ridge ran with the blood of brave men.

It was a slaughter that shocked both sides, those involved, and those watching.

Yarishlov shouted into his radio.

"Pull them back, in the name of the Motherland, pull them back, Deniken!"

Command and control was lost, but Deniken was already doing what he could to rescue his command.

The assault from Rechtern had been stopped.

1237hrs, Thursday, 25th October 1945, the Rail Bridge defences, Barnstorf.

It had all gone wrong.

Soviet infantry had moved into the vacuum created by the withdrawal of Bluebear and Hässler, and the veteran soldiers were already bringing the east end of the bridge under close fire, albeit carefully, understanding the nature of the ominous pile in the centre of the single span.

Yet more Soviet infantry were in the west entrance to the underpass, although understandably lacking in a desire to rush into an area containing munitions dressed with explosives and detonating cord.

Ramsey's unit was virtually surrounded, the enemy troopers across the river finding better positions, and returning fire on the covering 2nd Platoon.

Picking up the field telephone, he spoke quickly with Grayson.

"Captain, get Fielding to set the charges on the bridge now. Keep the Reds off him while he works. We have to blow that bridge. Clear?"

"Fielding isn't here, Sir. His sergeant is in charge and work is nearly complete. Hang on, Sir."

Ramsey risked a look at the west bank and saw Grayson shouting towards the pile of shells. He then rushed back to his main position.

Grayson's excited voice could be heard in the background, getting a quick heads-up from his man.

He took the telephone handset.

"Sir, give him four minutes. Then he can blow it. Just four minutes."

"Are all the 116th boys back over the bridge now, Grayson?"

"No, Sir, not all. Still some of the yanks hanging on at the east end, giving the engineers some breathing space."

Ramsey ducked instinctively, a mortar shell striking the ground to the left of his hole, showering him with earth and bits of vegetation.

"And what's your situation, Captain?"

"Holding, Sir. The main force was stopped south of town. Very messy, so I'm told. Aitcherson's on the spot and waiting to see what they do next."

Increased firing betrayed another attempt by the Guards infantry on the mound, the defensive fire slacker than before.

"Right. The underpass goes in two and a half minutes, got that?"

"Yes, Sir, good lu..."

Ramsey was picked up and turned over in mid-air, the force of the explosion removing both his boots, before returning him to virtually the same position.

The Sten was gone, thrown out of sight by the blast, which had also severed the cable on the field telephone, and tossed the set almost to the water's edge.

529

Testing his legs, Ramsey brought himself up into a crouch position, filling his right hand with his Webley revolver, and the left with his cane.

Picking his destination carefully, he sprinted forward, dropping in behind the tree stump he had considered wide enough to give him decent cover.

"Lads! Lads, listen in!"

Some men turned to their officer, others continued to pour fire into the attackers.

"We have to hold here. I will blow that railway in two and a half minutes. Keep your heads down. It will be an almighty bang!"

A few more eyes swivelled his way, and in those eyes he could see the fear of men approaching breaking point.

He thought fast, and rose to his feet.

"Lads, the Black Watch does not retreat! We will not retreat, so you will hold here, until I come back to retrieve this."

He rammed the cane point-first into the ground, the silver pommel instantly recognisable to every man of the old 7th.

Ramsey took off, ignoring the pain in his feet, as sharp splinters and stones cut his flesh.

He stumbled into the remains of Fielding, the man's unseeing eyes showing no pain, despite the unrecognisable nature of the rest of his body.

A few yards further on was the ignition point, two of the American engineers lying dead on the ground around it, protecting their work, even in death.

Ramsey made a final lunge. He threw himself left, but was thrown to the right, the impact of metal changing his direction in mid-air.

He screamed in pain, the rifle bullet having smashed into the same spot as the young German fanatic in Nordenham, and his already damaged ribs finding the butt of a Garand rifle.

With teeth clenched hard, to counter the excruciating pain, he retrieved his lighter, and lit the cord.

It fizzed and flared, making a noisy and obtrusive journey into the underpass.

Ramsey slithered back as best he could, every movement an agony, every movement moving him another inch towards safety.

He could hear Robertson shouting to the men, telling them to take cover.

'Urrah's' sprang from hundreds of throats, as the Soviet infantry equated the lack of fire with impending success over the defenders, surging forward in confident mood.

The IS-III's, unmolested, moved into view, the first tank racing forward towards its goal.

The det cord burned down, its final few seconds witnessed by a curious Soviet private, who suddenly realised that he was experiencing his last breath.

For him, and countless others, the world suddenly ended.

1239hrs, Thursday, 25th October 1945, astride Route 48, Barnstorf.

Yarishlov's tanks swept forward, conscious of the suffering of their infantry, and determined not to fail again.

Their fire was more accurate this time, enemy positions noted and marked, the SP guns and trailer weapons smashed one by one, until the Allied commanders pulled them back.

Yarishlov was interested in the enemy tank, determined to employ his own 100mm gun to good effect, satisfied that Deniken could manage the battle for the moment.

Behind him, the additional forces were already moving against the US defences on the Dreeke road.

To his left, yet more were pushing forward to the northeast, enemy fire slowing them but not stopping them.

To his front, somewhere, was the enemy tank that had killed so many of his comrades.

A jeep bounced up alongside and out sprang the muddy and bloodied infantry officer he had come to admire. Sparing a quick look at the jeep, he recognised it for the one that he had travelled in with Deniken so many days before.

"Comrade Polkovnik. My men have broken through and..."

The cataclysmic event that interrupted Deniken's report was later equated to a volcanic explosion.

The shock wave was immense, and both men feared for their ears.

A huge pall of smoke and flame rose from the railway line.

After a moment spent taking in the scene, Deniken spoke calmly.

"Well then, Comrade Polkovnik. We've wasted our time, and our men."

Both officers were horrified that so many lives had been lost in trying to take the rail bridge, only for it to be destroyed in front of their eyes.

The radio crackled in Yarishlov's ear, his attention mainly focussed on something darker in the dark greenery ahead.

Yarishlov listened to the message, the man's shock and disorientation evident, but still composed enough to make an important report.

The dark area grew slightly darker.

"The bridge is still up. Proceed, Comrade Deniken, and get away from this tank fast."

Deniken was momentarily surprised by the curtness, and then grasped the situation perfectly.

He leapt off the attractive target and ducked behind the jeep.

"Kriks, do not turn the turret. One o'clock, in the trees there, See it?"

Kriks looked.

"No... wait...yes...mudaks...the bastard has us cold."

"Driver, turn the vehicle to the right, millimetre by millimetre, carefully. Kriks, shout when you are on."

Yarishlov instinctively realised that the enemy tank had him, and was just waiting for a better shot, '*or maybe something else?*'

He quickly analysed the situation.

'*A better shot? What is better than me sat here in the open eh?*'

The T44 rotated slowly, the driver skilfully inching the vehicle into position.

"Stop. I'm perfect, Comrade."

The veteran tank commander spoke the words softly, not risking making his gunner jump with the command.

"Fire."

The two guns fired together, and both hit.

The 17pdr APCBC round struck the mantlet and flew skywards, the strike resounding inside the turret.

The 100mm AP shell struck the Glan bull on the right shoulder, transforming the heavy carcass into small pieces, and decorating the surrounding trees with bite-sized pieces.

Griffiths raged.

"You fucking pillock! It's still alive. Move back, Drives, smart about it."

"I sodding 'it it, Sergeant. Every shell but one 'it, and that was Drives' bloody fault."

"Shut up, you horrible excuse for a gunner. "

The banter hid the tension of the moment, the ammunitionless Comet no longer of any use, so Griffiths felt free to quit the field.

Uncharacteristically, Drives stalled the engine.

The crew said nothing, waiting for their experienced driver to sort it out. The engine turned, but refused to fire.

Griffiths watched the field to his front, studying the enemy tank, assessing if their recent target had worked out their position. He also watched the ground in front of their position, the Soviet forces spreading out, and, as he watched it all, Griffiths became witness to something truly awful.

Dunne, foaming at the mouth, eyes wild, had lost the plot, even to the point of producing his revolver, and threatening his own men.

Snatching the radio from the surprised radio officer, he spoke rapidly, issuing orders well beyond his comprehension.

"York-Six calling Trafalgar Leader, You may attack. That position is lost, over."

"Roger York-Six, Trafalgar Leader out."

Dunne returned the handset to the young captain.

"What have you done, Sir?"

"I've stopped the enemy, Captain Bracewell, that's what I've done, Single-handed, no help from any of you bastards. All by myself, I've won the fucking war!"

"But that's our positions, our men!"

"Long gone, Bracewell, I issued orders, don't you know."

"No you didn't, Sir."

"Silence, you mutinous bastard! How dare you disagree with me!"

"Get the aircraft back on and call them off."

The operator was fingering two perfect holes in the front of the comms pack.

"Set's fucked, Captain."

Bracewell looked at the destroyed radio.

"Then so are we all, Robson."

The sound of attacking aircraft drew his attention.

"Oh Jesus, so are we all!"

Others came to his aid, and a brief struggle took place. The revolver discharged twice more, before Dunne was wrestled to the ground.

Bracewell, his hand seared by the heat of the barrel, turned to the rest of the staff.

"I am relieving Dunne of his command."

Turning back to the signals corporal, he issued his first order.

"I'm the radio officer, Sir. There is no such message logged!"

The revolver spoke once, the hole immediately appearing in the canvas overhead.

"Consider yourself under arrest, Bracewell. I will have you court-martialled."

Suddenly, sure of his course of action, the radio officer leapt forward.

Dunn's radio conversation had been with Lieutenant-Commander Steele, officer commanding 822's Fireflies, and the overall leader of a two-squadron sortie by the recently formed Royal Naval Air Wing.

Accompanying him were his old comrades from the days of HMS Argus, the Corsairs of 853 Squadron FAA. Both squadrons had increased in strength, despite days of continuous combat, reinforced by men and machines from the training facilities, and survivors, recovered after the sinking of Argus.

Steele too, had heard the cry for help from Barnstorf, and had led his men into the air, despite the awful flying conditions, confident that their naval air experience in the unforgiving North Atlantic would carry the men through on their mission of support.

South of Barnstorf, 822 and 853 Squadrons found the enemy where Dunne had predicted.

Fig #69 - Immolation, Bloody Barnstorf.

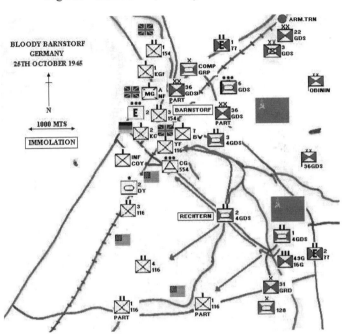

On the ground, the surviving tanks of Yarishlov's 1st Battalion scattered as the attacking aircraft were spotted. They tried to make cover in the woods, despite the presence of the enemy infantry.

RP3 rocket's, fired from the Fireflies, left criss-cross patterns in the air, most of the time ploughing up the sodden earth but enough hit to reduce the 1st Battalion to a shambles.

Tank after tank exploded, one tossed on its back, tracks still running, crew dead and dying inside.

One aircraft singled out the road bridge, three rockets destroying the structure, and the engineers who had laboured to preserve it.

Yarishlov's T44 was selected for particular attention, two of the rockets landing close enough to remove the tracks, sending pieces of it flying across the field.

Stunned by the shock wave, the tank Colonel fought back the nausea and tried to radio his units. His aerials had been carried away, so he tried in vain to contact men already dead or beyond caring.

Casualties amongst the accompanying infantry had been heavy enough, and they too sought cover in whatever was closest, large bodies of frightened men closing on the woods to the west and north-west, yet more investing the southern edge of Barnstorf itself.

Refraining from a machine-gun sweep, Steele called in the Corsairs, detailing the different sections into their own singular attacks.

853 Squadron consisted of nineteen aircraft, well over strength, a matter hidden from higher authority by the officers and men of the Royal Naval Air Wing, for fear of having them removed.

Five sections dived under Steele's instructions, his skill bringing each section in, staggering their assaults, and changing angles of approach to confuse any Soviet AA gunners.

Yellow section attacked the Russians to the west.

All but two of the Squadron's Corsairs had received the special field modification, which allowed a double load of the chosen ordnance to be carried under each wing, sacrificing range and speed for power of attack and maximum damage to the target.

Yellow section's four aircraft attacked in a slanted line, and conducted a textbook delivery of their payload.

Napalm.

Dunne had much to answer for, as the dropped tanks spread their awful load across friend and foe alike, turning the field and woods into an inferno, secondary explosions marking a grenade cooking off here, a mine there.

Blue section was next, their four aircraft immolating the Guardsmen heading north-west, the wall of fire falling just short of petrified Allied soldiers. Even then, the experience proved too much for some. Scot and American alike started to flee, panic bred panic, and within a minute, all the defenders were running for the Channel ports.

Yarishlov emerged from the turret, still reeling from the near misses, his eyes seeing much, but his brain struggling to comprehend what was in front of him.

536

Some yards away, Deniken's jeep stood unmarked, engine running.

Unoccupied.

Deniken had taken refuge in a small shell hole and had survived the attack on the T44, unlike his two comrades.

From the hole, he had watched as the first aircraft approached the mass of men, fear turning to abject horror, as hundreds of soldiers disappeared before his eyes, as the bright yellow wave seemed to engulf everyone in sight.

Now, he was focussed on his men approaching Barnstorf, willing them forward, looking at the approaching aircraft, knowing who would win the race for life.

White section, all but one of their aircraft modified, swept in line abreast, and dropped their Napalm just short of the buildings southeast of the railway line.

Whole lines of men were gobbled up by the greedy flames.

Deniken screamed in frustration and horror, beating the ground with his fists, as comrades from the old days were reduced to black pygmies by the unforgiving horror weapon.

Others, less fortunate, ran around the field and houses, streaming flames, their screams rising above all sounds of battle until some comrade or enemy gave them mercy.

Through his tears, Deniken saw a few dozen of his men still mobile, but retreating from the blackened fields.

Another group of aircraft, three this time, dropped their fiery loads around the Rechtern Bridge, ensuring that there was nowhere that he could look without seeing death at its most horrible.

Aloft, circling lazily, leaving others to watch for enemy aircraft, Steele was satisfied, his professionalism to the fore, his humanity shelved.

"Good job, Green Flight. Spot on the money."

Checking his target area, he called the Red flight leader and issued his final instructions.

537

The four Corsairs turned as instructed, circling to the west and approaching down the rail line, its metal tracks serving as a perfect marker for the attack.

Again line abreast, the four aircraft dropped sixteen napalm canisters on and around the west end of the rail bridge.

Grayson was groggy, a mortar shell having momentarily knocked him out.

Around him, men of his Gordon Highlanders fought alongside GI's from the 116th Infantry, as the engineers struggled to finish the job.

Many of the brave men had fallen, but the engineer unit's sergeant seemed to bear a charmed life, and was near to completion.

The napalm attacks on to the positions south and south-west had drawn many eyes, euphoria turning to sympathy, sympathy turning to fear, fear knocking on the door of panic.

Many an eye turned at the approaching four aircraft.

"Jesus Christ! They're going to attack us!"

Grayson leapt from the hole before finishing his words, loading the flare pistol, knowing he was too late.

"You stupid useless fucking bastards!"

Sixteen canisters detached from the Allied attack aircraft, hitting the ground within seconds of each other, and spreading their version of death amongst the Allied soldiers who screamed and cursed the already empty sky.

Across the river, Hässler was squealing with horror as the fire washed over everything.

Grayson disappeared in an orange wall, the rising fiery killer moving forward at high speed, engulfing everything and everyone the Master Sergeant could see across the Hunte.

"Rosie!"

Hässler had sent the wounded corporal back across the river on an unimportant errand, keen to get him away from certain death on the east bank.

Even Bluebear stopped fighting, the wall of flames drawing his eye, horrifying even a man whose style of fighting

538

brought him close and personal to the enemy in an extremely brutal and messy way.

Across the river, friends and comrades had been incinerated in the blink of an eye.

Some staggered around, enveloped in flames, lungs burnt by hot gases, unable to scream.

Others ran squealing noisily, their clothes and flesh falling from them as the sticky jelly did its horrible work.

Two Soviet soldiers, intent on nothing but self-preservation, dropped into the hole, not knowing that it was already occupied.

Death was waiting for them in its most horrible form.

Hässler watched horrified as Bluebear's tomahawk rose swiftly up and down, two blows for each disoriented guardsman, both faces quickly driven in, easily yielding to the heavy blows.

Still one lived, at least for the briefest of moments, a third blow ending his struggle for breath.

Wide-eyed, the Master Sergeant felt shock creeping over him, and punched his thigh in an attempt to break out of it.

Bluebear understood, and a large hand wiped itself across the German-American's face, the sound of the slap penetrating into Hässler's consciousness as much as the pain of the blow.

"Master Sergeant. Now is not time. Later we mourn. Now, we get outta of here."

The two men slithered out of the hole and down to the water's edge, moving to the north and away from the hell on earth behind them.

Yarishlov was unsteady on his feet, but made the journey anyway, supported by Deniken and Kriks.

Helping him into the jeep, Deniken climbed aboard as Kriks started the vehicle on its journey.

All around them, men of the Obinin assault force lay dead, killed by one of nature's most terrible forces.

None was recognisable.

And the smell.

Not even the rain could remove it.

539

An overriding taste of petroleum pervaded the air that they reluctantly dragged into their lungs, almost narcotic in its intensity.

Not as strong, but with their own special pungency, were the diverse smells of the burning, fuelled by rubber, wood, and man.

The sights were too awful, even for men used to the extremes of combat.

All three cried, the smoke undoubtedly playing its part, stinging their eyes, but their basic humanity was the larger contributor.

No guns, no explosions, no cries of pain.

The battlefield was silent now, the growing wind that distributed the fine ashes providing the soft steady accompaniment to the sound of the jeep's engine, gently cajoling the vehicle through the horrors of war.

All who would die had died. Those who were alive, too shocked to even talk, would survive the day.

Here and there, blackened soldiers and tankers shared cigarettes and canteens in silence, scarcely acknowledging the passing of their senior officers.

Moving on through the carnage, the rail bridge came into view.

Intact.

"Blue Three to lead. Those seagulls sound excited, Flight."

"Blue leader, roger. Now shut up."

Hall was trying hard to work out where the hell they were, the squalls and low cloud making any sort of navigation difficult for the one-man Typhoons of Blue flight.

The airwaves had been full of the sound of the Fleet Air Arm attack, the seagulls as they were affectionately called, calling in successful drop after successful drop.

Regardless of the urgency of the situation, Hall had to face facts. They were lost.

'Think it through man! Think it through!'

He summoned up the map in his mind's eye, ignoring the one in his lap, seeing his airfield, factoring in the wind, the speed, working the problem.

540

"Blue Two to leader, over,"

The train of thought was ruptured, and he responded in a clipped tone, convinced he had nearly solved the problem.

"Blue leader, Blue Two, this better be good, over."

"Skipper, that's a main road off to our right there. I think it's the 214, over."

Hall looked at the break in the clouds.

"Blue section, slow turn to port, execute."

The four aircraft turned lazily left, circling the break, examining the ground below.

"Blue leader to Blue Two. I don't recognise it, over."

Hall knew little of his number two, except he had been shot down twice in the German War, and had claimed three and one third aircraft destroyed.

"Blue Two to Blue leader. That town up ahead. See the five-point junction? That's Diepholz, Skipper. I went with a girl from there in June. That's Diepholz for sure, over."

The map almost leapt from Hall's lap, the paper pattern reflecting the junctions on the ground below. A swift look to the northeast was all he needed.

"Blue Leader to Blue Two, spot on Wallace, spot on. Blue section, turn to port, heading zero-four-zero."

The four Typhoons turned and applied the power again, following Route 51 north from Diepholz to Barnstorf.

'Intact?'

Deniken gave voice to their thoughts.

"It's intact."

The sight brought Yarishlov back to some sort of reality.

"We've done it, tovarich, we've done it!"

The infantry officer was already leaning across to the radio pack, seeking out Obinin to pass on the good news.

Yarishlov, coming out of his brain freeze, barked an order, forgetting the nature of his present company.

"Never mind that, Comrade. Order every available anti-aircraft gun here now. The allied fliers will be here, once they know it still stands."

Neither man would have believed that such an important structure had not even figured in the Allied plans before they

541

attacked, so imagining it as a priority target now that they held it in their hands was easy.

Deniken understood, and sent out the appeal, one that was taken up by other commanders, understanding the opportunity they had been presented with, as well as how fragile that opportunity could prove to be.

The SPAA weapons from 4th Guards Tank were the first to arrive, having been less than a kilometre away and already on the move.

They would have to suffice.

"Blue Three to Blue Leader, enemy tanks and vehicles, twelve o'clock low, hundreds of them, Flight!"

Four pairs of eyes looked down and forward, the sight as impressive as it was daunting.

Hall checked the map as he flicked the radio switch.

"Quartermaster, Quartermaster, this is Broadsword Blue leader, over."

An air controller with very little to control immediately acknowledged.

"Quartermaster from Broadsword Blue Leader. Enemy armoured force, approximately two miles northeast of Barnstorf, straddling Route five-one. Strength approximately two divisions, advancing south-west at speed, over."

A number of ears had heard the message, so no repeat was required.

"Roger Broadsword Blue leader..."

Hall's world went white in an instant.

A Soviet 85mm AA gun had fired a single speculative shot, the shell set to explode at a greater height.

None the less, the lump of metal passed straight through the aircraft, touching only one thing of significance; the radio's wiring.

Unable to contact 'Broadsword', or his flight, Hall waggled his wings and used hand gestures to pass on his orders.

The four aircraft formed line astern, Hall in the lead, and they dived upon the large Soviet force, the weather noticeably closing in once more.

Selecting the head of the column, Hall thumbed the button, sending eight RP3 rockets into the massed target.

Each rocket took lives and smashed vehicles, so concentrated were the lead echelons of the 3rd Guards Mechanised Corps.

Wallace followed on a slightly different line, diving lower still and adding his RP3's to the destruction. A secondary explosion, brought about by one of Hall's rockets, threw the Typhoon off track, and the Flight Sergeant caught a horrified, yet fascinating, glimpse as the body of one of the enemy soldiers flew high into the air, almost matching his height above the battlefield.

Full power and a rising stick took the Typhoon away from the sight, turning to port after his leader, the pitter-patter sounds of metal on metal showing that the lighter AA weapons were wide-awake and focussed.

Next in was Blue Three. McKenzie, the boy wonder, placed his rockets in the centre of the lead elements, wasting not one ounce of HE, flicking up and away to starboard to confuse the enemy gunners.

Blue Four, newly arrived with 182, an experienced Polish flyer, whose name was virtually unpronounceable, attacked and fired off his own rockets, even as the 37mm ZSU's caught him in a cone of fire.

The Typhoon kept on diving, adding Pilot Officer Jan Siesztrzewitowski and his aircraft to the destruction on the ground.

McKenzie and Siesztrzewitowski had made a huge contribution to the Allied defence, the dead and dying they left in their wake belonging to the irreplaceable 77th Engineer Brigade.

Hall elected to make a second pass before the weather closed in all together, and lined up his aircraft for another run.

Yarishlov's request for additional AA weapons had brought much of the 3rd Guards Mechanised's self-propelled mounts forward, and Hall paid the price of the increased firepower, his aircraft struck numerous times by the proliferation of ZSU-37's in the Soviet force.

Breaking off the attack, he could feel the difference in his aircraft, the normally powerful Sabre engine leaden, the manoeuvring worrying solid.

Hall screamed, first in terror, then in pain.

Two 37mm cannon shells struck his aircraft, immediately behind his seat, one passing through, the second exploding behind his seat, sending pieces of metal into his exposed side. The agony in his side suddenly secondary, as a heavy machine-gun bullet punched through the canopy and clipped his head.

Losing consciousness for a few seconds, he was unaware of other strikes on his aircraft. Although none was fatal, the Typhoon was a flying wreck.

Coming round and orienting himself, Hall knew he was badly hurt. Even though his vision was obscured by blood, the impairment did not stop him from seeing the gauges screaming their bad news, nor did it stop him from seeing or smelling the light blue smoke that began to fill the cockpit.

Thankful for the intact compass, the wounded pilot turned for home, hoping that his men would follow.

Wallace was already out of the fight, his aircraft clawed from the sky even as he lined it up for a second pass, his parachute opening just in time to prevent serious injury.

The Typhoon crashed into a small lake adjacent to the Am Sandhügel road, no trace of its presence left, save a few floating dead fish.

McKenzie, as ever the aggressive pilot, rapidly dropped lower, the streams of tracers missing by nearly a hundred feet above, the fuselage of the ground attack aircraft barely fifty feet above the ground. He fired, the Hispano cannons lashing out, chewing up men and vehicles, occasionally rewarded with a spectacular fiery display as something reacted badly to the stream of shells.

Pulling away, a single heavy-machine gun bullet struck his propeller, the change in note and handling instant and worrying.

Behind, McKenzie had left two of the ZSU's in flames, and eighty infantry and their transports out of the fight.

Turning for home, the young pilot, concerned by the weather closing in rapidly, increased his revs.

The damaged propeller protested, and he throttled back once more, losing height again, as he swept back towards Barnstorf.

In the strange light, the situation was clear, and obviously desperate.

The Soviet spearhead was approaching a huge hole, some three hundred or so yards from the rail bridge.

A cursory look at the river line showed McKenzie that the other bridges in the area were down, and that the Soviets were focussing on the rail bridge.

His eyes focussed on that bridge, straining to understand the nature of the pile on the centre. That understanding came in an instant, and he made his decision just as quickly, pulling back on the stick, rising rapidly, before side slipping to port and turning for the attack.

Yarishlov and Deniken had made their way over the bridge to the east bank, pausing for a moment to watch the engineer officer at work, delicately ensuring that no booby-traps were present, whilst painfully aware that the 3rd Guards Mechanised and 22nd Guards Rifle Corps were waiting on his best efforts.

Realising that their presence was placing increased pressure on the man, the two senior officers moved on.

Both men had seen combat in all its horrible manifestations, but what confronted them at the mound exceeded their experience.

The defenders had been overwhelmed after a bloody fight, a bestial affair that had left dead and dying men everywhere.

After receiving a report from an exhausted Starshina, the two followed the shocked man around the positions, seeing men locked in rigid positions, dead, and yet seeming still fighting each other.

Occasionally, a blackened pile transformed in the beholder's imagination, the mass suddenly identifiable as men burned beyond recognition.

The smoke was sweet and sickly, and had a smell that clung to verything it touched.

The Starshina stopped, feeling the need to identify one such abomination.

"That is my Major, Comrades. He was assisting these two wounded men when the flamethrower tank exploded."

There was no sign of the flamethrower tank in question, not that either officer dwelt to look for it.

The group of three burned men was more than awful enough to distract them, and they moved silently away.

545

A thudding sound caught their attention; regular, worrying, awful.

A Soviet soldier holding his spade continued to smash the skull of the cadaver he was kneeling on, the heavy blade now cutting into the shoulders, having destroyed everything down to that point.

The Scotsman's rifle was still in his hand, its bayonet through the throat of the Guardsman's brother, whose sightless eyes bore witness to the terrible indignations being visited on his killer's corpse.

Deniken gently took hold of the man's wrist, the wild eyes challenging him for an instant, until the moment drained from him, and he collapsed in tears.

Leaving the Starshina to get the man moving, the two moved on.

Another Soviet soldier sat with his legs crossed, every part of him shaking violently, as his system rebelled against his experiences.

In front of him lay his dead friend, both hands blown off, his stomach opened up by the explosive force of the grenade he had pulled to himself, in an attempt to save his comrades.

The sight and smell were both equally revolting.

They moved on again, through a field of corpses and body parts, comrades and enemy, smashed and broken by both the technology of the modern battlefield and other weapons of a more primitive nature.

On the top of the mound, the fighting had clearly been medieval in nature, close and bloody.

Both men recoiled from the sight of an enemy soldier, his throat ripped open by the teeth of his opponent, the Guardsman's bloody mouth still clinging to the torn flash, even in death.

A movement caught their eye.

Two Scottish soldiers sat on the floor, either side of their guard, a white-faced Corporal. All three were smoking British Player's cigarettes in silence, heads down, their eyes a thousand miles away.

One of the prisoners, an RSM, spared the Soviet officers a look, returning his gaze to the floor without comment.

A young Lieutenant, his lust for the glory of battle satisfied in spades by his first combat, walked shakily forward to report, holding a silver-topped cane.

Finishing his brief report, in which he detailed the loss of most of his company, the officer proffered the cane to Yarishlov.

"They fought around this, Comrade Polkovnik. It must be important for them."

The captured RSM looked up, this time, eyes keenly focussed on the object, the longing and desire evident in his eyes, something not wasted on Deniken.

He nudged the tank officer's arm, pointing at the man.

"So it seems, Comrade Leytenant."

All three looked at the battered Scotsman, recognising his hurt.

Taking leave of the stunned infantry officer, the two men moved slowly on.

Coming round full circle, Yarishlov saw a rifle poised, its bayonet held at the throat of a dazed Scottish soldier.

"Stoi!"

The rifle remained steady, the man ignoring the imperative.

"Serzhant, put down your weapon. Now! That is an order!"

Yarishlov got through the fog of hatred this time, the weapon relaxed, and the NCO acknowledged his presence with the briefest of nods.

"Are you alright, Comrade Serzhant?"

The NCO looked at Yarishlov as if he was a being from another planet.

"Do I fucking look alright, you stupid bastard?"

'That wasn't the brightest thing to say to a man who had been through hell, Arkady!'

"Comrade Serzhant Durestov, attention!"

The man stiffened automatically, and Deniken interposed himself.

"You will apologise to the Polkovnik immediately."

Durestov's mind cleared and he realised he was in a very precarious position.

"Comrade Polkovnik, my apologies. I have no excuse."

547

Deniken turned to the senior man, seeking his assurance that the matter had been attended to.

Yarishlov stepped forward, and took the Serzhant by the shoulders.

"Comrade Serzhant, your apology is accepted. Accept mine for asking such a stupid question."

Durestov looked confused. Yarishlov gripped him harder, and smiled.

"But don't make a habit of it with us Polkovniks. We're unforgiving bastards by nature."

"Yes, Comrade Polkovnik."

Yarishlov stepped back, and Durestov sprang to attention, saluting both officers.

As they moved on, Deniken spoke softly.

"Thank you for making allowances, Comrade Polkovnik. He is a good man; a wonderful soldier."

Casting an eye around the mound reinforced his view.

"Anyone who has survived this bloodbath has been through hell, Comrade Yarishlov."

The tank colonel had stopped abruptly.

A Soviet rifleman stood guard over two enemy soldiers who were busy working on the prone body of a third.

"Ramsey?"

The two Scots looked up, confused that the enemy officer knew the name of their commander.

They turned back quickly, doing their best to save the Major's life.

When the charges had exploded, Ramsey had been thrown fifty yards back towards the river.

His head had struck a tree as he flew through the air, the bloody flap hanging down the side of his skull, contaminated with green lichen, evidence of the unforgiving solid object that had caused his wound.

The left forearm was clearly snapped in two, his hand almost touching the elbow.

Both legs were missing below the knees, the tibias and fibulas, stripped of flesh, protruding for a few inches below the awful wounds.

Squatting beside the man he had met just once before, a lifetime ago, Yarishlov spoke softly to the Corporal who was about to bandage the bloody right stump.

"Will he live?"

McEwan did not look up.

"If ah can get the man tae the infirmary, then mebbe...Sah", he added after a moment's reflection.

His eyes took in the cane balanced in Yarishlov's hand, again, something not missed by Deniken, stood back from the vignette.

"What is inn-fer-mary?'

"A hospital, man! Doctors? Nurses?"

Yarishlov understood.

He took in the desperate sight of the battered man, part of his mind recalling their previous meeting, part of his mind wrestling with a problem.

The tank colonel stood, his sense of purpose affecting the group, Deniken suddenly aware that there was to be action taken.

"Comrade Deniken, I have need of your personal transport."

A silent question passed between the two, but Deniken knew enough of the Colonel to know he would not be about to do what he was about to do, if it wasn't the right course of action.

"I can get it no closer than the end of the bridge, Comrade Polkovnik."

A simple nod sent Deniken on his way.

Yarishlov switched to English.

"Come, soldier. Let us moving Mayor Ramsey to car."

The three men lifted Ramsey up, the unconscious man unaware of the journey he was undertaking. On reaching the bridge, the sound of the approaching jeep was welcome indeed.

The engineer officer considered reporting his closeness to completion, but decided against it. Sparing half an eye to the bloody sight that quickly moved past him.

Deniken moved forward with one of his men, relieving the Colonel of his burden.

Watching the wounded man being carefully loaded into the rear of the jeep, Yarishlov pulled out his notepad and penned a brief note, carefully ripping the end product from the book.

Pausing for a moment, he reopened the notebook and spent slightly longer writing another note.

Deniken attached a piece of white cloth to the shattered windscreen, one of the prisoners following his lead and doing the same the other side.

Yarishlov offered McEwan one of the pieces of paper.

"Show this to any Soviet mens. It is safe passage note."

"Thank ye, Sah. Thank ye from ma Major, too."

Yarishlov nodded as he wrapped something in the second note and it inside Ramsey's battledress pocket.

"And this is not for my friend eye."

'Friend? The commie bas is ma man's friend, is he?'

"Give this to your top officer."

"Aye, I'll attend to it, Sah."

McEwan's eyes strayed again to the cane, its closeness almost taunting him.

He was surprised when it grew larger, not realising that Yarishlov had held it out to him.

"This are Ramsey's, yes?

"Yes, Sah, that it is."

"Take it."

No second invitation was needed.

"Now go, soldier, and keep my friend live."

McEwan snapped to attention, the other Scottish soldier following suit, both men throwing up tremendous salutes as only the British Army could do to total perfection in the very oddest of circumstances.

Swinging into the driver's seat, McEwan waited for the other man to be settled next to Ramsey before letting out the clutch, and moving away.

Deniken stood beside Yarishlov in silence, both men watching the disappearing 4x4. One reciting a silent prayer to a God he didn't believe in, pleading for the life of a man he barely knew, the other, full of questions over what he had just been party to.

The prayer remained unfinished, the questions unspoken.

"Air attack!"

Experience gave both men wings, and they dropped into a nearby position, the horrible nature of its contents immaterial, its quality of cover paramount.

A single aircraft slashed in from the south, its cannon churning up the water before lashing the bridge.

The engineer officer disappeared in a burst of red, chewed up by cannon shells.

Both men hugged the bottom of the trench, expecting the stack of munitions to yield to the enemy attack.

Surprisingly, they did not.

AA weapons started rattling out as the aircraft circled for another attack, joined by anything on the ground that a soldier could point skywards.

The Typhoon swept in again, this time lower, leaving a vibrating trail in the water, as its turbulent wake and discarded shell casings disturbed the river's surface.

Yarishlov, stealing a look over the edge of the trench, could see the pilot clearly, so low and close was the Typhoon.

He watched fascinated as sprays of blood obscured the enemy flyer, the red Perspex hiding what lay within.

The pain was excruciating, as was the feeling of failure.

McKenzie had been hit by two bullets.

The one that caused his blood to squirt over the inside of the cockpit was the lesser of the two wounds; head wounds always bled profusely.

The other wound was more serious, a 12.7mm round having entered low through his right side and out the left hand side of his stomach, wrecking the pilot's bladder, and much else that was less vital as it journeyed through.

The Hispano cannons had fallen silent before their time, ammunition expended.

Pulling back on the stick, the young Canadian felt the Typhoon rebel as more strikes caused damage.

The propeller was now shuddering permanently, and the aircraft needed a permanent right pedal to stop it turning sideways.

Turning to port again, he felt the aircraft stagger under a hammer blow, a single cannon shell slamming into the side of the fuselage, and into the engine compartment.

The result was immediate and impressive.

The Typhoon caught fire, the shell hole emitting a long spectacular orange streak as damaged fuel lines fed an intense fire.

The same fire swiftly started to eat its way into the cockpit, and McKenzie's right foot was immediately affected, pushed forward, as it was, on the pedal.

Despite the pain, he kept his boot in position, his mind made up.

He turned the aircraft and lined up on the rail bridge.

Deniken was shouting at his men, knowing the aircraft was coming in again.

Yarishlov watched incredulously as the dying airplane drove onwards, guns silent, its fiery tail growing with every second.

In the final few seconds, the red smear in the cockpit became visible again, illuminated from inside by the growing fire that was obviously consuming the pilot.

None the less, the Typhoon held steady and plunged directly into the centre of the rail bridge.

The explosion was immediate, and devastating.

The noise was so loud that everything went quiet, those unfortunate to be too close clutched their ears, permanently damaged by the shock wave and intense sound.

Those who were closer still either clutched their wounds or lay dead.

Durestov, running away from the river, was transformed into a red smear on the earth, as the bulk of the Typhoon's Sabre engine briefly occupied the same piece of woodland as he did.

With his death, the Battle of Barnstorf ended, and to draw a fitting line under the battle, Mother Nature brought down her heaviest rain, and most violent thunderstorm.

Barnstorf.

A battle the Allies had most certainly lost.

A battle the Soviets had apparently won.

Except for the fact that no suitable bridge remained over the Hunte.

Except for the fact that thousands of their men lay dead upon the field.

And except for what would come next.

The allocation of blame often has more to do with your availability than your culpability.

Chris Coling

Chapter 101 - THE AFTERMATH

Eisenhower gripped the telephone, unable to grasp what McCreery had just said.

"Incredible. Really incredible. Our troops have done magnificently this week. Pass on a well done to your men, General."

Ike's face lost much of its pleasure as the commander of 21st Army Group relayed the butcher's bill.

Bedell-Smith, Hood and Rossiter had sat back, already satisfied with the events of the last few days, expecting McCreery's report to substantiate the original communications, confirming that the Soviet Baltic Front had been stopped.

Quite clearly, Eisenhower's body language and grim expression spoke of issues not previously communicated.

"I'm sorry to hear that, General, truly I am."

Only Rossiter had noticed Ike making notations as he listened.

"I will do what I can, and I expect I may well be able to give you some quality units soon. In the meantime, hold the line, General, and thank you again."

Eisenhower replaced the receiver and took a moment to reflect.

"Gentlemen, as we heard earlier, the Baltic Front assault along the Hunte River has been stopped," a natural pause as the commander licked his lips, "But only at great cost."

Consulting the note he had made, Ike passed on the grim news.

"The British 3rd Division was badly damaged, so too the 5th Guards Armored Brigade. Both the 29th Infantry and the 51st Highlanders have been wiped out, and in the case of the Scottish,

553

that leaves just a few artillery and support elements. The rest of the unit died on the Hunte River and beyond."

A respectful silence was observed before he continued.

"On the up side, it seems that they dealt the Communists a heavy blow. On the conservative side, the Reds lost over three hundred tanks and fifty thousand men in their whole operation."

Another look at the note and he could continue with confidence.

"Reports say that three British squadrons, two Royal Navy, and another from the RAF, were able to perform ground attacks against packed ground targets, with spectacular results."

It wasn't totally accurate information, but as good as he was going to get for some time.

Taking a cigarette from his pack, Eisenhower flicked open his lighter and drew deeply on the resulting rich smoke.

"Well then, it seems we have finally stopped the bastards."

His statement encompassed so much, from the incredible efforts of the ground and air forces, the Soviets own supply issues, and the continued intervention of partisan and Kommando units throughout Europe.

Such was the impact of the week's events, and McCreery's call, that no one noticed the unusual profanity from their Supreme Commander.

Raising his coffee mug, Eisenhower offered a toast.

"To all those men who have laid down their lives so far."

The four men drank quietly.

"Tomorrow, we will start the process of rolling them back."

He caught the enquiring look from Rossiter, and knew what was on the man's mind.

"Yes Sam, to the Polish border and beyond."

The human cost of stopping the Soviet attack on the Hunte went beyond the removal of some markers from the battle map; thousands of men were dead, and thousands more were hideously injured.

Ramsey survived his evacuation, his wounds dictating that he could no longer serve with his beloved Jocks. His removal from the front probably granted him survival, and an extended life way beyond the end of hostilities.

Hall survived a very ropey landing, his aircraft virtually folding in half as it came to rest. The Flight Lieutenant never flew operationally again, his partial blindness keeping him grounded and ensuring he survived the war.

Bluebear and Hässler stayed in the water, the incessant rain masking their progress to safety, eventually reaching the forward positions of the 3rd British Division.

Unwounded but both scarred by the brutal fight, they were returned to combat within the week.

McEwan, unharmed, and as dour as ever, joined the new formation of the Highland Division. He had no chance to tell Ramsey about the Russian officer, but remembered to hand over the man's note to an appropriate senior officer.

RSM Robertson and CSM Green were taken prisoner, and ended up in a Special Work Camp, deep in the USSR.

Flight Sergeant Wallace Gordon was badly beaten by his captors, but eventually made it to a Soviet prison camp, where he died in mysterious circumstances before the War's end.

Pilot Officer McKenzie failed to return from his mission and nothing was known of the manner of his death for some years.

The German officers, Strecher and Dieckhoff, were both wounded during the fighting, along with most of their men. Strecher was captured by the Soviets, and summarily executed. Kommando Friedrich ceased to exist.

Aitcherson survived the battle, and went on to join McEwan in the newly forming Highland Division.

Griffiths and his tank crew also survived the battle, and went on to greater glory on the North German Plain.

Rosenberg disappeared without trace.

Lieutenant Commander Steele lived for two days more. He was crushed by a fuel bowser as he lay snoozing on a grass bank outside his Squadron's dispersal building.

On the other side, the losses were worse and keenly felt, despite the capacity of the Soviet war machine to absorb death on a grand scale and still function.

555

The initial assault formations fared very badly, with both the 128th Tank Brigade and 31st Guards Rifle Division reduced to a handful of men and damaged vehicles.

Stelmakh's 6th Guards Heavy Tanks had not fired a shot in the battle, and yet consisted of only two vehicles and eleven men by the end of the battle.

The valuable 77th Engineer's and the 36th Guards Rifle Corps were both removed from the Soviet order of battle.

4th Guards Tank Brigade, Yarishlov's command, ceased to exist, its handful of survivors and running vehicles moved to fill in the gaps in other parts of 2nd Guards Tank Corps.

A large portion of the 3rd Guards Mechanised Corps was badly handled, a noticeable, but lesser level of damage inflicted upon the 22nd Guards Rifle Corps. Both units remained combat effective in numerical, if not mental, terms.

No Soviet aircraft made it back to base that day, and no pilots were recovered, the only survivors swept up and into Allied POW camps for the rest of hostilities.

Major-General Obinin received a visit from the NKVD, one that ended in suicide, his body being dumped in a roadside ditch.

Colonel Yarishlov was arrested, along with Lieutenant Colonel Deniken, the two taken away to Christyakov's headquarters to ascertain their culpability over the defeat.

Along the battle lines of the 1st Baltic Front, the red machine ground to a halt, exhausted, bloodied, and lacking many vital supplies.

The surviving formations held their collective breath.

Waiting, because experience told them that more was to come.

<u>2208hrs, Thursday, 25th October 1945, Office of the General Secretary of the Communist Party, the Kremlin, Moscow, USSR.</u>

"Disaster, after disaster, after fucking disaster!"

Beria was away in the East, so it was Molotov and Bulganin who had to endure the tirade.

"Our Soviet people, the glorious workers, have given these bastards everything they have asked for, and still they fail!"

He stood, slamming his palms on the old desk, making both men jump.

556

"Our Marshals and Generals fail continuously, our intelligence services fail continuously, our soldier's and worker's efforts wasted by the shortcomings of a few!"

Neither man could or would disagree; the floor belonged to Stalin.

"And this! What am I to make of this?"

Stalin picked up a folder containing a recently arrived report, sent by Beria using his personal code, product of his investigations into the Production issues.

The report detailed additional information on the recent liquidation of certain undesirable elements within one major chemical facility, liquidation that encompassed family members of all ages.

The son, wife, and two grandchildren of GRU Colonel General Pekunin had fallen victim to the overzealous approach of the local NKVD office.

That would have been wholly regrettable, had it not been for the additional inclusion of an NKVD assessment of the debacle that befell 3rd Red Banner Central European Front, mainly at the hands of GRU false assurances, emanating from Pekunin himself.

That made it something else entirely.

"Heads will roll!"

He returned to his chair and grabbed the telephone, the whole mount shuddering as he nearly knocked it flying.

"Get me NKVD Leytenant General Yegerov."

The wait was brief, but every second increased the malevolence of his thoughts.

"Comrade General Yegorov, I have orders for you. Your continued existence depends on their successful completion."

Such statements were bound to get the full attention of the hapless listener, and even an NKVD General knew his hold on position and life could be perilous when Stalin was on the warpath.

Both Molotov and Bulganin listened to the normal arrangements for arrests and executions that tended to follow ignominious defeats.

Their collective attention peaked as Stalin included names of men beyond reproach, silent surprise turning to silent incredulity.

Although talking on the telephone, the leader's eyes were fixed upon them, dealing with their doubts, staring them both down and into submission.

Their silent compliance was guaranteed.

"Immediately, Comrade Yegerov. Report to me when each arrest is successfully completed."

The phone did not return to its cradle, as Stalin placed another call immediately.

<u>2216hrs, Thursday, 25th October 1945, Office of Special Intelligence Projects, GRU Western Europe Headquarters, the Mühlberg, Germany.</u>

The phone rang, startling both occupants of the room, still working long after they could have retired to their respective quarters.

"Nazarbayeva."

"Good evening, Comrade Nazarbayeva. Do you recognise who this is?"

"Yes, and good evening to you, Comrade General Secretary."

The other occupant of the room, GRU Major Poboshkin, cringed automatically, burying his face deeper into the folder he had been reading aloud to his boss.

"I am giving you a direct order, Comrade Polkovnik. You will proceed to the office of General Pekunin and arrest him as an enemy of the state. Is that clear?"

Nazarbayeva was stunned, her mind reeled, for once in her life, her mouth worked without thinking.

"On what basis, Comrade General Secretary?"

Stalin, unusually, chose a softer path than that others had suffered on the rare occasions his orders were questioned.

"On my authority, Comrade Nazarbayeva. I possess real evidence that he may have deliberately sabotaged a military operation, and I also possess evidence that he has motive for doing so. Am I clear, Comrade Nazarbayeva?"

"Yes, Comrade General Secretary. I understand my orders."

Poboshkin could see from her face that Nazarbayeva did everything but understand what she had just been ordered to do.

"Good. Report to me immediately you have successfully detained him. An NKVD unit is on its way to relieve you of the prisoner as soon as possible."

The phone went dead in her hands, the empty electrical sound growing in intensity, as her mind tried to deal with the enormity of the situation.

'I have no choice. My orders are quite clear.'

Part of her laughed in mocking response.

'Your orders? Hiding behind orders, are you?'

Her stomach rebelled, and she spilt her dinner on the wooden floor.

"Comrade Polkovnik. What is wrong?"

She looked at her aide, barely recognising him, her mental faculties locked in confrontation.

'Orders are orders, and there is cause!'

'Really?'

She regained her composure, wiped her mouth, and stood up quickly, her hand automatically ensuring that her service automatic was in place.

"Comrade Major, retrieve an automatic weapon from the guard commander's rack, on my authority, and bring two of his men here now, similarly armed."

Poboshkin did not need to comment, his look drawing Nazarbayeva into further words.

"We have orders to arrest General Pekunin. Immediately."

Four minutes later, Nazarbayeva knocked on the door of Pekunin's office. The General was also working late.

"Come in."

The old man seemed genuinely pleased to see his protégé, although his smile faded a little when he saw her expression.

And the men she left outside the office.

"Welcome, Comrade Nazarbayeva. You have something to tell me, Tatiana?"

"I have orders, Comrade Polkovnik General."

She hesitated.

"If you have orders, then you must carry them out, Comrade Polkovnik."

"My orders are direct from the General Secretary, and they require me to arrest you immediately."

Picking up the Chinese puzzle box, he made a deliberate slow play of unlocking it, completing the first three stages, clearly a ploy to allow him to choose his words carefully.

"Then you must obey your orders, Comrade Nazarbayeva, for they were given to you, specifically, for a good reason. Otherwise our Socialist brothers of the NKVD would have been tasked with my detention."

"I am here to arrest you, and hand you over to them when they arrive, Comrade Polkovnik General."

Something changed in Pekunin's demeanour.

"And if I resist arrest, what will you do, Tatiana, eh?"

The woman in front of him showed doubt and indecision, her normally iron exterior suddenly brittle under the pressure.

"I will obey my orders, Comrade, and I will arrest you."

"And if I resist arrest, what then?"

Her hand reached for the Tokarev, its cold metal turning her arm to ice as she pointed it at her mentor and friend.

"I have orders to arrest you, Comrade Polkovnik General."

Pekunin reached for two things, placing the Chinese box and his favoured Nagant revolver on the table between them.

"Listen to me, Tatiana. I will not be arrested," he held up a hand to silence her protests, "There is no way I will place myself in the clutches of that NKVD snake Beria, you have to understand that."

She could, but could not find the words for the moment.

Pekunin continued.

"Before I resist arrest, take this," he slid the puzzle box across the table.

Their eyes met, the pain and anguish equal in both, the mutual feelings of respect and tenderness openly declared between them for the first time.

"It is my personal gift to you. Use it how you wish. Believe it, and believe nothing else, Tatiana."

Shouts developed on the edge of their consciousness.

"Clearly, our comrades of the Secret Police have arrived."

Tatiana had not taken her eyes off the box, despite the increased volume of an obvious disagreement outside.

"Comrade Nazarbayeva, you must now accept one final order from me."

She automatically clicked to attention.

"I will now reach for my revolver, and fire a shot into the wall beside your left shoulder."

She automatically inclined her head to the left, catching herself before she went too far.

"You will then ensure that the Chekist bastards cannot hurt me, or my family, further. Will you do this for me?"

She shook her head violently, relaxing her body posture.

"No, Roman Samuelevich, I cannot. You are a good man, and this is all wrong. All wrong!"

The external noise was now becoming overpowering.

"But you must, or we are all lost, Tatiana."

Pekunin picked up the revolver and aimed at the wall. Nazarbayeva, by reflex alone, brought up her Tokarev.

The door almost folded inwards as Lieutenant General Kochetkov burst in, brandishing his own weapon. Behind him, a scuffle between NKVD and GRU personnel was growing in intensity.

He saw the situation in the office quite clearly, but misread it totally.

His first bullet struck Nazarbayeva in the side of her right breast, passing through the soft tissue, and out again in an instant.

Pekunin's instincts made him change his target, one of his bullets taking Kochetkov in the chest.

Nazarbayeva, part in understanding, part in self-preservation, placed her own bullet in Pekunin, the impact knocking him back into his chair.

Through red teeth, he managed to speak.

"Not good enough, Polkovnik, make the next one better. Goodbye, and good luck. Now!"

He tried to raise the revolver, his strength ebbing with every beat of his heart.

The NKVD General finally swept into the room with most of his entourage, in time to witness a bleeding Nazarbayeva put a bullet through the head of the traitor, Pekunin.

The woman, tears, both of pain and of grief, streaming down her face, swivelled like a combat veteran, the Tokarev steady, aimed at the Chekist's head.

"Enough, Comrade Polkovnik, enough. You have performed magnificently," he gestured at her obvious wound, "And you have been wounded. Stand down now, and let my men take over."

His relief was obvious as the muzzle of the automatic lowered gently, the woman's gaze returning to the ruined features of her former boss.

Her mind worked fast, her hasty plan to use bluster and authority to secure her needs.

"Right, Comrade General. The wound is nothing, and we have work to do Comrade. You and your men secure these two vermin, and get them away. Have them photographed immediately. The Comrade General Secretary will wish to see the evidence of this night's work."

She slipped the safety on, and placed the Tokarev on the table.

"I have to report directly to Comrade Stalin straight away, so please get these two out of my sight immediately."

The NKVD officer was not about to be ordered about by some GRU pup, and certainly not a woman, until the mention of 'the' man, and the implied intimacy between him and the killer of Pekunin.

The woman bulldozed on.

"Mayor Poboshkin!"

Her aide arrived at the door, the evidence of a struggle quite clear on his face and uniform. The large glowing red weal, where his face had been struck, failed to hide his concern for his senior.

"Comrade Mayor Poboshkin. You are responsible for securing this room, once I have made my call to the General Secretary. No-one, repeat, no-one is to enter this room without the direct authority of," she looked directly at the senior NKVD man, the question hanging, and drawing him into the conspiracy.

"Dustov."

"Without the direct authority of Comrade General Dustov. Is that clear?"

"Yes, Comrade Polkovnik."

"Attend to your orders then, Comrade Mayor."

562

Addressing the NKVD officer, she pulled another chair over to the desk, and picked up the telephone.

"Once that is out of the way," she gestured at Kotchetkov's body, "I will inform the General Secretary that his orders have been carried out, and that you and your men have discharged your instructions to the letter."

"Thank you, Comrade Polkovnik."

Totally bamboozled and railroaded, Dustov organised his men, and the bodies of both GRU senior officers were whisked away.

Stalin took the call, listening to the brief details of Nazarbayeva's report.

"General Kotchetkov shot you? You are wounded, Comrade Nazarbayeva?"

Only Molotov now remained, Bulganin already on his way to the airfield to take a flight eastwards.

He waited as Stalin listened to Nazarbayeva's reply.

"None the less, I insist, you must have medical attention, Comrade Nazarbayeva."

Stalin's mind was working, wheels within wheels, priorities shifting, other possibilities occurring as he found himself smiling in unfeigned delight.

'Why not? Lavrentiy will enjoy it and competence earns its own rewards.'

"Comrade Nazarbayeva. It appears that you have removed the two most senior men within GRU West. That leaves us with a dilemma. Kotchetkov was the natural successor, and I am surprised that his treachery went undiscovered until now."

He reminded himself to encourage the NKVD to explore the late General's family, and uncover evidence of their undoubted complicity.

"You have created the problem, Comrade Polkovnik, so it falls to you to solve it."

Her wound was aching now, the blood clotted, and the adrenalin gone.

"How can I do that, Comrade General Secretary?"

"You will find a way, Mayor General Nazarbayeva, you will find a way. Now, tend to your wound, and organise your command. I will look forward to hearing your plans tomorrow."

The phone went dead in her hand.

Even though her mind suddenly filled with the implications of Stalin's statement, she acted on her hasty plan, opened the window, and dropped the puzzle box into the small shrub to its right, closing the window quietly.

She recovered her pistol and left the room, nodding to Dustov, leaving him in her wake. The troubled NKVD man was still wondering how exactly she had bulldozed him, but decided the details would not make his report to the Chairman.

On her way to the medical facility, Nazarbayeva recovered the box and put it in pride of place in her room, hidden in plain sight.

Bandaged and more comfortable, the new commander of GRU West returned to her billet and sat on her bed, eyes glued to the Chinese Box that Pekinun had so wanted her to take, as she began the process of unravelling what had just happened.

2258hrs, Thursday, 25th October 1945, Headquarters of 1209th Grenadiere Regiment, 159th Infanterie Division, Neuwied, Germany.

Oberstleutnant Gelben was a happy man. His command had still not moved forward, one of the few units that were still strangely uncommitted, as the 159th Division took its position in the line of defence.

That the 1209th Grenadiere was not committed was all due to his efforts, solely designed to ensure that his combat formation did not get in the way of anything his masters were planning.

Removing the competent Major in command of the 3rd Battalion had been a masterstroke, denying the Army his expertise, and demoralising the unit in one single stroke.

When the time of reckoning came, the Motherland would know he had done his duty.

His self-congratulation came to an abrupt end with an imperious knocking, the sounds author failing to wait for an invitation before stepping inside his private quarters.

One look at the man's face told Gelben that he had no future, other than that decided by the Feldgendarmerie Colonel.

"Pyotr Gelben, agent for the Communist State, I arrest you on charges of spying and murder."

The GRU agent considered his pistol, the comforting shape just beyond easy reach.

His eyes betrayed him.

"Agent Gelben, I will shoot you, but I will not kill you, and I do have such skills. You have some questions to answer, and answer them you will."

After a moment's delay, Gelben made his choice, and surrendered himself into whatever the future held.

Gelben was not alone, and other GRU agents found themselves rounded up, plucked from comfortable obscurity, and thrust into the limelights of interrogation and pain at the hands of silent, faceless, and uncaring men. However, some GRU agents were not detained, rather, left in place to be monitored, their contacts betrayed unwittingly as they went about the normal business of espionage, all of them to be subsequently offered a simple choice. Resist and die; assist and live. Many brave men and women chose the former option, but the majority chose the second, that being employment against their former masters.

2302hrs, Thursday, 25th October 1945, Headquarters, Red Banner Forces of Europe, Kohnstein, Nordhausen, Germany.

The staggering news had arrived as Zhukov and Malinin were trying to find some way of keeping the military initiative.

Alert orders had gone to the units arraigned above the Alps, preparing them to pursue the plan, once the command was given.

As always, supply issues were the bane of their plans, but one other area did suggest itself, and they were already sketching out the draft orders for the assault on the Moselle as well as a small-scale excursion into Denmark, something planned, but not of priority, now brought to the fore because of its low use of consumables.

The reports of the death of Pekunin had stopped them in their tracks. Each man mirrored the other, slumped in a chair, silently drinking warm tea.

They made eye contact as the sounds of feet, synchronised marching, coming closer, growing in purpose, and, in their opinion, increasing in threat.

565

The door burst open, the space filled by a Colonel of NKVD in combat uniform, PPD in hand, a man there to obey his orders to the letter.

Zhukov and Malinin stood in anticipation.

"Comrade Zhukov, I am commanded to relieve you of your command and accompany you to Moscow, where you must answer for your failures."

He did not wait for a reaction as, in his mind, if there were any, he would gun the 'Victory Bringer' down.

"Comrade Malinin is to retain his position until your replacement arrives."

The challenging look drew a curt response.

"And if I choose not to retain my position, Comrade Polkovnik?"

The officer's contempt was unconcealed.

"Then that has been anticipated, as your replacement is also already on his way here."

His eyes flicked down and narrowed.

"Surrender your weapons immediately," the barrel of the PPD reinforcing his request.

An NKVD Lieutenant slipped past him, and swept the two weapons up into his custody.

The two former commanders exchanged looks, in some ways shocked by events, in other ways stoically dealing with the expected result of defeat.

Again, marching feet, this time just two sets of boots, growing closer, and with that closeness a growing sense of foreboding swept over Zhukov.

The NKVD Colonel turned to look and clicked to attention.

"Comrade Marshal, the prisoners are secure. The command is yours."

"Thank you, Comrade Polkovnik."

Zhukov recognised the voice immediately, as did Malinin.

Konev stepped into the room, the expression bringing with it smugness and satisfaction on an epic scale.

"Ah, Comrade Zhukov."

He did not deign to recognise Malinin.

"Before you go, what other disasters have you left me to repair, eh?"

He picked up the notes the two had been working on, and quickly skimmed them.

"Too little, too late, Comrade. Your time has now passed."

Standing back, he nodded at the NKVD Colonel, who swept the two men out of the room, and away to await a flight back to Moscow.

When eating an elephant, take one bite at a time.

Creighton Abrams

Chapter 102 - THE SILVERBIRDS

It was a piece of theatre, worthy of one of Hollywood's best, and, even though he said so himself, Georges de Walle thought it brilliant.

'The Moonlight Sonata.'

The headquarters was silent and dark, the storm having passed as quickly as it came, the disappearance of the clouds now revealing the night sky in all its glory. The only illumination in the building was a reading lamp here and there, sufficient to track a safe path through the deserted desks and empty chairs, but not enough to overcome the artificial tension created by the music.

Guards were at a normal level around the headquarters, but not inside the building, where all was left quiet, save for those that had a part to play in the drama.

The visitor showed his papers for the third and final time and entered the building, immediately feeling his senses prick, roused by the semi-darkness, and the absence of activity.

And the music.

The gentle, yet sinister tones, of Beethoven's work permeated the senses, the mournful piano bringing different visions to those who could hear.

Kowalski moved carefully towards his goal, the door ajar, permitting a ray of light to escape, illuminating his path to Knocke's office, as the famous sonata moved into its second phase.

He pushed the door open, noting the figure of Knocke stood with his back to the door, framed in the window, the moonlight picking out the edges of the silent figure.

His senses were screaming, but he had a job to do.

"Come in, Comrade Kowalski, come in."

Knocke turned smartly and indicated the chair laid out for the purpose, relaxing into his own seat, flicking a Colibri

568

lighter into life, and lighting a cigarette, his face starkly illuminated by the flames.

Kowalski's heart thumped in his chest as he looked at the visage.

An emotionless face.

A sinister face.

A dangerous face.

In that face, Kowalski saw his end, and he knew something had gone wrong.

None the less, he determined to play the game to its bitter end.

"Knocke, you failed to assist the Soviet forces in the Alsace. My information is that you actively participated in their destruction."

Knocke's face remained impassive as Kowalski waited for some reaction.

"You know what this could mean? Your wife and your children? Do they mean nothing to you?"

Maybe it was the music, or possibly the moonlight, or even Kowalski's imagination, but something in Knocke's face made him suddenly afraid.

"My wife? My children? They mean everything to me, or, in my wife's case, meant everything to me."

The agent was confused.

"You don't know, of that I am sure, otherwise you would not be here, risking your neck for your masters."

Knocke opened the drawer to his right and selected a photograph.

"Kowalski, or whatever your name is, my wife was killed by the NKVD on October the 5th."

Kowalski knew he was a dead man walking.

"This picture was taken last Sunday."

The Legion officer flicked the photograph across the desk, where it came to rest perfectly, the image loud and clear, taunting 'Leopard' with its message of defiance.

Stood in front of the Unterlinden Museum was a family group. In the middle was Knocke, resplendent in his mixed uniform, French insignia and German medals comfortably mounted on a mix of uniform. Either side of him were two girls, young women, with their father's looks, and their father's eyes.

'I have been played for an idiot!'

569

The sonata drew to a close, its soft tones now not in keeping with the desperation that Kowalski felt.

"So, Herr Knocke, what now?"

The music stopped, the sound of the needle scratching constantly on the final circuit now became as threatening and sinister as the sonata had been, although unintentionally.

The tension grew, the scratching all invasive.

It stopped abruptly as De Walle lifted the arm off the record.

Kowalski jumped as the Frenchman's voice broke the spell.

"What happens now is that you work for us, Sergey Andreyevich Kovelskin. And if you do what is demanded of you," De Walle paused for effect, "Well, then you will get to go home and see Valeria and your son, Igor, when the war is over."

Shocked he may be, but the fact that the Frenchman knew specifics made his senses light off further.

De Walle knew he had his man, and nodded to his left.

Emerging from the shadows came Anne-Marie de Valois.

She placed a picture in front of the GRU agent, one he had seen before, of people he knew, and loved.

To another listener, her soft tones would have been soothing, possibly arousing.

To Kovelskin, they were the bitter gloat of a Harpy, cutting straight to his heart.

"Valeria and your son say hello."

Back in his jeep, Kovelskin sat in the front seat, as his driver had been ordered to take some boxes of important documents back to the headquarters, filling the back of the vehicle. He settled into silent thought, his commitment to the Motherland struggling with his commitment to his family.

Indeed, for the first time, he had to separate the two into different entities, knowing that to act in favour of one was to damage the other.

Noticing the driver's concerned look, he tried to smile, but found the act tested his powers of resilience.

"Is there something wrong, Sir?"

"Not really, Corporal, thank you."

Under the continuing scrutiny, Kovelskin shrugged, indicating that feminine intuition was indeed correct.

"Sir, do we need to get back to headquarters quickly, or shall I take the long route?"

The Major pondered that for a moment.

"Don't you have a date with soldier boy Logan tonight, Corporal?"

Gisela Jourdan made her play.

"Captain Logan let me down, Sir. I had promised to make him a meal in my quarters."

Leaning across to add to the drama, Jourdan spoke softly, and in a voice guaranteed to arouse sexual interest in a corpse.

"I arranged for fresh meat and vegetables, and a bottle of Moselle too," her foot came off the accelerator for the slightest of moments as she leant further over, "And my roommate is away for the night."

The subtle scent of the woman, the softness and tone of her words, the closeness of her body, collectively launched an assault on Kovelskin's senses.

"Such a shame to waste it all, Major."

'I need the escape of a woman's body.'

"True enough, Corporal. If that is an invitation, it is one I accept. Thank you."

At eight o'clock precisely, Gisela Jourdan drained the last of the second bottle of Moselle, one that had arrived with the Major.

They had rutted like wild animals until about an hour ago, when the last of four orgasms had sent Kovelskin into a deep sleep.

She had experienced two herself, and was glad her orders had now taken her down this path.

Deciding on a cigarette, instead of toast, for breakfast, Jourdan pondered the recent events.

Everything seemed fine, except for her nagging concern over one small matter.

The man had been offered a choice between his country and his family, and within a few hours, had betrayed his family with very little enticement.

571

That was a concern she shared when next she reported to the telephone contact known as 'Captain Logan', and one that he subsequently shared by a number of people with the OSS.

Europe was in darkness, in some places silent, in others the business of dying continued, although on a smaller scale, as the armies mainly drew back from each other.

Security at the Dutch airfield of Maaldrift was airtight, as the first of the aircraft made its approach.

At the same time as the tones of the 'Moonlight Sonata' played centre stage to the entrapment and subversion of Major Kowalski, the arrival of the bombers took place. The music would have been an eminently suitable backing to the arrival of the new aircraft, the latest boost to the Allied arsenal in Europe.

Each one came in alone, each too precious to risk to the vagaries of night air co-operation missions.

Deliberately timed at ten minutes apart, it took nearly two hours for the dozen aircraft to arrive, a further hour for them to be secreted away around the newly refurbished airfield, hidden from prying eyes in secure, but disguised buildings, built for the purpose.

Sergeant Riley, late of the Grenadier Guards, but now serving in a special duty company, grizzled to his comrades.

"I'm fucking cold."

A Welsh Corporal, Jones, another guardsman on light duties following injuries, could only agree.

"It's brass monkeys, so it is, Sergeant, brass monkeys!"

Blowing on his hands, Riley watched enviously, as the last of the big planes disappeared into a hillock that wasn't a hillock, the disguised doors closing on what was obviously a warm interior.

"So what the fuck was the fuss about, eh? Just another load of brylcreams arriving to eat all the fucking bacon, eh?"

Jones spoke with conviction.

"It's special they are, Sergeant. All silver and huge."

Riley spat in disgust.

"They all think they're special, Taff, the fucking lot of 'em."

"Sergeant."

The Grenadier guard looked down at the boy, his helmet almost sinking him into the collar of his tunic.

Guardsman Joseph Newton was eighteen and a half, and had not yet experienced any of the horrors that war had to offer.

"Did I not say speak when you are spoken to, Young Joe?"

Riley wondered if he were going soft, but he had a special affection for the young lad, keen as mustard, always with his head in the manuals.

"Sergeant, they are special, honestly."

Both NCO's knew better than to argue.

"OK, son, what are they then? Fortresses? Liberators?"

Riley dried up, as he exhausted his knowledge of US four engine bombers.

"No Sergeant. They're B29's, and they can fly higher and further than anything else in the world."

And that night, the first snows of winter fell.

This is, perhaps, the end of the beginning.

List of figures

Bibliography

Rosignoli, Guido
The Allied Forces in Italy 1943-45
ISBN 0-7153-92123

Kleinfeld & Tambs, Gerald R & Lewis A
Hitler's Spanish Legion - The Blue Division in Russia
ISBN 0-9767380-8-2

Delaforce, Patrick
The Black Bull - From Normandy to the Baltic with the 11th Armoured Division
ISBN 0-75370-350-5

Taprell-Dorling, H
Ribbons and Medals
SBN 0-540-07120-X

Pettibone, Charles D
The Organisation and Order of Battle of Militaries in World War II
Volume V - Book B, Union of Soviet Socialist Republics
ISBN 978-1-4269-0281-9

Pettibone, Charles D
The Organisation and Order of Battle of Militaries in World War II
Volume V - Book A, Union of Soviet Socialist Republics
ISBN 978-1-4269-2551-0

Pettibone, Charles D
The Organisation and Order of Battle of Militaries in World War II
Volume VI - Italy and France, Including the Neutral Conutries of San Marino,
Vatican City [Holy See], Andorra and Monaco
ISBN 978-1-4269-4633-2

Pettibone, Charles D
The Organisation and Order of Battle of Militaries in World War II
Volume II - The British Commonwealth
ISBN 978-1-4120-8567-5

Chamberlain & Doyle, Peter & Hilary L
Encyclopedia of German Tanks in World War Two
ISBN 0-85368-202-X

Chamberlain & Ellis, Peter & Chris
British and American Tanks of World War Two
ISBN 0-85368-033-7

Dollinger, Hans
The Decline and fall of Nazi Germany and Imperial Japan
ISBN 0-517-013134

Zaloga & Grandsen, Steven J & James
Soviet Tanks and Combat Vehicles of World War Two
ISBN 0-85368-606-8

Hogg, Ian V
The Encyclopedia of Infantry Weapons of World War II
ISBN 0-85368-281-X

Hogg, Ian V
British & American Artillery of World War 2
ISBN 0-85368-242-9

Hogg, Ian V
German Artillery of World War Two
ISBN 0-88254-311-3

Bellis, Malcolm A
Divisions of the British Army 1939-45
ISBN 0-9512126-0-5

Bellis, Malcolm A
Brigades of the British Army 1939-45
ISBN 0-9512126-1-3

Rottman, Gordon L
FUBAR, Soldier Slang of World War II
ISBN 978-1-84908-137-5

Glossary

.30cal machine-gun	Standard US medium machine-gun.
.45 M1911 automatic	US automatic handgun
.50 cal	Standard US heavy machine-gun.
105mm Flak Gun	Next model up from the dreaded 88mm, these were sometimes pressed into a ground role in the final days.
105mm LeFH	German light howitzer, highly efficient design that was exported all over Europe.
128mm Pak 44	German late war heavy anti-tank gun, also mounted on the JagdTiger and Maus. Long-range performance would have made this a superb tank killer but it only appeared in limited numbers.
2" Mortar	British light mortar.
39th Kingdom	See Kingdom39
50mm Pak 38	German 50mm anti-tank gun introduced in 1941. Rapidly outclassed, it remained in service until the end of the war, life extended by upgrades in ammunition.
6-pounder AT gun	British 57mm anti-tank gun, outclassed at the end of WW2, except when issued with HV ammunition.
6x6 truck	Three axle, 6 wheel truck.
Achgelis	The Focke-Achgelis Fa223, also known as the Dragon. One of the first helicopters.
Achilles	British version of the M-10 that carried the high velocity 17-pdr gun.
Addendum F	Transfer of German captured equipment to Japanese to increase their firepower and reduce logistical strain on Soviets

577

Adin	In Russian, the number one.
Alkonost	Creature from Russian folklore with the body of a bird and the head of a beautiful woman.
Anschluss	The 1938 occupation and Annexation of Austria by Germany.
Anthrax Bombs	Factual Japanese weapons, believed used against the Chinese by Unit 731. Both the US and Britain carried their own tests on the same weapon.
Aquitania, RMS	Cunard liner that saw service in both WW1 and WW2. She was scrapped in 1950.
B-29	The American Superfortress, high-altitude heavy bomber.
BA64	Soviet 4x4 light armoured car with two crew and a machine-gun.
Balebetishen	Roughly means respectable or respectable person.
BAR	US automatic rifle that fired a .30cal round. It was an effective weapon, but was hampered by a 20 round magazine. Saw service in both World Wars, and many wars since.
Battle of the Bulge	Germany's Ardennes offensive of winter 1944
Bazooka	Generic name applied to a number of different anti-tank rocket launchers introduced into the US Army from 1942 onwards.
Beaufighter, Bristol	British twin-engine long-range heavy fighter, saw extensive service in roles from ground attack, night fighter, to anti-shipping strikes. Also served in the USAAF in its night fighter role.
BergePanther	German Panther tank converted or produced as an engineering recovery vehicle to service Panther Battalions in combat.

578

Bletchley Park	Location of the centre for Allied code breaking during World War two. Sometimes known as Station X.
Blighty	British slang term for Britain.
Blue and Grey Division	The nickname of the 29th US Infantry Division.
Boyes	.55-inch anti-tank rifle employed by the British Army but phased out in favour of the PIAT.
Brandenburghers	Rough German equivalent of commando, who were trained more in the arts of stealth and silent killing.
Bren Gun	British standard issue light machine-gun.
Browning Hi-Power	9mm handgun with a 13 round magazine, used by armies on both sides during WW2.
Brylcreams	Slang expression for RAF aircrew.
Buffalo	British term for the LVT or Amtrak, the amphibious tracked vehicle that became a mainstay of the Pacific War, and featured in all major Allied amphibious operations from Guadalcanal onwards.
Bund Deutsche Madel	The League of German Girls, young females' organisation of the Nazi Party.
Bundook	Derived from the Indian language, slang for a rifle.
C47	US development of the DC3, known in British operations as the Dakota. Twin-engine transport aircraft.
Camel	US cigarette brand
Canso	RCAF designation for the Catalina.
Caudillo	Political-military leader, in this case, referring to Franco.
Cavalry	The German army had cavalry until the end, all be it in small numbers. The SS had two such divisions, the 8th and 22nd.

579

Centurion I	British heavy tank, equipped with the 17pdr and a Polsten cannon.
Chekist	Soviet term used to describe a member of the State Security apparatus, often not intended to be complimentary.
Chesterfield	American cigarette brand.
Chickamauga	A battle in the American Civil War, fought on 19th to 20th September 1863. It was a Union defeat of some note, and second only to Gettysburg in combined casualties.
Colibri	High-class men's accessories producer, initially specialising in cigarette lighters.
Colloque Biarritz	The fourth symposium based at the Château du Haut-Kœnigsbourg.
Combat Command [CC]	Formation similar to an RCT, which was formed from all-arms elements within a US Armored Division, the normal dispositions being CC'A', CC'B' and CC'R', the 'R' standing for reserve.
Comet	British medium tank armed with a 77mm high-velocity gun.
Corvette	Small patrol and escort vessel used by Allied navies throughout WW2.
Court of Bernadotte	The Court of the Swedish Royal Family.
Deuxieme Bureau	France's External Military Intelligence Agency that underwent a number of changes post 1940 but still retained its 'Deux' label for many professionals.
Douglas DC-3	Twin-engine US transport aircraft, also labelled C-47. [Built by the Russians under licence as the Li-2]
DP-28	Standard Soviet Degtyaryov light machine-gun with large top mounted disc magazine containing 47 rounds.

Duke of York	British battleship of the King George V class. Survived WW2 and was scrapped in 1957.
Dva	In Russian, the number two.
EBW	Explosive bridge-wire detonators.
Edelzwicker	Alsatian wine that is a blend of noble and standard grapes, and as a result is sometimes hit and miss, sometimes superb.
Elektroboote	A Type XXI U-Boat
ESM	Explosive Lens Maths. The complex array of calculations that come together to design the shaped charges in a nuclear device.
Falke	Infrared sighting system, installed on some German vehicles, especially useful for night fighting.
Fallschirmjager	German Paratroopers. They were the elite of the Luftwaffe, but few Paratroopers at the end of the war had ever seen a parachute. None the less, the ground divisions fought with a great deal of élan and gained an excellent combat reputation.
Fat Man	Implosion-type Plutonium Bomb similar in operation to 'The Gadget'.
FBI	Federal Bureau of Intelligence, which was also responsible for external security prior to the formation of the CIA.
FFI	Forces Francaises de L'Interieur, or the French Forces of the Interior was the name applied to resistance fighters during the latter stages of WW2. Once France had been liberated, the pragmatic De Gaulle tapped this pool of manpower and created 'organised' divisions from these, often at best, para-military groups. Few proved to be of any quality and they tended to be used in

low-risk areas.

FG42	Fallschirmgewehr 42, a hybrid 7.62mm weapon which was intended to be both assault rifle and LMG.
Firefly, Fairey	British single-engine carrier aircraft, used as both fighter and anti-submarine roles.
Firefly, Sherman V	British variant of the American M4 armed with a 17-pdr main gun, which offered the Sherman excellent prospects for a kill of any Panzer on the battlefield.
Fizzle	Failure of a nuclear device to properly explode, but which can result in radioactive product being distributed over a sizeable local area.
Flak	Flieger Abwehr Kanone, anti-aircraft guns.
Fuhrer-Begleit-Brigaden	German army armoured formation, formed from the Wehrmacht's Fuhrer Escort. Considered an elite formation, it was part of the Grossdeutschland detachments.
Gamayun	Creature from Russian folklore with the body of a large bird and the head of a beautiful woman.
GAVCA	Grupo de Aviação de Caça [Portuguese] Translated literally means 'fighter group', the 1st GAVCA serving within the Brazilian Expeditionary Force.
GAZ	Gorkovsky Avtomobilny Zavod, Soviet producers of vehicles from light car through to heavy trucks.
Gebirgsjager	German & Austrian Mountain troops.
Gestapo	GeheimeStaatsPolizei, the Secret Police of Nazi Germany.
Gitanes Mais	French cigarette brand

582

GKO	Gosudarstvennyj Komitet Oborony or State Security Committee, the group that held complete power of all matters within the Soviet Union.
Grease gun	US issue submachine-gun, designated the M3. Cheaper and more accurate than the Thompson.
Green Devils	Nickname for the German Airborne troops, the Fallschirmjager.
Greenhorn	An inexperienced soldier
Großdeutschland	German Army unit, considered to be its Elite formation. Sometimes mistaken for SS as they wore armband, although on right arm, not the left, as SS formations did.
GRU	Glavnoye Razvedyvatel'noye Upravleniye of Soviet Military Intelligence, fiercely independent of the other Soviet Intelligence agencies such as the NKVD.
Haft-Hohlladung magnetic mine	Often known as the Panzerknacker, this was a hollow charge magnetic AT mine.
Halifax, Handley Page	British four-engine heavy bomber
Hapsburg	European monarchy that ruled Austro-Hungary amongst other European states.
Harai Ritual	Harai or Harae are rituals for purifying and removing factors such as sin, uncleanliness, and bad luck from objects, places, and people.
Hauptmann	Equivalent of captain in the German army.
Hellcat Tank Destroyer, M18.	US tank destroyer armed with a 76mm gun. Capable of high speed.
Hero of the Soviet Union award	The Gold Star award was highly thought of and awarded to Soviet soldiers for bravery, although the medal was often devalued by being given for political or nepotistic reasons.

583

Hitler Youth [Hitler Jugend]	Young males' organisation of the Nazi Party.
Hohenzollern	Noble house of Germany, Prussia, and Romania.
Horsch 108	German transport that served throughout WW2 in a variety of roles from officer's car to ambulance.
HVAP	High-velocity armour piercing.
IL-4, Ilyushin.	Soviet twin-engine medium bomber.
Infected Fleas	Factual Japanese weapon. A load of infected fleas were dropped on Quzhou in 1940, resulting n the deaths of over 2000 people.
IR	Infrared, a technology that the Germans pursued late in the war.
IS-II	Soviet heavy tank with a 122mm gun and 1-3 mg's
IS-III	Iosef Stalin III heavy tank, which arrived just before the German capitulation and was a hugely innovative design. 122mm gun and 1-2 mg
JagdPanther	SP version of the Panther tank, armed with the 88mm gun.
JagdPanzer IV	SP version of the Panzer IV, armed with the 75mm gun.
Jeep	½ Ton 4x4 all terrain vehicle, supplied in large numbers to the Western Allies and the Soviet Union.
Job tvoyu mat	With apologies, this is translated in a number of ways, and can mean anything of the same ilk from 'Gosh' through to 'Fuck your mother."
Kalibr	Codename of David Greengrass, US Army Sergeant who was a Soviet Spy.
Kangaroo	Allied infantry carrier, either converted from a tank, mainly M4 Shermans and M7 Priest SP's, or

purpose built from the Canadian RAM tank.

Kar98K	German standard issue bolt action rifle.
Katana	The main sword of a samurai or Japanese officer.
Katorga	Soviet penal system, also accepted as a noun for a place of hard servitude.
Katyn	1940 Massacre of roughly 22,000 Polish Army officers, Police officers and intelligentsia perpetrated by the NKVD, Site was discovered by the German Army and much propaganda value was made, although in reality there was no sanction against the USSR for this coldblooded murder.
Katyusha	Soviet rocket artillery weapon capable of bringing down area fire with either 16, 32 or 64 rockets of different types.
Kavellerie	German translation of Cavalry.
K-Class Blimp	US Airship [dirigible] used in reconnaissance and anti-submarine roles
Kerch	Soviet peninsular that juts out into the Black Sea, known in English as the Crimea.
Ki-84	Japanese single-engine fighter aircraft, considered the finest fighter in the Japanese inventory.
King Tiger tank	German heavy tank carrying a high-velocity 88m gun and 2-3 machine guns.
Kingdom 39	The Fairytale Kingdom in Russian Folklore.
Kradschutzen	Motorcycle infantry, term also applied to reconnaissance troops.
Kreigie	US slang for a German prisoner of war.

Kreigsmarine	German Navy
Kriegsspiels	Wargames
Kukri	The curved battle knife of the Gurkha soldier.
LA-7	Single-engine Lavochkin fighter aircraft, highly thought of despite poor maintenance history.
Lavochkin-5	Soviet single-engine fighter aircraft.
Leutnant	German Army rank equivalent to 2nd Lieutenant.
Liebfraumilch [Liebfrauenmilch]	German semi-sweet white wine.
Lightning, Lockheed, P38	US twin-engine fighter, most successfully used in the Pacific Theatre.
Lisunov Li-2	Soviet licenced copy of the DC-3 twin-engine transport aircraft,
Little Boy	Uranium based fission bomb.
Luftwaffe	German Air Force
Lysander, Westland.	British single engine monoplane designed for Liaison activities, but best known for its use in ferrying agents into Occupied Europe.
M-10	Known as the Wolverine, this US tank destroyer carried a 3" gun with modest performance. It was subsequently upgunned in British service, and the more potent 17-pdr equipped vehicles became known as Achilles.
M13/40	Italian light tank with a 47mm gun and 3-4 machine-guns.
M-16 half-track	US half-track mounting 4 x .50cal machine-guns in a Maxon mount. For defence against aircraft at low level it was particularly effective against infantry.
M1Carbine	Semi-automatic carbine that fired a .30 cal round, notorious as being underpowered.

M20	US 6x6 Armoured utility car, which was basically an M8 without the turret.
M21	M3 halftrack with an 81mm mortar mount, providing mobile fire support.
M24 Chafee	US light tank fitted with a 75mm gun and 2-3 machine-guns.
M26 Pershing	US Heavy tank with a 90mm gun and 2-3 machine-guns. Underpowered initially, it had little chance to prove itself against the German arsenal.
M3 Halftrack	US standard half-track normally armed with 1 x .50cal machine-gun and capable of carrying up to 13 troops
M3A1 sub-machine gun	Often known as the Grease Gun, issued in .45 or the rarer 9mm calibres with a 30 round magazine.
M4A4	US medium tank, last of a number of developments, Armament ranged from 75mm through 76mm to 105mm Howitzer.
M5 HST	US fully tracked high-speed artillery prime mover.
M5 Stuart	US light tank equipped with a 37mm gun, and capable of high speed.
M8 Greyhound	6x6 Armoured car with 37mm main gun and 1-2 machine-guns.
Maior	German Army rank equivalent to Major.
Manhattan Project	Research and development project aimed at producing the first atomic bomb.
Market-Garden	Montgomery's failed plan to drop paratroopers and secure river crossings into Northern Germany, thus ending the war by Christmas.
Maskirova	Soviets have a fondness for deception and misdirection and

	Maskirova is an essential of any undertaking.
Matrose	German naval term for a common sailor.
Mauthausen	More properly known as Mauthausen-Gusen Concentration Camp, the camp grew to oversee a complex of Labour camps throughout the area. The high estimate of persons dying within the Mauthausen camp system is 320,000.
Maxon mount	A single machine gun mounting which could be installed on a half-track [such as the deadly M16 halftrack], or a trailer, by which means 4 x .50cal were aimed and fired by one man.
Maybach	German vehicle and parts manufacturer who produced the huge Maybach engines inserted in the Tiger I tank.
Merville Battery	German gun battery assaulted by the British 9th Para Battalion on D-Day.
Meteor F3, Gloster	British twin-engine jet fighter, which first flew in 1943.
Metgethen	Scene of a successful German counter-attack in 1945, where evidence of Soviet atrocities against the civilian population was uncovered.
MG.08	German WW1 machine gun. Many survivors were employed during WW2.
MG34	German standard MG often referred to as a Spandau.
MG42	Superb German machine gun, capable of 1200rpm, designed to defeat the Soviet human wave attacks. Still in use to this day.
Mills Bomb	British fragmentation hand grenade.

588

Minox	Gained notoriety as the first 'miniature' spy camera.
Mitsubishi Ki-46	Japanese twin-engine reconnaissance aircraft.
Mlad	Codename of Theodore Hall, Nuclear Physicist, and Soviet Agent.
Molotov Cocktail	Simple anti-tank/vehicle weapon, consisting of a bottle, a filling of petrol, and a flaming rag. Thrown at its target the bottle shattered on impact and the rag did the rest.
Moscow Crystal Vodka	Highest quality triple distilled vodka.
Moselle	Mainly white wine originating from areas around the River of the same name.
Mosin-Nagant	Russian infantry rifle.
Mosquito	DH98 De Havilland Mosquito was a multi-purpose wooden aircraft, much envied by the Luftwaffe.
Mosquito Mk NF30, De Havilland	British twin-engine night fighter.
Mosquito Mk VI, De Havilland	British twin-engine fighter-bomber.
Mosquito Mk XXV, De Havilland	British twin-engine light bomber.
MP18	A WW1 design sub-machine gun, often known as the Bergmann.
MP-40	German standard issue submachine-gun.
Mugalev	Soviet heavy mine roller gear, normally attached to T34 tanks.
Mustang	P51 Mustang, US single seat long-range fighter armed with 6 x .50cal machine-guns.
Nagant pistol	Standard Soviet revolver, very rugged and powerful using long case 7.62mm ammunition.
Natzwiller-Struhof	Concentration camp in Alsace.

Nebelwerfer	German six-barrelled mortar weapon, literally translated as 'Smoke Thrower' and known to the Allies as the Moaning Minnie, ranging up to 32cms in diameter.
NKGB	Narodny Komissariat Gosudarstvennoi Bezopasnosti, the Soviet Secret Police, separated from the NKVD in 1942 and absorbed once more in 1946.
NKVD	Narodny Komissariat Vnutrennikh Del, the People's Commissariat for Internal Affairs.
Normandie Squadron [Normandie-Niemen Regiment]	French Air force group that grew to three squadrons and served on the Russian Front throughout WW2.
OFLAG XVIIa	Offizierslager or OfLag No 17A, prisoner of war camp run by the Germans for officer detainees.
Operation Anvil	August 1944 landing in Southern France.
Operation Apple Pie	US project to capture German officers with specific knowledge about the Soviet Union's industry and economy.
Operation Berkut	Soviet land operation designed to push through the Alsatian plain and break into France via Colmar.
Operation Kurgan	Soviet joint-operation to employ paratroopers, Naval Marines, NKVD agents and collaborators to attack and neutralise airfields, radar, communications and logistic bases throughout Europe. Subsequently enlarged to include assassinations of Allied senior officers.
Operation Paperclip	OSS project to recruit German Scientist to the Allied cause post May 1945.
Operation Sumerechny	Soviet plan to remove German leadership elements from their

	prisoners. All officer ranks from captain upwards were to be executed.
Operation Unthinkable	Study ordered by Churchill to examine the feasibility of an Allied assault on Soviet held Northern Germany.
Operation Varsity	The largest single airborne operation of WW2, undertaken in March 1945, Varsity involved dropping over 16,000 paratroopers to the east of the Rhine.
OSS	US Intelligence agency formed during 2, The Office of Strategic Services was the predecessor of the CIA, and was set up to coordinate espionage activities in occupied areas.
P.O.L.	Petrol, oil, and lubricants.
Panther	German medium tank, considered by many, to be the finest tank design of WW2. Armed with a high-velocity 75mm, it could stand its ground against anything in the Allied arsenal.
Panther Tank	German heavy-medium tank carrying a high-powered 75mm gun and 2-3 machine-guns, considered by many to be the finest all-round tank of World War 2.
Panzer IV	German tank, which served throughout the war in many guises, mainly with a 75mm gun.
Panzer V	See Panther Tank
Panzer VI	See Tiger Tank
Panzerfaust	German single use anti-tank weapon. Highly effective but short ranged.
Panzerjager	Antitank troop[s] [German]
Panzerkanonier	Tank gunner
Panzertruppen	The German tank crews.

PanzerVIb	See King Tiger Tank
PE-2	The Soviet Petlyakov PE-2 was a twin-engine multi-purpose aircraft considered by the Luftwaffe to be a fine opponent.
PEM scope	Soviet sniper scope for Mosin and SVT rifles.
PIAT	Acronym for Projector, Infantry, Anti-tank, the PIAT used a large spring to hurl its hollow charge shell at an enemy.
Plan Chelyabinsk	Soviet assault plan utilising lend-lease equipment in Western Allies markings.
Plan Diaspora	Soviet overall plan for assaulting in the East and for supporting the new Japanese Allies.
Plan Kurgan	Soviet joint-operation to employ paratroopers, Naval Marines, NKVD agents and collaborators to attack and neutralise airfields, radar, communications and logistic bases throughout Europe. Subsequently enlarged to include assassinations of Allied senior officers.
Plan Zilant	The Soviet paratrooper operations against the four symposiums, detailed as Zilant-1 through Zilant-4.
PLUTO	Acronym for 'Pipeline-under-the-ocean', which was a fuel supply pipe that ran from Britain to France, laid for D-Day operations and still in use at the end of the war.
Pointe-du-Hoc	Cliff face and bunker position near Omaha beach, Normandy, assaulted by US 2nd Ranger Battalion on D-Day.
PPD	Soviet submachine gun capable of phenomenal rate of fire. Mostly equipped with a 72 round drum magazine but 65 rounds were

	normally fitted to avoid jamming. It was too complicated and was replaced by the PPSH.
PPS	Simple Soviet submachine gun with a 35 round magazine.
PPSH	Soviet submachine gun capable of phenomenal rate of fire. Mostly equipped with a 72 round drum magazine but 65 rounds were normally fitted to avoid jamming.
Pravda	Leading newspaper of the Soviet Union, Pravda is translated as 'Truth'.
PS84	Passenger Aircraft built at factory 84, the initial designation of the Li-2 transport aircraft.
PT-34	Soviet T34/76 with mine clearing Mugalev attachment.
PTAB	Each Shturmovik could carry four pods containing 48 bomblets, or up to 280 internally. Each bomblet could penetrate up to 70mm of armour, enough for the main battle tanks at the time.
PU scope	Soviet sniper scope for Mosin and SVT rifles.
Puma	German eight-wheel armoured car with a 50mm and enclosed turret.
Pyat	In Russian, the number five.
Ranger, USS	US Aircraft carrier [CV-4], Survived WW2 and was scrapped in 1947.
RCT	Regimental Combat Team. US formation that normally consisted of elements drawn from all combatant units within the parent division, making it a smaller but reasonably self-sufficient unit. RCT's tended to be numbered according the Infantry regiment that supplied its fighting core. [See CC for US Armored force equivalent.]

Red Devils	Nickname for the British Airborne troops, the Red berets.
Red Star	Standard issue Soviet military cigarettes.
Rodina	The Soviet Motherland.
Schmuck	A Jewish insult meaning a fool of one who is stupid. It also can literally mean the foreskin that is removed during circumcision.
Schwere Panzer Abteilung	Heavy tank battalion [German]
SDKFZ 234	German eight-wheel armoured car equipped with a range of weapons, the most powerful of which was a 75mm HV weapon. Of the four variants, the Puma with its 50mm and enclosed turret is probably the most well known.
Seagulls	Affectionate nickname for the Fleet Air Arm of the Royal Navy.
Senninbari	Japanese good luck charm given to soldiers, rooted within the Shinto religion. Each one carried 1000 stitches, each from a different woman. Typically, they were waist belts but could also be headbands, vests, and flags.
Shaska	A Cossack's curved sword.
Sherman [M4 Sherman]	American tank turned out in huge numbers with many variants, also supplied under lend-lease to Russia.
Shinhoto Chi-Ha	Upgraded Japanese battle tank, based on the Chi-Ha. The Shinhoto had a 47mm gun superior to the 57mm in its forebear.
Shinto	Japanese religion [Shintoism].
Shtrafbat	Soviet penal battalion.
Shturmovik	The Ilyushin-2 Shturmovik, Soviet mass-produced ground attack aircraft that was highly successful.

ShVAK	Soviet 20mm auto cannon that equipped aircraft, armoured cars, and light tanks.
Skat	German card game using 32 cards.
SMLE	Often referred to s the 'Smelly', this was the proper name of the Short, Magazine, Lee-Enfield rifle.
SOE	British organisation, Special Operations Executive, which conducted espionage and sabotage missions throughout Europe.
Spitfire, Supermarine.	British single-engine fighter aircraft.
SS-Hauptsturmfuhrer	SS equivalent of captain.
St Florian	Patron saint of Upper Austria, Linz, chimney sweeps, and firefighters.
ST44 [MP43/44]	German assault rifle with a 30 round magazine, first of its generation and forerunner to the AK47.
Standard HDM .22 calibre pistol	Originally used by OSS, this effective .22 with a ten round magazine is still in use by Special Forces throughout the world.
Starshina	Soviet rank roughly equivalent to Warrant Officer first Class.
Station 'X'	See Bletchley Park entry.
STAVKA	At this time this represents the 'Stavka of the Supreme Main Command', comprising high-ranked military and civilian members. Subordinate to the GKO, it was responsible for military oversight, and as such, held its own military reserves that it released in support of operations.
Sten	Basic British sub-machine gun with a 32 round magazine. Produced in huge numbers throughout the 40's.
Stroh rum	Austrian spiced rum.
Studebaker	US heavy lorry supplied to the Soviets under lend-lease, or built in the USSR under licence, often used

595

Stuka [Junkers 87]	as the platform for the Katyusha. Famous dive-bomber employed by the Luftwaffe.
SU-76	76mm self-propelled gun used as artillery and for close support.
Sunderland	British four-engine flying boat, used mainly in maritime reconnaissance and anti-submarine roles.
SVT40	Soviet automatic rifle with a 10 round magazine.
Symposium Biarritz	Utilisation of German expertise to prepare wargame exercises for allied unit commanders to demonstrate Soviet tactics and methods to defeat them.
T.O.E.	Table of Organisation and Equipment, which represents what a unit should consist of.
T/34	Soviet medium tank armed with a 76.2mm gun and 2 mg's.
T/34-85 [T34m44]	Soviet medium tank armed with an 85mm gun and 2 mg's.
T-44 [100]	Soviet medium tank, produced at the end of WW2, which went on to become the basis for the famous T54/55. Armed mainly with the same 85mm as in the T3485, a few were fitted with the devastating 100mm D-10 gun.
T-70	Soviet light tank with two crew and a 45mm gun.
Tallboy	British designed earthquake bomb, containing 12,000lbs of high explosive. It weighed five tons and proved effective against the most hardened of targets.
Thompson	.45 calibre US submachine-gun, normally issued with a 20 or 30 round magazine [although a drum was available.]

596

Tiger I	German heavy battle tank armed with the first 88mm gun, capable of ruling any battlefield when it was introduced in 1942.
Tokarev	Soviet 7.62mm automatic handgun [also known as TT30] with an 8 round magazine.
Trimbach	Quality Alsatian wine.
Trunnion	Heavy metal mounts either side of a gun barrel.
TU-2, Tupolev	Soviet twin-engine medium bomber. Extremely successful design that performed well in a variety of roles, the TU-2 is considered one of the best combat aircraft of WW2.
Type 97 Chi-Ha	Japanese main battle tank, armed with a 57mm gun.
Type XXI submarine	The most technologically advanced submarine of the era, produced in small numbers by the Germans and unable to affect the outcome of the war.
Typhoon, Hawker.	RAF's most successful single seater ground attack aircraft of World War Two, which could carry anything from bombs through to rockets.
U-Boat Type XX	30 such U-Boats were planned, but none produced during WW2. They were intended as pure supply boats, shorter than the Type XB but with a wider beam.
U-Boat Type XXI	Advanced U-Boat design capable of extended underwater cruising at high speed.
UHU	German 251 halftrack mounting an infrared searchlight, designed for close use with infrared equipped Panther units.
Unicorn, HMS	British light aircraft carrier and aircraft repair ship, seeing service throughout WW2. Scrapped in 1959.

597

USAAF	United States Army Air Force.
Ushanka	Fur hat with adjustable sides.
Vampir	German term for the ST44 equipped with an infrared sight, also used to refer to the operators of such weapons.
Venona Project	Joint US-UK operation to analyse Soviet message traffic
Vichy	Name of the collaborationist government of defeated France.
Vickers Machine-Gun	British designed machine-gun of WW1 vintage. Extremely reliable .303 calibre weapon, standard issue as a heavy machine-gun.
Vitruvian man	Da Vinci's sketch of a man with legs and arms splayed.
Wacht am Rhein	Literally, 'Watch on the Rhine', a codename used to mask the real purpose of the German build-up that became the Ardennes Offensive in December 1944.
Walther P38	German 9mm semi-automatic pistol with an eight round magazine.
Wanderer W23 Cabriolet	German vehicle designed for civilian use, sometimes pressed into military service, particularly as a staff car.
Wehrmacht	The German Army
Yakolev-9	Soviet single-seater fighter aircraft that was highly respected by the Luftwaffe.
Yakolev-9U	Soviet single-engine fighter aircraft, probably the best Soviet high-altitude fighter.
Zilant	Legendary creature in Russian folklore somewhat like a dragon
Zimmerit	Anti-magnetic paste applied to the side of German vehicles.
ZIS3	76.2mm anti-tank gun in Soviet use.
ZSU-37	Soviet light self-propelled anti-aircraft vehicle, mounting a 37mm gun.

Zuikaku

Japanese fleet aircraft carrier of the Shokaku class. Present at Pearl Harbor, she succumbed to air attack during the Battle of Leyte Gulf, sinking on 25th October 1944.

Zhukov's Army from a Hundred Lands

As Europe moved from September into October, a growing number of nations started to contribute more than good wishes to the Allied cause, prompting Zhukov to speak of the Allied forces as 'The Army from a Hundred Lands'.

Whilst the number was an exaggeration, the following will give the reader some information on the nations who slowly united against the spread of communism.

Fig #70 - The Allied Nations.

	Active Ground Forces	Active Air Forces	Active Naval Forces	Passive Ground Forces	Passive Air Forces	Passive Naval Forces
ARGENTINA	EUROPE	EUROPE				
AUSTRALIA	PACIFIC	EUROPE-PACIFIC	PACIFIC			
BELGIUM	EUROPE	EUROPE				
BOLIVIA				HOME SERVICE	HOME SERVICE	HOME SERVICE
BRAZIL	EUROPE	EUROPE				
CANADA	EUROPE-PACIFIC	EUROPE-PACIFIC	EUROPE-PACIFIC			
CHILE				HOME SERVICE	HOME SERVICE	HOME SERVICE
CHINA	PACIFIC	PACIFIC	PACIFIC			
COLUMBIA				HOME SERVICE	HOME SERVICE	HOME SERVICE
COSTA RICA	SERVICE UNITS			HOME SERVICE	HOME SERVICE	HOME SERVICE
CUBA	EUROPE				HOME SERVICE	HOME SERVICE
DENMARK	EUROPE				HOME SERVICE	HOME SERVICE
DOMINICAN REPUBLIC				HOME SERVICE	HOME SERVICE	HOME SERVICE
ECUADOR				HOME SERVICE	HOME SERVICE	HOME SERVICE
EGYPT				HOME SERVICE	HOME SERVICE	HOME SERVICE
EL SALVADOR				HOME SERVICE	HOME SERVICE	HOME SERVICE
ETHIOPIA	EUROPE				HOME SERVICE	HOME SERVICE
FRANCE	EUROPE	EUROPE	EUROPE			
GERMANY	EUROPE	EUROPE	EUROPE			
GREECE	EUROPE	EUROPE	EUROPE			
GUATEMALA	SERVICE UNITS			HOME SERVICE	HOME SERVICE	HOME SERVICE
HAITI				HOME SERVICE	HOME SERVICE	HOME SERVICE
HOLLAND	EUROPE	EUROPE	EUROPE			
HONDURAS						HOME SERVICE
INDIA	EUROPE-PACIFIC	PACIFIC	PACIFIC			
IRAN				HOME SERVICE	HOME SERVICE	HOME SERVICE
IRAQ				HOME SERVICE	HOME SERVICE	HOME SERVICE
LEBANON						HOME SERVICE
LIBERIA				HOME SERVICE	HOME SERVICE	HOME SERVICE
MEXICO	EUROPE	EUROPE				HOME SERVICE
NEW ZEALAND	EUROPE-PACIFIC	EUROPE-PACIFIC	PACIFIC			
NEWFOUNDLAND				HOME SERVICE		
NICARAGUA	SERVICE UNITS			HOME SERVICE	HOME SERVICE	HOME SERVICE
NORWAY	EUROPE	EUROPE	EUROPE			
PANAMA				HOME SERVICE	HOME SERVICE	HOME SERVICE
PARAGUAY	EUROPE				HOME SERVICE	HOME SERVICE
PERU				HOME SERVICE	HOME SERVICE	HOME SERVICE
POLAND	EUROPE	EUROPE	EUROPE			
PORTUGAL	EUROPE				HOME SERVICE	HOME SERVICE
SAUDI ARABIA				HOME SERVICE	HOME SERVICE	HOME SERVICE
SOUTH AFRICA	EUROPE	EUROPE-PACIFIC				HOME SERVICE
SPAIN	EUROPE				HOME SERVICE	HOME SERVICE
SYRIA				HOME SERVICE	HOME SERVICE	HOME SERVICE
UK	EUROPE-PACIFIC	EUROPE-PACIFIC	EUROPE-PACIFIC			
URUGUAY	EUROPE				HOME SERVICE	HOME SERVICE
USA	EUROPE-PACIFIC	EUROPE-PACIFIC	EUROPE-PACIFIC			
VENEZUELA				HOME SERVICE	HOME SERVICE	HOME SERVICE

NB - LIST DOES NOT INCLUDE ITALY.

Active forces = men & equipment supplied that forms fighting units, within the theatre indicated.

Service Units = manpower supplied, conditional non-combat use.

Home service = Also, using troops to relieve US forces in situ.

About the Author.

Colin Gee was born on 18th May 1957 in Haslar Naval Hospital, Gosport, UK, but spent the first two years of his life at the naval base in Malta.

His parents divorced when he was approaching three years of age, and he went to live with his grandparents in Berkshire, who brought him up.

On 9th June 1975, he joined the Fire Service and, after a colourful career, retired on 19th May 2007, having achieved the rank of Sub-Officer, Watch Commander, or to be politically correct for the ego-tripping harridans in HR, Watch Manager 'A'.

After thirty-two years in the Fire Service, reality suddenly hit, and Colin found himself in need of a proper job!

As of today, Colin is permanently employed doing night shifts for NHS Out of Hours service.

At this moment in time Colin has a wife, two daughters, one step-daughter, two step-sons and two grandsons, called Lucas and Mason, who are avid Manchester United fans, although neither know it yet.

Four cats complete the home ensemble.

He has been a wargamer for most of his life, hence the future plans for a Red Gambit wargaming series.

In 1992, Colin joined the magistracy, having wandered in from the street to ask how someone becomes a beak. He served until 2005. The experience taught him the true difference between justice and the law, the former being what he would have preferred to administer.

In his time, Colin has dabbled with keyboard, piano, and drums, but actually managed to get a reasonable note out of a trombone.

He always promised himself that he would write something but, apart from a short story or two, it never happened.

Until now.

Red Gambit was first researched over ten years ago, but work and life changes prevented it from blossoming.

Now it has become a projected six books, instead of one. As more research was done, and more lines of writing opened themselves up, the need for a series became inevitable.

Though the books are fiction, fact is a constant companion, particularly within the biographies, where real-life events are often built into the lives of fictitious characters.

Colin writes for the pleasure it brings him and, hopefully, the reader. The books are not intended to be modern day 'Wuthering Heights' or 'War and Peace'. They contain a story that Colin thinks is worth the telling, and to which task he has set his inexperienced hand. The biographies are part of the whole experience that he hopes to bring the reader.

Enjoy them all, and thank you for reading.

The Red Gambit Series
Opening Moves
Breakthrough
Stalemate
Impasse
End Game
Check Mate

Extras available on the website www.redgambitseries.com and also on www.facebook.com - group name 'Red Gambit'. [https://www.facebook.com/#!/groups/167182160020751/]

Please register and join the group or the forums. If on the website, remember only to visit the areas relevant to your book or you may pick up spoilers.

'Impasse' - the story continues.

Read the first chapter of 'Impasse' now.

In the absence of orders, go find something and kill it.

FeldMarschall Erwin Rommel.

Chapter 103 - THE SUNDERLAND

<u>1505hrs, Monday, 5th November 1945, the Western Approaches, approximately 45 miles north-west of St Kilda Island, The Atlantic.</u>

The Sunderland Mk V was a big aircraft, the four American Wasp engines giving her the power previously lacking in the Mk III.

Not for nothing was she called the Flying Porcupine, her hull bristling with defensive machine-guns, fourteen in total, manned by her eleven man crew. Such armament was required for a lumbering leviathan like the Short Sunderland, whose maximum speed, even with the Wasps, was a little over two hundred miles an hour.

In the German War, encounters with enemy fighters had been mercifully rare and, in the main, enemy contacts were solely with the Sunderland's standard fare; submarines.

This Mk V also carried depth charges and radar pods, making her a deadly adversary in the never-ending game of hide and seek between aircraft and submersibles.

Sunderland NS-X was out on a mission, having flown off from the Castle Archdale base of the RAF's 201 Squadron. The men had once been in 246 Squadron but, when that squadron ws disbanded, the men of NS-X, all SAAF volunteers, had been one of two complete crews to be transferred to 201 Squadron.

During World War Two, there had been a secret protocol between the British and Eire governments, which permitted flights over Irish territory though a narrow corridor. It ran westwards from Castle Archdale, Northern Ireland, across Irish sovereign territory, extending the operating range of Coastal

603

Command considerably, and bringing more area under the protection of their Liberators, Catalinas and Sunderlands.

The agreement was still in force.

NS-X had followed this route out into the Atlantic, turning north and rounding Malin Point, before heading into its search area around St Kilda.

A Soviet submarine had been attacked and damaged the previous day, somewhere roughly fifty miles west of Lewis, and the Admiralty were rightly jittery, given the importance of the convoy heading into the area in the next ten hours.

There was little good news.

The RCN corvette which had found and attacked the submarine was no longer answering, and was feared lost with all hands. Other flying boats and craft were assigned to the dual mission, all hoping to either rescue, or recover, depending on how fate had dealt with the Canadian sailors, as well as attack and sink the enemy vessel.

Flight Lieutenant Cox, an extremely experienced pilot, hummed loudly, as was his normal habit when concentrating.

Having just had a course check, and finding themselves a small distance off their search pattern, he eased the huge aircraft a few points to starboard, before settling back down to the extended boredom of searching for a needle in a choice of haystacks.

The Sunderland carried many comforts, including bunks, a toilet, and a galley, the latter of which yielded up fresh steaming coffee and a bacon sandwich, brought up from below by Flight Sergeant Crozier.

"There you go, Skipper, get your laughing gear around that, man. I'll take over for a moment."

South African Crozier wasn't qualified to pilot the aircraft, but that didn't trouble the old hands of NS-X. He flopped into the second seat and took a grip, permitting Cox to relinquish the column to the gunner.

"Skipper, I think Dusty is an ill man. He's wracked up on a bunk, looking very green."

Dusty Miller was the second pilot, and he had disappeared off to sort out a stomach cramp, about an hour beforehand.

"Too much flippin Jameson's last night, that's what that is, Arsey", the words came out despite having to work their way around large lumps of bread and bacon.

Rafer Crozier didn't much care for being called Arsey, but it didn't pay to point that out, for obvious reasons.

"Don't think so, Skip. Dusty was the only one to have the goose, wasn't he?"

The local procurer of all things, Niall Flaherty, had slipped such a beast to the camp cooks for a small consideration. In contravention of standing orders on air crews meals, Miller had wangled a portion of the well hung goose, prior to flight ops.

"Maybe you have a point, Arsey. Best we keep quiet then, eh?"

Another voice resonated through the intercom.

"Contact Skipper. Starboard 30. One thousand yards. Wreckage."

Flight Sergeant Peter Viljoen's crisp and concise report interrupted the great Goose discussion, as Cox wiped his hands clean on his life preserver, and took back command of the aircraft, releasing Crozier to crane his neck in the direction of the sighting.

"Contact confirmed Skipper, Starboard 35, One thousand yards. Wreckage, and lots of it too."

Cox spoke to the crew.

"Pilot to crew. OK fellahs, close up now, and keep your eyes peeled. Turning for a low level run over the site now. Sparks, get off a report to base right now. Magic, pass Sparks the position please."

Both radio operator and navigator keyed their mikes with an acknowledgement, as the port wing dipped to bring the lumbering seaplane around for a west-east run across the wreckage.

Whilst some of the crew used binoculars to probe the floating evidence of recent combat, others remained with eyes firmly glued elsewhere, seeking out the tell-tale plume of a periscope, or a glint of sun on the wing of an aircraft.

Nose-gunner Viljoen was first up again, professionally, and matter-of-factly, at first, then rising in pitch and excitement, as his eyes worked out the details of what he was seeing.

"Contact dead ahead, 500 yards. Dinghy in the water. Men onboard, Skipper, there's men onboard! They're waving!"

605

"Roger Dagga. How many?"

"Hard to say Skipper. Five, maybe more. Looks like a standard issue navy dinghy, and I will bet a pound to a pinch of pig shit that they are navy uniforms, Skipper."

The reason behind Viljoen's nickname was lost in time, but he was Dagga to everyone, including 201's Squadron Leader, although, in fairness, that may have been because they were brothers.

Sparks came back with a message, confirming the passing on of the location report, leaving Cox free to concentrate on his fly past.

His first sweep had been at full speed but, with the absence of any adverse reports, Cox turned his aircraft, and throttled back to permit closer examination.

He saw the waving men in the dinghy himself, and believed he saw others in the water, whose only motion was caused by the shifting of the sea.

'Poor bastards.'

"What's the latest on Dusty, please?"

A slight delay, and the metallic voice of Rawson, one of the gunners, responded with negative news.

The pilot did not welcome being single handed for the entire flight.

"Bollocks with an egg on top."

His favourite expletive, and one that always puzzled those who heard it.

"Arsey, I need a hand up here. Pass your guns onto someone will you."

"Roger, Skipper."

Crozier looked away from his waist guns, and saw Rawson moving forward.

"All yours, Tiger," and Crozier slapped the gunner on the shoulder, as he headed towards the stairs, that rose up to the flight deck.

Rawson had been nicknamed 'Sid' at a young age, for reasons best known to God, and his friends in Mrs Oosterhuis' class. That label survived until the first time that 246 Squadron's Operations officer had placed his initials up on the crew roster.

By the time those present had stopped laughing at G.R.R.R., 'Sid' was history, and 'Tiger' was born.

606

"Radar Contact, bearing 010, range approximately 95 miles, heading unknown, possibly south-south-west, Skipper."

Magic Malan's report was delivered in his normal impersonal style. The type VIc Radar set was supposed to be capable up to 100 miles in the right circumstances, and Flight Sergeant Malan always seemed to coax the best out of the equipment.

Cox thumbed his mike.

"Busby, fit in with you at all?"

After the slightest delay the Navigator replied.

"Position could tie in with the Stord, Skipper."

"Roger."

Stord was a destroyer of the Royal Norwegian Navy, one of the array of vessels converging on the area.

Crozier slipped into the second seat, a place he often occupied. He had failed his pilot's training, not on his ability behind the controls, but more on his inability with the required mathematics.

Lining up on the wreckage, Cox throttled back as much as he dared.

"Ok crew, Slow pass. Keep your eyes skinned."

As the big flying boat did a leisurely flyover, Dagga and the rear-gunner, Van der Blumm, confirmed the presence of Naval personnel amongst the survivors, as well as many bodies floating on the surface.

"Skipper, radar target has changed course, now confirmed at 90 miles, heading 190. She changed course after Sparks lit up the airwaves."

"Roger, Magic."

Standing orders no longer permitted the Flying Boat to touch down and recover the Canadians, but as the Norwegian Navy was coming to the rescue, it just meant a few more hours on the water for the survivors.

"Dagga, use the Aldis. Let them know we can't stop, but help is on its way. Witty, how long?"

Navigator Jason Witt was already prepared for the question, so his answer was immediate.

"Thanks, Witty. Four hours, Dagga. And wish them good luck. Sparks, send confirmed survivors at this location.'"

The Sunderland circled slowly, as the Aldis lamp blinked out the message to the men below.

607

"Skipper, message sent."

"Roger Dagga. Right, now let's find the bastards who did this."

For more, watch out for Book Four of the Red Gambit series, 'Impasse', which should be available by December 2013, on Amazon Kindle as a download, and createspace.com as a book.

Fig #71 - Rear Cover of 'Stalemate'

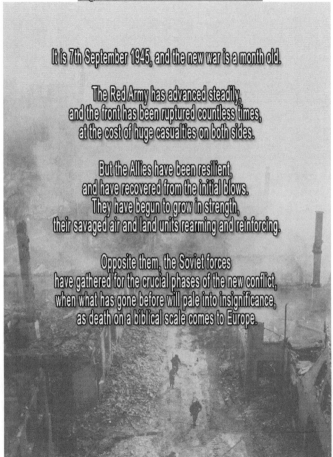